Sweet Songbird

Born in Essex, Teresa Crane still lives in a village in the north of the county. Married with two grown-up children, she began writing ten years ago. Her first novel, *Spider's Web* was published in 1980 and was followed by Molly (1982), *A Fragile Peace* (1984) and *The Rose Stone* (1986).

TERESA CRANE

Sweet Songbird

FONTANA/COLLINS

First published in Great Britain by
William Collins Sons & Co. Ltd 1987
First issued in Fontana Paperbacks 1988

Made and printed by William Collins Sons & Co. Ltd, Glasgow

For Andy and for Michele,
with my love

The splendid auditorium was packed. Tier upon tier of eager, animated faces were turned to the stage. Here and there a fan fluttered, shimmering in the dimmed gaslight that gleamed too upon the brilliant white of an elegant ruffled shirt, glowed upon the soft skin of a woman's bared shoulders, struck fire from a jewelled throat or wrist.

The terrifying rumours were true then; every seat in the house was taken.

'There's nobs in,' someone had said in the dressing room, suppressed excitement in the words, curiosity in the eyes that had flicked to Kitty.

Upon the stage, sequins glittering, the acrobats tumbled with professional grace from their pyramid, landing lightly, smiling their bright, empty smiles across the footlights. From where Kitty stood, transfixed with the paralysis of terror, she could see the sweat that shone upon their skin, smell its rank odour. Applause lifted and then died to an expectant silence as the orchestra struck a chord that slipped into a muted drumroll.

God in Heaven, she must be mad. What had possessed her ever to believe that she could step out onto that stage alone, face those avid, inquisitive eyes, fill that vast silence with the lift of her voice? Her throat was dry as dust, her heart thundering louder than the rattling drum.

Upon the stage a cat-like young man in spangled silk panteloons stood poised upon a swaying tower, arms above his head in the manner of a diver, every eye upon him. His handsome face was arrogant. This was his moment. Kitty tried to clear her throat, swallowed a choking cough as silence fell upon the opulent gilt and gold palace that was the New Cambridge Theatre. It seemed to her that the air that entered her lungs was dry as dust, hot as a furnace.

– Along the great shingled stretches of beach that were the Suffolk coastline the air on this fine autumn evening would be cool; cool and sea-washed and stirred as always by the fresh salt breeze –

The tower swayed. The onlookers gasped. Perfume drifted heavily upon the smoky air. From where Kitty stood she could quite clearly see the occupants of one of the boxes that abutted the stage. An impeccably dressed young man, a long-stemmed glass in his hand, leaned negligently in his chair, a half-smile on his face, as his eyes ran over the lithe body of the scantily-clad young girl acrobat who posed with a dramatic flourish near him. The eyes of the other three occupants of the box – an older man and two women, magnificently dressed, with almost identical nodding ostrich plumes adorning their piled, jewel-decked hair – were fixed in fascination on the handsome figure upon the tower.

– The sun would be gone, the vast, empty, light-washed sky still showing its glow in the west whilst the sea-horizon darkened to night –

The young man lifted his head and closed his eyes.

Kitty gagged on an agonized, nerve-induced cough. The muscle in her left leg, pulled painfully during yesterday's last, gruelling and all but disastrous rehearsal, twitched and throbbed. What was she doing here? How had it happened? Her almost paralysed brain refused to relinquish the vision it had conjured up of far-off peace, of the unchanging world of the Suffolk countryside.

In a blur of shimmering, vivid movement the young man launched himself into the air, somersaulting once, twice, three times. As he landed upon the boards, before the applause could start he leapt once more, tumbling and spinning at dizzying speed. The orchestra picked up the tempo of his movements as he circled the stage like a child's brilliant coloured spinning top, the strength and agility of his body apparently defying the common laws of gravity that bound other mortals to the earth. The excited audience were clapping now in time to the music, urging him on to greater efforts. With a facile grace that belied the sheen of sweat, the corded, strained muscles, he flipped from hands to feet, spun in the air, faster and faster. Kitty averted her eyes, the flashing movement deepening the chill, nervous nausea that threatened to betray her.

''Ere — 'Ave a sip o' this —' Pol's voice, Pol's square, roughened hand thrusting a glass at her. Gratefully she took it. On the stage the last flamboyant somersault brought the audience to its feet with a crash of applause.

Damn him! She had to follow that —! Suddenly, beneath the sick apprehension, something else stirred, heartening and familiar. She squared her shoulders, took a breath, gave the glass of water back to Pol with a perfectly steady hand. The customers had not come to see a brash young circus performer, however much of a showman he might be. They had come to see Kitty Daniels. And now, suddenly, the inspiring excitement seeped into her veins, coursing through her body, steadying her nerves, clearing her head. The acrobats streamed past her, chattering and laughing, pleased with their success. One or two sidelong, curious glances were thrown. Kitty ignored them. The audience had quieted. Pat Kenny was on her feet.

'And now, Ladies and Gentlemen, the moment you've — the moment we've all — been waiting for —'

The nerves that just moments before had threatened to incapacitate her were gone. She stepped into the lights.

'— It's my pride — my privilege — my happy prerogative — to present —'

She swaggered forward, saw the impeccably dressed gentleman's eyes open wide, caught the titillated, half-shocked gasps of the ladies.

'Miss — Kitty — Daniels —!'

Above the applause the orchestra struck up the familiar

introduction. And – would it have happened? she found herself wondering as she stepped to the centre of the stage – would I have been here if they had not died –?

PART ONE

1

Cruelly, and as seems so often the way of such things, upon that June day of 1863 when the grey waters of the North Sea reluctantly gave up their dead, those who were to be most affected by the tragedy were almost the last to hear of it.

The fishermen who had landed the gruesome catch clustered in silence upon the beach beneath the crumbling cliffs of the lost city of Dunwich and looked upon the sodden bodies in a shock of genuine grief that only barely masked a fearsome apprehension. In this isolated, close-knit community, that which affected one affected all; and who could tell what might come of this? The summer storm that had been the cause of the calamity had long since passed. The afternoon sun shone now, glinting upon the restless waters, the shifting wet shingle, the human bones that spilled grotesquely down the dark, eroded cliffs from the sea-devoured churchyard of All Saints. Its brilliance remorselessly illuminated the gaping, drowned faces, while above the still group upon the beach a gull soared, wheeling in the clear air, its cry a celebration of freedom and of the summer-bright beauty of the day.

The gaze of the two girls who lay in a sheltered spot in the brackened dunes a mile or so to the north followed the bird's sweeping flight. Kitty Daniels, lying in lazy comfort in a small, warm hollow in the sand, watched it with idle eyes as it drifted upon the peaceful air, a speck of living light against the vast blue spaces of the Suffolk skies.

'If you were a bird,' she said, her distinctive, husky voice low against the incessant wash of the North Sea tide, '– and

could go anywhere – anywhere you wanted – where would
you choose?'

Her companion – a small, neatly-built, pretty girl whose
fair hair framed a doll-like, delicately complexioned face
beneath the wide brim of her flower-decked sunhat – settled
herself more comfortably, arranging her pale muslin skirts
decorously and gracefully about her. 'Lor'!' she said, lightly,
her blue eyes crinkling to quick laughter, 'that's an easy
one! Almost anywhere away from this!' She waved a small
hand at the wild and windbeaten landscape that surrounded
them, the dismissive gesture encompassing the unchanging
and endless stretches of the beach, the long, creaming line
of the surf, the scrubland, the bracken, the distant salt flats
with their pools and inlets still now and reflecting the
peaceful sky. A curlew called from the saltings, the eerie
sound an echo of the hauntingly desolate countryside. 'London. I'd go to London. I'd build my nest in a tree in Hyde
Park and watch all the grand ladies and gentlemen parade
beneath me in their carriages –'

Kitty laughed softly.

The other girl tossed her head a little petulantly. 'Well,
what are you laughing at? You surely wouldn't want to stay
here?'

Kitty folded her hands behind her head, stretched long
legs that had been tangled in her skirt, stared into the
limitless sky. 'Oh, I don't know –'

'Oh, fiddle to that!' the smaller girl interrupted, and
laughed suddenly, the sound characteristically warm and
impulsive. 'We aren't staying here, I promise you that, Kitty
Daniels! So just make up your mind to it! I plan to marry a
gentleman of independent means with a town house in
Mayfair and a country estate in Kent, so that you and I need
never feel that beastly east wind again –!'

Kitty rolled onto her stomach and cradled her chin in her
hands. Her dun-coloured homespun gown, a little too short
for her rangy frame, was crumpled and dusted with sand,
her straight dark brown hair, escaping from its confining
pins, straggled, windblown, across her shoulders. 'Oh – I

don't know –' she said again. 'Tha'ss peaceful here –' She stopped then, faint colour glowing in her cheeks. Always she tried to be careful in her speech, emulating Anne's clear enunciation and trying to avoid the soft accents of Suffolk. Never, never would she forget the scorn of Miss Alexander, Anne's governess, when, at his daughter's insistence, Sir George Bowyer had indulgently agreed that Kitty, Anne's friend and playmate of childhood, the future companion of her young womanhood, should join her in the schoolroom of Westwood Grange. 'A servant's child, Sir George?' the woman had spoken as if Kitty had not been present, had spoken indeed as if the child had neither ears to hear the disparaging words, nor intelligence to understand them, 'Well – really – I must say that I hold out very little hope of improving the mind – or the behaviour – of a *servant's* child –'

Kitty now put the sound of the sharp, unpleasant voice from her. 'I like it here,' she said, 'it's all I know. I don't see why you should have taken so against it all at once?'

Anne's smile was amiably dismissive. 'You just say such things to provoke me, you know you do. Of course I've "taken against it". Lor', Kitty – we aren't children any more, to run barefoot on the beach or build castles in the sand! I won't – I will not! – spend the rest of my life buried here at the ends of the earth – and oh, for goodness' sake, Kitty,' she broke in on herself, her irritability as quick as her gaiety and as swiftly expressed, ' – do put your bonnet on! You'll finish up looking like a gypsy if you aren't careful.' She tossed the unadorned, battered straw bonnet that the other girl had discarded upon the sand across the small distance that separated them.

Kitty let it lie where it fell. She was looking out to sea, her dark eyes narrowed against the sun beneath their forcefully slanting brows. 'Strange.'

'What is?' Anne was combing through the tangled ringlets that blew against her cheeks, separating them with her fingers, tucking wayward strands beneath the flowered hat.

'This morning the sea was wild as winter. Yet just look

at it now.' Sunlight glistened upon long, swelling, white-topped rollers, glimmered diamond-bright upon the broken water, washed the vast horizon in light. 'It's like the mill-pond.'

Anne turned her back upon the water, drew her knees up beneath her flounced skirts and linked her hands about them. 'It's horrible,' she said, firmly. 'Horrible. It's always freezing cold, the colour of slate and choppy enough to make you seasick just looking at it! Oh, no. When I marry, Kitty, I shall make very certain that my devoted spouse lives nowhere near the North Sea! I shall not care if I never see it again, that I shan't. These salt winds are terribly bad for a lady's skin, you know.'

Kitty found herself smiling at the small conceit. 'Well – at least I don't have to worry about that, then!'

'Oh, but of course you do!' Anne was quick to turn, to reach a hand. 'A lady's – companion –' Kitty knew that it was not the first word that had come to her tongue – 'must be as careful of such things as her – as anyone. You shall not sit in my boudoir, Kitty dear, with a face scoured raw by the east wind! Nor –' she added, firmly, ' – with a skin as dark as a Turk's! Do put your bonnet on! If not for your sake, then for mine. Miss Alexander will take me to task as much as you if you turn up to lessons tomorrow looking like a Blackamoor!'

Sighing, Kitty sat up and reached for the despised bonnet. 'That makes me look a proper donkey,' she muttered, half under her breath.

'It,' Anne said, automatically.

Kitty turned her head.

'Not "that" – "it".' Anne threw up her pale hands in despair. 'Truly, Kitty, you must try to remember! You know how you hate for Miss Alexander to pick on you because of the way you speak. Do try. You mustn't say "that" – you must say "it" – *it* makes you look a proper donkey –'

There was a brief moment of silence. Anne bit her lip, trying not to laugh, for despite her occasional thoughtless-ness she was anxious above all things not to hurt this girl

who had been her friend, companion and stoutest strength
for as long as she could remember, and whose prickly pride
she had cause to know all too well. Kitty's brown eyes
crinkled. In a moment they were helpless, clinging to each
other, spluttering for breath through their laughter.

'I didn't mean –' Anne went off into another infectious
peal of helpless laughter.

'Stop it! Oh, do stop it!' Kitty buried her sun-bright face
in the crown of the offending bonnet.

They stilled at last, calmed to a quiet that was broken
still by an occasional breathless giggle. In the distance,
spray-hazed, a small, solitary figure had appeared, wandering
aimlessly towards them along the beach, stooping now
and again to pick up a stone and hurl it far out across the
water.

Kitty, watching, sobered.

Anne followed the direction of her gaze. 'Is that Matt?'

Kitty nodded. 'Yes.' As always, the sight of her young
brother had brought the faintest of shadows to her face.

'I thought he'd gone out in the boat with Papa and
Geoffrey?'

'No.' Kitty sat up, brushed sand from her bodice. 'Patrick
decided he wanted to go with the others after all. There
wasn't room for Matt.'

Anne's practised ear had caught the change in her
tone. Impulsively she leaned to Kitty, touching her hand
lightly. 'You really mustn't worry about him so much, you
know –'

The other girl moved her head sharply, in a half-impatient,
half-negative gesture. 'What else can I do but worry? Who
else is there to worry about him?' She stopped abruptly at
the expression on Anne's face. 'I'm sorry. I didn't mean that
the way it sounded, truly I didn't. You – your father – all of
you – have done so much for us both since Father died. But
– it isn't like family, is it? You must see that?'

'Papa loved your father dearly,' Anne said, a faint, stubborn hurt in the blue eyes. 'They were friends as we are
friends. They grew up together, as we did. They fought in

the war together. At Sebastopol your father saved Papa's
life. He never forgot it – you know that –'

Kitty, half-smiling, was shaking her head slowly back and
forth. 'Anne – Father was Sir George's servant. As I, for all
our friendship, am yours.'

Anne turned rudely from her. 'Oh, do stop it!'

Kitty, however, could be as stubborn as anyone. 'Not
speaking of it won't change it,' she said softly. 'Matt
and I have to look out for each other. We have no other
family –'

A rosy, petulant lower lip pouted. 'You're just being tiresome. And I won't hear another word. Papa couldn't have
treated you better if you had been my true sister –'

Kitty eyed the pretty, wilful face in silence for a moment
then, gently, she leaned forward and drew a fold of the soft,
pale muslin towards her, laying it across the coarse stuff of
her own skirt. The flared, expressive eyebrows lifted very
slightly, but she did not speak.

Anne snatched the fold of skirt away, her colour high.

Kitty sighed. 'Please – don't be angry. I don't mean to be
ungrateful. It's just that, for all your kindness, for all the
kindness in the world –' She trailed to a halt, watching the
oncoming figure. 'Blood, they say, is thicker than water.
And Matt is my brother. My responsibility.'

With another sudden, characteristic change of mood,
Anne laughed. 'I told you – you worry too much about the
little devil. He'll settle down. He'll be all right. It's your
own life you should be thinking about! Imagine what fun
it'll be when I'm married! I shan't move one step without
you, I swear!' She made a dramatic gesture. 'We'll travel,
how would you like that? All over the world! Well, Europe
at least. London – Paris – Rome –' She paused, giggled again.
'Oh, pooh! My geography's truly awful! I can't think of
anywhere else –!'

'Southwold?' Kitty suggested, straightfaced, 'Lowestoft?
Yarmouth?' The figure on the beach below was almost upon
them now, and clearly defined. She could see the dark,
straight hair, so like her own, the lanky, long-limbed frame

that Matt had inherited from their father as, to her chagrin, she had herself.

But from where or from whom, she found herself wondering bleakly and not for the first time, had her brother inherited those long, slim, thieving fingers that had landed him in trouble so often?

'Ugh! Just say the names and I smell fish. I really do! That's another thing – no fish. When I'm married to my fine gentleman we'll never eat fish again. And don't tell me you like fish –' Anne added, swiftly repressive, '– or I'll throw something at you!'

'Thee'll sit on a cushion and sew a fine seam,' Kitty quoted, smiling. 'And feed upon strawberries, sugar and cream –'

Anne wrinkled a mischievous nose. 'Sounds all right to me. Except the sewing bit.' The warm laughter pealed again. 'You can do that.'

Kitty laughed with her. The boy on the beach had seen them. He stood by the water's edge, lifted a hand. Kitty could sense, even at this distance, the wide, engaging smile. She acknowledged his greeting, then turned back to her companion. 'What about poor Mr Winthrop?' she asked, slyly.

Anne raised theatrical hands and eyes to Heaven. 'What about poor Mr Winthrop?'

'You won't even consider his offer?'

Anne's small shriek was halfway between horror and amusement. 'Consider it? Kitty – what in the world do you take me for? Consider marrying a man three times my age? Consider living in that great old-fashioned draughty barn of a house miles from anywhere with nothing but birds and bits of old stone for company? Heavens – Father's obsession for stupid, drowned Dunwich is bad enough – Mr Winthrop is a thousand times worse! It was, indeed, he who first infected Papa with this tiresome obsession. What the two of them find so absorbing about a heap of old stones on the seabed I can't imagine! Marry Mr Winthrop? Don't be absurd!'

'Your father would like such a match.'

'Then let him marry Mr Winthrop,' Anne said, pertly. 'I'm sure they'd be very happy together.'

Kitty smiled. 'He has your best interests at heart – your father, I mean.'

'Nonsense. He has his own interests at heart. What could be better – the boys to run the estate, his little girl a scant five miles away and safely out of trouble, and a boon companion who dotes on old bits of stone as much as he does! Lor' – can you imagine the gay times we'd have? Oh, Kitty, no – not Mr Winthrop!'

Kitty could not help but laugh. Below them Matt, shirt flapping in the cool breeze had turned from the water's edge and was toiling through the steep, shifting shingle towards them, the wind lifting his hair.

'I suppose that's where Papa and the boys have gone today?' Anne too was watching the approaching boy. 'Fishing up bits of Dunwich?'

'Yes. Some of the fishermen dredged up a piece of statuary yesterday. Sir George was anxious to find the place before tomorrow's high tide. Geoffrey and Patrick went with him.'

'They're as bad as he is.' Anne shook a gloomy head. 'Why can't they leave the blessed place alone? It's drowned and gone. And good riddance, as far as I'm concerned.'

Kitty looked out across the sun-struck sea. 'Have you ever heard the bells?'

Anne was impatient. 'Oh, of course I haven't! And neither, if you ask me, has anyone else. Because all the towers will have fallen long ago and all the bells buried themselves in the seabed. It's just a silly story. And I don't want to hear another word about it. Now – far more important – what are you going to sing for us tonight?' The change of subject was frank and brooked no contradiction.

Kitty shook back her hair, tried to stuff it into the battered bonnet. 'I don't know. I hadn't thought.'

'*The Green Willow*'s my favourite.' Anne half closed her eyes and sang a snatch of song in a small, breathless voice.

'Oh, young men are false and they are so deceitful, Young men are false and they seldom prove true –'

Kitty's voice joined in, strong and husky, ringing clear and true above the sea-sound. 'For rambling and ranging, their minds always changing, They're always a-looking for some girl that's true –'

'Oh, I do wish I could sing like you!' Anne watched as Kitty, a little ungainly, scrambled to her feet, then held out her own hand to be helped, contriving to lift from the sandy ground light and graceful as thistledown, her skirts swaying. 'I've never heard such a lovely voice. It's a gift from God, truly it is.'

Kitty's long mouth turned down. 'You think so? Then perhaps you'd like to have a word in His ear for me next Sunday? While He was handing out gifts I could have done with something a mite more useful.'

'Kitty Daniels!' Anne clapped a delightedly scandalized hand to her mouth. 'What a thing to say! Matthew!' She turned, laughing, to the boy who had just scrambled up the last stretch of sliding shingle to the dunes. 'Don't stand too close to Kitty – the thunderbolt meant for her might catch you too!' She squealed with laughter at her own joke. Brother's and sister's eyes met, not yet on the same level, though by the boy's lanky growth it was obvious that it would not be long before he overtook his tall sister. Kitty's gaze was daunting, the dark, winged brows – that gave to her face in repose a faint expression of mockery – lifted.

Matthew grinned easily, unabashed as always by any attempt of Kitty's to repress him. 'I shouldn't like ter see that 'appen.' His accent, unschooled by Anne or Miss Alexander held much stronger strains of Suffolk than did his sister's. Deliberately he exaggerated it. 'Tha'ss too bad when the good gits a-taken with the bad, i'n't it?'

Kitty did not answer. Her attention had been taken from him. She was staring southward, down the beach.

'We are talking of the musical evening,' Anne said. 'Kitty's going to sing *Green Willow*.' She brushed minute grains of sand from her skirt.

'Old Ben's coming,' Kitty said, puzzlement in her voice. 'And – that's Tom with him. And Will Hall. What on earth are they doing here at this hour?'

' – it should be a very pleasant evening. I shall play the piano. And the vicar's daughter has a passable voice, though not a patch on Kitty's of course. Matthew – if I persuaded Papa to let you attend – because we're sadly in need of decent male voices, and Geoffrey thinks it beneath him and Patrick screeches like an owl – if I persuade him, then will you promise me faithfully that –'

'Anne!' There was a strange sharpness in Kitty's voice. As she watched the hesitant approach of the men along the beach, an uncomfortable chill of foreboding had crept over her skin.

The men paused, some way away, conferred, shuffling their feet, averted their heads, reluctantly came on.

' –that you'll – behave yourself.' Anne paused delicately before the words. 'Papa is a patient man, no one knows that better than I, but –'

'Anne!'

The one, urgent word stopped her. She looked at Kitty in surprise. 'What is it?'

'Old Ben's coming. With some of the men.'

'Ben? What's he doing here? Surely it's a little early for Miss Alexander to have sent out a search party?' Anne's voice was still careless, but the apprehension in Kitty's had communicated itself surely to her brother. He turned his head, shaded his eyes, watching. The three stood in silence as the men climbed the low sandy cliffs from the wave-washed beach. As they came nearer and their faces were more clearly to be seen, the sea-filled silence stretched, hung all at once with awful apprehension.

Very, very slowly Anne reached for Kitty's hand. Kitty took the small fingers in hers. Her throat felt suddenly dry as bone.

They stood at last, death's reluctant messengers, their ragged, salt-stained shirts flattened by the wind to brown-skinned arms and torsos, canvas trousers string-tied, feet bare and calloused, spread toes turned into the sifting sand.

The two younger men avoided all eyes, casting their own down to the poor, windblown grass at their feet. The man everyone knew as Old Ben had a face of carved mahogany, set now into deep lines of sorrow. Anne's frightened gaze was fixed on his face: the dependable and loved face of a man she had known since childhood, a man who had told her her first tales of sea-monsters and mermaids, who had guarded her faithfully over the wild North Sea waters when her father had insisted that she 'try out her good Suffolk sea-legs'; a man who looked at her now with a depth of pity he made no attempt to hide. Stepping back from him she let go of Kitty's hand, brought both her own very slowly to her mouth. Her eyes never leaving the old man's, she shook her head, fiercely, as if to deny the very moment.

'What is it?' Kitty asked at last of the terrible silence. 'What's happened?'

(ii)

'Anne – Anne, please, won't you try to stop crying?'

The rage of grief in no way abated, as it had not abated in the hours since Anne Bowyer had collapsed, screaming, upon the sunlit sand at the news of the deaths of her father and brothers. In desperation, her own grief subjugated by concern for this girl who was as close to her as a sister, Kitty had tried everything she could think of to calm her, but to no avail. The bereaved girl was almost demented with shock.

'Anne – please stop it. You'll make yourself ill –' Kitty laid an arm about the shaking shoulders. In exhausted anguish Anne leaned weakly upon her, the helpless tears flooding still down the puffed and reddened face, her breath hiccoughing painfully in her throat. She moaned as she cried, like a small animal mortally hurt. The sound was awful. Kitty lifted a tired head, trying to ease her aching neck. So great was the disaster it was all but impossible to believe in it.

The big room was empty. Apart from Anne's racking sobs

there was no sound, neither from within nor from without the thick walls. It was, Kitty found herself thinking, as if the house, this great, ancient, weather-buffeted refuge of a house, itself mourned its dead. She shook her head at the thought, closing her eyes. It could not, surely, truly have happened? Today – a day like any other; busy, tranquil, exasperating, ordinary – could not have turned to nightmare at a stroke?

She shivered. The room, despite the summer evening sunshine that struck the distant sea to sullen, metallic light, was cold. Her arm tightened about Anne, and she made soothing, meaningless noises into the damp, disordered tear-wet hair. When the door opened she turned her head, quickly hopeful. Her brother Matt, white-faced and un-usually subdued, fidgeted in the doorway, his eyes flicking worriedly to Anne's distraught face and then sliding away.

Kitty closed her eyes for a moment. She had not herself realized how much she had longed to hand over the responsi-bility for the distressed and helpless child that Anne had become to some older and more experienced hand. 'Matt! Where in Heaven's name is everyone?' Her voice was strained and sharp. Anne wailed louder at the sound. 'The servants? Miss Alexander?'

'The servants are in the kitchen, the women that is. Miss Alexander told them to stay there till they were sent for. She's in the library, doin' somethin' with some papers. The men – they've gone down to the beach. To – to collect – the bodies.' Matt almost choked on the words. Understanding seeped slowly into Kitty's all but paralysed brain, and brought to her an added shock. Only pure chance had stood between her own brother and death. It was at the last minute that Patrick, Anne's young brother, had claimed his place with his father and brother on the ill-fated expedition that had cost them all their lives, taking Matt's place.

'Go and find Miss Alexander for me,' she said, gently. 'She ought to be here.' Under normal circumstances the woman who so resented and despised her would be the last person she would want to see, but at the moment any company,

any help, would be welcomed. Then as Matthew turned to go her eye fell upon a cupboard that stood beside the fireplace – an ancient battered thing that Sir George had once told her was as old as the house and in which he kept, she knew, as did everyone else on the estate, his share of the spoils of those moonlit expeditions by the village fishermen to which Sir George, a local magistrate and pillar of the community, turned a convenient blind eye. 'Wait.' She pointed. 'In the cupboard. Brandy. And a glass. Sir George kept –' She stopped, biting her lip, as Anne's frantic sobs, which had faded a little from sheer exhaustion, redoubled at the mention of her father's name.

Matt found an opened bottle and a glass, set them on the table beside his sister. Kitty with her free hand awkwardly splashed a large amount of the rich amber liquid into the glass. The pungent smell turned her stomach a little. 'Here, my love.' She put the glass to Anne's lips. 'Just a mouthful. It'll make you feel better –'

The girl sipped obediently, spluttered. 'That's better,' Kitty said soothingly. 'That's right. A little more –'

She held the glass steady. Anne drank again. With Matt's going heavy silence had fallen once more. Kitty felt numbed, helpless with disbelief. Anne had at last moved a little away from her and sat now, huddled into herself, still moaning softly in an awful, wordless way, like a beaten child. Kitty half-heartedly proffered the brandy again. Anne shook her head. Kitty sat for a moment, staring sightlessly into the glass. Then, almost without thought, she tilted her head and sipped the drink herself. It caught in her throat, burned her lips and her mouth. Then came the warmth, the spurious comfort, and she drank again.

It was the smallest of sounds that caught her ear. She glanced to the dark, open doorway to meet the level, sardonic gaze of the woman who stood there, silently watching. With no word and a world of contempt in each movement Imogen Alexander stalked across the huge, faded carpet, bent to the table and snatched the brandy bottle from it. With sharp, precise movements she went to the cupboard and replaced the bottle, clicking the door decisively as she shut it. Then she turned and surveyed Kitty with a contemptuous eye.

'I – thought it might help Anne –' Kitty found herself saying, unable to resist the goad of unspoken accusation.

The raised eyebrows, the downturned, dismissive mouth told her with no breath wasted upon words what Miss Alexander thought of that for an excuse. 'Miss Daniels,' the woman said at last in the clear, well-modulated voice that Kitty had come so heartily to detest, 'might I suggest that poor Anne needs rather more – mature – ministrations than you are able to offer?'

'I – yes. Of course –'

'The house, Miss Daniels, is full of servants – old and trusted servants – who have known Anne since the day she was born.'

'They – didn't come –' Always it seemed to Kitty that this woman could reduce her to the status of a half-witted child simply by lifting an eyebrow. The loathsome habit of calling her 'Miss Daniels' was in itself enough to reduce her to miserable confusion, as she was sure Miss Alexander knew. No one in her life before had called her 'Miss Daniels' but from the day that over Miss Alexander's furious and undisguised opposition she had been admitted to the schoolroom 'Miss Daniels' she had been, the words always spoken with a precise and frigid distaste: a strange and inverted insult – since Anne, the daughter of the house and Miss Alexander's true charge, was always addressed by her Christian name – that served, as the governess well knew, always to deepen Kitty's discomfort, her feeling of being an unwelcome intruder.

Miss Alexander strode now to the tasselled bell-pull that hung by the massive fireplace. 'They did not come, Miss Daniels,' she said, her voice chill with hard-tried patience, 'because you did not ring for them. They cannot read your thoughts.'

Kitty turned back to the sobbing Anne. In silence, arms folded, Miss Alexander stood guard on the fireplace, and the contraband cupboard. Kitty could feel those blue, scornful eyes upon her like cold shadows on a sunlit day. She kept her head averted.

The door opened. 'Yes, ma'am? You rang?' The white-faced, frightened servant girl looked at no one.

'Miss Anne needs attention. A dish of tea, perhaps, strong and with plenty of sugar. And a warming pan in her bed. At once, please.'

'Yes, mum.' The girl's whisper was scarcely audible.

'And tell Thomas I shall want to see him in a half hour or so. After we've settled Miss Anne.' Miss Alexander's voice was crisp and clear. 'He's to come to the drawing room.'

Kitty looked at her with an undisguised dislike that was threaded with disbelief. Did the woman feel nothing of grief, of loss? If she did it certainly did not show.

It seemed an age before Kitty was able to leave the fitfully sleeping Anne; she sat beside her until the last colour was fading from the sky; lavender to lilac, to rose-hued darkness over the sea. Wearily Kitty stretched her aching back. Very carefully and slowly then she stood, watching the sleeping girl. She could surely leave her now for a little? Just for long enough to slip downstairs to the kitchen? At least there would be company and some comfort there, a sharing of grief and shock. The great kitchens of the Grange, with their vaulted ceilings, their tiny, high arched windows, their mixed smells of yeast and herbs and the warmth of cooking, were her favourite place in the whole house.

The candles that should have lit the wide wooden staircase had not been kindled, but on the shadowed landing beneath where she stood light fell in a bright splash across the floor from the open drawing-room door. Kitty felt her way down the dangerously shadowed stairs, holding tightly to the great, worn bannister rail. At the open door she stopped.

' – to Southwold immediately.' Miss Alexander's voice, clipped and authoritative. 'The family solicitor must be made aware of what has happened at once. Here. This is his name and address. Do you read?'

Silence. A muttered reply.

'Then go to The Swan. The landlord will tell you. You may stay there the night and accompany the gentleman back here in the morning.'

'Yes, Miss.' The groom's reply was clearer this time, and rang with resentment at having to accept orders from someone he clearly considered to be little better than a servant herself. But then – Kitty thought – who else was there to give them, with Anne senseless in the room above and the house in a turmoil? She moved to the open door. The groom brushed past her without a glance. She stood, uncertain. Candlelight gleamed upon the polished lid of the piano. A recollection caused a sharp pang of pain; could it possibly have been only a matter of hours since that Anne had laughed so, and begged her to sing *Green Willow*?

'Miss Alexander –?'

The woman turned, fixed her with a piercing eye.

Kitty bit her lip. 'This evening – there was to have been a musical gathering –'

'Yes, Miss Daniels, I did remember.' The tone indicated clearly that Miss Alexander considered herself the only one capable of remembering anything in a world that had reprehensibly lost its grip on itself. 'I have sent word. I have also suggested that the vicar might call later this evening, and have suggested to Mr Winthrop that he might call sometime tomorrow.'

Kitty looked at her blankly. 'Mr Winthrop?'

'Of course. He is the family's oldest friend. And Anne will need the help and advice of a dependable gentleman.'

'Oh. Yes. Of course.' Kitty's brain seemed not to be functioning at all. She pressed a hand to her forehead. 'Anne – is asleep –'

Miss Alexander's expression changed not a whit. 'Good.'

'Miss Alexander?' Kitty hated the uncertain, almost pleading note in her own voice. 'Wh – what will happen now, do you think? I mean –' Her voice died.

The woman, tall, thin, austere in the black that had always seemed to Kitty to make her look close kin to a crow and that was now so chillingly appropriate, took a slow breath. 'To you? To Anne? To the house? Who knows? That very much depends upon Sir George's forethought – in which I have to say I have no great trust – and upon the new owner of the estate.'

'The new –?' Kitty stared. 'But – Anne, surely? The estate must go to her?' She stopped. Miss Alexander was shaking her head slowly and with heavy emphasis. 'What do you mean – "the new owner"?' Kitty's voice was weak.

Miss Alexander made a small, clicking noise with her tongue. She reached for the bell-pull. Kitty thought for a moment that she would not answer. Stubbornly she stood her ground, waiting, trying to still the strange, erratic beating of her heart. The governess turned back to her. 'The estate cannot go to Anne.' She spoke as if to an idiot child, slowly and clearly. 'It is entailed. To the male line. It may not pass to a daughter.'

'But – the Grange is her home!' The uncomfortable, irregular thumping of her heart had worsened. She could hardly breathe. 'Of course it must be hers.'

'No.'

'Then – who? Miss Alexander, *who*?' she repeated, when the woman did not immediately answer.

'Really, Miss Daniels, how should I know? The estate goes to her nearest male relative –'

'But she hasn't –' Kitty stopped, eyes widening in shock. 'Not that – that disgusting cousin of hers? Sir George couldn't stand him – he wouldn't have him near the place!'

'I hardly think, Miss Daniels,' the cool, hateful voice interrupted her, 'that this is the time or place for a discussion of the personal affairs of our employers. Now – if you will excuse me. There is much to do –'

Dumbly Kitty turned and left the room. On the vast, dark staircase she stood for a moment, struggling to adjust to this new blow. A stranger? To own Westwood Grange – the estate – the farms – the village? And a stranger, moreover, about whom the darkest of rumours had circulated; a rake and a gambler who had already all but beggared himself and squandered his own inheritance – to own all this? To take from Anne what should be hers when she had lost so much already?

Around her the house crouched in silence, brooding on injustice.

(iii)

It had never seemed reasonable to Kitty that one could hate – or for that matter love – another person on sight. But on the day that the foppish Percival Bowyer – now, thanks to blind providence and the wild North Sea Sir, Percival Bowyer, heir to a large slice of East Suffolk – stepped from his rented carriage, lifted a languid head and surveyed with open and scornful dismay the honest square red-brick front of Westwood Grange, she detested him. Small, slim, girlishly pale, he shuddered exaggeratedly. 'S'truth! What a perfect barn of a place!' He tucked his slender silver-headed cane beneath his arm, held out immaculately gloved hands to receive from the burly manservant who had scrambled from the carriage after him a small, snuffling bundle of fur with a wet, crumpled nose and venomous eyes.

'What in the world are we goin' ter do with this, my Barnabas? It looks more suited to house the Brigade of Guards than our poor selves, eh?' Smooth fair hair gleamed beneath his black silk top hat. The pale lavender and blue waistcoat, silk also, was displayed with elegance beneath an improbably well-cut frock coat. His dark trousers were immaculate and his boots, Kitty thought sourly, looked as if mud had never been invented. His attention entirely upon the ugly little dog, he neither moved nor glanced towards the household, assembled warily upon the wide steps that led to the great entrance hall of the Grange. The animal sniffled again, and dribbled disgustingly.

'Collins!' The word was sharp.

The manservant leapt forward, a large, snow-white handkerchief at the ready. The mustered servants and estate workers watched, their expressions ranging from amused astonishment to sardonic and downright disbelief. The animal attended to, the young man lifted his head, cast bored eyes over the assembly at last and, his gaze coming to rest upon a pale-faced Anne, made the weakest of efforts at a smile. 'Cousin Anne, I presume?' The vowels were so exaggerated, the tone so affected, that it was difficult to understand the words.

Anne stepped forward, bobbing something of a curtsey. 'Cousin Percival.' Her voice was subdued.

'Demmed pleased to meet you, m'dear.' He neither looked nor sounded it. 'Now – tell me – is there anywhere in this –' he cast his eyes to Heaven – 'god-forsaken place that a man might quench his thirst?'

'Why – yes – of course –' Anne stood confused. The doll-like young man had moved past her and was waiting at the top of the steps with ill-concealed impatience. She glanced around at the waiting, watching faces. 'Should you not like first to be introduced to –?'

A drooping, white-gloved hand flicked a bored dismissal. 'Later, later. You shouldn't, I'm sure, Cousin, wish to see me expire here on the doorstep?'

'Of – of course not –'

Kitty caught her brother's eye and the same caustic thought glinted between them. If wishes had been granted this day the precious Sir Percy would not survive to take another step. It was not, however, to be. The young man hefted the dog more comfortably in his arm, addressed himself entirely to Anne – as if, Kitty thought with a spurt of anger, the gathered household were of no more account than a flock of silly sheep to be herded aside and disregarded.

'The journey from London to Suffolk, m'dear, is an experience that should not be wished upon a dog, let alone one of such delicate disposition as meself. Ain't that so, my Barney?' He crooned to the dog as a mother might to her child. Kitty glanced at Cook. The woman pursed her lips and lifted her disbelieving gaze to the August skies. The men – servants, fishermen, men of the land – watched, faces impassive, eyes unreadable. 'I declare myself to be quite, quite worn out. Lead me if you will to a comfortable armchair and a large glass of madeira. All else must wait –' He preceded Anne through the front door and was swallowed by the gloom of the great house.

Embarrassed at the outright and careless offence offered to her waiting people, Anne, bright patches of colour upon her drawn face, glanced about her. Then she picked up her skirts and hurried after him.

She left behind her a silence edged unmistakably with anger, but coloured too with astonished hilarity. 'There's a poppet,' someone muttered, from behind Kitty. 'I allus did 'ear they bred 'em queer in Lunnon. Seems tha'ss true –'

'Poor little mannikin,' a woman's voice chimed in, mocking. 'P'raps 'e'll find Miss Anne's doll's 'ouse more to 'is taste?'

Kitty did not join in the general laughter. For all Sir Percival's limp-wristed foppery, his precious airs and graces, there had been something about that small-boned, handsome face that had disturbed her; a cruelty about the mouth, a hardness in the eye that no amount of affectation could disguise.

'Well.' Cook rubbed plump hands upon her vast, freshly starched apron. 'Seems we're not to be honoured with a word after all. So, seems we'd better be about our business. Tha'ss a pity the young man was so – tired –' She spoke the last word with a gently ironic emphasis that brought more laughter from the crowd. Talking amongst themselves they began to drift away in twos and threes. Kitty nibbled her lip. Such a beginning boded ill, she suspected – ill for the household and ill above all for Anne, already all but broken by the loss of those she loved, who would certainly bear the brunt of any difficulties created by the new master of Westwood Grange.

'Come, now, Kitty gel. Doan' look so down! Tha'ss not the end of the world, you know.' Cook's kindly eyes twinkled sympathetically. 'Come on down to the kitchen with us, eh? Tha'ss a good long time since you've honoured us with your company.' Her smile took any sting from the words. 'An' Miss Anne looks to be able to do without you for a minute or two –' She stopped suddenly, her hand searching in the capacious pocket of her apron. 'Lord above! My keys? I've lost my keys!' She stepped back, eyes searching the ground anxiously. 'I had them – I know I did. Ruby! Come, gel – your eyes is sharper than mine – help me look.'

The kitchenmaid obediently dropped to her knees and began to search. Others, too, bent their gaze to the ground. After a moment, however, Kitty lifted her head, scanned the faces about her and, heart sinking at the mischievous hilarity that lit a pair of dark eyes, pushed her way through the crowd to her brother's side. As she reached him another voice said, surprised, 'My kerchief's gone!' 'And mine! Right from round my neck!' 'My purse! Who has my purse?'

Kitty held out her hand.

Matthew laughed at her.

The noise around them had suddenly died. 'By God!' someone said. 'Matt Daniels up to his tricks again.'

There was a murmur. Some laughter.

Kitty was trembling with anger. 'Give them back,' she said.

Matt glanced about him, then made a pass with his empty hands and a red kerchief fluttered. A girl squealed. 'Tha'ss mine! You give that back, Matt Daniels!'

'Come and get it!' Matt was off, dodging through the crowd, chased by the girl who shrieked and tumbled after him. A leather purse flew into the air, a spotted kerchief dangled from the branch of a tree. Through the pandemonium Kitty stood like stone, watching as her brother eluded reaching, exasperated hands, danced like a wraith about the courtyard, dodging around the carriage and the patiently-standing horses, Cook's keys dangling from impudent fingers. Large Cook, red-faced, inadvisedly launched herself after him. 'Imp of mischief! Just wait till I lay hands on you!'

The horses moved uneasily. The driver fiddled nervously with the reins. The man who sat beside him – a giant with shoulders as big as an Essex barn, who had remained with the carriage to guard his master's luggage – reached across and with no ceremony twitched the reins from the man's nervous fingers and hauled sharply on them, quieting the beasts. Sir Percival's other manservant stood where his master had left him beside the carriage and watched the antics of Matt and his pursuers with a suspicious scowl. Matt dodged behind him. Cook, enraged, bore down on them both, hand upraised. Matt jingled the keys, grinning, and then was gone whilst with flawless timing the blow intended for him caught the manservant a buffet that all but knocked him from his feet.

The front door opened.

'Matt! Matt – enough!' Kitty's voice rose above the uproar, urgently.

Matt grinned at her, far beyond restraint now.

In the open doorway stood Sir Percival. Beside him, smooth malicious head bent to his, lips at his ear, was Imogen Alexander.

'Matt! Stop it!'

Matt ducked beneath a reaching arm, dodged behind a laughing girl, holding her shoulders lightly, using her as a not-unwilling shield. Behind him, heavily, Sir Percy's enormous manservant climbed down from the high driving seat of the carriage.

Kitty could only watch.

'Take him,' Sir Percival said, very crisp and cool, cutting the uproar to silence in a breath. The little dog, tucked still into the crook of his arm, yawned, showing yellow teeth. Imogen Alexander, her mischief done, glanced in small triumph about the chaotic scene and withdrew. Too late, Matt turned. A huge hand clamped upon his shoulder. He tried to pull away, twisting, still half-laughing. The man held him as he might a squirming puppy about to be drowned, and then, brutally, brought his free hand crashing down upon the boy's face. Blood spurted, bright in the sunshine. A girl shrieked. The man shook Matt, raised his hand again.

'No! Oh – please! Stop him! Matt didn't mean anything!' Kitty, tripping on her skirts as she scrambled up the steps, almost fell at Sir Percy's feet. 'Please!'

A small white hand, imperiously raised, stilled all movement. Matt, blood dripping from his damaged mouth, hung like an ill-strung puppet from the giant's fist. The man waited, his eyes, as were everyone's, upon his master.

Sir Percival's child-like fingers fondled the dog's head. Pale eyes travelled from the torn hem of Kitty's skirt to her distraught face. 'Your name?'

Behind him now Anne Bowyer stood, wringing her hands, the weak tears that were lately always so close to the surface standing in her eyes.

Kitty swallowed terror. 'Katherine Daniels.' Then, on a quick breath, as an afterthought: 'Sir.'

The light, heavy-lidded eyes were ice-cold in an expressionless face. 'And – that?' He indicated Matt with a contemptuous flick of his head.

'– is my brother, sir. He means no ill. I swear it. He's a boy, sir – high-spirited is all –'

Curved eyebrows lifted. 'So I see. And a thief to boot, I hear?'

'No!'

He waited a long time. 'Not the tale I've been told,' he said, pleasantly.

'Please –' Kitty was shaking. She clasped her hands together, if not to still their trembling at least to disguise it. 'It's a game to him, sir –' Not always, and not a soul there who did not know it. Please God, she prayed, let no one choose this moment to even past scores.

No one did. Warm, dusty silence rang with birdsong.

'Search him,' Sir Percival said, his voice still perilously easy, his hand, small, pale, fleshless, moving ceaselessly over the dog's long, soft fur.

With a rough hand the giant slammed Matt up against

the side of the carriage, held him there effortlessly, his
shoeless feet barely on the ground, as Sir Percival's other
manservant ran equally ungentle hands over the boy's body.
'Hah!' Triumphantly the man, tossing aside an assortment
of small objects, held up something that gleamed dully in
the light. Leaving Matt in the hands of the other man he
turned, ran to the foot of the steps and extended his hand,
upon which lay a shining silver coin. 'Mine, sir. You gave
it me yourself, if you remember, for –'

'Yes. Quite,' Sir Percival said.

'The little bugger must've filched it from me when 'e –
sorry, sir –'

Sir Percival had ducked his head to the dog, a pained
expression on his face. 'Really, Collins. Save your gutter
language for the gutter, if you will.'

'Yes, sir.'

The small, dapper figure straightened, walked down the
steps towards Matt and his captor. No one but Kitty moved.
Brushing aside the swift movement of Cook's restraining
hand she followed him and tried once again to interpose
herself between him and her brother, fell back at the look
he bent upon her.

'So – Matthew Daniels,' – all trace of the drawling, foolish
accent had gone – 'what have you to say for yourself?'

Matt said nothing, licked bloody lips.

'Tell me –' The man looked down at Barnabas, stroked
the dog beneath the chin. The animal stretched, raising its
head to the caress. Sir Percival lifted his cold eyes again.
'Are you not the same lad that was supposed to have been
attendant upon my uncle and older cousin on the day of
their' – he paused, delicately – 'unfortunate accident?'

'Yes.'

'Yes – sir,' the voice was steely.

'Yes, sir.'

'I see.' For a moment something close to a smile flicked
across the fine-boned face. 'A strange world, is it not? Had
you drowned in your young master's place you would not,
of course, be here today. And neither would I. It could be

said, could it not, that you did me a service by surviving?'

Confused, Matt glanced at Kitty and away. 'I – yes, sir. P'raps so.'

'I hope' – the voice was ice-cold – 'that you don't expect anything by way of gratitude, however?'

'N-no, sir.'

'Good.' Sir Percival made a sign to the servant who held Matt. Dangerously gently the man set him upon his feet. Sir Percival studied the boy for a moment, apparent interest in his eyes. Matt stood, head up, defiant; yet something in Kitty shrivelled in pain at the fear that lurked clear to be seen beneath the bravado. 'Are you familiar, Matthew Daniels,' Sir Percy asked at last, quietly, 'with the saying that those who are born to hang will never drown?'

'Yes, sir.' The boy's voice was a breath.

Sir Percival smiled again, and Kitty's heart all but stopped at the cruelty of it. The small man stepped forward, breathing in the boy's frightened face. 'I am your master now, boy. Would I not be failing in my duty if I did not discourage you – and others' – his flickering glance took in the silent assembly about them – 'from such a fate?'

'I – y-yes, sir.'

'Collins.' Sir Percival's voice lifted a little.

'Yes, sir?'

'My cane. I left it in the house. Fetch it.'

The man glanced at Matt, grinned wolfishly. 'Yes, sir.' He turned and ran towards the house.

Almost reflexively Matt began to struggle then, fiercely and with a strength born of panic. Then as suddenly, realizing the futility of it, he stopped, stood quite still, watching his tormentor with wide dark eyes.

His hand still moving constantly upon the dog's head, Sir Percival looked about him, his cold eyes moving, slowly, from face to face. 'Understand this. I am master here now, whether you will it or no. Watch well. And learn.' He nodded sharply to the giant who held Matt. With a sudden twist the man turned the boy towards him, trapping the dark head beneath his massive arm. With one hand he held him so;

with the other in a single apparently effortless movement
he ripped the shirt from the narrow, sunbrowned back. Kitty
heard someone, a girl in the crowd, sob, fearfully. Cook
muttered behind her. She stepped forward. 'Sir Percival – I
beg of you – it was a childish prank!'

The man did not even glance at her. His eyes were upon
the boy's exposed, curved back, the young spine clearly
defined, vulnerable as glass. 'You will all stay,' he said,
quietly. 'It will, I believe, do no one harm to have it clearly
understood who is master at Westwood Grange. And to
discover too that I will not tolerate as my uncle tolerated –'

'Here, sir.' Collins elbowed his way through the sullenly
silent crowd. In his hand he held Sir Percival's long, silver-
headed cane.

Sir Percival stepped back. For the first time the hand that
rested upon the dog's head was absolutely still. 'Lay it on
well, Collins. Teach the young villain that stealing is an
activity best avoided by an employee of mine.'

The beating was the most appallingly vicious thing Kitty
had ever witnessed. Matt had been beaten before – and for
much the same reasons – handed over to groom or bailiff by
an exasperated and over-tried Sir George. But never like this,
in public, as a spectacle and by a man who obviously took
his cue from his detestable master and sadistically enjoyed
the infliction of pain. The first blow broke the smooth,
child's skin. By the third Matt was screaming, the sound
blistering the hot summer air. By the time his screams had
reduced through anguished moans to silence, Kitty, her face
tear-drenched, her arms secured in grim friendship by two
white-faced labourers, had lost count of the strokes. Men
murmured angrily. Many of the women, young and old,
were weeping, heads turned, hands covering their eyes.
Collins, sweating, stopped for a moment, wiping his dripping forehead with his sleeve. Matt was silent, his breath
rasping like a dying man's. Kitty broke free of the hands
that restrained her and flung herself forward, catching Sir
Percival's arm in frantic hands. 'In the name of God, stop
it! You'll kill him!'

Pale eyes looked into hers. A hand gestured, negligently. With obvious reluctance Collins lowered the arm he had raised to strike again. The big man who had been holding Matt let him go and straightened. Kitty's brother, his back a bruised pulp of blood and torn skin, collapsed onto the cobblestones like a dropped sack of potatoes. As Kitty turned to run to him, a small hand, steel strong, detained her. 'Remember, girl, this time he got off lightly. Next time, if he survives the beating he gets, he certainly will not survive the hulks. No man, woman or child on this estate – my estate' – he emphasized the pronoun very slightly, the drawl back in his voice – 'will flout my will or the law with impunity. Cousin –' He turned to a pale, trembling Anne, her face tear-streaked, and smiled a little as she trembled from him. 'I'd be dashed grateful if you'd conduct me back to that excellent madeira?'

Cook it was who, infinitely gently and with a face like thunder, tended Matt. Kitty hovered about her as she bathed and poulticed the bloody mess that was the lad's back, whilst Matt's breath hissed through clenched teeth and the look in his eye promised murder and worse. When Cook had finished and gone back to the kitchen Kitty sat with her brother through the night, soothing the boy as best she could as he swung through childish, pain-filled sobs to outraged protestations at the injustice he had been dealt. 'It was a game – tha'ss all – a game – I was going to give it all back – I was!'

Kitty, gently, shook her head. 'Matt – Matt! How many times must you be told? Thieving is never a game.' And then, later, 'You should not have taken the coin. Will you tell me you were going to give that back too?'

Her brother, biting his swollen lip, turned his head away.

At last, with the dawn, he slept. But Kitty could not. She sat with him as the pearl-light of daybreak gave way to the bright sword-stroke of the rising sun. She was exhausted, her body aching as if she too had been beaten. Stiff and sore she struggled to her feet, flinching. The sky beyond the window was infinitely clear, the air sparkling fresh. The rising sun glittered dazzlingly upon the moving waters, as if nothing but good could exist in the world.

She walked a little-frequented track to the beach, not wanting to see anyone, not wanting to be seen. She had never, she realized, hated anyone before. But now as she thought of Sir Percival and his henchmen – yes, and the whispers of Imogen Alexander – hate curdled in her like sickness. What in the name of God was to become of them all in the charge of such people?

She almost fell over Anne, huddled in that very spot for which she herself had been making, the sheltered place in the lee of a ruined sea wall that had been their refuge in times of stress all their shared childhood. The sea crashed, cold and foam-laced, gleaming with light, a few yards from them. With no words Kitty dropped to the chill, tide-damp shingle beside the other girl, buried her fingers in the tumbling stones, feeling their wet smoothness against her skin.

With an obvious effort Anne roused herself at last. 'How's Matt?'

'In pain. But he's sleeping now.'

Anne looked bleakly into the shining distance. 'You must both come with me,' she said at last. 'You and Matt. We can't leave him here.'

Kitty looked at her, too tired to question. Anne's fair hair was disordered by the wind, her thin face that had been so plump and pretty, but that looked now like a waif's, was tear-marked. For the first time it occurred to Kitty that here was something other than Matt's trouble. 'What is it?'

'I'm to marry Mr Winthrop,' Anne said, tonelessly. 'As soon as may be. My – cousin' – she spoke the word bitterly – 'is assured that it is an excellent match.'

'What does he know of it? He only arrived a day since?'

Anne turned sadly weary eyes upon her. 'What did he know of Matt?'

Kitty, in her mind's eye, saw a smooth, bent head, pursed busy lips. 'Miss Alexander.'

'Of course. She is set upon making herself indispensable to our new master.'

'Well in that,' Kitty said with bleak satisfaction, 'she'll be disappointed. He'll use her and discard her –'

'– as he is discarding me. Oh, Kitty – he is worse, far worse, than we ever imagined he could be –' She bent her head in silence for a moment, fighting tears. Then: 'We'll leave,' she said, suddenly firm. 'You and I and Matt. We'll go together. Mr Winthrop is a kindly man. He will care for us.' There was a small silence. 'Kitty – you will stay with me? You always promised –' An urgency that was close to desperation threaded her voice.

Kitty nodded dispiritedly. 'Of course.'

They sat together in the sea-washed morning silence for a very long time. 'Do you know,' Anne said at last in a voice so low that Kitty could hardly hear it, 'that I have nothing now? Not a single penny, to take to Mr Winthrop. Cousin Percy says I am a pretty encumbrance he has inherited with the house. He says he cannot afford to dower me, as Father would have. He has – gambling debts, I believe –' She stopped, a catch in her voice. 'Oh – Kitty! – what if Mr Winthrop won't take me now – dowerless, penniless! What will become of us then?'

Kitty reached a comforting hand to hers, but said nothing.

2

In the event Mr Winthrop took a worryingly – not to say
unflatteringly – long time to decide that a dowerless and
orphaned Anne was as desirable a bride as he had found her
such a short while earlier. Whilst poor Anne drooped and
wept and huddled within her rooms in the changed house
that had for all her lifetime been her home, the old man
hemmed and hawed and prevaricated until it came to an
exasperated Kitty that she would like nothing so much as
to bang his head upon his own mounting block. Was it not
true that a bare three months before his heart had apparently
been set upon the girl? Yet now, given a chance to rescue
her from a situation that daily became more intolerable he
hesitated and hedged, talking of a decent time to consider
and to mourn, of changed circumstances and unforeseen
difficulties. Kitty found herself wondering, perhaps
uncharitably, if he were not hunting swiftly about the
district to discover if there were not some other girl on offer
whose father had not so inconsiderately died and left her
penniless.

'He will not take me,' Anne wept, disconsolate, 'he will
not! And then – what shall I do?'

'Nonsense. Of course he will. And – even if not – Mr
Winthrop isn't the only man in the world.' Kitty threw
back the curtains that Anne would have her leave draped,
cave-like across the windows. 'Why must you tie your hopes
to his coat-tails? Why, just a few weeks since – oh, Anne,
Anne, please – don't cry again. You have to stop. You really
must –'

But, at first, she could not. And small wonder, Kitty

sometimes thought, for all her bracing words, seeing the changes that had come so shockingly unheralded into her life and her circumstances.

Sir Percival Bowyer did not like Westwood Grange, and he made no effort whatsoever to disguise the fact. He did not like the rambling, old-fashioned house, its situation or the responsibilities that it brought. However, for reasons that were never made entirely clear but which were endlessly discussed in the servants' hall, always to his detriment, he and his appalling little dog were clearly determined upon making their home there – any hole, as Cook liked darkly to point out, being welcome to a hunted fox.

The quiet life of a Suffolk country gentleman was not, however, in the least to Sir Percival's tastes, and he went out of his way to ensure that he need not live it. Unable, under the same quirk of law that had caused him to inherit, to sell the place, he set determinedly about filling it with as many of his London cronies as he could entice for any length of time away from the drinking dens and gaming tables of town. To begin with he was fairly successful in this – a success that had its roots first in his guests' curiosity, secondly and perhaps more importantly in their eager willingness to live in some style for nothing, and thirdly in the weather. August and September were dry, warm months, mellow and beautiful, and the roads, if dusty, were easily passable. Week after week the house was full, riotous till long after midnight and dead till noon.

The estate, for this time at least, more or less ran itself, the year's planning and care already lavished and bearing fruit, the harvest good. As to next year – men of cottage and farm shook their heads. Time would tell but they had no great hopes. Sir Percival in his management veered characteristically from despotic decree to undisguised and short-tempered disinterest. He wanted his rents and his profits; he knew nothing and cared less about the efforts that needed to be made to secure them.

Day after day, week upon week, there seemed to Kitty to be a constant and dizzying coming and going in the courtyard that had once rung so rarely with any undue excitement: arrivals and departures of strange guests, with their valets and servants (who always managed, she noticed, to make themselves scarce if there were extra household tasks to attend to); strange horses in the stables. The servants grumbled, Sir Percy, uncaring, issued more invitations and Anne continued to wilt like a cut flower. Within a week the cellars were emptied and the call sent out for more – a call that was readily answered by those who had already marked out the new owner of the Grange as a likely customer for their night-run goods. Remembering Matt's beating, Kitty found herself reflecting bitterly more than once upon the gentry's interpretation of honesty as spirits and tobacco were welcomed to the cellars of the Grange, as well as bolts of silk for the ladies, a surprising number of whom braved the journey to the wilds of Suffolk to join the exiled Sir Percival and aid him in his efforts to spend his unexpected inheritance.

'The goings-on in this house,' Cook said one day, heavily, 'are no less than a scandal. With Sir George an' those poor lads barely cold in their graves –'

'Mrs Roberts.' Imogen Alexander's voice from the doorway was sharp and acid with sarcasm. 'When you are ready – some of Sir Percival's guests are in the breakfast room. Waiting – dare I say it? – for their breakfast.'

'Breakfast, is it?' Cook, one of the few in the house in no way in awe of the governess who, insidiously and in the absence of a mistress's hand, had taken over the role of housekeeper, swung ponderously upon her. 'Breakfast? At twelve noon? And where? Where is this – breakfast room?' She invested the last two words with a world of scorn.

Ruby giggled.

Miss Alexander quelled the girl with a glance. 'The breakfast room, Mrs Roberts, as you well know, is –'

'At the top of the stairs where the parlour used to be. An' where the parlour still is, as far as I'm concerned. Seems to me that did Sir Percy say so some of us'd be callin' cats dogs –'

Tight-lipped, Imogen Alexander left. Muttered words that sounded remarkably like 'stuck-up madam' followed her none too quietly to the door.

'I doan' know 'oo that woman do think she is –' Cook attacked her risen bread dough with fierce hands.

Kitty, come to the kitchen for a dish of soup to tempt Anne's failed appetite, tossed the straight, heavy hair from her eyes and swung the weighty saucepan onto the stove. 'She hopes, I think, that if – when – Miss Anne leaves Sir Percy will keep her on as housekeeper.'

Cook lifted her head. 'An' is there word of that?'

Kitty shook her head.

Cook sighed. 'Poor lamb. Who'd ha' thought – Oh, Ruby! Fir pity's sake, child! What ha' you done now?'

Poor Ruby, always clumsy but worse if hurried, had dropped on the flagstoned floor the great silver dish into which Beth, Cook's assistant, had been about to deposit the breakfast kidneys she had been frying. At Cook's angry tone Ruby flinched, picking up the dish with shaking hands.

Cook's own hands, flour-white, were lifted in despair. 'If you can't hold the blessed thing empty what in Heaven's name will you do with it full? Where's Thomas?'

Ruby, a frail, nervous girl, always easily cowed, blinked back tears. ''E's bin called away. Summat for Sir Percival. An' them others – them visitors – they're nowhere to be found. There's on'y me. An' Beth.'

'Well, I in't servin'.' Beth, a large, phlegmatic young woman with a round face and wispy fair hair, turned back with unshakable determination to the stove. 'I got enough ter do 'ere, an tha'ss a fact.'

Kitty smiled reassuringly at the trembling Ruby. 'I'll help. The soup isn't ready yet. Perhaps when it is Beth would run some upstairs to Miss Anne. Here – let me help with that dish.'

The parlour – now designated the breakfast room, furnished as such and the scene most days of a leisurely meal that might commence at any time between eleven and noon when the first yawning guests appeared and that could after a particularly energetic night go on to two or three in the afternoon – was almost empty. Kitty and the relentlessly nervous Ruby transferred vast dishes of bacon, kidneys, sausages and cold meats from the trolley to the side-tables beneath the window. Enormous baskets of bread and rolls and a great slab of fresh-churned butter joined them. Beyond the ancient, rippled glass of the window the day had turned grey and windy; heavy clouds billowed above the distant, white-capped water and seabirds hovered, beating against a gusting wind that was the early harbinger of winter. Ruby dropped a knife with a great clatter, sucked her bottom lip in a terror she seemed totally incapable of controlling.

'Let me.' Gently Kitty took the enormous silver teapot from the girl's shaking hands. 'You put the napkins on the table.'

Two young men, one dark as the other was fair and both of whom might from their dress and mannerisms have stepped from the self-same bandbox as Sir Percival himself, stood by the fireplace conversing loudly, ignoring the two girls as they would ignore the presence of any servant. A third – a long-legged, languidly handsome young man with soft, floppy hair and a dissolute face – slouched alone in an armchair. In contrast to his companions', his eyes, their expression unreadable, flickered once or twice from Kitty to Ruby, then remained on the nervous girl, speculative and unpleasant.

'– just a bit of a setback, that's all. The damned Yankees can't possibly win. The South's is a gentlemen's army. They cannot be beaten. They've got the officers, d'you see? And the officers have the devotion of their men. It can only be a matter of time. There's no question of that.'

'Well – Pa says we need the cotton. And jolly little of it's getting through –'

'It will, it will. Mark my words. The North can't win. Damned rabble of Republicans and freed niggers. Don't stand a chance.'

'I just hope you're right.' The fair young man was gloomy. 'I only know that at the moment we're losing money hand over fist, and Pa's talking about cutting my allowance –'

'God forbid,' said the languid young man from his arm-chair, his eyes still on Ruby. 'What happens to my profits at the card table if your Pa cuts your allowance?'

'You certainly cleaned me out again last night.' The words were rueful, but not particularly resentful, rather a comment upon an unfortunate and recurring Act of God, like rain-storms or colds in the head.

Kitty set the tea things upon a small table.

The dark young man stirred, pushed himself away from the mantelshelf where he had been leaning and regarded the food with growing interest. 'What do you think, Archie? About the war in America?'

The young man who sprawled in the armchair shrugged. He was still watching Ruby, quite openly. The girl was awkwardly and untidily attempting to fold a pile of napkins and set them upon the table. Aware of his unblinking regard the poor girl was almost paralysed with nerves. The young man smiled unpleasantly. 'The best thing that could happen so far as I see it,' he said lazily, 'is for the whole damned bunch of them to wipe each other out. What are they after all? Damned bunch of rebel colonials got too big for their boots – eh, my pet?' With a movement that was remarkably quick he reached for Ruby, his fingers closed about her narrow wrist and he pulled her to him.

She stood by his chair, trembling and silent, poppy colour in her small, childishly pretty face.

'Well?'

'I'm – I'm sure I don't know, sir.' The words were barely audible.

He laughed. 'Oi'm sure Oi doan' know, sor,' he mimicked.

The room had fallen silent. Very carefully and very quietly Kitty laid the plate she held on the table.

'Why don't you know, girl? Come to that – what don't you know? Or – what do you know?'

'Lay off, Archie. You're still drunk.' The dark man grinned, a little uncomfortably.

Archie considered that for a moment. 'Very probably true,'

he conceded at last, reasonably, 'but then, for Christ's sake what else is there to be in this most tedious of worlds?' His smile did not reach his jaded eyes. His hand was still locked about Ruby's thin wrist. Half-heartedly, and with a panic-stricken look at Kitty, the girl chose that moment to try to break away from him. The young man's long fingers tightened, and the girl let out a small cry of pain. He looked up at her with a small, fierce smile. 'So, come then, my pretty. What *do* you know? Eh?'

Ruby stood as if struck utterly dumb.

'Great God.' Archie's voice was suddenly ferocious with disgust. 'What a bloody place, eh? Even the bloody servant girls won't bloody fight back. It's the bloody end of the bloody world, that's what. No wonder poor bloody Percy's bloody pissed all the time.'

'Easy now, Archie –'

Kitty stepped forward. 'May I offer you tea, sir? Or chocolate, perhaps? Or there's ale in the pitcher, if you'd prefer, nice and cold?' Her voice was steady and cool; she kept her eyes levelly upon his, not bothering to veil the contempt in her own. 'Cook recommends the kidneys. Though I think you may find the bacon more to your taste.' She paused for a moment, then found herself adding with cool, utterly insulting emphasis, 'We've kept pigs for many years at the Grange –' But none as contemptible as you. The words, unspoken, hung in the air, ringing in the ears like a bell.

For a long moment the young man neither spoke nor moved. Then, very suddenly, he let go of Ruby's wrist so unexpectedly that in her fright she almost fell. She took several small, stumbling steps backwards, then stood, lost and indecisive, clasping her bruised wrist in her other hand, trembling visibly.

'Sir?' Kitty asked, softly.

'Get the hell out of here,' the young man said, tonelessly. 'We'll serve ourselves.'

'Yes, sir.' She signalled to Ruby with an almost imperceptible movement of her head, then turned to follow the girl from the room. As she did so Sir Percival, a yapping Barnabas at his heels, a chattering, overdressed young woman on each arm, entered the room.

'Wait, girl.'

Kitty froze. At the harsh words all conversation died. The focus of all eyes, despite herself she felt colour rise in her cheeks. Composedly she turned. 'Yes, sir?'

'Your name.'

'Daniels, sir. Katherine Daniels.' She spoke very clearly.

He held her eyes for a long moment.

'What's this?' Frowning, Sir Percival stepped forward. 'Is something wrong? Archie?'

Archie half-smiled, the threat in his eyes only for Kitty. 'Nothing, Percy old fellow. Nothing, that is' – his voice was very quiet – 'that I can't handle myself.'

Kitty, with iron will, controlled her shaking knees and left the room with creditable composure.

Angry though she was, she could not pretend that the undisguised animosity her own rashness had prompted from her master's guest had not frightened her a little. For two days she stayed out of the main house as much as she could, spending her time in the old nursery quarters on the top floor of the east wing, where Anne had now taken up more or less permanent residence. On the third day she visited her brother in his room above the stable. His back was healed – he had apparently recovered all his spirits with his health and was the same easy-laughing, feckless lad she had always known. Yet sometimes, when she saw his dark eyes fixed upon Sir Percival Bowyer's pale, delicate face, she suspected that the scars that her brother would always bear upon his back were not the only ones he carried. Sir Percival, on the other hand, seemed to have forgotten the whole incident – or perhaps it was that he was so assured of having established his mastery over the boy, and over the whole household, that he saw no need to reinforce it. He used the lad, much as Sir George had, to run errands and to help in the house, and even – so confident was he of a lesson learned – to wait upon those of his friends who had not brought with them their own servant.

'Quite a gentleman's gentleman I'm becoming.' Matt's voice was mocking, his smile subversive. 'See what a good boy I can be when I try?'

Kitty sighed. She mistrusted her brother in this mood.

He grinned at her. 'Well, cheer up. There's no call to look as if you'd lost tuppence and found a ha'penny.'

'It isn't what I might find that bothers me,' she retorted, grimly.

He lifted a shoulder, smiled his blithe, derisive smile. 'I'm sure I don't know what you mean, moi owd gel. Why – Mr Archibald Alliston gave me a shilling before he left – a whole silver shilling –' She could not tell at whom or at what his mockery was directed. 'Why should I thieve if I can get it for nothing?'

'Why indeed?' The name was slow in registering in Kitty's mind. She looked up, sharply. 'Archibald Alliston? Is that the young man they call Archie? – Tall, with fair hair that falls over his face?'

'That's the one.'

'He's gone?'

'Yesterday. Said he couldn't stand the place a moment longer, not even for the easy pickings at the tables. He's a fly one, that one.' There was a glint of admiration in the boy's eyes.

Kitty was herself surprised at how strong was the lift of relief she experienced at the news. She had not, remembering the look in Archibald Alliston's eyes, expected to be let off so easily. She stood up. The October wind swirled around the stable eaves, plucked the leaves from the overhanging trees, rippled the puddles left by two long days of rain. She stretched. 'The sky's clearing. Come for a walk with me, down by the sea – I've been cooped up for days –'

Two days later, at last, Mr Winthrop made up his mind. Out of the goodness of his heart and in memory of her dear dead Papa, he would take Anne, dowry or no dowry. The decision taken, he felt that it should be implemented as soon as might be considered decent and he suggested that a very quiet New Year's wedding would be appropriate.

Anne, upon hearing the news, burst into inevitable tears.

'Come, now, Anne my dear,' Miss Alexander said, lightly unfeeling, patting her hand. 'I know what very happy news this is for you. But do, my dear, try to contain your emotion –'

Anne's sobs redoubled.

Kitty, with nice restraint, held her tongue.

(ii)

As if the prospect of Christmas and a wedding – however quiet – were not enough to set the house upon its heels Sir Percival, venomously bored by the closing in of an early winter, decided upon a birthday party; his own, and that at the beginning of December.

'But – surely – no one will come?' Anne, surprisingly, had recovered her spirits somewhat. With a natural optimism that was, after the shock of the loss of her family, at last reasserting itself, she had come philosophically to believe that life as Mrs Winthrop might not be so terrible after all. She would be financially secure, virtually her own mistress, and it had been agreed that her beloved Kitty might accompany her to her new home. They would be free at last of the detested Miss Alexander, and – as Anne herself pointed out, an echo of the old, mischievous laughter in her voice – the ancient Mr Winthrop could not last for ever. Now she sat before her mirror, whilst Kitty brushed the loosened fair hair that clouded her shoulders. Outside a banshee wind howled bitterly, and the distant sea crashed. 'I mean – none of his London friends have been near nor by for weeks. They won't come at this time of the year, surely?'

Kitty shrugged. 'Who knows? All I know is that he – and that horrible dog of his – have been in the foulest of tempers lately. If having this blessed party cures that I'd be willing to put up with the whole of London coming!'

Anne giggled, then sobered. 'Oh, Kitty – I can't wait for us to get away from this place. Mr Winthrop isn't so bad.

He's kind, I'm sure. He'll be nice to us. And we'll have a place of our own again —'

Kitty half-smiled at the other girl's reflection in the candle-lit mirror, but said nothing. She knew Anne to be totally oblivious to the irritation that her easy use of the plural pronouns 'we' and 'us' could cause. The thought that Kitty might have separate needs and aspirations of her own rarely if ever occurred to her. Kitty continued with long, smooth strokes of the brush.

Of course it did not. Why should it?

Surprisingly — or perhaps not, considering the elaborate and luxurious provision that Sir Percival promised for his guests' comfort and delectation — many of his London cronies, perhaps diverted by the novel thought of a winter's weekend in the country, did accept his invitation.

Once again the Grange came to frantic life. There was linen to be found, rooms to be cleaned, beds to be aired and made up. There were stores to be laid in, food to be cooked, ale to be brewed. More Free Trade tubs rolled down the steps of the cellar. The farms and stables of the estate were raided for feed and space for the horses. Kitty found herself, like the rest of the household, run off her feet, ordered hither and yon by Miss Alexander, by Cook, by Anne herself. As the first guests began to arrive she joined the army of servants scurrying up and down stairs, along corridors, into almost forgotten parts of the old house, carrying coal, water, warming pans, bed-linen.

'It isn't fair!' Anne protested. 'You aren't a servant!'

'Of course I am. And I don't mind.'

Anne did not even pause for breath: '— And anyway, I need you here to do my hair.'

Kitty suppressed a smile. 'Don't worry. I'll be back later.'

Hurrying along an ill-lit passage in the east wing of the house, she almost cannoned into her brother. 'Matt! You startled me!' And then, sharply, 'What are you doing here?'

If he noticed the tone he gave no sign. 'The same as you. What a to-do, eh?' He grinned his wide, warm smile. In the last couple of months he had grown, was now, she realized suddenly, almost as tall as she was. 'Can't stop. See you at supper –'

Dinner was served to a dozen that night, and more guests were to arrive the next day, the day before the party itself. Whilst Anne and her cousin dined by candlelight in the Great Hall, Kitty was kept busy all evening helping a girl who had been brought in from the village to prepare more bedrooms. The long corridors of the east wing were dimly lit, and the candles set at intervals in sconces upon the walls guttered and danced in the chill draughts that crept through doors and windows and scurried like imps of winter through the darkness. Some blew out altogether. The bedrooms were lit by oil lamps which, long unused, flickered and smoked, sending elongated shadows dancing about the walls and bedcurtains.

'I doan' like this.' Rosie, the village girl, shook her head dolefully. 'I doan' like it one bit. Creepy, i'n't it? Fancy sleepin' 'ere!'

Kitty laughed a little, shook her head. 'You get used to it. Here – take the other side of the sheet. We'll make the bed quicker together. Did you bring the kindling for the fire?'

The girl shook a phlegmatic head. 'No one said nuthin' about no kindlin'.'

'Oh – well, all right – I'll make the bed alone. You pop downstairs for the wood –'

'What? All the way down there on me own? Not likely! I'm not goin' down them dark owd stairs on me own!'

'For goodness' sake!' Exasperated, Kitty regarded her, hands upon hips. She was tired now, and anxious to be done. Her back ached and her feet were sore. 'All right. You do the bed. I'll fetch the kindling.'

She sped down the dark passage. Halfway along, a door stood open. A shadow flickered in the splash of light. She had collided with the figure who emerged from the room as she passed before she could stop herself. Long-fingered hands caught and steadied her. 'I'm sorry, sir!' she gasped. 'It was my fault. I –' She stopped.

'Well, well, well.' The words were drawled. She looked into eyes that showed recollection and a spark of dislike, and her heart sank. 'Daniels,' he said.

'Y-yes, sir.' She had not expected to see him, had not heard his name mentioned, though she had found herself warily listening for it.

'What – Daniels?' Archie Alliston asked, softly, 'I have forgotten.'

Her mouth was dry. Something about the man, an unreasoning and capricious malice, terrified her. 'Katherine, sir.' She tried to keep her voice steady, despised herself for its trembling.

'And how old are you, Katherine Daniels?' His voice was still deceptively gentle.

'Seventeen, sir.'

'Seventeen.' He appeared to consider. 'Old enough,' he suggested softly, 'to have learned manners towards your betters?'

'Yes, sir.' She did not look at him.

He shook his head sorrowfully. 'But, no, sir,' he said. 'No, sir indeed.' He stepped back from the doorway. 'Well, Katherine Daniels, I have a job for you.'

'I'm – I'm already –'

'Yes?' His voice was cold.

Numbly she preceded him through the door. A small, battered trunk lay open upon the bed. Clothes were strewn untidily about the room, upon the bed, upon the chairs, upon the floor. 'Clear this up,' he said, pleasantly.

She hesitated, anger stirring, then seeing the expectation in his eyes, knowing with what pleasure he would report her insubordination to his host, she let prudence still rebellion. 'Yes, sir.'

He seated himself in an armchair near the fire, watched her with an unblinking stare that unnerved her as it had Ruby. But she did not – would not – let it disconcert her as Ruby had. Swiftly and neatly she picked up the clothes, folded them and stowed them in drawers and in the old-fashioned clothes press. When she had finished she stood before him, hands folded. The nagging ache in her back had developed into a stabbing pain. 'May I go now, sir?'

He got up, walked to the bed, reached into the trunk and took out a small box, which he upended. A shower of small items – a watch and chain, cufflinks, tie pins, collar studs – fell onto the counterpane. 'You haven't finished.'

She bit her tongue. Voices sounded beyond the door, then died. Tiredly she collected the things from the bed and put them in their appointed places on the dressing table. Then she stood silent, waiting. She was exhausted. She wanted nothing but to get away from this disturbing, undisguisedly vindictive young man. For God's sake what, after all, had she done that merited such malice – that could be the root of the cruel dislike she saw quite openly upon his face when he looked at her?

'Sullen,' he said, thoughtfully, eyeing her. 'Not all that much to look at either.' Insultingly his gaze travelled from the dusty hem of her skirt to her angry eyes. 'Pity.'

'May I go now, sir?' Despite her every effort her voice was threaded with fury.

He yawned affectedly. 'Go by all means. Go to the devil for all I care.'

She turned thankfully from him.

'But first,' said the young man to whom any show of independence in a woman offered personal insult, 'an apology.'

She stopped.

'I fear I left last time before you could make one. I'm sure you're ready to rectify that omission now?'

Her head went up. In the silence the fire crackled fiercely.

'Daniels!'

She did not speak.

'An apology.'

Her anger was ice-cold. She turned, eyed him levelly, knowing what she did, unable to prevent herself. 'An apology, Mr Alliston?'

'Yes.'

'No.' She saw the shock in his eyes, the unstable colour

that rose in his fair skin. She stepped forward, her diction
everything that Anne had ever taught her. 'I am no chamber-
maid, Mr Alliston, whatever you may think, to be bullied
and persecuted by you. I am Miss Anne Bowyer's companion
and personal maid.' She saw a flicker of disbelief in his eyes,
pressed on, the flame of fury crackling in her voice. 'And I
doubt that she would find it amusing that I should be treated
so by one of her own cousin's guests.' Stop it! a voice was
shrieking in her head. Why antagonize him further? 'You
talk of my learning manners towards my betters? May I
suggest, sir, that you could do with a few lessons yourself?'
She stopped then, knowing she had gone too far.

'Get out,' he said at last, his voice steel-hard.

She closed the door behind her very, very quietly.

He made her life a misery. No matter how she tried to keep
out of his way he was there, picking and carping, goading
her from behind cold eyes. She dismissed any thought of
going to Anne; it would be a needless worry to the girl, and
anyway there would be nothing she could do about it. She
did not even consider going to Sir Percival. There was
nothing for it but to hold her temper and her nerve, not to
allow Alliston his obvious design of her retaliation and
consequent disgrace. She set herself to take his slights and
veiled insults with a composure that, had she but realized
it, simply goaded him to further extremes. He had found a
pastime to ease the tedium between one gaming table and
the next: he would not easily relinquish it. She comforted
herself with the thought that he could not be here for long
– after the party he must surely tire of the futile game and
leave?

The day of the party dawned unexpectedly clear and
bright. The winter sun, low in the sky, dazzled the eye, and
the wind cut in from the sea like a knife. The household
was awake and about its business long before daybreak. By
midday Kitty felt as if she had already done two full days'
labour. Later in the afternoon she and Anne were dragooned
by Miss Alexander into helping with the decorations of the

Great Hall. Huge swags of greenery had been brought in from the woods, colourful paper flags were heaped haphazardly upon the floor. At the far end of the hall, beneath the gallery, estate carpenters were at work erecting a sham tower, complete with turrets.

'What on earth is that?'

Anne was agog with excitement. 'It seems that Cousin Percival saw a mock medieval tournament last summer. At the Cremorne Gardens. Tonight is to be –'

'– a mock mock tournament?' Kitty suggested with raised brows.

Anne, in exasperation that was not altogether feigned, slapped her arm lightly. 'Oh, don't be so tiresome! I think it might all be quite fun.'

Kitty did not allow herself to dwell upon the indecorum of such celebrations in a house whose last master was barely six months dead. If Anne chose to drown her grief in gaiety, no matter how tasteless, why question it? 'It should certainly be interesting.' She bent to pick up an armful of greenery. 'What are we supposed to do with this?'

'Some of it's to hang from the gallery. The rest is to be put in the window embrasures, so – to make it look like a woodland bower, you see?'

Kitty eyed the tall embrasure doubtfully. 'The gallery I don't mind. But I don't see why either of us should risk breaking our necks for Precious Percy.'

Anne giggled a little at the open use of their private nickname for her cousin. 'Why don't we get Matt to help? I saw him a little while ago –'

Kitty glanced round. Her brother was nowhere to be seen. 'Good idea. I'll get him.'

'Off you go then.' Arms laden with greenstuff, Anne started to ascend the stairs of the gallery. 'I'll start up here.'

Kitty hurried across the courtyard to the stables. The air was brilliant with cold, the lowering sun stark and red as blood in the bare branches of the trees. She stopped for a moment, watched as a flight of sea birds carved its way through the lucent winter sky. She started up the wooden steps that led up the outside wall of the stable building to her brother's little room. Ahead of her a robin sat upon the handrail, head cocked, watching her interestedly. She stopped, smiling. Took one more careful step. The robin hopped companionably ahead of her. Not wanting to startle it she moved quietly up another couple of steps. It perched upon the rail outside the door and twittered at her. Still smiling she slowly climbed the rest of the stairs. It did not move. It was still sitting there on the rail when she quietly opened the door.

Her brother's startled recoil as he flung round to face her screamed guilt with no word spoken. She stared at him. He had been standing at an open drawer of a battered washstand that stood beneath the skylight window. Guilt invested every line of his face and his body as he stood there, his hands clenched upon something that glinted in the sun-reddened light that fell through the window above him.

'What have you got there?' A lifetime's experience of her brother and his flawed talent embittered her voice.

He stepped back from her, put his hand behind his back. She walked to him, hand outstretched. 'Show me.'

He stood like a statue. His lean, slant-eyed face, so much like her own, and usually constantly on the brink of a smile, carried an expression of defiance that almost stopped her heart with dread. Not again. Surely not?

'Show me,' she said again.

'It's nothing to do with you.'

'And I suspect,' she said, tiredly, 'that it has — or should have — equally little to do with you. Show me.'

The authority of years told. Very slowly he brought his hand from behind his back. Something warm and smooth and heavy dropped into her extended palm. She looked, aghast, cold with shock.

The watch ticked quietly, the soft gold of its case glowed in the light of the sunset. She had seen it before. She lifted her head.

He looked away from the blaze of her eyes. 'He'll never

know I took it! He's drunk as seven lords already, and likely to stay so for days! He'll just think he's lost it –'

The crack of her hand upon his cheek was like the shot of a pistol. He stared at her, the imprint of the blow glowing like fire against the whitening face.

'What else?' she asked, quietly, and then, as he neither moved nor spoke, '*What else, I say?*' she screamed.

Sullenly he stepped back. She looked into the drawer. Cufflinks. A tie pin. Pearl studs. 'Great God,' she said, bitterly. 'You fool. You stupid – selfish – thieving – fool!'

His set mouth did not move, and yet he flinched, as if she had struck him again.

'Why him?' she asked. 'Why – of all of them – him?'

'I've been – looking after him –' he muttered. 'He has no servant of his own. Kit –' He looked at her, suddenly pleading, his face appallingly vulnerable, appallingly young. 'I swear he don't know he's got half this stuff! He wins it at the tables. An' – he leaves it about all over the place! I couldn't help myself. I swear it!'

She felt, all at once, as if every vestige of strength had left her. She sat down, very hard, upon the straw mattress of the slatted bed. The watch still ticked in her hand. 'We have to put them back. Now. Before he discovers they're missing.'

'No!'

'Yes!'

They stared at one another. Matt's eyes slid from hers.

Feverishly Kitty started to gather the trinkets from the washstand. 'You go over to the house: Anne wants your help in the hall. Tell her – tell her I've gone to see Cook about something.' She pulled her kerchief from about her neck, tumbled the things into it and tied a firm knot.

'No,' he said, quieter this time.

She glared at him.

'If –' he swallowed, '– if anyone's to take them back, it should be me.'

She surveyed him for a long, cold moment. Then, 'Yes,' she said, 'it should. But I can't trust you, can I? If you got your thieving hands on these things again God only knows what you'd do.' She picked up the kerchief. 'Now – hurry.'

She walked up the small staircase that led to the east wing bedrooms openly, kerchief swinging in her hand. Who, after all, would think to question her? There was no danger.

Stoically she ignored the frantic fluttering of her heart.

Outside Archie Alliston's room she paused, listening. All was quiet. Firmly she put a hand to the knob. There was no danger. She had every reason to be here. The fire to be laid. The bed to be turned down. There was no danger.

She pushed the door. It swung open.

The room was empty.

The pounding of her heart eased. She ran to the bed, pushing the door closed behind her as she went, hearing the latch click as it caught. She dropped the kerchief on the bed, fumbled with the knot. Chinking musically, watch and jewellery tumbled onto the counterpane, as they had before. Now; where had she put these things for him when she had unpacked the other day?

'Well. What – have – we – here?'

He was leaning against the door, bottle in hand. Her brain registered numbly that he must have been standing there, by the latticed window, when she entered the room. The opening door had concealed him from her.

She stood like a statue, mouth open, guilt personified.

He walked with drunken care to the bed, stood looking down at the glinting gold and pearl. 'A thief?' he asked at last, thoughtfully and interestedly, and tilted the bottle to his lips.

'No!'

He raised sardonic brows. The smell of brandy hung about him like a cloud.

'That is – I found the things. Found them! I was bringing them back!' Her scattered senses began to collect themselves. He had seen her – must have seen her – enter the room carrying these things. Whatever he might think, or guess, he could not possibly believe or prove that she had stolen them?

'Found them,' he repeated, and let the malicious amusement sound in his voice. 'Indeed?' The bottle tipped again.

'Yes.'

'Where?' The word was like a crack of a whip.

Silence.

'A pretty tale,' he said, his voice quiet again.

'Please – you saw me come in! You *saw* that I was carrying these things – bringing them back – you must have done! You can't pretend to believe I stole them –' She was on the verge of pleading.

'I?' he asked, gently. 'I saw?'

She stared at him in disbelief and fear. 'You know you did,' she whispered.

He said nothing.

She watched him, her heart in her throat. 'But – you will say otherwise?' she said, her tone half-questioning, wholly incredulous.

He lifted the bottle and drank again, deeply.

'But – why? Why would you do such a thing?'

Footsteps were hurrying down the corridor towards them. He walked, leisurely, to the door.

'Why?' she asked again, urgently, as if this one question were the most important in the world.

He opened the door. 'Girl!'

Rosie, hurrying past, stopped in alarm. 'Sir?'

'Fetch Sir Percival here. At once.'

Rosie threw a swift, inquisitive glance towards the white-faced Kitty. 'Yes, sir. At once, sir.'

He closed the door very quietly. Kitty stood as if turned to stone, watching him. 'You can't do this.'

'Oh, but I can.' He paused, smiled. 'I am.' He put the almost empty bottle on the dressing table, turned to face her, his handsome head limned bright against the bloodshot evening sky. 'You ask me why?' He paused. 'Had a man insulted me in front of my friends as you did, I might have thrashed him for it. I might have killed him. I – might – even have laughed. But – eventually – I would have forgiven him.'

'But for God's sake what did I say that was so – ?'

'It was enough!' The words cracked across hers, stopping her protest. 'To be insulted, publicly, by a slip of a girl? Oh, no. That, my dear, is utterly unforgivable.' He shook his head. 'Utterly. You spoke to me of lessons. Here is one you would do well to remember. You may take a man's heart if you can. You may squander his fortune and make three kinds of a fool of him. But you injure his pride at your peril.'

'Pride?' She spat the word, fatal temper rising, 'Pride? And what is pride without honour, Mr Alliston?' She stopped, fighting her fury, cursing her tongue that was in its own way as destructively unruly as her brother's thieving fingers. 'You know I did not steal these things –' she began more quietly.

He lifted a hand. 'Do I? And yet – there you stand, my poor possessions wrapped in your kerchief. What am I sup-posed to believe?'

'I told you,' she said, stubbornly, 'I found them.'

He looked at her steadily. 'And I asked – where?' And, in that instant, as clearly as if he had told her, she saw that he had known. Had known of Matt's weakness. Had known the boy would not be able to resist the temptation of easy pickings. He had hoped to trap her brother to spite her. And, beyond all his hopes it was she who had walked, blindly, into his trap. Her only escape would be to betray her brother. And that she could not do.

Silence hung between them. He waited. She stood stone-faced, saw drunken anger grow in him at her defiance, knew that she was damaging no one but herself with her bravado and was utterly unable to do anything about it.

Footsteps approached, rapidly.

'You speak of pride, Mr Alliston?' she asked, bitterly and softly. 'You don't know the meaning of the word.'

He lied, as she had known he would – as she knew he might not have done, had she held her temper and her tongue. He had come into the room, he said, and found Kitty taking things from the dressing table and hiding them in her ker-chief.

Kitty stood like a statue, saying nothing, looking at no one. What was the point? She was numb with shock.

Sir Percival was outraged. 'So. It runs in the family, does it? What have you to say for yourself?'

She looked, for the first time, directly into Archibald Alliston's eyes and said nothing.

'Dumb insolence won't help you, girl.' Sir Percival turned away. 'Take her to the cellars,' he said to the burly manservant who stood behind him. 'I can't spare anyone to take her to Southwold and the magistrates today. The slut shall not spoil my birthday.' He swung back upon Kitty. 'You learned no lesson, apparently, from what happened to your brother. You'll regret that, believe me. I doubt you'll like the way the magistrates will deal with you.'

Somewhere, distantly, Kitty heard Anne's voice, lifted in distress. Amongst the group of servants who had gathered by the door, attracted by Sir Percival's raised voice and Rosie's quickly-spread news, Matt stood, silent.

So they marched her to the cellars, her arm in the painful grip of the fearsome Collins, in her ears the buzz of voices as the onlookers, scandalized, delighted, whispered of bad blood and long-nursed suspicions.

The last sound she heard before the heavy door was locked and bolted upon her was the sound of Anne's voice – protesting, tearful. The last sight was of Matt's still, white face.

(iii)

She had no light and no protection from the biting cold apart from her everyday woollen dress, which served her ill against the dank and biting chill of her prison. The darkness about her whispered with terrifying life, shifting, scuttling, peering in curiosity and growing boldness at this unexpected intruder. At first, sunk in almost mindless oppression, she hardly noticed her physical discomfort: but before long, despite herself, the miserable cold roused her and she found herself to be shivering uncontrollably.

People had died of cold, so she'd heard. Well, so be it. Perhaps it would be for the best. Anything – even death, at this miserable moment – seemed preferable to the ordeal that she knew awaited her tomorrow.

Something near her moved, squealed as she kicked out at it. Nausea stirred. She had always hated rats.

With eyes that had grown accustomed to the darkness she looked around. Stout kegs and barrels, the night-run goods upon which Sir Percival and his cronies dined so well each night surrounded her. Afraid of the rats and the tangle of her long skirts she pulled herself to her feet, then scrambled up onto one of the barrels, tucking her feet beneath her, wrapping her skirt tightly about her legs and ankles. Though not comfortable, at least it gave some security. She sat in a stupor of cold and misery. Her brain seemed to have ceased to function altogether.

She sat so for an age. Above her, faintly, she heard the sound of music. It roused her a little. She moved her cramped limbs, rubbed her hands, wincing at the pain. How could it be – how could it? – that she, Kitty Daniels, should be huddled here, bereft, deserted, accused and with no reasonable defence, whilst above her strangers danced and celebrated as if there were no such thing as care in the world?

She wrapped her arms about her cold body. For the first time she felt the rise of tears.

'But I tell you – I insist –' the raised voice came from beyond the door – 'you know who I am. You cannot – shall not – deny me access to my own cellars.'

'I'm sorry, Miss, but you're wasting your breath. The master's instructions were –'

'I don't give a pin for his instructions!' Anne was doing her best, but even muffled as her voice was Kitty could hear that her attempted forcefulness was a pitiful failure. Timid tears sounded all at once in her voice. 'I – I insist that y-you l-let me speak to Kitty.'

Kitty clambered from the keg, and barking knees and elbow painfully in her haste, scrambled up the steps to the door. 'Anne?'

There was a moment's silence. 'Kitty! Oh, Kitty!' There was movement beyond the door, a banging upon the wood, and then a sharp, outraged exclamation. 'Let me go! How dare you!'

'Master's orders, Miss. No one – absolutely no one – to see or speak to the girl till morning. Now – you can run along like a good girl, or I can call someone down here to carry you. Which is it to be?' The man's voice was grim and brooked no argument.

'Kitty! Kitty – they won't let me see you! But – Kitty – I know you didn't – all right! – I'm going –' Anne's voice faded to silence.

Kitty stood for a long, lonely moment, leaning against the door, her forehead pressed hard against the ancient wood. It was a nightmare. It must be. None of this could possibly be truly happening –

At last she pushed herself away from the door, made her way back to the barrel, settling herself once more. Her head ached with terror and defeat. What would they do to her? What?

She huddled into herself, resting her forehead upon her drawn-up knees. The cold, perhaps mercifully, was dulling her senses, quelling her power to think, deadening even her fear a little. She closed her eyes, and for the first time since the confrontation with her brother that afternoon she allowed the tears to slide, cold and desolate, down her cheeks. It was a long, long time before they stopped.

The sound that roused her brought her heart to her mouth and, cold as she was, the sweat of fear to her forehead. She lifted her head, listening, ears straining. The party in the house above her was now in full swing – thumping feet, the sound of music, raised voices, laughter. Then through it all she heard it again – a harsh, grating noise, very close. The sound of breathing. Someone – something – moving in the darkness.

She felt a scream gather in her throat, and the rise of hysteria blocked her breath. She opened her mouth. Then – a glimmer of light, her whispered name.

'Kitty? Kit — where the devil are you?'

'Matt? Oh — Matt!' Trembling violently she threw her arms about the figure of her brother that had moved to her side, sobbing incoherently.

'Hey, steady now. Steady, moi owd gal. The guard will hear —'

With an enormous effort she calmed herself. They spoke on a breath, barely audibly.

'How did you get in?'

She sensed his grin in the darkness. 'The same way you're goin' to get out, owd gal. Sir Percy ain't the only one to like a bit o' the old duty free grog. There's more ways than one in an' out of here. Take my hand. Tha'ss right. Now — come on —'

Heart beating like a blacksmith's hammer she followed him through the darkness and along a vaulted tunnel to another, smaller cellar.

'There.'

A faint rectangle of light, glimmering with frosty winter stars, hung in the darkness above her head.

'Climb up here. Hurry now. We got to be well away from here by first light.'

Away. Strangely, the thought jolted her. 'Away where?'

'Jesus Christ!' For the first time her brother's young voice was not quite steady. 'Trust you to stand there askin' stupid questions at a time like this! Hurry up! No — wait — best if I go first. Then I can haul you up —' She saw a shadow swing from the barrel to the opening and wriggle through. 'Right. Now you. Give us your hand. Tha'ss right. Heave!'

She swung for a moment in mid-air. Then, with a convulsive twist she was through, blessedly free, gulping air.

'Come on.' Matt took her hand and they fled, past the house and onto the footpath that led by the shelter of the wind-blighted hedge to the sea. As they passed the windows of the Great Hall Kitty glanced in. Two men in shirtsleeves, each carrying another pick-a-back, were galloping the length of the room towards each other, to roars of drunken applause from the onlookers. The two 'riders' each brandished a sword, taken from the racks of such things that had decked the walls of the hall for nearly three hundred years. As Kitty watched, with blood-curdling yells they clashed, and one pair was sent reeling to the ground to more howls of approbation from the inebriated audience.

'Come on!' Matt dragged her behind him. Her feet tangling in her long skirts, she stumbled, then righted herself. Some way along the path, a safe distance from the house, her brother stopped abruptly.

'What are you doing?' Her voice was all but lost in the wash of the nearby sea.

'Wait here.' His voice, too, was indistinct. She peered at him through the darkness, confused. 'Look after this.' He had been carrying a bundle which he now thrust at her. 'Cook sent it. It's food and a change of clothes.'

'God bless her! But Matt – what?'

He was moving from her, melting into the darkness. 'Wait. Stay here. I won't be long.' He said something else then, something that in the crash of the water she did not quite hear. But moments after he had gone the sense of the words came to her, small cold sounds like pebbles in her head: 'A score to settle.'

'Matt!' she hissed into the wind-whipped darkness.

No reply.

She huddled there for perhaps twenty minutes, each of them the space of a small lifetime. She stood up, stamping her feet and swinging her arms to keep the cold at bay. It was a wonderful night, clear and cold and windy. To the landward side the huge bulk of the house reared, silhouetted black and solid against the sky, windows lit, the sound of celebration muted by distance, by sea and by the rising wind. The waters of the North Sea shimmered, chill silver beneath a hunter's moon, wave tops whipped to creamy foam. She stood for a moment looking northwards to where, two or three miles away, drowned Dunwich lay.

If ever she had been going to hear the bells of that drowned city, surely she would hear them tonight –?

When Matt came out of the darkness like a shadow she

jumped violently, her heart in her mouth. 'Where have you been?'

His teeth glinted like an animal's in the moonlight. 'Looking to our future,' he said. 'And repaying a debt.' She heard, very distinctly, the clink of coins.

'Oh, Matt!'

'Come on. We'll follow the beach south. We'd be best off avoiding the roads for a bit.'

She hurried after him, the wind plastering her skirt against her legs. 'Where are we going?'

'London, of course. Where else?' The coins clinked cheerfully again. Matt's voice was threaded with a wild excitement. 'If we can get as far as Colchester then I reckon they'll ha' lost our trail. We can catch a train from there.'

'Providing we can get that far.'

'Oh, we'll get there.' He threw back his head and laughed. 'Give or take a couple o' more minutes an' they're goin' to 'ave better things to think on than us.'

'What do you mean?' Kitty was having trouble keeping up with him. 'Matt — slow down! What do you mean?' For the third time she tripped over the heavy, sea-wet hem of her skirt. 'Oh, drat the thing! I can't walk like this! Wait —' She kilted her full skirt up, tucked it about her waist, leaving her long woollen-stockinged legs free. 'That's better. I — Matt! — what's that?' She had turned and was looking back at the house. 'Oh, my God,' she said.

The distant bulk that was Westwood Grange was lit now by more than the strung lanthorns and candles of the celebration. The upper windows of the west wing of the house — the windows of the rooms that Sir Percival had taken for his own — were lit by a lurid glow, a bloody light that, as they watched, flickered and flared and turned the silver moon pale by comparison.

She stared, aghast. 'Matthew,' she said at last, her voice lost in the sound of the wild sea-wind, 'what have you done?'

Beside her, her brother laughed.

3

They parted in anger three days later, in the stable yard of the Red Lion Inn in Colchester High Street. For two long days, as they had plodded southward, blown like fallen leaves before the winter wind, Kitty had struggled to keep a still tongue. On the second night they had taken the ferry from Felixstowe to Harwich and had spent the night in a small and insalubrious harbour-side inn. The next day they would make for Colchester, fifteen or so miles to the south-west – and there, Matt said, they could feel safe enough from pursuit to take the train to London.

'No,' Kitty said.

Matt looked at her, spoon poised halfway to his mouth. 'What do you mean – "No"?'

'I'm not going to London. What would I do in London?'

'Same as you'd do anywhere else.' Matt grinned. 'Only better, I reckon.' He touched the belt that encircled his narrow waist that held, buckled to it, the leather pouch that he never let out of his sight. 'We don't have to worry, Kit – we've enough here to see us all right for months –'

'No,' she said again, and shook her head miserably, 'I can't.'

'Can't what?' He was genuinely puzzled.

There was a long moment's silence. With the dirty spoon that was all they had been provided with to eat the unappetizing cabbage soup – the inn's only fare – she stirred the disgusting, watery liquid with no enthusiasm. 'I don't want anything to do with that money, Matt.'

He stared at her, angry disbelief glimmering in his eyes. 'Tha'ss plain daft,' he said, softly.

She shook her head, shutting her eyes for an instant. 'I can't help it.' Her nerves were strung to breaking point. She was close to tears. As they had trudged away down the beach two nights before, the wind-whipped flames that were devouring the house she had loved had reddened the sky behind them, a lurid, unnatural sunset at which she had refused to turn and look. But yet those flames had flickered before her eyes as she walked, danced in her dreams when she had at last slept, huddled in a hollow in the sand dunes, and curtained her sight every time she had looked at her brother. 'You should not have taken that money, Matt,' she said now, quietly. 'And you should not – oh, you should not! – have set that fire.' It was the first time the words had been spoken, though they had hung between them for thirty painful miles. She bowed her head, pressing her knuckles to her aching forehead. 'You should not,' she said again.

'By!' her brother said at last, his voice tight with anger. 'You do talk some rubbish sometimes.'

She shook her head.

He spooned more soup. 'I did it for you.'

She lifted a shocked, protesting head. 'For me?'

'Of course. I reckoned they wouldn't ha' been chasin' round lookin' for a runaway with a fire on their hands. Now would they?'

'They wouldn't have been looking for me anyway, not till morning. And – drunk as most of them were – perhaps not even then! Oh, Matt – how could you? What of Anne – Mrs Roberts – all of our friends? Supposing someone has been hurt?'

Unconcernedly he slurped the soup from his spoon. 'They'll be all right.'

'How do you know?'

He shrugged.

She shook her head angrily. 'I don't understand you. I'll never understand you.' She threw her spoon down, revolted at the smell that lifted from the dish, hungry as she was. 'You don't seem to care what you do.' Her voice had risen.

He hissed at her sharply. 'Keep your voice down, stupid! D'you want the lot of them to hear?' He jerked his head at a group of loud-voiced, rough-dressed seamen who lounged, talking, laughing and drinking, against the bar. 'I didn't hear you complain when I got you out of that cellar –'

That was too much. 'I wouldn't have damned well been *in* the cellar if it hadn't been for you!' Colour high she glared at him. A man in the group by the bar glanced at them interestedly, winked at Kitty. She ducked her head. 'I'm not going to London,' she hissed, quietly and determinedly.

Matt opened his mouth, shut it again, smiled that sudden, infuriatingly charming smile. 'You're tired,' he said, reasonably. 'We'll talk about it tomorrow. Are you going to eat that soup?'

Silently she pushed the bowl across the table to him.

They reached Colchester, set upon its hill above the placid River Colne, late the following afternoon. They saw the spires and towers of the town's churches long before they reached it; those last miles, Kitty thought, tiredly, must surely have been the longest she had ever walked? Wearily they trudged up the last hill, lined with fine, prosperous-looking houses, past the ruined town walls to where the roofless castle guarded the entrance to the wide, rutted High Street, the castle looking out as it had for so many centuries across the flat and fertile fields of north Essex. The High Street, continuing quite steeply uphill, was broad – traditionally market-place as well as highway – with a small Saxon market-church set island-like in the centre. The street's length encompassed many fine shops as well as several inns, as might have been expected of a thoroughfare that had served the thriving town since Roman times. The Red Lion, one of the largest of the taverns, was bustling with life. A group of red-coated soldiers were gathered beneath the arched entrance to the yard. Nearby, ostlers were rubbing down a matched pair of mudsplashed horses.

'Do you think we might get a room here?' Kitty craned her neck to look up at the ancient, overhanging, plastered storeys of the building. 'It looks big enough, but there's an awful lot of –'

'We don't need a room.' Matt swung the bundle he was carrying from his back to the muddy ground. 'Just something to eat and directions to the station. Ah –' Looking around he had espied a small coach, the words 'North Station' emblazoned upon it. 'Looks like we've come to the right place for that –'

The soldiers had been joined by two girls. They stood talking and laughing loudly, tilting their bonneted heads to look at the men, their impractically wide skirts belling about their legs, swaying as they moved. Kitty felt suddenly, mortifyingly, dowdy. She turned on her brother, her tone sharper than she had intended. 'Matt! I told you –'

The group moved off, pushing between Matt and Kitty as if they had not been there. One of the girls had a possessive hand upon the arm of a tall fusilier. Even through her anger Kitty noted with astonishment the frizzed hair, the artificial colour upon the girl's pointed face.

Matt jerked his head. 'We can't talk here.'

'We have to. I told you. I'm not going to London.'

She saw in his face then the same, fatal flash of temper of which she herself was so often the victim. 'Then stay,' he said. 'And good luck to you. I'll go alone.'

They glared at each other.

'Make way there!' A small open carriage drove under the archway and into the yard. Muddy water splashed high. Kitty stepped back.

Matt caught her arm. 'Kitty, don't be stupid! You have to come with me –'

'I do not.' Her blood was up to match his own.

'You've no money. Nothing. How will you live?'

'There's such a thing as work, Matt Daniels. Heard of it, have you?'

He flushed, angrily.

She snatched her arm from his hand.

'I'm going to the station,' he said. 'Now.'

'Go then. What are you waiting for?' She turned from

him, took a step towards the open tavern door, listening for his voice in argument, calling her back, waiting for his hand upon her shoulder. Neither came. At the door she turned, looked back.

Matt was nowhere to be seen.

She did not – could not – truly believe he had gone. She hung about the busy yard for half an hour, watching for her brother's gangling figure, convinced that he would not leave her like this, that when his temper had cooled he would be back with his quick, teasing grin, acting as if nothing had happened.

'Lookin' fer somethin'?' The voice was not friendly.

She jumped. A huge man in shirtsleeves and grubby apron glowered down at her, his small eyes suspicious.

'I – yes. My brother – we were – supposed to meet here.'

'Were you indeed?' The man leaned towards her. His breath smelled horribly. She stepped back onto the highly polished boots of a soldier, who swore and pushed her so hard that she stumbled from him. The big man caught her arm, more, it seemed to her, as if he believed her to be trying to escape him than to prevent her falling. 'Well, Miss – I don't mind people using my tavern as a public meetin' place – no, not a bit – just so long as they don't 'ang about gettin' under everyone's feet and spendin' not a farthin' piece. Be off with yer, now. This is a respectable 'ouse. We don't like your kind round 'ere.'

She looked at him, bemused. 'Her kind'? What on earth could he mean? He jerked his massive head graphically. 'Out.'

Miserably she walked beneath the arch and out into the now almost deserted High Street. It was very cold, and almost full dark. Lights had been kindled in the shop windows, the tall, pointed gas lamps glimmered in the street. People hurried past, heads down against the cutting wind. She shivered. Where was Matt? She glanced up and down the street, half expecting to see him hiding in a doorway, watching her discomfiture, laughing at her. She saw instead a soldier who leaned negligently against a street lamp, eye-

ing her with unflatteringly faint interest. It came to her then
in a surge of horrified embarrassment what the landlord of
the Red Lion had meant by 'her kind'. Colchester was a
garrison town, and a tavern yard was no place for an honest
girl to linger alone as darkness fell.

Avoiding the man's eyes – though to be sure he showed
no great interest in her – she crossed the street, hesitated
uncertainly on the pavement on the other side. Where to
now? She had nothing but a few pence in her pocket – barely
enough for a meal, let alone to pay for a roof for the night.

Where was Matt? How dared he leave her alone like this,
helpless and penniless in a strange town! That her anger
was not entirely just – she had after all told him to go – did
nothing to temper it. She straightened her shoulders, lifted
her chin. She was standing outside yet another inn, a tall,
square-built building whose sign proclaimed it 'The George'.
Giving herself no time for thought she pushed open the door
and marched inside. A few early-evening drinkers leaned at
the bar or warmed themselves by the fire. A girl was serving
at the bar, a thin, red-headed girl with bright eyes and a
ready smile. She looked at Kitty with some curiosity. 'Yes,
love?'

'I'd – I'd like to see the landlord, please.' Kitty tried, and
failed, to keep her voice steady.

Curiosity turned to faint sympathy. 'You all right?'

'Perfectly, thank you.'

The girl shrugged, losing interest. 'The old man's in the
yard.'

'Thank you.' She threaded her way to the door the girl
had indicated with an inclination of her head and followed
a long, dark corridor to the stable yard. The wind hit her
like a blast of pure ice. She shivered. The yard was empty.
Nonplussed, she stood in the lamplight, the courage that
had taken her thus far draining from her like water from a
holed bucket.

''E must 'ave gone upstairs.'

She turned. The red-headed barmaid stood behind her,
watching her. 'You want me to fetch 'im?'

'Y – yes please.'

The girl turned, then stopped. 'Job is it?' Sympathy again gleamed in her eyes. ''E ain't takin' anyone on,' she added gently, 'if that was what you were wantin'?'

'I – well – yes –'

The fiery head shook. 'We're overstaffed already. Business is a bit slack at the moment.'

Kitty's spine stiffened against such premature disappointment. 'I'd like to see him anyway, if you don't mind.'

'I don't mind, love. It's just it'll do you no good. An' he's bin in a bit of a paddy terday; I don't see 'im feelin' charitable.'

'Even so –' Kitty began, stubbornly.

A long finger poked beneath an improbably boned bodice and scratched unselfconsciously. 'Tell you what –'

'Yes?'

'The Cups – the big place up the road – they're lookin' fer someone. Leastways they were last I 'eard. They bin short 'anded ever since Betty Green an' 'er sister were took with the fever a coupla weeks ago. Bin downright terrible this year, it 'as,' she added, chattily, 'smallpox – scarlet fever – measles – people bin dyin' like flies this summer. Like – flies –' she added, relishing the words. 'Can't ever remember such a year! Why just last week –'

'Please' – in desperation Kitty stemmed the flow of words – 'this – "Cups" – where did you say it was?'

'Oh, just a way up the 'Igh Street. On the right. It's the biggest place in town, you can't miss it.'

'Thank you. Thank you very much.'

'Don't mention it, love.' A good-natured wink and the girl was gone.

The Cups was a large, prosperous-looking hotel standing towards the top of the High Street. By the time Kitty had reached it and plucked up the courage to push open the door the driving rain that had been threatening all day had at last begun. The place was clean, and comfortable-looking, with some small pretensions to grandeur. Brass fittings gleamed, wood shone with polish, and there was an air of much activity as maids dressed neatly in black and white scurried back and forth across the entrance hall. One glanced at her, eyebrows raised in supercilious question. Kitty stepped forward. 'Er – excuse me –?' The girl did not pause, but disappeared with a swish of her long black skirt into a room from which came the sound of a raised, impatient voice. Uncertainly, but determined, Kitty lifted her chin and followed.

She found herself in a large room in which chairs were being ranged in ranked rows before a low stage onto which a group of green-aproned men were trying to manoeuvre an enormous grand piano, supervised by a woman whose voice in her anxiety much resembled the squawking of an exasperated chicken.

'Oh, for goodness' sake be careful! – It's a musical instrument, not a sack of potatoes! And – Tom – I told you – the chairs in a semi-circle, so – not in straight lines. This isn't the parade ground and we aren't entertaining the Brigade of Guards. Yes?'

The abrupt, irritable word took Kitty by surprise. 'I – was looking for the landlord.'

The woman – small, plump, with an ill-tempered mouth – barely looked at her. 'My husband's away. As I know to my cost. He'll be back in –' She stopped, turned with a quick, nervously bird-like movement, eyeing Kitty suspiciously. 'What might you want with him?'

'I – I heard that there might be – that I might find employment here?'

The woman looked at her with a little more interest, brow furrowed. 'Well – we're looking for staff, yes. And it happens that we're hard-pressed at the moment. But I don't know –'

'Please. I'm new to the town, and I've no money –'

'References?'

Kitty stared at her, heart sinking. 'N-no.'

The men moving the piano were waiting, leaning on the instrument, watching her, openly listening. She flushed. 'Please,' she said again, softly, 'I'm a good worker, I promise you.'

'Well you talk pretty enough, that's for sure. Where you from?'

'A village – near Lowestoft. I was – a lady's maid. But – her father died and – she was left penniless – there wasn't enough money to keep the staff. We had to leave –' She cursed herself for not having thought of this, for not having a story ready. But the exigency of the moment oiled her tongue. 'My references – I lost them. On the journey. My bag was stolen.' She stood, lips trembling, unfeigned tears welling in her eyes. She could not – would not! – allow herself to be turned out into the strange streets and bitter weather that waited beyond the door of The Cups. She heard a small murmur of sympathy from one of the men.

'We-ell.' The woman pursed her lips. 'You look strong, I'll say that for you. Lady's maid, you say? We've nothing of that kind on offer –'

'I don't mind. I don't care what I do –'

'Kitchen maid's what we need –'

Kitty waited with bated breath, not daring to speak.

'All right then. I'll give you a try. Go and wait in the kitchen. I'll be along in a minute. But remember, mind –'

Kitty, turning to leave, stopped.

'– one step wrong, my girl, and you're out. Understood?'

'Of course.'

'Off with you then. I'll be there later.'

From that moment to the time she crawled thankfully into the narrow bed that had been set up for her in the cold attics beside those of the two other kitchen maids Kitty did not sit down once. Even her supper she ate on her feet, ordered hither and thither by first one and then the other, by Mrs Barlow, her employer, by Mrs Simkins the cook, by ex-Sergeant-Major Polliter who ran the dining room of The Cups as if it had been his Officers' Mess. After the meal had been served a recital took place, Miss Clara Saint regaling her enthralled audiences with songs so insipidly sweet – and so indifferently sung – that, tired as she was, Kitty found the sound, even from a distance, wore her nerves and her patience almost beyond endurance. When at last she was released from her labours and crawled into bed in the draughty attic the thin, anaemic tones of Miss Saint still rang in her ears, infuriatingly keeping at bay the rest she so desperately needed. Wind battered the ancient roof, sang in the chimneys, fluttered the curtains. Rain hurled itself in waves against the windows.

Where was Matt? Where was the brother she loved so dearly and had sworn so often to protect? In London by now, presumably, alone and vulnerable to God only knew what temptations; all too ready to learn the lessons that a city old in vice could teach.

Before the tears that gathered beneath her eyelids could fall, she slept at last, the sleep of the exhausted.

(ii)

She saw him – the brother she had given up all hopes of seeing again as surely as if he had been dead – just three days later. She could not, for a moment, believe her eyes. Sent on an errand by Mrs Simkins, she was standing at the counter of a butcher's shop in the High Street waiting her turn when through the multi-paned glass of the window she saw a group of flashily dressed and noisily laughing young men; and in the middle of them, laughing as loudly as any and dressed in as expensively bad taste, young Matt. It was a long moment before the paralysis of astonishment wore off – by the time she had fought her way to the shop doorway they were gone. But it had been Matt, of that there was absolutely no doubt. He had not, after all, gone to London. And if she had seen him once about the town she would surely see him again. She returned to The Cups more cheerful than she had been in days.

She could not for a moment pretend she was happy there. Her position was menial in the extreme – she scrubbed floors and cooking pans, peeled vegetables, washed up mountains of dirty dishes. She had no friend. She did not care. For the moment, she needed simply the security of a roof over her head and food in her belly. She laboured for the most part mindlessly, allowing the monotonous tasks to deaden thought, to exhaust her strong body until it wanted nothing but to eat and sleep and, above all, to obliterate any thought of the uncertain future. For the time being she lived from day to day, hardly thinking, hardly caring, and watching for Matt.

She saw him again one day in the market. He was with a lad a little older than himself, a boy with black hair, full red lips and eyes that never rested for a moment, flickering disturbingly from one object to another, from one face to another, never still. Kitty disliked him on sight. She and Matt stood awkwardly after the first stilted greetings.

'You – decided against London, then?' she asked at last.

He shrugged. 'Colchester's not so bad. There's a fair bit going on.'

His companion snickered. Kitty ignored him. 'I really thought you'd gone,' she said, quietly.

He had the grace to flush, then laughed uncomfortably, lifting a shoulder. 'Changed me mind.' She noticed that her brother, chameleon that he was, was already taking on the flatter accents of Essex, though in his tone he still retained the sing-song of Suffolk.

'I'm working at The Cups,' she said.

'Do you like it?'

'No.' Her voice was entirely devoid of expression.

'Then – why not come and join us?' Matt took her hand, suddenly eager. 'We're living out by the garrison –'

'We?'

He hesitated, glanced at his companion. 'Just – some mates I've met –' he said guardedly. 'It's good fun, Kitty – we have some high old times, I can tell you –'

'Oh?'

Her tone stopped him. He flushed again.

'And how do you finance your – high old times?' Her voice was low. 'Your precious new mates wouldn't be living on the money you – acquired – from Sir Percy, would they?'

'Oh, for God's sake, Kitty –!'

She shook her head.

'Well then,' he said, awkward again, but obviously intent against quarrelling, 'I expect we'll – see each other again?'

'I expect so.'

She turned and left them with no farewell, blinking against the sting of the winter wind that burned her eyes.

The next time she saw him was the week before Christmas. She was in the market, buying vegetables.

Matt was in the market picking pockets.

She knew the moment she saw him. He and the boy she had seen him with before were working together – the boy bumping into people, apparently clumsily, Matt with his charming, boyish smile admonishing, apologizing, brushing his victim down – Kitty flinched, turned to flee, and almost fell over a small child who was wandering behind her, dirty thumb in mouth, too-long skirts trailing on the littered floor. The child, falling, set up a howl like a banshee.

'Oh – I'm sorry! Poor little thing! I'm sorry –' Kitty dropped to her knees, set the child, scarcely more than a toddling baby, upon her small, uncertain feet, brushing the dirt and sawdust from her skirt. 'There, my poppet. Don't cry.'

The wails redoubled. The child, none too clean despite the obvious quality of her clothes, looked to be about two years old. Kitty glanced about her. No adult nor any older child appeared to claim the howling waif.

'Oh, come now!' On impulse Kitty bent and swung the child into her arms. 'It wasn't that bad –'

As suddenly as if a tap had been turned the tears stopped. The child looked at her solemnly for a moment before a smile like sunshine after rain lit the small face.

Kitty bounced her in her arms. 'There. That's better. Now' – she looked around again – 'whose little girl are you! There must be someone –' She stopped.

By the entrance to the market building a disturbance had broken out. A man shouted angrily. There was movement in the bustling crowds. The child in Kitty's arms seemed perfectly happy now. With damp fingers she clutched a handful of her rescuer's hair, making unintelligible but contented-sounding noises.

'Thief!'

Kitty winced.

'Thief! Stop him –'

She stood on tiptoe, looking for Matt. There was no sign of him or of his companion. The commotion by the doorway died. She let out a slow breath of relief. She stood for long moments waiting, listening for the shouts that would tell of her brother's apprehension. Nothing happened. The child stirred in faint protest at the tight grip of the arms that held her. With an effort Kitty relaxed. Matt, apparently, was safe for another day. Her immediate task was to discover the family of the urchin she held – she could not, in conscience, put her down and abandon her to her fate. She pushed her way aimlessly through the crowds, looking for someone who might be searching for the child.

'Mama,' the child said then, and a small, dimpled finger pointed.

Kitty glanced around. A woman stood by a fruit stall, haggling half-heartedly with the vendor over a sad-looking cabbage. She appeared to be surrounded by children. Twins of about eight years old played 'tag' about her, dancing from side to side, shrieking with noisy laughter, pulling her this way and that in their game, uncaring of her protests. Two smaller children squabbled equally noisily over a battered rag doll. Another was helping himself to an apple from the fruit stall.

'Hepzibar! Zacharius! Do stop! You're making me dizzy! You know my poor head –'

The two over-excited children showed no sign whatsoever of having heard her. She put a hand to her head. She was very small and slight, herself childlike, and her complexion was pale as washed linen. Her light blue eyes were set in a face that looked pinched and bruised with tiredness. The child with the apple squatted unconcernedly on the filthy floor and took an enormous bite from the fruit.

'That'll be another ha'penny,' the stallholder said, phlegmatically.

'Jeremiah! Come back here –!' One of the smaller children had grabbed the almost dismembered rag doll, dodged away from his mother and dived into the crowd. 'Jeremiah –!'

Kitty put out a long arm. To his astonishment Jeremiah found himself collared. With a bellow he tried to shake free. Kitty held on. Looking up he stopped struggling suddenly, regarding her with interest. 'That's our 'Becca.'

'Is it indeed?' The imp had a grin on him that the hardest heart could not have resisted. Kitty smiled back. 'Well, we'd best take her back where she belongs, hadn't we?' She shifted her grip from his collar to his hand, pushed her way through the crowd to the distracted mother.

'Rebecca!' At the sight of the child that Kitty carried the woman looked aghast and then glanced round, almost as if expecting to see the double of the child still clinging to her skirts. 'Rebecca,' she said again, faintly.

'I found her wandering over there –' Kitty released Jeremiah's hand and tried unsuccessfully to disengage the younger child's arms from about her neck. Rebecca clung like a limpet, bottom lip mutinous. 'Here's Mama,' Kitty said, gently. 'Go to Mama, now.'

The small body burrowed fiercely into hers. Nonplussed, Kitty looked at the other woman, who held out her hand. 'Come, 'Becca,' she said, no great conviction in the tone.

'No!' 'Becca roared. 'No-o!'

At that moment Zacharius, bored with the game he had been playing with his twin, gave her a fierce push that sent her sprawling on top of the child who had been contentedly munching his stolen apple. As if on cue pandemonium broke loose. The children screamed and fought. Their mother burst into helpless tears. Jeremiah made another bid for freedom. 'Becca, still in Kitty's arms, clapped her hands and crowed with delight.

'Enough!' Kitty said.

She might have been talking to a bunch of brawling monkeys.

'*Enough!*' With 'Becca still clinging with both arms about her neck she waded into the fray, dragging the furious Hepzibar off her squealing brother, clipping Zacharius' ear as she reached him and swinging Jeremiah off the ground as he dashed past her, depositing him in a safe corner where he was hemmed in by brothers, sisters and fruit boxes. 'What a performance,' she said, mildly.

The children stared at her. Their mother hiccoughed tearfully. Kitty turned to her, patting her shoulder a little awkwardly. 'It's all right. They've stopped.'

The woman let out a little, exhausted wail.

'You won't stop her now,' Zacharius said; the voice of experience.

Kitty ignored him. The crown of the little woman's head barely reached her chin. Sobbing, the woman leaned to the younger girl and Kitty found herself comforting her as she might a distressed child. 'It's all right – truly it is –'

The woman was crying tiredly, would not or could not lift her head. Curious eyes were turned their way. Kitty decided that enough was enough. 'Do stop it,' she said, her voice tart, 'please. You really must.'

The sharpness of her tone worked where sympathy had not. The woman lifted her pinched, tear-streaked face. Kitty busied herself with the buttons of 'Becca's coat, which were all buttoned to the wrong holes.

'I can't control them,' the woman said, unhappily. 'I can't. They'll be the death of me –'

'Well, wife? And what's this?'

The woman, small as she was, seemed to shrivel before Kitty's eyes. The man who stood before them, big as a barn, dark as a raincloud, waited, unsmiling.

'The children, Mr Isherwood –' she whispered, her voice all but lost in the hubbub about them, 'they misbehave – I cannot control them –'

The man frowned at the suddenly-sobered children. 'Becca buried her face in Kitty's neck. Jeremiah too moved closer to her and surreptitiously slipped his small hand into hers.

Piercing blue eyes in a florid, weatherbeaten face surveyed Kitty sternly. 'Have we met?'

His wife waved apologetic, ineffective hands.

'No,' Kitty said, unsmiling in the face of the man's own severity. 'My name is Kitty Daniels.'

'She – found 'Becca wandering –' the other woman stammered, '– and stopped Jeremiah –' She trailed to silence.

'Then I thank ye, Kitty Daniels,' the man said, heavily. 'The children are a handful sometimes. Mrs Isherwood finds it difficult. I thank you,' he said again.

'It's no trouble.' Kitty gently tucked Jeremiah's hand into his mother's, determinedly unclasped the baby's arms from about her own neck.

'Seems she's taken to you,' the man said.

Kitty smiled. 'Yes.' Gently she shook herself free of the child's grasping fingers, handed her to her mother. 'Becca's small arms reached and the wilful tears started again.

'I must go,' Kitty said, softly, to the mother, who looked herself as if she might cry at the abandonment. 'I work at The Cups. Cook will be waiting.'

The woman nodded, smiled a weak, pathetic smile.

' 'Bye, Jeremiah.' Kitty ruffled his hair, threw a swift smile at the other children and left.

In a strange way she was not surprised when Jonas Isherwood appeared two days later at the back door of The Cups, asking for her. He was a plain-spoken man, and made no bones about his errand. She could take his offer or leave it. He was a Mersea man, an oysterman with his own small smack and a few acres of ground which he farmed with his eldest son. His wife Martha, as Kitty must have seen, was poorly, very poorly; breeding again and not strong. For the past months, since the departure of the girl they had employed since 'Becca's birth, she had been left alone to cope with the house and the children, and the task was beyond her. Josiah had been much impressed to hear of the way Kitty had handled the children; in fact Martha herself had begged him to find the girl who had helped her so efficiently and ask if she might be willing to come and work for them. The pay was fair – seven guineas a year and found, and every Sunday afternoon free. His offer made, he waited, watching her. She wondered if he ever smiled.

Two days before she had seen Matt. He had been drunk as a lord and in company with two sharp-faced, red-lipped girls, each at least five years his senior. She had seen a ring glitter upon his finger that no honest money could have bought.

Yes, she said, she would take the post, and gladly. And if he would give her just a few minutes to speak to Mrs Barlow and pack her few possessions she would be ready to leave at once.

So it was that, just three days before Christmas 1863, Kitty Daniels rode out of Colchester on a jolting cart that reeked of fish and in the bottom of which a few gnarled, granite-coloured shells rattled, down St Botolph's, past an ancient-looking church with a great gateway beyond, up a hill and past a windmill that groaned as it turned and into the wide, windswept, waterlogged country that stretched to the coast and the island of Mersea, of which until today she had never heard.

As she huddled shivering in the bitter easterly gale she thought of the note she had left at The Cups for her brother, in case it should occur to him to look for her, and wondered, bleakly, if he would even notice she had gone.

4

Mersea Island, five miles long and a scant two wide, separated from the Essex coast by the tide-washed fleets and inlets of the River Blackwater, its only link with the mainland the ancient causeway known as the Strood – which was in winter months as often below water as above it – was a bleak place at the best of times. On the stormy December day that Kitty, huddled beside Jonas Isherwood on the high, unprotected seat of his ancient cart, rattled and jolted across the Strood with wind-whipped waves dashing and swirling almost to the horse's hooves and an early winter darkness clamping a bitter hand upon the flat and almost featureless landscape of the island, she thought she had never seen a place so desolate. So low-lying was the land, so encroaching the besieging waters whose lapping creeks and inlets reached greedy fingers into the scrubby marshland, that in the half-light the usually clear distinction between the two was blurred, and Kitty found it impossible to discern where the one stopped and the other began. The sea-wind stormed across the island unhindered, lashing the tough, flattened grass, howling in the bare branches of the few weather-battered trees. Every so often the cart rolled past a small, slate-roofed or thatched cottage huddled upon the edge of the marshland, the smoke from its hearth snatched low from its chimney by the demon gale, the faint, tallow-lit glow of its windows the very spirit of human comfort in the darkness.

'Do – do we have much further to go?' Kitty had to shout to make herself heard above the wild elements.

Jonas Isherwood did not take his eyes from the rutted road

along which the old horse picked its patient way, head down and unhurried. 'Couple o' miles.'

Beneath her heavy shawl she hugged herself, tucking her cold hands into her sleeves. They had moved a little way from the water now and were travelling flat, winter-tilled fields. 'Are we going to a village?'

He shook his head. 'Farmhouse. And cottage. Mile or so outside the City.'

The City? She glanced at his dour, uncommunicative face, surprised, wondering if she had misheard, but he elaborated no further upon his words. It was in fact a week before she discovered that to the islanders the village of West Mersea was known, and as far as anyone knew had always been known, as the City; though why a community of a few fishermen's cottages, oyster and winkle sheds and less than a thousand souls should be so called was a mystery.

Half an hour after this exchange, just as Kitty was despairing of any end to the cold and discomfort, Jonas clicked his tongue at the horse, the cart turned into a narrow lane and they were at their destination. She saw the house, at the end of the winding, hawthorn-hedged lane, some time before they reached it. It stood solid and four-square against the stormy sky, sheltered by a great evergreen tree – a holme oak, Kitty later discovered – that tossed and roared in the wind. As the cart clattered through the open gate that led into the yard Kitty noticed a small cottage, set to one side and unlit, though welcome light glimmered through the windows of the main house.

'Whoa! Whoa there –!' Jonas Isherwood drew the horse to a standstill outside the side door of the farmhouse. 'Amos! Amos – are ye there?' He turned to Kitty. 'Ye'd best get inside,' he said, not unkindly. 'Ye must be perished.'

She was. Stiffly, her bones brittle with cold, her body aching from the relentless jolting of the cart, she scrambled down from the high seat and stood for a moment outside the door, clutching her small bundle. Before she could knock the door opened, and a tall, slim figure, head haloed in gilded light, stood before her.

'Amos? Come on, lad – help me with Betsy. The poor beast's fair worn out.'

The tall young man lifted a hand in acknowledgement and, smiling, stepped past Kitty into the yard, the wind catching at his silvered hair and his shirt.

'She's here!' A small figure hurtled through the door and Jeremiah caught her free hand, swinging on it as if it were a dangling rope, grinning his imp's grin. She smiled back and, light as he was, lifted him, one-handed, off the ground.

'Jeremiah – please –' Martha had appeared behind him. Beyond her Kitty could see a large, cluttered room, dimly lit and untidy but at that moment the most welcoming sight she had ever seen. She allowed Jeremiah to pull her through the doorway as the young man, Amos, took the horse's head and led the tired beast off into the darkness. Martha shut the door, leaning hard against it in the wind. With Kitty into the room came a gust of winter, icy fingers of air that fluttered and swirled about the guttering candles and lamps and brought a puff of fragrant woodsmoke from the great open fireplace that warmed the disordered room.

Kitty found herself the focus of several pairs of eyes, regarding her with expressions that ran the full course from friendly greeting to – to Kitty's surprise – an unsmiling wariness that came close to hostility. The children she had met in the market were there – Hepzibar and Zacharius, sprawled upon the floor, bickering amiably over a heap of chipped glass marbles, Jeremiah still swinging in proprietory fashion upon her hand, 'Becca in her mother's arms, and the other little boy whose name she later learned was Daniel, who regarded her with solemn interest from behind his mother's skirts. At the big table sat a young woman of perhaps nineteen or twenty years, nursing a baby, a toddling child at her knee. It was this girl's striking eyes that regarded Kitty watchfully, flickering from her face to her ill-shod feet, their expression totally lacking in greeting.

Kitty smiled uncertainly. 'Hello.'

The girl nodded slightly but neither smiled nor spoke.

Martha Isherwood fluttered nervously between them.

'Kitty – you don't mind being called Kitty? – this is my
– that is Mr Isherwood's – daughter-in-law, Maria. She's
married to Amos – who is Mr Isherwood's son by his first
marriage. The two little ones are Joseph and Benjamin. They
live in the cottage that you passed by the gate – but much
of the time –' She trailed off.

Kitty waited for a moment to see if she were going to
finish the sentence, then said, a little formally, 'How do you
do?'

The girl nodded again, ungraciously. She was a strikingly
attractive young woman with a mass of dark hair and a
strong, discontented mouth. Kitty, remembering the tall,
gilt-headed young man she had met at the door, found
herself thinking they must make a handsome pair. Certainly
the two little boys were the prettiest she had ever seen, the
older one with his mother's dark eyes and his father's fair
hair, the younger also blond, and blue-eyed, his cherub face
bright with laughter. Yet there was about both children a
faint air of neglect – dressed as they were for bed yet still
their hair held the tangles of the windy day and their hands
were grubby.

'And – Hannah must be somewhere –' Martha Isherwood
looked vaguely about her.

'In the kitchen. Gettin' supper.' Maria's voice was harsh,
low-pitched.

'Oh – yes, of course. Hannah's our maid –' Martha's voice
was nervously distracted as she tried to disentangle 'Becca's
sticky fingers from her hair. 'She's a good worker, really –
but no good with the children. Well – you can't expect –'
As before, she seemed to lose track of what she was saying.
'I'm – so glad you agreed to come –'

There was a short, awkward silence.

On the floor the bickering had changed its nature and was
reaching quarrelsome proportions.

'You did!'
'I didn't.'
'You did!'
'I didn't, I tell you! I gave you exactly the same!'

'Zach! Hepsi! Please –'

Predictably they took not the slightest notice of Martha's ineffectual exclamation.

'You didn't! You've got more! You cheat! The red one's mine – give it me –'

'It isn't. I won it!'

The opening of the door and the entrance of Jonas and his son on another swirl of wintry air put a stop to the hostilities as if the draught had blown out a candle. And Kitty took note that the children, if they disregarded their mother, certainly held their father in more respect. She turned, colliding as she did so with the young man Amos who, laughing, caught her elbow to steady her. He was more than a head taller than she, and very slight, though his shoulders were wide and the work-hardened hand on her arm was strong. He smiled down at her. Damp silver hair fell across his wide forehead. He flicked it back. His naturally fair complexion was burnished by sun and wind and in the dark face he had the very bluest eyes she had ever seen, fringed with lashes as long as any girl's. Absurdly and embarrassingly, for one strange moment she could not look away. Then, 'I'm – I'm sorry –' she stammered.

He smiled, white teeth in that weather-brightened face, and stepped back from her, crossed to his wife, stood smiling down, his hand on the soft down of the baby's head. Maria scowled up at him.

Martha was speaking. Kitty turned. 'I beg your pardon?'

'Your room – you'll want to rest before supper –'

'Oh, yes. Thank you.' She felt suddenly tired, and overwhelmed by them all. Her hair was a bird's nest, her face still painful with cold, as if the wind had flayed the skin from it. 'I should certainly like to tidy up.'

'I'll show you. Hepzibar, take the baby –' Martha dumped the child into her reluctant sister's lap and straightened, smiling shyly at Kitty. 'This way.'

She picked up a lamp and led the way through a door and up a steep flight of stairs. A narrow, windowless landing flanked by closed doors ran the length of the house. At the end of the landing another short flight of steps, almost ladder-like, led to a low door. The attic room beyond was tiny, with an uncurtained dormer window about which the wind shrieked and whistled, wood-lined walls and ceiling and a very small fireplace in which, blessedly, burned a few coals. The room was barely large enough to hold the bed, washstand and tiny bedside table that were all its furnishings. Martha opened a little door next to the fireplace to reveal a deep, slope-ceilinged eaves cupboard. 'You can put your things in there.'

'Thank you. I don't have much.'

'Supper's ready when you like. We've been waiting.'

Not for the first time it occurred to Kitty that she had no idea of her standing in the household. Mere servant? Nursemaid? Companion? 'I won't be long,' she said a little awkwardly. 'If I could just take a few minutes to tidy myself?'

Martha's hands fluttered. 'Of course – of course – please – don't worry. When you're ready –'

As the door closed behind her Kitty dropped, sighing with relief, onto the bed. She felt bone-tired. Her back and buttocks ached from the uncomfortable ride from Colchester. She sat for a moment, very still, eyes closed, breathing deep and steady. Wind buffeted the window. Rain had started now, hitting the thick glass like handfuls of flung gravel. She opened her eyes. There was a chill in the room, the coals that burned in the grate barely warming the cold air. Suddenly and determinedly brisk, she reached for her bundle, undid it and hunted for her hair brush. A jug of cold water stood upon the washstand. She poured some into the bowl, splashed her face and hands, rubbed them dry with the coarse towel that hung on the rail of the stand. Then, brush in hand, she set about unpinning the heavy brown hair and brushing out the tangles, watching herself in the big, old-fashioned, damp-specked mirror that hung above the washstand. Her hair sparked and flew. She brushed harder, letting the long, smooth strokes soothe her, closing her mind to thought.

And there slipped into unwary consciousness a picture of a pair of very blue eyes in a weather-darkened face, of windblown silver hair heavy across a wide forehead.

She stood absolutely still for a moment, staring at herself, her winged brows drawn to a ferocious frown. Then, with fingers brusque to the point of roughness, she twisted her hair into a thick brown rope which she wound deftly about her head, tucking in the stray strands, patting and smoothing with long, square-tipped fingers. She brushed the dust from her skirt with her hands, settled her shawl about her shoulders, looked for another long, repressive moment at the thin-faced reflection in the mirror, then turned and left the room once more to face the Isherwoods. The ones she had expected – and the one she had not.

(ii)

As she had herself recognized, Kitty's status in the Isher-wood family was an ambivalent one. She was not a member of the family – yet neither was she entirely a servant. Everyone but the maid Hannah, a surly, orphaned child of thirteen years who clearly resented the advent of another voice to order her about, called her Kitty; everyone, that is, but Maria, who rarely addressed her directly and never at all by name. In a very short while Kitty came to accept the other girl's ungracious lack of friendliness and shrug it off – indeed it seemed simply to reflect Maria's relationship with the rest of the world. Even for her handsome husband – whom Kitty, though she never admitted it to herself, took great pains to avoid – she rarely had a smile or a soft word. To Kitty herself it seemed that her place in the household was as housekeeper, nurse, governess, chief cook, occasional bottle washer and general factotum. In those first days after her arrival her largely self-appointed task – made so by the fact that Maria Isherwood seemed utterly incapable of doing any appointing of her own – had been to organize the family's Christmas – a bare three days away and, she had discovered to her horror, next to nothing done. At first wary of Maria's reaction – Amos' wife, after all, might have been the natural successor to the ailing Martha in the running of the household – she soon realized that the girl had no interest at all in the task, and so the day after her arrival she set a resentful Hannah to help her clean, polish, sweep and scrub the main rooms of the house. In daylight she had discovered it to be every bit as ill-kept as it had looked in the lamplight; and yet the old house itself, though fallen a little from former glory, was spacious and attractive and worthy, Kitty thought, of rather more than the neglect that had clearly been its lot for the past years. Built a hundred years before for a prosperous oyster merchant, it stood square and solid beneath its ancient tree, outhouses and stabling forming a cobbled courtyard at the back, where stood the well that supplied the house with sweet water. Apart from the cottage a few hundred yards away there were no neighbouring buildings, and grass- and marshland swept to the distant estuary. The village of West Mersea – the mysteriously named 'City', and the only village of any consequence on the island – lay a mile or so away, and it was from the City's beach, known locally as a 'hard', that Jonas, Amos and a couple of village lads worked the oyster grounds in Jonas' eleven-ton smack, the *Girl May*. On those three cold December days Kitty threw herself wholeheartedly into the task of preparing the house and its inhabitants for the coming festival. She was up with the menfolk in the dark, pre-dawn hours, rousing sleepy, protesting Hannah – who in the past, having first fed the master and his son and seen them on their way, had been in the habit of creeping back into the warm pallet in front of the kitchen fire that was her bed – and if she rested for more than half an hour between then and the time she fell exhausted into bed she counted it as time wasted. She also discovered that in hard work and weariness there was some antidote to the heartache caused by the fact that throughout those days and the days that followed there came neither sign nor word from her brother. That her frantic activity also kept her mind from dwelling upon Maria Isherwood's disturbingly attractive husband was something she tried not to think about.

The house gleaming, she set the older children to gathering evergreens for decoration. Christmas Eve was spent cooking and baking in the big, warm old kitchen, a task which she enjoyed immensely, despite the fact that the whole tribe of young Isherwoods, of whom she was already becoming very fond indeed, showed themselves determined to congregate to watch her efforts and steal what they could of the results. Martha spent the first half of the day fluttering ineffectually about her, making in her eagerness to help an easy task difficult. In the afternoon, however, she was, to Kitty's somewhat shamefaced relief, overcome by what she described as 'one of my headaches' and was easily prevailed upon to retire to bed. The children too tired at last of the novelty of Kitty in the kitchen and disappeared in ones and twos to get up to the devil knew what mischief elsewhere. Hannah had been sent on an errand to the village – a trip from which Kitty already knew from experience she would return at her own pace and in her own time – and 'Becca alone was left, sitting happily occupied on the flagstoned floor, two spoons and a pan lid her absorbing toys.

Kitty did not hear the door open. Her first intimation of Amos Isherwood's presence was his quiet voice. She jumped, and barely prevented a baking pan from slipping from suddenly untrustworthy fingers.

'This kitchen hasn't known such smells since my mother died,' he said.

She smiled diffidently but neither replied nor looked at him. Like a boy he dipped his finger into the cake mixture and licked it appreciatively. When Jeremiah had done the same thing a few short moments before, Kitty had chased him around the kitchen in mock outrage, brandishing a wooden spoon. Now she turned her head, pretending absurdly not to have seen, bending to the baby and fussing with the child's multi-layered clothes.

Amos walked to the small window and peered out into the wild December afternoon. 'Well, Kitty Daniels,' he said, directly and unexpectedly, 'what d'you think of us all?'

'I – I like it here. Very much,' she stammered, taken aback.

He leaned by the window, watching her with those desperately disturbing blue eyes. She lifted 'Becca, perched her, straddled upon her hip.

'You'll like it better in the summer,' he said. ' 'Tis pretty then. The marshes full of flowers, an' the seabirds flyin' –'

'Yes,' she said, 'it was so in Suffolk.'

He half-perched on the table, long leg dangling. 'There's bathin' machines on the hard in the summer. City folk come here on holiday –' He grinned suddenly, white teeth gleaming. 'If they don't recognize anythin' else I reckon they recognize the smells.' He laughed outright at her questioning look. 'London muck – the sweepings of the streets. We use it to fertilize the fields about here.'

She wrinkled her nose. He laughed again. 'Grows good 'taters.' He grinned. Then, restless, he slid from the table and walked to the window again. 'It sometimes do seem that the winter'll never end, don't it?'

She allowed herself to watch him for a moment. The dull, rainwashed light shadowed a profile that was clear-cut and flawless, a golden head struck upon a coin of lead.

'Amos, lad.' Jonas stood, unsmiling as always, in the open doorway. 'Given up for the day, have ye? Roof of the byre's mended? Betsy fed?'

'Why, no, Pa. I was just goin' to do it.' Amos reached for the heavy jacket that hung inside the kitchen door.

Jonas watched him shrug into it with austerely knitted brows and a forcefully displeased gaze that seemed to Kitty to be out of proportion to the deed. She had already noticed some tensions between the two men – the father a man of few words, hardworking, an authoritarian, the son perhaps a shade less than industrious, but easy-going and, it seemed to her, eager to please. It was strange too that this same sharp attitude was mirrored in Amos' relationship with his difficult wife; several times over the past few days Kitty had found herself wondering what kept those two together.

Amos and Jonas gone, she settled 'Becca back on the floor,

put the cake in the oven and swung the big black kettle onto the hob. Three days' hard work had, she reflected, made an almost miraculous difference to the old house. The brass shone, the wooden furniture gleamed with polish, the whole place smelled differently, fragrant as it was with the mingled smells of soap and polish and the tang of woodsmoke from the warming fires she had lit in every room. She glanced about the great, warm kitchen. That too had been tidied and reorganized. She spent a small glow of satisfaction. 'Becca returned her smile and waved the wooden spoon in the air, to the grave peril of her left ear. The sight of the child reminded Kitty of poor Martha and her headache. A little guiltily she realized that it must be all of two hours since Martha had retired to her bed. She picked the baby up again. 'Let's go and see Mama, eh?' she crooned, bouncing the child in her arms. 'Poor Mama – let's go see how she feels –'

The door of the bedroom stood slightly ajar. Kitty, arms clasped about the child, pushed it with her foot. 'Mrs Isherwood?'

There was a small, surprised sound, half gasp, half exclamation. 'J – just a moment –'

Too late. The door had swung wide. Martha Isherwood, still fully dressed, half reclined on the bed, her already cumbersome body, in the fourth month of pregnancy, propped up by pillows, her startled white face turned towards Kitty. In one hand she held a glass. The other, which pathetically and vainly she was trying to conceal beneath the pillows, held what Kitty instantly recognized as a gin bottle. There was a short, embarrassed silence.

'I'm – I'm sorry –' Kitty felt as if it were she who had been caught in indiscretion. Her cheeks burned. 'I – came to discover – if you'd like a cup of tea –'

With the careful precision of drunkenness Martha leaned down and placed the bottle upon the floor on the opposite side of the bed from where Kitty stood. Then she sat bolt upright, still holding the half full glass, her untidy head held rigidly upon her skinny neck in a pitiful travesty of pride.

'Yes, please,' she said, voice and manner that of a child at a birthday party, 'I should like that very much.'

Face still bright with embarrassment, Kitty beat a hasty retreat, closing the door quietly behind her.

As she turned from it she heard, unmistakably, the creak of the bed and then the unsteady clink of glass on glass.

(iii)

Matt's silence throughout the Christmas period, though far from unexpected, nevertheless caused Kitty a heartache that she tried to assuage in hard work. She ran the surprised household like clockwork, receiving one day early in January dour thanks and congratulations from Jonas Isherwood that both astonished and delighted her. She had no idea if he knew of his wife's drinking – for as the weeks went by she came to realize that the incident on Christmas Eve had not by any means been an isolated one – and did not feel it her place to broach the subject. Neither was it ever mentioned between herself and Martha. Her good sense told her it was none of her business and best left alone; but as time went on she discovered within herself a real if sometimes exasperated fondness for Martha Isherwood despite her slipshod, ineffectual ways and nervous manner, and she could not help but worry about her. For herself she was not unhappy. She got on well with and was extremely fond of the children who were her charges, her duties in the house were not so onerous as to cause her any problems. The strange bitter-sweetness of her feelings for Amos Isherwood – much as she tried to deny them, much as she castigated herself – did not at that time induce unhappiness. He was Maria's husband, the father of her children. Nothing could possibly come from any warmth she might feel for him. But yet this was her first infatuation, and the sight of him, the sound of his voice, the glimmer of his smile could lighten a day and lift her heart, however much she might try to deny it. The only real cloud on her horizon was her worry for Matt. Several times she considered going in to Colchester on her free afternoon to find him, but each time pride prevented her: if he bothered to look for her he would find her – if he did not it could only be that he did not care what became of her. Stubbornly, each time she crossed the Strood in Jonas Isherwood's cart going to Colchester to shop for the household she told herself that she would not go looking for him. He must come to her.

And to her unutterable delight, graceless and winning as ever, in the middle of frost-sharp February he did.

The day was crisp and clear. Jonas and Amos were at the oyster beds in the *Girl May*, the twins were at school in the village, Jeremiah and Daniel miraculously occupied at some task their father had set them to be finished by his return, and 'Becca was with her mother upstairs. Kitty devoutly hoped that the 'medicine' that Martha was undoubtedly taking for her 'headache' was not also being poured down the child's throat to keep her quiet. She was drawing water from the well and filling the big tank that stood by the kitchen door when footsteps startled her and she looked up to see the familiar, lanky form, so long looked for, coming across the yard towards her. Very, very carefully she put down the slopping pail and stood waiting for him, head high, the pleasure that she felt at the sight of him fiercely suppressed.

Not so with Matt. Ignoring her lack of welcome, he grinned his wide, blithe, irresponsible smile and his arms went out to sweep her almost from her feet.

'Kitty! Moi good owd Kitty!' The Suffolk accent was comically exaggerated for her benefit. He gave her a smacking kiss, stood back, bright-faced, to look at her. 'You're thin,' he pronounced. 'What's the matter? Don't they feed foreigners on this godforsaken island?'

She could not, of course, resist him – could not resist his good nature, his utter refusal to take note of her displeasure, the breath of home and another life that he brought with him. He did not stay long that first time, but left promising to visit again soon which, much to her surprise, as bitter winter moved on into a cold and changeable spring, he did, and often. He rarely came into the house, except occasionally to perch, restless as some bird of passage resting in midflight, on the broad windowsill of the kitchen, watching her as she busied herself about her tasks. Often, despite the weather, they would stroll to the City hard and watch as the oystermen, in from the layings, unloaded their precious catch.

'Why do they do that?' Matt asked one day, idly, as he saw a crab crushed ruthlessly beneath a massive sea boot.

'The crabs eat the young oysters.' Kitty drew her shawl tighter about her shoulders against the bite of the inevitable wind. 'Crabs, limpets, whelks, starfish – they call them five-fingers around here – they're all the enemies of the oyster. Mostly they're culled on board, as the men empty the dredges. The crabs they kill, as you see. But they'll often bring the starfish in. They make good fertilizer, and the farmers will pay a fair price for a sackful.'

They stood in companionable silence, watching the men and boys working. By the water's edge a group of small, dirty, tough-looking children played, intent upon the smooth pebbles they were using as five-stones. Two out of the three boys in the group wore soldiers' uniform trousers, cut off at the knee, a common sight in an area where cast-offs from the garrison were a cheap source of clothing – and the only girl sported a bright red army jacket from the same source. Matt grinned. 'Little tykes. I wouldn't like to meet them in a dark alley.'

After the undeniable awkwardness of his first few visits almost the old easy relationship had been established between them, perhaps because by common consent whilst talking often of Suffolk and their shared past neither ever mentioned the particular chain of events that had brought them here, and by the same token neither did they discuss Matt's present obviously dubious way of life. He looked well fed and was well, if flashily, dressed; and if the shadows beneath eyes that betrayed more of experience than his fourteen years should encompass spoke of lack of rest and perilously intemperate living, Kitty had the good sense to keep a still tongue and her worries to herself. He had come to her, and of his own accord. To probe and – inevitably – to censure would surely drive him from her, and that thought she could not bear. Only once did she ever mention, obliquely, her concern for him. Sitting in weak March sunshine in the shelter of a still locked and shuttered bathing hut, her eyes upon the Isherwood children as they roamed the hard looking for shells and small pebbles, she said into a long silence that had fallen between them, 'Matt – I'm sorry that I don't come to you as you do to me –'

He stopped her with a quick movement of his hand, the customary laughter fleetingly gone from his young face. 'Don't think of it.' He paused. 'It's best you don't.'

She knew how hard it must be for him to admit that to her. 'Matt?' she said again.

'Hmm?'

'If you should ever –' She stumbled over the words, uncertain how to express herself. 'That is – if you should ever find yourself in – well – trouble of any sort – you'd come to me, wouldn't you?'

'I won't be.' The voice was jaunty again, but she could not see his face as he leaned to toss a well-aimed stone at a great gull that had been strutting with arrogant unconcern nearby. The bird rose with an elegant lift of wing and a most inelegant and irritable squawk. 'Don't worry. I can take care of myself.'

'Well of course,' she said quickly, 'I know that. But – just in case – you promise me?'

He regarded her, the dark, graceless eyes veiled. 'I promise, moi owd Kitty,' he said.

But if both knew quite well of the things that Matt kept from Kitty, only Kitty knew of the growing heartache that she kept from her brother; for as the months went by and the marsh flowers that Amos had spoken of budded and bloomed so did Kitty's infatuation for the tall young man with the silver hair grow, painfully and frighteningly, and no amount of common sense or self-castigation could stop it. Thrown together as they so often were, she had little chance to fight it. Each glimpse of the cornflower eyes, the tall, wide-shouldered figure, the bright hair turned a knife of excitement in her that was, she knew, as absurd as it was unforgivable. She truly did her best to avoid him, was all but dumb in his presence, denied herself even the indulgence of fantasy; yet within her it seemed to her that the thought of him was always there, an ineradicable part of her. How it could have happened that this unknown young man who was husband to the sullen, flamboyantly lovely, but unloving Maria could have so effortlessly enslaved her was beyond her – his days were spent either on the *Girl May* or working in his father's fields, hers in the house or with the children. Yet when he was there, she knew it with sure instinct, and when he was not she was bereft.

It was not until the beginning of a still-cold April that she discovered a delightful and unsuspected common ground with him.

The children were fractious – all day it had drizzled from leaden skies that had seemed to rest squarely upon the chimneys of the house, keeping spirits down and tempers up, and still with dismal darkness creeping across the flat, watery landscape the rain showed no sign of easing. Cooped up indoors all day the twins had become progressively more quarrelsome, Jeremiah more wilful, Daniel more put-upon and 'Becca more peevish. Long before, Martha – now a bulky and uncomfortable seven months gone in her pregnancy – had given up the unequal struggle and retired to her room and her own particular comfort. Kitty sent up one of her brief regular prayers that this child should not be born with gin in its veins instead of blood and set about entertaining her difficult charges. At last, after a quiet game had degenerated into a chaos of fisticuffs and name-calling and Jeremiah had determinedly wriggled his way through the telling of Little Red Riding Hood, thus spoiling the story not only for himself but for everyone else, she remembered the battered upright piano that stood, never to her knowledge used, in the front parlour. Briskly she sent Hannah to light the ready-laid fire and herself kindled the candles that were set each side of the music stand on the piano. The children, ready to be bored before she started, trailed into the room after her, Hepzibar dumping the unfortunate 'Becca onto the floor and leaving her to stagger on uncertain legs to a nearby chair upon which she attempted dangerously to clamber, while her sister gazed dolefully out of the window at the rain. Kitty ran her fingers experimentally over the keys. To her surprise the instrument was remarkably tuneful. With one finger she picked out a tune remembered from happy childhood days at the Grange.

'Wass' that?' Jeremiah appeared at her elbow, one small fist poised above the piano keys which, before she could answer his question, he proceeded to thump discordantly. Her patience stretching like a very worn thread, Kitty slapped his hand away sharply. 'It's a song about a soldier,' she said. 'A not-very-nice soldier.'

Jeremiah brightened at that. 'Sing it to us,' he demanded.

The day had not been one for pleases and thank yous. Kitty let discretion oust valour and ignored the preremptory tone. She struck a soft chord.

'Oh, soldier, soldier, won't you marry me, With your musket, fife and drum?' She paused. 'Oh – no, sweet maid, I cannot marry thee, For I have no coat to put on –'

Hepzibar had abandoned her disconsolate staring out of the window and had turned, interested. Jeremiah on the other hand was put out by such girlish stuff. He sniffed, and banged the piano keys again, in a high, tinkling, discordant chord. Kitty determinedly drowned it with a strong martial one of her own and sang again, the tempo briskly marching. 'So *off* they went, To her *grand*father's chest, And *brought* him a coat, Of the *very, very* best, And the soldier put it on. – Oh, –'

The other children were drifting towards the piano now, Hepzibar automatically stooping and swinging the baby 'Becca into her arms as she passed.

'– soldier, soldier, will you marry me –'

By the third verse they were all singing. By the sixth they were making up unlikely articles of clothing so that the song should not come to an end. At last, laughing, Kitty slowed the accompaniment to a dirge. 'Oh, no, sweet maid, I cannot marry thee –' She paused. Her audience watched her with bated breath. 'I've a wife and a child of me own!'

That brought the house down. 'Sing us some more!' shrieked Jeremiah, swinging from the piano lid.

'Yes! Please, Kitty –!'

'Well,' Kitty said, 'something a little quieter I think. Why don't you be my little birds –' She played a pretty, simple tune, sang softly, 'I open wide my dove-cote door. The pigeons fly out and away they soar. They fly to green field and spreading tree – that's right, flap your wings – fly about the room, and then come home to roost – But soon to their roost they fly once more, And then I close tightly my pigeon-house door.' She caught hold of Jeremiah, the most enthusiastic of the little birds and hugged him tight.

'Sing it again! Sing it again!'

She sang it again. And again. And might well have been singing until midnight had she not, turning, caught sight of Amos standing still as a drawn figure by the door, the lines of his face bright in the light of the lamp he carried, and stopped, almost choking, in mid-bar.

'Oh, please – don't stop –'

'I was – playing with the children,' she said, stupid with surprise and shock.

'Yes. I heard.' He walked into the room, set the lamp upon the table. He moved always, she thought, with grace. She took her hands from the keys and folded them, very still, in her lap. His bright head gleamed in the rain-dark room. He smiled delightedly, his blue eyes persuasive. 'Would you sing something for me? You've a lovely voice.'

'I – thank you –' She had no control whatsoever over the deep flush of colour that rose in a tide from her throat to her cheeks. She turned from him, back to the piano. Cleared her throat. She loved to sing, and he had asked her. She could, after all, make a small gift to him.

Astonishingly, the children quieted.

'Her father bin a noble knight, Her mother bin a lady

bright –' She sang the sad little love song – that she and Anne had laughed so often and so heartlessly over – as if it were the story of her own life into a silence that was absolute and spellbound. As the last note died, reluctantly she raised her head. He was watching her, the brilliant eyes sober, bright and questioning. She looked away. There was a small, strange silence.

Then, 'Do you know this one?' he asked, and sang in a light and pleasant tenor, 'As I walked down a fair London street, A charming little oyster girl by chance I did meet, And into her basket I slyly did peep, For to see if she had any oysters –'

Picking up the simple tune as he sang, through the second and third verses she picked out, softly, a few accompanying chords. By the end, more boldly, she had mastered the tune. The end of the story, telling how the oyster girl, having outwitted her would-be seducer, picked his pocket and left the tavern paying his bill with his own money as she went, delighted her and she threw back her head and laughed unrestrainedly, forgetting for the moment the burden of her shyness with Amos.

He was riffling through a pile of old, damp-marked song sheets. 'Let's try something together – ah yes, this –' He set a sheet before her on the music stand, his arm brushing hers. 'Zach – light another lamp. There's a good lad. Now, Kitty – let's have a note –'

She struck a chord and their voices rose harmoniously. 'On Richmond Hill there lives a lass, More bright than May Day's morn –'

The communion was absolute, the mingling of their voices as instant and intimate a contact as if they had clasped hands. As she sang, so his voice blended perfectly with hers, the pretty, lilting melody complementing their improvised harmonies. As the song ended first Hepzibar and then her twin and the others applauded noisily. 'More! Sing some more!'

Amos smiled down at Kitty. 'You choose.'

The warmth of her delight in him shocked her. She shook

her head, her smile fading. 'I can't. I'm sorry. I have to get supper.' She heard in her own voice the odd and unnecessary brusqueness of nerves, saw the brief flash of surprise in his eyes.

Jeremiah pouted. 'Oh – oh!' And, 'Oh, please, Kitty,' Hepzibar begged.

Kitty stood up, closing the piano lid, her movements jerky. 'I'm sorry. Perhaps another day.'

In the dark hallway that led to the kitchen door his soft voice stopped her. 'Kitty?'

She stood for a moment, hand on the door handle, ridiculously and humiliatingly unable to turn to face him. When she did she knew her smile was wooden, her tone brittle. 'Yes?'

'It's my birthday – next week. I wondered – well it's so long since we've had a musical evening – there's been no one to play the piano since Ma died, you see –'

Kitty gave a quick little shake of her head. 'I doubt that your father would –'

'Oh, but yes!' he rushed on, 'of course he would. Please, Kitty – it'd be such a pleasure for us all.' In his enthusiasm he had moved very close to her. For a panic-stricken moment she was afraid he was about to take her hand. She backed against the door. 'That piano was my mother's. She had a lovely voice too, though nowhere near as good as yours – Pa used to love to listen to her. And the children – they'd enjoy it, too, now wouldn't they? You could teach them some songs –' He stopped, waiting, watching her, his face openly and boyishly pleading. 'Please?'

Trapped, she could do nothing but agree. 'I – well, yes, of course' – she stumbled over the words – 'if you'd really like to, and if your father agrees.'

'Oh, he will, I'm sure he will! Thank you.'

His smile, had he known it, was more than thank you enough. Kitty left him standing there, shut the kitchen door firmly and decisively in his face and set about the pots and pans with a clatter that might have been heard in Colchester.

5

(i)

Rather to Kitty's surprise Jonas did indeed agree with no argument and even with pleasure to the idea of a musical evening. And to her almost equal astonishment the next few days were the happiest she had spent since leaving Suffolk. Blithely unpredictable as always, the Isherwood children took to her singing lessons like small ducks to water. All but Jeremiah had reasonably tuneful voices, and what he lacked in musicality he made up for in volume and enthusiasm. There was a certain amount of brotherly and sisterly squabbling regarding the choice of solo voices – the children being nothing if not supremely confident in their own abilities – but this was soon settled by the choice of a solo each, and the rehearsals continued relatively peacefully. When Matt called to take her for a walk on Sunday in weather that had at last turned enjoyably spring-like and warm he remarked upon the change in her.

'Why shouldn't I be happy?' she asked in response to his comment. 'I'm settling down here. I like it. It suits me.'

He glanced about him, his mobile face caustic. 'This dead-and-alive hole?'

She made a quick, only half-playful lunge at him, clipped his ear smartly. 'Yes. And there's no need to be rude. We can't all be gay blades.'

He looked at her, curiosity in his eyes. 'You really like it here?'

She shrugged. 'Yes,' she said, staunchly.

'But – don't you ever feel – well, cut off? Lonely?'

She shook her head. 'Why should I? The family are always –'

'I'm not talking about the family. I mean – you work for them, don't you? However fancy they wrap it up. I mean – mates –' Ever restlessly energetic he vaulted in a single exuberant leap over a stile, and then waited with some impatience and no offer of help as she followed him, necessarily more decorously. 'Mates,' he repeated, as they strolled on in the sunshine, 'someone of your own. What goes on here? Are the islanders friendly?'

'I wouldn't exactly say that.' She bent to pick up a piece of twig, switched it idly in the grass as she walked. She saw no reason at all to tell her brother that apart from the fairly civil but meaningless exchanges she shared with the tradesmen who called at the house she had barely passed a word with anyone but the Isherwoods since the day she had arrived. 'They tend to keep themselves to themselves.' And no reason either to mention the covert glances that she knew followed her when she took the Isherwood children down to the hard to play, the sudden silences that fell as she passed, or walked into a shop. What did it matter? She was bound to be an outsider in this ancient, almost tribal community, with its rivalries and its gossip. She was perfectly content to be so. And happier, certainly, than she had been these many months.

It took an incident two days before the much-anticipated birthday celebration to show her, however, that old scars had not, as she had been too ready to believe, entirely healed and that her peace of mind was as fragile and easily shattered as fine-blown glass.

Late one afternoon, with pale April sunshine lighting the distant seascape and touching the new-budding trees with gold, she turned from the small kitchen window from which she had been watching the children playing in the yard to find Amos standing, quiet and still, in the doorway behind her. She started violently. He stepped forward with a quick gesture of concern. In his hand he held several sheets of music. 'I'm sorry. I didn't mean to make you jump.'

'It's all right. I didn't hear you, that's all.' As always the sight of him stirred her to a turmoil that affected voice and nerves and drove her to fury at her own weakness.

'I wondered if you'd got a minute spare to run through these with me?' He held up the dog-eared song sheets.

She forced a smile. 'Of course. If you'd like.' She walked briskly past him and led the way to the parlour and the piano. Slim, bright fingers of sunlight probed through the west-facing, latticed windows. She perched uncomfortably upon the piano stool, back ramrod straight.

'It's a fine evening,' he said.

'Yes.'

'I told you, didn't I, that the island was a prettier place when the sun shone?'

'Yes.'

Her monosyllabic replies apparently disturbed him not at all. 'Just wait till summer comes. You'll never see a finer sight than sails on the Blackwater in the summer sun.'

She did not reply, but busied herself at the piano, clearing the music stand of music, settling herself upon the stool, clearly dismissing his attempt at friendly conversation. He watched her for a moment, his expression entirely unreadable. Then he came close behind her, leaned over her shoulder as he put a piece of music upon the stand. 'Let's try this one, eh? It's *The Pretty Ploughboy*. D'you know it?'

She played a quiet chord. 'Yes. I've heard it certainly –'

And then, despite her stubborn defensiveness, the miracle happened again; they were instantly absorbed, all restraint falling from them as they shared the gift of music. Within minutes, in easy companionship, they were playing and singing, laughing at a wrong note, a stumbling phrase, enjoying again that extraordinary communion of spirit as their voices rose in impromptu harmonies.

'It was early, early, in the spring, When my true love went to serve his king –' Laughing he snatched the song sheet from its rest and tossed it on the table. 'No, no. Not that one. It's too sad. And anyway – it's got no tune at all. Try this one –'

The sun dipped to the mainland skyline, shimmering in

lucent glory upon the distant waters, painting the skies with an artist's palette of red and gold. In the breaks in their music they could hear the shrieks of laughter of the children as they played outside and, distantly, the sound of a herd of lowing cows as they plodded heavily to the milking parlour; while here within the sunlit room the music wove an enchantment that brought, fleetingly, happiness such as Kitty had all but forgotten could exist. Her voice rose, strong and clear and beautiful, perfected and tuned by her desire to please the young man who watched her, smiling his pleasure, sun-gilded head turned towards her, cornflower eyes intent – not, for this precious moment, another's husband and father to her children, but simply the object of all Kitty's desires, all her first, fierce, tender infatuation.

'That was grand!' he said when she had finished. 'You'll sing it for us on my birthday?'

'If you'd like me to.'

'I should say so! Oh – and that reminds me – Pa asked' – he was sorting once more through the sheets of music – 'ah – here it is – I'm sure you must know it –'

As she stared at the piece of music he placed before her the laughter and the happiness fled from her as if it had never been. She sat like a statue.

He did not notice. 'You know it?'

'Yes.' Her voice sounded peculiarly distant in her own ears. She cleared her throat, violently, laid wooden fingers to the piano keys, fluffed the introduction inharmoniously and had to start again. 'All round my hat I will wear the green willow –'

The drawing room at the Grange. Anne's fair, laughing face. Her brothers – her now-dead brothers – chaffing her for her slight, child's voice. 'Let Kitty sing! Let Kitty –!' Sir George, bluff and hearty, with his dogs and his guns, his contraband brandy and his endearing passion for a long-lost city. Then Anne's face again, as she had seen it that day on the dunes above Dunwich, stunned and desolate with grief. 'Oh, young men are false and they are so deceitful –' She stopped singing abruptly, in mid-breath. A few bars later, with treacherous tears blinding her, she stopped playing also and sat, rigid, fighting the waves of misery and homesickness that crashed over her.

'Kitty? What is it? What's the matter?'

She hardly heard the words. Blindly she stood, stumbled away from him to the window, resting her head upon the wooden frame and crying like a heartbroken child. 'I'm sorry,' she tried to say, her voice hiccoughing with the helpless violence of her tears. 'I'm sorry –'

He was beside her. With no thought and no predesign she turned to him, to the human comfort of his arms, his soft, consoling voice. It seemed the most natural thing in the world. It was several long minutes before the storm passed. She stood trembling then, tear-drenched eyes closed against the rough warmth of his cotton shirt. Then, slow and dreamlike as the transition between sleep and waking she became aware of where she stood – within the close circle of his arms, his heart beating steadily and strongly beneath her wet cheek. Aghast, she tried to pull away. With no effort he held her. She felt, light as the touch of a butterfly, the brush of his lips on her disordered hair. Beyond her own trembling she could sense his; even in her inexperience recognized the surge of excitement that was its source. She lifted her head to protest, and could not, caught by the expression on his sun-darkened face as he looked at her, by the dramatic line of bone, the brilliance of the blue eyes.

A moment before he bent his head to her she knew he would kiss her, and she could no more have stopped him – or herself – than she could have stopped her own breath. With all her helpless, innocent first love in her eyes she watched him, waiting. His mouth was warm, and unexpectedly soft as a girl's, yet oddly and excitingly demanding. Nothing – not Anne's ill-informed if interesting speculations, nor the hasty and entirely unsatisfactory experiments with Tom, the stable lad at the Grange, had in any way prepared her for this assault on her senses – an assault of savage sweetness such as she had never known could exist. For the space of perhaps a dozen heartbeats they clung together, enmeshed in the golden light that poured through the window, before he released her and stepped back, his sun-bright face flushed.

The kitchen door slammed. 'It's mine, I tell you! It *is*!' Sounds of a scuffle, and a muffled crash. An aggrieved shriek. 'I'll tell Kitty of you! I will!' A lifted, tear-filled voice. 'Kitty! Kitty!'

'Kitty –' Amos began, softly and fiercely.

The howls from the kitchen grew louder, punctuated by sounds that could only mean a stand-up fight.

Her eyes never leaving Amos' intense face, Kitty backed away from him.

'Ki-tty!' Another crash.

With no word to Amos Kitty turned and fled.

A new kind of agony now. No longer the half-acknowledged, childish longing for a lovely, unattainable object, but an obsessive memory she could not erase, a restless physical need, the more painful for not, in her innocence, being clearly defined, coupled with a shame so deep she hardly knew how to face him, or the others, certain that her sin – for sin it certainly was to lust so for Maria Isherwood's young husband – must clearly show, burned upon her face like the brand of whoredom she had read of in the Bible. It was as if the touch of Amos' lips had opened some fearful Pandora's box of emotions and longings, the existence of which in all of her nearly eighteen years she had never even suspected. She had not known it possible to want anything – need anything – as she now wanted – needed – Amos Isherwood's touch. It was her nightmare that she might betray herself, crawl to him, beg him, embarrass them both with the appalling intemperance of her feelings. For certainly, of course those moments in the parlour could not have meant to him what they had to her. With her stupid, childish weeping she had simply aroused in him an understandable desire to comfort which, in the warmth of the moment, had translated itself to a transient lust. What man with Maria Isherwood to warm his bed would so much as glance at skinny, inexperienced Kitty Daniels? And with that bitter thought came another unwelcome emotion; jealousy gnawed her, despicable and deadly. What in God's name, she found herself wondering wretchedly, was happening to her?

The musical evening, so happily anticipated, was for her and, she assumed, for Amos a purgatory of embarrassment from which she could not escape soon enough, though everyone else, even the difficult Maria, seemed to enjoy it greatly. Kitty played and sang mechanically, eyes riveted to the music before her, every nerve in her body painfully aware of Amos, standing tense as a strung wire next to her. On the rare occasion she glanced at him he avoided her eyes. In the intervals between songs he went immediately to Maria, perching upon the arm of her chair, even once sitting on the floor at her feet, a sight that no matter how she tried to prevent it turned a bitter blade in poor Kitty's heart. By the end of the evening she had decided in her own mind that she must leave. To endure the cruel torment of his close proximity was more than she could bear. She could not, of course, go immediately – Martha's child was due in about four weeks, and Kitty suspected that to abandon that strangely lonely woman at this stage might trigger disaster – but as soon as may be she would go. Matt still talked occasionally of London and of the high old times they'd have just as soon as she saw sense and agreed to go. Perhaps it wasn't such a bad idea after all.

On that cool, windy night of Amos' birthday, standing at her uncurtained attic window watching in bleak envy the small, flickering light that gleamed fitfully from an upstairs room in the cottage by the gate, Kitty, miserable tears sliding down her face, resolved to speak to her brother soon about leaving for London in a couple of months' time.

(ii)

Determined as she had been, however, at the moment of making that decision, Kitty's suggestion to Matt was never made. It was just four days later – four days in which an almost desperate Kitty retreated into a shell of silence, barely acknowledging Amos when they chanced to meet – that he, face unusually forbidding, stepped quietly into the kitchen where she was preparing the family meal and closed the door firmly behind him.

She stared at him, knowing the blood to be draining from her face. Then, very carefully, she put down the spoon she had been using and clasped her hands very firmly before her. She would not have him see their trembling. She did not speak.

'Lost your tongue?' he asked, harshly.

The roughness of his tone took her entirely by surprise. She blinked, took a sharp breath.

'Well?' A disturbing, pent-up anger was clear in his voice, in the brilliance of his eyes.

'I – no – of course not –'

'Well, you could ha' fooled me these past days. Not good enough to talk to, am I?'

'Amos – please –!' She was shaking now, her brain and tongue paralysed by his presence and his unexpected anger.

He stepped closer, only the width of the table between them. 'You playin' with me?' he asked, very quietly. 'Are you? You the kind of girl likes to make a fool of a man –?'

'No! Of course not!' He came around the table towards her. Incredulous, half-frightened, she stepped back from him. And yet she was aware of something else – aware that beneath her confusion and distress her heart had taken up a steady, driving beat of intense excitement. She loved him, oh, how she loved him! And he was here – his angry attention concentrated upon her alone. The thought flashed into her mind that she would not care if he struck her. The recognition of that appalled her. She lifted her head fiercely. 'Don't come a step nearer! Don't dare!'

He stopped. Had she been a little more experienced she might have recognized the flicker of calculation in his eyes. Then he turned away, hands spread upon the table, shoulders hunched almost to his ears.

She held herself rigidly from him.

He lifted his head at last. 'God, Kitty – I'm sorry. Truly I am. It's only that – since the other day –' He shook his head, his face a boy's again, pleading, 'I couldn't stand it that you might hate me –'

'Hate you? *Hate you!*' There was a small, incredulous sob of laughter in the words. 'I don't hate you.'

Something gleamed again in his face and was gone. She caught her breath, knowing that she had betrayed herself.

From above their heads a weak voice called, 'Kitty?'

'God Almighty!' Amos said, voice ragged with frustration.

'Kitty!' Martha's voice was querulous.

Kitty cleared her throat. 'Coming.'

'Kitty – wait –' He caught her hand as she turned. 'We can't leave it like this. You know we can't. Meet me. Tomorrow. We have to talk –'

She stared at him wordless.

'Five Acre Barn,' he said, his voice low and rapid. 'You know it?'

She did not reply.

Almost he shook her. 'Kitty! Do you know it?'

'Yes.'

'Tomorrow afternoon. About three. I'll meet you. Pa's going into Colchester, so we'll be in by then.'

'I –'

'You'll be there –' The words were imperative, only barely a question.

Of course she would not. The suggestion was outrageous.

'Kitty –! You'll be there!'

'Yes,' she said.

How she got through the endless day she never could afterwards recollect. After an all but sleepless night she had climbed tiredly from her bed determined not to keep the tryst; but one glance at Amos' unsmiling, questioning face in the soft light of an April dawn before he and his father left for the *Girl May* undid all those hard-won resolutions at a stroke. As the day wore on she swung exhaustingly upon the pendulum of her emotions, swinging from a wild anticipation that took no count of right or wrong to an utter determination not to go. Then, as the hour approached, the innate and uncompromising honesty that was her pride and her bane forced her to admit it – since he had spoken those words, 'You'll be there,' she had known that she would be, and that no power on earth would stop her.

She left the house at a few minutes to three, the basket that was to be her excuse if questioned swinging in her hand. Half a mile along the track from the house she struck out across the fields to where the barn known as the Five Acre stood, on a rise of ground overlooking the wide Blackwater, sheltered by a grove of wind-twisted oak trees. The day was fine and clear, high clouds scudding across the blue vault of the spring sky, their fast-moving shadows dappling earth and water beneath them. Out on the water stood the wing-like sails of the oyster fleet, very close together, hardly moving as they dredged with the tide, their manoeuvres like the stately, esoteric patterns of a dance of which only they knew the steps and the purpose. She watched for a moment, her eye caught by the peaceful beauty of the scene. Seabirds wheeled and called above the little smacks. A mile or so away the smoke from the clustered chimneys of the City drifted fragrantly in the air.

By contrast to the bright day the lofty interior of the vast barn was dark, cool and still. She paused at the wide empty doorway, its cavernous, dusty depths awaiting the year's harvest. A bird fluttered about the soaring, ancient beams of the roof. Gleams of sunlight, sharp as bright needles in the gloom, glinted through holes in the tiles of the roof and the planks of the wooden walls.

'Amos?' Her uncertain voice echoed to the vaulted roof.

Silence hung like a curtain. Dust motes stirred, shimmering in the air about her as she stood, tense and waiting.

Her heart sank. He wasn't there. He hadn't come. Had probably never intended to come –

'Amos? Are you there?'

There was a flash of movement in the shadowed darkness,

and there, smiling, he was. Against all real hope, all expectation, he was waiting for her.

She knew and did not care that all the longing and love she felt for him was in her face as she turned to him.

Neither spoke. In a few long strides he reached her, caught her shoulders with quick strength, pulled her to him, covering her face, her hair, her neck with kisses. Drowning in the excitement of it she clung to him, her hands in his hair, on the wind-roughened skin of his face, touching his features with her fingertips as if struck blind and seeing him with her touch. When they drew apart they were both trembling, and the silence was a strange one: what words now could explain, excuse, debate?

He retained a hold upon her hand. 'Kitty,' he said softly at last, and then again, 'Kitty.' And it was as if that simple repetition of her name were enough to settle all arguments, answer all anguished questions. 'Lovely, lovely girl.'

She shook her head, blushing.

'Oh – yes. I thought so the very first time I saw you, with that wild, white face and lovely eyes –'

Wordless she reached a hand to his face, touched his lips, warm and soft, lightly with her finger. The scuttling, whispering darkness of the barn enclosed them. They might have been alone in creation. She thought she had never seen anything so truly beautiful as his face, shadowed and smiling. And in that moment the world's judgement mattered not a fig. 'I love you,' she said, simply, and there was such relief in the saying of the words that she could have sung with sheer happiness. 'I love you,' she said again.

He laughed softly, teasingly, throwing back his head. 'And I thought you hated me!'

'Of course I didn't,' she said and then, with strange and gentle perspicacity, 'You knew I didn't.'

Perhaps wisely, he did not reply to that, but drew her, unresisting, deeper into the darkness to where a pile of dry, fragrant hay was piled against the wall. Laughing still, he sank back into it, pulling her after him. At the last moment, however, she let go of his hand, and as he lay, arms wide, smiling up at her she sat almost decorously beside him, straight and still, her long legs tucked beneath her spreading skirts, her hands clasped in her lap.

He folded his arms behind his head, narrowed his eyes as he watched her. 'Take down your hair,' he said abruptly, then as a soft afterthought, 'Please.'

She did not move.

The long, tangled lashes flickered, veiling but not hiding the bright devil of excitement in his vivid eyes. 'Please,' he said again, the intense word as much command as plea.

She could not resist him. At that moment she would have done anything he had asked. Slowly she unpinned the heavy coils of hair, shaking them out onto her shoulders, veiling her face as she bowed her head.

He reached a long arm, coiled an uncompromisingly smooth and straight lock about his finger. Then he reached further, tangling his hand painfully into her hair, pulling her to him. She did not fight him. He pulled her on top of him, then as they kissed rolled over so that his body pinned hers beneath it. As suddenly as a leap of flame a searing excitement took her, wiping her brain clear of everything but the fiercest desire she had ever known, a wild conflict of submission and aggression that melted her body beneath his whilst her long, strong fingers and sharp teeth matched his force with a strength and wildness of her own. He shuddered, burying his face in her disordered hair. She felt his fingers at the buttons of her bodice and she stilled, biting her lip, fighting a small lift of panic.

'Kitty –' he said. 'Kitty – help me –'

Never in her life had her breasts been bared to a man's eyes. That alone – the expression on his face as he looked at her – before he had touched her swelled them and engorged the teats. With lips and tongue then he teased her, until, arching her back, she moaned a little. He transferred his mouth to hers, stifling her breath, taking her wet nipples between roughened thumb and forefinger, squeezing and pulling lightly and rhythmically with a relentless, practised, sweetly painful force. The waves of excitement that took

her were all but unbearable. Then he pulled away from
her and was kneeling above her, the dramatic, gilded head
outlined in the light thrown by the dipping sun through the
doorway, his face in shadow. Their wild movements stilled
for a moment. She lay waiting, trembling, for the first
time afraid. His eyes never leaving hers, he reached to her
disordered skirts.

She moved her head sharply, in an almost unconscious,
panic-stricken negative.

'It's all right,' he said in a voice that beneath its gentleness
was threaded sharp with excitement. 'I won't hurt you. I
promise. I won't do anything to hurt you. I want to see you,
that's all. To touch you. I won't hurt you – I promise I won't
hurt you –'

Almost hypnotized by his voice and the brilliance of his
eyes she lay, still as a rabbit that is prey to a stoat. She did
not move as he pulled her skirts to her waist and deftly
untied the tapes of her drawers. As if from very far away she
heard her own voice, 'No – please –' Another whisper in the
whispering darkness.

He took no notice. His swift hands moved with sure
confidence and then she lay all but naked in the darkness,
the warm air cold as shame upon the pale, fine skin of her
belly and thighs. She was shaking now, uncontrollably, with
fear and with that intolerable excitement that his touch
induced in her.

'There, now. Gently. Gently –' Fingers, lips, tongue,
feather-light, shockingly arousing. Never had she dreamed
of such pleasure, of such enslavement to touch and sensation. He knelt above her, mastering her, and affording her,
she realized as she lay beneath his knowing fingers, the
extremes of pleasure that for the moment he denied himself.
A tide of delight rose mercilessly from his manipulating
fingers, and she abandoned herself to a climactic violence
of pleasure and pain that burned in her body like fire, a fire
that fed upon itself, demanding and addictive. She reached
for him, crying his name. He held her for a moment as she
drifted in darkness upon waves of weakening sensation.

Then, 'Now –' he said, and his voice was harsher, more urgent. 'Now, pretty Kitty – you'll help me, won't you? See – like this –' He guided her hand, smiling into her astonished, half-frightened eyes. 'Ah, no – don't cover yourself. Let me see you. Now – kiss me –' He too was now all but naked, his slim body a flame of white in the darkness. 'Kiss me there – and yes! Like that! – don't worry – you won't hurt me –' And the darkness of that strange afternoon deepened and became more complex as she explored his willing body and watched its power pulse and grow and then spend itself beneath her hands and questing tongue. She had not dreamed herself capable of such things – guilt and shame crouched within her, waiting – waiting for the inevitable aftermath of such sin, waiting to lift a leering head and promise the punishment that must surely follow such wickedness. Yet as she lay beside him, her face buried in his naked shoulder, she could not bring herself to regret. She loved; with her body and her soul she loved. That, surely, could not be entirely wicked? Yet she was downcast and silent as, avoiding his eyes she dressed and recoiled her hair about her head, and he noticed it.

He lifted her chin with his finger. 'What's this?'

She shook her head, eyes downcast.

His smile, had she seen it, held a small glint of gentle triumph. 'Silly girl. Tell me.'

She turned from him. 'You know. You're married –'

'You knew that when you came here this afternoon. Yet still you came.' The tone had a sudden, hard little edge to it that turned her back to face him, anxiously.

'I didn't mean –'

He stopped her mouth with his, the momentary harshness gone. 'Of course not. Darling Kitty – pretty Kitty – listen to me. My marriage to Maria is no marriage. You must know that? The moment I saw you I knew you'd understand me as she never could. We're doing no one any harm, you and I. How could we be?' He stopped, watching her intently. She shook her head, bemused. 'You'll meet me again? Here?'

She hesitated for only a moment. 'Yes.' There was a

finality about the word that frightened her a little – yet
there was no other answer she could give.

He relaxed, smiling again. 'I'll let you know when.'

'Yes.'

He kissed her again. 'We'll have to go. You first, I'll follow
in ten minutes or so. We must be careful.' The words were
matter-of-fact. Dimly she perceived that the deception had
begun.

She nodded, turned to leave, then stopped, driven to saying
just once more those words that she had denied herself
so often, the words that made wrong right and excused
everything. 'Amos, I love you.'

She saw the flash of his smile in the shadows before she
stepped into the world beyond the cool darkness, submitting
herself to the swordstroke of light and warmth beyond the
door, and refusing for a moment to consider the fact that
not once in all their whispering and lovemaking had he used
those words to her.

Her world became dominated by Amos, her days measured
by the times of their meeting, her life ruled by her desire
for him. She prevaricated shamelessly, to herself no less
than to others, in order to see him, however briefly, to touch
him, and also to convince herself that what they did was
not truly wrong. So consuming was her reckless infatuation
that such considerations as pride and honesty, until now
her touchstones, weighed little against it. There were of
course occasions when the sharp teeth of guilt and doubt
gnawed like rats in a far dark corner, when her good sense
and dignity struggled to reassert themselves; but a swift,
hidden smile, a glimmer in the lucent eyes as he looked at
her and she would be lost again. There were times when
she wondered if her feelings and her deceptions were not
too transparent, for she was ill-used to subterfuge. Was it
her imagination that Maria's hostility to her had deepened?
That the resentful glances that she had grown used to
receiving from the charmless Hannah now seemed to hold
an unpleasantly sly and knowing gleam? But when such

worries assailed her she reassured herself that it could not be so. Her conscience might be sleeping, but it was by no means dead, and if she jumped at shadows she had at least the sense left to see those shadows for what they surely must be – the reflections of her own guilt. In her heart she knew that what she and Amos were doing was wrong, and could come to no good end. In moments of honesty she knew there to be no future for her with him. Yet this first passion of her young life so ruled her that she told herself she did not care. She lived for the day and for the sight of Amos, for their swift glances and their bitter-sweet hours in the great barn that had become their haven. Her tender conscience she salvaged with that magic word 'love' – they loved, so what they did could not be judged by the yardstick exercised by ordinary people in ordinary situations. Her suspicion that she was not the first nor likely to be the last to use this perilous reasoning to justify the unjustifiable did nothing to prevent her clinging stubbornly to it. On the gale-swept day in May that she surrendered her body to him, fully and willingly, she felt no added burden of guilt. He had her soul already in his keeping; to yield her body to his pleadings and so assuage their fierce hunger for each other was a small thing by comparison. They lay together afterwards and listened to the wild summer rain that lashed from the sea to fling itself in fury at the great wooden walls of the barn, and in the storm-filled silence she seemed to hear the words 'I love you' so clearly in her heart that almost she could convince herself that he had spoken them.

During the first days of June, with the oyster fishing season finished till autumn and the spring's lambs growing plump upon the sea-girt grasslands, Martha Isherwood, in drawn-out anguish and almost at cost to her life, bore to Jonas another lusty son, Thomas Paul. The prolonged and painful labour, culminating in the barbarously agonizing, life-and-death struggle of birth, appalled and frightened Kitty. During the week that followed she and the slatternly midwife from the City fought to keep the guttering flame of life burning in the pallid creature who lay unmoving in

the big bed, showing interest neither in her newborn child
nor in the tiresome ministrations of those who fought to
save her. Despite a spent lack of co-operation on her
patient's part, Kitty refused to give up. Stubbornly she stayed
by Martha, talking, cajoling, scolding, forcing the exhausted
woman to take broths and soups, refusing to listen to her
feeble protests. And then as summer settled in at last to the
world beyond the latticed windows and the swallows and
martins swooped, calling, about the eaves of the old house
the ebbing tide of Martha's strength was stemmed and,
painfully slowly at first, her health began to improve.

It was not until three weeks after Thomas Paul's birth,
with Martha at last on the slow road to recovery, that Kitty
realized with something of a pang that her own eighteenth
birthday had passed, unmarked and unnoticed, the week
before. It being no one's fault but her own – she having
neglected to mention her birthday to anyone in the house
– she could hardly complain, and anyway any self-pity she
might have been tempted to indulge in was completely
dispelled by the arrival on the following Sunday afternoon
of her unchangingly unpredictable brother with a gift of a
shining jet necklace with matching earrings and brooch and
a bunch of flowers large enough to have decked the whole
of Mersea church.

'Matt! They're lovely! Thank you so much!' She held the
necklace to her throat, turned this way and that, admiring
her reflection in the glass front of the kitchen dresser.
Judiciously she had refrained from enquiring as to the source
of the gift.

He grinned, pleased. 'Come on – put them on – let's
show these bumpkin islanders what a pretty girl looks
like –'

They strolled together down the lane towards the village.
It was a perfect day; for once there was a mild land-breeze
that, soft with the fragrances of early summer, lacked the
chill knife-edge of the easterlies. It sighed, softly, through
the tall, waving grasses that rippled in the sunshine as if
mimicking in play the movement of the distant waters on

the calm estuary. A lapwing lifted almost from their feet as they passed, and wheeled, calling eerily, above their heads, whilst high above it a lark spilled her golden torrent of song through the sunlit air to the earth below. They stopped for a moment and leaned upon a ramshackle gate, looking in companionable silence across the glimmering waters to the mainland with its picturesque lifts of tree-mantled land and its tall church spires. 'Well –' Matt turned from the view, restless as always, and leaned on his elbows, his back to the gate, one heel hooked into the bars, his dark head tilted to the sun. 'When are you going to change your silly mind and come to London with me, moi owd Kitty?'

She glanced at him in surprise. It had been some time since he had mentioned any thought of leaving. She had over the past months assumed that he had become as settled in Colchester as she was on the island. He moved his head, avoiding her eyes. She frowned a little, feeling a small stirring of unease, noting for the first time a certain tension about him, a strained tautness about his face that was at odds with his usual easy laughter. She shook her head. 'I –'

'Oh, all right, all right, I was only joking.' He turned again, drummed his fists lightly against the wood of the gate, his voice, his stance, everything about him, suddenly too careless, too studiedly casual.

She watched him for a moment longer. She knew him too well. 'Matt? Is something wrong? I mean –' All the old anxieties that had been lying in ambush, camouflaged by distance and by a certain amount of deliberate self-deception, sprang to life, full blown. 'You aren't in some sort of trouble?'

'Oh, for Gawd's sake!' The edgy exasperation that under-lay his grin was ill-concealed and did little to reassure her. ''Course not! Hey – by the way' – the words came in the same breath, blatantly changing the course of the conversation – 'tell me something – you been having any trouble with that Amos? Heard a few things about him the other day – he bothers you, you let me know, eh?'

She blinked at him abstractedly, half her attention still taken by her concern for him. 'What? What do you mean? What have you heard?'

'Oh, come on – you must know?'

'Know what? Who have you been talking to?' He had her attention now.

'On the way back from here last time I stopped off at The Rose – you know, the big place at Peldon, t'other side of the Strood?'

'I know it.' Strangely she found her throat to be dry. She cleared it, nervously.

'There's a girl there – Maisie Biggs – nice little thing. Well, we got talking and I told her where you worked.' He lifted his eyebrows, whistled a little, shook the fingers of his right hand as if they had been burned. 'By, did she have some things to say about Amos Isherwood!'

'Things? What sort of things?' Somewhere in the pit of her stomach a small twinge of acid discomfort had flared, unpleasantly bringing saliva to her mouth.

He turned and looked at her, dawning surprise in his eyes. 'You mean you really don't know? The lad's a regular tomcat by all accounts. Why do you think there's not a village girl'll work for the Isherwoods? If there was one who wanted to, her family wouldn't let her, so says Maisie. The last girl – the one before you – he got her in the family way and they threw her out. And it isn't the first time, neither, why – that snooty old wife of his –'

Kitty's hands, that had been lightly clasped on top of the gate were clamped now to the splintered wood as if to life itself. She heard her brother's voice, struggled to follow the words, as if from a great distance: '– laughing stock of the island, Amos Isherwood and his rutting ways – got his come-uppance when Maria's father escorted him to church with a shotgun –'

It was as if she had known. Had he laughed, she found herself wondering somewhere in a small, agonizingly cool corner of her mind, to find her so easy?

'– and according to Maisie there's dark alleys in Mersea

that the lad wouldn't venture down alone. Half the fathers and brothers on the island are after him —'

His voice went on, but she heard no more. Cold waves of humiliation washed through her, making the blood rush in her ears so that her brother's voice rose and fell eerily, blinding her eyes so that the sunlight that had been so golden and welcome a short while before seemed harsh and hurtful.

'Gawd, Kit —' Matt said, heedlessly relishing the joke of his knowing more about her employers than she did, 'did you really not know? I know you said the islanders were close-mouthed, but this really takes the biscuit — Here —!' He stopped suddenly, frowning. 'He hasn't tried anything on, has he —? I mean to say —'

She wanted to scream. She wanted to cry. She wanted to cover her ears and her eyes and never to hear or see anything ever again. She stood, calm and still, even, faintly, smiled. 'Not a thing. I suppose I can't be his type.'

Easily reassured, he shrugged. ''Course he's a good-looking cove, I'll grant him that. Not surprising they fall for him like skittles, eh?'

'I suppose not.' With an effort of will that all but drained her she pushed herself away from the support of the gate. 'Matt — do you mind if we go back? I don't like to leave Martha for too long.' To her own utter astonishment her voice was perfectly cool and normal.

He shrugged. 'We can go back now if you like.' He hesitated, and though Kitty was now too distracted to notice it, the too-confident over-brightness was back in his voice: ''S'a matter of fact I wouldn't mind getting back a bit earlyish myself.' He winked, swaggering. 'Got to see a man about a dog.'

They turned back towards the house. Kitty walked in silence. Now that her shocked brain had started to work again she realized that she did not for a moment doubt Matt's gossip. Nor was she stupid enough for one moment to doubt the relevance of the story to herself. It was as if some small part of her had known, had always known, that her flawed lover with his sapphire eyes and hard, knowing hands would in the end prove himself the punishment for her sin. As she walked collectedly beside her brother, in the small, stubborn corner of her soul that had remained untouched by Amos Isherwood's charm, she cringed, flinching from her own folly and self-delusion. A handsome face, an ounce of attention, and she had come running like a bitch to snapped fingers. The warm tide of humiliation rose higher. Then, somewhere in the recesses of her aching heart a very small voice asked – perhaps not? Perhaps, with me, it was different?

Then why, asked the plangent voice of common sense, tart with the relief of release after so long in thrall, has he never once told you he loved you? For you well know he never has –

Her brother seemed entirely unaware of her abstracted silence. He chattered on – only vaguely did she register what he was talking about – a mysterious deal, the big one – enough to set them up – take them at last to London –

'Yes,' she heard herself saying. 'Perhaps you're right. Why not London? A new start entirely –'

'Dead right.' He was pleased. 'Just give me another couple of days. Then I'll let you know – well, here we are –' They paused at the gate, in the shadow of the cottage in which lived Amos and Maria. In the tiny garden little Joseph played, hunkered to the ground, his attention entirely taken by the heap of stones around which his solemn private game was centred. Kitty averted her eyes sharply from his fair, sun-gilt head.

'I'm sorry?' Her brother had spoken, but she had not caught the words.

Grinning he jerked his head towards the cottage. 'I said keep a weather eye out for matey there.' He raised the dark, wing-like eyebrows that were so much like her own. 'I'd hate to have to sort him out. He's bigger than me.'

Stiff-lipped, she laughed with him. 'I will,' she said.

She faced Amos in the barn, their barn – and who else's? she had wondered bitterly as she had walked across the fields – quiet-voiced, all her pain in her eyes and in the bleak line of her mouth. 'Amos – why didn't you tell me about – about the others? About the girl you got pregnant?'

He moved towards her, easy penitence in the summer-bright face, confidence in his reaching hands. 'Kitty –'

She stepped away from him. 'Why didn't you tell me?' she asked again, flatly.

He half turned from her, his shoulders lifting in a shrug of quick exasperation. 'What would have been the point?' The soft mouth was petulant.

At least, to her relief, he had not bothered to deny or try to excuse. She looked at him for a long, bitter moment, words teeming in her head, refusing utterly to order themselves and come to her tongue. Blindly and without speaking she turned from him.

The hand that seized her arm was not gentle. 'Where d'you think you're going?'

With a violence born of self-disgust at the effect that his touch still had upon her she wrenched herself free. 'Leave me alone.' But, strong as she was she was no match for muscles toughened by fishing and farming. He held her with ease. Incensed, she fought him as he pulled her to him; and felt how her struggles inflamed him. 'Amos, let me go! Let – me – go!'

He turned her to him, his hands brutal on her shoulders, shaking her, then holding her, arms pinned to her side, helpless. 'Tell me, Kitty – pretty Kitty –' he said, his voice low and trembling with that familiar excitement that communicated itself to her through his touch like the running line of flame that devours a fuse, 'tell me why you are so angry? What has changed? What has truly changed?'

She trembled in his hands, speechless.

'I'll tell you, shall I? You've discovered that you were not the first. Is that so terrible? Did I ever pretend otherwise?' He shook her again, like a boneless doll. 'Did I?'

Bleakly she shook her head.

'Then why the commotion? For God's sake – I have a wife and children – you knew that – yet it did not stop you –'

This time in fury she did manage to pull away from him. Her smoothly sun-browned face was poppy bright. She turned from him. 'You never loved me.'

'I never said I did.' It was wholly reasonable, wholly hurtful.

She flung around to face him. 'How many others have there been? How many others like me, who were weak enough, stupid enough to be gulled into playing your games with you –?'

His shrug was totally dismissive.

Her spoiled love was like a sickness, tainting body and mind; she was powerless against its malice. 'I hate you!' she spat.

Had he not laughed she might never have touched him again. But he did and, goaded beyond control, the tinder of her temper flaring balefully, she hit him with every ounce of strength she possessed powering the blow. Her knuckles, more by luck than intent, caught his mouth and she felt sharp pain as his teeth caught her skin, saw the bright blood blossom upon his lips. With a grunt of anger he reached for her, pinning her arms to her sides, trapping her struggling body with his own. Locked so together they tumbled, thrashing, to the dusty floor, Kitty taking the brunt of the fall with Amos' not inconsiderable weight on top of her. He took no notice of her cry of genuine pain. With savage, excited strength he pinned her beneath him, stopping her cries with his mouth. She tasted his blood, salt and warm. Felt the treachery of her own body, knew herself even now to be incapable of denying him this final act of aggression and submission. She stilled, panting. He lifted his head, looking at her with triumph in his eyes. 'I thought I loved you,' she said, softly and scornfully, 'I really believed I loved you.'

He took her then, with self-absorbed force and she neither resisted his violence nor denied him his pleasure. Instead she rode herself upon the thrusting waves of his strength in an abandonment to lust that was all that was left of her blighted love. When he had done she very composedly stood, wiping his blood from her mouth with her handkerchief, re-coiling her disordered hair, re-ordering her clothing. Then she stood looking down at him. He lay upon his back, utterly relaxed, watching her through half-closed eyes, obviously confident still of his hold upon her. Neither of them had spoken.

Her voice was soft and clear, hard as diamond. 'I shall leave as soon as I can,' she said. 'But I shan't run away from you. I'll wait until my brother and I are ready to go. In the meantime' – she paused, her face expressionless – 'if you so much as touch me again, Amos, I'll kill you. I promise it.'

And, seeing the sudden flicker of the girlish lashes, the astonished and wary expression in the blue eyes, she had at least the empty satisfaction of knowing that he believed her.

(iii)

Her bravado lasted less than an hour before crumbling into miserable self-pity and a total inability to think clearly. At first she waited for Matt, watching for him, rehearsing how she would tell him that she had decided at last to go to London. But a week passed, and then two and he did not come. She was not particularly worried – he had left it longer than this between visits on other occasions – but found herself in the grip of torpor, will-less and dispirited, from which she could not break free. She lived as she had lived before, ate and drank and spoke as she had done before – even occasionally smiled, though rarely laughed; but it was as if something within her had died and in its passing had taken something of herself with it. She tended to Martha and the children, looked after the house, tried to ignore the sly question in Hannah's eyes that followed her too closely and too often.

Hannah it was who turned the knife in the wound – deliberately? maliciously? Kitty neither knew nor cared – by breaking the news that Maria was pregnant again. The news, just a week after the scene with Amos in the barn, woke many emotions; jealousy, self-disgust, and above all, fear. Foolishly it had never occurred to Kitty that she too could easily suffer the fate and public humiliation of the girl who had been her predecessor. Supposing she should be pregnant? The belated thought terrified her. She lay awake for long, anguished nights, begging God to spare her that, anything else – any punishment – she would accept; but please, oh please, not that. For two weeks her life became an intolerable, drawn-out agony of waiting. By the end of that time, with her period a scant day late, she was convinced that the worst had happened and was ready to die of it. When the proof came, late that night, that she was not after all carrying Amos' child she cried impassioned tears of relief and gratitude and then slept the sleep of the dead for the first time in weeks.

It was as well that she did – for it was in the seeping, pearly, pre-dawn light of the following day that her brother came, hunted and desperate. She woke to the rattling sound of pebbles against her window. She lay for a moment, groggily confused, eyes still throbbing and swollen from the tears of the night before. The sound came again. She slipped from her bed and opened the window. Matt's marked face, white as alabaster, stark in the pale light, stared up at her. Even in the half-darkness she could see the blood, the purpling bruises.

'My God! Matt! What –?'

'Ssh!' Every line of his body was desperation. 'Kitty – I have to talk to you –'

'Wait. I'll come down. Go to the front door. Hannah sleeps in the kitchen.'

Her fingers like thumbs, she pulled on her woollen robe and, still fighting the loosened plaits of her long hair, fled down the stairs to the door. He was waiting outside, shivering, running blood.

'Good God!' she said, horrified, and reached to pull him in.

With surprising strength he resisted her. 'No.' He was far gone in exhaustion and pain, yet the intransigent obstinacy she knew all too well and that had got him this far, battered as he was, showed in the line of his bloodied mouth. 'Can't stay. Have to get away. Came to –'

'Matt!'

'Came to say goodbye an'' – he grinned twistedly, staggered a little, righted himself – 'an' to borrow – some money –'

'Matt, for Heaven's sake let me at least tend to those cuts –'

'Can't. Too many people know about you. Someone'll put two an' two together an' start lookin'.'

'Who? Who's looking for you?' The sinking of her heart put sharpness in her tone.

Once again the grin was crooked, distorted by crushed lips, but it was recognizably Matt's. 'All the world an' his wife. Friend. Foe. The law' – his knees buckled again and he leaned against the wall – 'and the lawless. I've really done it this time, moi owd Kitty. Like you always said I would.' He pushed himself away from the wall, made a gallant attempt to stand upright. Through the heartbreaking bravado she could all but smell his terror.

She stared at him. 'Matt – what were you thinking of? Coming here. If they guess – anyone who wants you only has to stand guard on the causeway –'

He drew a massive, trembling breath. 'Had to say goodbye, didn't I? Couldn't just go off – not like before. Don't fuss. I can swim.'

'In that condition?' She was appalled. 'Matt – surely it can't be as bad as that? What – what have you done –?'

He shook his head. 'Nothing they won't cut my throat for.' He tried again to grin, but looking at him in despair Kitty knew that he was not joking. He was next to delirious with pain and exhaustion. If she let him go like this she knew instinctively he stood no chance at all. The thought cleared her head; suddenly, for the first time in weeks, she was herself again, quick-thinking and positive. She caught him firmly by the shoulders, propped him against the wall. 'Wait here. Don't move.'

'What're you doing?' His speech was getting more slurred with every word.

'I'm coming with you. The skiff's on the hard by the church. If we take that we'll be in Salcott in half an hour and Maldon by noon. No one will catch us then. Wait!' she exhorted him again, fiercely and unnecessarily, and sped indoors.

The mile-long journey to the beach, encumbered by her injured brother and the small bundle of possessions she had hastily thrown together, seemed like ten. As the sky grew progressively and threateningly brighter, and the ghostly, transparent summer moon faded, she tried to hurry Matt, knowing that only one inquisitive early riser could be their undoing. Bravely, but almost at the end of his tether, he hurried his stumbling steps. When at last they reached the skiff it was all he could do to tumble aboard and collapse like a heap of bloody rags in the scuppers. Single-handed, desperation lending her strength, she kilted her skirts about her waist and pushed off, then scrambled inelegantly aboard and laid hold of the oars. At the far rim of the world the first crimson light of morning bloodied the moving waters.

'Well,' Matt said, uncertainly, from somewhere near her feet, 'it's off to London at last, eh?' He paused. Then, 'About bloody time, an' all,' he said, and passed out.

PART THREE

PART THREE

1

The darkness, emphasized here and there by the infrequent, pale wavering nimbus of a gas lamp, but for the most part unrelieved as pitch, showed no obvious signs of an approaching dawn. Huddled in filthy discomfort upon a dirty sack of potatoes, Kitty glanced up at the stooped back of the sleeping cart-driver and wondered at his ancient horse's undisturbed and steady progress, unguided, through the narrow city streets. Blinkered head down, great fringed plodding feet sure upon the slick unevenness of the cobbles, the animal toiled, the dilapidated cart, punitively loaded, groaning and clattering behind it, the all-but-unconscious driver, head drooping almost to his knees, swaying to the movement. For what seemed like hours now, sleepless beside her slumbering brother, Kitty had watched in alarmed fascination as the figure perched high above her had lurched perilously from side to side, seeming always to be on the very point of being pitched clear to the cobbles below, yet always, miraculously, righting himself with no apparent conscious effort nor any break in the stentorian snoring which sounded trumpet-like even above the ear-splitting clatter of the iron-shod wheels on the road. For herself – dirty, exhausted, and desperately uncomfortable – she could not help but envy the man his improbably sound repose, as she envied Matt his apparent ability to sleep anywhere and under any circumstances. By the shafting light of a street lamp she glanced at her brother. The two weeks since they had left Mersea Island, despite their privations, had seen his battered face return to something like normality, the bruises fading, the cuts healing, though the deepest of them, high on his cheekbone, still showed red and angry and promised a certain scar. He could consider himself lucky, she thought now, grimly, that this was, so far as she could ascertain, the only lasting damage incurred by the savage beating he had suffered.

The reason for the attack and for his flight from Colchester she still did not know and had, in face of her brother's stubborn reluctance to divulge it, given up questioning. With an often barely conscious, injured boy on her hands the first few days of their journey had in any case been such a nightmare, involving as they did the simple, basic need for survival, that such questions had been an irrelevance in a world dominated by the search for food and for shelter.

The first three or four days, until Matt's condition had improved enough for him to travel, had been spent hidden in a barn on the mainland a mile or so from the village of Tolleshunt d'Arcy. During that time they had lived frugally upon the few pence that Kitty had brought with her – for, needless to say, Matt's pouch with its precious hoard of stolen gold was gone, together with the ill-gotten rings and stickpins she had so often seen him wearing – and upon the produce of Kitty's own wits and determination. And indeed, after the months in thrall to Amos and her own infatuation she had found herself almost welcoming that challenge, and her ability to rise to it. During those days she had discovered within herself a strength and a ferocity of will that she had herself found astonishing. Doggedly she had tended her brother's hurts, guarded him through the endless, friendless nights while he slept, foraged for them both as if born to the vagabond life. She had coaxed life-giving milk from the cows who peacefully grazed the unknowing farmer's pastures, had stolen eggs from his wife's chickens and early apples from his orchard. Once she had ventured to the village to expend a few precious coppers upon bread and cheese, and on the way back had, with smiles and winks and a quick, lascivious kiss that had promised more on account than she had any intention of paying, shamelessly blandished a scrawny rabbit from a young poacher who evidently thought his supper well lost for a few moments' counterfeit of laughter and love. With a mocking self-derision Kitty had thanked Amos Isherwood for that rabbit – six months before, she would have gone hungry. Remembering, she mused now – not for the first time – on the undeniable fact that the girl who had seen Matt through those first, harrowing days and had since shepherded the at first subdued youngster along the forty or so difficult and penniless miles to London bore scant relationship to the one who had shared Anne Bowyer's tears of grief in her bereavement a long year ago. She tilted her tired head, closing her eyes for a moment. A year? Dear God, it felt like a lifetime –

She flinched and grabbed for the side of the cart as one of the wheels mounted a kerbstone and crashed down again with a particularly bruising jolt. Matt stirred, muttering, and was still. In the sky now it seemed to her that at last she could discern the first herald of the coming day, not strong enough yet to be described as light, but the faintest lessening of darkness, which allowed the dense bulk of the buildings around them to loom, mysteriously shadowed, above the lumbering vehicle and its load of fresh vegetables bound for London's Covent Garden Market. They had been more than relieved at last to meet with a driver who had not greeted their request for a ride with a lifted fist or boot. ''Course, me old ducks,' the wizened, weather-beaten gnome of a man had said with a wide, discoloured grin, 'climb aboard. First class passengers on the 'taters, second on the carrots –' And, despite the bone-shattering discomfort of the unsprung cart, they had been grateful – for their rumbling bellies and blistered feet had been quarrelsome companions for the past few miles.

Kitty shifted again, trying in vain to find comfort. The now rapidly paling sky showed clearly the buildings that towered above her, crowding in on the narrow streets, leaning, it seemed, towards each other as they reached like dying plants towards the cleanliness and light of the sky. Kitty sighed, and tried to dismiss a too-well-remembered vision of wide, light horizons and a vaulted, wind-cleansed sky.

Since they had left the flat Essex countryside and entered the first outlying areas of the suburbs of the city an oppression had settled upon her that she knew to be due to more than just the uncharitable and depressing hour. And as they had progressed into the maze of endless, cluttered streets that was the East End of London she had been aware of optimism and confidence draining quietly from her, leaving a vacuum all too easily filled by uncertainty and apprehension. It had seemed in the circumstances a simple and obvious plan to journey to the capital, where surely there must be work, and where surely no enemy would think it profitable to search for them. But now, rattling in solitary discomfort beside her sleeping brother through strange streets that smelled squalidly of night-odours and the droppings of horses, suddenly she could not be so brave. What if work were not so easily come by? What were they to do, friendless and penniless in an environment that must be innately and inimicably hostile? Far from any fear that anyone might search them out and do them harm, it seemed to her in that bleak moment a far greater possibility that, together or separately, she and her brother might well disappear unnoticed into the sea of uncaring humanity that she sensed about them, drowned as surely as had been Sir George and his sons in the North Sea waters. Miserably for a moment she huddled, close to sudden tears. Then, with an enormous effort she straightened her back and flexed her aching neck, trying to throw off such morbid fancies. If she gave up now, before they had started, then what chance would they have? The cart was bound for Covent Garden Market; well and good – there must surely be casual work in a market? Enough, anyway, to keep them from starvation until such time as they could find more permanent employment?

That her brother undoubtedly had other ideas concerning their future was a fact that for the moment she resolutely ignored.

She became aware that their pace had slowed, and craning

her neck saw that it was because they had come up behind
another cart, smaller than their own, piled high with vegetables and cut flowers and drawn by a shambling donkey.

''Ay, Charlie!' – a woman's voice, raucous and brassily
good-humoured, its owner nothing but an enormous
shrouded bundle half-seen in the darkness – 'Wake up, yer
silly bugger! Afore that flea-bitten nag o' yours 'as yer in
bleedin' Billin'sgate!'

'Piss orf, Berth.' Charlie did not move; his voice, mildly
at variance with his words, issued from his still apparently
sleeping form. 'Silly cow.'

The woman, unoffended, shrieked with laughter and
clucked at her donkey. From a side lane another cart issued,
and another.

''Mornin', Charlie.'

''Morning, Alf.'

'Where's the Missis then?'

'Orf sick. Legs is gorn agin. Sunthin' awful.'

'Sorry to 'ear that, Charlie. Give 'er me best, eh?'

'Will do.'

They turned into a wider thoroughfare; handcarts here,
and women with loaded baskets over their crooked arms or
balanced upon their heads. Others carried stacks of shallow
baskets for sale, or trays of trinkets. The slow-moving river
of humanity was fed constantly by the tributaries of the
side lanes and alleys as the market traders headed for their
day's labours, calling greetings and more-or-less friendly
insults, braving the chill half-dark with coarse camaraderie.

Matt stirred and stretched. Jumped awake, wincing.
'Ouch! God Almighty – I feel as if I've been kicked by a
horse!' With unfeigned difficulty he struggled to a sitting
position. 'Bloody Hell!' he said, with pious depth of feeling.

Kitty smiled faintly but said nothing. The streets through
which they were passing were wider now, and less depressing. She looked around her with growing interest. By the
lifting dawn light and the pale flicker of the now more
numerous gas lamps she saw the ancient streets of the City
of London with their top-heavy buildings crowded together,

huddling as if for support and protection whilst here and there a grand new edifice stood, four-square and ornate, proud offspring of the new and burgeoning iron-age of industry. The roads were teeming now with slow-moving market traffic — coster-carts, porters, donkey-barrows, shawled women with their flower baskets — and she guessed that they must be nearing their destination. She watched in faint and unkind amusement as Matt painfully unfolded his long, cramped legs, cursing beneath his breath, before he lifted his marked young face to look about him with quickening interest. 'Well, well,' he said, softly. 'So here we are at last, eh?'

'Looks like it.' She had to smile. 'Not quite the way we planned to arrive?'

He grinned back, his teeth a gleam in the darkness. 'S'pose we might as well get off this bone-shaker and walk?'

Kitty shook her head. 'Not yet.' Something that their benefactor had said in his exchange with the woman he had called Berth had registered in her subconscious and now surfaced smartly. She edged closer to Charlie who now, thoroughly awake at last, had taken the reins in his hands and was guiding the plodding old horse through the dense traffic.

'Er — excuse me?'

He neither turned nor answered.

She raised her voice, shouting against the opposition about her. 'Excuse me, Mr — er Charlie?'

This time he glanced across his shoulder. 'Yes, ducks?'

'I wondered — I heard you say that your wife was poorly. I thought — could you do with some help? For the day at least?'

He pondered, sucking his lower lip noisily through his hideously discoloured teeth. 'S'madder o' fact —' He paused, glanced at her, warily appraising. 'Can't pay more'n a tanner —'

'That's all right.'

'— fer the both of yer.'

She hesitated at that. 'Ninepence,' she said, firmly.

He wavered, shrugged, grinned his grimy grin. 'Ye'r on.'

She nodded, relief flooding her. It was better than nothing. And certainly better than the mischief idle hands might bring to Matt.

They were moving now along a road which, suddenly and unexpectedly, gave onto the vast market square. Kitty stared, aware too of Matt's wide eyes beside her. She had never in her life seen such a place. The great market building with its grand arched entrance, its colonnades and arcades, dominated the paved square, on the far side of which stood a large but simple church whose columned portico complemented that of the market building perfectly. Kitty's first bemused glance took in the tall, elegant gas lamps, the shops and taverns that lined the market place, the enormous theatre building beyond church and market – but the thing that most riveted her eyes and opened her mouth in a small breath of amazement was the turmoil of activity that seemed to fill every far-flung corner of the square.

Even at this hour Covent Garden Market was a swarming ant-heap. It seemed to her that every conveyance that had ever been invented clogged the Piazza and the streets that led into it: barrows and carts of every size, condition and description, battered gigs and wagons, even to her astonishment an elegant carriage, the uniformed driver, his expression supercilious, riding high above the heads of the crowds, and beside him a mannikin child, black as new-mined coal, sumptuously attired in silks and satins the peacock colours of the East, his teeth flashing like jewels in his small ebony face as he beamed down on the apparent chaos about him. As the carriage slowly passed, a great rocking galleon on a heaving human sea, Kitty caught a glimpse through the curtained window of a pale, haughty face shaded beneath an enormous hat which was decked itself with flowers and fruit as any of the stalls being set up close by. As they stopped to let the vehicle pass a movement caught her eye within a pile of baskets stacked against the wall. Seemingly of its own volition a large basket rocked, rolled a little on the pavement and then, to Kitty's

amazement, disgorged a small boy who, apparently totally
unaware of the crowds about him – as indeed they appeared
unaware of him – rubbed his eyes sleepily, stretched, brushed
a little at his crumpled, ragged clothes and, his morning
toilette apparently accomplished, sauntered off across the
square. As Charlie's cart struggled on past the portico of the
church she saw him again, in company with another half a
dozen or so waifs, drinking from the pump that stood beside
the church. Others of their kind dodged about the crowd, all
reaching hands and cajoling voices.

'Want some 'elp ter set up, Mister?'

'Need an 'and wiv yer basket, Missis?'

'Spare a copper, Guv?'

'Git orf.' Charlie, voice still mild, took a casual sideways
swipe at an importuning lad and Kitty winced as leather
rapped knuckle and the boy snatched his hand away from
the horse's reins with an exclamation that meant nothing
at all to Kitty but which raised Matt's expressive eyebrows
almost to his thatch of hair and brought from Charlie a
muttered, 'Filthy little bugger.'

'Watch yer back terday, Charlie –' The half-laughing
warning came from a huge, cheerful-looking porter who
strode beside the cart, a great swaying tower of baskets
balanced upon his head. 'That's one o' Croucher's lads if
I'm not mistook.'

Charlie shrugged, heaved on the reins. 'Right-o, me old
ducks. 'Ere's where we start.'

They had drawn up not in the market building itself,
within whose deep and shadowed arcades Kitty could see
carts and wagons far bigger than theirs being unloaded, but
in the Piazza, not far from the church. Stacked in a nearby
doorway were some trestles and planks. ''Eave-o, lad. Give
us an 'and,' said Charlie, and – reluctantly – Matt clambered
from the cart and, with a speaking glance at his sister, bent
his back to the trestles.

The stall set up, Charlie produced a large umbrella –
which he called, a little confusingly, a 'gingham' – and set
it above them. Then he showed Kitty how to stack the fruit

and vegetables the best to display them. 'Careful now, girl
– good stuff at the front, see? Doan' want ter put the punters
orf, do we? That's the ticket. An' if yer serves, yer serves
from the back, see?' She nodded, and carefully set about her
task. He watched her for some few minutes then, apparently
satisfied with her efforts, he scratched his dirty neck with
a long black fingernail and said, 'Right – you two can carry
on, can't yer? Got ter see a man about a dog. Won't be two
shakes. If anyone wants me –' he added over his shoulder,
already pushing into the crowds, 'tell 'em I'm in the
Mar-Kwiss –'

Kitty stared at his departing back blankly. 'The what?'
she asked her brother.

He snorted with laughter. 'The Marquis. The pub we
passed on the way in.' He stood beside her, fidgeting, his
bright dark eyes narrowed against the rising sun as he took
in the scene about him, one long, narrow finger resting
pensively upon his lower lip. Alarm bells rang very loud and
clear in Kitty's ears. She reached a firm hand.

'You stay right here, you hear me? Help me with these
carrots –'

For one moment he stood, as if poised for movement, an
eager young animal sensing the wilderness and hearing its
call. Then he relaxed and, shrugging, he reached for a carrot,
rubbing it absent-mindedly upon his already filthy shirt
before taking half of it at one bite.

Kitty hid her relief. 'Stack them,' she said, 'don't eat
them.'

Of course there was no hope – and in a small honest
corner of her heart she knew it – that she could keep him
by her side all day. As the late August sun rose in the sky
and the customers began to arrive Charlie reappeared, his
stained grin a little wider, his gait noticeably more unsteady.
Business was for a while brisk and Kitty was kept busy
replenishing the display of fruit and vegetables. By mid-
morning, despite the welcome shade of the gingham, she
was unpleasantly warm, her clothes stained and sticky with
sweat. The market place was like an oven and great, disgust-

ing bluebottles buzzed about the foetid pile of rotten mer-
chandise that had gathered in the gutter near them. Charlie
– finding urgent business once more with the man who
owned the dog – disappeared again in the direction of The
Marquis and came back a couple of hours later with what
he himself described as 'a bit of a shake in me pins' – which,
more honestly translated, meant that he could barely stand
on his feet. By now the rush was over. Kitty settled him on
the battered chair that was set by the stall and in no time
he was asleep, head sunk upon his meagre chest. She could
not resist the thought that had Charlie met up with a less
honest companion for the day he might have ended up much
the poorer for it.

'Vi'lets, dear? Buy a bunch o' pretty vi'lets?' The light,
sing-song voice came from beside her. 'On'y a penny.
'Apenny the little 'uns. Vi'lets?' The girl was little more
than a child, pale-faced and undernourished, but with long-
lashed eyes the colour of the wilting flowers she was trying
to sell and a pretty, beseeching smile.

Regretfully Kitty shook her head. The girl turned away,
stopped as she found herself confronted by Matt's agile,
lanky form that had moved – faster, Kitty thought sardonically, than it had all day – from behind the stall to block
her way. In her brother's long fingers, shining in the
sun, was a bright copper penny. 'What else do I get for
this?'

The girl giggled. 'Don' be cheeky!'

Kitty opened her mouth to remonstrate with her brother
– for there was but one place the penny could have sprung
from, and it had no business in Matt's fingers getting itself
spent on violets – and then, glancing in some disgust at the
snoring Charlie, shut it again. Damn it, if the man cared to
pass half the day in a drunken stupor he'd be lucky if a
penny were all he lost.

'Come on, now' – Matt's voice was warm and wheedling
– 'take off that owd bonnet. I'll bet you've got hair as pretty
as summer sunshine hid under there?'

'Ooh – get on wiv yer!'

Kitty's attention was drawn from her brother's sly wooing by a smattering of applause from a small crowd that gathered, not far from the stall, upon the steps of the church. Standing on tiptoe she saw a small, flying figure that tumbled and spun in the air, landing neatly and precisely upon dirty bare feet before spinning again into a dizzying succession of cartwheels and handsprings which drew appreciative cries from the audience. Thin and supple as a whip, long hair flying, the boy's every movement was graceful as a cat's. Kitty watched the display in fascination. Almost faster than the eye could follow he flipped into the air, over and over like a spinning coin, to land on his hands, steady as a man might on his two feet; Kitty glanced wryly at Charlie and corrected the thought – steadier than some. Bare, dirty feet bouncing about his lifted, tousled head, the urchin ran like a monkey around the circle on his hands and then with no apparent effort flipped himself into another flawless somersault.

'Matt, look! Did you see –?' She stopped in mid-sentence. Charlie snored unconcernedly. And Matt was nowhere to be seen.

Her mouth tightening upon a spurt of anger, she turned back to the spectacle. Let the untrustworthy little devil go. Why should she play nursemaid? When did it ever stop? But a darkness had fallen on the day just as surely as if the hot August sun had slid behind stormclouds – a darkness that was deepened when her practised eye noted a new activity amongst the growing crowd about the young acrobat. To an innocent eye it might have meant nothing – two or three small street arabs squirming through the crowd to get a better look at the entertainment – but with Matt for brother Kitty knew differently and saw all too clearly the swift fingers, the pattern of movement, the perilous dance of theft. Then, as she watched, one of the urchins whistled, sharply, and disappeared, fast as a lizard under a stone. Ponderously, sweating in his heavy uniform, the Beadle came, leaning upon his staff, mopping his florid face with a large, dirty handkerchief.

The young pickpockets had disappeared, like smoke before the wind.

There came another burst of applause as the acrobatic entertainer finished his display with a dazzling string of somersaults, and the chink of coppers as the more generous onlookers tossed coins into the lad's cap. Kitty looked around for her errant brother, one worried eye upon the portly Beadle. There was no possibility, she knew – and had to admit had known all along – that her brother would be able to resist such temptation as faced him here. The Beadle had moved on now, was standing in earnest conversation with a stall-holder on the far side of the square. Kitty hoped fervently that if her brother were thereabouts the man might prove as stupidly unobservant as he had a few moments before.

And in that, in her innocence, she erred badly; for a very few hours later she and her brother were to learn in painful fashion that the law was far from the primary danger that faced Matt and his nimble fingers in this harsh new world they had entered.

(ii)

With the waning of the afternoon, custom all but died. Here and there about the square early leavers began to clear their stalls, leaving their fly-blown rubbish in foul-smelling heaps behind them. Charlie slept on, Kitty's half-hearted attempts to wake him irritably brushed away. She sat upon the high kerb, her back against a lamp post, and dozed a little, her irresistibly heavy eyelids and suddenly leaden limbs clear legacy of an uncomfortable and sleepless night. With the new philosophy that had been forced upon her by the past fugitive weeks she closed her mind to the uncertainties of the future and relaxed, enjoying, simply, the blessed warmth of the sun on her face. When, however, that sun dropped with unexpected speed behind the steepled rooftops and the long, cool fingers of the lengthening shadows brushed her skin to goosebumps, she jumped awake. Charlie had not moved. Matt regarded her with laughing eyes. 'The Sleeping Beauty awakes,' he said, 'though Prince Charming seems to have had something of an accident –' He rolled mischievous eyes towards the snoring Charlie.

'Where –?' she began, and then stopped, her quick anger dying almost as it was born. What was the point? She scrambled stiffly to her feet, brushing the dust from her worn and grubby skirt. The scene around them resembled in more ways than one the aftermath of battle. The shadowed market building rang eerily with the echo of men's voices; and with the evil-smelling detritus of the day littering the square the scavengers were already at work. Ragged children, male and female, lean as skinned rabbits and gaunt as death foraged about the disgusting heaps, squabbling viciously over the pickings, stuffing themselves voraciously with the maggot-ridden market leavings that had festered all day in the hot sun. Kitty was appalled. She could not imagine such hunger. She turned away, sickened. All the neighbouring stalls were cleared. The Piazza was quiet. On the shallow steps close at hand two dirty little street arabs regarded her with interest. She leaned towards Charlie. 'Wake up! Charlie – wake up!' Suddenly uneasy, she looked at her brother. 'It's time we were going. We have to find somewhere to sleep.'

He grinned at her, blithe and mischievous, for all the world as if there were no such place as Colchester and no still-bloody scars upon his face. Clearly, as he laughed and shoved his hands into his pockets, she heard the jingle of coins. 'We're safe for the night,' he grinned, 'not to worry. What's your fancy? Champagne and oysters?'

Heartsick, she turned from him. Ninepence she had earned, if lucky, by the labours of the day. What indeed did that merit but scorn? Strongly, and – perhaps strangely – for the first time, resentment welled. 'Charlie!' Her husky voice was suddenly harsh, and she kicked ill-temperedly at the leg of the sleeping man's chair. 'Wake up!'

He jumped, wagged his head groggily. 'What's up?'

'Everyone's gone. And we've to be off too.' She planted

herself firmly before him, determination in her eye. 'You owe me a shilling,' she said, flatly.

'What?' That woke him, spluttering. 'A shillin'?'

'That's right.'

'A tanner, I said –'

'Ninepence, you said. And help, you said – not running the whole damned stall by myself while you drank yourself stupid with your mates. A shilling.' She was aware, as he must have been, of interested onlookers. The two urchins on the steps had been joined by three or four others. They sat, tiered like a theatre audience, openly watching the entertainment. Perhaps oddly, far from abashing her their presence goaded her further; she well knew how clearly she could project her low-pitched voice. 'There's two of us and one of you –' She paused, added drily, 'Less than one of you.' The watching children sniggered. 'Now. You want that cart loaded so you can get off home to that poor old wife of yours? We'll do it. For a shilling.' She held out a dirty, flat-palmed hand. 'Anything else, Charlie, and we might find it in our hearts to hinder rather than help. Now, you wouldn't want that, would you?' She was aware of her brother's dark, astonished eyes upon her. She did not look at him. 'Well?'

The man pulled himself unsteadily to his feet. 'Well, I'll be buggered,' he said mildly, and reached for the tin that held the day's takings. ''Ere.' A shining coin spun in the air and Kitty deftly caught it. 'Now,' Charlie said, mournfully, 'give us a quick 'and, eh? She'll top me proper if I gets 'ome late.'

They loaded the cart for him and Matt held the patient horse's head whilst Charlie, with some difficulty, climbed aboard. As they watched the vehicle lumber across the square it seemed to Kitty that its driver was asleep again before it had turned into the shadows of Southampton Street. She felt an absurd sense of melancholy. Charlie and his cart may not have been much, but they had been all the friendship offered them so far in this daunting city.

They stood for a moment, brother and sister, side by side,

looking after the departing cart. 'Well,' she said at last into the quiet. 'Here we are. What do we do now?' Suddenly aware of a strange quality to her brother's silence, she glanced at him. He had half-turned from her and was looking towards the steps of the church. The expression on his face spun her to face the sidling, malevolent threat that had crept up on them like disease, or death. She caught her breath. Perhaps two dozen ragamuffin boys had gathered, ragged, barefoot, hardfaced. As, despite themselves, both Matt and Kitty fell back a step the urchins fanned out silently and surrounded them, pinning them with the wall to their backs. In the centre of the threatening half-circle a boy of about Matt's own age regarded them with intent, hostile eyes. His growth was stunted – in height and reach Matt outmatched him by inches – but there was about him an aura of embittered strength and cunning that chilled Kitty's blood. The boy's eyes, in a face death-pale, were black as the pit, ancient with spite and experience, his unkempt hair lustreless and dark as soot. Beside him, impassive, stood the young acrobat, wand-thin and graceful, utterly venomous.

There hung a long, still moment of silence.

'Well, me ol' chinas –' The black-haired boy took a light, menacing step forward. His voice was flatly conversational. ''Ere's a thing, eh?' He let the words drop into the silence like stones into a cold pool, and like ripples on dark water the sound echoed faintly out into the all-but-empty square. His eyes were upon Matt, direct and deadly. 'A fine wirer. Good, too – I'll grant 'im that. But' – he paused – 'a bit, as yer might say, unwelcome, eh? Very, very unwelcome.' The slow words were spoken with such unmistakable threat that Kitty's skin crawled. With a sharp jerk the dark head flicked up and the black, lightless eyes moved to Kitty and then back to Matt. 'Sarf Bankers, are we?' he asked, softly. 'That it? Yer a long way from 'ome, mateys, a very long way. Yer got yer nerve, I'll say that for yer. Where's yer bullies, then? Scarpered, 'ave they? Bust me if I blame 'em, eh, lads?'

A small ripple of sycophantic laughter rustled and was

still. The boy stood waiting. 'Well?' he said sharply after a moment.

Helplessly Matt shook his head. 'I – I don't understand you. I don't know what you mean.'

A small, tow-headed brat crouched upon the steps not far from Kitty let out a discordant shriek of laughter. 'Ay – joo 'ere that? Oi doan unnerstan' yer – It's a pair o' friggin' country bumpkins!'

'Shut up, Weed.'

The child subsided, still snorting unpleasantly.

The eyes now held a light of malicious interest that if anything Kitty found even more unnerving than the undisguised hostility of a moment before. 'You sayin' you ain't Sarf Bank?'

'I tell you I don't know what you mean.'

''E don't know what I mean,' the other boy said, mockingly mournful. 'Poor little bastard. 'E don't know what I mean.' The boy turned to his audience, affecting a drama of gesture and voice that brought another ripple of laughter. 'What d'yer fink o' that, my bullies?' With a speed that had Kitty's heart jumping in her throat he spun to face Matt again, a pale, bony finger levelled like a blade at the other boy's throat. 'But yer knows abaht dippin', doesn't yer, cully? An' yer bin workin' the market, 'aven't yer?' He waited. ''Aven't yer?'

Matt's shoulders lifted in the faintest of shrugs. 'Yes.'

'An' no one does that, country-boy dipper – straw-arsed fine wirer! – wivaht talkin' first ter Croucher! That right, lads?' The last three words, in contrast to the ferocity of what had gone before, were conversationally mild. Answering grins flitted across dirty faces.

There was an expectancy, an anticipation in the air that Kitty could sense, and it terrified her. She stepped forward. 'Please, I'm sure that –'

'Shut yer mouth, Duchess.' The tone was still deceptively mild. 'One at a time, if yer please. We'll deal wiv you later.'

'Watch 'er friggin' tongue, Crouch,' a reedy voice piped. 'She'll cut yer froat wivaht gettin' near yer!'

Shouts of laughter greeted this witticism. Croucher's eyes did not leave Matt's face. 'So –' he said, ignoring Kitty, 'I s'pects we can settle this like genn'lemen, eh?'

Matt relaxed a little. 'Yes.'

A narrow, grubby hand reached, palm up.

Matt frowned.

The thin, grimy fingers snapped and rubbed, indicating impatience. 'The lot,' Croucher said. 'Fer good will, like.'

Matt shook his head.

'Matt! For God's sake! – give it to him! What does it matter?'

Slow colour was creeping into Matt's lean face. He shook his head again, mouth set.

'Oh dear. Deary me. Goin' ter be difficult, are we?' The wicked eyes rolled, drolly. ''Ow did I guess that was goin' ter 'appen, eh? 'Ow did I guess?'

'Yer juss too sharp fer yer own good, Crouch.'

'Fer the dipper's good, yer mean,' said another voice, grimly amused.

'Matt!'

Kitty's voice distracted her brother; he shifted his stance, glancing at her, and in the blink of an eye his antagonist was crouched suddenly a scant two yards from him, bare feet spread upon the dusty ground, the fingers of one hand crooked, tense and clawlike, the glint of steel in the other, weaving and glimmering, slicing in a deadly arc before Matt's dumbfounded eyes. Matt leapt backwards, almost falling over an abandoned box. Recovering his balance he steadied himself, eyes fixed upon the flickering needlepoint of the knife.

'We don't – take kindly – to any ol' – Tom – Dick – or bleedin' 'Arry – workin' our market – do we boys?' Each phrase was emphasized by a lethal, flashing pass with the knife, inches from Matt's sweating face.

The sound that rose from the watching youngsters was a primitive growl of anticipation and rapacious excitement that turned Kitty's stomach with fear. Here, she knew instinctively, was something more malevolent, more truly

and brutally savage than anything she had ever encountered
– or even envisaged – in her life before. The boy Croucher,
still grinning with wolfish enjoyment, jumped at Matt utter-
ing a short, staccato barking sound as if in spiteful play,
then leapt back. Dark blood dripped from Matt's jaw, and
the knife's gleam was sullied. Kitty flinched, her hand to
her mouth. For a moment Matt stood like a statue, his eyes
riveted as if in fascination upon his tormentor, making no
attempt to defend himself.

Croucher barked again.

Matt blinked, flinching.

'Go it, Crouch! Slit 'is gizzard!'

The smaller boy moved again, supremely confident, quick
as a cat. But this time, with the lanky agility that Kitty
knew so well, Matt sidestepped, avoiding the attack and –
as much by luck as by judgement – caught his opponent a
buffeting blow on the ear as he did so.

The openly surprised Croucher staggered a little, spun to
face Matt and dropped into his threatening crouch again.
He was smiling no longer. He sidled closer. The knife,
cradled loosely within his small, flat palm, held deceptively
lightly, wove a glimmering pattern in the air. Twice, experimentally it flashed, a lethal gleam in the shadowed light;
but this time Matt, with less apparent effort, stayed beyond
the blade's reach. Sudden silence had fallen upon the
watchers. Kitty glanced around. Eyes avid for blood watched
every movement. Here and there a brow furrowed. Then
with that same strange little barking sound Croucher attacked, in a flickering fury of movement that had Matt
stumbling back before its force. The arm he raised to protect
his face was blooded twice, and deeply, before his opponent
fell back. The onlookers growled again, satisfied.

'Cut 'im up good, Crouch.'

'Cripple 'im, Croucher.'

Croucher fell back, the grin back in place. His eyes flickered to his rapacious supporters.

It was a mistake.

With a swift, deft movement that took even Kitty by

surprise, Matt was upon him, his long-fingered hands banded in a grip like steel about the other boy's wrists as he used the advantage of his greater height and strength to contain the threat of the knife. They swayed so for a moment, locked together in a fierce, hostile embrace. Then with a vicious twist Croucher was free again, and the shining knife-arc divided them once more. Yet the smaller boy was unbalanced. Gracefully Matt sidestepped the blade and his hard, bunched knuckles took the other boy high on the cheekbone, drawing blood. Croucher hissed like an angry cat and slashed awkwardly at his dancing opponent. Matt avoided the cut with ease and fell back, big hands spread open and wary before him, eyes watchful.

There was a movement now, Kitty saw, within Croucher's watching tribe; a shifting of feet, a worrying restlessness. That Croucher's victim should show a good account of himself had in no way apparently featured in their plans, and they were clearly not impressed. She clenched her hands nervously; nothing, it seemed to her, short of a miracle, could save them now. Whichever way the fight went they were lost, for the concept of fair play clearly figured nowhere in this struggle, and if Matt did not finish it quickly – and the likelihood that he could finish it at all was remote, despite his courageous defence – then he would be overwhelmed, not just by Croucher, but by this venomous mob of young devils who were not about to stand by and see their leader bested.

Croucher moved again, leaping in to the attack with practised skill. Matt dodged, stumbled, and the two crashed to the ground almost at Kitty's feet. Matt's left hand was clamped desperately about the wrist of Croucher's knife-hand, his right was buried, deeply and painfully, in the sooty black hair. For a moment the knife hovered perilously at his throat, but then once again his greater strength began to tell and inch by hard-fought inch the smaller boy's arm was forced back, as was his head, dragged brutally backwards by Matt's fierce grip on his hair. Croucher's face twisted in pain; with a strong, convulsive movement he broke Matt's grip and twisted free, his knee in Matt's groin.

As he did so the knife spun from his hand and skidded clattering past Kitty into the gutter.

She turned. Yards from her a small, wicked face snarled, daring her to try. The knife lay between them, honed like a razor and with a point ground as viciously as a needle's. For the space of a drawn breath she faced the rat-faced urchin, then she threw herself forward, snatched at the knife and in one movement turned, calling 'Matt!' as she tossed it to her brother's hand. Almost before it had left her hand she felt the monkey-weight of the child on her back, felt the terrifying strength of its bony fingers upon her throat, smelled its stink in her nostrils. Staggering, she fell, carrying her burden with her. Those terrible, fleshless fingers with savage sureness probed for her eyes. She screamed. Then, suddenly, the world was still. Her attacker, with one last cruel raking of her face with sharp nails, was gone. She sat up, dazed.

Within the closed circle of watchers Matt knelt. On the ground beside him, locked painfully there by the grip of Matt's hand in the thatch of black hair, was Croucher. But what held him there most surely, and held too for the moment at least the poised and menacing crowd of watchers, was the rock-steady knife-point that rested bloodily on his dirty, stretched neck.

'Well, now,' Matt said, very softly. 'Shall we talk?'

Silence.

Matt's dark head wagged sorrowfully. 'Manners!' he said, gently, and a trickle of blood wormed its way across the grimy skin of Croucher's throat.

Croucher spat a filthy word, the sound strangled.

Matt sighed. 'Tha'ss a shame, you don't seem to be hearin' so well,' he said, pleasantly. And the knife slid, infinitely menacing, to Croucher's right ear. Blood again, like dark rubies, dripping. 'There. Is that better?'

His captive's instructions were explicit, and obscenely impossible to carry out.

Incredibly, Matt grinned. 'You do have a fine turn of phrase, I'll say that for you.' He lifted his head, looked slowly round the ring of faces. In the sudden silence a pigeon lifted from the ground of the square, wings clapping in the still, warm air. It landed ponderously upon the pumphead, its beady eyes regarding the scene with detached lack of interest. A short distance from them Kitty saw, to her astonishment, that the tiny, scavenging children still swarmed about the piles of discarded fruit as if nothing untoward were happening. Nothing, it seemed, could distract them from their frantic and pathetic search for sustenance.

Matt took his time. Kitty watched him, breath held. 'Seems to me,' he said at last, as much to the watchers as to his captive, 'that there's been a bit of a misunderstanding.' About his mouth there was still the faintest quirk of a smile.

One of the crowd, oddly, tittered.

Croucher was very still, black eyes wide and unblinking on Matt's face.

'Seems to me –' Matt said again, more soberly this time, and directly into those savage dark eyes, 'that – bein' on the same side, so to speak – it don't make too much sense, you an' me scrapping like cat an' dog?'

A faint tremor ran through the small, tense body, the faintest shadow of relaxation.

'Let's get straight.' Matt might have been holding a friendly conversation with a mate over a pint of ale. 'This is your patch, right?'

Imperceptibly, the dark head moved in assent.

'An' you thought I was hornin' in – that I was a' – he paused – 'member of the opposition, so to speak?'

Again the movement.

'Wrong on both counts. Seems to me – if you'd given a feller a chance to ask, civil-like – that you were the gent I was lookin' to meet.' He let that sink in for a moment. The knife-point had not moved by a fraction. 'Now. I'm sorry our acquaintance has started so' – he paused again, and his long mouth twitched – 'unfortunate –'

Another snigger from the audience.

'– but I s'pose that can happen to the best of us. Me and my sister, we're' – he crinkled his eyes a little, frankly now playing to the gallery; and it was working. Quite distinctly Kitty could sense the lessening of the hostility around them – 'lookin' for work,' Matt finished, innocently. The phrase brought more laughter which quickly choked to astonished silence as, easily and slowly, Matt sat back on his heels, releasing his captive, and smiling his crooked, infectious grin. Casually he reversed the knife in his hand, held it, bouncing upon its slender blade, hilt first towards its owner, who had twisted to face him. 'Any ideas?'

The moment hung on a fragile thread of tension. Kitty, breath and heartbeat suspended, stood as if rooted to the spot. Then, slowly, the small grimy hand reached for the knife. Matt relinquished it. Hardly glancing at it Croucher tossed it, spinning, into the air and caught it, hefting it lightly and thoughtfully in his hand. 'You an' the Duchess,' he said at last, pensively, 'lookin' fer work, you say?'

Shakily, Kitty opened her mouth.

'Yes,' Matt said.

There was the smallest of silences. Then Croucher's face split into a ragged, evil grin. 'Plenty of that around here,' he said.

(iii)

'No!' Kitty said for the dozenth time, dogged anger in her voice. 'I won't stay here! I won't live like this!' She jerked her head, indicating the dirty, sparsely furnished room. 'I won't, you hear?' She turned her back on her brother and stared through the uncurtained window to the cheerless vista of filthy alleys below. Age-blackened buildings, their fabric rotten, their squalor exacerbated by the hopeless grime of poverty, huddled together around a nest of darkling streets and alleyways so narrow that they rarely felt the warmth of sunlight. On a sultry day such as today, with heavy stormclouds resting almost on top of the smoke-blackened, decaying chimneystacks, it looked to her like the worst vision of Hell. 'I won't,' she said again, miserably.

'Kit –' Matt's voice showed the strain of an argument repeated to the point of quarrelling. 'I keep telling you – we've no alternative. Not at the moment. And it won't be for long, I promise you. At least we're safe here – we've food, and shelter –'

'Safety? Shelter?' She flung to face him, her expression incredulous. 'Here? Are you mad? Safety in a den of thieves? Shelter in a filthy, crawling pigsty that's home to more villains than a dog is to fleas? I'd as soon take refuge in a snake-pit!'

'Kitty!'

'Matt, no! I won't listen to you! We have to get out now! Now! Or God alone knows what will happen to us!'

He gestured angrily. 'And go where? Do what?'

'I don't care! Anywhere – anything – but this! Oh, Matt, can't you *see* what will become of us if we stay?' She was almost in tears. 'You'll become a hardened thief – hounded, hunted, never safe – flogged and sent to the hulks if – when – you're caught. And I –?' She stopped, said quietly, 'What of me, Matt? What will become of me?' It was the first time she had uttered the words openly, and they gave him pause.

He shook his head, held out an awkward hand. 'Nothing'll happen to you, Kit. I'll look after you.'

She pulled away from him. 'Oh?' The single syllable was bitter, her smile entirely mirthless. 'Well, that's a great comfort, I must say.' She turned back to the window. When she spoke again her voice had changed – it shook with an intensity of fear and loathing that brought him quickly to her, his hands on her shoulders. 'I don't want to live like a rat in a drain,' she said. 'And I won't – Matt, I won't become a whore! Have you seen them out there? Have you seen their eyes – their faces!' She was trembling, as if fevered.

He swung her to face him, his eyes fierce. 'You? A whore? What're you talking about?'

She wrenched herself from his hands. Tears of anger and of fear smeared her angular face. In the three days since they had accompanied Croucher and his gang back to the slums of Whitechapel that were their sanctuary and their home these thoughts had haunted her. Whilst Matt had set off each morning in company with the young thieves to 'work the market' she had stayed here, huddled in this hateful room alone, looking fearfully into a hateful future, afraid to leave, afraid to stay, afraid for her brother and even more afraid for herself. She had seen and heard the activities about her, knew with certainty the trade of the women who flaunted their diseased charms in the doors and alleys of the shambles that were the back streets of Whitechapel. Corruption bred in the very air – and Matt was breathing it. 'What else can there be for me here?' she asked now, hopelessly. 'What?'

He looked at her, nonplussed. 'Kit – we can't leave now. Not just yet. I've promised to stay for a while. There's a man – Moses Smith – he runs things round here. P'raps he'll find something for you? But we can't go. Not yet. We've nowhere to go. No friends. No money.'

'I'd rather be friendless in the street than sheltered here!' The words were violent.

'That's easy enough to say.' He was fighting to hold his temper. He flung out his arm, long finger pointing. 'Have you seen what's out there? Do you know what you're saying? We wouldn't last twenty-four hours on our own, I tell you!'

'We could try!'

'No!'

They glared at each other. He regained control of himself first. 'Kitty – I'm sorry – I know how you hate it' – almost, ruefully, he smiled – 'tha'ss not exactly what I had in mind for myself. But for now it's all we've got. We've food and a bed and a roof over our heads. And whatever you might say, tha'ss better than nothing. I've had to say that we'll stay for a bit –'

'Why?'

With open hands he pacified her. 'Kit – Croucher needs me. He has to pay dues to this Moses Smith, and his takin's are down. He can do with a bit of what I'm bringing in. And

– Kit, listen to me – he knows every wrinkle, every dodge there is! We can use him, p'raps. Make a killing, quick, then get out. Set you up in a little shop somewhere –'

In despair she turned from him. 'Oh Matt!'

The door opened. Weed jerked a sour head. 'You're wanted dahnstairs. Mr Smiff's 'ere.'

Kitty glanced a sharp enquiry at her brother.

'The man for the rent,' he said. 'And – Kitty – if we know what's good for us, we'll pay it.'

The place to which Weed led them Kitty had never been in before. It was in the foundations of the tenement – a long, low cellar with weeping, arched walls and roof and a damp flagged floor. It was lit by smoking tallow candles whose acrid smell lay upon the dank air like scum on dark water. There were benches set along the walls, and low tables. On one side the benches were occupied by the child thieves and mendicants that Kitty had seen in the market. Here and there she recognized a face. Most of them greeted her brother – with, it seemed to her, some respect – her they ignored. For the first time she realized that Croucher's disreputable battalion was not exclusively male; here and there a grimy ribbon, a pathetically tidied head of long, no doubt louse-infected hair bespoke a girl-child, though in no other way, either in signs of cleanliness or softness did they betray themselves from their fellows. Their faces were as hard-eyed, as fearsomely sly as any other to be seen about the room.

As Kitty and Matt were shepherded into the vast cellar by an impatient Weed and waved to a seat beside Springer, the acrobat, who neither glanced at nor acknowledged them, they were followed in by a woman in her late twenties who was escorting a frail-looking but strikingly attractive girl a little older than Kitty herself. She had seen them both before from a distance. They lived, she believed, on the floor above the room she shared with Matt. The pretty one, slight, golden-haired and blue-eyed, looked death-pale and extremely unwell. Her friend, a buxom brass-blonde whose dark eyebrows were at surprising and violent variance with her hair, supported her solicitously and settled her on a bench not far from where Kitty sat. There were others too, men and women, that she had not seen before. She glanced at Matt, raising questioning brows, and he leaned to her.

'That's Pol, and Lottie,' he said, indicating the two girls. 'They both work for this Smith bloke too – seems just about everyone does. The chap next to them's called Squirt. He's a bouncer' – he caught her puzzled look, '– steals from shops. Kids on that he wants to buy something, then nicks whatever he can lay hands on while the shopkeeper's occupied.' He paused, running his eyes over the oddly quiet assembly. He indicated with a movement of his head a small, well-dressed whippet of a man who leaned negligently against the wall behind Pol and the wilting Lottie. 'That's Johnny Sly. Best dragsman in London, so Crouch reckons –'

'Matt – must you talk their ridiculous language? Dragsman?'

Matt was patient. 'He relieves carriage and cab-passengers of their excess luggage by climbing up behind and cutting the straps –'

'Very public-spirited,' she said, dourly. 'Tell me – is there anyone here who isn't a thief?'

He shrugged. 'Must be, I s'pose. Moses Smith runs some legitimate business – well, sort of anyway. He's got a Song and Supper Rooms somewhere round Bethnal Green – that's where Pol and Lottie work –'

'What's that?'

'Just what it sounds like. A kind of theatre where you eat. Or p'raps it's an eating house where people entertain you – I don't know.'

'And that's all that goes on there?'

'What d'you mean?'

'It seems unlikely,' she said quietly, 'that anything this Moses Smith is involved in can be that straight.'

He shrugged, and turned away from her. She brought her attention to Croucher's unusually silent street arabs. She had picked up some of their names now – or rather their nicknames, for none appeared to be blessed with such a luxury as a true Christian name. Weasel was the rat-faced boy who had faced her over the knife and had been ready, she knew, to kill her for it. Tater and Gasser were brothers and looked it, brown-haired and pale-eyed, their mouths twin hollows of blackened, rotting teeth. Og the Shaller was a slight, hauntingly pretty child with a clear, piping voice and a vocabulary that would shock a docker; he was, according to Matt, the most accomplished young mendicant to be found between here and Poplar, often bringing home from his West End haunts more in his begging box than Croucher's best thieves made in the market at far greater risk. He could not, she thought, be more than eight years old. Beside him sat an ugly urchin that Kitty surmised upon the evidence of a grubby scrap of ribbon that dangled from the lank and filthy hair to be a girl. As she studied her some sixth sense told the girl she was being observed. Venomous eyes flickered to Kitty's face, and the child scowled menacingly. Kitty hastily looked away. Of all the threats of the past few days she still found these poisonous children the most difficult to come to terms with. Around her subdued conversations whispered along the cold walls. There was a strange air of tension amongst the gathering that kept the children fidgeting and voices hushed. Then, as a door at the far end of the cellar opened all sound died and in total silence three men entered.

The first two were bully-boys, enormous, ugly men with the faces of pugilists and bodies that seemed to fill the cellar with their bulk and brutish power. The third man was of medium height, pink-faced, entirely bald and grotesquely fat. He was dressed fastidiously, the quality of the dark, broadcloth coat and snow-white linen obvious even in the ill-lit cellar. In his lapel he wore a single dark red rose. Kitty watched as he took his seat, alone, at a small table upon a low dais at the far end of the cellar, whilst the other two men took station behind him, their brutal faces blank. The fat man laid his tall top hat carefully on the floor beside him, glanced about him with a cherubic smile. 'Greetings, dear children.' His voice was smooth as syrup. 'Are we all here?'

A murmur of assent ran around the cellar.

'Good. Then to business, I think. Croucher?'

Croucher slipped from his seat and scuttled to the dais. He was carrying a leather pouch which gingerly he set upon the table before the fat man. It struck Kitty that she had never until now seen the boy move with less than arrogance; yet here, beneath the false benevolence of Moses Smith's flinty smile his cocky confidence had, it seemed, deserted him entirely. He stood a pace from the table, head lowered, and by his side his right hand twitched convulsively, the fingers rubbing and snapping together in uncontainable nervousness. Moses surveyed the boy thoughtfully for a moment before, with a tiny, dimpled hand, delicately upending the leather bag. Coins rang upon the table top. Silence again. Then, with a faint expression of distaste, Moses prodded at the little heap of coins with a small, pink-tipped, beautifully manicured finger, sliding them one from the other, lining them up, his expression pensive. At last then he lifted his head, and it seemed to Kitty that Croucher had to make a physical effort not to cower before the pale, questioning eyes.

'What's this?'

'Rent, Mr Smith.'

'Rent.' Cold light eyes raked the trembling boy, then switched to the other children who sat, still as stone, eyes downcast, upon the bench. Moses drew a deep, regretful breath. 'Rent,' he said again.

'Business 'asn't bin too good, Mr Smith. Honest it 'asn't. There just don't seem so much gelt abaht in the market, like —'

'Then try somewhere else, Croucher. Try somewhere else. Do you think I run a charitable institution here?' The voice was soft, the beatific smile still in place. Kitty shivered, and to her own surprise found herself feeling positively sorry for the dreadful Croucher. 'The South Bank bunch still seem to be doing all right, or so I hear. Isn't that so, Bobs?'

The largest of the pugilists stationed behind the chair nodded. 'Yes, Mr Smith.' Kitty had the distinct impression that he would have chanted the same response had the fat man told him to cut his mother's throat.

'So –' The small eyes moved back to Croucher. 'This is the second quarter running, Croucher my lad. It isn't good enough. Is it?'

'No, Mr Smith.'

For a long moment, infinitely menacing, the man held the boy's eyes with his own. Then, suddenly, he relaxed, leaning back in the protesting chair, snapping his fingers at Bobs who leaned forward and swept Croucher's offering into its pouch. 'One more chance, Crouch, my lad, one more chance,' Moses said, jovially.

'Thank you, Mr Smith.'

The chill glance flickered again to the benches and back. 'You can't tell me that there isn't someone here, Croucher, who isn't ready as paint to step into your dirty little shoes? There's always someone. Don't get me encouraging them, Croucher. You wouldn't like that.'

'No, Mr Smith.' Tight-mouthed, Croucher turned, to be stopped by small, snapping fingers.

'Wait.'

Croucher waited.

Pale eyes searched the room, rested upon Matt. 'I hear you've a new recruit?'

'Yes, sir.'

'Bring him here.'

Croucher turned, jerked a head at Matt. His expression was ferocious.

Matt, slowly, stood.

'Here,' Moses said, gently.

There was a small rustle of expectation from the watching children. Calmly and in his own time Matt walked the length of the cellar, stood before the table, relaxed, hands loose at his side, dark head tilted.

Moses looked at him for a long time. 'They tell me,' he said at last, pleasantly, 'that you fancy yourself as a bit of a smart fine-wirer, yes?'

Matt lifted a shoulder.

Moses frowned. 'Well?'

'Yes.'

'Yes – Mr Smith,' Bobs said, evenly.

Matt looked at him, mouth derisive. Kitty held her breath, praying. Her brother left his reply just long enough to make the pause insulting. 'Yes, Mr Smith,' he said, civilly.

Moses smiled, leaned back in his chair. 'Show me,' he said, and waved a small, pudgy hand. 'I'm sure that Bobs must have something about his person that you could – procure – for me?'

One of the children giggled nervously. Kitty saw an expression close to distaste flit across the good-natured face of the girl Pol. The other girl was leaning back against the wall, eyes closed, taking no interest in the proceedings. Bobs stepped down to face Matt, flexing hands as big as hams. For the first time his expression showed some faint interest.

Matt backed away from him, grinning placatingly, hands spread before him palms up. 'Now easy, Mr Bobs – I can see you're not the kind of feller to take kindly to having his watch lifted –'

Bobs grunted, and advanced.

Matt danced away from him. Chairs and benches scraped as, miraculously, the floor area was cleared to something of an arena.

Moses watched the play, smiling.

Bobs lunged forward. Swift as a moving shadow Matt ducked beneath a massive reaching arm and came up behind the man, who turned and lumbered after him. Matt dodged again, ducking and weaving, grinning hugely. Not once did the grasping hands come near to holding him. He was enjoying himself. Playing to the watching crowd he led the man a dance up and down the cellar, onto the dais and off again – even once using the still-smiling Moses as a shield – and Kitty was reminded vividly of his performance on the day that Sir Percival Bowyer had arrived at Westwood Grange. And of its consequences. She glanced around, worriedly. The girl called Pol winked at her and nodded approvingly in Matt's direction. There were smothered grins, the occasional chuckle.

'Here, Bobsy, here I am —' Matt leapt onto a long bench, ran its length lightly, scattering its occupants, then leapt to the floor. In two swift strides he was at the table in front of Moses Smith. In his hand he held the filthy scrap of crumpled material that served Bobs as a handkerchief. Bobs gaped. With a great pantomime of fastidious revulsion, Matt dropped the thing upon the table. A spontaneous gust of laughter swept the room. Moses too was openly laughing, his pale eyes running tears which he mopped delicately with a scrap of fine lace. 'You'll do, my lad, you'll do. It seems that our Croucher has done something right at last.'

Matt grinned, half-bowed, mockingly, and turned to walk to his place beside Kitty. Halfway down the length of the cellar, however, the focus of all eyes, he stopped, as if suddenly remembering something. Turned. 'Ah — I almost forgot —' Lightly he ran back to the table, made a deft pass with his hands and a watch spun before Moses Smith's eyes heavily and slowly upon its chain, the gleam of rose-gold warm in the chill, flickering shadows of the cellar.

The room fell to absolute silence.

Kitty held her breath. Matt — Matt? Why must you always do it? Why can you never let well alone?

Very slowly, the smile gone from his face, Moses reached for his watch. Matt held onto the chain for a fraction of a second before, with a regretful twitch of his lips, he let it go.

Moses surveyed him thoughtfully. 'Thank you.' He laid the watch upon the table.

Matt, apparently totally unaware of the tension around him, walked jauntily back to Kitty and slipped into his seat.

Moses turned his head. 'Johnny,' he said to the man Matt had called Johnny Sly, 'I trust your — business — had gone a little more successfully than friend Croucher's?'

The slight, dapper man went to the table and tossed a heavy purse upon it. 'Yes, sir. That it 'as.'

'Good. Good.'

And so it went on. One after another Moses' minions paid their 'rent' and were congratulated or castigated according to their contribution. Thieves, forgers, beggars, prostitutes; in this part of the city all were under Moses Smith's protection and all paid dearly for the doubtful privilege. In whispers from the irrepressible Matt, Kitty learned names and occupations. 'Tha'ss the Bentall brothers. Best fences in the area. And Clanger there – he's a bit faker –' He grinned at her expression. 'Counterfeiter,' he supplied.

'Pol Taylor. Lottie Andrews,' Moses called.

Pol stood alone.

Moses waved an impatient, pudgy hand. 'Both of you.'

Pol's wide mouth tightened, but she did not argue. Gently she offered an arm to the other girl who climbed wearily to her feet and made her way painfully to the far end of the cellar. With a faint, scornful flick of the wrist Pol tossed a handful of coins onto the table.

There was a very long silence. Then, sorrowfully, Moses shook his head. 'Won't do, Pol.'

'It's all we got.'

He smiled his cherubic smile. 'I don't believe you. And neither does Bobs. Do you, Bobs?'

'No, Mr Smith.'

Pol, for all her bravado, was obviously very frightened indeed. Lottie, barely able to stand, was it seemed beyond fear. She stared, her great violet-coloured eyes blank.

'Lottie, yes,' Moses conceded. 'Perhaps it's understandable –'

'P'raps?' the word was sharp as Pol's temper ousted good sense. 'P'raps? Fer Gawd's sake, Mr Smith – be 'uman! The girl's just 'ad a bleedin' miscarriage! She nearly died! 'Ow much trade d'yer reckon she's managed in that state? It's all she can do ter stand on 'er feet at the Rooms. You ask Midge – she'll tell yer –'

'It isn't Lottie I'm concerned with.' It seemed to Kitty

that there was some slight warmth in the eyes that the man turned on the sick girl, a shadow that disappeared entirely as he turned back to Pol. 'But you? What's your excuse? You've had a miscarriage also?'

'I've bin lookin' after 'er.' The words were sullen.

'I see.' Absently Moses played with a copper coin, spinning it, watching it until it stilled on the table, the sound still ringing in the ears. He lifted his eyes. 'I shouldn't like to think, Pol, that you were trying to swindle me. Doing a little – trade on the side? Pocketing the profits?'

'I swear to yer, Mr Smith –'

He held up a sharp hand. She fell silent. 'Just a friendly warning, Pol. Just a friendly warning.' He leaned forward. 'Now, I suggest that you leave Lottie to take care of herself and get about your own – about my – business. Do I make myself clear?'

Rebellion died. Pol avoided the small, pale eyes. 'Yes, Mr Smith.'

'Get off with you.'

The two girls stumbled back to their places. Moses Smith's eyes surveyed the cellar, came to rest, unerringly, upon Kitty. Kitty felt sudden cold sweat start upon her skin.

'It seems,' the man said, pleasantly, 'that we have another stranger in our midst?'

Every eye in the room turned upon poor Kitty. She saw a flash of understandable relief cross Pol's face, tinged with an unexpected sympathy.

'Here, girl.'

Kitty felt Matt tense beside her. She touched his hand in light warning, then composedly stood.

'Here.'

She stepped into the open space before the table.

'Name?'

'Kitty Daniels.' She hesitated: '– sir,' she added.

'And what contribution, Kitty Daniels, are you making – or thinking of making – to our small and happy community?' The words were peaceful.

'I've – only just come, sir.'

'Ah. I see.' He tapped small, regular teeth with a pink
fingernail. 'But you have, I assume, some – talent' – the
word was faintly mocking – 'that you intend to put to our
mutual good advantage?'

'I –'

'She's my sister, Mr Smith.' Matt was on his feet. 'She –
helps me.'

'Helps you?' Fine brown brows were raised. 'My dear
young man, anyone in less need of help I doubt I've ever
met.'

'We work together,' Matt said, doggedly.

'I see.' The silence was cold. Then, 'I don't believe that
that is enough,' the fat man said, regretfully. 'Indeed no.'

Kitty kept her head up and her mouth closed. What was
there to say?

Moses eyed her contemplatively. 'We carry no passengers,'
he said.

'I'll work,' she said. 'I'm strong.'

He raised his eyebrows again, maliciously expressive. A
man laughed.

'We could do with an extra pair of 'ands at the Rooms, Mr
Smith.' Kitty recognized Pol's voice from behind her.
''Specially with Lot still poorly.'

Moses considered, then, ponderously, nodded. 'I believe
you've hit it, Pol. See to it.'

'Yes, Mr Smith.'

Moses heaved himself to his feet. 'Well, my children,
regretfully I must leave you. I have other members of my
unruly family claiming my attention.' Surprisingly lightly
he stepped from the dais and past Kitty towards the door at
the end of the cellar. His bodyguards, impassive as ever,
followed. By Matt, Moses stopped. Gold gleamed in the
smoky air. 'I believe firmly in the rewards of labour' – the
silken voice was pleasant – 'and I greatly admire skill. I
would advise you, however, in friendship, never – ever – to
try that trick again.'

And so he left, leaving Matt to stare, astounded, at the
valuable gold watch that had been deposited in his open

palm, and Kitty, cold with fear, to wonder at her sudden conviction that she and her brother had flown, like helpless flies, into the web of a great, obscene spider.

2

Smith's Song and Supper Rooms was very far from being
the most salubrious establishment in London, and bore little
resemblance except in name to its distant cousins in the
West End that were patronized by the Bohemian rich and
their idle sons. Smith's was situated just a mile or so from
the teeming alleys of Whitechapel, in Stepney, close to the
docks, its entrance in a narrow street known as Blind Lane,
a long, cobbled alley that ended abruptly as a dead end in
the foetid waters of an ancient, disused canal. Part of the
building had seen past service as a warehouse, and it was in
this lofty, barnlike structure that the low stage had been
constructed, its apron jutting into the large room that had
tables and chairs packed closely about the dirty, sawdust-
covered floor. At the opposite end from the stage was a long
bar, scarred and stained. There were some pretensions to elegance in the cheap glass gas chandeliers that lit the hall and
the motheaten and mildewed velvet drapes that disguised
the stark brick-and-timber structure of the place. Since there
were no windows the impression a customer received when
he walked through the curtained door and down the wide,
shallow steps into the body of the hall, was of a kind of timeless night, always dimly gaslit, always shadowed, and bearing
no relationship at all to the realities of climate or light in the
world outside. Even at those rare times when the midday sun
of summer slid reluctant fingers of warmth into the filthy
alley that was Blind Lane, within the rooms the shades of
night defied the truth and confused the senses. Not that the
frequenters of the Rooms found anything to complain of in
that – for most of the criminals, pimps and ruffians that made

up the bulk of Moses Smith's patrons the bright light of day was no more their natural setting than it was for the sewer rats that scuttled below the floorboards and fed from the kitchen scraps, or the bats that roosted in the crumbling belfry of the half-ruined church that could be seen from the end of the lane across the dark stagnant waters of the disused canal. The remainder of the clientele were seamen from the ships berthed in the nearby docks, for the most part simple and lawless men, as ready to spend their money as they were to break a head or cut a throat.

The entertainment that drew them to the place night after night was varied. George Milton, baritone, was a man who had seen better days, most of his professional life having been spent delighting the ears of the favoured rich in the ballrooms and parlours of the fashionable streets of Mayfair until his eye for the ladies led him once too often into temptation and his engagements – and his income – had been abruptly terminated. The only other regular on Smith's bill was Potty Masters, a stand-up comic with a repertoire of the filthiest jokes in London and a pleasant enough voice in which he rendered songs so coarse that it had been known even for his villainous audience – who liked nothing so much as to join him in his rousing and vulgar choruses – to be occasionally taken aback by the grossness of the words they were singing so gustily. It was normal too – and popular – for a member of the audience to take his turn in front of the footlights – to say nothing of his chances on the mood of his fellows, which could turn from benign to merciless in the blink of an eye. The girls who worked in the Rooms under the eagle eye of Midge Corelli would occasionally give a turn – and by far the most popular of these was Lottie Andrews, whose small, sweet voice and lovely face had been known to quiet the rowdiest of audiences. Sometimes too an itinerant ballad singer, of which there were hundreds roaming the streets of London earning a pittance from singing their own compositions and dreaming dreams of fortunes and famous clients that were rarely realized, might drop in and try his luck.

When an apprehensive Kitty first entered the place in company with Pol her impression was of a dark world so totally alien to anything she had ever known that it might have been the jungles of the Amazon or the harsh fastness of the desert.

'S'all right, love.' Kindly Pol, with sure instinct, divined the reason for her hesitation. 'You'll soon get used to it. Come on – I'll take yer to Midge –' Halfway across the hall, weaving expertly between tables and chairs in the half-darkness, she stopped. 'Word in yer ear before yer meet 'er –'

'Yes?'

'She's' – Pol hesitated – 'a bit of a rough diamond, our Midge.' She grimaced a little. 'Not to be picky about it, she can be a right bitch, though 'er 'eart's in the right place if yer can find it. Thing is – well – she don't 'old with airs an' graces in 'er girls. Know what I mean?'

Kitty had already been the recipient of enough spiteful mockery to know exactly what she meant. 'I can't help the way I am,' she said, woodenly, 'or the way I speak. It doesn't affect my work or my strength. It's no one's business but my own.'

Pol watched her for a moment longer, reflectively. 'Suit yerself, gel. Can't say I didn't try. Come on.'

Midge Corelli was everything that might have been expected of a woman who could run such an establishment in such a district with neither trouble nor interference from either the rough customers who were her neighbours or the arguably rougher customers that were her clientele. Though Kitty managed not to betray it, the woman terrified her from the moment she fixed her with a sharp unfriendly eye and snapped to Pol, 'Jesus! Where did Moses pick this one up from?'

'She's stoppin' at the Market Row lodgin's with us. 'Er brother's the new dipper.'

'Oh, yes.' The gaze became if anything even chiller. 'I've 'eard about 'im. Sounds like a bunch o' young trouble ter me.' The eyes narrowed unpleasantly. 'Cocky little bastard from all accounts. Runs in the family, does it?'

Kitty jumped. Her cheeks were suddenly scarlet. 'I – no.'

'Well, it better 'adn't. Or I'll skin yer, straight. An' that's a promise.'

Kitty believed her.

Her new employer eyed her for a moment longer with undisguised disdain before turning back to Pol with a dismissive gesture. 'Fer Gawd's sake get 'er down to 'Arry's place an' tog 'er up. She looks like a bleedin' moultin' crow at a funeral. I'll leave 'er with you. Show 'er the ropes. Any trouble, report to me.'

'Yes, Midge.'

Midge barely glanced at Kitty. 'Cash for the togs'll be stopped from yer wages.'

Kitty said nothing.

'Get orf.' As the girls reached the door she stopped them with a sharp word. 'Pol?'

The girl turned.

''Ow's that good-fer-nothin' Lottie?'

Pol shrugged. 'Bit better today. She'll be all right.'

Midge nodded. 'Silly little bitch. Tell 'er Luke was askin' after 'er last night. An' tell 'er 'Arry's got a good bit o' blue velvet down the shop. She can 'ave it if she gets back on 'er feet, stupid little cow.'

'I'll tell 'er.'

Outside the door Pol grinned widely at Kitty. 'Midge 'as got a real soft spot fer Lottie.'

'She has?' Kitty's voice was doubtful.

Pol laughed outright. 'Come on – I'll show yer round 'ere first, an' tell yer what's what. Then we'll make tracks fer 'Arry's place. We ain't got much time.' She waved a hand. 'Waitin' at tables is the main thing, though we all takes our turn at servin' be'ind the bar –'

Bemused, Kitty trailed around behind her, her confused brain only taking in half of what she was being told. 'Meals and drinks – especially drinks – more profit, y'see – smile at the customers – don't keep 'em waiting – don't be cheeky and keep out of trouble. Trouble starts, you call fer Midge or fer Bobs. Watch the table customers – they're spendin' more, they expect service. An' whatever else you don't do, watch the big table by the stage. Moses' own, and you'd better just jump if he's there. Another thing – Moses don't drink the same rubbish 'e serves to the payin' customers. 'E an' Luke Peveral 'ave their own private supply downstairs.'

An ice of misery seemed to have encased Kitty's heart. She couldn't work here. She could not.

'You better come an' see the kitchens. Mornin', Belle –' If Pol noticed her companion's unhappy silence she gave no sign. Her greeting was to an enormous woman who was standing at a stained, dripping sink peeling a small mountain of potatoes with filthy hands. The kitchen smelled foul and looked as if no one within a mile of it had ever heard of soap and water. Belle grunted bad-temperedly, hardly glancing at Kitty. Kitty blinked away visions of the huge, warm old kitchen at the Grange with its appetizing smells and rows of gleaming brass and copper utensils and allowed herself to be towed back to the darkness of the Rooms. Pol was still talking. 'There's two performances a night. Reg'lar, that is. Sometimes there's more. Depends.' She stepped up onto the low stage, with its draped velvet curtains and battered upright piano. 'George Milton's our regular at the moment – watch 'im, 'e's a nice enough bloke, but 'e's got more 'ands than an octopus – mind you,' she grinned, not unkindly, ' 'e probably won't bother you. Likes 'em with a bit o' meat on 'em does George. Somethin' ter get 'old of. An' Potty Masters is the other – Gawd, 'e can be funny that lad, when 'e's 'ad a few. Mind you, 'e's fallen flat on 'is stupid face a coupl'a times lately. Don't know 'ow much longer 'e'll be with us. Moses don't take kindly ter riots, an' when the customers start ter throw things it ain't far off.' She grinned cheerfully again. 'Lot sings sometimes. Pretty little voice she's got.'

Dumbly Kitty followed her onto the stage. Standing next to the piano, very slowly she extended a finger and touched the battered, closed lid.

'Don't know 'ow she does it meself.' Pol had planted

herself in the centre of the stage, hands on hips, and was surveying the huge, empty hall. 'Scare the piss out of me, it would. You play that thing?'

Kitty jumped, snatched her hand from the piano as if it had been burned. 'No,' she said.

'Right – well – I think that's the lot. Apart from –' Pol stopped. Kitty, suddenly aware of a touch of awkwardness in the other girl's manner, waited. Pol was looking at a door set in the wall beside the stage and hung with tawdry velvet. Then, saying nothing, she turned abruptly. 'Come on. Let's go see 'Arry.'

She led the way into the street, exchanged obscene pleasantries with the two bruisers who guarded the door. At the end of the lane they turned into a broad, busy thoroughfare lined with tall brick buildings grimy with soot and the dust of the street. Sweatshops, warehouses, tenements and factories stood shoulder to shoulder, looking at the world through the blank, dirty eyes of their narrow windows. Kitty still felt overwhelmed by these city streets with their noisy, laden traffic, their pale, scurrying pedestrians, their filthy gutters and littered pavements, the squalor glimpsed through arch and doorway behind the façade of commerce. She followed Pol, pulling her skirts from the grasp of a half-naked beggar-child, almost falling over the outstretched legs of a man who huddled in a doorway, a gin bottle clutched to his breast. She drew a quick, shocked breath at sight of his face – the suffering of the damned could surely bring no more despair than she glimpsed in the ravaged eyes? So many times this same countenance could be seen, in every doorway, on every street corner – desperate, forsaken, perishing by slow inches and no hope of salvation. Such sights almost paralysed her with terror; always she was aware that this was only one short step down from where she and her brother stood. Almost running, she hurried after Pol, followed her into a narrow lane and through an archway into a cobbled court-yard, two sides of which were formed by derelict stable buildings and the third by a wall of smoke-blackened brick in which was set a door; above this hung the three brass balls that were the sign of the pawnbroker.

As Pol pushed the door open somewhere at the back of the shop a bell rang.

''Arry? It's Pol. Got a customer for yer.'

There came a rustling from the shadows, and Kitty jumped as a voice close at hand said ill-temperedly, 'Nae need to shout, girl.' A tall, pale, stooping man with a lugubrious face and a head of thinning sandy hair shuffled towards them. He wore carpet slippers, crumpled trousers, a collarless shirt and a shabby, ill-fitting jacket that hung upon him like rags upon a scarecrow.

'Got somethin' pretty for a new girl?' Pol asked cheerfully.

Harry surveyed Kitty doubtfully, sniffed, and with no word scuffed his way back through the cluttered shop to a curtained archway. Pol grinned and jerked her head, indicating that Kitty should follow. The room to which the man led them smelled abominably of that stale and nauseous odour peculiar to old and unwashed clothes. On two sides of the room long rails held every conceivable type of attire – men's, women's and children's. A third was lined with deep shelves which held shoes, boots, hats, bags, gloves, belts and umbrellas. There were boxes of cheap jewellery, tumbled into tawdry heaps that gleamed garishly in the dim light. Scarves there were, and feathers and shawls. In the centre of the room stood a bare, dirty table and beside it a tall, fly-specked mirror. Harry looked again, dolefully, at Kitty. 'I've not much'll suit. She's gey tall.' He spoke with the reluctance and difficulty of a man who spent much time in his own silent company and preferred it to the garrulousness of others.

Pol skipped along the rails, twitching a skirt here, a sleeve there. ''Ere – try this. An' that looks as if it might – no, 'Arry's right – you are a bit lanky, ain't yer? Ah, this looks more like –' She pulled a dress of scarlet from the rack, shaking out the creases, threw it on the table. 'You can wear red, I reckon, you bein' dark – or green o' course, green'd look good. 'Ow about this?' She held up a dress of cheap

emerald satin that shrieked in protest at the garish red of
its trimming. 'Gawd, don't I remember this? Fanny 'Awkins,
wasn't it?' She did not bother with the unlikely possibility
of an answer from Harry. 'She was tallish, as I remember it.
Do you well, I reckon –' She held the dress out to Kitty,
who mutely shook her head. 'Try it,' Pol said, firmly, 'it'll
be a bit short, but the customers don't mind a bit of ankle,
eh, 'Arry?' She giggled. Harry sniffed.

Kitty picked up the abominable dress, and held it to her,
looking in the mirror. It was cut so low as to have almost
no bodice at all. The skirt finished, ludicrously, just below
her knees.

Pol pulled a disappointed face. 'P'raps not. Gawd, girl, 'ow
tall are you? Try the red.'

Kitty picked up the scarlet dress. Its shoddy satin shone
like new-shed blood, cheap glass beads edged the wide, low
neck and small frilled sleeves, teardrops in the uncertain
light.

'Well, try it on.' Pol was impatient. 'We ain't got all day.
An' at least it looks as if it'll cover yer bloody knees.'

Embarrassed, Kitty clutched the dress to her, looking at
the impassive Harry.

Pol shrieked with unconcerned laughter. 'Oh, don't mind
'im. 'E's seen worse than you can show 'im, eh, 'Arry?'

'Aye.'

'An' 'e's not about ter leave us in 'ere alone, are yer, 'Arry?'
Harry shook his head.

'Trustin' bastard, aren't yer?' Pol asked, pleasantly. 'Now,
come on, Kit – do yer stuff. Time's gettin' on –'

Awkwardly Kitty turned her back on the watching man,
fumbling with the buttons of her skirt. Stepping from it and
clutching her blouse to her breasts she scrambled into the
scarlet monstrosity, dragging it up over her ragged, grubby
petticoats. Then, her fingers thumbs with embarrassment,
she dropped the blouse and struggled to slip her arms into
the scarlet sleeves.

Pol shouted again with exasperated laughter. 'Good
Gawd! Such maidenly modesty's never been seen 'ere before,

eh 'Arry? It's no good, love — you'll 'ave to take that bleedin'
thing off —' And to Kitty's horror she stepped towards her
and with swift movements unlaced her bodice and stripped
it from her, leaving her naked to the waist. Not altogether
unkindly Pol laughed again. 'Christ in 'Eaven, what yer
makin' all the fuss about? You ain't got that much to 'ide!'

Mortified, her cheeks of a colour with the awful dress,
Kitty slipped her arms into the sleeves and stood as Pol
buttoned her up and stood back. 'There. Not bad. Not at all
bad.'

Kitty stared aghast at her reflection. 'I can't wear this,'
she said, faintly.

''Course yer can. It looks a treat. Shame yer 'aven't got a
bit more on top — that was made fer a girl a bit more blessed
than you —' Pol twitched at the all-but-empty bodice with
dirty fingers. 'P'raps we could pad you out a bit? Anyway —
like I said — the colour suits yer —'

'It does not. It's awful.' Kitty hated the shaking desperation of her own voice. She swallowed noisily.

''Course it isn't.' Pol was just a little injured. 'It's just
what the doctor ordered.'

Trembling, Kitty glared at the figure in the mirror,
freckled, bony shoulders all but naked, small breasts bared
almost to the nipples by the sagging neckline, the gaudy
skirt, flounced and flared like garish tiers of flame about her
long legs. 'I look like a whore,' she said, flatly and miserably.

There was a brief, edged silence. ''Ere.' Pol picked up a
worn black shawl and tossed it about her shoulders. 'That
better?'

Kitty clutched at it. 'I still don't like it. Isn't there something else?'

Pol sighed, commendably patient. 'If there is, ducks, we
don't 'ave time ter look for it. The Rooms open in 'alf-'our.
If we ain't there, Midge'll 'ave both our guts fer garters. Got
a pair of boots, 'Arry?'

It took a full ten minutes to find a pair of battered black
leather buttoned boots that came anywhere near Kitty's
long, lean feet. 'Thank Gawd fer that!' Pol breathed an

exaggerated sigh of relief when at last Kitty found something she could walk in that did not cripple her. 'You sure they're all right? I tell yer – yer feet are goin' ter kill yer quite enough on their own account withaht yer boots givin' 'em an 'elpin' 'and.'

Kitty, aware of rough kindness, nodded. 'They're all right.'

'Good. Put it on the slate, 'Arry, will yer? Midge'll stump up. Kitty – you ain't got time ter change – 'Arry – stuff 'er other gear in a bag, eh?'

A few short weeks before, Kitty would no more have contemplated walking through a crowded public place dressed so than she would have contemplated cutting her own throat.

She pulled the black shawl closer about her shoulders, took the paper bag from Harry's hands with no word of thanks and followed Pol out into the street.

(ii)

Unsurprisingly Kitty at first found the work at the Song and Supper Rooms every bit as disagreeable as she had expected; what she had not bargained for, however, was the additional strain of a complete physical exhaustion that left her too tired to sleep. For the first week she lived in a miserable daze, lying each night desperately sleepless in her bed – when at last she reached it in the early hours of the morning – dreading the day that must follow, and with it the ordeal of facing once more Moses Smith's villainous customers. It seemed to her that the place had deadened heart and brain – it was as if both her courage and her wit deserted her the minute she stepped across the threshold into that unnatural night. She was cursed for her clumsiness, ridiculed for her apparent obtuseness and bullied by just about everyone, including the other girls.

'Stand up to 'em, love.' Pol did her best, her heart touched by the other girl's obvious unhappiness. 'Give 'em a bit back. They'll soon give over –'

'I can't, Pol, I can't!' Kitty shook her head wretchedly. 'I'll never get used to it —!'

Her new friend surveyed her with worrying soberness. 'You'd better. An' quick. There's a lot worse Moses could set you onto if 'e 'ad a mind.'

Kitty, who even in her present state had eyes in her head, could have no doubt as to the other girl's meaning. Compared to some other establishments that Moses Smith ran — notably the brothel a little further down Blind Lane, known as The House — the Song and Supper Rooms was a lady's tea party. When Pol left her she sat alone in the dismal room she still shared with her brother in Market Row, her face buried in her hands. Never could she remember feeling so utterly alone, or so terribly afraid. Matt she saw infrequently — in characteristic manner he had taken to the perilous life of a street arab as if born to it, had even found his way into the special if untrustworthy favour of Moses Smith — and he faced her intransigent unhappiness with a predictable and infuriating optimism; 'You'll get used to it, owd Kitty. 'Course you will. Tha'ss not so bad. An' tha'ss not for long —'

'How long?' she had asked, for the dozenth time, 'Matt — how long?' And he had shrugged again, and laughed again, and turned the question with a joke again.

She took now a long, shaking breath. The sounds of the building came to her through the insubstantial walls. A dog yelped. Quarrelling voices were raised. A woman shrieked. A man's voice growled a curse and there came the unmistakable sound of a blow. Somewhere a child was whimpering, dismally and with no pause for breath. With a quick, fierce movement Kitty stuffed her fingers in her ears, pressing them in painfully hard, making the blood roar in her head, screwing up her eyes as if to shut out for ever this world that she so hated. She would not be part of such a place. Of such a life.

But she was. Apparently inescapably, she was.

Miserably, and without bothering to take off the hateful scarlet dress that seemed to her to be the badge of her enslavement she threw herself onto the stinking, unmade bed, drew her knees to her chin and prayed for sleep that she knew would not come.

Such utter misery, however, could not last. She was young, she was healthy, and in the way of such things as the days moved on she found if no kind of contentment at least some acceptance of her situation, and gradually, at last, her spirit and good sense began to reassert themselves. As she became more used to the work she made fewer mistakes and was therefore subject to less abuse and mockery; and given her stubborn refusal to rise to their jibes the girls of the Rooms grew at last bored with her lack of response and tormented her less. Then, one night, during her stint behind the long bar, stung to retaliation by a particularly coarse taunt, she found her tongue at last and, encouraged by Pol's approving eye, gave an account of herself that brought grins to the faces of her surprised and discomfited victim's companions. After that life became easier, as she discovered a hitherto unknown talent for defensive and acid retaliation; and if her vituperative tongue did not make her popular it kept the customers at a distinterested arm's length and that was all she asked – for it had been a very few days indeed before Pol's reticence regarding the velvet-draped door by the stage was explained. Beyond the door was a steep flight of dark stairs, at the top of which were half a dozen ill-furnished bedrooms – 'for private entertainment' was the euphemism used. If Smith's Song and Supper Rooms was not exactly a brothel, in the sense that The House was, it seemed to Kitty to come close.

But Pol dismissed her first fearful questions with a wave of her hand. 'Honest, love, you won't 'ave ter worry. Midge – she won't 'ave 'er girls forced. Moses? – yes, I'd put nothin' past that bastard. But Midge is no meat-merchant. You want ter use the rooms – yer use 'em, an' yer pays yer dues, ter Midge an' ter Moses. But – yer don't? – that's all right too. I tell yer – I've never known a girl forced. Not 'ere. What goes on up at the 'Ouse – 'oo knows? But not 'ere. You got ter face it, Kit' – Pol's good natured face was unusually sober

– 'you could 'a done a lot worse. Yer want to ask Lottie what can 'appen to a girl what doesn't know when she's well off.'

'What do you mean?'

Pol shrugged. 'Couple o' years back the silly little sod took it into 'er 'ead that she was too good fer poor old Stepney. Went off up West, she did.' She grinned, sardonically. 'Lookin' fer fame an' fortune. Joined an 'ouse in the 'Aymarket – all silks an' satins an' French perfume, know what I mean? Entertainin' the gentry.' She made a swift, coarsely explicit gesture. 'Well, I tell yer – she was back 'ere before yer could say "Jack Robinson". An' carryin' a few scars, too.' She leaned towards Kitty, wagging her finger. 'At least round 'ere if a girl gets a good beatin' it's 'cos 'er feller's drunk, or mad at 'er. 'E don't string 'er up an' do it fer pleasure, with 'is mates watchin' an' 'is trousers round 'is ankles! I should coco. I'd 'a' bleedin' brained 'im meself, title or no title. So just think on – there's worse things in this world than waitin' on tables at Smith's. An' worse things that can 'appen to a girl than what goes on upstairs, an' all. In the 'ouse Lottie was in they 'ad these peep'oles – oh, all right, me lady, I'll shut me mouth. I'm just tellin' yer, that's all –'

That Pol herself was not averse to using the draped door Kitty knew and accepted as being none of her business; the first time she saw her brother slip through it with a pretty sharp-faced girl called Biddie in tow she was ready to skin him alive. He took her castigation philosophically, and on his first free evening headed straight back to Smith's, Biddie, and the draped door. Kitty, wisely, gave up. She had problems enough of her own to worry about.

One of them was Lottie.

The root of Kitty's problem with the girl lay buried deeply in Lottie's jealously possessive character. From the first she had shown antipathy towards Kitty, but from the moment kindly Pol had befriended the newcomer openly, it was obvious that Lottie had set her face firmly against her, an attitude that became more open and more obviously hostile as the sick girl began to regain her strength. Frail, lovely, oddly spoiled, Lottie had a stubborn streak in an otherwise rather unstable character that made her cling like a limpet to those upon whom she depended, and defend with fury against any threat, real or imagined, to her own position. Kitty she marked as an enemy from the first time Pol smiled at her, and there seemed to be little that Kitty could do about it. At first, sympathetic to the girl's ill-health and insecurity she had, despite snubs and scornful rejections, gone out of her way to be pleasant and to try to allay the other girl's fears and suspicions, but to no avail. Lottie – intense, emotional, vulnerable, indulged – woud have none of her friendly overtures. And so Kitty at last found herself shrugging and leaving well alone. Lottie's irrational fears and jealousies were not of her making, whatever the other girl might think.

'Leave 'cr be, Kitty.' Pol was gentle. 'She's a queer fish sometimes. She'll come round.' Kitty, smiling, said nothing. But aware of the naked hostility in Lottie's lovely eyes when she looked at her, she knew better. Yet in truth, Lottie's fears about what she saw as Kitty's intrusion between herself and Pol were utterly groundless. Pol and Lottie were the very closest of friends and Kitty's coming made no difference to that. It seemed to Kitty that pretty, dependent Lottie was everything to Pol – friend, sister, darling, spoiled daughter. She petted and scolded her, watched over her, reassured her. Within days of meeting them Kitty became aware that on only one issue were those two utterly divided – and perhaps unsurprisingly, that issue was a man.

Kitty knew of Luke Peveral by reputation for some time before she saw him. It seemed that everyone at the Song and Supper Rooms was ready and eager to illustrate his or her intimacy with Moses Smith's most illustrious customer with a story, often patently exaggerated and tinged, according to the teller, with admiration, envy, sycophancy or – in the case of most women – that faint, defensive derision that bespoke strong physical attraction. Luke Peveral, it appeared, was the Supper Rooms' idea of a gentleman. He was also a master thief – one of an aristocracy of crime whose contacts in the world beyond the stinking midden-slums of the East End gave him access to the kind of ill-gotten spoils of which most of the habitués of Smith's only dreamed.

One successful assault, so it was said, by Luke Peveral and his sidekick, a tiny ex-jockey called Spider Murphy, upon the bastions of wealth and privilege and the White-chapel fences could close their doors for a fortnight. He was run by no one – not even Moses – though word was that a few had tried, to their own eventual regret. The double tongue of gossip worked its usual confusion over the man – Peveral, said some, was ruthless, tight-fisted, unfriendly and arrogant – yet others would have him easy-going, generous, unassuming as a girl. Upon one point only did all tales tally – Luke Peveral was a womanizer. Upon which grounds alone, Amos Isherwood hovering at her shoulder, Kitty disliked him before she ever had laid eyes upon him. But she could not deny a certain curiosity, for from none of the contradictory stories did any clear picture emerge, and the contradictions were personified in the attitudes of Pol and Lottie. Pol clearly disliked the man – it would not be too strong indeed to say that she hated him. Lottie, on the other hand, jumped to his defence always with a passion that spoke for itself.

For the first couple of weeks that Kitty was at Smith's Luke Peveral was 'away on business'. With any other of Midge's patrons Kitty had very soon learned that this would have but one interpretation. Not so, it seemed, however, with Luke Peveral. 'No such luck, love.' This, disgustedly, from Pol. ' 'E's too fly fer the bloody coppers. 'E's probably in the country somewhere, enjoyin' the 'ospitality of whatever poor bugger 'e's next goin' ter rob blind. Champagne an' caviare an' lah-di-dah chit-chat, then bang! The 'ouse-guest's gone, an' so's most of 'is Lordship's family heir-looms.'

'He really does that?' Kitty remembered Sir Percy's com-panions at the Grange, and the idea did not seem so far fetched.

' 'E really does that.' Pol's voice was unimpressed. 'So can a monkey climb a tree. It don't make 'im clever.'

'So he must make a lot of money?'

'So it's said.'

'Then – why on earth does he live round here?' With her own and only burning desire being to get away, Kitty could not for her life understand anyone staying of their own accord.

'Because it's safe, stupid,' Lottie said. ' 'Ow many coppers 'ave you seen fingerin' people's collars around 'ere? Luke's among friends 'ere. Where else would 'e go? 'E knows where 'e's well off.'

'I see.'

'You see nothing.' The other girl's voice was flatly contemptuous. 'Come on, Pol – you promised you'd give me an 'and with the blue –'

The only other information that Kitty picked up about the mysterious Peveral was that he lived in or around the derelict church that could be seen on the other side of the canal, but that no one appeared to know exactly where, and he guarded that privacy with a blunt intransigence that daunted the most persistent of curious souls. He might, Kitty thought sardonically, stay in Whitechapel as Lottie said because he was amongst friends – but he seemed ready to go to some lengths to prevent those friends from coming too close. If Luke wanted company he came to the Rooms, if he did not he stayed at home, and was disturbed at peril. Not even Lottie, who quite clearly had more than a passing acquaintance with the man, knew exactly where he lived.

Her first meeting with the man about whom there was so much speculation occurred one evening in September, and it was not particularly auspicious.

It was a cold evening, and raining – a threatening harbinger of a hard winter that the weather had turned so early. From the moment that she arrived at the Rooms she was aware of an extra bustle in the air, an odd edge of excitement. For the first time Kitty could remember the large round table that was always set ready upon a low, curved platform that

abutted the stage was occupied. One of the occupants was
Moses Smith, his bulk encompassed by an enormous chair
especially constructed for the purpose.

'Gawd, gel!' Pol was uncharacteristically flustered.
'Where yer bin? She's spittin' rivets –!'

She was interrupted by Midge who bore down on them
like a man o' the line, all guns blazing. 'Where yer bin, yer
lazy cow? What time d'yer call this? Two bob docked fer
Friday. Think I pay yer ter keep lady's hours, yer idle slut?
Now, stir yer stumps before I chop 'em off. Pol – get be'ind
the bar before there's a riot. You' – she glared at the quailing
Kitty – 'take over the tables 'ere. Luke wants Lottie ter
sing. An' 'e's spendin' 'ard ternight, so what 'e says goes.
Move!'

Pol swung away. 'Keep yer eye on the big table. Keep 'em
'appy. Lot'll 'elp.'

For the next ten minutes Kitty was rushed off her feet.
The place was full, the customers hungry and possessed
of their usual prodigious thirst. At seven the lights were
dimmed, the primitive footlights flared smokily and the din
quietened a little as the small, nondescript pianist whose
name Kitty had never learned slid across the stage and took
his place upon the stool and George Milton, a fine figure
still, despite advancing years, in his cutaway black tail coat
and frilled shirt, his fine mutton-chop whiskers as grey
and luxuriant as his hair, took the stage. Though his best
performances were undoubtedly behind him he was a popular figure, and an impressive one. As he stood, and bowed,
from the audience came a roar of encouragement, and then
comparative quiet. Kitty glanced nervously towards the big
table. Lottie, she saw, stood attentively beside Moses' huge
chair. Reassured, she scurried to the bar to fill the order for
another table. George's voice lifted, 'I dream of Jeannie with
the light brown hair –' Somewhere in the crowd a drunken
voice was raised in conversation, and was furiously hissed
to silence. 'I see her tripping where the bright streams
play –' Kitty stood for a moment, watching and listening,
half-smiling, the music filling her mind, lighting and

warming her unhappy soul like sunshine on a winter's day. 'Many were the wild notes her merry voice would pour –'

A long, clawlike hand gripped her arm painfully. 'What in 'ell's name d'yer think you're doin', madam?' Midge's low voice grated with fury. 'There's empty bottles on Mr Smith's table! Get on over there!'

'But – Lottie's there –'

'Lottie's with Luke ternight. Get going.'

Panic-stricken, she stumbled through the crowd to the table where a scowling Moses awaited her, pudgy fingers beating an ominous tattoo on the table top. 'And about time too. More champagne.'

'Yes, Mr Smith.' With barely a glance at the other occupants of the table, but hotly aware of Lottie's maliciously amused eyes upon her, she turned and nearly tripped down the step, saving herself awkwardly. Lottie laughed, very softly, very spitefully. The applause for George had died, and he stood clearing his throat for his next song.

'I haven't seen that one before.' A light, pleasant voice, idly conversational. 'New?'

'New and stupid,' Moses said, sourly, and Kitty knew that the words were for her. The other man laughed, and Lottie's laughter chimed with his.

She all but ran to the kitchen. 'Champagne for Mr Smith!' A few moments later, two unopened bottles balanced precariously upon a tarnished silver-gilt tray, she wove her way carefully back to the table.

George was in good voice. Now, with feeling and enormous volume he was inviting Maud to come into the garden. Kitty hovered nervously at Moses' shoulder with the champagne. He was watching the singer, a benign smile upon his face. He clicked his fingers impatiently at Kitty, not looking at her. 'Open it.'

The heavy green bottles shook, very slightly, on the tray. Kitty had never in her life opened a bottle of champagne. 'I –'

'Allow me.' A long dark hand reached and wrapped itself

about the neck of one of the bottles. 'One of my very few
real talents.'

She found herself looking into a pair of narrow eyes,
night-black and fringed with a tangle of dark lashes that
almost obscured the mocking gleam beneath them. Almost,
but not quite. Kitty stiffened, hearing the echo of his unkind
laughter, an odd spurt of antagonism spurring temper. She
put the tray with the other bottle on it firmly upon the
table. Too firmly. Moses glanced at her, frowning. Lottie
smiled. The dark eyes mocked further. The only other person at the table – a tiny, wizened man with a face wrinkled
as a walnut who sat a little distance removed – noticed
nothing. His eyes were fixed on the champagne bottle as
they might be on his hope of Heaven.

'That will do, Kitty. But watch, next time. I am not used
to waiting for service in my own establishment.' The silky
voice always seemed to Kitty just half a note from threat.

'Yes, Mr Smith.'

'And try not to fall down the step.' The voice was falsely
solicitous, as were the narrow eyes. This, Kitty suddenly
knew, was Luke Peveral. With no further ado, mentally she
ranged herself with Pol.

'I'll do my best,' she said, as coolly as she dared, and was
rewarded by the quick flash of surprise that crossed a face
as dark as a gypsy's, and hawk-nosed. To be honest she
could not deny his attraction. The man's impact was almost
physical.

Amos chuckled at her shoulder.

'Excuse me,' she said.

He sensed her antagonism, and it amused him. Lottie, on
the other hand, had suddenly ceased to be amused. She had
stilled, ice-cold and wary, watching.

Composedly Kitty walked away from them. Biddy, Matt's
light o' love, tripped past with a jug of rum and a couple of
mugs. None too gently, Kitty caught at her arm. 'Do me a
favour?'

Biddy cocked a suspicious eye. She was under no misap-
prehension at all as to Matt's sister's opinion of her. 'What?'

'Take over these tables – the ones in the corner and the big one? I'll –' She had been about to offer a bribe. In time, at the expression on the sharp-featured little face, she stopped.

'Luke Peveral's table? Gawd, not 'alf. 'Ere' – she shoved the jug and mugs into Kitty's hands – 'these are for the Jack Tars over there. Watch 'em, they're all 'ands –' and Biddy was off, patting her hair and smoothing her bright, swinging skirt over her hips like a girl who had just sighted her lover.

Kitty served the seamen, deflected their drunken amorous advances and busied herself with the other customers. On stage now Potty Masters was aiming his act almost exclusively at the group about Moses' table, his swift patter a dextrous mixture of sly ingratiation and acid-sharp humour. In this vein he could not be bettered. He had, Kitty knew, consumed the best part of a bottle of gin in the half-hour before taking to the boards, and his performance was correspondingly good; one day, she thought, he'll fall off that stage and break his neck, and laughter will be his epitaph. Luke was smiling at Potty's story of a gentleman cracksman who met his match at the hands of one of the more unscrupulous of the fair sex. Kitty found herself studying him. He was, she judged, about thirty years old, tall and leanly built, his skin dark, his thick, longish hair black as the berries she remembered from the autumn hedges of Suffolk. Unusually, at a time when beards and moustaches were fashionable and prevalent, he was clean shaven, but long dark sideburns sharpened an uncompromising line of jaw. He sat easily, his body relaxed to utter stillness, long hands resting unmoving on the table. At that moment, as if sensing her regard, he turned his head, swiftly. The narrow, guarded eyes were shielded by dark, lowered lids and tangled lashes, but he smiled, amused and mocking, to catch her eyes upon him. Furious with herself she turned quickly away.

'Pint o' porter, love, please. A man 'd die o' thirst around 'ere an' no one any the wiser.'

'Sorry –' She hurried to the bar. The climax of Potty's act was approaching – always he ended with a ribald comic song. Tonight's offering was particularly salacious. There were roars of approval and shouts for more. 'Give us *The Old Man an' the Milk Maid*, Potty –'

'*Black Maria's Curse* –'

'Same agen, girl.'

''Nother pint, love.'

'Rum fer me an' gin fer the little lady –'

'Pie an' mash on ternight?'

She scurried about her tasks. Matt signalled with a friendly wave from the bar. She nodded. As always she had to trust that he had enough common sense not to try his cocky skills on the hardened members of this brotherhood of villains and under Moses Smith's very nose –

'Ssh!'

'Sh-shh!'

A sibilant hush fell. She turned. Poised upon the stage in the uncertain glow of the footlights, Lottie looked a princess from a fairytale. She had let down her golden hair and it fell, curling, about her pale, shadowed face and smoothly rounded, pearly shoulders. Her eyes were wide and limpid, incredibly blue in the smoky light and fixed upon the only man in the room of whom she seemed aware. Luke leaned back in his chair, raised a glass, brimful and sparkling, in gentle salute, and drank from it. To the side of the stage a man passed a comment and guffawed loudly. Luke stirred very slightly and turned his head. Silence fell.

The piano tinkled, a little off-key. Lottie lifted her head, fixed her eyes on some point above the heads of her attentive audience, her hands clasped before her like a child's. 'Sweet maiden, where do you go this day –' Kitty did not know the song, but gathered from the expressions around her that it was a well-liked favourite in Lottie's repertoire. 'Kind sir, I travel in love's lost cause –' Lottie had a good voice, true but light. It did not fill the spaces of the hall around her but rather dropped into the quiet like small, fragile, chiming notes of glass hanging upon a summer breeze. Kitty stood as if turned to stone, watching the small figure on the stage, fighting something so unexpected, so bitter and so terrifyingly strong that it all but took her breath away.

'And if my love should be waiting there –'

Very, very carefully Kitty put down the tray she had been carrying, then straightened, breathing deeply. It struck her like a blow that this feeling that had so suddenly assaulted her was envy, pure and deadly. To her horror it came to her with sudden, astonishing force that in that brief moment she would have seen the other girl dead and stepped over her corpse in order to stand there in her place and sing.

'Then nothing will part us again, oh no, oh nothing will part us again.'

Kitty turned her head away and found herself looking directly into a pair of dark, disturbing, narrow eyes. The look was speculative.

She turned away.

'No, nothing will part us again.'

(iii)

'Can anyone sing?' Kitty asked Pol next day, apparently casually, 'at the Rooms, I mean?'

Pol was patching a ragged skirt. She bit through the thread, held the garment doubtfully up to the light. 'This damn' thing's fallin' ter bits. Don't know why I bother. Yes, I s'pose so. If yer can sing – yer can sing. Why?'

'I –' Kitty shrugged a little, gazed at the tattered skirt as if it were the most fascinating article she had ever come across. 'I can sing,' she said abruptly.

'Yer can?' Pol stopped, and turned her head, interested. 'Yes – yer've got a nice enough speakin' voice. You ever sung in public?'

Kitty shook her head.

Pol stood up, held the skirt to her, shaking out its crumpled folds. 'Why not 'ave a word with Midge? Catch 'er in a good mood – yer never know –'

'Pol.' Lottie stood in the doorway. 'Moses is downstairs. You comin'?'

Pol sighed, reached for the pile of coins she had set upon the table. 'Good old Moses. Gives it with one 'and, takes it back with the other. Wish I 'ad 'alf 'is style. You comin', Kit?'

Kitty glanced at the stone-faced Lottie. 'No. I'll come down with Matt.'

'Right-oh. See you later.'

The thought would not leave her. It was as if that blinding, unexpected moment of envy as she had watched Lottie upon the stage had shown her a door beyond which, if she could but find the key and open it, lay hope in a hopeless world. And yet, for fear, she could not bring herself to approach Midge. Each day she rose with the determination to do so, each evening her courage failed her and, cravenly, she held her tongue. Pol did not mention their conversation again – obviously she had not taken Kitty's diffident claim seriously – and so Kitty wrestled alone, torn between a dream that as the days wore on came close to an obsession and the intimidating and terrible fear of failure. Yes, she could sing, she knew it. But here? On that stage? Before that audience? Nothing in her life had prepared her for that. And each evening as she watched George Milton's sure and confident handling of his difficult audience, or suffered for Potty when his drink-inspired genius failed him – as it was doing more and more often – and he lost them, it was brought home to her forcefully that more than mere talent would be required to survive more than five minutes on that stage, and she doubted herself.

She found herself studying the performers. George simply dominated his audience apparently effortlessly with his presence and his fine if failing voice. Potty, on a good day, slyly invited them into a camaraderie of shared obscenity or provoked them into a conspiracy of laughter in which he was the leader. Yet more and more she saw the effort of the performance telling upon him, and ever more often he failed, and was himself mauled by his merciless followers.

Lottie on the other hand relied instinctively upon her fragile beauty and undisguised vulnerability to beguile the savage beast that lurked beyond the footlights. It did not always work, and Kitty was quick to notice that Lottie rarely sang if Luke were not there to quell with that dark, uncharitable glance any graceless interruption. Despite herself she could not deny that she watched these two, and with mixed feelings, Lottie's ill-will notwithstanding, yet the sight of the girl's total and obvious infatuation with Luke Peveral she found painful, recalling as it did her own experience with Amos Isherwood. When Luke was near Lottie's eyes followed him as if she could never have enough of the sight of him. His word and his desire were the limit of her world. That he treated her as he might a pet or a favoured child seemed not to worry her at all. If he wanted her, she was there, ready; if he ignored her she submitted, watching and waiting for the crumbs of his attention.

Kitty, with memories fresh enough still to bring the warm flush of humiliation to her cheeks if recalled, found herself fostering a slight, unwelcome sympathy for Lottie and an often exaggerated hostility towards Luke. Not, she knew, that her attitude to either of them mattered – Lottie detested her, and Luke barely knew she existed – yet nevertheless she often found herself angry both for and at Lottie for her submissive acceptance of Luke's casual and capricious treatment of her. There was no doubt that she was by no means the only woman in his life, and he made no attempt to hide the fact. Though usually when he availed himself of the services provided beyond the draped door – which he did, if not often, at least at fairly regular intervals – Lottie was his chosen companion, there were many others eager and ready to claim his attention, and his resistance to their charms, Kitty noted acidly, could not be described as strong.

She herself kept out of his way. She also kept her feet firmly from any path that might lead to that draped door and the squalid rooms beyond – and to her surprise, as Pol had predicted, no one forced or even questioned her. There were more than enough willing and warm bodies about Smith's Song and Supper Rooms for a cool, unwilling fish to slip through the net almost unnoticed. The place had a

good name – as in everything else, Moses ran it according
to his own lights and his girls were known to be clean, safe
and willing, a rare thing in this part of the world. If the tall,
odd-looking girl with the stuck-up voice wanted to stay out
of the game, who cared? Who, indeed, would want her?
Everyone knew that Moses only kept her on to humour that
rascal brother of hers –

Yet she knew that here was just one more difference, one
more cause for resentment against her – another reason to
hesitate before rashly stepping onto that stage and exposing
her soul to the whips of their scorn. She could have no
illusions; if, as she feared, she failed, there would be no
tolerance and less pity for a girl that most considered arrogant and unfriendly. Her downfall, she knew, would afford
positive and heartless pleasure to others than Lottie, and
the knowledge daunted her. Two full weeks after her conversation with Pol she still had not approached Midge. She
would wait, she told herself, despising herself for her weakness, until the time was right.

In this, however, she reckoned without Fate, Lottie's
spite and – again and infuriatingly – without her brother's
mischief.

The evening, she always remembered afterwards, began
on a sour note. A seaman, drunk, picked a fight with another
and thirty seconds later there was a throat cut and a body
to dispose of. Sickened, Kitty averted her eyes as the dripping
corpse was unceremoniously bundled out of the door and
towards the river, another mutilated, nameless obscenity to
be washed with the tide, unmourned, to an unknown grave.
The killer, bloody knife still in his hand, watched with
puzzled, drunken eyes.

'Get rid of him,' Moses said.

Bobs, with the faint look of interest that only the prospect
of violence could bring to his face, lumbered forward. Kitty
turned away. Moments later apparent normality had returned and the Rooms buzzed again with rough talk and
laughter – yet it was as if the violence had stirred something,
like mud at the bottom of a clear pool of water, that hung

dangerously in the air, sharpening voices and edging glances. Matt, together with Croucher and the acrobatic Springer, the only three of the urchin gang that Moses would allow in the Rooms, stood by the bar. From the corner of her eye Kitty saw Luke Peveral appear in the doorway, smiling, lifting a hand in greeting to an acquaintance.

She did not see her brother move.

A moment later there came through the hubbub a crash, a sharp, painfilled cry and then sudden silence fell. She turned, and froze. Luke Peveral's dark face was savage. He held Matt in a vice-grip by wrist and elbow, the arm twisted to breaking point behind the boy's back. Matt's face was agonized. She took a step forward. A firm hand gripped her and dragged her unceremoniously back, the fingers biting painfully into her arm. 'Leave it!' Pol hissed into her ear. 'You'll do more 'arm than good.'

Luke twisted harder. Matt let out a shriek of anguish.

'You stupid little bastard.' The light, hard voice was quiet, yet the words carried to every corner of the watching room. 'I'll teach you to try to thieve from me.'

Matt shook his head. 'I was only –'

'You were only,' Luke supplied pleasantly, emphasizing his words with another tightening of his grip, 'attempting to relieve me of a watch of which I am inordinately fond.'

Matt was very still. To Kitty, watching, it seemed that the slightest move might break the abused arm. The boy's teeth were clamped into his lower lip. Luke held him so for a moment, then very slightly relaxed his grip. It was a mistake. With a sudden, agile twist Matt was free and diving for the door. But not fast enough. Like a striking snake Luke's hand shot out, catching the boy by the collar, all but ripping the shirt from his back in the violence of the movement, and jerking him back into the man's strong grasp. The vicious pattern of welted scars that marked the pale skin of the young back shone ugly in the light. There was a moment's quiet, then Luke let Matt go so suddenly that the boy staggered a little. A lean, dark hand flashed, clipping the boy's ear painfully. 'Nothing I can do to you that hasn't already been done from the looks of it. Learn a lesson, lad. Never try to out-harlot a better whore. You're good. Use your skills on those that know no better.'

Matt rubbed his ear ruefully. Moses was pushing his way through the crowd, Bobs at his heels. Matt glanced at their coming, apprehensive.

'What's going on?' Moses' brow was thunderous.

Luke smiled easily. 'Nothing, old friend, nothing at all.'

'But —'

Luke put a hand under the fat man's elbow, guiding him to the round table, winking at Matt as he went. Matt stood staring after him, a strange look in his expressive eyes. Kitty began to elbow her way towards him. Moses lifted a plump, imperative finger. 'Girl! Here!'

She stopped.

'Champagne,' he said. 'Now.'

'Yes, Mr Smith.'

When she returned with the bottle Lottie was standing, alone and unnoticed, behind Luke's chair. She looked unhappy and ill-tempered. As before the room had apparently reverted to normal, yet still that thread of brutal excitement occasioned by blood and the stimulation of violence seemed woven into the smoky air. When the lights dimmed and Potty Masters, in braces and baggy trousers, his shirt hanging out like one of Croucher's urchins, slouched onto the stage, the sound that met him was more a growl of anticipation than applause. Kitty flinched. Poor Potty was in for a bad time tonight. And from the look in his eyes and the set of his shoulders he knew it. George Milton was nursing a sore throat. His was the stage, with no help or support. He struck a stance, eyed his audience, could not, for Kitty, disguise his terror.

'I say, I say, I say —'

'You've said enough. Get orf!'

Roars of applause.

'Give us a chance, gents —'

'What, another? What d'yer take us for, Potty? Yer soddin' gran'pa —?'

''E probably was,' called some other wit from the back. 'That accounts for Potty.'

The laughter was vicious.

Pathetically and obstinately Potty tried again. ''Ave you 'eard the one about the copper 'oo's mother fucked a –'

''Eard it? I bleedin' told you it –' They were not going to give him a chance. A pie sailed through the air, and caught him on the chin. The place exploded into dangerous hilarity. More missiles were hurled. Moses was making testy movements with hs hand. 'Get off, man! Get off! Before we have a riot!'

Potty stood his ground for one bitter moment before retreating under the hail of pies, potatoes and other projectiles. Reaching the edge of the stage he turned suddenly, and fled to safety. But not before Kitty, aching with sympathy, had caught sight of his tears.

Midge stepped onto the stage. 'Gents – please –'

The uproar continued.

'Where's George?'

'We – want – George!'

'Send for George!'

'We want a bloody song! That right, lads?'

A shout of approval.

'Then bloody sing it yerselves. George is sick.' Midge was not intimidated.

The invitation was taken up happily and inebriatedly in several corners of the room. One man clambered onto the stage and struck a drunken pose. 'Dear Mother, I remember well – the parting kiss you gave to me –'

Someone blew a loud raspberry and made a filthy gesture. Feeding on its own excesses the mob shrieked with laughter.

From the corner of her eye Kitty saw Lottie bend to Moses' ear and whisper, earnestly.

On the stage Midge was fighting a losing battle for control.

Moses crooked a small finger at Kitty, and Lottie smiled. She knew, before she reached him and bent to hear his words, what he would say.

'Lottie tells me that you can sing?'

Dumbly she shook her head.

'Oh, yes!' Lottie said. 'She told Pol an' me. She's told everyone. Bragging about it, she was. Makin' us other girls out to be nothin'.'

Kitty opened an astonished mouth.

Moses Smith's eyes were dangerous. 'That so?'

'No!' she got out, 'no, I didn't –'

Satisfaction in her face, her mischief done, Lottie turned aside. 'All mouth,' she said. 'That's what I thought.'

Trembling with fear and humiliation, Kitty could say nothing. Moses' small mouth had tightened. The chaos about them grew. 'It seems to me,' he said, 'that you and your brother are two of a kind after all. I'll deal with him – and I'll deal with you – later. I'll teach you to brag when you've nothing to brag about. To set trouble among my girls. You see if I don't.'

She was aware suddenly of Luke Peveral's eyes upon her, not mocking now but oddly pensive. From behind him Lottie grinned at her, purely and triumphantly malevolent. The red mist of temper shimmered behind her eyes. 'I can sing,' she said.

'What?' Moses had half-stood. He looked at her. The faintest of smiles glimmered upon Luke Peveral's gypsy face and was gone.

'*I can sing!*' she shrieked above the hubbub. Already she was regretting it. Already her throat was tightening in protest, dry as the dust of the desert, but she faced him, head up. 'I can sing,' she said again. 'Try me.'

His face was pink with anger. 'By God I will!' he snapped. 'They'll save me some trouble. They'll bloody tear you apart!'

She watched him step up on the stage beside Midge. The drums of pure panic were thundering in her ears. What had she done? What in God's name had she done?

Moses held up his hands for silence, and such was his power a semblance of silence fell.

'Give us a song, Mose?' The muffled cry came from the back. A ripple of laughter echoed through the crowd.

'Better than that, lads. A treat for you –' All eyes were on him. He gestured, widely. 'A new talent. Discovered here, right here, under our noses –'

'Under Moses' noses –' The drunken wag was at it again.

'– and you, my lucky fellows, are going to be the first – the very first – to hear her. Ladies and gents – I give you your own – your very own – Kitty' – he hesitated, shrugged, his voice dropping – 'whatsername.'

Hands pushed Kitty forward. She stumbled onto the stage. She had never experienced such terror. The lights blinded her, the swirling smoke clawed at her throat. Her appearance, for the moment at least, had quieted the crowd. Moses grinned at her, savagely, and stepped from the stage, leaving her alone. Like an animal waiting to pounce it seemed to her that the audience crouched, one breath, one pair of eyes, one rapacious appetite for defeat and failure. Her mind was a perfect blank. Neither word nor note of music came to her frantic brain. She cleared her throat nervously.

'That's a start,' said someone, sniggering like an ill-behaved child.

'I can do that,' said another, and the hall immediately echoed to a thunder of cleared throats.

She stared down at them, suddenly furious, filled with contempt. Stupid children. That indeed, was what they were. Stupid, unpleasant, destructive children –

Somewhere in her head the thought sparked a memory; a sullen, bent-on-mischief face and then the sudden lighting of interest –

Giving herself no time to think or consider, she marched to the piano. If they could do no better than to act like children, then so she would treat them. She struck a crashing, martial chord. Unexpectedly, utter silence fell. Beyond the uncertain flare of the footlights she caught a brief glimpse of narrowed, gleaming eyes.

'Oh, soldier, soldier, won't you marry me, With your musket, fife and drum –'

They couldn't believe it. She saw crooked, surprised grins appear. A few started to beat time with their hands and feet.

'Oh, no sweet maid, I cannot marry thee, For I have no' –
she paused, cocked her head cheekily and waited for the
space of a drawn breath – 'coat to put on.' Her expression
was entirely innocent. Incredibly and capriciously, they
loved it. The roar this time was of approbation. Her voice
strengthened. Across Moses Smith's face she saw flit a
variety of expressions – disbelief, amazement, interest, and
finally a small smile of delighted satisfaction. Beside him,
Lottie scowled. Kitty coarsened her voice and winked salaciously. 'So *off* they went to her *grand*father's chest and
found him a coat of the very, very best –'

It was unlikely that any nursery song had ever been sung
with such swagger, nor indeed with such wanton innuendo
and suggestion. She left the piano and strode across the
stage, scarlet skirt swinging about her long legs. An excitement had taken her, irresistible and vital, lifting her, concentrating its force in voice and gesture as with fierce enjoyment
she commanded the attention of this dangerously feckless
audience. Without changing a word she transformed the
innocent children's song into a bawdy ballad, and the customers loved it. The applause as she finished was all but
deafening, and the sweetest sound she had ever heard. She
stood suddenly abashed, a little of the excitement ebbing.
She looked at Moses, uncertainly. He was on his feet, gestur-
ing excitedly, encouraging her – ordering her – to sing again.
The room fell to quiet. Instinct told her that she could not
continue at this pitch of excitement. A little apprehensively
she walked to the piano and settled herself on the stool.

' 'Tis the last rose of summer, left blooming alone –' The
atmosphere could not have been more different. Yet, as if
spellbound, still they listened. 'All her lovely companions
are faded and gone –' The sadly plaintive notes echoed to
the smoke-blackened beams. She lifted her head, her heart
and soul in the melancholy words. And she held them, and
she knew it, and nothing in her life had ever brought such
happiness.

3

(i)

She could hardly believe the change in her life. Overnight it seemed that Fortune, whose face for so long had been wantonly turned from her, smiled and beckoned at last. From the moment that she stepped from the stage to be offered a brimming glass of champagne by a beaming Moses, her perfidious world took its cue from its master and the near-outcast became by the fickle magic of success a courted celebrity. Those who would not have greeted her nor willingly given her the time of day before were suddenly eager to claim long-standing friendship. But not for long – for the past hard and lonely months had not gone for nothing, and it was a new Kitty who faced this fresh situation coolly, keeping her head and guarding her heart, knowing well that no matter what they now said to her face, behind her back they still used the spiteful epithets of resentment. She neither courted nor wanted such untrustworthy popularity, though in shunning it she realized that she aroused still more hostility. She did not care. Indeed she hardly thought about it. Her whole existence in those first weeks was bounded by and concentrated upon those few minutes each night when she stepped upon the ill-lit stage to sing: for Moses, delighted at the unexpected gift from the gods that had sprung from such an astonishingly unpromising source, overrode her first slightly panic-stricken protests and installed her upon his bill of attractions the very day after that first triumph. And so the door that she had glimpsed had opened, and she had indeed, to her delight and astonishment, discovered paradise. In the exhilaration of performing she experienced an emotion that towered far above mere happi-

ness, and that for the moment at least absorbed and out-
weighed all other considerations. Yet paradise, as always,
had its serpent and in this case the devil's flaw proved to be
the nerve-wracking fear that beset her each time she stepped
out to face her audience.

'Gawd, Kit!' Pol had said in some awe after that first
night, ''ow did yer do it? It was like watchin' someone else
up there –'

'It was like being someone else,' Kitty had replied with
simple truth. And so it was. It was as if when she stepped
into that smoky circle of light some other Kitty Daniels –
braver, stronger, strangely nerveless – inhabited her body
and took over her mind. And, unable to analyse or explain
this extraordinary transformation, she at first lived in terror
that the gift, if gift it were, might leave her as suddenly as it
had come, and that she would one day find herself marooned
alone and defenceless before the voracious creature that she
faced each evening as she walked onto the stage. For despite
the joy she found in performing, her first image of her
audience as a predatory beast red in tooth and claw persisted.
Neither its enthusiastic plaudits nor its new-found admiration fooled her into believing that it would not be just as
entertained by her humiliation and failure as it was by her
success. She did not easily forget the tears on Potty Masters'
face.

Indeed there were many, she knew, who would be positively pleased to see her come to grief as quickly as she had
come to success – for, not surprisingly, pretty Lottie had
many loyal supporters and in the perhaps inevitable rivalry
that arose between the two girls – on Kitty's side unsought
and unencouraged – bad feeling was exacerbated and malice
fostered. There were times when Kitty strongly suspected
Moses' gleeful fat hand in the promotion of the jealous
competition between Lottie's supporters and her own – for
the Song and Supper Rooms did not suffer on account of it,
quite to the contrary – more tables were packed onto the
crowded floor and the price of happy insensibility went up
by a ha'penny a tot. But the real and open break with Lottie

came when George Milton fell sick and Kitty found herself billed as the Rooms' main attraction – 'The Songbird of Stepney' – and as such was excused the drudgery of waiting on tables. And the other girl's rage was fed further when Moses made it clear that his new and unlikely star attraction, whilst she was no longer required to be at the hoi polloi's beck and call, would certainly not be allowed to wriggle out of her duties altogether; her place now was with Moses and his guests, and to that end she was required to join them at the round table each evening an hour or so before she took the stage.

This last Kitty found a doubtful privilege at best, and one she would happily have surrendered to her rival, given the chance. Acutely nervous, she would sit for the most part in silence, answering when spoken to, deflecting with equal determination Moses' disgustingly fulsome jollity and any faint and very occasional laconic interest on the part of Luke Peveral. From time to time other guests joined them, men whose hard eyes, rough voices and expensive gold jewellery betrayed their profession clearly, but more usually it was Peveral's company in which she found herself. She sensed that he knew of her dislike for him and sensed equally that it amused rather than offended him – indeed she knew that it tempted him on occasion to mischief. The pernicious charm that she so detested and which she observed him turn upon every other female who approached within yards he never used upon her, a small mercy for which she was thankful. On the other hand, with her nerves tight enough to snap, in face of his disconcerting mockery and occasional downright provocation she often found it difficult to keep a civil tongue in her head; and she sensed that he knew that too. She was in truth sometimes alarmed at how frequently she experienced the urge to slap the sardonic, gypsy-dark face very hard indeed. The tone of their relationship, such as it was, was well and truly set, and the fickle nature of Moses' favour proved, on a night just a few days after that first, memorable performance and before she had been excused the chore of waiting at the crowded tables, when she turned to find herself the subject of that intense, narrow gaze, and he snapped his fingers casually, as he might to call a dog to him. The rise of anger at his arrogance almost choked her. She stood, mouth tight, defying him for the space of several seconds before, slowly, chin high, she moved to his side. 'Yes, Mr Peveral?'

He leaned back in his chair, surveying her. Only the blandly provoking expression upon his face betrayed the degree of his inebriation. 'I have to ask, sweet songbird. What in the hell's name are you doing wearing that dress?'

She stared at him, totally bereft of words.

Luke turned to Moses. 'She looks like the village maypole,' he said, mildly, and for all the world as if Kitty were stone deaf.

Moses shrugged and spread his hands. 'So she's thin –'

Not far away Lottie had paused by a nearby table and was openly listening, the faintest shadow of a smile hovering about her mouth. Kitty's cheeks were of the colour of the detestable dress. 'I –'

Luke grinned amiably, still addressing Moses. 'So what? That doesn't mean she has to look like a string bean in a rage. You know what they say – "the nearer the bone, the sweeter the meat" –'

Moses sniggered. 'You fancy 'em skinny, do you?'

Luke shrugged dismissively. 'Not particularly.'

Outraged, Kitty drew breath and opened her mouth.

Luke looked at her, apparently innocently unaware of her fury. 'I really would suggest that you get yourself something decent to wear. Something a little less' – he paused, and added delicately – 'violent.'

Finding her voice at last, she interrupted him. 'Do you think,' she said, softly and clearly, her husky voice shaking in her unsuccessful attempt to control her anger, 'that if there had been anything decent to wear within ten miles of this – establishment' – both the pause and the word were trenchant with disgust. She saw, too late, Moses' head lift sharply, his brows drawing together thunderously – 'that I shouldn't have found it?' Her momentum carried her on,

'Do you think that I'd choose to walk around looking like – like a dockside whore?' She stopped then, suddenly aware that she had gone much too far, and equally suddenly sick with fear. Moses' face was suffused. Luke's normally guarded eyes had widened, surprised almost to sobriety. There was a very small silence.

Moses, in his anger, was struggling to his feet. 'You little bitch! Who the hell do you think you're talking to!'

Luke, swiftly and placatingly, put out a hand to stop him. 'Moses, no –' His eyes flicked back to Kitty and in them she read faint puzzlement – as if, she thought bitterly, some inanimate object had grown teeth and bitten him. 'Easy, Moses. It wasn't her fault.'

Obscurely, and despite the fact that she was almost rooted to the floor with terror, she found his defence of her almost as intolerable as his earlier heartless carelessness. She glared at him. A sudden flicker of amusement in his eyes, he turned from her and aimed the full battery of his facile charm at Moses. 'Easy, Moses,' he said again, and jerked a long, comradely thumb. 'Wring the songbird's neck and she won't sing too well, eh?'

But Moses was not to be so easily placated. 'Brass-faced little slut.' His round face gleamed with the sweat of anger. His small hand shot out and fastened itself with surprising and hurtful strength about Kitty's wrist. She flinched, but had the sense not to enrage him further by trying to pull away. 'Nothing but bloody mischief, you, from the day you came. Too bloody good for us, are you? Eh?' His grip was agonizing.

Tears of pain standing in her eyes obstinately unshed, she shook her head.

'Come on, now, friend.' Strangely, for all the disarming amiability there was a new, almost warning note in Luke Peveral's voice. Firmly and surprisingly he leaned forward and laid a long, forceful hand upon the pudgy wrist that, extended by the force of Moses' grip upon poor Kitty's wrist, looked fit to burst from its frilled, diamond-studded cuff. 'Be fair. It wasn't her fault. Leave it now.' The two men's eyes met for the briefest of moments. Kitty felt the biting pressure of the short, powerful fingers relax a little. As if sensing it, Luke leaned easily back in his chair, grinning again, drawing Moses into a close and cleverly woven net of masculine camaraderie. 'Women!' he said, the lift of his shoulder mocking. 'Tempers, tantrums and only ten pence to the shilling, most of 'em. Not worth the effort of slapping them around. Save your energy, man. Let her get up there and do her act. The customers are waiting.'

Furious, she glared at him. The faintest flicker of impatient warning lifted the dark brows.

Moses let her go. 'You'll apologize first, girl.'

She fixed her eyes somewhere upon the empty air between the two men. 'I beg your pardon,' she said, her tone completely devoid of expression.

She felt Luke's eyes on her. Turning, she heard Moses, his mood changing mercurially, suddenly sputter with laughter. 'Did you hear that? God Almighty! "I beg your pardon," the little bitch says – cool as you like! Bugger me if I can make that one out –'

Moving from them, Kitty did not hear Luke's reply. Neither did she see the look of pure hatred bestowed upon her by Lottie. The incident had passed, and was not mentioned again, except indirectly when Midge brusquely informed her that she was to visit Harry's again. 'Get yerself a couple of outfits. Tell 'im it's on Moses.' She hesitated, the next words obviously coming hard. 'You're ter tell 'im you're ter choose 'em yerself,' she said.

This time she was luckier – a more leisurely hunt through Harry's cluttered, evil-smelling back room turned up a gown of musty black velvet trimmed with tarnished metal buttons and tattered silver ribbon. She spent days refurbishing it – letting down the hem, taking in the bodice, tucking and tacking and darning until she was satisfied, and for the first time in her life she sent up a small prayer of thanks for those detested sessions she had spent with her needle at Anne Bowyer's side under the repressive eyes of Imogen Alexander. The other dress she found was of dark green satin, in good repair, if a little short, with a wide skirt and big, sweeping sleeves.

'Blimey, where did 'Arry find them?' Pol asked in wonder, blinking at the magnificence. 'Bloody Buckingham Palace?'

Kitty smiled. Pol wandered further into the room, stood watching as Kitty neatly and quickly unpicked a worn seam and pinned it together again. 'Bloody perishing, isn't it? Can't remember such a winter, freezes yer marrer. 'Eard about the poor little bleeder upstairs, did yer?'

Kitty, her mouth full of pins, nodded. A small child who lived on the floor above had been discovered the day before by his mother, frozen to death in his bed. The malnourished little corpse still lay there, in a room occupied by seven brothers and sisters, waiting for the frantic mother to scrape together the necessary funeral fees. 'We got a collection goin,' Pol said. 'Poor little sod ought to be buried. It ain't right. 'Ello, what's this?'

Kitty removed the pins from her mouth. 'A couple of songs someone dropped into the Rooms for me to look at.'

Pol stared at her. 'Gettin' famous, are we?' she asked, amiably caustic.

Kitty flushed a little. 'No. No, of course not. It's just – the man writes songs for a living and has heard me sing –' But while the words were dismissive she could not deny to herself that this proof of her growing popularity had pleased her. The songs were second-rate, and she could not use them, but it was flattering nevertheless to be treated thus, as a true professional. The thought brought upon its heels another – a remembered, bitter comment about people getting too big for their boots, and a pair of blue eyes bright with spite. 'Pol?' she asked, quietly, laying down her needle-work for a moment on her lap, 'Lottie – why does she hate me so? Why won't she even try to be friends? What have I ever done to her?'

Pol stared at her in open amazement. 'You kiddin' me on?'

'No. No – of course not. I really don't understand. I don't want –' Kitty stopped.

Pol shook a bright, brassy head. 'What you want's got precious little to do with anythin' so far as our Lottie's concerned. Lottie's Lottie, an' that's the way she'll stay. She 'ates your guts, an' to be honest by 'er own lights 'oo can blame er'? There's nuthin' yer can do about it.'

'But —'

'Ferget it, Kit,' Pol said succinctly, 'you're on an 'idin' ter nuthin'. Just stay out of 'er way if yer can. She might look like some kid's fairy doll, but she's got a funny streak in 'er, our Lot. A very funny streak.'

With Christmas just a month away Kitty found herself working as hard as she ever had, and thoroughly enjoying it. With experience and practice her voice strengthened and her confidence grew, though she had come to believe that she would never curb the paralysing bouts of pre-performance nerves that assaulted her each evening. As the bitter weather continued, George Milton's abused constitution refused to institute a quick recovery from his bout of illness and Kitty became, day by day, more established as Smith's star performer — and this despite the fact that, as yet, few women enjoyed such status. She worked hard extending her repertoire, with the willing help of the ailing George whose generous, almost fatherly attitude, delighted and touched her.

Her brother Matt could not get over his sister's new-found glory.

'Who'd 'a' thought it, moi owd gal?' He still often used that affectionately exaggerated Suffolk accent to her, though now in normal speech it was more often than not overlaid by the flat London accent, as his vocabulary was laced with the pithy Cockney slang. 'You'll 'ave your owd face on a broadsheet next, you see if you don't! I heard the Guv'nor say the other night as how he reckons you've got the makin's of real talent —'

Kitty lifted her head in a swift, impatiently irritated movement. 'For heaven's sake, Matt — just because that awful Spider calls' — she hesitated — 'Mr Peveral "the Guv'nor" does it mean you have to? And –' she added, honest peevishness showing itself, '– does it take Luke Peveral's word to show my own brother if I have or haven't got some talent?'

Matt grinned, infuriatingly knowingly, and did not bother to reply.

She looked at him, a faint worried line fine-drawn between her brows. Lately, to her already strong dislike of Luke Peveral had been added a growing unease about his – as she saw it – unhealthy influence upon her brother. For if she had escaped the net of the man's doubtful allure, Matt most certainly had not. Since the day that Luke had caught him trying to pick his pocket and had shown such unexpected clemency the boy had been all but enslaved; Luke Peveral was his hero, and – more disturbing to Kitty – his model, his boyish devotion and admiration rivalling the faithful Spider's. Luke, obviously aware of the boy's hero-worship, treated him with a casual and tolerant amusement, accepting, it seemed to the infuriated Kitty, her brother's devotion as his natural due, and doing nothing whatsoever to discourage the growing close association between Matt and Spider – an association that seemed to her to promise nothing but trouble for her brother.

'Matt –' she said now, abruptly, 'do you think it's a good thing for you to be seeing as much as you do of Spider Murphy? The man's a notorious drunkard, and his –' She stopped. Matt had unfolded his lanky frame and stood, towering above her, shaking his dark head.

'Don't,' he said. And oddly the word stopped her in her tracks. 'Spider's my friend. He's all right. And anyway – even if he weren't – it's none of your business.'

'But –'

'But nothing, moi owd Kitty.' There was steel beneath the usual affection, and in the dark sharp glance. 'You got to face it, Kit. I'm not your baby brother any more. You're makin' your life, an' I don't interfere with that. If you want us to stay mates – you got to do the same for me.'

'But Matt! Can't you see? – If you get too involved with these people we'll never get away! Never be free –!'

'Get away?' His voice was suddenly soft. 'Who wants to get away?'

'I do!'

He watched her for a long, long moment. Then he shook his head. 'But I don't, Kit. And I never will. You have to face it. This is where I belong. Whether you like it or not.' All trace of the spurious accent was gone. His mouth was hard.

'No,' she said, 'I don't believe that. I'll never believe it.'

He was struggling with his temper, trying to hold it, trying to prevent sharp words from becoming a quarrel as they so often had before. 'Kit – listen to me. I'm sorry. I know what a disappointment I've always been to you. But I can't help what I am –'

It was a match to tinder. 'And what's that?' The words were bitterly angry. She glared at him. 'Say it, Matt. Tell me what you are? And as you say it – think of Father. And of Sir George, who did his best for you. And of me –'

He flung away from her. 'I can't help it!' he said again, his voice shaking. 'Why won't you understand that? I can't help it! Kitty – I couldn't stop myself thieving any more than I could stop myself from breathing, or growing! Why can't you see that? No matter what happens – I'll never be able to stop –'

'I don't believe it! I won't believe it!' She caught his arm. 'Matt – please – listen to me! I've discovered something I can do, and can do well. Can't you see what that could mean? Eventually I might be able to get out of this rat hole and earn us an honest living. Oh – I know it won't be yet – I need experience, and I need to find how to get away from Moses. But I'll do it! I will! And it won't be an easy life, I know that too – but surely, anything's better than this? How long, Matt, before you're caught? How long before they send you to Newgate, to tread the wheel? Do you want that? Do you? Matt – somewhere there's a chance for us – I feel it, I know it – but if we're going to take it you have to promise to give up thieving –'

'I can't.' The words were flat. 'Will you listen to me? I'm telling you – I can't. Not now. Not ever.'

'Is that what your precious Luke Peveral's put into your head?' she asked, bitterly. 'Is it? And you'd listen to that — that thief — before you'd listen to me —?'

'For Christ's sake, Kit, will you stop this? It's nothing to do with the Guv'nor. It's to do with me! Me!' He was shouting now. 'Leave me be, will you? Stop trying to change me! I know what I'm doing! I know what I want. And you'll break both of us if you try to stop me!'

She stepped back from him. She was shaking violently with anger and with a disappointment so brutal she hardly knew how to contain it. In the past weeks small dreams had dared to grow, like fragile flowers defying the frosts of March. Somewhere, sometime, a new life. A life without the threat of the whip and the treadmill and the iron bars of Newgate hanging over her brother's head. Her dread for him was often fierce as physical sickness. He stared now, defying her, miserably unable to explain himself any further, apparently obstinately unwilling to listen. Remembered words, words she struggled time and again, unsuccessfully, to keep from her memory rose, soft and deadly in her head — 'Are you familiar, Matt Daniels, with the saying that those born to hang will never drown?'

'You should have gone that day,' she heard herself say, bitterly and softly. 'You damned well should have drowned with them. Before you disgraced your father's name and broke my heart —'

White-faced, he stepped back from her, as if she had struck him.

The unforgivable words streamed from her like helpless tears. 'You're worthless! You always have been! It's your fault! All of it! Everything that's happened — your fault! Don't you dare — don't you ever dare! — come to me for help again! Stay with your good-for-nothing, pitch-fingered mates! See if I care! I despise them and I despise you —!' She stopped, appalled at her own words. His face was bleached with pain and anger. Without a word he turned and left her.

The breach was deadly. For days they treated each other like the strangers they had become and barely spoke. Kitty, aware once more of the damage done by an unruly temper and an even more unruly tongue, was utterly miserable. But yet she could not bring herself to take the first step to reconciliation – if indeed such a step were possible. She snapped at Pol, flared up at kindly George. When Moses, prompted by the practical Midge who pointed out that the long trip from Market Row in still-bitter weather could hardly improve Kitty's voice, offered her a room of her own – at twice the rent – in a lodging house not too far from the Rooms she jumped at the chance. The move, however, was not a particularly good one, for though it afforded her the privacy that she had longed for it cut her off from Pol and from Matt and made reconciliation with her brother even more unlikely. His intransigence, somewhat unfairly, she used to fuel the fire of her dislike for Luke Peveral; the man was a pernicious influence and – totally unable to accept Matt's own explanation of his compulsion to thieve – she chose to believe that her brother's hero-worship of a man steeped in corruption was to blame. Hurt and miserable, she threw herself into her work, learning new songs, practising movement and gesture before the long, fly-specked mirror in her room. And each night she sang, and each night she became for those few, too-short minutes, that other Kitty Daniels, and was transiently happy. She was learning, slowly, the trick of handling her difficult audience, and her fear, though still fed and kept alive by nerves each night, retired like a small, sharp-clawed creature to the corner of her mind, patiently awaiting its opportunity to spring.

To her astonishment it was Luke Peveral who intervened at last in her quarrel with Matt.

It was a fortnight before Christmas. The winter had been a dreadful one so far and promised no better. There had been riots, brutally suppressed, in the streets of the city by a starveling population calling for bread to fill their bellies and the bellies of their dying children. They received, these helpless dregs of a prosperous nation, whose average expectance of life was less than twenty-three years, earnest lectures upon thrift and self-help and the evils of drink. And, when these failed lamentably to cure the bad habits of protest and riot, vicious prison sentences and a close acquaintance with the whipping post and the treadmill were substituted for sanctimonious words. Standards, after all, must be maintained in society, and the poor kept in their place. The thieves and whores of Stepney and Shoreditch felt little if any sympathy. Starvation and disease were the old enemies. You cheated them if you could, as you cheated any and everyone else. It was the way of things. To protest was a waste of time and of precious energy. What was the use? What politician was interested in filling the bellies of the unfranchised poor, or of clearing the festering rubbish from their streets, or ensuring a clean and healthy water supply? What votes would that buy? As soon protest to Lucifer that he should clean up hell. And so, on the whole, the unrest passed the criminal fraternity by, and the weather and the high price of food simply added another unpleasant dimension to the struggle to survive.

Sitting at the round table, Kitty heard the subject discussed quite often – for Moses had firm views on the subject; in his view the rioters should get back to their sweatshops and leave the streets to those who knew what to do with them. Civil unrest meant an uncomfortable number of regular policemen and special constables on the streets, and that was bad for business. If people were indeed starving to death, what the dickens were they about, wasting time in marching the streets and besieging an unsympathetic Parliament? Were they going to feed their children better from Newgate?

Kitty sat one night half-listening for at least the dozenth time to the aggrieved Moses' complaints and watching in fascination the young man who, sitting beside Luke Peveral, was with swift confident pencil-strokes transferring the ranting Moses to the pages of a sketchbook that lay on the table before him. A recently acquired drinking-partner of Luke's, he had been joining the company assembled around

Moses' table for the past few nights, always with his sketch-book and pencil at the ready.

Luke, openly amused at Moses' conservative reaction to the crisis, was mildly and mischievously egging him on. 'You can't expect a man not to protest when, after working in intolerable conditions for intolerably long hours, he has to stand by and watch his children die as the pittance he's earned goes up in the smoke of high prices and extortionate rents. Can you?'

Kitty noted a little acidly that Luke's sympathy, such as it was, did not apparently extend itself to the hundreds of thousands of women in the same boat.

Moses twitched disgustedly at such idiotic notions. 'You should start a Mission, my boy, that you should! Teach the poor bastards how to take care of themselves, eh? Pass on a few of your skills. I don't see you starving, eh, Jem boy?'

The young man beside Luke lifted his head at the sound of his name and smiled a little abstractedly. He was perhaps a year or so older than Kitty herself, fair and slight with a pleasant, boyish face and thick straight hair that flopped over his eyes and lay in shaggy untidiness on his neck. He obviously had not been listening to the conversation.

'Luke's about to start a self-help Mission for the poor of Stepney,' Moses said, grinning hugely.

Jem smiled back. He had an extremely nice smile, Kitty thought, vivid and warm, that brought bright life to his face. 'Well, he's sure helped me out once or twice, Mr Smith –'

He had the strangest accent she had ever heard – a soft, not at all unattractive drawl that Pol, very impressed, had told her had its origins in the Confederate States of America. 'There's some sort o' shindig goin' on out there at the moment,' she had said, at Kitty's questioning, '– or so Luke told Lot, anyway. An' 'e's bin fightin' in it. Funny, in't it? Don' look no kind of soldier ter me. But, Gawd, – 'ave yer seen 'im drink? 'E can do that all right, 'parently 'e told Lot 'e'd found 'imself fightin' on the wrong side and scarpered. Don't make a lot o' sense ter me. But 'e's a sweet little thing, ain't 'e? An' as fer them drawin's of 'is – bloody marvellous they are! Got a name fer it, too –' she had added, giggling. 'James Beauregard O'Connell if yer please. Sounds like the bleedin' Kings of Ireland, don't it?'

Kitty watched him now as he picked up his pencil again. Already several of his sketches and charcoal drawings were pinned about the walls and behind the bar, to the much-denied but quite obvious delight of his villainous subjects. The pictures were like nothing that Kitty had ever seen before – neither the heavy and rather lifeless oil paintings that she remembered adorning the dark walls of Westwood Grange, nor the stylized, minutely detailed book illus-trations to which she was used. James O'Connell's art was a bold, inventive affair of undisciplined line and quite start-ling life. It astonished Kitty that from a few apparently random lines, boldly drawn, a vital and astonishing likeness could appear. For days she had been trying to gather the courage to engage the intriguing young man in conversation, but had not yet managed it. She craned her head a little now, to see what he was doing. The face upon the paper smiled, defiantly sweet, desperately vulnerable. Lottie's face. Kitty looked sharply away and caught Luke's eyes upon her. Before she could turn from him he leaned towards her. 'How long are you going to let your poor little sod of a brother eat his heart out?' he asked, pleasantly.

She blinked, too surprised, almost, to be angry. 'What?'

'Oh, I think you heard.' He reached for his glass of wine, sipped it, watching her over the rim.

'I – don't know what you mean.'

The long mouth tucked itself in at the corners and he made a small gesture of exasperation. 'Suit yourself.'

She waited for a moment. He said no more. Annoyed at her own defensiveness, she found herself saying sharply, 'It takes two to make a quarrel.'

'And one to finish it.'

She was silent.

Unusually soberly he watched her. 'He's a child,' he said, unexpectedly. 'You aren't. And I'm not talking about age alone. I don't know what the fight was about. I do know he's unhappy. You're all he's got.'

'It's his own fault if he's unhappy,' she said, stubbornly.

'Very possibly.'

Oddly, she could not leave it. 'He knows where I am.'

He said nothing.

She fiddled with her glass of watered wine, staring into its pale depths, the sudden recollection of her brother's white, drawn face choking her to silence.

'What did you fight about?' Luke's voice was neutral. She could not tell if he were truly interested or not. She glanced at Moses and away. Luke did not miss the look. 'He can't hear. What did you fight about?'

'His thieving,' she said, flatly, and lifted her head to look with direct dislike into the narrow, guarded eyes. 'I hate it. I always have. I always will.'

He nodded, slowly and thoughtfully. 'I see.'

'I don't think you do.'

Infuriatingly and imperturbably he half-smiled.

'I promised our father I'd care for him,' she found herself saying, miserably, 'and I've tried – I have tried – but –'

'But I don't see how you can keep that promise if you aren't speaking to him?' The practical words were quizzical.

'He doesn't want me to.'

'Are you quite sure of that?'

The battered upright piano was being pushed to the centre of the stage, its candles lit. Kitty felt the sudden, inevitable onslaught of nerves. Her hands were ice-cold and clammy. 'Yes.'

'You're wrong.'

She shook her head. Her throat was closing. This was the night. This was the night when her voice would desert her. She stood up, shakily.

Luke leaned forward. 'You're wrong,' he said again, gently. 'Spider knows. He talks to Spider. Whatever you said to him it all but broke him. Can you stand that? He won't come to you. If you want him back whole you'll have to do the asking. Tell me, little songbird –' The eyes narrowed further, their gleam inquisitive. 'What the hell was it you said to him?'

You should have drowned with them.

She started at him in silence, biting her lip.

He leaned back, letting her go.

She escaped onto the stage.

She knew he was right, and characteristically, having admitted it, she acted upon the knowledge immediately. As she stepped from the stage the second time that evening she saw Matt pushing his way through the crowds towards the draped door, his hand in that of a tall, red-headed girl with a dirty neck and a wide gap between her two front teeth. Biddy had not lasted long. Quickly Kitty slipped through the crowd to cut him off, acknowledging applause and congratulations as she went.

He faced her with flat hostility in his eyes.

'I'm sorry,' she said, clearly and directly. 'What I said was unforgivable. And I didn't mean it.' She steadfastly ignored the glances and open eavesdropping of an interested audience. She kept her eyes and her voice very steady, willing him to respond, to take the olive branch she offered. 'I'm truly sorry, Matt – I can't say I understand – but I'll try. If you'll let me. I can't bear for us not to be friends.'

For one terrible moment she thought he was going to push past her. Then he grinned, and the sheer relief on his face made her want to hug him. 'You got a bloody temper on you like a poisoned cat,' he said, 'tha'ss your problem.'

'That's true enough.' She smiled back at him.

The red-headed girl tugged at his hand, scowling sullenly. She could not have been more than thirteen years old.

'Got to go,' he said. 'See you tomorrow?'

'Yes.'

He raised a hand and left her.

Kitty felt a light touch on her arm. 'Everythin' all right?' Pol asked.

Kitty nodded, smiling.

'Take a look at this –' Pol proudly displayed a much-fingered sketch of herself, head thrown back and laughing. 'What a bloody lad, eh? Drunk as a lord 'e is, an' still drawin' like mad —!'

Kitty glanced towards the table. Jem O'Connell was the centre of a small admiring crowd. Luke sat a little apart, drinking alone. He caught her eye, smiled a little and, with the smallest of movements, toasted her with his glass.

Against her better judgement – almost, indeed, before she had realized what she was doing, she smiled back.

During those two weeks that led up to Christmas Jem O'Connell became something of a fixture at the Rooms, and a very popular one at that. He was a good-natured young man with an apparently unlimited capacity for alcohol and a true artistic eye that perceived life and beauty in the most uninspiring of subjects. His energy and enthusiasm were infectious, and to all appearances inexhaustible; with a bottle of Moses' whisky under his belt he would take to the stage in fine style, his preferred speciality being the minstrel songs and negro spirituals of his native land. On extreme occasions he could reduce himself and his audience to tears. There was, however, little danger of his taking Kitty's pride of place at the top of the bill. Soon after her reunion with Matt Kitty at last shyly plucked up the courage to engage him in conversation and was delighted to discover that he warmly welcomed her tentative advances and in no time they became real friends. Within the first hour of their acquaintance she felt she had known him all of her life. He was amusing, articulate and companionable, and his talent enthralled her.

To discover that this admiration was mutual surprised and delighted her. Despite Pol's friendship she had been lonely over the past months; discovering a warm comradeship with Jem O'Connell meant a great deal to her. He spoke to her of Paris and of the new wave of artists who were doing their impertinent best to revolutionize the world of art. Names of which she had never heard – Gustave Courbet, Paul Cézanne, Edouard Manet – slipped into his conversation often enough for her to become familiar with them and to share in some small part his enthusiasm and respect for what they were trying to do. These, she gathered, were the men in the forefront of the battle to wrest the goddess Art from the entrenched bastions of the Establishment where she had been languishing in mortal decline for some time, and to restore her to robust health with the common people. Realism was a word he used often – he had no time for past conventions and styles. His passionate ambition and vowed determination was to go to Paris and study with and under these new masters — but for the moment at least he showed no sign of doing anything but making Smith's his permanent home.

Where he got his money from Kitty did not know – certainly he never charged a penny for the drawings that he gave away so generously. The rumour amongst the girls was that an irregular income from his family accounted for his pendulum swing every now and again from open-handed near-wealth to utter and cheerful poverty. When he was in funds he would treat the world and his money slipped through his fingers like water from a holed bucket. Broke again, he was reliant upon Luke, who would grin and cough up without a word. It intrigued Kitty, this unlikely friendship between the older, cynical, much tougher man and the young artist whom he appeared to protect – and occasionally bully – as he might a younger brother. It seemed that Luke Peveral, also, perceived much of worth in the young American. She wondered if it were true that Jem was a refugee from the distant war that the young men at the Grange had talked of and that still tore his country in two. Certainly it seemed to her that sometimes she sensed a shadow of sadness in him, quickly hidden, that was out of character with the light-hearted Jem she knew. And somehow she never cared to question him about it. If he wanted her to know, he would tell her. For now she was happy with his friendship.

Meanwhile, Luke Peveral continued to surprise and confound those who would try to dissect his character and his

motives. Two days after Christmas he prevailed upon Moses
Smith, to everyone's astonishment not least Moses' own,
to close the Supper Rooms down for an evening so that
all and sundry might accompany Luke on the 'threepenny
steamer' that plied London's river to the Cremorne Gardens
to celebrate – he said – the feast of St John and his – Luke's
– birthday. The occasion was a special Christmas Gala,
which the bills proclaimed to be the Greatest Ever Held
and which would include sideshows, circus turns, outdoor
dancing if the weather permitted, brass bands and fireworks.

Though she would never have admitted it openly, Kitty
had never been so excited in her life. She leaned on the rail
of the boat beside Jem, drinking in this view of the city in
which she had lived for so many months and of which she
had seen little and knew less.

The air was cold and clear, the early winter dusk already
ringing with frost. The flag- and lantern-decked little
steamer chugged steadily against the tide, dark, foam-
flecked water churning from its bows. Two children waved
from a bridge; like a child herself Kitty waved back. Beside
her, watching her, the young American grinned, and she
laughed a little, unquenchable excitement in her eyes and
in the strong lines of her face. The great buildings of London
slid past, mysterious and romantic in the chill twilight. One
by one Jem pointed them out to her.

'– and oh, whatever is that? It looks like a palace –'

'That's your Houses of Parliament. You've never seen
them before?'

'No. Heavens, aren't they magnificent? Are they very old?'
They both at the same moment recognized the incongruity
of her ingenuous question to a foreigner. Kitty blushed a
little. Jem smiled.

'Pretty old, I think. But thirty years or so ago there was a
fire, and a lot of the building had to be rebuilt –'

Fire. For one unguarded moment the flames that had
licked from the windows of Westwood Grange flickered in
her memory. Matt, Matt – why did you do it? She shook her
head clear of such thoughts, leaned her elbows upon the

rail, standing on tiptoe, straining her eyes into the dusk. 'Oh, doesn't it all look pretty with the street lamps alight? It's like fairyland! Do tell me – have you been to the gardens before? Do you know them?'

He nodded.

'What are they like?'

He turned to her, propping himself against the rail, his perceptive, artist's eyes intent upon her face. 'They're like fairyland too,' he said, smiling again.

She smiled back, glad that he had chosen her company, glad too that for once he appeared to be stone sober. Which was a lot more than could be said for Luke Peveral. She glanced to where he stood a little way along the deck, holding court with easy, and perceptibly drunken charm, Lottie clinging like a pretty limpet to his arm. As Kitty watched, Luke, gently but firmly, tried to disengage himself. Lottie, fragile as a flower and tenacious as the toughest bramble, would not be disengaged. Luke did not persist. Kitty wondered, not for the first time, at the odd contradictions in the man's character. 'Is it really Luke's birthday, do you know?' she asked Jem.

The American shrugged. 'I don't know.' He paused. 'But if the man says so –'

She turned back to contemplate the glimmering fairy lights that were reflected in the moving waters. 'He's a strange man, isn't he?'

She was unaware of the quizzical look in his eyes as he watched her. 'He sure is.'

'Have you noticed – everyone seems to see him differently?'

'He's been good to me. He's a pretty grand guy as far as I'm concerned.'

She nodded, apparently absorbed in her study of the water. 'You don't like him?'

That brought her head round, sharply. 'I didn't say that.'

'No. Of course not.' The tone was wry. Jem O'Connell, for all his youth, was no fool where women were concerned. He was watching her with a friendly sympathy that she entirely failed to recognize, and his smile was touched with a faint self-mockery.

'I can't say I care one way or the other.'

'No,' he said again, soberly, 'of course not.'

She brought her eyes back to his face, suspiciously. 'Are you laughing at me?'

'Just a little, I suppose.'

'Why?'

He hesitated. Shook his head, smiling that warm smile. 'Because for someone who doesn't care one way or another you seem to be asking a lot of questions.'

She shrugged. 'The man just seems to be a bundle of contradictions, that's all. I mean – look at all this. However did he get Moses to shut the Rooms?'

'Who knows? When Luke sets his mind to something he's pretty hard to resist.'

'Is he?' Her voice was cool. 'I wouldn't know. He seems quite resistible to me.' Once again she missed the amused and friendly sympathy in his glance. 'It must be costing him a fortune.' She could have kicked herself – why not just let the subject drop?

'I don't guess he cares how much it's costing. This last little' – Jem hesitated – 'trip – seems to have set him in funds for a bit.'

'So they say.' And – she thought – it wasn't all they said. The week before, Luke had disappeared on one of his expeditions to lighten the pockets of the rich. When he had returned a couple of days later it had been obvious that it had been a successful one. It had been obvious too – according to Pol – that it had been a dangerous one. As Luke had celebrated his profitable raid with unusual gaiety and even more unusual wildness, Pol had shaken her head grimly. 'That must 'a' bin a close shave.'

'What must?'

'Look at 'im. I 'aven't seen 'im like this in a few long months. Sure sign. You can bet your boots 'e nearly got 'is collar felt this time.'

And Kitty, watching, had seen what she meant. Beneath

the reckless high spirits had lain a thread of strain that had shown itself in a shade too much carelessness, a shade too much laughter, a shade too much generosity, that had culminated in this madcap trip.

'Pol thinks he nearly got caught this time,' she said, now. 'Now there's a lady who really doesn't like him.'

The inference of the gently teasing emphasis was not lost on her. She maintained a dignified silence. Mischievously he let it stretch for a full minute before, relaxed and easy, he changed the subject. 'By the way, Miss Songbird' – he often used the nickname Luke appeared to have coined for her – 'I haven't had a chance to tell you how very handsome you're looking this evening –'

She glanced at him again, half-suspecting mockery, but his smile was genuine, his eyes warm. 'Thank you.' Slightly self-consciously she made a small, unnecessary adjustment to the claret-coloured ribbons at her throat. The little, plumed grey velvet bonnet that so nearly matched with the sweeping cloak-coat known as a paletot which she wore over her wide-skirted claret wool dress had been a find she had not been able to resist, despite the expense. Her visits to Harry's over the past few weeks had been funded by the generosity of Smith's customers to their favourite artist. Even after Moses had extracted his dues and his rent her savings were slowly growing. When she had found this outfit it had been with only the faintest tinge of guilt that she had plundered the precious pouch she always wore for safety pinned to her petticoat and decked herself in the second-hand finery of a respectably fashionable young woman, as different from the clothes she and the other girls who worked in the Rooms would normally wear as was chalk from cheese. Her needle had gone to work again, and her reward had come when she had joined the excited gathering outside the Rooms this evening and had noted the small, astonished silence that had greeted her appearance.

'Good Lord,' Luke had said, straightfaced and already pleasantly and determinedly inebriated. 'The Songbird in her plumage. I give you good day and welcome, ma'am.' But

beneath the flippancy had been a gleam of approbation that
to her own disgust had pleased her.

Jem touched her arm lightly. 'We're almost there. See –
there's the landing stage.' The steady chug of the engines
was slowing. Ahead she could indeed see the landing stage,
decorated with bunting and lanterns. Excitement took her
again.

Cremorne Gardens at first sight, decked and lit with the
trappings of Christmas looked, as Jem had said it would,
truly like fairyland. From the moment she passed beneath
the huge illuminated star that lit the impressive entrance
from the King's Road Kitty was entirely dazzled. The
twelve-acre gardens were dominated by the graceful,
pagoda-shaped bandstand in their centre, with its wide,
tree-sheltered open-air dancing platform. The lilting strains
of a waltz lifted above chatter and laughter. On the floor
couples danced, swaying and spinning in each other's arms,
the wide skirts of the women lifting and swirling like multicoloured upturned flowers upon a summer stream. Around
the dance floor were small columned grottoes, most of
them already occupied, whilst above them the small private
rooms that had given the gardens a name rather less than
respectable glowed with soft light behind draped curtains.
The thronging crowds were gay and out for enjoyment. The
red coats of soldiers, every bit as bright as the dresses and
shawls of their female companions, contrasted well with
the more sober attire of their non-military brethren. Kitty
had never seen such a scene of colour and movement, never
felt the infection of sheer, boisterous energy that can be
generated by such a gathering. Jem had his sketch book out.
Kitty grabbed his arm. 'Come on! You'll get lost!' and,
laughing, he allowed himself to be towed along behind the
others. Kitty, clasping his hand, caught a brief glimpse of
her brother's impish, grinning face before with a lifted hand
he disappeared with Croucher and Springer into the crowds.

Moses had evidently not given everyone the night off.

'Hey, look! Wait, Kitty – I must get that –' Jem's sketch
pad was out again and his pencil flew as he caught the

picture of a trio of gaily dressed entertainers in pantaloons
and gypsy-style blouses who danced upon stilts high above
the sea of top hats and bowlers and pretty, feather-decked
bonnets to the sound of a clattering barrel organ. A tiny
monkey dressed in scarlet pantaloons and a bright green
jacket leapt upon Kitty's shoulder, chattering volubly and
shaking a tin of coins in her face. Surprised, she gave a small
shriek and the creature bared its tiny yellow teeth in a
caricature of a grin.

'Here – take yourself off –' Jem dropped a coin in the tin
and the little animal leapt from Kitty's shoulder onto a
soldier's broad, scarlet-clad back. The gaily-painted barrel
organ thundered deafeningly on. Kitty and Jem pushed their
way to where the others had gathered in front of a striped
Punch and Judy booth. Moses, Kitty saw, was almost apo-
plectic with laughter as the repulsive puppet pulverized first
his wife and then his ugly baby with his truncheon. Only
once before had she seen this traditional performance – one
Christmas, when a travelling Punch and Judy man had come
to the Grange – and she had no better liked it then that she
did now.

'Well, Songbird – and what do you think of my birthday
treat?' Dark eyes, all but hidden in their tangle of lashes,
strangely sober in a smiling face.

'It's lovely,' she said simply, 'I've never seen such a place.'

'London knows how to enjoy herself.'

'Yes.'

Lottie, utterly lovely in blue velvet, a gift from Luke as
she had made certain everyone knew, appeared beside him,
catching his arm, eyes venomous upon Kitty. 'You promised
we'd dance –'

He allowed himself to be drawn back into the laughing
crowd.

Pol bounced to Kitty's side. ''Ave yer seen the circus acts?
Blimey – I don't know 'ow they do it! There's a girl over
there walkin' a bleedin' tightrope over a cageful of the
'ungriest-lookin' brutes of lions you've ever seen! Come on,
come an' 'ave a look –'

'A drink, everyone. There's wine, and there's ale by the jugful –'

''Oo's comin' ter see the two 'eaded lady –?'

'– bloody fortune-teller knew more about me than I know meself! Christ, it was creepy, I don't mind tellin' yer – fair gave me a turn –'

'– there's our Springer doin' 'is bit. Best bloody tumbler in London Town is our Springer –'·

'– come an' 'ave a ride on the elephant with me – I ain't goin' on me own, no fear –!'

'A dance, Miss Kitty – I insist –' She found herself, laughing, in Jem's arms. They were of a height, and he danced lightly and well. She found herself wondering where he had learned to dance so. Since they had arrived at the gardens he had been drinking steadily and the light in his eyes was reckless. Faster and faster they spun. Breathlessly she clung to him, her tuition under the effete but strict eye of Anne's dancing master standing her in good stead as the sweep of her wide crinolined skirt and the skilful swooping speed of their progress cleared a space in the centre of the floor and the other dancers stopped to watch, laughing and applauding. Joining in the spirit of the thing, the band increased the tempo. Upon a sudden surge of delighted and delightful excitement Kitty spun and spun in Jem's surprisingly strong arms, his smiling, reckless face the only focused thing in a world of light and colour that spun past her dazzled eyes like a host of shooting stars. At last, upon a grand, triumphant chord, they were done, and were awarded a burst of generous applause from the onlookers.

Jem swayed a little on his feet. He did not release his hold on her. His eyes, light and clear as water, held hers for a long, smiling moment, then, 'Christ!' he said, with feeling, 'I need a drink.'

'The fireworks will be starting soon. Let's find a table.'

Seated and with welcome drinks to hand, they watched as the world perambulated past them. Both were still breathing heavily from their exertions on the dance floor. Catching each other's eye, they burst into spontaneous laughter.

'That was fun,' Kitty said.

'It sure was. Exhausting – but fun –'

They giggled again. 'Haven't danced like that in a long, long time,' he said, and as if some sudden memory had taken him by surprise Kitty saw a flash of such pain in his face that she flinched from it. He sat rigid for a moment, as if frozen, then he reached for his glass, drained it at a gulp and sat staring sightlessly at the empty glass, all laughter and all joy gone from him.

'Jem! Jem – whatever's the matter?'

Painfully he dragged himself back to her, looked at her with blank eyes. She saw the almost physical effort with which he shook himself free. 'It's nothing.'

She did not know what to say.

He shook his head, buried his face in his hands for a second, elbows on the table. 'It's nothing,' he said again, his voice muffled.

Something about the slump of his shoulders, the almost childish vulnerability of the bared, bowed neck brought an aching lump of sympathy to Kitty's throat. She reached to him, gently took his charcoal-stained hand in hers. 'Funny kind of nothing,' she said.

He lifted his head. His hair was like a bird's nest.

'Might it not help to talk?' she asked, softly.

His eyes were fixed, blindly, upon their linked hands. She wondered what he was seeing.

'Jem? Can't you tell me? Is it – something to do with home?'

The pale, blue-green eyes lifted to hers. 'Home?' he said, and shook his head. 'My home, Kitty, had the misfortune to find itself slap in the middle of a battlefield. It doesn't exist any more. Not one brick is standing on another.'

'I'm – sorry –' The words were hopelessly inadequate.

He shook his head. 'Don't be. For even if it were still there, there'd be no place for me. Ever. I am my father's only surviving son. And my father would burn the place down with his own hands before he'd let me pass the door. And I don't blame him.'

To her horror she saw the glint of sudden tears in the lantern light.

'Jem – I didn't mean to pry. If it upsets you too much –'

He did not seem to hear her. He continued speaking in that clear monotone that was nothing like his usual speech. 'My brothers are dead. My father is crippled. My mother's heart is broken. And I broke it.' He reached for the whisky bottle, poured a great tumblerful. Kitty made a half-hearted gesture, a small plea for restraint, then watched helplessly as he poured it down his throat. She was horrified at the bottomless chasm of tragedy that had yawned so suddenly at his bleak words.

'My sister tells me all of this,' he said after a moment, wiping his mouth with the back of his hand and eyeing the bottle longingly. 'She makes sure I know it. Because – understandably – she hates me.'

'Oh – surely not!' Kitty's protest was half-hearted and she knew it.

'Oh yes. And I don't blame her. I don't blame any of them for hating me. I pretty well hate myself sometimes.' The liquor was getting to his tongue. He frowned a little.

She could not sit silent. 'But – none of it can have been your fault. It was the war, surely, that destroyed your home?'

He lifted his head. 'Ah yes, Songbird. The war destroyed my home. But I – I destroyed my family.'

She sat in silence now, not knowing what to say or how to comfort. He reached for the bottle again, missed it and gave up. In the distance the martial strains of a brass band echoed. People hurried past, faces eager and expectant. 'Here they come! Oh, don't they look just fine!'

'Slavery,' Jem said, clearly, 'is an abomination. I have always believed so. Even as a child I could not accept that the people who worked for me, waited upon me, cared for me, could be owned body and soul by a master who could buy and sell them like cattle, breed them like pigs, work them like oxen and flog them like dogs. Oh no' – he had caught the startled look in Kitty's eyes, 'my father did none of those things. He was a kindly and civilized man. He loved his people, and treated them fairly. But he owned them. And I couldn't stand that.' The last, low words were threaded with such pain that Kitty touched his hand again, unable to find words. He looked at her with entreaty in his eyes. 'How could I fight for that? How could I? How could I defend something that I knew to be wrong, that I'd always hated from the bottom of my heart?'

She shook her head. 'You couldn't.'

'But I should have done. I – should – have – done! I should have died with Baxter and Lee and Bobby-Joe at Gettysburg –'

The band was closer, the steady, rhythmic beat of its drums pulsing like a heartbeat through the air, an occasional triumphant bugle note sounding distantly above the uproar.

'That's ridiculous,' Kitty said, as firmly as she could manage.

'It may seem so. But it's the simple truth.' He was staring into some distance that bore no relationship to the time and the place that was now. 'Yes, it was the war that destroyed my home. But I destroyed more than that when I marched to war on the wrong side. I was at Gettysburg too. Fighting against them. How do I know it wasn't my bullet that shot away Baxter's face? Or caught Lee in the belly so he took three days to die? Or – God help us all – lodged in my little brother's throat so he choked on his own blood?'

Struck with horror into silence she looked at him. The band crashed past them, brave and gaudy in the flickering flare of the lantern light, scarlet and gold and gleaming black, precision in movement, the pride of a nation. Neither of them tried to speak until the sound had died and the crowd had moved on. The respite gave Jem a chance to pull himself together. The colour, slowly, was returning to his face, the tension drained from him and he ran distracted fingers through his thick, straight hair that flopped over his eyes like a child's. He poured a very small tot of whisky and sat looking at it, twirling the glass in his charcoal-grimed fingers.

'What did you do?' Kitty asked at last, very gently.

'Do?'

'You're here,' she said.

He smiled, a small, downturned, bitter smile. 'What do you think I did? What any right-minded, cowardly son-of-a-bitch would do. I ran away. I deserted. Left the ranks. Made of myself an outcast who can never go back. And my sister writes to me, and sends me the money that my mother cannot bear to send herself and makes me pay for it by telling me – in detail – all the family news.'

'What will you do?'

He lifted eyes clear as rainwater and filled with pain. 'I shall go to Paris,' he said, and grinned, harshly. 'And starve in a garret. What better do I deserve?'

In helpless friendship she took his hand again. There was a sudden swishing noise and a great, gasping breath of awe from the watching crowd as a rocket rose and burst in the frost-clear sky above them, showering the night with fiery light.

And that was the picture that remained with Kitty from that evening; Jem's young face, bleached and sobered with pain in the multicoloured, magical light of the fireworks that lit and patterned the sky with beauty – that and the sudden, adult understanding that she was not alone nor unique in misery and that, perhaps oddly, that thought was in itself some consolation.

(ii)

A month later he left. The city of which he had spoken of so often – Paris – his destination.

'You will write?' Kitty asked, sad to see her friend go.

He kissed her lightly upon the cheek. 'Of course I shall.'

And – just once – a couple of weeks later, he did, a hastily-scribbled stained note written upon some café table and containing an address in the Quartier Latin and the news that he was well and happy and at the time of writing three parts drunk.

'Not much changes, does it?' Pol asked, grinning at the

thought. Then she sobered, and shivered. 'Christ, what a night! It's black as Newgate's knocker out there, an' thick as me Mum's pea soup. No wonder the customers ain't turning out. Not so sure I should 'a done meself.' The Rooms were all but empty. A couple of drinkers stood by the bar, and a sailor snored, his head upon a table. A group of girls sprawled at a table near the bar, bored and restless. 'Not worth openin' ternight.'

Midge thought the same. 'You girls might as well get off. We're doin' nuthin' ternight, an' I ain't payin' you lot ter sit around on yer fat arses. Get off while you can still see where y'er goin'. See yer termorrer.'

'Mingy bitch.' Lettie Robson, a newcomer to the Rooms, gestured, wickedly obscene, at Midge's departing back, turned to her friend Rosy, who Kitty suspected to be Matt's latest light o' love. 'Comin' up Blackfriars, Rose? Never know, we might strike lucky – make ourselves a bob or two –'

Pol watched them go. 'Rather them than me in this lot. I dunno about you, but this weather gives me the devil's creeps. Come on – I'll walk part the way with yer –'

Kitty shook her head. 'Would you mind if I waited a bit? I wouldn't mind running through a couple of new songs while I've got the place to myself. Give the customers a treat –' She nodded, grinning, at the snoring sailor.

'Suit yerself. See yer tomorrer then.'

In fact, over an hour later, Kitty rather regretted her refusal of company. Wrapping her shawl about her head and shoulders she said goodnight to Bobs and his companion, who were settling down to a game of cards as they took up their guard duty for the night, and stepped into the lane. Pol had been right. The fog that crept in dense, poisonous billows from the river and blanketed the streets and lanes of Stepney was of exactly the colour and consistency of pea soup. Nothing in the cold, swirling mists of the Suffolk and Essex coasts had prepared her for a London fog. A little taken aback, she stood for a moment by the door, clutching the shawl tighter, straining her eyes into the disorientating foggy darkness. The corner of the lane had disappeared entirely, as had the glimmer of water at the canal dead-end of the road. A single gas-light hung, disembodied, above her head and cast distorted shadows upon the soot-laden wall of dripping fog. It was very cold. For one moment she considered staying where she was, and utilizing for the first time the doubtful comforts of one of Midge's upstairs rooms. Then, from behind her she heard the murmur of gruff voices and a sharp burst of laughter, and that idea dismissed itself out of hand. She was safer in the fog. Clutching her shawl tightly to her throat, she stepped warily into the darkness.

It was a nightmare. As the choking yellow stuff closed claustrophobically about her she found that her sense of distance and of direction had entirely deserted her. She groped for the wall. Surely – surely? – the corner that led into the main street must be here somewhere? She took a few more uncertain steps forward, stumbled on the slick, filthy cobbles. Behind her the lamp that had marked the doorway of the Rooms had disappeared, extinguished entirely by the smothering fog. She stood still for a moment, fighting a losing battle with her nerves. Where in God's name was the corner? It surely shouldn't have been this far? She groped into darkness again, and felt nothing where she had been certain there should have been a wall. Paralysed, she stopped. In which direction was she facing? Remembering the stagnant, stinking waters of the canal she did not know if she should go back or forwards. She stood fighting the rise of panic. When a small dark figure scuttled from the gloom and touched her arm it was all she could do to prevent herself from shrieking aloud.

'S'all right, Guv'nor. It's the gel. Kitty.'

She recognized, with a surge of relief she had never thought to experience at the sight of that particular, walnut-wrinkled face, the child-sized figure of Spider Murphy. A week before, visiting her brother, she had found Spider sprawled, dead drunk, upon her brother's bed. Wearily, she had taken Matt to task. Matt had shrugged good naturedly. 'Leave him. He's got nowhere else to go. The Guv'nor'd half

kill him if he caught him in this condition. He has to go on
a binge every now and again, that's all. He'll be all right in
an hour or two.' The incident had done nothing to endear
the little man to her. She jerked her arm from his hand,
turned as a taller shape loomed beside her.

'Well, well.' There was the inevitable amusement, laced
with surprise and – she thought – the faintest thread of
exasperation in Luke Peveral's voice. 'I thought all the birds
had sensibly flown? What's the Songbird doing still here?'

'I stayed behind,' she said tartly, resenting his assumption
that she should explain herself to him, 'to try out a couple
of songs.'

'Very creditable.' He had lifted his head, like an animal,
scenting the air, listening. His voice was abstracted. Somewhere in the darkness something clicked and clattered.
Spider faded into the fog. There was a spiteful shriek and a
giant cat sprang past them into the darkness. Luke relaxed a
little, regarded her with an expression of faint exasperation.
'But not a good night for it,' he added, mildly.

She did not feel that called for an answer. She made to
turn from him.

Very firmly he gripped her elbow. 'You're going the wrong
way.' His voice was quiet, and pleasant.

She stopped. She was in no position to argue. They stood,
dark statues in the swirling fog. The man was watching her,
and there was no doubt now as to the clear exasperation in
the line of the straight, hard mouth. Annoyance stiffened
her back. 'If you could just show me the way to the corner –?'

He regarded her for a long moment, still in silence. Then,
'The corner,' he said regretfully, 'may not be a good idea.'

She was aware that a very uncomfortable sensation was
making itself felt in the pit of her stomach. A strange tension
emanated from the man, an aura of danger and of violence
that had nothing to do with the eerie, smothered silence of
the dripping night. She suddenly discovered that she was
very frightened. 'What do you mean?' She had lowered her
voice, but it was still too loud. Instinctively she knew it,
and instinct was confirmed by the warning, spasmed grip of

his hand upon her elbow and the quick glance that he flicked into the darkness. His face was shadowed, beads of moisture hung about his dark, bare head like glittering gems. 'I just want to go home,' she said, and succeeded – just – in keeping the tremor from her voice.

From somewhere to the right of them came the single, clear sound of a footfall, then silence. Luke's hand dropped from her arm and he stepped back, his head tilted again in that animal-like, watchful stance. Spider scuttled silently from the gloom, whispered something and was gone. Luke turned as if to follow him, then stopped, took a swift step back to where she stood. 'For once in your life,' he said, agreeably, close to her ear, 'do as you're damned well told without arguing. Come.'

She came. She could not, in reason, see anything else to be done. As if some sixth sense were guiding him he led her swiftly into the fog. They passed the light that guarded the door of the Rooms. Remembering the threat of the rank waters of the canal she hung back. Unceremoniously he pulled her after him, jerking her almost from her feet. They reached the canal which cut across the lane and ran on through a dark canyon of walls that channelled the foul-smelling fog as a gulley might channel filthy water. A small, sloping, perilously muddy path led through the mass of decayed vegetation that clogged the steep bank.

'Mind where you're putting your feet.'

The quiet warning was entirely unnecessary. The footing was treacherous in the extreme, the way narrow. Brambles scratched and tugged at her skirt, the black, fog-wreathed, disease-ridden waters waited. She watched where she was putting her feet. And baulked when she found herself with one of them upon a slender, muddy, bouncing plank that precariously spanned the water and led into deep and fog-blanketed darkness.

'I'm not going over that.' Oddly, she could not bring herself to speak in a normal tone of voice, but found herself whispering absurdly, like a conspirator over a keg of dynamite.

'I'm afraid you are.'

'No.'

A small, impatient silence. 'You aren't going to have hysterics, are you?'

'Certainly not!' she snapped. 'And neither am I going to drown. In fact I'm not moving another damned step until you tell me what's going on!'

'Here and now?'

'Here and now.'

'Don't be stupid.'

'Is it stupid to want to know where I am – where you're taking me –?' The hissed words were furious. 'To want to know what this ridiculous charade is all about? I tell you I won't move another step until you've explained!'

'Please yourself.' In the short breath it took to speak the brusque words he released her hand and melted like a wraith into the fog. Silence closed about her. Anger, so often the cause of her downfall, this time came to her aid. Almost too furious to be frightened, she gathered her muddy skirts to her knees and turned in preparation to make her way back along the bank.

In a small flurry of movement he materialized beside her again. Something slid into the water almost at their feet, and ripples glimmered. She thought of rats, and shuddered.

'I'm sorry,' he said.

She waited.

'It's hardly the time to tell you the story of my misspent life –'

'Just this bit,' she said grimly.

'Won't you just trust me?'

'A strange word to use.'

She caught a reflexive glimmer of amusement on his face at that. 'Kitty – truly –' The amusement was gone and the words were deadly earnest. 'I can't explain because I'm not certain myself. We may be playing cat and mouse with shadows. But there's mischief abroad tonight. Bad mischief. And I don't want you caught in it. I've had word someone's looking for me. An old – acquaintance –'

'What has that to do with me?'

'Nothing at all. Unless he thinks that a girl walking alone from the Song and Supper Rooms might have some information as to the whereabouts of his old friend Luke Peveral.' He let that sink in, added softly, 'He's a very unpleasant man. With some very unpleasant mates. I don't think you'd enjoy meeting them.'

'Why should they bother with me?'

'Why indeed?' The words were heartfelt. Despite the cold she flushed. 'Do you want to go off on your own and find out?'

She shook her head.

His teeth gleamed in the darkness of his face. 'Then it's the plank after all, I'm afraid. Or the night spent camping here.' He held out his hand. She took it. It was warm, and rock steady. The smile glimmered again. 'That's the ticket.'

She followed him, the sweat of fear freezing upon her skin, over the narrow, bouncing plank and then on into a maze of foul-smelling alleys. They moved in silence. Once they stopped and he drew her close to him in the shelter of a doorway, his head cocked, listening. Quite close by someone coughed, the despairing emptying of consumptive lungs. Luke relaxed, guided her around the heap of rags that huddled in the gutter and pushed on. Quite soon after that the fog thinned a little and she found herself recognizing landmarks. They had made a wide sweep and were approaching her lodgings from the Whitechapel direction. The fog, though lightened a little, still hung about them in a noxious curtain. Luke strode confidently on, not slowing his steps to hers. She scurried beside him, cursing beneath her breath the great swaying bell of a skirt that hampered her every stride. She did not see his smile. At the door of her lodging house he stopped and faced her. She became suddenly aware that their hands were still linked.

'I'm sorry,' he said, 'if you were frightened. It was probably for nothing. I've been known to jump at shadows before. But better safe than sorry.' He still held her hand as if it were the most natural thing in the world.

'Thank you,' she said.

He smiled, inclined his damp dark head and was gone.

And she was left reflecting not on the bizarre and frightening events of the evening but on the treacherously pleasant recognition of the warmth in his usually guarded eyes as he had smiled at her, and the disturbing feeling of his hand in hers.

4

Two days later, Luke Peveral – and Kitty – discovered that
Nemesis had indeed been lurking in the fog that night. But
the first person that it overtook, as the yellow murk still
lay upon London's dirty roof-tops and crept along her narrow
streets, was Spider Murphy.

Kitty it was who found him, sprawled upon her brother's
bed, at first sight apparently once again drunk as a lord and
dead to the world.

Then she saw the blood.

'Oh, my God!' She ran to him, stopped, appalled at the
unrecognizable, purpling mass that was his face. She stood
for a moment, her hands pressed tightly to her mouth,
quelling nausea. The little man muttered, the words indis-
tinguishable, bleeding tongue lolling on all but toothless
gums in a wrecked mouth. His right arm was twisted grotesquely by his side. His clothes were in shreds. There
seemed to be no part of him that was not bruised or bloodied.
One eye was swollen shut, the pupil a smeared gleam between the puffy lids.

'Spider – for God's sake! – what's happened?'

Her voice roused him. He caught her hand with his left
one, half-lifted himself in agitation. Blood and spittle
streamed down his unshaven chin as he gabbled. He stank
of blood and urine and worse.

'Don't try to talk. Lie still. I'll get help.' She broke away
from him, fled to the door. Where was Matt? Or – Pol!
Blessed thought. Pol would know what to do.

She flew up the dark, narrow stairway, burst into the
room that Pol and Lottie shared. 'Pol, quickly! Something

awful's happened to Spider! He's in Matt's room. He's hurt! He's bleeding – oh, please, come and help –' She stopped.

Pol, unflustered, untangled her plump, bare legs from the crumpled bedclothes, ran her hands through her bright, tousled hair and reached for a dirty robe. 'Gawd, gel, where's yer manners? Didn't anyone ever teach yer ter knock at doors?'

'I'm sorry –' The words were, in the circumstances, perfunctory. The memory of Spider's shattered face overrode all other considerations.

The naked man at Pol's side – stocky, dark and hairy as a gorilla – struggled to a sitting position and grunted angrily.

'S'all right, love,' Pol said to him soothingly, 'it's a friend o' mine.' She stood up, belting the crumpled gown about her heavy, lush body, raised only half-amused brows at Kitty. 'This'd better be good.'

'I'm – I'm sorry, Pol, truly I am – but – Spider's in an awful state. He's been beaten half to death from the look of it – oh, please, do hurry – I came to see Matt, but he's off somewhere – and Spider – he's bleeding so badly –'

'All right. All right.' Pol's voice was steady and sensible. 'I'll come down an' take a butcher's. Oh, fer Gawd's sake!' – this to her irate, hairy swain who, in a picturesque state of arousal, had swung his bare feet onto the floor and was complaining bitterly and forcefully at this interruption to his pleasures. 'I'll be back. Keep it warm for me.' She ushered Kitty through the door. Kitty almost fell back down the steep stairs. When the two girls reached Matt's room it was to find that Spider had somehow dragged himself from the bed and was crawling across the floor to the door.

'Bloody 'ell,' Pol said with feeling, 'you bin arguin' with a bloody steam roller or somethin'?'

Spider gargled in his throat, his one eye desperate.

''Ere – give us an 'and ter get 'im back on the bed –' Pol and Kitty struggled to lift the little man. Spider fought them every inch of the way, still trying to get to the door.

'Spider, for God's sake!' Kitty was terrified to touch him, in case she hurt him more. 'We're only trying to help you –!'

'Ellerguvner,' he said.

'What?'

'Guv – ner.'

'Yes. What about him?' Unpleasant things were happening to the hairs at the back of Kitty's neck.

He stopped struggling. His small, fearsomely strong left hand gripped hers, his one good eye was fixed upon her face. His damaged mouth simply would not obey him. It was agonizing moments before, with a superhuman effort, he enunciated, relatively clearly, 'Warn – him –'

Kitty's stomach, already queasy, shifted again. 'Warn him of what?' She did not want to warn Luke Peveral of anything. She did not at that moment want anything to do with Luke Peveral ever again. She did not want anything to do with anyone or anything that could reduce a man to this bloody, dehumanized pulp.

'They know – where 'e is.' Blood bubbled, pink and frothing. There was another long, struggling silence. 'I – told – 'em. They'll – skin 'im. 'E don't know –' He could not go on.

'Shut yer mouth.' None too gently Pol hauled him almost single-handedly to the bed. 'You tryin' ter kill yerself? Kit – we need some rags. An' some clean water. Be still, will yer!' This, furiously, to the struggling Spider. ''Ave I got ter tie yer down?'

He was still holding onto Kitty's hand. His one eye was pleading. 'Tell – 'im! They'll – kill 'im!'

'How can I? I don't know where he is!'

He pulled her to him. Revolted, she put an ear to the bloody cavern of his mouth. 'Church,' he said, and shook her. 'Church!'

'Yes – I know the church – at least –'

He pulled her close again. 'Rope.'

'What rope? Spider – what rope?'

'Bell –' He gave an odd, bubbling sigh. His eyes closed. For a second it seemed that he had stopped breathing. Then 'Go,' he whispered, and '*Go!*' he screamed, terrifyingly, with the last of his strength.

She was horrified. She stood, trembling, looking at the unconscious body.

Pol sat back on her heels, looking at her. 'You goin'?'

'I – no! I can't!'

Pol glanced at the gasping Spider, then back at Kitty.

Kitty shook her head. 'Pol – how can I? It's nothing to do with me – I don't even know where I'm supposed to go –'

'Yer can see the church across the canal from the Rooms.'

'I know. But –'

Pol looked back at the bleeding, recumbent figure. ''E worked awful 'ard ter get 'ere. I s'pose 'e was lookin' fer Matt to 'elp 'im warn Luke?'

'I suppose so.' What had Luke Peveral risked, to see a girl home through the foggy darkness, when he could himself have been safe off the streets? 'Pol – I can't go, can I? Not alone –' She hesitated. 'Would you come with me?'

Pol shook her head. 'Nope.'

'Well then –'

'You're right. To 'ell with Luke Peveral. 'Elp me with Spider –' Pol leaned forward. Kitty stood one moment longer. Spider moaned, turned his head, opened one blood-shot eye and fixed it in entreaty upon her.

'All right,' she heard herself say. 'All right. I'll try.'

She regretted the words the moment they were out of her mouth, and as she hurried through the familiar, gloomy streets towards Blind Lane at each step she was on the point of turning back. How was she supposed to find Luke Peveral with only the sketchy information Spider had passed on? What was she to tell him? Supposing he wasn't there?

Supposing someone else was.

That last thought gnawed like a rat in her mind. The men who had so brutally maimed Spider would surely not waste time in getting to their real quarry? How long had it taken Spider to get to Market Row? She lifted her skirts, half-running. She must be mad. She must be!

The amber sky was weighted to the rooftops by the fog. The light, such as it was, was yellow, as if the world were sunk below the evil waters of a sulphurous sea. People hurried past, heads down, collars up, hands deep in pockets. The whores in the doorways, their lacklustre charms muffled beneath ragged, threadbare shawls, watched her go by with disinterested eyes. She turned at last into Blind Lane. As she had expected at this time of day it was deserted. The far end of the alley, where lay the canal, was swathed in evil, ochre-coloured fog. She was running in earnest now, heart pounding, breath rasping in her chest. And while the question still hammered her – why in God's name was she doing this? – yet she knew, remembering Spider's smashed face, the anguish in his one eye at his betrayal of Luke, that there could be no turning back now.

She reached the canal. There was the path along which Luke had led her two nights before, and there, a little way along, hidden by a corner, the plank. And across the water, almost lost amongst the smoke-blackened, mostly derelict buildings, she saw an ancient, squat grey tower with a boarded-up belfry of rotten wood perched upon it. If Pol were right, this was Luke Peveral's unlikely hideout.

She had to stand for a moment, regaining her breath and trying to control the trembling of her legs before she started across the perilous bridge. A short way downstream the decomposing body of a dog moved sluggishly in the water, set in motion by God knew what disgusting agency. The stench was vile. She edged carefully out along the unstable plank, swayed dangerously for a moment, threw herself forward and in an awkward, scrabbling dash was over. She scrambled up the bank, heedless of the mud and the clawing brambles. In the alleyway beyond she hesitated. Which way? She could no longer see the church. The alley in which she stood, a bare few feet wide, ran ahead between towering, sooty walls for perhaps fifty yards, and then met another running at right angles across it. She flew to the corner. Stopped again. The church had seemed to be to the right – she turned right, ran for perhaps a hundred yards, only to find herself in a cul-de-sac, dark and well-like beneath high, blank-windowed warehouse walls. Panic muffled her heartbeat. Despite the cold she was uncomfortably hot, and sweat channelled, prickling, down her back. On a doorstep a child sat, half-naked in the cold, face vacant, thumb stuck in a mouth that was rimmed with running sores.

'The church?' she asked him. 'Is there an old church near here?'

He stared at her, neither moving nor blinking.

She turned and ran back the way she had come. A raw-boned dog, scavenging in the squalid, streaming gutter that ran down the centre of the cobbled alley, joined happily in the game, tail wagging. Unable to avoid it, she sprawled in ungainly fashion upon the dirty ground, grazing her hands and banging her knee painfully enough to bring the rise of tears. Helpfully, the dog climbed all over her, licking her face.

'Get off! Get – off – me!'

She scrambled to her feet, dashed a scratched and dirty hand across her face. The choking smell of human refuse rose from the foetid gutter. She ran again, turned left and found herself in a wider lane. In a jumble of rooftops she glimpsed the belfry. Her heartbeat slowing a little, she hurried on, turning corners, followed her nose, losing the landmark of the tower, finding it again – and then, suddenly, there it was. Turning a corner she found herself in a dark, narrow lane, one side of which was formed by a great, windowless grey wall. In the wall was a single, arch-shaped wooden door. She craned her neck. Silhouetted against the grim yellow sky was the derelict belfry.

There was no one in sight.

Heart thumping, she approached the door. Gingerly pushed it open. 'Hello?'

Her voice sounded frail in the cold silence. Her heart sank. This could not possibly be the place. She was standing in a vast, gloomy porch, shadowed, silent, bitterly cold. The dirty wooden ceiling high above her head was hung with cobwebs, the stone walls gleamed, chill and damp, the place smelled of abandonment and neglect. Apart from the door through which she had entered there were two others – a big one, facing her, which obviously gave onto the body of the church, and a small one to the right which she assumed led to the tower above. Both were firmly and securely boarded up. In the corner, hanging through a trap in the ceiling, were two moth-eaten bell-ropes. To her left, in the thickness of the ancient wall, was an alcove, ornately screened, which looked as if once held a life-sized statue but which was now empty. That was all.

'Hello?' She heard the strain in her own voice. This could not, surely, be the place? She had made a mistake. Spider's warning would not after all reach Luke Peveral, and it was her fault. She stood for a long moment, tensed against the terrible cold of the derelict building, listening. Her knee throbbed where she had fallen, and her hand stung painfully. She put it to her mouth and sucked the sore place. The silence was unbroken, except for the disturbed flittering of wings high above her. The musty, neglected stillness was oppressive. She turned to leave; and as she did so her attention was caught by the faded, coloured bell-pulls in the corner.

'Rope,' Spider had said and, 'Bell –'

Moving slowly she stepped to the ropes. They hung motionless, dirty and threadbare. There were no cobwebs on them. Gingerly she put out a hand and then snatched it away. Metal-tongued giants hung soundless above her, massive in their rotting cages. If she should set them in motion . . . Her skin crept coldly at the thought. The bell-ropes hung, still as death.

Rope. Bell –

Luke Peveral, at possible risk to his own skin, had seen her safe through an unsafe night.

Bronze monsters waited above to give strident voice to her error – or worse, to burst from weakened bonds and crash down through the rotten fabric of the tower –

She reached to the nearest bell-pull, then at the last moment changed her mind and tugged the other one, hard.

Absolutely nothing happened.

She stood weak with relief and anticlimax. Her heart was

thundering in her ears. Absurdly, she was trembling and though her feet and hands were frozen, sweat trickled again uncomfortably down her back and between her breasts. She waited a long moment. Nothing. No echo of sound, no movement. Emboldened, she reached for the second rope.

'I really shouldn't do that. You'll wake the neighbours.'

She nearly died of shock. She spun round, breath choking in her throat. Luke Peveral stood, grinning warily, in the alcove not three feet from her. As she turned, his quick, narrow glance took in her wrecked appearance and his smile faded, but his voice was cool and pleasant as ever as he said, lightly, 'Wasn't it Benjamin Franklin who said "Three may keep a secret if two of them are dead?" Am I right in suspecting that if you are here half of London has found me?'

She could not for a moment force her voice past her almost paralysed vocal chords. 'Something like that,' she said, shakily.

'Tell me.'

She took a breath, spoke rapidly: 'Spider's at Matt's. He's been beaten, terribly. He's badly hurt. Whoever did it was looking for you, and Spider couldn't hold out – he told them – he asked me to warn you –'

The smallest of smiles, warm and genuine flickered and was gone. 'And so you have. Who of the two of us is more surprised, do you think?'

She could not stop the small, shaky laugh that brought.

He stepped to her, took her arm. All traces of levity had vanished. 'First things first. I want you out of here, and right now –' He stopped. They both heard it; the sound of running footsteps in the lane outside, a sharp, barking voice.

Luke moved faster than she could think. He caught her wrist and pulled her into the alcove. Cut at right angles into the thickness of the wall, hidden by the ornate screening that decorated the front arch, was a narrow opening, barely eighteen inches in depth. He turned sideways, slid into it, then held out a hand to her.

There were other harsh voices now, outside the door.

She took the extended hand and slipped after him into the shadowed darkness. In a moment she stood upon an ancient-looking twisting stone stairway, winding upwards, dimly lit by high, slit windows.

'Come on!' He leapt ahead of her. She bunched her skirts above her knees and scrambled after him. Panting, she almost fell through the small wooden door that he held open for her at the top of the stairs. He slammed it behind her, locked it, pocketed the key.

She gaped.

She was standing in a large chamber, beautifully proportioned, and panelled in wood. At one end was an enormous open fireplace, in which blazed a great log fire. The door through which she had just flung herself was in the corner of the room, set into the panelling, almost impossible to see. A huge, round, beautifully patterned stained glass window lit the room with its jewelled colours. In the wall opposite the fireplace was a huge door, massively barred. But it was the contents of the room that held her for one incredulous moment almost rooted to the spot, and staring. The place was a treasure-house, an Aladdin's cave; soft, rich rugs glowed upon the floor, luxurious furs thrown over the huge couch that dominated one end of the room, elegant, comfortable furniture glowed in the light of the fire, as did marble statues, the pictures that adorned the walls, the delicate glass and china.

The ill-gotten rewards of deceit and theft. Even in that fraught, astonished moment she knew it. 'What is this place?'

Luke brushed past her and in a couple of long strides was across the room and kneeling in front of a massive ebony bookcase. 'Abbot's room. This church used to be part of a priory. Ah –' He straightened, and at the bare touch of his hand the huge piece of furniture seemed almost to float away from the wall, revealing another small, panelled door. He grinned a little. 'An appropriate time to examine the good priest's cellars, I think. This way.' He held out a hand to usher her through the door. From far away came a violent crashing sound. 'They're breaking into the church,' he said, and glanced at the great barred door at the end of the room, 'so at least Spider didn't tell them about the back door. They'll have a bit of trouble there, I should think.' He looked back at her still, frightened face. 'The guided tour,' he said, gently, his eyes encouraging, 'starts, I'm afraid, of necessity in the cellars.' He moved his fingers, beckoning her into the darkness. The violent sounds from below were louder.

She ran across the room to him. A waft of freezing, evil-smelling air hit her. After only a moment's hesitation she stepped through the door and found herself upon a small, flagged platform from which steep stone steps led downwards. Luke followed her. On the wall just inside the door was a dusty shelf upon which lay several candles, one in a tarnished brass holder. He took a box of matches from his pocket and, with a perfectly steady hand struck one, lit the candle in the holder and pocketed the others. Then he turned his unhurried attention back to the bookcase. Using a small handle on the back he guided it soundlessly back so that it concealed the doorway, then he knelt and pulled a small lever. The massive piece settled upon the floor like a rock. 'Take God Himself to shift that.' He shut and barred the little door.

'You're very well organized,' Kitty said.

She saw the glimmer of his smile. 'Be a daft rat that didn't have a bolthole.'

Darkness had settled about them, momentarily blinding despite the candle. Kitty stood quite still, waiting for her eyes to adjust. Oddly, for all the panic that had preceded this moment she was unafraid. With light, sound too had been cut off. They stood for a moment in a cold circle of stillness. The candle guttered and danced. Luke's shadow loomed upon the wall, his hawk's face was limned in gold by the flickering flame he held.

Soundlessly he turned and led the way down into darkness.

(ii)

She had a brief moment to be amazed at her own calmness. As if this madness were part of the most everyday occurrence in the world she followed him, stepping carefully, steadying herself with a hand upon the damp, rough surface of the cold wall. From below she heard the sound of water dripping. Luke lifted the candle above his head. Shadows lurched upon the curved walls.

'Watch the steps. They're a bit slippery.' His voice echoed eerily within the confined space.

'Where are we?'

'We're going down into the crypt. It runs under the building next door and then joins the sewer that runs under the road.' He sensed her reaction and she heard the smile in his voice. 'You're right. Not the sweetest place in the world. But if you can stand it – and if the waters aren't too high – it's a damned sight safer than facing our friends up there.'

She had not missed the qualification. 'And what if the waters are too high?'

'Then it's a bit stickier.' His voice, though still cheerful, had lost the smile. 'We choose between swimming and sitting and twiddling our thumbs until it's safe to go back upstairs.'

There was, she thought, little point in voicing the obvious question as to how they were supposed to know when that magic moment had arrived. 'Are you sure they can't follow us?' she asked.

'Certain.' The word was confident. Luke paused, turned, watched her by the light of the candle. 'Even if they knew of the existence of the door – which I'm sure they don't – it'd take a steam roller to move that bookcase. Don't worry. We're safe down here.'

'Am I allowed to know from whom?' There was a small touch of bravado in her voice. 'If I'm going to die young, oughtn't I to know why?'

A cold draught wafted up the stairs, bringing with it a foetid whiff of soiled and polluted water. He turned and started on down the stairs. 'Some years ago I made some rather – unorthodox – arrangements concerning an ex-partner of mine. He'd tried to gammon me once too often. I thought it might suit us both if he spent the rest of his life in rather sunnier climes. He didn't appreciate my efforts. Damned ungrateful of him.'

'You shopped him?'

'Yes.'

'And he was transported.'

'Yes.'

'And now he's back? And is looking for you?'

'So it would seem. Funny – I'd never have thought he had it in him. Life, he got, so he isn't back here courtesy of Her Majesty. Botany Bay must have toughened him.'

'And now he wants to kill you.'

His laughter was grim. 'That, I imagine, is the least he wants to do.'

'So he's not going to give up?'

'I imagine not – not until –'

'Until what?'

She sensed his shrug. 'Not until one of us is dead. That's right.'

In silence she followed him down into darkness.

A few minutes later they reached level ground. Luke lifted the candle high. They were standing on wet flagstones beneath a vaulted stone barrel of a roof. The air was thick with the suffocating stench of the sewer, that fouled the throat and curdled the stomach. The light flickered upon several ancient stone tombs that were lined against the wall. As Luke moved forward there was a sudden scrabbling sound, and an offendedly indignant squeal. Rats. Kitty's skin crawled. For one moment she considered seriously the alternative of facing the men upstairs. At least the terror there was in light, and air. The reeking darkness bore down on her like the weight of all evil.

'Are you all right?' Luke's voice held a small, sharp edge.

'Yes.'

'Come on, then, this way.' He led her forward, through a

series of low arches. Kitty put a hand over her nose and mouth, trying to filter the foul air. The awful, scurrying rat-sounds were all round them. Small, vicious eyes gleamed, sinisterly red in the candlelight. Her legs were shaking, and her skin was cold as the hand of death. 'God,' she muttered, behind her hand, 'I h-hate rats.'

His cold hand tightened on hers. 'It's all right. They can't hurt you.'

'I kn-know –' Her teeth were chattering.

'Can you go on?'

Glad of the darkness that hid the sudden craven rise of tears, 'Yes,' she said.

A few minutes later they had reached the end of the crypt and stood in a long, brick-built, dripping tunnel. By the light of the flame that Luke carried Kitty could see that the curved walls were in ill-repair and covered for the most part in a spectacularly evil-looking slime. She could also see that the slow-moving river of filth that they enclosed reached from wall to wall and even encroached upon the stone floor of the crypt. The foul stuff must have been more than waist deep.

'Shit!' Luke said, beneath his breath, with bitter feeling, betraying in the one word his disappointment at the height of the flow.

Unexpected hysterical laughter gurgled in Kitty's throat. Her stomach was heaving. 'That's what it is all right,' she said. 'At least, most of it.'

He coughed with laughter. Stood for a long moment surveying the disgusting river of ordure. 'Kitty – do you think you could – ?'

'No!' She shook her head, gestured at her wide, heavy skirts. 'How could I?'

'It's a few hundred yards, that's all. Then it empties in the canal –'

'You go,' she said. 'In these skirts I'd drown. And without them I'd freeze to death. You go. Get help –' She grimaced over her shoulder. A rat scuttled.

'Plan number two,' he said.

'What's that?'

He jerked his head back at the crypt. 'We make ourselves comfortable and wait.'

She lifted skirts already sodden with the sewer-filth that polluted the floor. 'We make ourselves what? Truly, Luke Peveral, I'm coming to believe that you must have a very peculiar sense of humour!'

He laughed, gave her his hand. 'Let's go and find ourselves a coffin.'

They moved back into the crypt, away from the nightmare stream. The smell, however, followed them, clinging about them, as tangible, it seemed to Kitty, as the London fog that wreathed the streets above them.

'Here —' Near the steps down which they had come was a large, flat tomb, ancient, begrimed, littered with rat dirt, the inscription indecipherable in the weak light. 'Sorry, friend,' Luke addressed the occupant drily, 'we won't be with you for long.' He took Kitty by the waist. 'Jump —' He deposited her on top of the tomb, vaulted up after her. 'We'll be dry here at least and out of the way of our four-legged friends.'

'This —' Kitty muttered, tucking her legs beneath her skirts in a vain attempt to warm them, 'is getting to be too much of a habit.'

'What?'

'Nothing.' She settled herself as best as she could, her back against the wall. She felt as if a part of her brain had ceased to function altogether. Since the moment she had found Spider, beaten and bleeding upon her brother's bed, an understandable air of unreality had stalked events.

Luke set the candle beside her, crossed his long legs and rested his hands loosely on his knees. They looked at each other in silence.

'Now what?' Kitty asked, her voice fragile in the dripping quiet.

He considered, soberly, for a moment. 'Well, since this is hardly the time or place for a seduction —' Mischievously he left a small, half-questioning pause before settling more easily against the wall, long hands resting upon his bent knees. 'Why don't you tell me the story of your life?'

'– and so we came to London. Matt fell in with Croucher at Covent Garden and – you know the rest –'

A rat rustled across the floor. The small remnant of candle burned steadily. Her eyes were used to the light now, and she could discern every expression on his face. Even the vile smell seemed to have diminished a little, though she realized that this too must be because she had become used to it.

She wondered, dispassionately, why in all her narrative she had made no mention of Amos Isherwood.

He tilted his head. He had listened to her story intently, with hardly any interruptions. 'You've had some bad luck.'

She glanced at him sharply. She could not let that pass. For a moment the warmth of comradeship that during the telling of her story had enclosed them as the light from the candle enclosed them, cooled, as the candle might flicker in a cold draught. 'No. It's had nothing to do with bad luck. Our misfortunes have stemmed from one thing and one thing only. Matt's thieving.'

Amos smiled knowingly in the darkness. She ignored him.

'It wasn't his fault that old Sir What's-his-name and his sons drowned.'

'No.' Her voice was obstinate. 'But after that.'

The silence was broken by the irregular dripping of water from the roof. 'You really do hate it, don't you?' he asked at last, quietly.

'Yes I do!' Her voice was suddenly violent. 'All of it. It isn't even just a case of honesty or dishonesty any more. I hate the squalor. I hate the fear. There's no pride in any of it!'

'There's not a lot of pride in starving either.'

'There are other ways to eat.'

He cocked a sardonic brow. 'You think so? You believe, do you, in the pride of honest labour, the commendable sweat of a respectable man who slaves for others to see his children starve?'

Shaken by the depth of bitterness in the words she did not reply.

He shook his head. 'You've got it wrong, Kitty. The people you so easily despise – including me, including your brother – they may be everything you believe they are – they may be vicious, and cruel, and frightened and degenerate. They may be worthless. They may deserve no more than the lash or the hangman's noose. But think. What kind of society has produced these people? Are they not also, in their way, victims? Victims of a society whose sternest judgement and punishment is visited upon those unfortunate enough to be born poor? What greater crime is there than being penniless? For nothing more than that thousands upon thousands of souls are condemned to the harshest of hard labour, to the most atrocious living conditions that man could envisage, to disease, to hopelessness and to death. They watch their loved ones die – their wives, their husbands, their children. And for their inability to save themselves from the quicksand of poverty into which others have thrown them they are castigated, preached at, despised. Do you wonder that half the population of Stepney is three parts drunk most of the time and on the sharp side of the law all of the time? What else would you have them do? Have you seen the sweatshops? No hard labour in Newgate can touch them, take it from me. Have you seen the girls – girls no older than you – blinded, and stooped like old women? Burned and scarred by phosphorus? Do you blame them, then, for selling their bodies? Have you seen the children making boxes for a ha'penny a gross – and a glass of water and a crust of dry bread stopped out of their wages?'

She was staring at him in astonishment. He stopped. Spread his hands, studying the nails. Lifted his head again.

'Matt didn't have to do any of those things,' she said, quietly.

'No. And neither, if you're asking, did I.' The unusual

passion had died as quickly as it had flamed. 'Of course, you're right. Matt and I – we're the other kind. Born to hang.'

'Don't say that!'

His brows lifted. 'Sorry.'

She shrugged.

'Matt can't help it,' he said.

'That's what he said.'

'Believe him. He knows.'

'I don't understand it.'

'No. I don't suppose you do.'

'It would have broken Father's heart.'

Silence.

'I promised I'd look after him –' she said, her quiet voice all but lost in the still darkness.

'And so you have.'

'Not well enough.' She was fidgeting with her sodden woollen skirt, pleating it with her fingers, smoothing it out.

'I'm sure he wouldn't agree with you.'

She could not repress a smile. 'What's so different about that? Matt agrees with very little I say.'

They fell to silence. After a moment, a little defiantly, she said, 'Your turn.'

'What is?'

'The soul-baring. I've told you about us. Now it's your turn.'

'You mean – what's my excuse?' The tone was bantering.

'If you like.'

'I can think of more interesting subjects to talk about,' he said, a little tentatively.

She maintained an obstinate silence.

'Very well.' He dug into his pocket and produced a fresh candle, lit it from the guttering remnant in the holder. As he carefully forced the new candle in the melted, dying stub of the old she studied his dark, closed profile. He sat back. The candle stood, tall flame bright and steady between them. His eyes were fixed upon it, thoughtfully. For a moment she thought he was not going to continue. Then,

'Once upon a time,' he said, 'there was a princess, fair and very beautiful.' His voice was light. She did not know if he mocked her or not. 'She lived in splendour and comfort in a great house in the country. She dined off silver platters and drank from the finest crystal. Dressed in silks and in satins, she rode in a carriage behind the finest pair of matched bays in the county. She was kind and she was gentle, and she was very much loved.' He paused. Kitty sat, watching and waiting, still and quiet as a mouse. 'But yet – there was something missing in her life. She did not know herself what it was, you understand – she only knew – something missing – something important –' The dark, deeply shadowed eyes lifted to Kitty's face. 'And then the gypsy came.'

It occurred to Kitty that he had told this tale before. She waited.

'He was handsome – oh, yes, the finest-looking man the princess had ever seen was the gypsy. And proud as Lucifer. And wicked as the hounds of hell.' His eyes had drifted from her and were fixed once again upon the candleflame. 'But of course the princess didn't know that. She saw the handsome face, the splendid body, the proud glance and was stricken with' – for a second his long mouth twitched into an entirely mirthless smile – 'lust.'

He fell silent. When the silence lengthened Kitty could not resist saying, as she knew she was expected to, 'What happened?'

'Don't be silly, Songbird. What do you think happened? She lay with the gypsy one night under the stars. And for one night of pleasure reaped a short lifetime of misery. When it was discovered that she was carrying his child she was turned from her father's door. Naturally enough she fled to her lover. And he beat her and humiliated her and treated like a dog the child that she bore him.'

'No!' She could not prevent the shocked word.

'But yes.' His voice was flat, nervelessly composed. 'And so you see, from very different backgrounds you and I have something in common, do we not? We are both misfits

– over-educated, under-capitalized and with expectations beyond our station. And each of us has been born with a talent. You can sing. I can thieve, as a good gypsy should. How can you hold that against me?'

'Is it true? They were your parents?'

'Yes.' He gave a small impatient jerk of his head, flicking the dark hair from his eyes. She had the sudden impression that he regretted embarking on the story. He turned to her, and his face had changed. The Luke she knew, the man whose arrogance and carelessness had so antagonized her was back. 'You want to know the end of the story?'

'No.'

He ignored that. 'They didn't live happily ever after. He killed her.'

She caught her breath. 'Oh, my God!'

'God had very little to do with it actually. It had rather more to do with strong spirits and a long, sharp knife.' His bravado had failed him a little.

'You were there?'

'Yes.'

She sucked her lip. 'How – how old were you?'

He shrugged. 'Eleven – twelve?'

The thought struck her wordless. She put a hand to touch his. He allowed it to rest there for a brief, oddly courteous moment before, unable to accept her sympathy, he disengaged himself. The candle was leaning a little. Tallow dripped, one-sidedly. Absentmindedly he pushed at it with a long fingernail.

'You must have hated him,' she said.

That brought his eyes to hers. He shook his head. His expression was sombre. 'No.' He paused. 'I wanted to. For a while I thought I did. But then I realized –' He poked at the candle again, face shadowed.

'What?'

'Then I realized that – no matter what – I loved him –' The words came painfully. 'I wanted to hate him. I wanted to kill him for what he had done to my mother, and to me. But I couldn't. For a word from him I'd've crawled on my belly. I did everything I could to make him notice me. He never did.'

In the darkness that gathered in the corners something stirred and was still, like a small breath of evil. Luke drew one knee up to his chin, linked his hands around it. 'One day, Songbird,' he said softly, 'I'll have a son. And he'll love me as I loved that devil of a father. No matter what I do, no matter who I am, he'll love me. And I'll show him what it is to have a father. We'll put it right.'

She waited, then, 'What did you do?' she asked.

'The day after he was killed in a tavern brawl I left. I was good with horses. I'd had a good, if rather eccentric, education from my mother. I talked, thanks to her, like a young gentleman. I made my way.'

She stretched her legs a little, glad at the lessening of the disturbing tension his story had engendered. 'So. Here we arc – both making our way.'

He smiled at her, and she saw the gleam of it in the candlelight. 'And yours, Kitty Songbird, could be a very good way indeed if you play your cards right.' She got the impression that he was only too pleased to change the subject.

'What do you mean?'

'Oh, come now – what modesty! What do I mean? What do you think I mean?' He grinned again. '"My soul is an enchanted boat, Which like a sleeping swan doth float, Upon the waves of thy sweet singing –"'

She laughed delightedly. '"And thine doth like an angel sit, Beside the helm conducting it, Whilst all the winds with melody are ringing –"' She had capped the quotation before the possible inference of the words had struck her. She stopped.

'What ever would poor Percy think,' he asked of the awkward silence, lightly, 'to hear himself quoted in a sewer?'

She laughed a little. Fidgeted, arching her back to ease its ache. 'Luke?'

'Mm?'

'How – how much longer, do you think?'

He shook his head. 'Give it a little longer.'

She nodded uncertainly. The bitter cold was numbing her.

'Tell me something.'

She looked enquiringly.

'You aren't thinking of singing for Moses Smith forever?'

Her eyes were suddenly wary. 'I – hadn't thought about it.'

'More fool you, then. You're good. You know you are. You've a lot to learn. But it's coming. It shows.'

'Thank you.' The words were dry.

'If you ever' – he paused – '*when* – you want a bit of help moving on, come to me. One good turn deserves another. I've got friends that might help.'

'What sort of friends?' Her voice was guarded.

He gave a small bark of laughter. 'Not the sort to worry you. Perish the thought. I do have some law-abiding acquaintances, you know. Have you ever heard of a man called Patrick Kenny? He opened a place called the New Cambridge about – oh, eight months or so ago. It's doing very well.'

She nodded. 'George mentioned it. But don't be silly. Patrick Kenny wouldn't be interested in me.' She hesitated. 'Would he?'

His chuckle brought a blush of mortification to her cheeks. 'Let's wait and see, shall we?' He reached into his pocket, took out a watch, tilted it to the light of the candle. Then he slid to the floor, held out his hands to help her down.

Her heart had started to thud uncomfortably. 'Now?' she asked.

'Now,' he nodded.

(iii)

He tried to leave her halfway up the stairs, with the candle and instructions to wait.

'No,' she said.

'Kitty – please don't be stupid. You know as well as I do that there's a chance they'll be waiting –'

'So – what good will it do me to be trapped like a rat when they come down here – ?'

'There's no reason they should.'

'Unless they guess you'd been warned. Don't you think they might check? I'm not staying here alone. I'm coming with you.'

He argued no further. Silently he led the way to the top of the steps. 'At least,' he whispered, his eyes sardonic in the candlelight, 'you'll allow me the doubtful privilege of going first?'

She did not bother to answer.

He blew out the candle, set it down and very, very gently lifted the bar of the door. Noiselessly then the door swung open. The warm, acrid smell of burning seeped into the tunnel. Luke was hunkered down, feeling for the lever of the bookcase. Very carefully he pulled it. Fractionally the enormous piece of furniture lifted from the floor. Kitty thought her heart must stop beating altogether.

There was no sound.

Infinitely slowly Luke eased the bookcase from the wall. When the gap was a few inches deep he stood for a moment, head cocked, listening, before sliding his lean frame into the narrow gap.

Kitty's knuckles were at her mouth. She heard the faint rustle of Luke's movements, smelled again a drift of fragrant smoke, then almost jumped from her skin in terror as there came a violent flurry of movement, a choked cry and then silence. She stood as if turned to stone.

'It's all right. You can come out. But don't scream.' Luke's voice, very quiet.

She pushed the bookcase. It floated as if on air away from the wall. 'Why should I –?' She stepped into the room, and stood aghast. It had been utterly wrecked. Furniture and pictures were smashed, books and papers ripped and smouldering in a heap in the fireplace. Broken glass and china crunched underfoot. Cheated of their prey, Luke's enemies had indulged in a mindless orgy of destruction. There was a strong smell of urine. But what riveted her eyes was the horror that lay sprawled upon the bed, still twitching, the blood pumping from a gaping hole in his throat.

She opened her mouth.

Luke tossed the bloody knife he was holding onto the soiled bed and was by her side in a second, his blood-smeared hand clamped on her shoulder. 'Not a bloody whimper!' he hissed, and jerked his head downwards.

Her eyes widened. 'They're here?' Her voice was a breath.

'Almost certainly. Waiting downstairs. They'd left him here in case they missed me.'

Sickly she turned her back on the ghastly thing on the bed. 'What are we going to do?'

'What we should bloody well have done in the first place,' he said. 'We're going through the sewer.'

'But –'

'No buts. Wait.' Swiftly and quietly he strode to a wardrobe in the corner of the room. The doors had been smashed open. Clothes lay like heaps of rags on a market stall, strewn upon the floor. He bent and sorted through them, tossed her a shirt and a pair of trousers. 'Here – put these on –'

She stared like a halfwit.

'For God's sweet sake, girl!' The words were taut with edgy impatience. 'You said yourself – you'd never get through that muck in those skirts. Get them off!'

The good sense of his words was apparent. She thought of her heavy, full skirts dragging her down into that mire and shuddered.

'Hurry!'

She snatched the clothes, turned her back on him. He did not even notice. He had turned from her and was surveying, hard-faced, the wreckage of the once-lovely room. She scrambled awkwardly out of her own clothes and into his. Lean as Luke was, the waist of the trousers was inches too big and the legs too long. She bent and rolled them up to her ankles, then stood clutching the loose waist of the trousers. Luke turned, and his strained face split into a quick grin. 'Here –' He tossed her a wide leather belt. She buckled it tightly about her waist, bunching the trousers. They felt very strange, stiff and heavy and confining. She picked up the jacket he had tossed her. 'I'm ready.'

He was watching her, the smile softer. 'You make a handsomer lad than your brother,' he said. 'And as game a one too it seems. Right. Off we go.' He slid back behind the bookcase. Feeling incredibly ungainly in the unaccustomed clothes, and with the dead man's eyes boring like hot needles into her back, she followed.

Beyond the crypt the sewer breathed its poisonous miasma at her. She stood trembling, shaking her head. Luke's hand, cold and strong, held her steady. Breast-high the filth invaded her. She sobbed a little, biting her lip.

'Not far. It really isn't far. Hold on. We're nearly there.' Luke sounded as sick as she felt. 'Hold on –'

She could not. She knew she could not. It was impossible to keep her footing. She would fall, she knew, and drown in the unspeakable obscene darkness – for the dozenth time she slipped and only Luke's strength prevented her from plunging into the stinking depths. Her hair, unpinned, hung down her back and plastered itself across her face, heavy with filth. She retched. Her limbs felt trapped by the nauseous quagmire.

'Steady – see – we're almost there –'

Ahead, incredibly, was light. Sobbing, she almost stumbled again. Floundering, she regained her balance, and the part of her mind that remained clear of the blindness of panic thanked God and Luke Peveral that she was not wearing the clinging skirts that would have undoubtedly dragged her down. The candle that Luke held, head-high, blew out. Faint grey light invaded the stinking tunnel.

'We're nearly there – nearly through – that's a brave girl –' She did not feel brave. She felt defiled. Defeated.

Long minutes later, hardly daring to believe it, she found herself wading between the beslimed banks of the canal. Never had the fog-heavy air of Stepney seemed so pure.

Convulsively she gulped it into her lungs. The stagnant canal-waters that had so revolted her earlier might have been the crystal spring-waters of Eden. She retched violently. Luke was coughing beside her. When her stomach had ended its rebellion she splashed her arms and her clothes, trying to clean off the worst of the filth. She was suddenly aware that she was freezing cold and shivering violently, her teeth chattering in her head. Luke, as bedraggled and dirty as she, and in as bad a way, held out his hand. 'Just a little further. Blind Lane isn't far. Midge will see us right.'

They clambered with difficulty up the slippery bank and stumbled upstream. Kitty had lost one of her boots. Brambles tore at her, broken glass lay in ambush for her bare foot. 'Luke, please – wait!'

He shook his head. 'Keep going. We're almost there.'

She followed him blindly. Fog still wreathed Blind Lane. She leaned against the wall, exhausted, as Luke's fists thundered upon the door of the Rooms. 'Open up! It's Luke Peveral! Open up, for Christ's sake –!'

'What the bleedin' 'ell?' Bobs stood, blinking in astonishment. He turned from them, wrinkling his prizefighter's nose in disgust. 'Christ's bleedin' teeth!'

Luke pushed roughly past him, dragging Kitty with him. 'Get Midge! Quickly, man!'

Kitty snatched her hand from his, sank onto the nearest chair and covered her filthy face with her even filthier hands. She felt indescribably befouled. Tainted. She would never be clean. The dead man's eyes bored still into her brain.

She could not even cry.

An hour later, bathed, fed and with a quarter of a bottle of Moses' best brandy poured unceremoniously down her throat, she was in bed. Moments before she drifted into brandy-induced, nightmare-ridden sleep it occurred to her that she was almost certainly the first of Midge's girls ever to sleep in one of these beds alone. And probably the last.

No one saw or heard from Luke Peveral for the best part of ten days. Having delivered Kitty to Midge and seen her safely cared for he had left, and disappeared, so it seemed, from the face of the earth.

Four days later the bodies of two men were fished from the Thames. They had been neatly garrotted, apparently by the same hand. No one came forward to identify the bodies.

Three days after that a man was found hanging beneath Blackfriars Bridge – a man in his thirties, the police surgeon hazarded, with skin darkened by a foreign sun and the shackle-scars of a convict on wrists and ankles. No one enquired too closely into his death, either.

Spider smiled painfully at the news, delivered through the obscure grapevine of the underworld, and applied himself with more appetite than normal to the mash that Pol pushed between his crushed lips.

A few days later Luke Peveral sauntered into the Rooms as if he had never been away. Obviously aware of the buzz that ran around the hall at his appearance, he grinned, greeted a friend, joined Moses at his accustomed table.

Lottie shrieked and flung herself upon him. Over her head he looked to where Kitty sat, death-still and suddenly pale as ivory.

'Good evening, Songbird,' he said, gently. 'Not too late for the show, am I?'

It was just a week after that, that Oliver Fogg first appeared at Smith's Song and Supper Rooms. And set in motion a chain of violence and death that was to affect them all.

5

(i)

Kitty, her sensitivity heightened by the horror of that bizarre day of bloodshed and murder, noticed straight away that Luke Peveral had a wary eye upon the unsettling stranger who sat alone at a table in a corner near the bar, one bony hand nursing a half-empty glass, his expressionless, cadaver's face in shadow. When the two men's eyes first met in the smoky, dimly lit atmosphere she was certain that she detected upon Luke's face that faint flicker of surprise that denotes unexpected recognition; then in the blink of an eye it was gone, but she noticed that Luke turned his chair a little, to keep the gaunt stranger in his field of vision. He said nothing, however, and no one else seemed to know the man. For a week or so he was a regular visitor – spending little, eating nothing, sitting all night nursing a single drink, never speaking, his eyes coming back time and again to the table where Luke sat with Moses. He and Luke rarely exchanged glances and never a word, and yet more and more strongly as the days passed Kitty became convinced they knew each other. And always, it seemed to her, they faced each other, watching.

It was one day a couple of weeks after Luke's reappearance at the Supper Rooms that Moses at last noticed his guarded gaze and sensed his distraction. He turned to follow the direction of Luke's gaze and frowned. 'That the cully Midge was talking about?'

Luke shook his head. 'Midge?'

'Sits all night, she reckons, dumb as a duck an' don't spend a tanner.'

'Possibly.'

Something in his tone caught Moses' astute ear. 'You know him?'

Kitty, her first performance done, sipped her watered wine and listened. For a variety of odd and, even to herself, confusing reasons she had hardly spoken a word to Luke in the past couple of weeks. The strange camaraderie of those hours in the foul-smelling crypt had for her been brutally overlaid by the violence of the events that had followed. Her worst, and strongest, recollection of those nightmare hours were the staring eyes of the man that Luke had so apparently casually killed, and the awful, scarlet spread of his blood. That three other men had died since had drawn a curtain of horror between herself and the man with whom in such strange circumstances she had exchanged confidences and quoted Shelley, one she found impossible to draw aside. She found herself, often, watching his hands; narrow, dark, strong. Hands that had killed – how many times? He had tried to thank her for her part in his narrow escape. She had accepted his thanks so woodenly as almost to constitute an insult. He had not bothered with her again. He sat now, pensive, long steady fingers wrapped around the slender stem of his wine glass.

'Well?' Moses was puzzled.

Luke nodded. 'Yes. As a matter of fact I think I do. His name, if I'm not much mistaken, is Oliver Fogg. He is – or certainly was when last I came across him – a policeman of no great repute.'

'A copper? Here?' Moses' outrage could not have been greater had he been St Peter facing Lucifer at the gates of Heaven.

Luke, smiling a little at the fat man's choler, nodded.

'By Christ! Why didn't you tell me? I'll have him hanged, drawn and quartered, see if I don't!'

Luke shrugged. 'Why bother? Better the devil you see than the one you don't. Perhaps he's just taken a fancy to our Songbird's singing?' He raised an unnecessarily mocking brow in Kitty's direction.

'Do you think it's you he's after?' Kitty asked, directly.

'Maybe.'

Moses leaned forward, great stomach pressing against the table. 'Don't be so modest, my friend. Who else would he be after? We must do something about this.'

'You could always cut his throat.' Kitty, her eyes upon Luke, had spoken the words almost before thought. She herself heard – and too late regretted – the harshness of the tone.

Luke gave her a long, unfriendly look. 'Lend me your tongue and I will,' he said, gently.

Moses looked from one to the other impatiently. 'Who needs to cut throats? I can arrange such things. If there's one thing Moses Smith can do for a friend it's preserve his privacy on his own patch from the pryings of the scum of the Metropolitan bloody Police Force! I've got' – he winked a small eye – 'contacts in high places. Very high places. Constable Fogg –'

'Sergeant, I believe –' Luke interpolated mildly.

'Sergeant – Constable – Moses Smith pays good money to keep them all off his back and off the backs of his friends. This – Fogg – breaks the rules –'

'One of his habits, as I remember,' Luke said, thoughtfully.

'He should mind someone doesn't break his neck. I'll get a message sent, sharp. You won't be bothered again, Luke my boy. And – this Sergeant Fogg' – Moses invested the words with enormous scorn – 'will likely find himself with his eye in a sling and his flat feet back on the hard pavements of the South Bank –'

Luke shrugged again, smiling, his eyes flicking to the sinister face of the man who watched from the shadows. 'If you think you can?'

Pleased, Moses leaned forward to slap his knee in friendship. 'My pleasure, my boy, my pleasure. Trust Moses. Coppers? I own 'em. All of 'em. Have no fear – we'll get that ugly face out of here in two shakes of a Manx cat's tail.'

He was true to his word. Two evenings later the table in the corner was empty – and within another two Kitty had forgotten the man's existence, for, to her astonishment, and despite the indefinable strain that lay between them, Luke kept his lightly given promise of reward for her help, and she stepped onto the stage to find herself performing before the shrewd and calculating eyes of Patrick Kenny, whose name was synonymous not just with one of London's most successful and popular new music halls, but with many others that were fast establishing themselves all over Britain. Here was a man who could, with his influence and his flare for the recognition of talent, make or break a performer overnight.

He looked bored.

Forewarned, through Midge, by Luke, Kitty had taken especial care with her appearance – the black velvet dress had been steamed and pressed, a precious paste necklace borrowed from Pol at her throat, with matching earrings swinging beneath her precariously piled, upswept hair that was decked with softly waving white plumes. As she stood nervously awaiting her cue from the pianist she saw Luke lean to his guest and pour the magnificently moustachioed impresario a glass of champagne. She hoped fervently that it was not his first. The man did not look very impressed by his surroundings – and who could blame him? she wondered gloomily, fighting jangling nerves. What possible method of persuasion could Luke have used to get the man into this den of drunkards, thieves and whores? It was much later that she realized that other talents than her own had been nurtured in such surroundings, and if he did look out of place in his well-cut evening clothes, cane resting with his white gloves and black silk top hat on the table beside him, it was certainly not the first time Patrick Kenny had visited such an establishment and it would be unlikely to be the last. That did not, however, mean that he had to enjoy it. He accepted the brimming glass from Luke, tilted his head and fixed a gimlet eye upon Kitty.

She swallowed. She had a nerve-induced lump in her throat that felt the size of a tennis ball.

The pianist played a slovenly introduction, striking two wrong notes in quick succession.

Trembling like a leaf in a gale she launched herself into the haunting and popular ballad that told the story of dead, sweet Alice and her Ben Bolt, back from the sea.

Patrick Kenny looked, if it were possible, even less impressed than he had before.

Half an hour later, shaking no less, she presented herself at the table. She knew she had not done well. Her nerves had shown, and had threaded her top notes with uncertainty. She had fidgeted upon the stage like a performing child –

The dapper Mr Kenny rose courteously and offered his hand. 'Miss Daniels.'

She took it briefly, and in a flash of nervous hysteria wondered if she were expected to kiss it. 'Mr Kenny.' Despite the nerves she managed to settle herself fairly composedly in the chair opposite him, and smoothed her skirt. Then she lifted her eyes directly to his face. 'I'm sorry,' she said, straightforwardly, 'I didn't sing well, I'm afraid.'

She saw a faint gleam of appreciation in the shrewd eyes. 'No, you didn't,' he said, pleasantly. 'But – you have a good, perhaps the word is unusual? – voice. I might argue that your performance lacked – somewhat – a little fire?'

'I was very nervous.'

'So I guessed.'

She folded her hands in her lap and waited.

'Luke tells me that you have aspirations to' – he waved a wry hand at their surroundings – 'tread a wider stage?'

'Yes.'

'He tells me too that he thinks you capable of it. And I value his opinion.'

She shot a quick, surprised glance at Luke and then wished she hadn't. He was regarding her dispassionately – disappointedly? – as he might, she thought with an irrational spurt of anger, an unsatisfactory insect impaled upon a pin.

'However' – Kenny paused upon the fateful word – 'however I cannot of course take his word alone for it, and upon your performance tonight –' He stopped, stroking his moustache doubtfully.

Her heart sank to her shabby boots. She had had one chance, and that provided by Luke Peveral. And she had made a mess of it. She kept her own eyes steadily upon Kenny's flamboyantly whiskered face, swallowed chill and bitter disappointment – and in her determination not to show her distress missed altogether the import of the man's next words.

'– and we'll see how you go from there. A little more experience – a little more panache – and who knows? Not that I'm promising anything, mind – you must understand that –'

'I – beg your pardon?'

He stopped, surprised.

'I didn't – I didn't quite catch what you said?' She saw the gleam of Luke's amused smile from the corner of her eye and glowed with embarrassment.

Patrick Kenny was politely and commendably patient. 'My small establishment in North London. I said I'd try you there. For two weeks to start with. Seven and sixpence a week, and supper, starting next week.' He turned courteously to Moses. 'As long of course as that does not incommode Mr Smith?'

'Mr Smith,' Luke interrupted smoothly, 'has already agreed that Kitty may be released to work elsewhere.' Kitty was staring, dizzily. Luke leaned forward, poured more champagne for Kenny. 'Seven and six, supper and a cab home,' he said, reasonably.

Kenny arched an injured eyebrow. 'Now, Luke –'

'Come now' – Luke spread those dark, well-shaped hands – 'you can't expect the girl to walk halfway across London?'

Kitty would have walked to and from the North Pole. She opened her mouth to say so.

Kenny made an exaggerated gesture of surrender. 'Very well, very well. We'll make it seven shillings, supper and a cab home. Well? Are you willing?' He looked at Kitty.

'Oh, yes! Yes, of course!'

He leaned back. 'Well and good. That's settled then. Luke – you can get a couple of bottles of this excellent champagne

for me, if you would? Where you find such stuff is beyond
me –'

Luke grinned. 'It's beyond the Excise men as well.' He
glanced then at Kitty and she understood that a bargain had
been struck, a debt paid.

'Another bottle!' Moses lifted a hand. Lottie appeared
by his side. She was wearing a dress that Kitty had not
seen before, and one she would have wagered her soul had
never seen the grimy interior of Harry's doubtful empor-
ium. It was of vivid sapphire satin and fitted the girl like
a second skin before flaring to a full, graceful skirt. Her
shoulders were bare – in fact for all the concealment the
dress offered, cut as it was to reveal her white, swelling
breasts almost to the nipple, she might, Kitty thought a
little sourly, have been naked to the waist – indeed the
effect contrived to be somehow even more provocative
than if she actually had been. She saw Moses' eyes
linger upon the expanse of smooth, blue-veined skin as
his arm slipped about the girl's supple waist, and her own
skin crept as a fat little hand openly caressed the girl's
breast. 'Another couple of bottles, my dear. And – bring a
glass for yourself –'

'Yes, Mr Smith.' Lottie's blue gaze was fixed upon the
fat man's face as if her hope of salvation might be found
somewhere behind those hot, almost lashless eyes. Kitty
glanced at Luke. He was watching the byplay through narrow eyes, his mouth straight and unsmiling. Lottie turned
without so much as a glance in his direction. When she
returned with the bottles and the glass she brought them to
Moses, leaning across him so that her bared breasts pressed
against him and the fall of her hair brushed his face. He did
not look displeased with the experience. He dragged a chair
to the table beside him, fondled her buttocks. 'Sit here, Lot.
Next to me.'

'Yes, Mr Smith.'

Kitty, a little pensively, accepted her glass of champagne.

'A toast,' Luke said. 'To the Songbird of Stepney. Our
very own star of the music halls.' Kitty suspected mockery

beneath the sober words and threw him a dark glance of exasperation.

Patrick Kenny raised his glass, and to his credit his lack of conviction was not as obvious as it might have been.

Glasses were lifted. All eyes were turned to Kitty – all that is except Lottie's. She, perched on the edge of her chair, was leaning against Moses as if without his support she might slip helplessly to the floor, and her doll-like gaze was for no one but him.

(ii)

'Pol? What's Lottie up to with Moses?' Kitty was stitching industriously at the green dress, adding a couple of swathes of glittering braid to the skirt and sleeves.

Pol was attempting to clean a pair of tarnished silver slippers, purchased from Harry for an exorbitant three shillings. 'It's called playin' both ends against the middle, if I'm not much mistaken. ''Ere – I'm not sure I can get this all off –'

'Don't worry. They'll be fine – they're looking much better already. You mean – Moses and Luke –?'

'Seems like it, don't it?'

'But – why? I mean –' Kitty bent to her work, frowning in ferocious concentration. 'I thought it was Luke she was after?'

'Don't fool yerself. It is. Ask me, it always will be. But that Jack the lad ain't about to be tied down, is 'e? She's tried one way. Now she's tryin' another.' The brassy head lifted. 'Seems she thinks 'e's got 'is eye on someone else,' she added, quietly.

That brought Kitty's head up quickly. At the look in Pol's eye she flushed deeply. 'Oh, don't be silly! I don't even like Luke Peveral. And he doesn't like me. I was forced into a position where I had to help him. He was forced into a position where he owed me a favour. That's it. That's all.'

'It is?' Pol's voice was openly caustic.

'It is.' The words were brusquely firm and declared that

the discussion was at an end. She went back to her sewing.

Pol watched her for a quiet moment longer, her kindly face serious. Then she held the slippers up to the light, examining them. 'Well, I'm bloody glad to 'ear it, girl. Bad enough to 'ave Lot moonin' over that good-fer-nothin' bastard, without you startin'.' Her eyes flicked back to Kitty's face, straight and sober. 'Watch 'im, Kit. 'E's nothin' but trouble, an' always will be. An' Lot makes a pretty bad enemy –'

Kitty stood up, shook out the dress, held it to her, inspecting her reflection critically in a broken slither of fly-specked mirror that was propped upon a shelf. 'Lot can have him,' she said firmly. 'And welcome to both of them. You can tell her that from me.' She turned, the skirt of the dress flaring about her legs. 'I've got other fish to fry, Pol. I'm going to sing. I'm going to sing on the stage of the New Cambridge Music Hall. I'm going to convince Mr Patrick Kenny that I'm the best thing that's come his way in many a long year. I'm going to get out of this rat-hole, Pol, and I'm never coming back!'

Pol was watching her affectionately, half-smiling. 'Yer know? – I almost believe yer.'

Kitty turned back to the mirror, holding the dress. 'Believe me,' she said, flatly.

To Kitty's delight Pol – to whom, in Pol's own words, Midge 'owed a few favours' – got the evening off to be with her on her first night at the Queen's Music Hall in Enfield, North London, an establishment that had grown, as had many such, from a public house famous for its 'Saturday night sing-songs' to be a fully fledged theatre, albeit still with a bar.

'Thought yer might like someone to 'old yer 'and an' cheer yer on a bit,' Pol said, obviously gratified at Kitty's pleasure, 'an' I can give yer an 'and ter get ready, if yer'd like?'

'I'd love it.' She hesitated. 'You're sure Lottie won't mind?'

'If she does, that's 'er problem.'

'I'm sorry. I just don't want to cause trouble between you.'

'You don't. She does,' Pol said, succinctly. 'She don't own me, no more than you do. I go me own way.'

Kitty grinned. 'I've noticed.'

'So – 'ow yer feelin' about it all?'

'Terrified.'

Pol laughed. 'What yer goin' ter sing?'

'I thought – the flower girl's song' – Kitty hummed the first few notes of the popular tune *Won't You Buy My Pretty Flowers* – 'then *The Soldier's Tear* – that always goes down well, God knows why, and then – providing they haven't booed me off the stage by then – I thought something from *The Bohemian Girl*.'

'Sounds good.'

Kitty took a quick, suddenly nervous breath. 'Oh, Pol! Supposing I can't do it! Supposing –'

'S'posin' nothin',' the other girl interrupted firmly, 'You'll knock 'em dead. You'll see. Now' – she stood up – 'get yerself a good night's sleep. I'll see yer termorrer.' At the door she stopped. 'You all squared with Moses? It ain't like 'im ter lose 'is star turn without kickin'.'

Kitty grimaced. 'He's kicking.'

Pol raised questioning brows.

'He's docking me half my wages.'

'Bloody 'ell,' Pol said, sombrely, ''ow d'yer ever break free?'

'If I ever find out, I'll let you know.' Kitty's face was grim. 'And that's a promise.'

She suffered the next day the worst bout of nerves that she had ever envisaged, let alone endured. The first sight of the theatre – two or three times the size of the Supper Rooms, with a balcony and boxes that glittered with gilt and sparkled with tall mirrors, a large stage that projected into the audience who sat at small, candlelit tables, and an orchestra pit that looked to her to be the size of another stage in itself, all but frightened the life from her. It was all an awful mistake. She couldn't – she couldn't! – do it. She'd never

sung with an orchestra – she didn't know how – no one
would hear her – she'd forget her words –

The afternoon rehearsal was a scrappy, mediocre affair,
neither a true disaster nor any great success. The orchestra
leader was a pompous little man with thin, greased hair and
pockmarked skin. He was not, he made it clear from the
start, about to be ordered about by any chit of a female from
Stepney.

'Please – I wondered – just there – wouldn't it be better
with just the piano – ?'

'Nonsense, Miss Daniels. Allow me to know my business.
The whole orchestra, if you please.'

'Well, if you think so?'

'Seems ter me yer'd better start standin' up fer yerself,'
Pol said, gently. 'You're doin' the singin' after all.'

'Oh, Pol, how can I? I'm a nobody! Next but one from the
bottom of the bill! I'm supposed to do as I'm told and be
grateful for it! Oh, Pol – perhaps I never should have tried.
Oh, I could kill Luke Peveral for getting me into this!' she
added, with sudden and violent illogic. 'It's going to be
awful! I know it is!' She had been given a tiny corner of a
squalidly untidy shared dressing room, her little patch no
more than a rickety chair, a stained and chipped shelf and
a mirror. She stared now into the damp-marked glass, oblivious of the cheerful bustle around her as a group of Italian
acrobats, chattering at the tops of their voices, limbered up
in the restricted space and helped each other with their
make-up and their gay, spangled costumes. Beyond the reflection of her own white face she could see their kaleidoscopic movement, and beyond them another splash of bright
colour in the peasant costumes of the dancing Bartlett sisters
who wrangled between themselves, as they had been
wrangling all afternoon, their sharp unpleasant voices
scraping nerves already raw.

'Don't talk so bloody daft.' Pol leaned towards her, re-
adjusted a dark ringlet that had just been taken from its rag
and showed every sign of wanting to revert to its natural,
rain-straight habit. From the direction of the stage came a

sudden burst of laughter and a roar of applause. 'I'll never ferget that first night at Smith's – yer did it then, yer can do it again –'

Kitty tried to smile with frozen lips. God in Heaven, if she were always to suffer this agony of apprehension before she stepped upon a stage, was it worth it? Why didn't she give up now?

And do what? a small, drily practical voice that was all that was left of her composure asked sharply. What is there for you if you fail? Whoring? Thieving? Dying, diseased and destitute in a Whitechapel alleyway?

'Corelli brothers. You're on.'

'I'm next,' she said, around the lump in her throat. 'I think I'd better go to the lavatory again.'

Ten minutes later she stood alone in the wings watching the handsome acrobats with their broad, muscled shoulders, their shining black hair, splendid moustaches and bright, gleaming smiles as they took the plaudits of the audience, bowing gracefully, princes of the moment. They ran lightly past her, laughing and chattering, their dark skins agleam with perspiration.

The applause died to an expectant, murmuring quiet.

From where she stood she could see a segment of the audience – lifted, smiling faces, candlelight glimmering in bright eyes. She stood straight and still, awaiting her introduction. The thundering of her heart quieted. Her trembling stopped. Excitement lifted. From one moment to another her raw nerves calmed, her confidence blossomed and there was nothing – nothing! – that she wanted so much as to step out onto the brightly lit stage with its crudely painted backdrop and cheap draped curtains.

'– and so, ladies and gentlemen – for the very first time at the Queen's Music Hall –'

She lifted her head, clasped her hands lightly before her.

'– give you the Songbird of Stepney –'

She stepped into the light.

'Miss – Kitty – Daniels!'

The applause was enthusiastic, but only politely so. She

walked confidently onto the apron of the stage, smiled brilliantly at the Master of Ceremonies, then at the orchestra
leader, and then, with a lift of pure happiness, at her audience.
She felt their reaction, felt the warmth they offered in return
for that smile. And as she stood calmly awaiting the first
notes of the orchestra she knew with utter certainty that she
had found the place in which she belonged, the way of life she
wanted above all others. In that moment of brilliant clarity it
seemed to her that here was her home, her natural environment; and all she had to do to claim it was to sing.

   She gave the performance of her young lifetime. She sang
with a joy and verve that infected her audience and had them
banging the tables for more. She caught sight of Pol, in the
wings, shouting and clapping with the rest, her face alight
with generous happiness. It was over too soon, too desperately soon; she could have stood upon that stage and sung all
night. She took a curtain call, and then another. The Master
of Ceremonies beamed at her, made a small circle with thumb
and forefinger to indicate his approval. On a crest of excitement she left the stage at last, knowing she had succeeded,
knowing that the last of her doubts were gone, knowing above
all that away from the repressive and violent atmosphere of
Smith's she had lost her fear of her audience.

   'Bleedin' marvellous! Bloody, bleedin' marvellous!' Pol
threw her arms about her and smacked a kiss on her cheek.
'What did I tell yer? Blimey, girl, you did a job an' an 'alf
there! I'm proud of yer!'

   Kitty allowed herself to be ushered to the empty dressing
room, sat a little unsteadily upon the rickety chair. Her ears
were still ringing with the echoes of applause. She looked
at Pol. 'Did I really go down as well as it seemed?'

   Pol laughed. 'Well, I told yer – it was bloody marvellous!
No 'oldin' yer now, eh?'

   Kitty smiled. Her heartbeat was slowing, the pitch of her
excitement dying. A man's baritone, rich and strong, echoed
from the stage. She envied the unknown singer. She wanted
to be out there again, beneath the lights, and bathing in the
rapt attention of the audience.

Half an hour later she took the stage again, with the rest of the company, for the finale. As one by one the performers stepped forward to take their bows she found to her horror that she was listening jealously to the volume accorded each artist. To her delight she received not only prolonged and appreciative applause, but a small nosegay of flowers presented with a gallant flourish by the smiling Master of Ceremonies. The curtain came down once, swept up, and down once more and it was over. The artists left the stage, talking amongst themselves. No one spoke to Kitty, though she was the recipient of one or two curious glances.

'Miss Daniels –'

She turned to find the Master of Ceremonies bearing down on her. 'Well done, Miss Daniels, wonderfully done!'

'Thank you.'

She stood and spoke with him for a few minutes. In the hall beyond the curtain someone had started playing the piano and the audience was singing.

'– the contract will certainly be extended. And perhaps, next week, when Ventro the ventriloquist leaves us we could give you another spot – an extra song or two –?'

'That would be lovely. Thank you.' She left him. The Corelli brothers swept by her, volatile tempers up, arguing volubly, seeming on the point of blows. Pol was nowhere to be seen. Kitty went into the dressing room to pack up her few belongings. The Bartlett sisters were sprawled upon every chair, half-naked, their discarded costumes strewn all over the room. One of them leaned to the gaslit mirror, wiping her painted face dispiritedly with a piece of dirty flannel. Upon a shelf stood an open, half-empty bottle of gin.

'Wan' a tot, ducks?' A woman past the prime of youth, her doll-like face painted on over a skin crazed with wrinkles, her fiery hair darkly grey at the roots, waved a chipped mug a little uncertainly at Kitty. She was naked beneath a soiled robe that had fallen open as she moved and which she made no move to fasten.

Kitty, picking her way through the room, shook her head. 'No. Thank you.'

The woman arched sardonic, please-yourself brows, poured herself a hefty drink and passed the bottle on. Another, younger girl walked across the room to proffer her own mug, her bare breasts swinging heavily as she moved. As she passed Kitty she flicked dismissively at the small bunch of flowers that she still held. ''Ad a better offer, 'ave we ducky?' Neither the voice nor the gesture were particularly friendly.

Kitty shook her head.

The other girl laughed, unpleasantly knowing.

Before Kitty could respond the door opened and a spotty-faced boy put his head round the door. 'Miss Daniels? Some cove ter see yer –'

'What's 'e like, Spotty? Look a good performer, does 'e? Could 'e manage two of us, d'yer think?'

''Ere, Spot, lad, come an' 'ave a taste –' One of the girls bared a large breast and manipulated the nipple with her fingers, making lascivious kissing sounds as she did so. The others roared with laughter as the lad's fine, marked skin burned to his ears.

'Never mind 'er, Spotty, take a look at mine –'

''E don't like tits, do yer, Spot? 'E's an arse man. I can spot 'em a mile off! 'Ere, Spot – what'd yer like ter do with this –?'

Kitty fled.

Spotty banged the door behind him. 'Bleedin' whores.'

'You said –?'

'Over there.' He waved a hand and left her.

From the dressing room came a gust of drunken laughter. In the shadows a tall figure moved, stepped forward. 'Congratulations.'

An infinitesimal silence. Then, 'Thank you,' she said.

Luke Peveral wore an impeccably cut black tail coat and trousers, black satin waistcoat, snow-white ruffled shirt. He carried a cane, top hat and gloves.

She eyed him dourly, determinedly unimpressed. 'Are you looking for Cinderella?'

He grinned. 'That altogether depends on what the time

is. If it's too close to midnight then any old ugly sister will do.'

She had to laugh. The excitement of the evening was still singing in her blood like wine. In an odd way Luke's being here did not surprise her, nor did his changed appearance. Violence and death suddenly belonged to another world.

'You got the flowers?' he asked.

'They were from you?'

A smile flickered. 'You've got Johnnies queuing up already?'

She shook her head. Looked round.

'I took the liberty,' he said, 'of treating the dragon Pol to a cab home.'

'And she went? Didn't you have to rope and tie her?'

'I used a little persuasion.'

She looked a sharp question.

He lifted a shoulder. 'I told her it was none of her damned business if you had arranged to come to dinner with me without consulting her,' he said, imperturbably.

'You – what?'

'You heard. Shall we go?'

'Supposing I say no?'

'Then you'd be a fool. You'd also miss one of the best dinners London has to offer. It isn't every day you'll find yourself invited to Whistler's, my girl.'

'What's Whistler's?'

He shook his head, tutting mockingly. 'Such ignorance! Such shocking ignorance! The only way you get to find out is to come. I'll show you.'

Whistler's was a restaurant. It was more than a restaurant – it was the night-time haunt of the rich and the famous and of those who liked to rub shoulders with riches and with fame. On seeing the discreetly elegant façade of the place, with its gleaming, gaslit windows, its brass polished to gold and its uniformed lackey waiting impassively to hand her from the hired hackney, Kitty shrank back, genuinely terrified. 'I can't go in there!'

'Of course you can. Don't be such a baby.' Casually Luke gestured as the cab door opened and the poker-faced doorman held out a white-gloved hand. 'After you.'

Silently she stepped onto the pavement. As he joined her and took her arm she hissed at him through clenched teeth, 'Luke!' He took no notice. With a bland smile and a hand firmly upon her elbow he steered her through the door and into the elegant and crowded interior.

At the top of a shallow flight of steps they were met by a splendid personage, smooth-haired, smooth-faced and dressed every bit as fastidiously and expensively as Luke himself. 'Ah – M'sieu Peveral! So nice to see you again, M'sieu! Your table waits –' Shrewd eyes flicked to Kitty, summed her up and found her wanting. 'Ma'mselle.' His bow was brief and chilly.

She nodded and, head high, followed Luke between the crowded tables, astonished at the number of people who lifted a hand or called a greeting to him. She was painfully aware of the scuffed velvet of her gown and of the cheap brilliance of her gaudy stage jewellery. But when they reached the table and Luke, turning to her with a warm smile, brushed aside the supercilious mannikin's half-hearted attempt to settle her in her seat and solicitously saw himself to her comfort, her selfconscious unease vanished like a mist in sunshine. She was Kitty Daniels; the new Kitty Daniels. Today she had stood upon a stage and held a thousand people in the palm of her hand. She did not need diamonds. She glanced up at Luke and caught a look of amused appreciation in his eyes.

'Something to drink, m'sieu?'

'Of course. Champagne,' Luke said.

'Of course.' The disapproving maître d' handed a large leather folder to Luke and managed to deposit one in Kitty's hands with the air of a man knowingly casting pearls before swine.

She opened it. Sat frozen, with all her facile self-confidence oozing from her. She lifted panic-stricken eyes to Luke over the huge, elegantly decorated, floridly handwritten, indecipherable menu. With easy charm Luke reached across the table. 'You've done quite enough hard work for today. I insist that you do no more. You'll allow me?'

She let the menu slip from her fingers. 'As long as you don't intend to drink my champagne for me as well,' she managed, half-heartedly, and was rewarded with a quick smile. As he spoke rapidly to the maître d', the old Kitty stood suddenly by her shoulder, scolding, aghast – what in Heaven's name was she doing in a place like this with a man she did not like – a thief, a killer and God knew what else besides –

She watched him pour the golden, frothing champagne into two tall glasses.

A man she did not like?

He too was watching the sparkling stream, face intent, hand steady.

A thief, and a killer.

Somewhere the mocking shade of Amos chuckled, and warned caution.

Too late.

She drank much too much champagne. The food was the most delicious she had ever tasted, the atmosphere heady, the high-strung excitement of the day had already wreaked havoc with her usual good sense, and the undoubted danger that lurked across the table, smiling and patient, added a zest to the evening that urged her to recklessness. The excitement of her small triumph at the music hall had not died – it bubbled through the occasion as did the bright sparkle of the champagne that she found herself drinking as if it were lemonade. And why not? she found herself asking – it sharpened her tongue and her wits, drowned the embarrassment of shoddy velvet and shoddier paste. Drowned too that tiresome warning voice to which she was tired of listening. With what more appropriate beverage could she celebrate the birth of the new Kitty Daniels?

Luke ordered more champagne.

Around them handsome men and elegant women conversed, flirted, laughed and argued. Kitty tried not to stare. The glittering gowns, the fire of gemstones dazzled her. Jewelled hair and jewelled bosoms, jewelled wrists and jewelled fingers – she glanced at Luke. With unerring instinct he leaned across the table, picked up the posy of flowers and held them to her cheek. 'Better than diamonds,' he said, and for once he was not smiling.

She saw a lovely, well-dressed woman at the table next to them glance across, her eyes wide and interested on Luke's face.

Kitty tried not to wonder if Luke had ever brought Lottie here – Lottie who would stand out, a beauty in any company.

'You sang the wrong songs tonight,' he said, pleasantly and musingly.

She could not have been more surprised had he dashed cold water in her face. 'I – beg your pardon?'

'I said you're singing the wrong songs. Your voice is too good – too strong – for those wishy-washy parlour songs. You need something of your own – something with a bit more character –'

Quick irritation flared, fuelled by champagne. 'I see. My performance lacks character?'

'Did I say that?'

'It sounded like it.'

He did not give an inch. 'If that's what you want to hear.'

'What do you mean?'

He shook his head. 'Let's change the subject.'

'Not until you tell me what you mean.'

'I think that had better wait till you're in a more receptive mood. I don't fancy being brained by a champagne bottle, thank you. Especially not when I've paid Gaston's exorbitant prices for it. For the moment let's leave it that you're obviously the best thing that's happened to that fleapit for years, and I shall be very surprised if friend Kenny doesn't know it by tomorrow. I should shut your mouth, if I were you,' he added mildly. 'There's a cab coming.'

'You – you liked me?'

He sighed. 'You prickly idiot! Of course I did! How could I not? Would we be here if I didn't?'

'That rather depends on what we're here for,' she snapped without thought, and regretted it the moment the words were out.

His expression was solemn, his eyes pure malicious mischief. 'I don't think I understand what you mean?'

She flushed. 'Well – I mean –' All at once she found herself questioning whether champagne were quite the wit-sharpener she had felt it to be.

'You mean,' he asked gently, 'that my intentions might not be strictly honourable?'

She struggled with good manners. 'Yes,' she said.

'You're right. They aren't. Not in the least.' His eyes were wary.

An orchestra, hidden in a verdant jungle of palms and aspidistras, had started to play. She watched them for a long moment, as if they were the most totally absorbing sight in the world. Then she brought her dark eyes to meet his.

He nodded, regretfully. 'I'm afraid so. I'm just the bastard you thought I was.'

For perhaps the first time in her life she was utterly dumbstruck.

He waited, politely, for the space of a few moments. 'Aren't you going to say something? Throw something? Walk out?'

She shook her head.

'Well,' he said lightly. 'Am I supposed to know if that's a good thing or a bad?' His face was intent, the narrow black eyes disturbingly steady.

She hunched her shoulders a little, and looked down into the glass that she was holding as fiercely as if it were an anchor in a suddenly storm-blown world. Furious with herself, she tried to control the sudden lunatic hammering of her heart, the savage rise of excitement that, surely he must see, must sense thundering through her body.

The silence stretched on.

'Kitty?' His voice was soft. She recognized that persuasively caressing tone; Luke Peveral was an accomplished expert in a field in which Amos Isherwood had been a raw novice. 'Aren't you going to say anything?'

In desperation she wished she had not drunk so much champagne. That there were not so much noise ringing about them. That she did not so much – so very much – want to be alone with him. To touch him. To have him love her. She shivered at the thought, confused, afraid and aching with need for him. 'The other night –' She found herself speaking the thought aloud, and stopped.

His face closed. 'Yes?'

She lifted her eyes to his face. 'You killed a man,' she whispered, and the sound, all but lost in the noise about them, echoed in her head like a clap of thunder, accusing and unforgivable.

She saw the fractional hardening of his mouth. 'If I hadn't, he would have killed me.' His voice was still, even and pleasant. He might have been discussing the food they had just eaten.

'I – yes, I know –'

'So. What would you have had me do?'

She sucked her lip, biting it hard, staring at him, wondering how in God's name the conversation had taken this dangerous turn, unable in her confusion to sort the right words from those that tumbled in her brain and so, damningly, saying nothing.

He shook his head, laughed shortly and entirely mirthlessly. 'If it's dead heroes you're after, Songbird, you're in the wrong shop. So, that's that. Serves me right, I daresay. Just one small thing. Has it occurred to you that it would have been more than me they killed? You think they'd have patted your pretty little head and sent you home?'

'No.'

Luke lifted his hand and clicked his fingers sharply to a hovering waiter. 'My bill, please.'

'Luke –' she said, miserably.

He turned a cold, waiting face.

'Oh, God!' she said, looking back down at her clasped hands, very close to tears, her face sombre, all the joy of the day leeched from it. 'I don't know. I don't know anything.'

In the silence the chatter and the sound of music rose and fell like the tide of an invasive sea.

'I'll take you home,' he said.

Numbly she followed him, clambered into the hackney beside him, held herself rigidly from him as the cab lurched forward. In silence they rode through the darkened streets, slipping in and out of the pools of light and dappled shadows thrown by the street lamps. She sat stiffly, hands clenched in her lap. The happiness and excitement that had so buoyed her had drained from her, leaving her empty and utterly miserable. As the cab rattled smartly around a corner Luke leaned with the movement and his arm brushed hers. She drew back, huddling into the corner. He sensed her recoil and himself shifted slightly, leaning away from her, staring out of the window.

In the secret darkness she watched his profile. In her blood and her bones and in the aching of her body she felt her need for him. The thought of his touch, of the strength of him, left her all but defenceless.

She shrank back further into her corner.

He sat, his head turned from her as in silence he watched the night streets of London pass. She glanced again at that dark, forceful profile, then looked quickly away.

A woman leaned against a lamp post, aged young face limned by the light, half-bared bosom gleaming. She watched the cab pass with an impassive face.

The horse's hoofs clopped eerily upon an empty sweep of cobblestone.

After what seemed a very long time, Luke said, quietly, without turning, 'I'd like you to accept that I'm sorry. That I would never have subjected you to this evening had I realized just how much you hate me.' His voice was absolutely calm, devoid of any expression. 'I'm afraid I must admit to a habit — a regrettable habit — of not seeing, not accepting, those things I don't want to.'

'I don't hate you.' Her voice was a breath, close to tears. 'I don't.'

He shrugged. 'What I am then. It comes to the same thing.'

For perhaps the space of a dozen heartbeats she fought the terrible tangle of her emotions. Then, 'Luke!' she said, desperately, 'I don't hate you! You surely know that!' Faint bitterness threaded the words. What was she doing?

He turned sharply to look at her. She saw the straight line of question drawn between the sardonic brows, saw the lean, hard lines of his gypsy's face, the straight, sharply defined mouth. She looked away from him. He waited, tense and graceful in his corner, like a cat, she thought, waiting to pounce on the stupidly gullible mouse and swallow it whole.

'You're right,' she said, clearly, staring straight ahead into the darkness, 'I do hate what you are. But I don't care. I – don't – care –'

The tension held him still. He watched her narrowly.

She was sitting very straight now. She could not look at him. With an odd, defiantly prideful movement she lifted her head. 'Would you – take me home with you?'

Still he said nothing. Still he watched her, frowning.

Her cheeks burned in the darkness. If revenge for humiliation was what he wanted he had it now. 'It doesn't matter. I thought perhaps –'

He reached a hand to her, cupped her chin and turned her face to him. The warm strength of his hand set her trembling. Tears rose. Angrily she tried to pull away. He held her strongly, hurting her, studying her face in the moving lamplight. She stilled. Watched him. She knew – had known in her heart since the first time she had laid eyes on him – that this was the most exciting man she had ever known, or was ever likely to. It was sheer perversity to deny it. And sheer stupidity to ignore the danger he represented; in that, if in nothing else, Pol was undoubtedly right. The fingers that had held her painfully relaxed. He moved his hand. His flat, hard palm caressed her cheek. There was a moment when she could have pulled back. She did not. She had made her first mistake with Amos in innocence and ignorance; so be it – she would make her second with her eyes wide open. Thief, killer, heartbreaker – she would not, could not now, let him go. She turned her face, pressed her lips gently to his open palm. For what seemed a very long time they sat so, the simple gesture an end and a beginning with no words spoken, the contact a point of fire and of promise between them. When he kissed her it was as she had known it would be – feared it would be – from the first time she had seen him. The touch of his mouth vanquished her; she was as much his as if they had already lain together and loved. He lifted his head. In the darkness she could not see his face.

'You're sure,' he said, no real question in his voice.

She traced the lines of his face with her finger. 'I'm sure.'

The porch of the derelict church was dark. Luke took her hand and guided her surely to the secret entrance in the alcove. There he paused to light a candle and they climbed together the narrow winding stairs. At the top he unlocked the little wooden door and stepped into the room ahead of her. Heart thumping, she followed. The candlelight flickered about the lovely, tranquil room. The embers of a fire glowed in the hearth. Moonlight filtered through the great, jewel-coloured window. Nothing of the carnage or the wreckage of violence that she remembered remained. She stood still for a moment, looking round, outfacing horror.

He watched her.

She took a slightly shaky breath.

Very carefully he put the candle upon a small table. Shadows leapt.

'Would you like a drink?'

'No. Yes. Just a small one –'

She saw his smile. He splashed golden liquid from a heavy glass decanter into two glasses. 'Come and sit near the fire.'

She took off her gloves, folded her shawl, perched on the edge of the armchair nearest the fire. Taking the glass from him she touched it to her lips. Caught her breath. Midge had poured this down her the day of the horror. Anne had choked upon it on another day of misery. She put the glass down abruptly.

'What is it?'

'I don't like brandy. I'm sorry.'

'Would you prefer something else?'

'No. Thank you.'

He put his own glass down and came to her, stood before her, his hands held to her. She took them. He pulled her to her feet, her body against his. She closed her eyes. His hands were in her hair. She felt the relief as the heavy coils, unpinned, fell about her face and shoulders. She lifted her face to him.

They came together in a sudden violence that was as much like the rage of birth, or battle or sudden death as love. He took her, and she abandoned herself to him and to the fierce pleasure and exquisite pain that his body inflicted upon hers. He watched her, afterwards, by the light of the fire, leaning on one elbow, brushing the long, damp strands of hair from her face. His skin was slick with sweat. 'I was rough. I think I hurt you. I'm sorry.'

She shook her head, smiling.

He leaned and kissed her, gently; her parted lips, her nipples, her belly.

'You – weren't disappointed?' she asked.

He nipped her with sharp teeth. She jumped. 'Terribly,' he said. 'Try a bit harder next time –'

They made love again, more tenderly and with less fierce urgency, watching each other, touching and whispering and gently pleasuring. Afterwards they lay sprawled upon the bed, arms and legs and hair entangled, the dying firelight gleaming upon sweat-smooth skin. She dozed, and awoke to find him leaning above her, watching her. As her eyes opened he kissed her, a long, tender, almost passionless kiss that drove the treacherous blade of love deeper into her heart than all their lovemaking had done. He tangled his hand in her hair, sprawled beside her.

She slept.

It was morning when she woke, a spring morning of sunshine that filtered through the stained glass of the great window and dappled the room with colour. She watched Luke as he slept, his bandit's face closed and dark and sharply beautiful, black hair tousled upon the pillow, the skin of his body swarthy against the bleached sheets, a man who had loved her; a man she knew not at all. Across his shoulders – something she had sensed with her fingers last night in the darkness – ran a brutal pattern of silvered, long-healed scars, the marks of a merciless beating and the explanation, perhaps, of his unexpected clemency to Matt. Once, she knew, such a sign of violence and pain would have revolted her.

She watched him for a very long time. Watched the rise of his breath, the flicker of the thick lashes. Watched the long hands that rested, relaxed upon the fur coverlet. Hands that could thieve without conscience, kill without pity. Hands that had explored her body and roused her to a savagery that she blushed now to remember.

His eyes flicked open, and she saw instant, total awareness. 'Good morning.'

'Good morning.' She kissed him.

He lifted a hand to her face, touched her cheek gently, then, a hand in her hair, pulled her, less gently, down on top of him.

(iii)

They could not, did not indeed, attempt to keep their new relationship from the world. Often Kitty would find Luke waiting for her in the cab that brougt her home from the music hall. Sometimes they would go to her room, more frequently to his. Their lovemaking did not lose its fire; the meeting of their minds was a little more wary. Both of them were as aware of the things that held them inexorably apart as they were of those that drew them together. But for now the day was enough. Frequently they would go to Smith's for supper, where sometimes Kitty would allow herself to be persuaded to sing. It was never suggested by either of them that more permanent living arrangements should be made. Indeed Kitty found herself positively shying away from the thought; as her popularity grew and her hopes bloomed brighter, she had other things to think of than the doubtful permanence of any relationship with a man like Luke Peveral. The sight of him, the touch of his hand, fired her as nothing had ever done before, and in her new wisdom, that for the moment was enough. Tomorrow must take care of itself.

The world on the whole was not enchanted by the arrangement. Pol was openly disgusted that Kitty − as Pol saw it − had fallen after all for the flawed charms that had been the downfall of so many others. Spider, who since she had risked her own skin to warn his beloved 'Guv'nor' had begun to show some small warmth towards her, cooled off considerably and regarded her with new suspicion; anyone, Kitty guessed, who might in any way prove a weakness in Luke would be anathema to Spider. Matt too was overtaken by a surprising and, to Kitty, positively comical attack of brotherly concern and questioned this relationship with a man whose way of life was, he pointed out, even more unorthodox than his own.

She was torn between laughter and exasperation. 'You can talk! Matt Daniels, if you aren't the greatest hypocrite under the sun! You go your way, you said, and I'll go mine! Well, I've done it − and it's none of your damned business!'

He had the grace to look faintly abashed. 'Still, Kit − I mean, you know how I feel about the Guv'nor, it isn't that − but −'

'But nothing. I know what I'm doing,' she said with no regard for the truth at all, 'so let's change the subject.'

Lottie's reaction was predictable, yet in her own way the girl retained her dignity which Kitty could not help but admire. There were, oddly, no tempers and no tantrums. She simply acted, so far as it was possible, as if neither Luke nor Kitty existed. Luke she could not entirely ignore, for whatever else he was to her he was still one of Moses' best customers and as such entitled to service. Kitty she could, and did, which distressed Kitty not at all. After a while, against common sense, she even managed to convince herself that Lottie bore her no real grudge beyond the damage done to her pride, though sometimes she caught a look in the other girl's eyes that belied that comfortable conclusion, a disturbing flash of bitterness that would gleam and be gone in a second. Yet to all outward appearances the girl had little to be bitter about, for if she had lost Luke's precarious favours she looked to be in the process of gaining a protector of – in her world – even more prestige and power, albeit with less physical charm.

For her single-minded pursuit of Moses Smith was showing surprising signs of success. With Kitty away she was once more entrenched as the Song and Supper Rooms' only female entertainer. The songs she sang so sweetly she now sang for Moses, the forget-me-not eyes turned to him as if he were the only man in the world. His every wish she would anticipate, his most salacious and public fondling she would accept with the docility of a beautiful doll. He had only to snap his fingers for her to be by his side. Whether the fat man was truly taken in by this sudden upsurge of apparent devotion Kitty doubted, but like most men he was willing to be flattered by the slavish attentions of a lovely woman, whatever her motive; and, she suspected, the fact that Lottie had for so long been Luke Peveral's woman, far from detracting from her charms in Moses' eyes, actually enhanced them.

And so, slowly, as the weeks passed and summer crept, sluggishly hot and sticky, into the yards and alleys of the East End, it became accepted that Lottie was Moses' private property and Moses himself did nothing to discourage the idea. Kitty, however, was not the only one to be surprised when, in June, with rumours and fears of cholera creeping about the sweltering streets, Lottie left the room she shared with Pol and joined Moses in his spacious apartment over a warehouse in Wapping. The general feeling amongst the girls at the Rooms was that their Lottie had done bloody well for herself, and good luck to her. Only Pol was depressed.

'Nothin' good'll come o' this. You mark my words.'

'How can she stand it, I wonder?' Kitty did not voice the words, After Luke.

Pol shrugged. 'Money in 'er pocket. Frills an' furbelows. Three square meals a day. Somethin' ter be said fer it, I s'pose.'

'But – Moses! Of all people! He's – he's so cruel!'

Pol lifted a single brow, her gaze direct. 'Aren't they all?'

'Not like that.'

'Different 'orses run different courses, Kit. It's easy fer you – you've got what Lottie wants.' The words were spoken with neither rancour nor accusation but nevertheless Kitty found herself flushing. 'Don't blame the girl fer makin' the best of what's left.'

'I didn't mean –'

Pol patted her hand. 'O' course you didn't. I know it. Lot doesn't. Best thing fer you ter do is keep mum an' stay out of 'er way. She pretty well 'ates you. She don't want your pity nor yet your opinion on what she's doin'. I 'ates ter say it, but if I was you I'd watch me back fer a good long time yet.'

Kitty laughed, a little uncertainly. 'Oh, come on – that's a bit steep – surely she can't carry a grudge for ever –?'

Not long after that conversation such reasoning was apparently confirmed as an obvious but nevertheless surprising reason for Lottie's move revealed itself. She was pregnant and, amazingly, Moses was to allow her to keep the baby, even proudly claiming paternity. A man should have a son, he said, beaming at Luke, his eyes a shade malicious.

The thought of Moses Smith as a proud father turned Kitty's stomach more than a little. But within days of the news her own life had again changed dramatically and she had little time to dwell either on Pol's warning or on Lottie's changed fortunes.

6

Kitty's birthday -- that had passed all but unmarked the year before – was in this year of 1865 a much more significant event, made so in the main by Luke's characteristically idiosyncratic birthday present.

Matt it was who brought the message to her that Luke – and her present – awaited her at the Song and Supper Rooms, and who waited, as agog with curiosity as was Kitty herself, to escort her there at the extremely odd hour of two in the afternoon. Matt, no matter how she badgered him, would say nothing of what was going on at the Rooms. It was a fine warm day that, in the countryside, or in the wider avenues and green parks of more fashionable London, would have been a delight. Here, however, no breath of air stirred the suffocatingly close atmosphere and the heat pressed down on the shabby houses and dirty streets with the force of a furnace. Bluebottles buzzed, heavily and repulsively, everywhere about the streets and gutters, spawning their filth, carriers of disease and death as were the rats that scurried in sewer and cellar and the stinking, undrinkable water that as always was taking its summer toll of life. The misery of cholera, this year as every year, stalked London's streets – this time an epidemic even worse than usual, that struck young and old with brutal impartiality whilst those that lived in comfort and comparative safety spoke of the Hand of God, and the sweet water supply that would have saved so many from an unspeakably filthy death was much discussed but still not forthcoming. Kitty pressed her handkerchief to her nose and drew her skirts about her ankles. A small, undernourished child watched her with

lacklustre eyes, not bothering to brush away the flies that
crawled upon his dirty, bloodless-looking skin. A little way
along the street more flies buzzed in a cloud about a costermonger's fish cart. Even through her handkerchief Kitty
could smell the stomach-turning stench that hung in the
air about the barrow. On the corner of Blind Lane an Italian
ice-man dispensed ha'penny ices from his barrow to a
scrabble of eager urchins. A sweep, black and sweating and
reeking of his trade, stood beside the barrow in conversation
with the ice-man, gleaming teeth and scarlet tongue bright
against the soot-ingrained darkness of his face.

The interior of Smith's seemed even darker than usual
after the brilliance of light outside, and the atmosphere
was heavy with last night's smoke and ale fumes. The
distinctive, unpleasant smell hit Kitty as she stood at the
top of the steps waiting for her eyes to adjust to the dim
light. In a moment she saw Luke: he was leaning against
the piano, at which sat a small, dapper man she had never
seen before. Spider lurked, as always, in the shadows behind
him, and Midge and Pol sat at a table, a bottle between
them. The place was otherwise empty.

Luke lifted his head and saw her. She watched him as he
came towards her, moving with that singular grace that was
so much a part of his attraction. Reaching her, he took her
hand and kissed her lightly on the cheek. 'Happy birthday.'

'Thank you.' The sight of him, the touch of his hand,
lifted her heart and quickened her pulse.

'Come. There's someone I want you to meet.' He led her
by the hand to the stage where stood the small, sprightly
looking man who had been seated at the piano. He had
shrewd eyes and a crooked-toothed smile. 'Barton Wesley,'
Luke said. 'Barton – here she is – Kitty Daniels.'

'How do?' They shook hands. Wesley beamed. Bemusedly,
Kitty smiled back.

'Barton,' Luke said, 'is – in a manner of speaking – part of
your birthday present.'

Kitty's smile became even more puzzled. 'He is?'

He grinned at her. 'Sit here and listen. And don't say a

word until you're spoken to!' He perched her upon the edge of the stage and sat beside her. Barton Wesley sat down at the piano, flexed his fingers a little theatrically and began to play, and then to sing, his accent an atrocious stage Cockney, his delivery abominable.

'Me muvver was a lady, Me farver was a sport –' He paused. The piano trilled.

At least – Kitty thought – he can play the piano, even if he can't sing –

'I was drug up not far from 'ere, In Jago's grimy courts –' the reference to this most notorious area of Shoreditch was accompanied by dramatically rolled eyes.

Kitty glanced at Luke in half-exasperated question. He put a long finger to his lips and directed her attention back to the stage.

'I found I 'ad a talent, Which 'elps me wiv me bread – it 'elps me cos I 'elps meself, Just like the Good Book said –' Wesley winked, wickedly, the tempo of the piano picked up jauntily. 'I'm Dick, I'm Dick the Dipper, the smartest lad in Town, You've seen me in the 'Dilly, Just walkin' up an' down, You've never felt me fingers as their little game they've played, But when you get back 'ome again, your watch you'll 'ave mislaid –'

'Luke –'

His finger this time was laid on her lips. 'Ssh. Listen.'

Wesley was off again, playing for all he was worth to his small, but appreciative audience. Kitty could not help wondering how he had the gall to sing at all with such a voice.

'I wouldn't say I'm honest, But I wouldn't say I'm bent, Compared to some I knows round 'ere' – he paused, jerked his head knowingly in Luke's direction, winked mischievously at Pol and Midge – 'I am the perfect gent! Some bullies can paint pictures, Some others Shakespeare played, It 'appens I can lift a purse, That's 'ow my fortune's made!' He jumped from the piano stool and strutted across the stage, thumbs hooked in his braces. 'I'm Dick I'm Dick the Dipper –'

'This is my birthday present,' Kitty said.

'Part of it. There's more. Ten guineas worth.'

'You were robbed,' she said, drily. 'What am I supposed to do with it?'

'Wait. I'll show you.'

She subsided, joined in the applause at the end of the little man's performance.

'You want the other one now, squire?' he called to Luke.

'In a minute.' Luke stood, pulled Kitty to her feet. 'I've something to show Kitty first.' And with a firm hand on her elbow he guided her towards the draped door beside the stage.

Midge said something inaudible. Pol shouted with laughter. Kitty disengaged her arm. 'Oh, no you don't. It's my birthday, Luke Peveral, not yours!'

He laughed, propelled her forwards again. 'You've got a dirty mind, girl. I'm surprised at you.'

'It must be something to do with the company I've been keeping,' she said and once again, determinedly, shook her arm free.

He stopped. Turned. Eyed her pensively. 'You walk,' he said, 'or I carry you, birthday or no birthday. Which?'

She lifted her narrow shoulders. 'Fair enough. I walk.' She preceded him through the door.

At the top of the stairs he opened a door and ushered her into an empty room. The windows were shut and it was hot as an oven, yet smelled strangely and unpleasantly damp. She wrinkled her nose. The furnishings were basic – a narrow bed, a washstand upon which stood a badly cracked bowl and a chipped enamel jug and a wardrobe with a large mirror which she noticed was strategically placed opposite the bed. The carpet was threadbare. A single, bloated bluebottle buzzed against the window, mindlessly seeking escape. Sunlight gleamed through the holes in the dirty lace curtains. On the bed was a heap of old clothes.

'There,' Luke said.

'What? Where?'

He walked to the pile of clothes, picked up the shabby, oversized cap that lay atop them, slapped it on her head at a cheeky angle and turned her to face her reflection in the mirror. 'There.'

'Luke, for Heaven's sake! – What do you think you're up to?'

'Dick the Dipper,' he said, 'wears a cap. And – a pair of trousers' – he pulled from the pile a pair of ragged, much-darned trousers, '– a shirt' – a patched, shabby shirt, '– braces and, of course – a weskit' – a small stained waist-coat flew through the air. Willy-nilly she caught it, her eyes stormy.

'You aren't –' she said slowly, advancing on him, the cap tilted rakishly over one eye, 'for a moment suggesting – that I should – that I should wear these rags?'

'Just that,' he said. 'I'm always telling people you're quicker on the uptake than you look.'

She swiped at him with the waistcoat. He grinned.

'No,' she said.

'Try them.'

'No!' The word was grim.

The smile faded a little. Very seriously he took her hands in his, forcing her to look at him. 'Just give yourself a minute to think about it, Songbird. All right – it may turn out to be a stupid idea – but it may, it just may, work for you. I've bought *The Dipper* for you. Barton has another, just as good – *Monty from Mayfair* – now, just think about Monty – dress suit, top hat, cane –'

She was staring at him. 'But – Luke! I couldn't! It's – well, it's scandalous! Women can't wear men's clothes on stage or off!' She broke off, staring at him.

'Well, now,' he said softly, seeing the growing understanding, the dawning of excitement in her eyes. 'Is that so? So, why shouldn't Kitty Daniels be the first? I've told you – your voice is too strong, too individual for those half-witted parlour ballads you sing. Leave them to Lottie and her like. Pretty girls with pretty voices are ten a penny. If you're going to make it you have to be different.'

Wryly she held up the ragged trousers and surveyed them. 'Oh, I'll be that all right!'

'Kitty – I've seen you in boy's clothes – Do you remember what I said?'

She shook her head. 'I was a bit preoccupied at the time.'

'I said you made a handsomer lad than your brother. And you did. The idea's been nagging at me ever since. Come on – if only for a bit of fun – try it now. Put these things on and come downstairs and give *The Dipper* a go.' He grinned, pulled her lightly to him. 'Don't I deserve at least a bit of a show for my ten guineas?'

She tilted her head to look up at him. Laughed suddenly. 'Why not?' She moved away from him and began to undo the buttons of her bodice.

He watched her for a moment, thoughtfully. 'Seems to me you could do with a little help with that?'

She let her hands drop to her sides, looked at him with provocative solemnity. 'Dear Lord, how very easily distracted you are, Luke Peveral!'

Some considerable time later she stood before the mirror, staring in a kind of apprehensive delight at the long-legged, barefoot urchin who looked cockily back at her. She had stuffed her heavy hair into the cap that was set at a careless angle on the back of her head.

'I'm Dick, I'm Dick the Dipper –' As she had seen Barton Wesley do she hooked her thumbs into her braces and swaggered a little across the room. Then she stopped, flushing self-consciously. 'Luke – I can't! – I just can't be seen like this!'

'Why ever not?' He was sprawled easily upon the bed, his arms tucked comfortably behind his head. 'You look bloody marvellous. Suits you a damn sight better than those silly frills and furbelows –'

'Well, thank you very much.' The words were swiftly caustic.

'Don't be daft. You know what I mean. Look at yourself. It could work. Couldn't it?'

She stepped back to the mirror. Studied her image for a

long silent moment. Lifted her chin. Struck an attitude. Then, 'Yes,' she said quietly. 'Yes, I think it could.'

He swung his long legs from the bed. 'Right. Let's give it a go.'

Spider, Matt, Barton, Midge and Pol were gathered around yet another bottle at a table near the stage. It took a second for Kitty, lagging a few self-conscious steps behind Luke, to realize that now another table was occupied: Moses Smith and Lottie sat together with a group of men, Moses' friends, many of whom Kitty recognized and whose presence now pulled her up sharply, her confidence plummeting. She turned to flee.

'Oh, no you don't!' Without looking at her, Luke caught her wrist in an ungentle grip and towed her forward, raising an unconcerned and friendly hand to Moses and his friends in passing.

'Where yer bin, yer naughty boy?' Midge wagged a knowing finger. 'Took yer long enough, the pair o' yer, didn't it?'

He bent and kissed her. 'Rome wasn't built in a day, Duchess. And Dick the Dipper took some convincing.'

'I'll just bet 'e – she – did.' She grinned, salaciously.

'Still –' Firmly Luke drew Kitty forward from where she had been trying to hide behind him. 'Here he is. Ladies and Gentlemen – may I introduce London's newest sensation – Kit Daniels as Dick the Dipper –'

Kitty stepped into the light. Pol gasped audibly. Matt's eyes widened.

'Bloody 'ell!' said one of Moses' guests, reverently, and 'Jesus!' said another, rather less so.

Kitty, drawn willy-nilly into the public gaze, lifted her chin and stuck her hands in her pockets, striking a cocky pose.

Barton Wesley was on his feet. 'Bloody marvellous! You dog, Luke! She looks bloody marvellous!'

Pol, with an intimacy that bespoke a rapidly formed relationship, slapped his wrist admonishingly. 'Bloody cheek. What language! There's bloody ladies present!'

Barton was already heading for the stage and the piano.

'Come on, ducks – let's give it a try –' He played the simple melody. Kitty hummed it. It was a straightforward tune and the words easily memorized. Already she was beginning to feel more at home in the strange clothes – in fact was finding them surprisingly comfortable after the restrictions of tight bodices and long, hampering skirts. Her bare feet spread themselves firmly upon the dirty boards of the stage. She thought of Matt, of Croucher, of the acrobatic Springer. She thought of the way they moved, of the young pride and arrogance in them. Of the reckless mischief and careless courting of danger. She swaggered to the front of the stage. 'Me mother was a lady –'

She brought the house down. Two of the men at Moses' table leapt to their feet, clapping and howling like banshees. Pol, too, stood, beaming and applauding, and Luke held up a dark hand, thumb triumphantly up. But if anything it was the look on Lottie's face that most attested triumph.

Chilled, Kitty bowed and smiled and accepted enthusiastic congratulation, and wondered just what she had done to earn such hatred.

The manager of Queen's was unimpressed. 'If I'd wanted a street arab on the bill I'd have gone out and got one. There's plenty out there.'

'Just watch her,' Luke said, mildly reasonable. 'Give her a chance. You wouldn't want Mr Kenny to know you'd upset a good friend of his, just for the sake of a few minutes, now would you?'

'That was unforgivable!' Kitty hissed at him later, waiting nervously in the wings as the grumbling pianist, dragged unwillingly from a profitable dice game backstage, thumped ungraciously at the piano, peering bad-temperedly at the music she had given him, and the grim-faced manager settled himself out front in the empty theatre. 'If I'm going to make it I'll do it without blackmailing people, thank you.'

'If you're going to make it,' Luke said, evenly, 'then you're going to have to take every small advantage that you can. If you're going to get to the top, Songbird – and if you aren't aiming for that, you aren't the girl I take you for – you're going to have to learn to fight. With every and any weapon that comes to hand. Right – off you go – you're on.'

'Where are you going?'

He smiled placidly. 'To join our friend out front. Just to make sure he pays attention.'

Kitty never knew how much of the manager's rather suddenly acquired enthusiasm for her new act was genuine reaction to her performance or how much it owed to Luke's smiling, steel-eyed presence beside him. Neither did she care. The outcome was that she got his permission to try it out in public, and that was enough.

Late that afternoon, too excited to keep still, she wandered restlessly about Luke's room, tinkering with ornaments, straightening pictures, plumping cushions. 'He did like it, didn't he? I mean – he didn't have to be that enthusiastic, did he? And the pianist – he isn't easily impressed, I can tell you – he came straight up to me afterwards and said –'

Luke laughed, cutting into the nervous stream of words. 'I know that he said. I was there, remember? And, yes – of course they liked it. Now – Doctor Peveral diagnoses a bad case of nerves, Miss Daniels. Come here and let him deal with it.' He was lying, relaxed, on the bed, watching her, his eyes amused.

She stood fingering an exquisite figurine, looking at it with sightless eyes. 'Barton's had an idea for a new song – a new personality – a highwayman with an eye for the ladies. It'd make a lovely costume, wouldn't it?'

'To say nothing of a lovely fee for Barton.'

She turned quickly. 'Oh, Luke, no! I wouldn't expect you to pay for this one.'

He smiled, lazily. 'You can pay me back when you're rich and famous. But on one condition.'

'What's that?'

Purposefully he patted the bed beside him. 'Like any good businessman I want something on account. Now. Come here.'

She looked at him for a moment, smiling, the tension leaving her. 'Give me a moment.'

A small, dark flicker of something close to anger showed in his face and was gone. As she walked past him to the door of the small water closet he reached to catch her wrist. She stood, looking down at him, waiting. 'That Pol's a bad influence on you,' he said, his voice light, his lashes veiling his eyes.

'I don't think so.'

He said nothing. Neither did he release her.

'Luke,' she said, gently, 'just a little while ago you were telling me I should aim for the top. Success might be a little difficult to achieve, don't you think, with a fatherless child tugging at my apron strings? Be sensible.'

The mischief in his smile did not quite reach his eyes. 'There's no such thing as a fatherless child. Come. I'll show you.' He tugged gently at her wrist. 'It takes two.'

Equally gently but greatly determined, she disentangled herself. 'I shan't be a minute.'

They made love in the jewelled light of the great circular window, the kaleidoscopic shift of colour patterning the bedclothes and the smooth pale skin of their bodies. She lay afterwards with her head on his shoulder, the feathered sweep of her long hair dark upon his chest, a faint furrow of thought between her eyes. 'Talking of Pol –'

'Were we?'

She ran a finger across his chest, along his jaw, round the line of his mouth. 'Well if we weren't we are now. What do you think's going on between her and Barton?'

Luke yawned. 'No idea.'

She dug a long, sharp finger into his ribs. 'Don't be so dense. You must have noticed?'

'Noticed what?'

She drew herself up onto an elbow, absently tickling his jaw with a lock of her own hair. 'That Pol's interested in Barton.'

'Then look out, Barton.'

She pinched him lightly. 'Don't be horrible. Pol's my friend.'

'Is she, now?' He turned his head on the pillow to look directly at her. The lightheartedness had suddenly gone from the conversation, and she could not pretend that she did not know why. She sustained his look, returned it levelly. Her face was sober. The unasked questions hung between them as they had for days – ever since Pol had taken her to one side and explained, flatly and forcefully, what could be achieved with a small piece of sponge doused in vinegar, and what could be the consequences of ignoring such advice. She had not at the time been able to bring herself to pursue Pol's caustic inferences, but they had lain and festered in her mind ever since.

'Luke?' she asked him now, abruptly.

'Mm?'

'The child that Lottie lost last year – just before we came –' The room seemed suddenly very still. 'Was it yours?'

He did not reply for a very long time. She lay in stubborn silence, waiting.

'So she said,' he said at last.

'Did you have reason to doubt it?'

Silence.

'Luke?'

'Oh, for Christ's sake!' His voice was tense. 'How should I know?'

She looked down at him, her face serious. 'Luke. Be fair.'

'All right,' he said, his eyes cool. 'Yes. I think it was mine.'

'And if – if Lottie had carried the child to full term – if it had been the son you so much want – would you have married her? Or at least recognized the child as yours?'

The silence this time was angry.

'Luke?'

'For God's sake! What difference does it make? The child was lost.'

'It made a lot of difference to Lottie.'

'Kitty – none of this is your business.'

'Isn't it? You don't like it that Pol explained to me how to – how to avoid having a child. Do you?'

'It isn't natural.'

She stared at him. He turned from her, eyes half closed in the dappling light.

'You confuse me,' she said at last.

He half-smiled, bitterly at that. 'I confuse myself.'

'You encourage me – help me – to be a success – and yet, what you really want –'

He caught her shoulders. 'Leave it.'

'You're just playing at it really, aren't you? Humouring me.' She had not thought it out before, had not seen the logic that practical Pol had instinctively devined. 'You don't really believe I'll stick it, do you? You're waiting for me to fail – no, to tire of it, perhaps –'

He pulled her roughly to him. 'Shut up. Just shut up.' He stopped her mouth with his. She fought him for a moment, and then, as he mounted her, dark face vivid above her, all doubts and all questions were lost in their loving, and, fatally, she let the moment pass.

(ii)

Ably assisted by the debonair Monty in cunningly cut dress suit, top hat and cane, Dick the Dipper took the Queen's audience by storm. To see a girl dressed as a handsome boy tickled the jaded public palate; that the girl had the talent and personality to carry it off so well enhanced their appreciation, and they showed it. They loved her.

Just two weeks after the Dipper first sauntered onto the Queen's stage Patrick Kenny, accompanied by Luke, paid a visit to the dressing room one night after the performance. Kitty sat alone, removing the dirt stains from her face, her feet and legs still bare beneath Dick's ragged trousers. She had tossed the cap aside and her hair hung down her back, straight as a torrent of rain. She turned as the door opened, scrambled to her feet as she saw the identity of her unexpected visitor. 'Mr Kenny!'

'Sit down, my dear, sit down. Don't let me interrupt you. I came merely to express my congratulations and admiration. A brilliant idea brilliantly executed. And wonderfully suited to that extraordinary voice of yours. Well done. I'm delighted.'

Kitty flushed, pleased. 'It was Luke's idea actually.'

'And a pretty splendid one.' Kenny seated himself astride a rickety-legged chair, folded his arms along its swaying back, rested his chin pensively upon them, watching her speculatively. She returned his gaze as composedly as she was able. Her heart was thumping like a trip hammer.

'The question is,' he said, 'where do you go from here?'

She said nothing. Behind Kenny, Luke winked.

'I could, I suppose, throw you straight to the lions of London and hope for the best,' Kenny said at last, as if talking to himself. 'However – it seems to me to be rather early days for that. I should like to give you just a little more experience first.'

She waited. Luke leaned negligently by the door, watching.

Kenny sat back, reached into an inside pocket and withdrew a long cigar. He offered it first to Luke, who refused it with a smile and a shaken head. The impresario then drew from his pocket a small implement that gleamed soft gold in the lamp light.

Kitty held her patience.

Kenny cut the cigar, made a small ceremony of lighting it, blew the smoke in a fragrant cloud to the ceiling. Only then did his eyes come back to Kitty. 'I have a small company touring the provinces at the moment. A six-week tour, two of which have passed.' He drew on the cigar again. 'The tour can't be said so far to be an unmitigated success. It needs a boost. It also needs a couple of replacement artists, owing to the unfortunate circumstances brought about by the fact that my leading female singer has chosen a most inconvenient moment to elope with the Great Margico's assistant.' His eyes gleamed. 'I do hope they neither of them ever plan to work in the theatre again. It occurs to me that this might be as good an opportunity as any for you to get a little more experience and to try out your new act on a wider and more varied audience. What do you say?' Before she could open her mouth he lifted a quick hand. 'It's understood, of course, that if you make a success of this — if the provincial audiences like you as much as the East End does, then you get a crack at the Cambridge.'

'The Cambridge?' she said.

He smiled. 'Brighton first. You'll go?'

'When do I leave?'

He beamed. 'The end of the week.'

Luke came with her to the splendid new Victoria Station, to see her on her way. He had made no demur, had in fact seemed genuinely pleased at the chance that had come her way. Since their conversation about Lottie and the baby it seemed to her that he had been bending over backwards to convince her that her suspicions were unfounded. Or perhaps, she had found herself wondering once or twice, to convince himself.

Crowds swarmed through the busy booking hall, whistles blew, doors slammed like pistol shots, steam shrieked to the echoing roof: the regular chuntering of the great steam engines as they drew in and out of the long platforms was all but drowned by the sound of the frantic human activity that surrounded them. Silently nervous, Kitty clutched the battered suitcase that an impressed Pol had lent her and looked around.

Luke took her arm. 'Platform Two,' he said. They pushed through the crowds, stopped at the barrier. 'Where's the girl who's supposed to be going with you? The magician's assistant — what's her name?'

Kitty consulted a scrap of paper she carried. 'Miss Fleur Harcourt.'

'Where are you supposed to meet her?'

'On the train. First carriage. Oh, Luke!' With a sudden movement not far removed from panic she flung her arms about his neck. 'I do wish you were coming with me!'

He put her from him gently. 'I can't. You know I can't. But I'll come and see you. I promise. In three weeks' time – in Manchester –'

'Three weeks? Why so long?' The moment the question was out she wished she had not asked it. His face had assumed the expression she most hated, as if a shutter had closed upon it, guarding all thought.

'I've something planned,' he said.

She stepped stiffly back from him. 'Be careful.'

'I'm always careful. Now – Let's find the first carriage, and Miss Harcourt.'

She trailed behind him along the platform. The first carriage was empty.

'She'll miss it if she doesn't hurry.' Luke stowed her suitcase on the rack, turned and took her hands. For a moment the awkwardness of parting held them in silence. 'You've got the address to go to in Brighton?'

She nodded.

A whistle shrilled. 'I'd better go.' He kissed her lightly and stepped from the carriage, swinging the door shut behind him. She leaned at the window and watched the tall lean figure walk down the platform. He would not, she knew, wait for the train to leave. At the barrier he turned, raised his hand and was gone. Nervously Kitty settled herself in her seat. She had admitted to no one, not even Luke, that this was the first train journey she had ever in her life undertaken. Matt's insistence that trains could travel at fifty or sixty miles an hour she had dismissed as his usual extravagant exaggeration. A little distractedly she wondered now just how fast they did go.

On the platform the guard called, blew his whistle. As the train, puffing like a great dragon, began slowly to pull away, the carriage door flew open and a girl with the most unnaturally red hair Kitty had ever seen flung herself into the moving train. She slammed the door behind her, muttered an obscenity of the kind that Kitty had rarely heard from a man's lips, let alone a woman's, threw a string-tied paper parcel onto the rack and then sprawled into a seat glaring at Kitty as if whatever disaster had caused her nearly to miss the train were entirely her fault. Kitty's heart sank. The girl's plain, pale little face was the most bad-tempered she had ever seen.

'Miss – Fleur Harcourt?' she asked, tentatively.

Unpleasantly, the other girl barked with laughter. 'Florrie,' she said.

Kitty extended a hand. 'How do you do? I'm Kitty Daniels.'

'That so?' The red-headed girl completely ignored the outstretched hand, neither did she return any other greeting. She slumped into the corner opposite Kitty and scowled out of the window, where the countryside streamed past at a dizzying rate. 'Bleedin' Brighton,' she said.

The journey passed almost entirely in silence.

Brighton was brisk and breezy and – for the time of year – rather cold. Kitty, with Florrie trailing, grumbling, behind her, obtained directions at the station and set off for the address at which she had been told that digs had already been taken for them. To her surprise she was discovering herself rather to be enjoying the adventure of being out in the world on her own – though she had to admit that she wished the experience might be shared with someone a little less ill-tempered than the sour Miss Harcourt. Her consternation was considerable, therefore, when she discovered upon reaching the address they had been given – a small, unkempt house in a narrow back street some considerable distance from the sea and, they were to discover later, from the theatre – that she and her travelling companion were to share a room.

'But – is there no separate room available?' She surveyed in dismay the tiny, shabby room to which they had been shown.

'It's all there is. Take it or leave it.' The woman who ran the establishment, who had introduced herself brusquely as Mrs Moulder, sniffed. She was extremely fat and her soft, pale skin looked as if it had never seen the open light of day. Her colourless hair straggled from an ill-constructed bun and she smelled of stale sweat and staler cooking. Kitty took a small step back from her. 'One room, they said. Lucky to get it, too, the measly price they pay. Real actors now' – she crossed her muscular arms over her vast bosom and eyed the two girls repressively – 'they're diff'rent. Proper gentlemen we get here when there's something decent on at the Palace.' She looked them up and down. 'Variety, is it?' she asked dismissively.

Kitty admitted that it was. Florrie, who had ignored the entire exchange, flopped gloomily onto one of the narrow, uncomfortable-looking beds.

'Hmmp!' The sharp, disapproving sound left no doubt as to the woman's feelings about Variety. 'Well – I'll have you know we allow no hanky panky here, young women. You make your own beds and clean your room and be home within fifteen minutes of curtain or you'll find yourselves locked out. That clear?' She did not wait for a reply. 'Breakfast's at eight. High tea at five, if you pay extra for it. You behave yourselves, we'll get on. You don't, and you're out.' And with that uncompromising warning she left them.

Kitty stared after her, speechless.

'Stupid old bitch.' Florrie struggled to a sitting position. ' 'Ere –?'

'Yes?'

The other girl's expression was suddenly wheedling, 'Wouldn't 'ave such a thing as a tot o' gin about yer person, would yer?'

Kitty shook her head.

Florrie grunted, flung herself back onto the bed, turning her back.

Grimly Kitty set about unpacking.

Two hours later the girls were at the Palace Theatre for their first, hurried rehearsal before taking their place on the bill the following night. They were greeted with a marked lack of any interest or enthusiasm – a negative attitude rather than a positive one, Kitty quickly concluded; the company were not particularly hostile, they simply could not care less one way or another. Morale at the moment was evidently not at its highest. The two girls were each allocated a grubby corner of the women's dressing room. Florrie was introduced to the Great Margico, who nearly fainted when he saw her. 'A boy! I need a boy!'

'Well, 'ard cheese,' Florrie said, dourly, 'you're stuck wiv me. Mr Kenny's orders. 'E's pissed orf wiv your boys an' their nasty little 'abits. Anyone got a tot o' gin?'

To her surprise Kitty found herself almost at the top of the bill, sandwiched between Barney and his Incredible Singing Dog and Mr George Bonnard, the Famous Nigger Minstrel. The latter she watched at rehearsal, his being a name she had heard from George Milton, and was disconcerted when her mildly friendly overtures were completely rejected.

'Don't mind him, love.' Barney fondled his little dog, straightening the tinselled ruff about its neck. 'He hasn't got over losing Miss Lilly Colrane to a magician's assistant. Understandable, I suppose.' He smiled a maliciously wicked little smile. 'She was his wife.'

She survived. More – she loved it. For the first time in her life she was alone and relying solely upon her own resources and she was delighted to discover that, hardship and discomfort notwithstanding, she thoroughly enjoyed it. Her act was popular from the very first performance – more and more often as her technique and confidence improved she found herself the recipient of the most enthusiastic applause of the evening – something which did little or nothing to endear her to the other members of the company. She accepted that philosophically; what mattered was that each evening, despite the petty squabbles and inconveniences of the day she renewed that special relationship between herself and her audience that invested the most squalid of surroundings with magic and gave purpose to the dreariest of days. It was a hard school, but an effective one. Florrie Harcourt's constant and sullen presence notwithstanding –

for wherever they went it remained accepted practice that they should room together, probably, Kitty concluded, because no one else could bear to spend their leisure hours, such as they were, to the tune of the girl's constant, ill-tempered grumbling – she very much enjoyed this, her first taste of theatre variety. As the days and then the weeks passed she found herself an accepted member of the company; was astonished to find herself the object of some friendly – and some not so friendly – envy.

'Oh, come on, ducks,' Barney said, grinning his disbelief at her expressed surprise, 'you know how good you are. You can't expect the rest of us to be happy about spending the rest of our lives treading the boards in Scunthorpe or Margate while a chit of a lass like you swans off to the bright lights?'

She protested politely, and hugged entirely to herself the pleasure that the man's words gave her. Barney was a true professional, and his opinion in such matters was not to be taken anything but seriously.

In Manchester, the week before they were due to move to a small theatre in Bethnal Green, in East London, Luke came to see her. She spotted him immediately in the audience, ran to him almost incoherent with excitement when he came backstage after the show.

'Well, well,' Florrie said, acidly, eyeing Luke with the first faint interest that Kitty had seen her display since they had first met. 'All right, Miss Show-off – 'ow many more surprises 'ave yer got for us?'

'Luke, Luke! I've missed you so! What did you think? They loved the Dipper, didn't they? Funny – in the south they seemed to prefer Monty. How's Matt? Have you seen Pol –?'

He stopped the words with a kiss, swinging her almost from her feet. They spent two perfect days together; she did not ask him about the activities that had kept him away for three weeks, nor about the source of the money he spent so freely, and he of course volunteered nothing. She was so pleased to see him, so delighted to have him with her again that for the moment she told herself she did not care. For now she was happy to live for the day and let the morrow care for itself.

He left Manchester two days before she did. They'd be together again once the company returned to London – for while they were performing in Bethnal Green she could return to her old room in Stepney.

She did not confide her own thoughts about that.

In Bethnal Green they played to the most appreciative audiences of the tour. Kitty was utterly amazed, and rather pleased, to discover that in returning to London she felt almost as if it were a homecoming. Luke came to almost every performance. Matt and his friends graced the balcony one night and Pol too managed an evening off to see her. But the happiest surprise of all came on the last night, when a so-familiar yet almost forgotten face appeared, with a smiling Luke, at the stage door after the performance.

'Jem!' Kitty threw her arms about his neck. 'Jem O'Connell! What in the world are you doing here?'

The young American hugged her, laughing delightedly, rocking her back and forth.

'A celebration,' Luke said, 'would seem to be in order. And for more reasons than one.'

Kitty glanced sharply at him. His narrow eyes gleamed with laughter. 'I saw Pat Kenny today. He sent a message. He wants to talk to you. Tomorrow, in his office –' He stopped.

She waited, breath bated.

'The New Cambridge,' he said. 'You're in, Songbird, you're in.'

(iii)

How the three of them finished up in a dockside drinking den at two o'clock in the morning she never afterwards remembered. Carried along by the men's exuberance and her own excitement she protested not at all at being swept from place to place in a giddy progress that was marked on the part of her companions by the emptying of an unlikely number of bottles of strong spirits and on hers by singing until she was all but hoarse. She was lifted onto chairs, onto tables, onto bars, and she sang. And the pimps and the prostitutes, the dockers and the seamen, the bully-boys and the swell-mobsters sang along with her. Once, in the shadowed crowd, she caught sight of a face that tweaked her memory uncomfortably – a cadaver's face, gaunt and unshaven, with disconcertingly bitter eyes. She glanced at Luke. He had one arm about Jem's slim shoulders, in his other hand was the inevitable glass. When she looked back at the crowd the face had gone.

They clattered through the night amidst a mob of friends and drinking acquaintances. It was not until they found themselves, in the early hours of the morning, seated at a quiet table in a corner of a sprawling dockland pub that Kitty at last had a chance to talk privately with Jem.

'Jem, it's so good to see you again! How was Paris? And the painting? Have you come back to us to stay?'

He shook his head. She noticed that through a hard night's drinking, despite the smile on his lips, his eyes had remained quite disturbingly sober. 'I'm on my way home.'

Luke was at the bar, getting drinks. As always, wherever he went in this mood, it seemed, he had discovered friends and was engaged in entertaining them. A roar of laughter almost drowned Jem's words.

'But I thought –?' She stopped, uncertain what to say.

He smiled, sadly. 'The war's over, Kitty. It's finished.'

It came to her with something of a shock that she had neither seen nor read a newspaper in a year. 'I didn't know. What – what happened?'

'You mean who won?' He played with his glass for a moment. 'No one.' He lifted the glass, drained it in a movement.

She watched him.

He pushed the glass aimlessly around a pool of ale on the table top. 'My Pa died,' he said at last. 'I thought – that is – I can't leave Ma and Cecilia to cope alone. God knows what's left, but I have to try –'

Kitty remembered what he had said of his mother and sister and their feelings towards him when they had spoken in the Cremorne Gardens. A small frown furrowed her brow, but she did not speak.

'I have to try,' he said again, for all the world as if she had voiced her doubts.

She covered his hands with her own. 'It'll be all right. I'm sure it will.' In her own ears her voice did not exactly ring with conviction.

He shrugged. 'Well, if they won't have me back' – his smile did not quite disguise the pain behind the words – 'Paris will always be there, I guess.'

Some noisy altercation was taking place at the bar. Kitty heard Luke's ringing laughter. She glanced to where he stood, easily leaning against the bar, head tilted provocatively. She could sense the mockery in his stance from where she sat. He did not even glance her way. The burly, red-faced docker to whom he was speaking said something, and Luke replied. The onlookers at the bar howled with laughter again. The big docker's colour heightened further. Smothering a faint unease, Kitty turned back to Jem, who had spoken and was awaiting her reply. 'I'm sorry?'

He was watching her, strangely intent, the pale, clear eyes searching her face. 'I said – you, and Luke – I wasn't surprised.'

She found herself flushing. Looked down at her clasped hands.

'You're sure you know what you've taken on, Songbird?' The words were light, but the expression in the pale eyes was serious. 'That's one hell of a – Great God! What the devil's he up to now?'

The uproar at the bar had reached riot proportions. The docker that Luke had so obviously been baiting was drunkenly stripping off his waistcoat and grubby shirt, revealing even grubbier underclothes. He was built like a bear and had hands the size of hams. 'Oh, yes? You an' 'oo's bleedin' regiment, gypsy?'

Luke was still laughing, but his face was dangerous. Kitty

half-rose in her seat. Jem put out a swift hand to restrain her. He shook his head. 'He won't thank you.'

There was a sudden clattering and scraping of chairs. Miraculously a space appeared in the centre of the room. Men clustered, grinning, to watch the fun. A small rat-faced man had leapt onto the bar and was taking bets.

'Two to one against the gypsy!'

'A guinea on Rozzer!'

'Five that 'e don't stand up two minutes. I've seen Peveral fight before.'

Luke, unhurriedly, had stripped off his jacket and kicked off his shoes. Not once did he glance in Kitty's direction. She suspected he had forgotten her existence. His dark hair slicked down across his forehead, the narrow gaze was intent. He showed no sign whatsoever of the enormous amount of alcohol he had consumed. The other man, too, faced a little disconcertingly by this suddenly dangerous-looking opponent, seemed to have sobered.

The two men circled each other warily.

'Can't we stop it!' Kitty asked of Jem.

He shook his head.

A roar went up as the huge Rozzer leapt suddenly at Luke, who sidestepped lightly, chopped painfully at the other man's kidneys and then was across the sawdust floor, poised and waiting before the heavier man could turn. He grinned wolfishly, made a little, mocking, beckoning motion with his hand. Like the bear he so much resembled the other man charged furiously at him. Again Luke dodged, but this time not quite so smoothly, and a fist like a hammer caught the side of his head, rocking him. In one movement he ducked and turned acrobatically, coming up inside the other man's guard. The sound of knuckle upon bone made Kitty flinch and she closed her eyes. When she opened them again blood had appeared on Rozzer's broad face, and Kitty remembered the heavy ring that Luke invariably wore and saw it suddenly and for the first time as less an ornament than a weapon. Luke had stepped back and was standing easily, waiting, his dark face alight with the reckless enjoyment of the moment. Kitty turned her head away. Jem's hand touched hers. Another roar brought her eyes back to the conflict despite herself. Rozzer had Luke in the bear's grip of one arm, whilst with the other he was pummelling the slighter man's body with brutal force. With a strange, twisting movement Luke turned, and ducked and – incredibly – his heavier opponent flew over his shoulder and crashed to the floor.

The silence of astonishment held the room. The man who had put his money on Luke grinned happily. Luke himself stood back from his prostrate opponent, bouncing on the balls of his feet, half-smiling, eyes watchful.

Rozzer lay on his back, winded, his feet tangled in the wreckage of a smashed chair. For a moment he seemed totally stupefied, then with an enraged growl he rolled over and came to his feet with surprising speed. Instead of retreating, however, Luke stepped straight into the enraged attack; in a blur of movement he blocked the blow that was aimed at him, caught the man's flailing arm and once again the unfortunate Rozzer soared, somersaulting, into the air to crash with painful force onto a table that disintegrated into splinters beneath him. The shouts of the crowd held laughter now. This was better than a circus act.

'What's the matter, Rozzer, can't yer keep yer feet?'

'Come on, Rozz – my old woman'd do better'n that!'

Very slowly Rozzer pulled himself to his knees, head hanging, great shoulders heaving as he struggled to gain his breath. One of his supporters leant to him, as if to help him to his feet. The big man stood and slowly turned.

In his hand now he held a great metal hook, a tool of his trade, a shocked Kitty guessed, used to help haul the great sacks of carcasses the dockworkers handled. He lifted it. The spike wove a brutal pattern before Luke's still face. The man who had handed it to Rozzer stepped back, a small grin of satisfaction on his face.

Where the knife came from Kitty did not see. Nor, she was certain, did anyone else. One moment Luke stood empty handed. The next a blade glittered, slender and lethal, in his fingers, lightly held.

She caught her breath, heard that same exhalation from a dozen throats. The men around the arena shuffled back a little.

Rozzer had frozen where he stood. The knife spun in the air, glimmering, as Luke tossed it up, reversing it, catching it delicately by the razor-sharp blade, standing poised to throw as Kitty had seen stage performers do.

'Aw, come on, gypsy –' one of the onlookers asked, uneasily, 'is that fair?'

Luke did not move a muscle. 'Drop it,' he said to Rozzer, softly. The laughter had gone entirely from his face. It was stone hard now, and frightening.

Rozzer stared at him. Sweat streaked his broad, florid face, his eyes glinted still with the red fire of rage.

'Drop it,' Luke repeated, very quietly.

With a roar the other man leapt for him, his brute strength carrying him and the lethally swinging hook across the short distance that divided the two men. Luke moved swiftly. Kitty saw the flashing movement of his hand and the glint of flung metal. The hook nicked Luke high on the cheekbone. A scarlet thread of blood appeared. And then the other man was down, howling, clutching his shoulder, the hook skittering away across the sawdust floor. Quick as thought, Luke stepped in before anyone could stop him and brutally flicked the knife from where it had buried itself up to the hilt in the flesh of the other man's shoulder. Rozzer shrieked. Kitty flinched. Unhurriedly Luke wiped the blood from the blade and the knife disappeared as magically as it had earlier appeared.

Rozzer moaned.

'Fair fight,' someone said. 'Rozzer pulled the 'ook first.'

There was a murmur of assent. Rozzer groaned as several pairs of unsympathetic hands hauled him upright. 'Best get Doc Aherne.' The barman, entirely calm, was wiping down the bar. 'If 'e isn't too pissed ter stand upright that is. 'E'll patch 'im up.'

Luke picked up his jacket, brushed it off, shrugged into it. He seemed utterly composed, the rhythm of his breathing barely altered. Only the high stain of colour in his dark face betrayed him, and the slender thread of blood upon his cheek. That, Kitty thought, fighting nausea, and the light of pure excitement in his eyes.

She watched him as he came towards her. Those dark eyes were a little wary as they met hers, yet still gleamed with that unholy excitement. No one could doubt that he had enjoyed this short, violent encounter, that he had so cavalierly provoked. She looked away from him.

'My apologies.' His voice was cool. 'If you'll spare me one more moment I'll see the landlord about the damage.'

As he walked away she caught Jem's eyes on her, and knew that he guessed her feeling surely. He took her hand. 'He's a violent man, Kitty,' he said, 'from a violent background. He can't help it.'

Matt's excuse. She said nothing.

'He's had to fight since he could walk. Dog eat dog. He lived in a world where the strong survive and the weak go to the wall.'

And he enjoys it. Still she sat in silence.

The warm pressure of his thin hand was comforting. 'You'll never change him, Kitty.'

'I know.' She did not see, beneath the sympathy, the strange shadow of sorrow in the pale eyes.

'Right, that's settled. Time to go, I think.' Luke had materialized again at her side. She knew from his eyes that he sensed her horror – sensed it and rejected it. She trailed behind him to the door, all eyes upon them. As she passed through the door and turned to hold it for Jem, who was warily bringing up the rear, a face in the crowd behind them leapt out, unsmiling, watchful, puzzlingly familiar. A face she had seen before, this evening, in another crowd, in another tavern.

Minutes later, as she ran down the deserted, darkened street, hurrying to keep pace with the men's long strides, the name associated with that face clicked in her mind like a key unexpectedly fitting into a strange lock.

Oliver Fogg.

7

(i)

Kitty told Luke about Fogg the next day, when she met him to tell him of the outcome of her meeting with Patrick Kenny. He frowned, pensively. 'You're sure?'

'Certain. It isn't a face you easily forget, is it?'

'Interesting.'

She watched him. Neither of them had touched on the potentially explosive matter of the fight. Luke, when he had greeted her, had acted as if nothing more than usual lay between them. Kitty, who, since Jem was staying with Luke for the duration of his short stay, had had the quiet of a long night alone to brood upon the violent events of the evening, knew neither how to broach the subject nor, if she were honest, what she would say about it if she did. She did not want to quarrel. Neither did she want to express openly the revulsion she felt, for fear of the breach it might cause between them. She understood well that what Jem had said the night before was the truth; Luke was a man who had lived since birth in a harsh and perilous world. The casual acceptance and use of violence was not to be wondered at in a man of his background and occupation. But the disturbing fact was that in her heart she knew that no matter how she loved him she would never learn to accept that – as she could not, try as she might, close her eyes to the way in which he earned his living.

'I'll keep an eye open,' he said now, referring to Fogg. 'So – what news from Kenny?'

The excitement she had been tamping down since she had left Kenny's office stirred again. 'I'm to be given a spot next month at the New Cambridge.' Her attempt to sound casual failed dismally. 'Mr Kenny says the act needs polishing a bit – the Cambridge is no penny gaff – if I can make it there –'

'You'll have London at your feet.'

'Well – not quite that. But it's a start. A marvellous start. If I can do it.'

'Sure you can. No question.' Jem, who had been sitting quietly at a table with chalks and paper, stood up now and presented her with the drawing he had been working on. 'There. A farewell present. To remember me by when you're famous.'

She stared in delight. 'Jem! It's lovely!'

'I sketched it last night, while you were on stage. You like it?'

'I love it!' Impulsively she kissed him. 'It's the Dipper to the life! Though you flatter him a bit, I think!'

'Not at all.' Jem took the drawing back and looked at it for a long moment. 'Not at all,' he repeated, then, tossing the paper onto the table, he stretched lazily. 'Well, if you two don't mind I'm off for a farewell stroll round my second favourite city. I'll see you later, down at the Rooms.' He slung his cap at a rakish angle upon his fair head, raised a hand. 'Don't do anything I wouldn't do –'

When he had gone the silence was long and faintly uncomfortable.

'Something worrying you?' Luke asked softly at last.

She looked at him, a thousand words crowding her tongue, a thousand protests, arguments, pleas. 'No,' she said.

He tilted her chin, kissed her lightly. 'Then let's do what Jem so thoughtfully left us to do. Come to bed.' He stepped back, hands held up placatingly. 'All right – do what you have to do first. But hurry.'

After their lovemaking they lay in silence for a long while, Luke's head cradled upon Kitty's shoulder, her fingers in his thick, straight hair. Kitty had given up all thought of tackling him about what had happened the night before. The opportunity had passed, as he had no doubt intended.

'What are you thinking about now?' he asked.

She hesitated. 'I wanted to ask your advice.'

'What about?'

'Luke – I have to get away. From here. From Moses.'

'Yes,' he said, quietly.

'Will he let me go, do you think?'

He rolled away from her, onto his stomach, came up onto his elbows, dark hair flopping into his eyes. 'He'll let you go.'

'What makes you think so? Moses seems to believe that he owns anyone and anything that comes within five miles of him – anyone but you, that is. But I won't let him stop me. I can't. I'm leaving. And' – she glanced a little nervously at his calm profile – 'I want to take Pol with me, if she'll come.'

To her surprise he threw back his head and laughed. 'God, girl, you don't believe in doing things by halves, do you?'

She did not reply to that but there was stubborn resolution in the set of her mouth. 'Luke – I've thought about it – thought about little else over the past few weeks. I won't stay here. He'll have to kill me to make me stay.'

He opened his mouth to speak. She rushed on.

'Matt won't come – I know that – nothing will persuade him. He's got what he wants.' She tried to suppress the bitterness in her voice at that. 'At least he thinks he has. I can't change him. But I can't let him stop me.'

'He wouldn't want to.'

She turned her head on the pillow. 'I know.'

'I believe he thinks that he'd be no good to you. That he'd spoil your chances.'

'And I believe it's got more to do with an itch to thieve and that girl he's fallen for.'

'Sally-Anne? They're still seeing each other?'

'Yes.'

'He'll find himself in trouble with Moses there if he isn't careful. Moses doesn't take kindly to anyone messing with the girls in The House.'

'I know. I've told him. He won't listen.'

'P'raps I'd better have a word?'

'You can try, but I don't think even you could influence him over this. He says he's in love. Perhaps he is.'

Luke grinned. 'For the third time this month?'

She did not respond.

In one of those strange, gentle gestures that from him always struck her to the heart he reached a long finger to her face, stroking it. 'Don't worry, Songbird. I'll handle Moses for you.'

She turned her head. The heavy gold ring on his finger glinted in the light. She sat up abruptly, folding her long legs to bring her knees up under her chin, clasping her hands about them. 'No.'

He lay back, his face expressionless.

She shook her head, her hair veiling her eyes. 'No,' she said again, 'can't you see? I have to do it myself.'

His eyes were cool, as was his voice. 'Don't be stupid, Kitty. I've told you – in this world you have to use any weapon that comes to hand. I'm your weapon against Moses. To hell with your pride. I'll sort Moses out. He'll let you go.'

'And Pol?'

'Ah. That might be a bit more difficult.'

'I'm not going without her,' she said, and was mortified at the frail catch of uncertainty in the words.

In the event she found herself confronting Moses Smith rather earlier than she would have wished, and on the fat man's own ground. She did not even know if Luke had got round to talking to him.

It was some time since Kitty had been summoned to one of Moses' 'quarterly meetings' in the cellar – her new status, both as entertainer and with regard to Luke Peveral had spared her that. She was surprised therefore to find herself and Matt peremptorily summoned some few days later. She had no time to consult with Luke, nor indeed with anyone else, and it was with some misgving that she obeyed. She did not at the moment dare to do anything else, for the last thing she wanted to do was openly to antagonize the man.

Reluctantly she had come to accept that only with Luke's influence behind her would she be able to break free; despite the promptings of common sense she still harboured the hope that Pol might be allowed to leave with her. Not that Pol allowed herself to harbour such false hopes. 'Don't take the chance, love – you'll cock it up fer yerself if yer try it. The old bastard won't let me go, you can bet yer boots. 'E won't be 'appy at losin' you – 'e'll keep me ter spite us both, you mark my words.' But Kitty had determined not to give up so easily; so now, if the brusque summons from Moses caught her unaware and unnerved her more than a little, at least it looked likely to take matters from her hands and force the issue one way or another. It might as well be now as later. It was with some determination in her step that she set out for Whitechapel.

She should not, she afterwards realized, have been surprised to discover that it was not she who had stirred up the hornet's nest of Moses' anger, but her brother.

She suspected that Matt knew, or guessed, more of the reason for the summons than she did from the moment she slid into the seat beside him, squeezing onto the low bench between him and Croucher. The dimly lit cellar was exactly as she remembered it from that first evening that now seemed so long ago – even the faces were the same, except that Pol now sat alone, brass-blonde head tilted a little tiredly to the mildewed wall. Lottie, of course, was no longer required to attend such gatherings.

'What's this all about?' she whispered to Matt.

He shrugged, a little too carelessly. He had hardly greeted her. Springer, seated at his other side, cast him a single disgusted look and sniffed.

She peered at her brother suspiciously. 'Matt?'

'How should I know?' His face looked a little pale in the half-light. His fingers fidgeted with the ragged strands of cotton at his cuff.

'You haven't –?' Kitty's question was cut short as all sound suddenly died as Moses, Bobs, and another bruiser, a particularly unpleasant man known as Dyce, who, she had heard, brutally and efficiently policed the brothel known as The House, entered the cellar. Kitty heard her brother's sharp-indrawn breath. His eyes were fixed on Dyce, and the last vestiges of colour had left his face.

Moses was in no good temper, and it showed. His plump pink face was bereft of expression, his small red mouth pursed. His eyes were flat and cold as a snake's as he seated himself and stared about the room, his eyes flicking coldly from face to face with no sign of warmth of greeting. Dyce and Bobs stationed themselves one each side of his chair. Moses barely looked at Kitty; the chill gaze slid across hers, fixed upon her brother and stayed there. She felt Matt tense beside her as he lifted his chin and returned the man's look. Kitty's heart sank to her boots. The silence was tense.

'In this organization,' Moses said, at last, quietly, 'a warning is given only once. I believe that you all know that. I will not be cheated. I will not be crossed. I will not be disobeyed. Matt Daniels. Here.'

Awkwardly Matt stood. With brave composure he walked into the open space before the dais, where he stood, head up, watching Moses.

Kitty was trembling, fear turned her stomach. Matt, oh Matt, why must you always do it? It was like an oft-repeated nightmare.

At a sign from Moses Bobs stepped forward and caught the boy from behind, holding him by the elbows, twisted savagely back. Matt did not struggle, nor did he take his eyes from Moses'. Dyce stepped to him. He was a brute of a man with a vicious, pock-marked face and the strength of a bull, as many a girl in The House would testify.

Moses spoke very softly. 'Matt Daniels, did I not, just a week ago, and for the second time, forbid you The House?'

Matt did not reply.

Almost casually Dyce backhanded him across the mouth. 'Speak when you're spoke to.'

'Yes.' Blood dribbled from Matt's lip and dripped onto his grubby shirt.

'And have you obeyed me?'

Matt hesitated. Dyce lifted a hand. 'No,' Matt said.

'No.' Moses' voice was deceptively mild. He surveyed Matt for a long moment. 'Can you give me one good reason,' he asked, suddenly sharp and hard, 'why there should be one rule for Matt Daniels and another for everyone else?'

Matt was watching him as if mesmerized. Kitty could see his fear and his brave attempt to hide it. He shook his head.

'And yet – that would seem to be your opinion, boy. This is not the first time you have defied me, that you have presumed upon my good nature and my favour. It will be the last. I told you to stay away from The House, and to stay away from Sally-Anne.' He glanced around the cellar. 'Matt Daniels,' he said, cruelly derisive, 'thinks he can have for nothing what other men pay hard-earned money for.'

Unexpected, painful colour flooded Matt's face. His bloodied lips tightened, but he said nothing.

Moses' eyes came back to him. 'Every whore in that house pays dues to me, boy. And Sally-Anne's a whore like the rest of them. How can she pay her dues if she's giving it to you for free?'

Desperately Matt shook his head.

Moses pressed savagely on. 'Sally-Anne's been with me for four years. Since she was twelve. And the most willing whore I've had – no tongue, no trouble – that right, Dyce?'

'Yes, Mr Smith.'

'An' what happens now? Along comes Mr Cleverdick Daniels, and the girl finds herself in trouble. Eh, Dyce?'

Dyce grinned. 'Yes, Mr Smith.'

Matt looked at him, wrenched suddenly upon his held arms. 'What have you done to her?'

'Ask yourself what you've done to .her, lad,' Moses snapped. 'That's a bit more to the point, isn't it? What Dyce did was hurt her, and on my orders. What you've done's far worse than that.'

Matt was struggling wildly now, tears on his face. 'You bastard! I'll kill you!'

Kitty sat rooted to the spot. She caught Pol's eye, sympathetic and warning.

Dyce, at a sign from Moses, struck Matt hard once, and then again, across the face. The boy reeled back, still held by Bobs.

'Tell me, Matt,' Moses said, very softly, 'what the buggery do you think you've been doing here? I mean – we all like to take the little ladies for a ride, don't we? But – fair's fair! The poor little bitch thinks you love her – least, that's what she told Dyce. Wasn't it, Dyce?'

Dyce grinned again. 'Yes, Mr Smith.'

Matt had stopped struggling. He stood, slim and rigid in Bobs' grip, his face a picture of ineffectual rage and hatred. 'I do,' he said.

Moses shook his head mournfully. 'Oh, no.' His eyes flicked to Dyce. Dyce spat on his hands, rubbed them on his dirty shirt. 'You can't love Sally-Anne, Matt – She's mine – And I won't have you – putting ideas in her head – that don't suit me. You hear?' At each pause Dyce's great fist buried itself in Matt's lean stomach. Matt screamed. Moses talked inexorably on. 'You behave yourself a while – show me how sorry you are – and maybe, sometime – you'll be allowed back at The House – but you'll take whatever girl's offered – and it won't be Sally-Anne. Understood? Enough, Dyce,' he added.

Matt hung, silent, from Bobs' huge hands. After a moment he lifted his head. Moses was waiting for him. 'I asked if you understood?' The steel chill of his voice gave notice that Matt Daniels had forfeited his untrustworthy favour for ever. Matt nodded. Kitty looked down at the cellar floor, not to see the expression on his face. Moses' next words almost stopped her heart. 'You will not, of course,' he said, 'be leaving with your sister. That goes without saying. You owe me, Matt Daniels, and you'll pay. You stay.'

His words caused a stir about her. Eyes turned to look at her. Moses' gaze was still fixed upon Matt, but there was a hint of malice in his face that she knew was directed at her. If pressure from Luke were forcing him to let her go he would make her suffer first if he could. That, she suddenly saw, had been the reason for his summoning her to witness Matt's humiliation and punishment.

Moses jerked his head at Bobs. 'Let him go. He's going to be a good boy now. Aren't you, Matt?'

Bobs let go of Matt's arms. He staggered, righted himself, wiped the back of his hand across his still bleeding mouth.

Moses, at last, turned his attention to Kitty. 'After all I've done for you, girl?'

She said nothing.

He shrugged. 'Never let it be said Moses Smith wasn't soft-hearted. You want to go? Go. Just remember – anyone asks, it was Moses Smith gave you your first chance.' He turned to leave.

Kitty stepped forward. 'Mr Smith!'

He stopped. Kitty saw Pol's frantic gesture to silence, and ignored it.

'Yes?'

'Pol – I'd like Pol to come with me.'

He turned very slowly, eyed her for a long moment. 'I see. And what does Pol have to say about it?'

'She'll come if you'll let her.' Doggedly she held his eyes, refusing to be intimidated.

'Will she now?' The small, unfriendly eyes turned to Pol. 'I'm surprised at you, Pol. You and me go back a long way.'

'That's true,' Pol said, sourly.

'Mind you' – he mused for a moment – 'getting a bit long in the tooth now, I suppose?'

Pol flushed very slightly, and bit off a sharp retort. The faintest gleam of hope had appeared in her eyes.

'Was a time when I might have felt different – but, well, I can't deny Lot's had a word in my ear –' He turned suddenly to the wary Kitty. 'Tell you what I'll do. Pol wants to go with you – she can go –'

She did not believe it. She waited, and was not disappointed.

'– for a price, of course,' he added smoothly.

'A – price?'

'Well of course. By way of compensation, as you might say.'

Kitty held his eyes, 'What sort of price?'

'Well – let's see – she might be on the shady side of thirty, but there's life in her yet, and she's strong.' He might, Kitty thought bitterly, have been talking of a milk cow. 'Midge'd miss her if no one else did. Let's say – fifty guineas?'

She stared at him. 'You're joking!'

He shook his head.

'I can't – you know I don't have fifty guineas!'

His small mouth quirked mockingly. 'You don't say? Well that's that then. Fifty guineas is my price.'

The light had gone from Pol's face. Kitty's temper stirred. 'Thirty,' she snapped.

'Forty-five.' He was grinning, now, enjoying the entertainment.

She hesitated. 'Thirty-five.'

He laughed. 'You got thirty-five guineas?'

She shook her head. 'I'll get it.'

'Not a penny less than forty.'

She glared at him. 'Done!'

He opened a plump white hand, pointed to the palm, 'Cash on the barrel. Before she leaves.'

'You'll have it.'

'I will. Or Pol stays where she belongs.' Moses turned and left the cellar, Bobs and Dyce at his heels. Muttering amongst themselves, casting sidelong glances at Kitty and Matt the others followed. Pol, the last to leave, smiled ruefully at Kitty. 'Forty guineas? Soppy thing – where you goin' ter get forty guineas?'

'I'll get it.'

The other girl laughed a little, shaking her head sadly. 'Not much of a bargain fer you, girl. I'd ferget it were I you.' Still smiling, her eyes sombre, she left them.

Kitty looked at Matt. He had until now been standing, with an effort, in the middle of the floor, where Bobs had left him. Now he moved painfully to a bench, and dropped down onto it, his arms crossed over his bruised torso.

She moved to him, touched his shoulder lightly.

He lifted his head.

'We'll get you away, too,' she said, uncertainly, 'eventually.'

To her surprise he shook his head, his face set. 'I'm staying. And not on Moses Smith's say-so either.'

'Matt – please – if it's the girl – you'll do more harm than good –'

'Leave it,' he said.

She shut her mouth.

He grinned a little, split lips seeping blood. 'It's not just that. I'm going to be big, Kitty. Big as the Guv'nor. And when I am – I'm going to kill Moses Smith. Very slowly.'

She knew at last from experience when to argue and when not. 'Tell me when,' she said, grimly, 'I wouldn't want to miss it.'

She would not ask Luke for the money, and there was no one else she could go to. When her temper cooled she had to admit that her impulsive acceptance of Moses' deliberate challenge had been foolhardy. 'I'll save it,' she said, as confidently as she could, to Pol. 'It means you'll have to wait a bit before you can join me, but I'll do it, I promise.'

'What'll you be earning at this Cambridge place?'

'A guinea a week to start with.' A fortune she had thought it.

'Well, that's all right then,' said Pol, gently mocking, 'providin' yer don't want ter eat, dress or live anywhere – roll on a year or so –'

Kitty looked at her, miserably. 'Oh, Pol – I'm sorry –'

Pol patted her hand. 'It's all right, yer daft 'a'porth. You tried. That's what counts. You bloody tried. An' I won't ferget that.'

(ii)

Her disappointment about Pol and her worries about Matt notwithstanding, Kitty's spirits were high as she set out with an advance from Patrick Kenny in her pocket to find herself somewhere decent to live at last. Not even the days that she spent tramping London's grimy streets and crowded pavements could dampen them. A week or so later – a week of knocking on strange doors, inspecting rooms that ranged from the squalid through the cheerless to the barely adequate, she found herself in Pascal Road, a narrow residential street in Paddington, not far from the great station. The paved street was quiet and respectable-looking. The houses – built perhaps twenty years before – were small, the front doors opening directly onto the pavement. Most had lace curtains hanging at meticulously cleaned windows. The tiled doorsteps were burnished red, to vie with each other, gleaming crimson. She counted the doors. Number twenty-three was as clean and neat-looking as its neighbours. A small flowering plant blossomed at one of the lace-draped windows and another stood by the scrubbed and polished doorstep. Faint hope stirred. She knocked.

'Yes, dear?' A diminutive woman opened the door, tilting her head to look at tall Kitty. 'Can I help you?'

'I've come about the room.' Beyond the little woman Kitty could see a long hall that in the shadows gleamed with polish, and narrow stairs, carpeted with a well-brushed runner. An indefinable smell, compounded of soap and polish and the fragrance of flowers, came to her nostrils. The smell of a well-kept, well-loved home.

The little woman stepped back. 'Yes, of course, dear. Come in. I'll show you.' She had little black eyes, shiny as boot-buttons, and an equally small, turned-up nose. Her movements were quick and bird-like. She was, Kitty surmised, not all that much older than she was herself. 'This way, dear. Any preference, front or back?' The woman bustled up the stairs, stopped, laughing, halfway: 'Oh, I suppose I should introduce myself?' She spoke very fast, hardly seeming to take breath between sentences. 'Mrs Buckley. Amy Buckley. A widow, I am. Now – what do you think, front or back? I've two rooms going, you see, I'm moving downstairs and letting off the top.' She led the way

up the narrow stairs, still talking breathlessly. 'With poor
Mr Buckley gone, you see, I need to do something – something to bring in a bit of money. He left me the house, you
see, but nothing to go with it – not that I'm complaining,
mind you. Oh, no, I wouldn't complain. Worked hard all his
life, he did, and no one could argue about that. Now –' She
paused on a tiny landing, lit from fanlights above the two
doors that stood one each end of it. The landing was permeated, as was the rest of the house, with the fresh and
clean smell of soap. 'Which would you prefer, front or
back? The front's a bit bigger, but the back's quieter. Prettier,
too, I reckon. Looks out onto the gardens you see –'

'Might I see the back?'

''Course, dear, this way.' She led Kitty to one of the doors
and threw it open, standing back. 'There.'

Kitty stood like a statue. It seemed to her to have been an
age since she had seen such a room, welcoming and homely.
Roses scrambled across the wallpaper and over the plump
eiderdown that covered the bedspread. Crisp and pretty pink
curtains hung at the narrow window. Roses there were too
upon the jug and bowl that stood on a sparklingly clean
tiled washstand in the corner. She walked to the window.
A long slender strip of garden marched in parallel with its
neighbours to a fence, beyond which ran a narrow, linking
alleyway. The garden was a patch of grass with a tiny path,
straight as a ruled line, beside a washing line upon which
blew Mrs Buckley's immaculate washing. The path ran
beneath the spreading branches of what looked like an apple
tree to the wooden gate that led to the back alley. She felt
Mrs Buckley's small presence at her shoulder. 'Mr Buckley's
pride and joy was that little garden,' she said a little sadly.
'I try to keep it nice. For him, like.'

'It's lovely.' Kitty turned. 'And so's the room. I really don't
need to see the other. Your advertisement said three and six
a week?'

'That's right, dear.' The little widow glanced up at her,
bright and birdlike again. 'Though if you think that's too
much I could probably see my way to –'

'Oh, no. I can manage that.' On a guinea a week – unheard of riches – Kitty knew herself to be well off, even though she was committed to saving up for Pol.

Amy Buckley seemed as pleased as she was herself. 'Well, good, that's settled then. I'm sure we'll suit. Felt it as soon as I saw you. You've got references, of course?' This last was said with a beaming smile and no question in the tone.

Kitty hesitated. 'References?'

The little woman's smile faded. 'Well – I can't say I'd considered taking any young woman without references.'

Kitty wondered, dourly, what sort of reference her present landlord would give her. 'Please – I can pay in advance if you'd like – it really is the nicest room I've seen.'

'Haven't you someone who'd stand for you?' The poor little woman was obviously distressed at Kitty's disappointment. 'I'm a woman alone, you see – I really must be careful.'

'Well yes, of course, I can see that –'

'You've got work?' The words were hopefully expectant. It came to Kitty that Mrs Buckley was trying as hard as she was to find a way out of their difficulty. But here, of course, could be another stumbling block.

'Yes,' she said, and then, quickly, to get it over, 'I sing. On the stage.'

'Sing?' Amy Buckley repeated. 'You sing? On the stage?'

Kitty's sinking heart settled lower. 'Yes. But truly, Mrs Buckley, it's –'

'But how lovely! Good Heavens! A real singer! Oh, the lovely times that Mr Buckley and I had at the Music Rooms down the street! A fine voice, he had, Mr Buckley, a fine voice. I used to love to hear him sing.' She blinked, swallowed, looking vaguely astonished at her own emotion. 'We've a piano in the parlour. I'd be pleased to have you use it any time –'

'You mean – you'll take me? Even without references?'

'Oh, I don't see why not, dear, do you? We'll give ourselves a couple of weeks and see how we do, shall we? No obligation on either side of course.'

'Of course.' Relief welled in Kitty. 'And thank you.'

'Now — why don't we go down into the scullery and have a nice cup of tea?' And you can tell me all about yourself —'

In the event it was a lot harder to leave Stepney than she had anticipated — not that she had the slightest regret at turning her back at last on the dirt and squalor that she so detested, but saying goodbye to Matt and to Pol was quite another matter. And not made easier by the fact that both of them seemed quite surprisingly — and, it occurred to Kitty, quite callously — ready to see her go.

'It's what you've wanted, moi owd Kitty,' Matt said. 'What you've been working for all along. You deserve it. And you aren't going a million miles away, are you? I dare say your Mrs Buckley isn't such a dragon that she won't let your brother visit you, is she?'

'She isn't a dragon at all.'

'Well, then! — And anyway, the Guv'nor isn't moving house as far as I know, is he? So I daresay we'll still be seeing a fair bit of you?' He grinned, and with some difficulty winked. His right eye was still all but closed, a legacy of Dyce's fists, the bruise around it fading now to ochre and blue. Since his outburst in the cellar he had mentioned neither Moses nor the girl Sally-Anne, and Kitty had thought it best to steer clear of the subject. She had long ago given up trying to force her brother to confide in her.

She sighed. 'Matt — be careful?'

He flicked back the hair from his brow, the faintest irritation in the gesture. ''Course.'

If Matt's equanimity at her impending departure did not particularly surprise her, Pol's did — and hurt her not a little as well, though she did her best to hide it. Pol's theme was, sensibly, much the same as Matt's. 'You aren't takin' ship for bloomin' America, yer know. We'll be seein' plenty of one another, you'll see.'

'Yes, of course.' Her friend's apparent unconcern disconcerted Kitty. Her voice was subdued. 'Pol — I'm so sorry I couldn't get Moses to let you come with me.'

'Think nothin' of it, love. When yer don't expect nothin'

yer can't be disappointed, can yer? Want an 'and with yer packin'?'

A few days later, escorted by Luke, she piled her few possessions in a hackney and at last left Stepney for good. No one came to see her off, there were no last-minute tears or goodbyes. It was strangely anti-climactic and not at all somehow what she had expected. She stared stonily from the cab window. Luke, beside her, cast an amused glance but thankfully held his tongue.

When they reached Pascal Road, Amy Buckley, hearing the cab, opened the door with a wide smile that faded a little when she saw Luke.

'I – oh, Miss Daniels – I thought you'd be alone –'

'This is a friend of mine. Mr Peveral.'

'How do you do?' Amy Buckley worriedly bobbed a neat little head at Luke. He looked very big and very out of place indeed in the little hall. 'A gentleman friend. I didn't know you'd be bringing a gentleman friend.' The little woman fussed nervously with her spotless apron.

Kitty cast a quick, fiercely warning glance at Luke, knowing his acid humour, ready to kill him if he so much as opened his mouth.

She need not have worried. 'Mrs Buckley!' Warmly Luke held out his hand and bent his most charming smile upon her. 'I'm so very pleased to meet you.'

'Why – charmed I'm sure.' Suddenly cherry red, Amy Buckley took his extended hand and then dropped it like a hot cake.

'Miss Daniels has told me all about you – and about your delightful house. It seems she was very lucky to find you.'

'Oh, I wouldn't say that –'

'Oh, but yes, Mrs Buckley.' The narrow, dark-lashed eyes crinkled beguilingly. He lowered his voice a little, laid a confidential hand lightly upon her arm. 'Miss Daniels needs a friend, Mrs Buckley. Someone kindly and sensible, who'll look after her. I suspect – I greatly hope – she may have found that someone in you.'

Kitty winced and cocked a derisive eyebrow. Luke, surely, was laying on the charm just a little too heavily.

But no — Luke, as always, had gauged his victim to a nicety. Blushing like a poppy, Amy Buckley beamed. 'Well, do come in both of you.' She glanced up at Luke with an eye that could only be described as coy. 'If you wouldn't mind carrying Miss Daniels' case, Mr —?'

'Peveral,' he supplied easily. 'And of course not, Mrs Buckley. That's what I'm here for.' Grinning, Luke waited as Kitty fetched her reticule from the cab, then stepped back for her to precede him through the door. As she did so she thought she saw the curtain at the front bedroom window twitch. She glanced up sharply. An indistinct figure drew back.

'You've let the front room, then, Mrs Buckley?' A faint, unreasoning disappointment stirred. She had already, perhaps absurdly, come to think of number twenty-three as home. She did not want to share it so soon with a stranger.

'Yes, dear. Just yesterday. Nice enough young woman. Very quiet.'

They had arrived at Kitty's room. Luke looked round approvingly. Kitty thought of his own eccentric taste in accommodation and could not prevent a smile. 'Very nice, Mrs Buckley,' he said. 'Kitty was absolutely right. What a pity the front room is taken. I might have been tempted to take it myself.'

'Mr Peveral!' The little woman was quite delightedly scandalized. 'I couldn't see my way clear to taking a gentleman lodger. Oh, dear me, no!' Her small hands had begun their agitation with her pinafore again. 'Mr Buckley would never have approved of that!'

Luke turned to her. 'That,' he said with a smile, Kitty thought, that might have charmed a winkle from its shell, 'is my loss entirely, Mrs Buckley.'

Amy Buckley was blushing again. 'I'll — go and make some tea,' she said, and fled.

Luke, behind the door, was convulsed with laughter. Kitty slapped him none too gently with the gloves she was carrying. 'You pig! Poor Mrs Buckley! You're not to tease her, do you hear? Poor little thing –'

Luke gurgled but could not speak for his repressed laughter. Kitty stifled her own, holding onto severity. 'You really are a pig! Stop laughing – she might come back!'

He struggled for composure.

The door at the other end of the landing opened.

Kitty stood, half-laughing, hands on hips, watching Luke. 'Honestly – you think that all you have to do is to turn on that disgusting charm of yours and half the female population will drop dead at your feet –'

'While the other 'alf spits in 'is eye,' a familiar voice put in, caustically, from the door.

Jaw dropping, Kitty turned. Pol lounged, brassy head cocked at the familiar, affectionately mocking angle, laughter in her eyes.

'Pol! What are you doing here? How –?' Kitty stopped. Her eyes travelled beyond Pol to the open door at the other end of the landing. 'You?' she asked, faintly. 'It's *you*? In the other room?'

'That's right. Me. Large as life an' twice as awkward,' Pol said, grinning widely. 'An' with a whole envelope full of forged references at that. Thanks for the tip.'

'But – how? How did you get round Moses?' Kitty intercepted the small, significant glance that flicked between Pol and Luke. She turned to him. 'Luke? You did it? You paid Moses off?'

Luke smiled, said nothing.

'That's what 'e did all right.' Pol's voice was light, as if even now she could not bring herself to speak warmly of the man she had always so disliked.

'Oh!' Kitty stepped towards Luke, hugged him fiercely. 'Oh, thank you! Thank you! I'll pay you back, I promise, every penny –' She turned. Pol held out her arms. Kitty flung herself into them. 'Pol! Pol!' The two girls held each other, laughing and crying together. 'Oh, I thought I was going to be so lonely and miserable without you – and I thought you didn't care.'

'Goodness gracious me!' Amy Buckley said, uncertainly, from the top of the stairs. 'I came up to tell you that tea's made. And to introduce you.' She looked from one to the other, puzzled, yet obviously pleased at the happiness in their faces. 'Seems I don't have to?'

Up to the terrifying night that she opened at the New Cambridge Kitty found herself working harder than she had ever believed possible. Until now she had worked instinctively; now the professionals took over and she discovered how much she had to learn. In a cold, bare rehearsal room she worked and reworked her act under the shrewdly critical eye of Patrick Kenny himself, rehearsing every note, every step, every movement until she could have screamed with the frustration of it all.

'No, no, Miss Daniels! Can't you see? You've got to move about more – use the whole stage. Get down to the front there – involve your audience! And exaggerate, Miss Daniels – exaggerate! Get that chin up – stick those elbows out! Good Christ, you're supposed to be the cockiest pickpocket in town, not a sneak-thief who pinches pennies from old ladies! Jesus, Mary and Joseph! Smarten up! Swagger a bit! That's better –'

Sometimes she thought she hated him. Sometimes she knew she would never be able to face the vast stage and huge, intimidating, critical audience with which he so often threatened her. She lay sleepless through the long hours of the night, staring into darkness, hearing the echoes of that carping, critical voice, seeing nothing ahead but disaster and humiliation.

'For God's sweet sake, Miss Daniels – how often must I say it? Stop creeping around like a beaten child! Stand up straight! Get your shoulders back! And *sing*, girl, *sing*! Don't whine – oh, Christ, you aren't snivelling now, are you?'

'No.'

'Good. Right – back to the beginning. Start over in that corner and come towards me –'

If it had not been for Pol and little Amy Buckley she was sure she never would have stuck it. Pol it was who held her hand, wiped away her tired tears, mocked her gently and encouraged her fiercely when the mockery failed. She also showed unexpected skill with her needle and was invaluable in helping with costumes and props.

'You'll be there, won't you?' Kitty asked, anxiously, 'to help me dress?'

Poll grinned. 'Try ter keep me away!'

Time and again Kitty had tried to thank Luke for his magnificent gesture in paying off Moses so that Pol could join her. The debt, she knew, went beyond the money it had cost him, yet he brushed her thanks aside and utterly refused to discuss any idea of repayment. If, however, he had hoped – not unreasonably – that his gift might have made some difference to Pol's unflattering opinion of him, he must have been disappointed. Though unreservedly grateful, she with bland obstinacy reserved her right to dislike him, and made no secret of it. And Kitty sometimes thought that Luke admired her for it. She visited him at least twice a week, oases of pleasure in a grinding round of hard work. Their lovemaking was as fierce and as pleasurable as ever and in it she found the antidote to the fears and worries that beset her when faced with what seemed to her as Patrick Kenny's heartless persecution.

'Don't be so silly, Songbird!' Luke kissed her nose lightly, brushed warm lips along the line of her jaw. 'He wants you to be a success, that's all. And it doesn't grow on trees, to be picked with no effort. You don't get more than one chance in this business. You flop, and that's that. No second go. Kenny's putting his own reputation up with yours, you know – and he has more to lose than you have. Listen to him. He knows what he's doing.'

'Well, I just wish he'd stop shouting for a minute every now and again while he's doing it,' she said, gloomily unconvinced.

Inexorably the night grew closer and, as surely, Kitty's nerves grew taut as strung wire. The night before her debut

at the Cambridge Pol insisted upon pouring a large tot of
the detested brandy into her tea.

'Ugh! I can't drink this!'

''Old yer nose!' Pol said, firmly, 'it'll 'elp yer sleep. Yer
don't want ter go on stage lookin' like a bleedin' ghost, do
yer? Sorry, Mrs B,' she added and without waiting for protest.
Their friend and landlady, Kitty was astonished to note, was
in her determinedly respectable way toning down Pol's
vocabulary considerably – a feat which a few short weeks
before Kitty would have believed impossible.

She woke the next day, after a night of broken sleep, to
the low-slanting red sun of a late autumn morning, the first
crisp touch of winter in the steamed window panes and the
cloud of her breath on the air. It surprised her. In her
preoccupation she had hardly realized how the year had
advanced. She lay quite still for a long moment. This, then,
was the day. By this time tomorrow she would know what
the vastly different and more sophisticated audience of the
New Cambridge thought of her. Success tonight could mean
an open door to fame, prosperity and safety. Failure could
condemn her to a return to Smith's Song and Supper Rooms
and the shackles of poverty.

With a sudden, determined briskness she threw back the
bedcovers and braved the unexpectedly chill air.

Her success that night went beyond even her wildest and
most private dreams – a success, she realized later, that was
aided and abetted by an audience already strongly predis-
posed towards her.

'There's nobs in,' she heard someone say, excitedly, ten
minutes or so before the curtain went up. 'They've packed
the place. Pat Kenny's jumping about like a monkey with
pepper up his you-know-what –' The speaker, a young girl
in the spangles and tights of an acrobat, cast a quick, inquisitive glance in Kitty's direction as she flitted gracefully past,
but said nothing directly to her. Earlier Kitty had seen her
nursing a tiny, undernourished baby who lay, now dis-

regarded, in a cardboard box in the corner of the dressing room.

'Nobs?' Kitty asked uncertainly of Pol's reflection in the mirror. 'What does she mean, nobs? What's she talking about?'

Pol tweaked a lock of hair. 'Sit still. Your bloody 'air's 'ard enough to 'andle without you jumpin' about like a scalded cat. Luke's invited a few friends, so I 'ear – oh, come on, don't be daft' – she sensed Kitty's stiffening, had caught the swift, concerned glance in the mirror – 'not them kind of friends. Gawd girl, give 'im credit fer some sense! No – I 'eard 'im tellin' Mr Kenny 'e'd arranged a party fer some of the toffs 'e knows. The West End mob 'e 'angs about with.'

'Oh, God!'

'Come on – what's the difference? Toffs – dockers – they're all the same underneath. They'll take one look at them long legs o' yours an' that will be that, you mark my words. They'll love yer. There. Yer look top notch. I'll get the other outfit out.'

'We only have four minutes to change,' Kitty fretted.

Pol was unruffled. 'That's all right then. We only need three.' The dressing room was empty now. The neglected baby mewed in the corner. Music sounded in the distance. Pol grinned into the mirror encouragingly.

'Kit Daniels. Call for Kit Daniels.'

Shakily Kitty stood. Pol kissed her. 'You'll be just fine.'

Not until much later, in a dressing room crowded with strange faces and with an enormous glass of champagne in her hand, did Kitty dare to admit to herself just how terrified she had been until the moment she had stepped onto the stage. But then the magic had worked, and now it did not matter. This time her success was solid and incontrovertible. If she could arouse the audience of the New Cambridge to a pitch of enthusiasm where they simply would not allow her to leave the stage, then there could now be few barriers left between herself and what had seemed to be her unlikely ambitions. She did not fool herself – she knew what lay ahead involved hard work and no few heartaches, but the chance was what she had wanted and now, with the wildly enthusiastic roars of applause still ringing in her ears, she knew she had gained it.

'Splendid, m'dear. Absolutely splendid! An' very fetchin' too, if I might say so! Luke, old lad – where have you bin hidin' such a treasure?' The speaker was a tall, thin young man with a beak of a nose and a monocle that dropped from his eye every time he opened his mouth to speak. 'By God! I haven't enjoyed myself so much since Mackney opened at the Alhambra! And I must say, m'dear, you're a great deal prettier! A very great deal!' He snorted with laughter, then with elaborate courtesy removed the white carnation from his buttonhole. 'Please – a small token of me undyin' admiration –'

Kitty accepted the flower, smiling, laid it beside several others on the table before her.

'Out of the way, Barty old boy. Let the dog see the rabbit! Ah – and there she is! Beauty, talent and that rare – *je ne sais quoi* –' A stocky man, red faced, white haired and with the most magnificent set of snowy whiskers Kitty had ever seen, bent to give the surprised Kitty a smacking kiss. 'Ain't ready to consider marryin' a besotted old man, I s'pose? That'd show the young 'uns, what? Percy Roland. Your devoted slave, Miss Daniels.'

'Sir Percy,' someone said, drily, 'still doesn't let the grass grow under his feet, does he? God only knows what he was like at thirty –'

'Roly!' Luke came through the crowd, smiling easily. 'Leave her alone, you old dog!'

The old man's eyes twinkled with mischief. 'Aha! That's the lie of the land, is it? Might have known it, you gypsy barbarian!' He turned back to Kitty. 'Dear child – just re-member – if ever you need to be rescued from this savage, just call on me. My sword is at your service at all times.' He winked salaciously.

She laughed. 'I'll remember.'

More champagne was poured. She drank it thirstily.

'Kitty! Wonderful! Hit of the season! I knew you could do it! We'll draw up a contract tomorrow –' Patrick Kenny swooped on her. Dapper as ever and not a hair out of place, yet she sensed his genuine excitement.

'Contract?' Luke said, wagging a gently admonishing finger sorrowfully. 'Tut, tut, tut. Not the time nor the place to talk business, my friend. And anyway – we aren't sure we want a contract –'

We? Kitty sat bolt upright, head tilted, straining her ears in the hubbub to catch the words of the conversation now being carried on above her head.

'Oh, come now, Luke – who took the chances?'

'There were none to be taken. You knew what you had.' Luke's smile was easy, his voice friendly, yet there was a hint of steel somewhere about it.

Kitty looked sharply from one to the other. 'Luke!'

'My dear Miss Daniels – or may I call you Kitty? I'm sure we're going to be just the greatest of friends. We might as well start as we mean to go on, yes? Standen D'Arcy – theatre and music critic for – oh, Lord knows how many unnameable rags – well, we all have a poor living to make, don't we? So delighted to meet you –' She found her fingers taken delicately in a small white hand, raised to red, full lips. The diminutive, effeminate Mr D'Arcy simpered at her. 'Aren't you just the teeniest bit curious to know what I'm going to say about you tomorrow?' he asked, archly.

At that precise moment she was in fact much more interested in what Luke and Patrick Kenny were saying about her over her head. She gave in, however, gracefully. The purveyor of information to Lord knew how many unnameable rags was clearly a personage to be courted, and unfortunately he knew it. She patted the chair beside her. 'Of course, Mr D'Arcy. Do come and tell me.'

(iii)

It was astonishing, after that first breakthrough, just how quickly the snowball of fortune moved, gathering momentum, drawing to Kitty as it went both the privileges and — inevitably — the disadvantages of sudden fame. She was besieged by those who wanted to court her, dress her, write songs for, or articles about her. She became almost overnight the fresh focus for those idle and usually well-heeled gentlemen of all ages who made an enjoyable way of life out of pursuing the darlings of the theatre; the newer and more outrageous the better. They got as short shrift as did the over-enthusiastic tradesmen. If they were amusing — and, to be fair, a lot of them were — she had no objections to being amused; any other expectations were swiftly dashed — though she could not help but suspect with an amused exasperation that their restraint had more to do with Luke Peveral's shadowy presence in her life than with any respect for her or her wishes.

In one thing she was adamant — she would not allow herself to be winkled out of Pascal Road. If it was good enough before the New Cambridge, it was most certainly still good enough now. In the short time she had been there it had become a comfortable home and a stable base, and her friendship with Pol and with Amy Buckley was very precious to her. Pol, who was still unabashedly and, Kitty suspected, more successfully, pursuing Barton Wesley, was now officially her dresser and went everywhere with her. When, in the week that followed that first triumphant night, Patrick Kenny, at Luke's insistence, installed Kitty in her own private dressing room, complete with day bed, mirrored dressing table and with the picture of the Dipper that Jem had given her in pride of place on the wall, Pol it was who, with razor tongue and an utter disregard for rank or station, defended her privacy and kept unwanted visitors from the door. For, of course, unwanted visitors there were, by the baker's dozen; it did not take Kitty long to discover that the bright blade of success was sharply double-edged. Inevitably there were drawbacks. If she were too tired or too busy to give an interview, a critic would damn her as arrogant. If she resisted the too-forceful charms of a young man of flawed reputation, that did not always stop him from speaking of her as if she had not. None of it worried her. She was, in the months that followed, truly happy for perhaps the first time in her life. Success bred in her a confidence that in turn bred further success. Her relationship with her audience – almost the most important thing in her life, certainly the mainspring of her performance, improved with each passing day. It was for them she worked, to them she dedicated every effort, and they instinctively knew it, and they loved her for it. She gave them unstintingly of herself, and in return they strengthened and stimulated her. She added to her repertoire – Bertie, who suffered unrequited love for Carrie, the costermonger's daughter, came into being, together with a dashing cavalryman, Stacey by name, who strode the stage in gallant scarlet and was the scourge of the Frenchies and the darling of the ladies.

'Do you think I'll ever get to wear a dress in public again?' she asked Pol one day, half-laughing. 'I'm afraid if I walked onto the stage in a gown no one would recognize me!'

The weeks and the months sped by. She signed a short-term contract with Patrick Kenny, but not until after she had had a few sharp words to say about the man's infuriating tendency to confer not with her but with Luke – a tendency that Kitty knew to be not the least discouraged by Luke himself. It caused the first real discord between them for some time, and the air did not clear for days, due mainly to the fact that, once temper had slipped the curb on Kitty's tongue, she as always found it impossible to hold back, and what had started as fairly reasoned argument soon deteriorated to passionate quarrelling.

'You don't own me, Luke! Stop trying to run my life!'

He was as angry as she. 'You'd have done well without me, I suppose?'

'I didn't ask for anything! You can't say I did! What you did, you did – for God knows what reasons of your own. Am I supposed to pay for that for the rest of my life with my freedom?'

'Is that what you think? Is it?'

'What else is there for me to think? You treat me like a

child! – Get on the stage, Kitty, and sing to the nice people – don't worry your pretty little head – I'll manage all the grown-up things.'

'You sound very grown-up at the moment, I must say!'

'Luke – you have to understand! I want some say in what I do, in what I am. That isn't too much to ask, surely? You and Barton might have created the Dipper – but you didn't create me! It's bad enough that Pat Kenny and people like that appalling little D'Arcy man think they can run me; to have you doing it too is just too much! How do you think I felt when Pat told me you'd already virtually negotiated that contract without once consulting me? Two inches high, that's how! And I won't have it!'

'I didn't think you'd want to be bothered with such details.'

'Well, think again! And stop interfering!'

She knew she had gone too far. She did not see him for days. Three evenings running she allowed herself to be escorted by surprised and delighted young Johnnies to the smartest restaurants in the West End. Hoping to see him. Hoping, more to the point, that he would see her. See that she didn't care. On the fourth, alone, she finished up as she had always known she would in the dusty porch of St Bartholomew's, tugging nervously at the bell-rope that hung in the corner.

'Well, well. The prodigal returns. Where's the sackcloth and ashes?'

Miserably she pulled a face. 'I'm sorry,' she said. 'I'm sorry. I didn't mean it.'

He eyed her with frank and exasperated amusement. 'Don't tell such fibs. Of course you did.' Strong arms, warm mouth, lean body that fed her hunger and slaked her thirst. They made love in the firelight and then again in the dawn, and all was well.

Until the next time.

One aspect of her new life brought her nothing but pleasure. She, who had never in her life owned more than two dresses at the same time and never one that might be described as fashionable, now discovered that it was positively expected of her that she should invest in a wardrobe as varied and fashionable as possible. The full crinoline, that had never really suited her, was now evolving into the elegant bustle – a style very well suited to Kitty, with her long legs and narrow hips, though her lack of curves and strong-boned face still kept her, she was the first to admit, from being regarded as a popular beauty. From light-hearted, modish, Second-Empire Paris a foam of frills and flounces were imported. Wisely she resisted them, refusing to be forced into styles that she knew did not suit her – and in another area of her life her confidence grew again as she learned to take decisions and stick to them.

In the early spring of 1866, Lottie was delivered, full term, of a child, a little girl that she named Poppy. Pol, who despite Lottie's earlier coldness to her had never lost her affection for the other girl, was there to help both before and during the difficult birth, and for her friend's sake if not for her own Kitty was happy at the reconciliation. Pol it was who told her of Moses Smith's unlikely delight in the unexpected role of father.

'Anyone'd think the thing'd never bin done before. Mind you, she's a pretty little thing, the kid. Accordin' ter Lottie Moses is talkin' of makin' it legal. Mind you – pigs might fly – needless ter say 'e 'asn't named a day!'

But – astonishingly – he did. With that odd quirk of respectability that so often resides in the least respectable of souls, Moses Smith decided to make an honest woman of the mother of his child – and so it was that in midsummer of that year, with two great countries of Europe, Austria and Prussia, on the brink of war, with the telegraph cable that was to link Britain to the United States nearing completion and with the music halls of London gaining in popularity every day, Kitty found herself back at Smith's Song and Supper Rooms celebrating the most improbable wedding of the year.

She pondered, that afternoon, as she watched the festivities, on the strange and timeless magic of such occasions.

Animosity and resentment seemed for the moment forgotten – Moses had greeted her, beaming, as if no sharp word had ever passed between them, though Lottie had not spoken to her. Hardship and deprivation, the fear of the law and its punishments that more usually haunted these streets had given way for the time being to celebration. As the bride, looking more beautiful than Kitty had ever seen her in a dress of cobweb lace sewn with tiny pearls, and her fat, perspiring husband were escorted through the cobbled streets and lanes from the church, the world and his wife turned out to greet them. On every street corner barrels of ale and of porter had been set out. Men, women and children staggered happily as they called down the blessings of Heaven on the happy couple. Flower petals and tiny scraps of coloured paper made a colourful blizzard in the stinking alley of Blind Lane. Moses beamed, a father to his people, his malice stored in darkness for the day. His bride, pale and beautiful, looked at Luke Peveral with a defiance in her eyes that no one noticed but Kitty.

The Rooms were packed. For a while Kitty found herself an embarrassing centre of attention – not a soul there but had heard of her success and wished to assure her that never a doubt had there been as to its certainty. When she realized that through no fault of her own she was causing almost as much stir as the bride and groom she hastily disengaged herself from the crowd and tried to shrink into the relative obscurity of a darkened corner. Over the heads of the crowd the bride's eyes met hers, cool and expressionless, and she knew that nothing, whether real or imagined, had been forgotten or forgiven.

It did not, of course, take long for the party to become predictably riotous. Kitty, seated at a table beside Luke with Pol and Barton Wesley, winced at a rendering of *Polly Perkins* so off-key as to be painful, but bearing in mind the bride's already intemperate hostility declined to improve on it herself. A space was cleared on the floor for dancing, and the pint mugs of porter began to line up on the piano and the pianist got into the swing of the celebrations. Nearer at hand, Barton was already at that happy stage of inebriation that had stilled his usually rapid tongue and put a picturesquely silly smile more or less permanently on his face.

Pol leaned towards him. 'Nice do, ain't it?'

'It certainly is.' The words were more than a little blurred at the edges.

'Married,' she said, thoughtfully. ''Oo'd 'a' thought it?'

Barton shook his head sagely, still grinning like an idiot.

Kitty, knowing Pol, was watching and listening, stifling laughter.

Pol sighed. 'Nice idea, ain't it – marriage? Sort of – romantic?'

A spark of panic had appeared in the little man's eyes. 'Sort of permanent, too,' he managed, remarkably soberly.

Pol leaned closer, took his hand in hers, turned it over as if to read his palm. 'Aw, Bart – just think. 'Ome an' 'earth. Kids. Slippers by the fire.'

He was staring at her, owlishly appalled. 'W-would you like another drink?'

Straight-faced, she leaned back in her chair, reaching for her empty glass. 'Not half. I thought you'd never ask.'

As Barton pushed his way into the crowd Kitty laughed. 'You shouldn't tease him so.'

'Why not? Does 'im good. An' one o' these days I'll get 'im so pissed 'e'll propose, you see if I don't.'

'Kit! Kitty, moi owd gal! There you are! I've been looking all over the place.' Matt swooped upon Kitty, caught her hand. 'I'm going to dance with my famous sister. Don't mind, do you, Guv'nor? – come on, Kit – let's show them how it's done –'

It was deliberate, she knew – dancing and breathless she could not ask awkward questions of him. She had not seen much of him in the past months, but rumours had reached her – rumours that she prayed had not reached Moses – that he still courted his Sally-Anne, despite – or perhaps, she thought, knowing him, because of – the obstacles. 'How are you?' she shouted, above the music.

'Fine.'

'Keeping out of trouble?'

'Trouble? Me?' He swooped her into his arms, whirled her around the floor. 'Don't know the meaning of the word.'

When she returned to the table Luke stood a little way off, talking earnestly to Spider. Barton snored, his head pillowed uncomfortably upon the table. Pol nursed Poppy, a tiny, delicately beautiful child, murmuring to her softly, protecting her from the crush about them.

Kitty parted the shawl that covered the child's face and looked at the perfect, doll-like features. 'She's lovely.'

'She is that. 'Ow's Matt?'

'Same as ever.' Kitty offered a finger to the tiny, grasping hand. 'Oh, Pol – I do hope it isn't true he's still seeing that girl – he's storing up such trouble for himself – and still he won't listen, still he won't come. It's like – it's like talking to a stranger –'

Barton mumbled and moved. His arm slipped, dangling, from the table.

'Oh, blimey, just look at 'im. 'Ere – Kit, 'old the baby fer a minute, would yer? I'd better straighten 'im up before 'e does 'imself a mischief.'

Kitty received the warm little bundle, settled the child safely in her arms. Someone had staggered onto the stage and was roaring a drunken and riotously obscene song. Pol heaved at Barton's slight, utterly unconscious body. Kitty bent to the child, adjusted the shawl about the tiny, flower-like face then, some sixth sense warning her, she glanced up to find Luke standing across the table from her, eyes and face totally inscrutable us he watched her. Oddly, a faint, uncertain pulse, something like a flutter of fear, began to beat in her throat. Hastily she leaned towards Pol. 'Here, you'd better take her –' and she handed the child back.

Someone had struck up an energetic polka on the piano. She stood up briskly, holding out her hand to Luke. 'Let's dance?'

They went back to his room long before the celebrations, that looked set to continue into the following day, had even begun to wane. They walked the narrow streets that were

still littered with the detritus of the day, clambered precariously across the wooden plank and walked the canyoned
alleys down which Kitty had fled in panic that day so
many months before, to the church. Behind them flitted the
watching shadow that was Spider.

'Where does he live?' Kitty asked, in curiosity. 'Where
does he sleep?'

Luke shrugged. 'He has places.'

'But – no home?'

Luke shrugged.

'But – that's a pretty awful life, isn't it?'

'It's what he wants. I've tried to change him. He won't
listen. He's doing what he wants to do.'

'Looking after you.'

'I suppose so; yes.'

'Why?' There was real curiosity in her sideways glance.

'I saved his life once. He thinks he owes it to me.'

'It's more than that,' she said, positively.

He turned her into his arms, kissed her. She closed her
eyes and snuggled to him. She was pleasantly light-headed
from the wine she had drunk. They strolled on.

'Someone –' he mused, 'was it the Greeks? I can't remember – someone used to believe that if you saved a person's
life you became responsible for them. They belonged to you
– you became' – he paused – 'irretrievably entangled.'

They had entered the dark porch. 'Do you remember the
first time you came here?'

She shivered a little. 'Yes. Of course.'

'You probably saved my life that night.'

She shook her head. 'You'd have got away somehow.'

He smiled faintly. 'Such touching faith, Miss Daniels –'

They slipped into the alcove, started up the stairs. Suddenly then Luke's hand was an iron grip upon her wrist, his
voice a breath in her ear, all mockery gone from it. 'Wait!'

She saw it too. Above them a faint light filtered into the
stairway through the open door.

She sensed rather than saw the finger he put to his lips.
Silent as a menacing shadow, he continued up the stairs.

She waited for a tense moment before, unable to remain behind, heart pounding and head suddenly and uncomfortably clear, she followed.

Luke stood like a statue by the door. She looked past him. Sprawled on the rug by the empty fireplace lay the body of a man.

Kitty put a hand to her mouth.

Then she saw the empty bottle that had rolled a little way from the lax, open hand.

Jem O'Connell stirred, snorted, lapsed again into unconsciousness, dead drunk.

8

(i)

It took three days properly to sober up the young American, three days during which he slept a lot, wept at least once and divulged not one word of what had happened to bring him back, and in such a state.

'Leave him,' Luke said. 'What he wants us to know he'll tell us in his own good time.'

But he did not. Neither then nor later did Kitty learn the details of Jem O'Connell's last and obviously harrowing trip home. Remembering their conversation in the gardens, there was a lot at which she could guess but she, like Luke, respected Jem's silence and did not question. Just once he spoke, bitterly and close again to tears, of the helpless vulnerability to hurt that could be inflicted by love, and it occurred to Kitty that his treatment at the hands of his mother and sister had deeply damaged an open and loving nature. It would be a long time, she thought, before Jem O'Connell would be ready to give his heart into the hands of a woman and once again leave himself open to such pain. His mother and sister had rejected him – how brutally could only be judged by the depth of his distress. Whatever had happened, it had driven him from home for good. He was on his way back to Paris, he told them, and this time to stay. 'At least,' he said with a flicker of a smile, 'a man can drink himself to death there in good company and with no interference.'

That possibility, a concerned Kitty felt, was not in fact as remote as could be wished. Not even the ravages that Jem suffered after that first spectacular bout of drinking that had left him unconscious on Luke's floor could keep him from determined and almost self-destructive intoxication; she suspected too that he had discovered the doubtful pleasures of the Oriental waterfront bars, where more than alcohol was offered as a way to oblivion. His talent he wantonly neglected. In the three months between that unheralded and drunken arrival and his equally abrupt if slightly more sober disappearance just after Christmas Kitty never once saw him pick up a paintbrush. It surprised and hurt her more than a little that he left without saying goodbye, except by means of a brief, self-mocking little note in which he apologized for the outrageous inconvenience to which he knew he had put them and promised, sooner or later, to be in touch if and when he was ever sober again.

'I suppose he's gone back to Paris?' Sadly Kitty fingered the pens and pencils he had left behind, which she had seen him use so often and with such skill. She had grown very fond indeed of Jem O'Connell and had found it painful to watch his degeneration over these past months.

'I wouldn't be surprised.' Luke folded and refolded the note, tossed it in the fire and watched it burn. 'He has friends there, after all.'

'He has friends here.'

He said nothing.

The anger of frustration and worry sharpened Kitty's voice. 'Some friends. Seems to me they're the kind that will help him drink himself to death rather than hinder him!'

He shrugged. 'You have to let a man go his own way.'

She lifted her head sharply at that.

He did not notice.

It was an irony that, during those months that Kitty found herself helplessly watching as Jem drowned himself and his talent at the bottom of a whisky bottle, her own star had risen beyond any expectation or dream she had ever dared entertain. She had completed her first contract with Kenny and had signed another. She had been delighted and astonished to discover that she could now command a salary of thirty guineas a week – an absolute fortune to one who had once scrubbed floors for seven a year and worked a long hard day in Covent Garden for a shilling. She was able now to pay Pol a regular salary, and had found a niche too for Barton, as secretary, songwriter and general factotum. Matt, stubbornly, refused her help. He was unreservedly pleased for her and proud of her. But he would not join her. And finally she realized she would have to give up. Matt would do what he wanted and nothing would stop him.

To Luke's amusement she still would not leave Pascal Road for more splendid accommodation. For her, the little house had become more a home than any she had ever had, and she needed nothing grander. She, Pol and Amy Buckley were the firmest of friends, living together in easy companionship. Number twenty-three was a haven for Kitty, a place where she could be herself and where warmth and undemanding affection were assured. Amy looked after their physical well-being with the skill and pleasure of a born mother – Kitty often felt saddened for her that there had been no little Buckleys to appear before her husband had died of fever the winter before. Pol was Kitty's strong right hand, a happy combination of mother, friend, sister and maid, whose sense of humour rarely failed and whose loyalty was absolute. Kitty happily used some of her new-found wealth to make them comfortable; no longer did Amy Buckley have to scrape and save to provide a meal each evening. They ate and drank of the best. She bought comfortable furniture for the sitting room, a sewing machine for Pol. She filled the bunker in the back yard with coal. Just before Christmas she took Amy and Pol to the wonderful new showrooms of Messrs Swan and Edgar at Piccadilly Circus and bought each of them a fashionable new outfit as a Christmas present. She enjoyed spending money, and spend it she did.

But for every penny spent there was a penny saved. Kitty Daniels was never going to be poor again, on that she was determined. Her thrifty saving was, she knew, another thing that amused Luke. When she tried to pay him back the money he had paid to release Pol he grinned. 'Put it in your moneybox, little miser. It means a lot more to you than it does to me.'

Jem left them in January, with bitter winds scouring the city and Croucher and his mates working the 'shaller dodge' – begging, half-dressed and half-frozen in the winter streets. At this time the relatively new music halls were perhaps the most popular and expanding entertainment in London, and the prospect of fame and fortune upon its stage was no longer for Kitty simply a dream. Fortunes were being made overnight by those with the talent and the strength to exploit the possibilities. At the top of the tree a hundred guineas a week and more could be earned, and of course for a pretty girl the lure of a liaison, or even in some cases a marriage, with wealth and title, was the glittering lure that was to lead some to brilliant fortune but many more to disillusion and obscurity.

Kitty had her admirers, and she learned very quickly to play the game that was expected of her with skill; but for her still the reality of her complex and often difficult relationship with Luke precluded the possibility of any other. And Luke's reputation was such, she soon discovered, as to keep the most persistently amorous swain at bay, no matter what his place in society. But though the addiction of his powerful attraction still held her fast, their life together was far from peaceful, and at the beginning of a cold February they had a very typical quarrel, blown from nothing to something in a second and, once started, all but impossible to stop.

Kitty was not at her best – she always suffered depression for a couple of days before her monthly period started, and the strain of performing on stage at these times inevitably stretched her nerves and shortened her temper. Their lovemaking that afternoon was brief and for her less than satisfying. She wished she had the strength at such times to explain, to refuse him, but though often she made the resolution she never carried it through. She lay on her stomach, her head pillowed on her crossed arms. When Luke spoke she stirred, a little sleepily. 'Sorry?'

He was sitting on the side of the bed pulling his shirt over his head, and his voice was muffled. 'I said how long are you thinking of staying with Kenny at the Cambridge?'

'I don't know. I haven't really thought about it.'

'Well, you should, don't you think?'

She swallowed the first stirrings of irritation. 'I will,' she said, mildly.

'Soon.'

Exasperated she lifted her head. 'Luke – for Heaven's sake! I wish you wouldn't lecture me! Do I go around telling you what to do and what not to do?'

He paused, one foot poised above his trouser leg. 'There's no need to be so touchy.'

'I'm not!' she snapped.

'I'm only trying to help.'

She relented. 'I know. I do know. But – as I said – the truth is I don't know quite where I want to go from here. Pat wants me to extend the new contract –'

'So he told me.'

Firmly she quelled the renewed spurt of irritation the inference of the casual words aroused.

'You could get more elsewhere,' he said.

'We don't know that. I might get less.'

'Not if you play your cards right.'

She ducked her head again, not looking at him, praying for patience. 'Luke – I'm not playing cards! I'm living my life. Or trying to. I don't want to take too many chances too soon.'

'I can understand that I suppose but you must surely see that –'

She interrupted him. 'The one who took the chance was Pat Kenny. I feel I owe him something. I can't just up and walk off –'

'Nonsense.'

Her mouth clamped shut. The uncertain temper that so plagued her prompted words that she would not speak. In silence she sat up and began to dress with quick, angry movements.

'Why not try Morton at the Canterbury?' He seemed
entirely unaware of her anger.

'Don't be silly. I'm not sure I'm ready for that yet.'

'If you aren't ready now, you never will be.'

Grimly she wrenched at outrageously expensive white
silk stockings. Why were the damned things never long
enough? Four petticoats were strewn, crumpled about the
floor. Her heelless buttoned boots lay where she had kicked
them off on the rug before the fire. Grumpily she scavenged
for her clothes. 'Perhaps later on in the spring,' she said,
sweetly reasonable.

'Perhaps that will be too late?'

That did it. 'And perhaps,' she said very precisely, 'that's
my business?'

He treated her to a long, cool look. She turned from him
and began to struggle into the voluminous petticoats. She
glanced at the clock that ticked quietly on the mantelshelf.
In two hours she was due on stage. She was late.

'You have to move on,' he said.

'I don't have to do anything I don't want to do!' There
was open challenge in her voice. Absurdly angry she
struggled into the violet velvet, bustled daydress that
seemed determined to fight her very inch of the way. 'God!
Why must women be so afflicted with buttons and bows
and bloody trimmings? What's the matter with this damned
thing?' She fumbled with the last of the fastenings, snatched
the matching jacket from a nearby chair.

He would not give an inch. 'Kitty, do stop being so childish. We have to talk about this –'

She straightened to face him. Shook her head. 'No, Luke.
We don't have to talk about it at all. I have to think about
it and I have to make a decision. This is my business. Mine!
Do I try to tell you what to do? Do we hold a board meeting
about every decision you take?'

He made an irritated, dismissive gesture. 'That's different –'

'It bloody isn't!' She stormed to the mirror, brush in hand
and with swift, angry movements swept her straight hair

into a severe centre parting and pinned it into a bun at the
nape of her neck.

He watched her, and she saw in the mirror his effort at
self-control. 'Fair enough,' he said, coolly.

She said nothing. Cursorily she finished her sketchy
toilette. Glanced again at the clock. 'I'll have to go.'

He nodded.

'Will you be there tonight?'

'I don't know.' The chill was there, barely beneath the
surface.

She paused at the door. 'Please yourself.' She shut the
door very quietly behind her.

A dozen steps up the road she wanted to turn back. But
she did not.

(ii)

In her oversensitive mood the quarrel, silly and slight as it
was, upset her badly. That evening she was absent with Pol,
downright distant with poor garrulous Barton. In her head,
as so often, she argued with the absent Luke, finding too
late the reasoned words that had earlier eluded her, firmly
saying all the right things –

'It's almost time,' Pol said.

'Thank you.' Why hadn't she kept her stupid temper?
How had she been reduced to such childishness? And why,
oh why, couldn't Luke learn that she had to be independent
– didn't need or want to be looked after like some kind of
backward infant?

'Miss Daniels. Miss Daniels. Five minutes, please.'

She stood up, peered at her transformed self in the mirror,
picked up her top hat and cane. Tonight she would speak
to him. Tonight she would be all reason and charm but she
would make him understand. Tonight, when he came – if
he came – she would, oh she would keep her temper –

Two hours later she sat before the same mirror and knew
that her resolutions had been for nothing. Luke was not

coming. She felt restless now, and full of that strange energy that her stage performances seemed to generate within her. Despite her earlier depression and despite Luke's absence she felt stimulated and exhilarated. The audience had loved her. She had taken three curtain calls. She could barely sit still now as Pol brushed out her hair, the echoes of applause still filling her ears.

'Went down well ternight from the sound of it.' Pol brushed her hair with long, soothing strokes.

'Yes.' She leaned back and closed her eyes, trying to relax. Why should she care if Luke chose to sulk?

'They liked the new verses?'

'Loved them. I must remember to tell poor Barton. I'm afraid I rather snapped his head off earlier.'

Pol smoothed the heavy hair with her hand, bound it into a loose knot. 'What's goin' on ternight? You comin' 'ome? There's a cab waitin'.'

'Yes, I think so. Luke's' – she hesitated – 'busy.'

Pol did not comment. 'You could do with an early – 'oo the 'ell's that?'

The sharp rap sounded again at the door. 'Mam'selle Daniels?' An assured voice, heavily accented.

Pol's eyes met Kitty's in the mirror, eyebrows raised. Kitty shrugged. 'Be a dear – get rid of him for me?'

Pol went to the door and opened it a crack. 'Can I 'elp you?'

'I wish to see Mam'selle Kitty Daniels on a matter of the most extreme importance. You'll please tell her?'

From the mirror Kitty gained an impression of a square, heavily handsome face, eyes of velvet brown beneath shining hair black and smooth as jet, and a picturesquely neat Imperial moustache and beard. The man's accent was magnificently Gallic.

'Miss Daniels isn't available.' Pol's voice was brusque. She didn't care for foreigners.

'But no! I insist! I tell you I have something of very great importance to discuss with her –'

'Tomorrow,' Pol said firmly.

'But tomorrow, Mam'selle, may be too late! I really must see her –'

Pol was having some difficulty in shutting the door. Kitty saw with some amusement the toe of a shining boot planted firmly in the opening.

'Well, 'ard cheese,' Pol said, pleasantly enough, and pushed harder.

'Mam'selle!' The word was urgent. 'I implore you! A chance, simply, to introduce myself –'

The opening had been reduced to a crack no more than three inches wide. 'Introduce away,' Pol said, agreeably.

'I am Charles Parisot. Mam'selle Daniels will undoubtedly know of me –'

Pol glanced at Kitty, who shook her head. 'I think not, Monsewer,' Pol said, drily.

'But yes! Of course! I have many theatres and café concerts – in Paris and in Bordeaux – my name is known throughout Europe!'

'Not 'ere it isn't.' Pol, putting all her considerable strength into the effort, was winning the battle of the door.

On impulse Kitty smoothed her hair, drew her loose gown around her. 'All right, Pol.' She winked. 'Let him in.'

Pol looked at her in surprise.

Kitty shrugged. 'Why not?'

'Mam'selle Daniels!' With exaggerated gestures the Frenchman entered, elegantly and gallantly bending over her hand, snow-white gloves, silver-topped cane held with his top hat in one hand, a single bright diamond on the hand that held hers. 'I come to tell you – you are a wonder! An enchantment! Parisot – even Parisot! – is smitten! What style – what panache –!' He placed a rose on the table before her, reached for her hand again, pressed his lips not to her knuckles but to her open palm. Over the bent head Kitty's eyes signalled hilarious disbelief and Pol screwed her face up in open laughter.

'– When my good friend Kenny tells me he has discovered a sensation, I tell myself – phut! The Irishman exaggerates again! But no. This time every word he speaks is truth.

Mam'selle Daniels – I come to tell you – you are wasted here! Wasted!' He straightened. He was still holding her hand. Gently she disengaged it. He looked regretful, but did not openly protest. 'Mam'selle, I have something of enormous importance to put to you –' He looked round and indicated a nearby chair. 'I may sit?'

'By all means.' The man's every word was accompanied by gestures of such immoderation that Kitty found it difficult to take anything he said very seriously.

Parisot drew a spindle-legged chair very close to hers. 'Europe – Paris – *La Ville Lumière* – awaits you, Mam'selle!'

Kitty kept a perfectly straight face. 'Really?'

He sat back. 'You joke with me?'

'Of course not, M'sieu. But – forgive me – this is a little sudden, is it not?'

He smiled a small, utterly charming smile. 'Mam'selle – great passions are always sudden, are they not?'

She could not help but laugh. 'I suppose so.'

'But of course. Love does not wait upon convenience, Mam'selle. And Paris will love you, as you will love Paris. You know my wonderful city?'

She shook her head. 'No.'

The beringed hands spread, the eyes rolled dramatically. 'Ah – but then I envy you! For what an experience you have to come! To see Paris for the very first time – and in the spring! To walk her streets, to feel her heart beat – Mam'selle Daniels, Paris is a flower of a city! The centre of Europe! The jewel in the crown of the world! And now – this year – her glory is doubled by the efforts of our Emperor! You have heard of the Great Exhibition?'

Kitty shook her head again. 'No.' Despite herself she was fascinated by the flamboyance of the man, the odd, almost irresistible warmth he exuded.

He leaned forward again. 'In the summer, Mam'selle, Paris is to be the scene of the greatest exhibition the world has ever seen, or will ever see again! Art! Music! Culture! Science! The wonders of our modern world! All the elegance, all the knowledge of man will be there – and to see it will come the cream of Europe, and beyond. Crowned heads, Mam'selle – the Czar, the Kaiser, your own dear Queen – and you – you, Mam'selle Daniels! – shall be part of it all!'

She stared at him, bemused, still half-laughing. 'M'sieu –!'

'No, no!' He held up an imperious hand. 'Say nothing! A word spoken swiftly will always be regretted!' He paused. Kitty wondered if he ever spoke in anything but exclamations. His next words, spoken softly and persuasively, the dauntlessly charming smile flitting once more across his face, seemed to prove that he did not. 'Come to dinner with me, Mam'selle! We will speak of it! I will persuade you!'

She had to laugh. 'M'sieu Parisot, I'm afraid –'

'Ah, but no! You will not – you cannot? – refuse me, Mam'selle? A few short hours in your delightful company is all I ask. I will tell you of Paris. I will tell you of my theatres. I will tell you of the sensation you will cause in my wonderful city –!'

'And will you tell me, M'sieu, of your wife and beautiful children?' she asked, gently mischievous.

He looked surprised, even a little hurt. 'But of course!' He smiled, wickedly. 'I have daguerreotypes.'

She considered that. 'Which you don't, of course, carry upon your person?'

He shrugged. 'Ah, but no, Mam'selle – they are –'

'– in your hotel room?' she finished.

'But yes.'

'I thought they might be.' The man entertained her enormously. She laughed suddenly, coming to an impulsive decision. Let Luke think she was moping alone over cocoa and biscuits! She held out her hand. 'Dinner? Yes – why not?' She wagged a stern finger. 'Daguerreotypes and hotel rooms? Definitely not.'

'Mam'selle,' he said collectedly, 'your good sense is exceeded only by your beauty. I'll wait while you dress.'

'Outside,' she said, firmly.

Mournfully he nodded. 'Outside.'

'The funny thing is that I think it's really all true!' Kitty told Pol later, curled in an armchair before the dying fire in the little sitting room of number twenty-three. Amy had gone to bed long ago – it had amused Kitty to find Pol, dozing but determinedly waiting, when she had arrived home. 'He really does have theatres in Paris and Bordeaux. And there really is to be a great international exhibition in Paris this summer. And M'sieu Parisot really is going to open a new theatre – the Moulin d'Or – to coincide with it –'

'An' I s'pose 'e really does 'ave a wife an' children, too?'

Kitty spread expressive, Gallic hands. 'But of course!' she said, her voice heavily accented, and giggled. The champagne had been very good indeed. 'The children are at school in England, and he really did have pictures of them. Oh, Pol – I rather like him. Once he stopped trying to get me into bed with him he was very nice. He even got round to admitting that the reason that he's over here looking for someone to open at the Moulin d'Or in the summer is because the girl he originally booked had been poached by one of his rivals. He threatens a duel!' She laughed again, then sobered, and sat for a moment looking into the glowing embers of the fire. 'Paris,' she said pensively.

'You really think 'e's serious? About givin' you a job? I mean 'e's not just – you know – after the other?'

Kitty grinned. 'Oh, that too, if he can get it. But – yes – I think he's serious.'

'An' are you?'

The expression on Kitty's face was faintly defiant. 'Luke tells me I should take some chances,' she said. 'Why not this one?'

'Seems a long shot?'

Kitty lifted a shoulder, turned her gaze back to the fire. 'That doesn't stop me thinking about it, does it?'

Charles Parisot laid seige to Kitty as if he were a general determined to bring about the downfall of a citadel. He came to the theatre each evening, he sent flowers and outrageously expensive perfume, he entertained her, whenever she allowed him, to dinner. His light-hearted charm amused her, as did his declarations of devotion. She adamantly resisted all his efforts to get her into bed. She asked Patrick Kenny about him and was reassured that yes, he was indeed what he said he was and more. 'He's one of the greatest showmen in France, if not in Europe. If you can stay out of reach of those hands of his he could do a lot for you. But – a word in your ear – watch his wife!' Kenny grimaced, unsmiling. 'Believe me, that lady could – and would – tear you apart with her bare hands if she thought you were after Charles. At least one aspiring star I know of felt the brunt of Madame's anger and won't ever forget it. And neither will she work again.'

Luke, too, was amused by the flamboyance of the French-man, obviously, Kitty observed a little wryly, in no way seeing in him a rival for her affections. His arrogance, she thought, sometimes could be quite breathtaking. Their quarrel, such as it was, had been patched up a couple of days after it had happened, and Luke was in her dressing room when Charles Parisot's first gigantic bouquet was delivered.

'Good God!' Luke said mildly. 'Do you think he's robbed Kew Gardens? They surely couldn't all have come from the same shop?'

'M'sieu Parisot doesn't do things by halves.'

'I can see that.' Luke leaned back in his chair, watching her as she removed her stage make-up. Monty Montague's black silk top hat was perched at a rakish angle on his head. Luke was in high good humour. Kitty strongly suspected he was planning a fresh coup. 'Would it be ungallant of me to ask just what M'sieu is after?'

She laughed. 'Much the same as any other man. Except –'

'Except?'

'He's serious about this job in Paris. He's been let down – he badly needs a replacement, and quickly. He really does think I'm the one.'

'You should take it,' he said, positively.

She quelled irrational disappointment. That she was considering the Frenchman's offer she had not told Luke – she had half-hoped that when she told him he might try to dissuade her. 'Isn't it a bit soon?' she asked, perversely. 'I'm only just getting established here.'

'My dear Kitty – poor Jem was right about one thing if about nothing else – Paris at the moment is the centre of civilized Europe. A successful season there would make you.'

She turned back to the mirror. 'You wouldn't miss me?'

'I didn't say that.'

She dabbed furiously at her face.

'Take it, Kitty,' he said, 'it could be the chance of a lifetime. And that is what you want – isn't it?'

She went to dinner again with the Frenchman three evenings later; by the end of the evening he had agreed to give her ten days in which to make up her mind whether or not she would accept his offer. She hoped that that might cool his more personal pursuit, but it was not to be. The next day more flowers arrived, together with a note suggesting that she might like to meet him that evening after the performance, for dinner at his hotel. She read the note, then re-read it, her long, square-tipped finger tapping thoughtfully upon the table.

Pol snorted. 'What does the feller think – that yer floated upriver on the last 'igh tide? Dinner at 'is 'otel indeed! You aren't goin', are yer?'

Kitty shook her head. 'No, I'm not. But I don't think I'll tell him that. M'sieu Parisot really does have to be shown that I'm interested in his job not his splendid person – if he won't accept that, I shan't go to Paris anyway. I shan't reply. It won't do him any harm at all to expect me and to kick his heels alone tonight.'

In the event, however, it appeared that Charles Parisot's ardour had been cooled some other way. Just before the evening's performance a small boy in the claret and blue uniform of the Great Royal Hotel knocked at the dressing-room door. 'Note for Miss Daniels.'

Upon the claret-edged, pale blue notepaper Charles had apologized, picturesquely and profusely, for having to cancel their engagement at the last moment. An affair of great importance had cropped up and, regretfully, for now and for the next few days he would be, with extravagant regret, unavailable.

'Well –' Kitty tossed the note upon the table. 'That takes care of that anyway.'

Pol grinned irrepressibly. ''Is wife probably turned up.'

Kitty was searching through her purse for a coin to give the messenger boy. 'If I thought that was true I'd turn a cartwheel better than one of Springer's. Nothing could suit me better. Here.' Smiling, she handed the lad a sixpence.

'She did,' he said.

Kitty blinked. 'Who did? What?'

'The Frenchie's wife. Turned up.' The boy grinned, slyly pert. 'What a to-do! She was the third Madame Parisot we'd seen in as many weeks – an' a likely fourth was lunchin' in the dinin' room with 'im. Never saw anyone move so fast in me life.'

Kitty surveyed him, thought in her eyes. 'You mean – the *real* Madame Parisot turned up? From Paris?'

'The very same.' He grinned again. 'Unexpected-like. Large as life an' twice as mad.'

'And she's staying with him? At the Royal?'

'That's right.'

'Tell me –' Kitty had dipped into her purse again and was toying with a sixpence. 'You wouldn't know if they're dining at the hotel tonight?'

'Oh, yes. Took the message meself.'

Kitty handed him the other sixpence. 'Thank you. Thank you very much indeed.'

When she arrived at the Great Royal later that night the dining room was thronged with diners and the meal – as she had planned – was well under way. She had taken great care with her appearance – her dark red velvet gown, if not exactly demure, was restrained and she had had Pol coil her hair severely at the nape of her neck and confine it in a dark silk hairnet. Her only jewellery was a slim golden chain that Luke had given her. She looked, she thought, the very personification of respectability.

'I on'y 'ope yer know what yer doin',' Pol had grumbled for the dozenth time. 'This Madame what's 'er name don't sound like a lady ter be trifled with.'

'I'm not going to trifle with her.' Kitty had patted her hair sleekly to her head. 'I'm simply going to try to make sure that her husband stops trifling with me!'

Now she handed her velvet cape to the waiter who hovered questioningly at her side. 'M'sieu Parisot's table, please. He's expecting me.'

'Yes, madam. This way.'

She followed him, threading her way through the crowded tables. In a far corner of the room she could see her prey. Half-hidden by a monstrous aspidistra, Charles Parisot sat with his back to her approach. Opposite him sat a statuesque and striking woman in vivid emerald silk. A mass of black hair was piled in a glittering tower upon her head. Her bare, sloping shoulders were magnificent. Diamonds glittered at throat and ears. Fierce dark brows arched above enormous eyes, Spanish-dark. She looked, Kitty thought, quailing suddenly, a prima donna straight from the stage at Covent Garden. She took a breath, then swooped upon the table. 'Charles, my dear – I'm so sorry I'm late!'

She saw the shock in his eyes, the almost terrorized glance he threw at his wife. She turned, smiled her warmest smile. 'And you, surely, must be Charles' wife? I couldn't be mistaken – Charles has spoken of you so often – I truly feel as if I know you. Are you here to visit the children? Charles has shown me their pictures – such lovely little things! Little Marie has your eyes, has she not? Charles, you naughty thing' – she felt a nervous hilarity bubble at the frozen look on the man's face – 'why didn't you tell me that Madame Parisot was going to be here? I would have tried much harder not to be late!' She laughed a little – easy to do with the elegant and assured Charles Parisot staring at her for all the world like a goldfish stranded a very long way from its bowl. She proffered her hand to Madame Parisot, let quite genuine admiration show in her eyes and voice. 'Madame, it's a pleasure to meet you. Charles never stops speaking of you. Now that I've met you I must say that I can see why.' She stopped then and waited, patiently polite.

Charles, with an effort, collected himself. 'Chérie – this is Mam'selle Daniels. I have told you of her –'

'Ah. Yes. Of course.' Madame's English, like her husband's was meticulously correct if heavily accented. 'How do you do?'

'I'm well, thank you.'

Charles was still struggling somewhat. 'Kitty – Miss Daniels – I –'

She regarded him, artlessly questioning. He subsided. His forehead was beaded finely with sweat.

'Mam'selle Daniels' – Madame's voice was as velvet dark as her eyes – 'you had perhaps arranged to meet my husband this evening?' Her glance flicked to Parisot who all but physically flinched from it.

'Why, yes.' Kitty was innocence personified. 'I assumed we were to talk of the contract. I can't make up my mind until I know – oh, Charles!' She turned. 'I'm so sorry! Did I make a mistake? I was so sure that your note said tonight –?'

'I – sent another note –'

'Another?'

'Explaining –' He made a weak gesture towards his wife.

'You sent a note to the theatre?'

He nodded.

'There! That's that scatterbrained Pol again! She must have forgotten to give it to me. And – I've interrupted your meal together. Oh, I'm mortified – I'm so sorry!' She made a small, prettily apologetic gesture not to Parisot but to his wife.

Madame's glance held in its depth a distinct and astute gleam of amusement. 'You would care to join us perhaps?'

'Oh, no – I couldn't –' Kitty had made no move to rise.

'But yes' – the gleaming eyes flickered again – 'I have a feeling that we might find we have much in common, Miss Daniels.' The tiny, diverting moment of conspiracy passed Charles Parisot by completely. He looked bemusedly from one to the other.

'Well – if you're sure –' Kitty replied, smiling.

Smiling in return, Genevieve Parisot raised a long, commanding finger. '*Garçon!* Another place, *s'il vous plaît . . .*'

Luke was gratifyingly and amusedly admiring. 'So – having now established a bosom friendship with Madame Parisot –'

'Genevieve,' Kitty corrected him, grinning.

'– then poor M'sieu is snookered by the pair of you?'

'Something like that.' Kitty was unsympathetic. 'And the bonus is – I really do like Genevieve very much indeed. And I think she likes me. And now she knows I'm not after her husband there's no reason why we shouldn't be good friends.'

'You scheming little cat.' He pulled her to him. 'I'd never have guessed you had it in you to be so devious.'

She laughed softly. They were lying naked upon his bed. He kissed her breasts, gently rubbing the nipples with his lips, bringing the immediate, almost unbearable excitement to her body. She caressed his back, her fingers brushing lightly the scars of the long-healed welts that criss-crossed his wide shoulders. 'My father,' he had said, brusquely, when she had brought herself to question him. 'Who else?' And again, and not for the first time, she had found herself wondering that the man who had had such a father should so desire a son.

'I think,' she said, after a moment, as he lay with his head pillowed upon her bare shoulder, 'that I might go to Paris. Will you mind?'

He lifted his head. She saw the gleam of his eyes in

the half-darkness. 'Of course I'll mind. I'll go mad with loneliness.'

She turned and nipped the smooth skin of his upper arm with her teeth.

'Ouch!' He pinned her to the bed, kissed her hard.

She emerged from his embrace, gasping and laughing. They wrestled playfully for a moment in the firelight before settling down again, bodies relaxed against each other. It was at times like these that sometimes her treacherous heart wondered why she ever fought him, why she simply could not be content to be with him, to bear for him the child that she knew he wanted. But then, as always, her logical head had the answer. It was impossible. It would never work. Quite apart from the storms that so frequently shook their relationship, what would happen to her – and to the child, if they had one – if he were taken? Or if – as must be more than possible – he simply one day did not return from one of his perilous enterprises? The thought was beyond bearing, but it had to be faced. Until she knew that she could accept his way of life unquestioningly she could not so commit herself. And sadly she knew in her heart that such acceptance would probably never come. How could she bring into the world a child with an unrepentant and notorious criminal for a father? What sort of life would they ever have? Love was not enough; she wished with all her heart that it were. She reached for him, drew him to her, kissed him fiercely, closing her eyes.

(iii)

Kitty had certainly meant it when she had declared her liking for Genevieve Parisot, and was delighted when it became apparent that the feeling was mutual. The stylish Parisienne was unlike any woman Kitty had ever come across before. She was acutely intelligent, utterly independent in thought and deed and had about her a chic that made every other woman in a room she entered look dowdy. She in her turn made no secret of her admiration of Kitty and her talent.

'Oh, but of course, chérie! Charles is right!' she enthused after having seen Kitty on stage. 'You must – you must! – come to Paris! I tell you – you will be the sensation of the greatest season our lovely city has known!'

They went shopping together and in her positive way Genevieve left Kitty in no doubt whatsoever as to what she thought of her new friend's dress sense. '*Mais non!* A horrible shade of pink! It makes you look like a great gangling schoolgirl! Try this one – ah, see how much better! But – so – a little off the shoulders. Madame! Here, please –' She clicked imperious fingers. The small assistant hurried to her. 'This may be altered so –?'

'Yes, madam.'

'But Gené!' Kitty protested, 'I'll feel as if I'm walking about half-naked – and the price!'

'Oh, pouf! You'll get used to it. You have lovely shoulders. When you stand up straight, that is. And you have the money. What is it for but to spend?'

Poor Charles, outmanoeuvred and faced with the fait accompli of their conspiracy, gave in with his Gallic shrug and more or less good grace and stopped his pursuit of Kitty. But he was adamantly set upon taking her to Paris, and the time for decision had to be soon.

Kitty vacillated. Though she had said to Luke that she would probably go, she still had not truly made up her mind to it. Charles wanted her to open at his new theatre on April the first, the same day as the Great International Exhibition was to open, and he had to have her answer soon, for that was barely a month away. Yet while she knew that on the one hand there could be no doubt as to the dazzling boost a success in Europe's most glittering city could bring to her career, on the other the fear of the loneliness and disappointment of failure daunted her. Genevieve, in her eagerness to impress her new friend with the splendours of the city that she herself so loved, had almost succeeded in frightening her away altogether. The picture of Paris that Gené painted

– a city of brilliant distinction, of cosmopolitan charm and gaiety, of exacting demands and a constant, restless search for novelty, a city all but dizzy with its own prestige and glamour – simply intimidated poor Kitty into a state of nerves she had not suffered since the Dipper had made his first appearance on the stage of the Queen's. How could she hope to make her mark on such a place? And yet – both Charles and Genevieve obviously had faith in her, and why should they be wrong?

'If I did go,' she said to Pol one day, curled before the fire at number twenty-three, a half-gale rattling the window panes and flinging rain almost horizontally along the narrow street, 'you would come with me, wouldn't you?'

Pol had laid a tray with teapot and cups upon a little table. At Kitty's words her hand stilled for a moment. Then she reached for the milk jug.

'Pol?' Kitty was puzzled at the silence.

'Well, now.' Pol poured the tea, straightened and handed Kitty a cup. 'That, to be honest, is a question I was rather hopin' wouldn't get itself asked.'

'Why ever not?'

Pol was looking uncommonly embarrassed. A faint flush stained her cheekbones. She perched on the edge of a chair, balancing her teacup.

'Pol? What is it?'

'Well, it's like this, Kit –' Pol hesitated, then, blushing sheepishly, blurted rapidly, 'Barton an' me – we're gettin' 'itched – an' we reckoned as 'ow, if yer went ter Paris, well, yer could do without me fer a bit an' we'd get some time on our own. Jus' – well, jus' ter sort of get used ter the idea I s'pose –'

'Oh Pol! Pol, that's wonderful news!' Kitty was on her feet, flinging her arm about her friend's neck and kissing her. 'I'm so happy for you! When is it to be?'

'As soon as we can. A month or so. Just somethin' quiet –'

'Oh, and if I go to Paris I'll have to miss it!' Kitty stopped, sobering. 'But then – if I stay – I suppose you'll be leaving anyway? How strange it will be without you!'

'Oh, come on, now – don't be daft. I just won't be livin'
'ere that's all. I doubt we'll go a million miles away! Yer
won't get rid o' me that easy! It's just that – well, fer this
summer, while y'er gone, if y'er gone, that is, it'd be nice
to 'ave some time on our own, that's all. Yer do see, don't
yer?'

'Of course I do. Of course.' Oddly, Kitty felt the sudden
burn of tears behind her eyes. She blinked and swallowed,
sat back on her heels, shaking her head. 'And to think I
didn't know! Didn't notice! Have I been so involved in my
own affairs? Oh Pol – why didn't you tell me?'

''E on'y got round ter poppin' the question a couple o'
days since – an', well, I bin waitin' ter see if yer made up
yer mind about Paris.'

'You and the rest of the world.' Paris with no Luke, no
Matt – and now no Pol. A city full of strangers, and all of it
to do again. Round went her thoughts in the same old circle,
mice on a treadwheel.

'I'll make up my mind tomorrow,' she said.

She spent the following afternoon, as she spent so many
afternoons, as if afraid to waste the time that she sensed
was so precious to them, with Luke in his room. He had
been away, his recent plans come to fruition, and he had
returned as she had seen him once or twice before, high-
strung and tense; too high-spirited. He had kept up a merciless flow of acerbic conversation until they had gone to bed,
had made love with a wildness that had driven her beyond
reason or thought and then, naked and restless, prowled the
room, a glass of brandy in his hand. Not his first, she
suspected.

She watched him for a long time, saying nothing.

He wandered back at last to the bed and sat beside her,
his dark hand resting upon her flat stomach.

'The Peelers,' he said lightly, 'aren't always as stupid as
they look, are they?'

'You were nearly caught.' There was no question in the
words.

He smiled, savagely and with no trace of mirth. 'I was, as you say, nearly caught. Perish the thought.'

Her heart had taken on an odd, uneven beat, unpleasant and disturbing. She hated the look in his eyes.

'But I wasn't.' His sudden compulsion to speak of it apparently deserting him, he stood up abruptly and went back to the table where the brandy bottle stood.

'What happened?'

He raised his glass, tossed back the contents in one smooth movement. 'Nothing. Nothing happened. I got away.'

'One day,' she heard herself saying softly, the unspeakable finding its voice at last, 'you won't. What then?'

He turned to face her. The lean, handsome lines of body and face were blurred in the dim light of a cloud-heavy, cold day. His eyes were totally shuttered. 'That won't happen.'

'How can you know?'

He shrugged.

She shook her head upon the pillow.

He refilled his glass, came back to the bed, stood looking down at her.

'Did you know,' he asked, 'that I once did a stretch?' He smiled self-derisively. 'A "tailpiece in the steel"?'

'No.' There was soft astonishment in the word. The thought of Luke in prison was like the thought of the wind caged.

He swirled the liquid in his glass, watching it. 'Death couldn't be worse,' he said. 'You are reduced to the level of an animal. No – it's worse than that, for an animal doesn't know its own degradation. No animal can be forbidden the right to communicate with its own kind, to sit, to stand, to sleep, to wake in its own time and its own manner. The first thing they do of course is to strip you – and in doing that they quite deliberately take from you everything that gives you identity, that gives you pride, that declares that you are a man as they are, God curse their souls.

'Their aim is to make of you a thing, a nothing – they control you every moment in everything you do. You may not speak, you may not smile, you may not blow your nose or make water without their permission and under their prying eyes. You may not greet a friend. You may not look directly at them, for that is insubordination. But neither must you cast your eyes too far down, for who knows then what thoughts you might be concealing?' He paused. She had never in her life heard such a bitterness of hatred in a voice. 'They confine you in a cell not much bigger than this bed, they shut the door with a sound like the knell of doom, and they lock you in. On their side of that door are the punishment cells, the whipping post, the manacles and the treadwheel. The oakum to pick till your fingers bleed and rot. The stones to break till you're crippled. The coal sacks to sew. The bread and water diet. On your side there is nothing. Nothing but enslavement and deliberately inflicted humiliation.' He lifted his narrow eyes from their contemplation of the glass and saw the look of horror in her eyes. As if waking, he shook his head a little, turned from her, slumped forward, elbows on knees.

A helpless, impossible rise of anger and pity held her. She wrapped her fingers around his strong wrist, feeling the warmth of it, the throb of his pulse beneath the thin skin. 'Then for God's sake, stop it, Luke! Stop it while you can! Before you're taken again, and this time they kill you! You're an intelligent man – you don't have to thieve!'

Relentlessly gentle, he disengaged his wrist from her grip. 'You think not?'

'No!'

'And I say – yes! I know nothing else!'

'Then learn! Others do –'

'Others are not me.'

'Oh, don't be so pig-headedly – arrogantly – stupid!' She turned her head from him to hide the tears. 'It's no good even talking to you, is it? You'll go on and on, doing things your own way – until you're caught and flung into one of those bloody cells you're so afraid of –' She stopped, herself shocked at the word she had unthinkingly used. She heard his sharp breath, saw the stiffening of his back. 'Luke –' Her voice was pleading. She turned back to him.

He moved away from her, his face expressionless. He stood up, heading for the bottle again. 'I've told you. They won't catch me again.'

'I'm glad you can be so certain.' It was her turn to be bitter.

'God help the copper who tries to take me in,' he said.

She stared at him. 'You'd kill –'

He nodded.

'– or be killed.'

'Yes.'

A strange emptiness suddenly seemed to have dulled her emotions and stilled her tongue. She sat up and reached for her clothes.

'You've always known that,' he said, his voice hard.

'Yes,' she said, 'I suppose I have.'

'You have to accept it.'

That brought her head up. 'No, Luke. I don't.'

She finished dressing. He pulled on trousers and a loose white shirt and returned to the bottle. Standing before the huge mirror that hung above the fireplace, she busied herself with her hair. 'I'm thinking of having my hair cut,' she said, simply to break the silence that had clamped suffocatingly on the room. 'It's such a nuisance on stage.' And – God! she thought, I could be talking to Pol, or Amy –

'Don't.'

She shrugged. 'I'll see.'

His reflection appeared, very close behind her. 'I like it as it is.' His breath smelled of brandy.

'I said – I'll see. Shoulder length it'd be a lot easier to handle.'

'I don't want you to cut your hair.'

She knew he was three parts drunk. She knew she should humour him. 'It's not up to you, Luke. It's up to me.'

Angrily he leaned across her to put his empty glass on the mantelpiece. 'For Christ's sake, girl, must you make a bloody issue of every single little – ?' His forearm caught the massive mirror. It creaked ominously.

'Luke!' She grabbed him and pulled him back. The great mirror teetered and toppled, turning over in the air to crash on its back upon the hearthrug. The glass, still in its frame, shivered to a cobweb of broken images. They stood looking down at it for a long moment of shocked silence.

'Seven years' bad luck,' she said at last, shakily, looking at his face in the silvered kaleidoscope of reflecting shards. 'Isn't that what they say?'

He laughed, and it grated her nerves, chilling her. 'A glass that size? A lifetime, I'd say. At least a lifetime.'

It was evident when he came to her dressing room that night that he had been drinking steadily since the afternoon. He was dressed as he had been then, in loose white shirt open at the neck, black trousers and boots. He had never, she thought, looked so much the gypsy. Nor had she ever seen him more handsome. When he came into the room she was seated at her dressing table contemplating with an exasperated frown a small mother-of-pearl box which lay before her. He threw himself onto the day bed, stretched out his long, booted legs. In one hand he held a small silver flask. Pol scowled at him. With an undisciplined grin he reached to pat her buttocks. 'Hello, Pol, my love – when are you going to desert that itinerant songsmith of yours and run away with me?'

'That'll be the day.' Pol threw a disgusted glance at the flask.

He grinned, toasted her with it, took a swig. 'Pol,' he said unrepentantly to Kitty, 'doesn't approve of me.'

'I'm not surprised. I'm not sure I do myself at the moment. Don't you think you've had enough?'

'No.' He smiled beatifically.

She turned from him, picked up the pretty little box. 'Pol – do me a favour, would you? Take this down to the doorman and ask him to give it back to the Honourable What's-his-name when he calls? I can't possibly accept it. Flowers are one thing – but diamonds?' She tilted the little box, peered into it a touch uncertainly. 'I suppose they are diamonds?'

With a turn of speed that entirely belied his previous studied laziness Luke unfolded his lean frame from the day bed and was by her side, long finger touching very lightly the earrings that glittered, rainbow-brilliant, in the box. 'They're diamonds all right,' he said, picking one up and holding it to the light. 'Ye gods – Le Parisot's going to town, isn't he? I shouldn't let your friend Gené see these –'

'They aren't from Charles.' Kitty took the earring firmly from him and almost threw it back in the box. 'They're from the Honourable' – she quirked a sharply mocking brow – 'Ernest Belcham. His father owns half of Somerset, so he tells me. He's a pest with more money than sense and even more self-esteem than money, and that's saying something. He thinks he can buy anything he wants and he's never learned to take "no" for an answer.'

Luke took the box from her, stood with it in his hand, angling it so that the stones that rested within it caught the light and sent shafts of fire flashing about the room. 'Are you sure you want to give him "no" for an answer?'

She knew his perversity at these times. She removed the box from his fingers and snapped it shut. 'I'm sure,' she said, crisply. 'Pol –' She held the box out to Pol. Before Pol could take it the door swung open, with no knock. Framed in the opening stood a young man, foppishly dressed, a silk handkerchief drooping elegantly from his frilled cuff, a diamond pin glimmering in his matching creamy silk cravat. His soft, already thinning sandy hair fluffed above puffy, tired eyes. His mouth was that of a petulant child. He ignored both Luke and Pol.

'Kitty –' He stepped delicately into the room, holding out both hands to her. 'You were divine this evening.'

'Thank you.' Kitty tried to temper the tartness of her tone, but she made no move to take the outstretched hands.

Luke, an astonished and entertained half-smile that Kitty

very strongly mistrusted playing about his mouth, stepped to the wall and leaned there, watching, flask in hand.

'You got the baubles I see. But – you aren't wearing them! Naughty girl! Here, let me –'

She stepped back from him. 'Mr Belcham,' she said, very firmly indeed. 'I don't know what you're doing here – I did instruct the doorman that I was very tired tonight –'

'And I, m'dear, instructed him that I was very rich,' the insufferable Mr Belcham interrupted.

Kitty ploughed on, '– and that I wanted no visitors.' She saw the young man's bloodshot eyes flick for a moment to Luke. Luke smiled, pleasantly. Faint colour rose beneath the boy's thin skin. Kitty frowned ferociously at Luke, turned back to the Honourable Ernest. 'However, since you are here it will save Pol a journey. I was about to ask her to return these to you.' She held out the box. 'I really cannot possibly accept them. It's out of the question.'

The petulant mouth pouted. He made no move at all to take the box. 'But, dammit –'

'But nothing, lad,' Luke said softly. He had pushed himself away from the wall and stood, relaxed and infinitely dangerous-looking, arms folded, still smiling. 'Do as you're told. Take them and leave.'

Kitty spun on him. 'Luke – please! Let me handle this!'

'Just who is he?' The boy's colour was high. 'What's this to him?'

'Nothing,' Kitty said.

Luke's smile was tranquil.

Kitty still held the box. 'Mr Belcham' – she made no attempt to hide her exasperation – 'will you please take these? You must know that I can't accept them –'

'I know no such thing. Why, Gertrude Daley had a sapphire ring as well! Come now, Kitty, stop bein' so tiresome. Put the damn' things on like a good girl and come and have supper –'

She took a breath, praying for patience. 'Mr Belcham – perhaps I should make the situation brutally clear? I don't want the earrings. I don't want supper. I don't, I'm afraid, want you. So please – take your toys and run along. Perhaps,' she added tartly, 'if you hurry you'll catch the end of Miss Daley's performance. The Berkeley's just a short cab ride from here, and they have a late performance tonight I believe.'

'I don't want to see Gertie. I want to see you.'

His likeness to a spoiled child at that moment was quite remarkable. Almost it made Kitty laugh. She shook her head in amused amazement. 'Mr Belcham –!'

'Time,' Luke said conversationally, 'to put an end to this, I think.' In two long strides he was beside the young man, towering over him, a light hand on his shoulder. 'Out.'

The Honourable Ernest, outraged, struck at the hand that rested upon his perfectly tailored shoulder. 'I say, sir! Take your hands off me! Kitty – who is this bully-boy?'

'Luke, will you please leave this to me?' Kitty caught his arm. 'Go home. I'll come later.'

Luke ignored her. He had been, she realized despairingly, looking for an entertaining diversion, an outlet for his nerve-bred mischief, and here it was. 'This bully-boy, my little maggot, my snot-nosed Little Boy Blue, is Luke Peveral.' His voice was tolerant and friendly. 'Remember the name – Luke – Peveral.' He had taken the young man by his cravat, held him so, one handed, and with each word shook him, sharply, as a terrier might a rabbit.

'Luke!' Furiously Kitty pulled at his arm – steel-like tendons, rock-like muscles – she might have been a kitten nipping at the heels of a stallion.

'By God, sir, I'll have you horsewhipped for this! See if I don't! Let go of me –!' The Honourable Ernest was struggling fiercely, arms flailing in ungainly fashion, fists swinging full inches from Luke's grinning face. 'Let go of me, I say!'

'Only if you promise to be a good little maggot and run along home to Mummy.'

'Luke, will you for Heaven's sake –!'

The Honourable Ernest let out a squeal of rage and lashed out with a well-shod foot, catching Luke more by accident than design a sharp crack on the shin. Taken by surprise, Luke let go of him and stepped back. The sandy-haired young man, in an ill-advised fury of temper, launched himself at Luke.

Kitty flung the box she still held to the floor, shouted like a fishwife at the top of her voice. 'Will the pair of you stop this! Get out of here! Both of you!'

Luke met the Honourable Ernest's senseless rush with a short, almost casual but entirely ferocious jab with his left fist. The boy shrieked and reeled back. His nose gushed blood. Luke stepped lightly after him. Once, twice, three times, his fists connected brutally with the boy's face. The younger man staggered, making no attempt to strike back at Luke, trying only ineffectually and pathetically to protect himself from the remorseless blows. Luke slapped him, open-handed, caught him as he staggered and slapped him again.

Kitty's temper snapped. She grabbed the first thing to hand and leapt forward, eyes blazing with anger. 'Luke! Get back!' The heavy candlestick she had picked up threatened him.

He grinned at her, totally impenitent, totally out of control. He let go of the younger man's shoulder. With a groan Belcham slumped to the floor. Luke rubbed his knuckles, still grinning. The Honourable Ernest was making the odd, blubbering noise of a painfully crying child.

There was a knock at the door.

'Keep back,' she said to the still-poised Luke.

He held his hands above his head in a mocking gesture of surrender, stepped back against the wall.

Another knock, louder.

'Oh, Lord, Pol – see who that is – and for God's sake don't let anyone –'

Too late. Tentatively the door had opened to reveal a small, dark man holding pad and pen. 'Miss Daniels? I'm from the *Daily*' – he stopped, the smile sliding from his face, interested eyes taking in every detail of the scene – '*Argus* –' he finished. 'And I see you are already engaged. So sorry to have troubled you –' His quick black eyes were everywhere, taking in every detail. 'I'll come back some other – more convenient – time –'

Kitty lowered the candlestick. 'Wait!'

But he was gone.

Luke threw back his head and laughed.

Kitty bent to pick up the mother-of-pearl box, all but hurled it at the Honourable Ernest. 'Take them. And please leave. As I earlier asked you to.'

The boy scrambled awkwardly to his feet, sobbing. One eye was closing, blood was everywhere. 'I'll have the law on you!' He retreated from Luke, his limbs shaking. Tears were streaming down his face, mingling with the blood that smeared his skin and flecked his handsome clothes. 'I'll see you punished! I'll see you hanged! I have friends! Influential friends!'

Luke smiled derisively, reached into his pocket for his flask, tilted and drained it.

Still sobbing, the beaten man left. Kitty held the door open, making a small sign to Pol. Pol's mouth set stubbornly. 'Yer needn't think I'm leavin' yer with this drunken –'

'Please, Pol, go.'

Reluctantly, Pol left. Kitty leaned against the closed door and looked at Luke. 'You despicable bully,' she said, quietly. 'Is violence your answer to everything?'

The smile flickered from his face, but he said nothing.

'You're brutal and you're cruel,' she said, very clearly. 'You're self-centred and self-indulgent. You're arrogant. A barbarian. Your answer to everything is to lash out at someone weaker than yourself. You coward. I pray some day you'll find a man who can stand up to you. Who'll beat you to a pulp. You deserve it. But at least, thank God, I won't be there to see it.'

A pulse was beating rapidly in his jaw. His dark eyes had narrowed to fierce slits, glinting danger. She – miserably, intolerably angry – was beyond fear.

He stepped forward. Murderous anger, drink-fuelled,

burned in his face. She had no chance to avoid the crashing, back-handed blow that sent her reeling across the room to smash painfully into the wall. She tasted blood. He came after her in brutal rage, hauling her upright, shaking her with a violence that threatened to break bones. For a moment, in real terror, she struggled. Then he let her go. She stumbled, righted herself, supporting herself against the wall. They stared at each other in numbed silence. Then 'Get out!' she said. '*Get out!*'

He slammed past her, nearly knocking her off her feet, crashed the door almost from its hinges. She stood in the silence that followed his leaving, very still, trembling, fighting collapse. She felt the trickle of blood upon her chin. She touched it with her finger, looked bemusedly at the scarlet stain. Shakily she moved to a chair, sat down. Her head rang with pain and with the echoes of his awful violence. Slowly she bowed her head, burying her face in her hands, the tears flowing uncontrollably. For a long time she sat so, crying desolately, weeping for herself, weeping for Luke, weeping for the precious thing he had finally and utterly destroyed. She heard the door open, sensed Pol's presence, felt a hand softly on her shoulder. Still crying, she leaned on the girl's soft body, her arm about her waist, sobbing as if her heart would break. Pol held her, rocking her, wordless. The storm passed at last. Kitty, sniffing, groped for a handkerchief, mopped at her face, her breath catching frequently and painfully in her throat.

'Bastard,' was all Pol said, but the tone of her voice grated in Kitty's ears. Then, 'Feelin' better?' she asked.

Kitty nodded, shakily.

'Could you manage a cup o' tea?'

'Oh, yes. Please.'

After Pol had left Kitty examined the wreckage of her face in the mirror, gingerly touching her swollen, bleeding lip. Her head ached terribly and try as she might she could not control her trembling. She looked awful. On the floor still lay the candlestick with which she had threatened Luke. As she bent to pick it up the tangle of her hair fell across her face. She sat up, straightened her back, pushing the long hair out of her eyes. She sniffed, dashed her hand across her bloody mouth. She'd get her hair cut. Tomorrow. Or the next day. Some time, anyway – before she left for Paris.

PART TWO

PART TWO

1

Paris, during that spring and summer of 1867, was the undisputed, glittering Queen of Europe. The wild prodigality, the opulence, the gaiety and the squalor – all were part of the most intriguing and vibrant capital in the world, and some would say the most libertine. At all hours the wide new boulevards of Georges Eugène Haussmann – designed as much to give a clear field of fire to the authorities in case the unfortunate Parisian habit of insurrection should again manifest itself as to delight the eye – were thronged with the carriages of the rich and the fashionable. The pavements too were colourful with promenaders, seeing and being seen, ostentatiously flaunting wealth and position, gossiping and flirting, spending money with an extravagance that defied both reason and conscience in a city where the unhoused poor starved in the gutters. In the Paris that had been so splendidly rebuilt for the Second Empire at the cost of the common people, a costume from Monsieur Worth could cost anything over sixteen hundred francs, whilst the girl who sewed it would be lucky to earn two or three francs a day to stave off starvation. At Magny's, at the Aux Trois Frères Provinçaux, at the famous Maison Dorée or the even more distinguished Café Anglais, five or six courses might be served to a clientèle looking in this as in everything else as much for novelty and new experience as anything so tedious as simple nourishment, whilst in the ever-more-crowded poorer districts starveling children begged in the streets. But such was life in *La Ville Lumière* – and most people, rich and poor alike, with a shrug accepted it; life had always been so. The rich were entirely absorbed in the intrigues, the extravagances and the cut-throat rivalry that comprised their social lives; the poor, according to their natures, in either slaving for a pittance or emulating a large number of their so-called betters in living off their wits. As with most other major European cities of the time squalor was, on the whole, their lot and alcohol their escape.

For those with money, however – and these the city attracted like an exotic flower might the bees that were the emblem of the Emperor – Paris, wanton beauty that she was, was irresistible. Life was frenetically gay – by day a call, a drive in the Bois, perhaps a teatime tryst, a scandalous gossip at a café table, and by night a ball, a masque, a banquet, a visit to the opera, the ballet, or the theatre where the audience was there as much itself to be seen as to view the performance. And each night too an opportunity for a flirtation, a liaison, the possibility of love, real or imagined, bought or given freely for a reckless hour. This was a time and a place of restless searching – for fortune, for love, or what might pass for love, for new sensations, new enthusiasms. Overnight a name might be made – one week the handsome young Léotard risking his neck upon the high wire of the Cirque de l'Impératrice, the next the delectable Theresa, adored star of the café-concert, with her charming, salaciously ribald songs.

Into this vortex Kitty was thrown, dizzy, excited and on occasion half-dead with fright. After that disastrous evening – a comprehensive and highly imaginative account of which had duly been reported in the *Daily Argus* – her one thought had been to get away, to put as great a distance as possible between herself and Luke Peveral. The Parisots had been more than happy to oblige. Within a week she was installed with them in their splendid and elegant apartment on the Rue de Rivoli, not far from Charles' new theatre, the Moulin d'Or. The theatre was in itself a revelation to Kitty; its baroque exterior resembled a palace rather than a place of entertainment, its opulently gilded, velvet upholstered and draped interior was an extravagance of gold and crimson. Within a day of her arrival, sets were being built – a replica of a London street for Dick the Dipper, complete, to her amazement, with a real horse-drawn omnibus; a country lane, lamp-lit, with real trees through which rustled a gentle breeze for dashing Jack Blade the Highwayman. Charles Parisot laughed at her astonishment. 'But – chérie! – you are in Paris now! What else would you expect?'

'Charles, it must be costing a small fortune?'

He spread careless hands. 'But of course.'

Most mornings she spent shopping with Genevieve in arcaded shops so lavishly stocked and extravagantly priced that she could scarce credit her own eyes, whilst her afternoons were given over to rehearsals under Charles' friendly but critical eye; and only now did she truly appreciate the hard work Pat Kenny had forced her to do those months before. Her contract with Charles, running from April to October, was a generous one – a thousand francs a week and a pressing invitation to stay with them in the apartment on the Rue de Rivoli. She had the guest suite – a bedroom, a small sitting room and a tiny bathroom; nothing could have been more pleasant. The rooms were comfortably and elegantly furnished, the Parisots' carriage was put at her disposal. At the theatre she had her own dressing room and an experienced dresser to help with her costumes – a small, dark, excitable Parisienne who could not have been more in contrast to Pol had she tried. Kitty's only regret at the speed with which the move had been accomplished was that she would miss Pol's marriage – her first task in Paris was to fill a trunk with the most beautiful linen to be found in the city and send it to the happy pair as a wedding gift. Apart from the disappointment at missing the wedding she was only too pleased to have got away from London, for a while at least. Luke's display of violence had frightened and disgusted her, had brought to the surface in the most shocking way those differences between them that she had tried so hard to ignore but that she had always feared in the end would defeat their love. She would not – could not – live with such a man.

But it was in vain that she tried to forget him.

In the two weeks before opening she worked hard indeed to prepare herself for this new and exacting audience. It had been decided that it was perfectly acceptable for her to perform in the main in English – anything English being, as it happened, at this moment considered the height of chic in Paris – but Charles believed it would be well taken if she could perform at least one or possibly two songs in French, a language of which she had only the sketchiest knowledge, and so, added to the usual hard work of rehearsal was the mental strain of singing in a language not her own. She fell into bed each night worn out, her brain overstimulated, her body often aching with fatigue. She found herself suffering nausea that prevented her from eating properly – obviously a physical result of the stress she was living under but a worrying one since, slim as she was, she could ill-afford to lose weight. Yet no matter how she drove herself or how tired she was, Luke awaited her each evening in her lonely room, in the vast, empty bed, his mocking voice in her ears, his dark gypsy face and brilliant smile vivid in the darkness behind her closed lids. Stubbornly she resisted him. She would not contact him. She would not, willingly, see him again. She remembered her passion for Amos: that had eased with time and so would this. The disaster of their relationship had to be stopped, and it had to be stopped now.

But in the dark and lonely nights she cried, and often.

It was a full week before she remembered her intention of contacting Jem.

'An artist? Pouf –!' Genevieve made one of her graceful, expressive gestures. 'There are thousands in Paris! Most of them causing trouble –!'

'But – an American? There surely can't be many Americans? And I have an address – an old one it's true – but he might still be there, or someone might know where he's gone –'

Genevieve regarded her with kindly, thoughtful eyes. 'It's important to you?'

Kitty remembered the warmth of friendship. 'Very,' she said.

'Then – certainly we must try. Charles knows many people. But' – she held up an elegant hand to stop Kitty's eager thanks – 'I don't promise anything. He could be anywhere. You don't even know if he's still in Paris.'

But he was. Just two days before both the Moulin d'Or and the Great Exhibition were due to open their doors to an eager public, and with no less excitement and last-minute panic afflicting the one than the other, a harassed Charles presented Kitty with a grubby scrap of paper upon which was scrawled an almost indecipherable address. 'It may not be him, but the name is right, and he's an American –'

'Oh, Charles! Thank you!' She threw her arms about his neck and kissed him. Over the past few days, the hope of finding Jem, of renewing their friendship, of opening her heart at last to someone who knew so much of her relationship with Luke had greatly cheered her. 'It must he him, surely?' She glanced at the clock. 'May I take the carriage now? I'd so like to find him as soon as possible.'

'But of course' – Charles raised a detaining hand as she turned to go – 'but take Gustave with you. He's a good lad. And big.' He flicked the paper she held with his finger. 'The Left Bank can be a strange place. I want my new star to be in one piece for the opening night!'

(ii)

Half an hour later, peering uncertainly through the carriage window at a tall and indescribably dirty tenement building as squalid as anything she had encountered in the stews of Whitechapel, she understood her mentor's concern. The inevitable gang of street urchins had materialized by the carriage door as if by magic. Gustave's whip cracked, and Kitty winced as one of the youngsters screeched. The ragged waifs withdrew a little, scowling. One small boy, his face and bare shoulders a mass of running sores, picked up a stone and made to hurl it at the carriage. The whip cracked again and the child yelped savagely as a lace of blood appeared upon his upraised arm.

'Gustave! *Non!*' Kitty scrambled inelegantly from the high step of the carriage. Gustave, an enormous young man with the physique – and, Kitty suspected, the sensitivity also – of a bull leapt down beside her, whip in hand.

'*M'sieu m'a prié de vous protéger,*' he said stubbornly. '*Ils sont méchants, les gamins!*' He raised the whip again, threateningly, at the children. A small girl spat, accurately and scornfully. Gustave snarled and reached for her.

'Gustave – no! Please! Stop now!'

There was no misunderstanding the tone of her words. Reluctantly the young man straightened. The girl smirked saucily at him and made a small, foul gesture. Kitty's months of coping with Croucher's urchins stood her in good stead. With long, bony fingers she clipped the surprised child's ear, hard. 'Enough! *Tais-toi!*'

The girl scowled threateningly. Kitty took her by the shoulders and swung her to face her, held her there, one long, commanding finger held before the dirty face. The child quieted and stood, watchful. Very slowly Kitty reached into her reticule and took out a coin of the lowest denomination she could find – she did not, she told herself grimly, want to be responsible for murder – and held it in front of the little girl. Pale, watery eyes fixed upon it. 'M'sieu O'Connell,' Kitty said quietly, 'Jem O'Connell. *Il reste encore ici?*'

The child neither moved nor spoke. The eyes that were fixed upon the coin did not flicker. Kitty closed her hand about it, hiding it. 'Jem O'Connell,' she said, firmly.

A bigger boy pushed his way from the back of the crowd, sly eyes on Kitty's closed fist. 'Jem O'Connell –' he said eagerly, reaching. '*Oui – oui! Il –*'

With the shriek of a banshee the girl turned on him, leapt upon him with fingers extended like claws, raking his face. They rolled on the floor, fighting like two ferocious small animals, vicious and with intent to cripple.

'*Madame?*'

At a tug on her sleeve Kitty looked down into a grubby, cherub's face with eyes as old as sin. '*L'Américain? Vous cherchez l'Américain?*'

Even Kitty's limited French was up to that. '*Oui*,' she said. On the ground at her feet the boy, stronger and longer of limb, had overpowered his still — screeching opponent and, his fingers tangled in her long greasy hair, was trying to bang her brains out on the pavement. Kitty turned back to her small informant. '*Où est-il?*'

A dirty finger pointed to a door, then up to the first floor, to an uncurtained window whose shutters were hanging loose and behind which Kitty was sure she discerned some movement. '*Voilà*,' the child said.

Kitty held out the coin. Almost before the movement was complete the urchin had snatched it and was gone, scampering down the street at incredible speed and disappearing around the corner into a maze of alleys and tall, shuttered buildings. Gustave grinned, kicked casually at the still-fighting children on the ground and said something in rapid French. The boy rolled off his smaller opponent and in a moment the whole yelling horde had poured off down the street in pursuit of the boy with the coin.

Kitty looked up. A pale face had appeared at the window the child had indicated. '*S'il vous plaît*,' she said to Gustave, awkwardly, '*restez ici* —' She waved a hand. 'I won't be long.'

He nodded, impassive now, leaned against the great wheel of the carriage, arms folded across his broad chest.

Inside the tenement it was dark and smelled sourly of cats and of urine. A steep and narrow flight of uncarpeted stairs led to the first floor. The bannister was perilously rickety and several of its supports were missing. A little nervously she climbed, and found herself standing outside a peeling door on a dark landing. More stairs led upwards into the unappetizing mysteries of the upper floors of the tall building. She hesitated for a moment, then lifted her hand and rapped firmly with her knuckles upon the door. There was a moment's silence, then the faint sound of movement.

Kitty waited.

Nothing happened. She knocked again, sharply. 'Jem?'

This time after a minute or so the door opened a crack to

reveal a small, slovenly girl with an abundance of mouse-coloured hair and the slanting eyes and high cheekbones of an eastern princess in a face pinched with hunger and possessing that slum-pallor that Kitty recognized all too well. Her expression was sullen. She did not speak.

Kitty cleared her throat awkwardly. 'Please –' she said, 'er – *s'il vous plaît'* – she stumbled on the words – *'je – je cherche* Jem O'Connell.' She spoke the name very clearly and rather loudly, as if, she realized, embarrassed, she was addressing a backward child. She coloured beneath the girl's hostile stare. 'Jem O'Connell,' she said again in a more normal tone.

The lovely slanting eyes did not so much as flicker. Behind the girl, through the narrow opening of the door Kitty could see a room of almost indescribable squalor. A stale smell of food, unwashed bodies and strong tobacco hung on the air, mixed with the tang of paint and of varnish. Kitty swallowed, an unpleasant stirring of her stomach bringing bile to her mouth. 'Jem O'Connell?' she said again, anxiety and uncertainty sharpening her tone despite all her efforts to keep her voice even. 'Please – does he live here?'

From the other side of the door came movement, a crash, and an incontestably American profanity. 'Lucette? Who the hell is that?' Jem's voice, slurred and a little husky but unmistakable.

'Jem? Jem – it's me – Kitty. Kitty Daniels, remember?' Kitty waited, then 'Jem?' she called again.

Very slowly the door swung wider, revealing the room in all its sordid chaos. The only furniture was a small table covered in stained and ragged oilcloth and two unmatched and battered chairs. On the floor in a corner lay a mattress, the grimy bedclothes tumbled and unmade. The rest of the room was a shambles of canvases, paints, brushes, dirty rags, boxes of odds and ends. Framed in the doorway, blinking in astonishment, stood Jem – not quite the fresh-faced, boyish Jem that Kitty remembered so well, but Jem nevertheless; his straight fair hair grown shaggily shoulder length, his unshaven face thinned to fragile planes and angles, his pale, green-blue eyes bloodshot. 'Kitty?' The word was spoken in astonished disbelief.

'The very same.' Kitty held out both her hands to take his. Leaned to kiss him. 'Lord – what have you been doing to yourself? You're all skin and bone!' Beneath the gaiety her voice trembled slightly.

'I've been – unwell –' Distractedly he ran his hand through his wild, dirty hair. 'Kitty! It's really you!'

'It's really me.'

'And – just look at you – you look wonderful!' His eyes took in her smart afternoon suit, the little hat with its curling feather. 'A full-blown Parisienne no less! And you've cut your hair – what on earth are you doing here?' The sentences were disjointed. Kitty received the distinct impression that her unexpected appearance had completely confounded the young American. He shook his head again in astonishment, glanced over her shoulder. 'Luke – is he with you?'

She shook her head. 'I'm in Paris alone. Working. I open at a new theatre – the Moulin d'Or – the night after next.'

Gradually he was regaining control of himself. 'But that's marvellous!' His smile was one of genuine pleasure, and was at last something unchanged from the Jem she knew. He reached for her hands again and held them. 'Kitty Daniels! I'll be double-damned!' She suddenly realized he smelled strongly of drink.

The girl who had opened the door moved to his side, her face truculent. Almost insultingly she let her eyes wander from Kitty's well-shod feet to the small curling plume on the velvet hat. Kitty found herself blushing furiously. Jem slid an arm about the girl's waist. 'Kitty, this is Lucette –' He spoke to the girl in swift, easy French.

The girl lifted slanting eyes to Kitty's face and made a small movement of her head that might – or as easily might not – have been construed as greeting.

There was a moment's undeniably awkward silence. Then quite deliberately the girl turned her back and walked away, into the room. Jem pulled a mild, apologetic face, and opened the door a little wider. 'Come in. If you can stand it!'

At close quarters the room proved even more of a shambles. Kitty hesitated, aware of Jem's embarrassment. 'I've – come at a bad time –' she said, 'I should have warned you –'

He shook his head. 'Of course not.' Lucette stood by the window in sullen silence. Jem glanced at her in exasperation. She glowered at him. Kitty looked around. Canvases were stacked everywhere. Sheaves of drawings were strewn upon the table and upon the floor. In the far corner empty bottles lay where they had obviously been tossed, and left, some of them broken. Jem followed her gaze and grinned a little shamefacedly. There was another small, difficult silence. Then Jem spoke questioningly to Lucette in French. She grunted. He snapped in reply. Reluctantly she turned from the window, walked to a shelf, took down a ragged purse. Scowling ferociously she took from it two bank notes, separated them and made to put one back. Jem's dirty, paint-stained fingers closed about hers and he deftly possessed himself of both the notes, which he held up with the air of a conjuror producing a rabbit from a hat. 'We celebrate,' he said.

Kitty shook her head. 'Jem – it really isn't necessary. I only –'

He stopped her with upraised hand. 'Enough. I insist.' He grinned suddenly and bowed, mockingly but affectionately, in Lucette's direction. '*We* insist,' he corrected himself. 'The Café Barrette awaits, in all its doubtful splendour. Kitty, it is so very good to see you – I want to hear all the news. All of it.'

They sent the carriage – whose presence outside his front door caused Jem much genuine hilarity – back to the Rue de Rivoli, much to Gustave's indignation, with a message of assurance to the Parisots that Jem would see Kitty safely back. Then they set off through the chill, bright March streets for Jem's favourite café. It was Kitty's first visit to the Latin Quarter, and it was an experience she never forgot. The streets were crowded – students, artists, the Bohemian idle and the curious rich all jostled shoulder to shoulder. The bar to which they went was one where he and Lucette were obviously well known. Jem was greeted with good-natured camaraderie by staff and customers alike. In the corner of the crowded room a dark-haired young man with a neatly trimmed beard held court as he sketched the scene before him. As Jem passed the artist raised a friendly hand in salute. 'Olà, Yankee –' His eyes ran appreciatively over Kitty.

Jem grinned. 'Olà, Claude.' He pushed his way to an empty table. Kitty and Lucette followed. Lucette had spoken not a single word on the walk to the café. She settled herself now, very close to Jem, her face still set in sullen lines, her mouth clamped tight shut as a trap. Jem glanced at her face, sighed a little, then brightened as he turned to Kitty. 'Now. Absinthe and news, Songbird – not necessarily in that order.'

Over the strong drinks Kitty told him of all that had happened since he had left London. Her relief at seeing his familiar, friendly face, however changed, in this unfamiliar and intimidating city, at speaking to someone who knew her – and Luke – so well broke down all barriers of reserve. At her brief and shaky description of the violent scene in the dressing room that had caused the final rift with Luke, Jem reached for her hand sympathetically, whilst Lucette sulked jealously beside him.

'And you didn't see him again?'

She shook her head.

'Didn't give him a chance to apologize?'

She cast him a disbelieving look. 'Apologize? Luke? He doesn't know the meaning of the word.'

He had taken his hand from hers. Pensively he was watching her, turning his glass in his hand on the table with little, regular movements. 'You've probably done the right thing. Giving it all a chance to blow over. When you get back –'

'No!' She was herself surprised at her own vehemence. She shook her head. 'No, Jem. I've made up my mind. There's no going back. There can't be.'

'I doubt Luke sees it that way.'

'I don't care what Luke sees. I'm finished with him. I can't stand it any more. The uncertainty. The fear. The violence.' She caught her breath. Tears were very close. 'I can't stand it any more,' she repeated, and took a too-big mouthful of absinthe, nearly choking herself.

'But – you still love him. Don't you?' Jem's voice was so soft it was barely audible above the noise about them. His eyes were strangely veiled.

It was a long time before she answered. 'I don't know,' she said, bleakly. 'Sometimes I think I hate him. Sometimes I think I'll die without him. Is that love?'

'Sounds to come pretty close to me.'

She shook her head. 'I want no part of it. Luke and I are finished, Jem. I swear it.' She smiled a small, self-mocking smile. 'He's probably forgotten all about me by now. With half the female population of London ready to fall at his feet, he doesn't need me.' To break the tension of the moment she sipped her drink again, pulled a face. 'Jem, this is absolutely gruesome! How can you drink it?'

He picked his up, tossed it back at a gulp, linked his hand to hers again, laughing. 'I, my sweet Songbird, can drink anything!'

Lucette, shut out, looked from one to the other, her eyes lingering on their linked hands. Kitty tried to draw away, but Jem would not let her. His light eyes were suddenly challenging upon the French girl. Kitty, recognizing all too well the signs of a stormy relationship, shook her head fiercely at Jem.

Suddenly and without a word Lucette stood, and leaving her drink untouched stalked away from the table.

Kitty watched her go, troubled. 'That was silly,' she said quietly, 'and quite unnecessary. We've upset her. I've upset her. I wouldn't have done that for the world –'

He stopped her. 'Don't think about it. She's a good kid and she's seen me through some bad times. But she doesn't own me. She knows that, or she should. We have an arrangement. She has to learn to stick with it, or quit. Don't worry about Lucette.' The tone of his voice indicated clearly that the subject was not open to discussion. She watched him for a moment, sensing again that deep reserve that she was sure was rooted in the savage wound caused by his own betrayal of his family, and by their rejection of him. Impulsively she squeezed the paint-stained fingers that still held hers. 'Oh, Jem – I'm so glad I found you! Please – don't be angry if I ask – is there any way I can help you? I have money now.'

It was too clumsy. He shook his head sharply. 'No.'

'But – I'd really like to. We're friends, aren't we?'

'I won't take your money, Kitty.'

'But why ever not?' She was exasperated. Hadn't she just seen him take Lucette's? Where was the difference?

He shook his head stubbornly. 'Leave it, Songbird. Just leave it. As you say – we're friends. Let's keep it like that.'

She gave in. Shrugged. Changed the subject. 'You're painting again, at least?'

'Yes.'

'I'm glad. I was afraid you'd given up.'

'I nearly did. But Paris took it upon herself to change my mind.'

'I believe,' she said, only half joking, 'that you're in love with Paris. No woman stands a chance against her.'

'You could be right.' He drained his glass. 'I've changed my mind.'

'What about?'

'Your offer of money –' She opened her mouth. He stopped her, grinning. 'You can buy us another bottle,' he said.

For more than an hour, then, he talked, entertainingly and fluently, telling her of his life in Paris, painting a picture far removed from the opulent extravagance of the city Kitty had so far seen, speaking with fire and enthusiasm of the brotherhood of artists who fought to break the iron grip of established rules and confining formulae, of poets and writers who struggled to expose the decadence of a society whose glittering surface barely disguised the rottenness at its core, and of young and gutter-tough insurrectionists who worked for revolution and the rule of the common man. It was a world away from the Imperial balls, the *demi-mondaines* who rode in their carriages in the Bois, the salons, the cafés, the bright lights of the Rue de Rivoli.

'I love this damned place, by God I do – but I think it's heading for trouble. It's like a powder keg just waiting for the match. La Pavia wears a million francs worth of jewels on a single dress while men, women and children die in poverty outside her door. Half the city's been torn down to make way for Haussmann's boulevards – for shops, and gardens and homes for the rich. And the displaced poor have nowhere but the gutter to lay their heads. The whores of the rich feed their cats on caviare while the children of the poor starve.' He tossed back the contents of his glass, shook his head. 'It can't last.'

'But isn't it like that everywhere? Hasn't it always been?'

'I suppose so.'

'You honestly think there'll be revolution in Paris again?'

He shrugged. 'I wouldn't be surprised.'

'What would you do?'

He appeared to consider the question seriously. 'Sit here, drink absinthe and watch,' he said.

She laughed. 'And paint pictures of it of course.'

'Of course. Which reminds me – you'll be going to the Exhibition, won't you?'

'Oh yes, as soon as I can.' It was time to go. She reached for her gloves, stood up.

He took her arm to escort her through the crowded bar. 'Let me know when. I'll introduce you to my own little corner of it.'

She turned to stare at him. 'You're exhibiting? At the Exhibition?'

He grinned, tousled his hair in that boyish gesture she so well remembered. 'Hardly. The Establishment hasn't softened to that extent! No –' He pushed open the swing door, stood back for her to pass through it. Joining her on the pavement he tucked her arm into his. At their feet a man worked with pastel chalks upon a paving stone, creating a masterpiece that would be washed out by the first shower of rain. 'Have you heard of something called the *Salon des Refusées*?'

She thought for a moment. 'Yes, I have. Charles mentioned them. A group of artists, weren't they, who set up their own exhibition when the Salon refused to exhibit them? Didn't the Emperor give them some money or something?'

'That's right. Well – that same group is setting up a salon outside the main Exhibition. Manet already has his own pavilion. So has Le Courbet. A group of us, not so well known, have decided to do the same. Who knows?' He winked down at her, laughing. 'I might even sell something. And if I do –' He caught her elbow and swept her across the busy street at peril to both their lives. 'We'll drink our next absinthe at the Maison Dorée, and that's a promise!'

On the first of April 1867, in inclement weather, the Great International Exhibition of Paris opened its doors to an enthralled world that found beyond the Grand Entrance of the great glass and iron structure that had blossomed on the Champ de Mars on the Left Bank of the Seine a wonderland of the arts, the sciences and of modern technology. There were exhibits from all over the world – everyone, from France's close neighbours Britain and Germany to the far-flung countries of Japan and China, had contributed something of their art, their culture, their way of life. There were gardens from Persia, a Chinese tea kiosk, a fire engine from Turkey. There were machines that wove cloth, that made hats, gloves, shoes – indeed it seemed that for every human requirement there must surely in the vast sprawl of kiosks, pavilions and mock factories be a machine. The Americans, their young giant of a nation struggling to recover from the civil war that had so recently devastated it, sent amongst other things a complete field service, or 'ambulance' as it was coming to be called – an exhibit that aroused at the time little or no interest. The Prussians, on the other hand, were presented with an award for their prize exhibit – the biggest object the world had ever seen; Herr Krupp's gigantic fifty-ton gun was capable of firing a shell that in itself weighed as much as two small cannon. The Parisians smiled politely, yawned behind their hands, unsurprised that their bombastically militaristic neighbours had produced something of such little taste, and moved on.

On that same day Kitty Daniels' first performance in Paris was received rapturously by the first-night audience of the Moulin d'Or. Within twenty-four hours all Paris was talking of her; it was fashionable to be English, and Kitty was English; it was even more fashionable to be novel, and in her dashing masculine clothes, with her boyish long-legged figure and her swinging short hair she was certainly that. There was not a ticket for her performance to be had in all of Paris. Charles was ecstatic, Genevieve complacently pleased. Kitty was quite simply astonished – astonished, and of course delighted. The hard work had paid off, she was a success. For now she could stop thinking about a future that to her at that moment seemed so unclear that she could neither plan nor worry. For a few short weeks she could drift on the tide of this happy success. Then she would see.

As she had promised, she visited Jem and his friends in their cramped little pavilion on the Avenue Bosquet. She came to them straight from the main Exhibition, the scale and splendour of which had stunned her.

'Have you seen it?' She had thrown herself into the proffered chair and kicked off her shoes, wincing as she wriggled her cramped, silk-clad toes. 'It's the most fantastic thing I've ever seen! There's food and drink from just about every country in the world! And there are factories, and houses – and the Kaiser's sent the most enormous gun –' She stopped for breath. Jem was openly laughing at her. She pulled a childish face at him. 'And I'm going up in one of M'sieu Nadar's balloons if it's the last thing I do! They say you can see the whole of Paris –'

Jem sketched a small, gallant bow. 'From what I hear, Mam'selle, the whole of Paris is queuing to see you!'

'Oh, nonsense!' But she was pleased, and he could see it, and they smiled at each other in friendship.

She glanced around the crowded little room. 'God, I'm tired! My poor feet are –' She stopped. 'Jem! Did you do that?'

Lucette looked down from the canvas, vibrant and full of life, love in her slanting eyes and the sweet curve of her mouth.

'You like it?'

'Oh, it's lovely! It's every bit as good as those pictures you showed me the other day – the ones by that famous friend of yours –'

He laughed. 'My dear Kitty – that famous friend was Claude Monet, and whilst I appreciate the compliment I doubt its foundation in truth. But I'm glad you like the picture.' He grinned, mischievously. 'You wouldn't like to buy it, would you? Only a hundred francs –' He had shaved and trimmed his hair. The few good meals to which she had managed to treat him and the silent Lucette over the past few days showed in his face.

She did not reply for a moment. She stood, looking thoughtfully at the picture, the germ of an idea moving in her mind. 'I might at that,' she said, lightly. 'I'll see.'

Returning to the apartment in the Rue de Rivoli an hour or so later, she hurried to Genevieve's elegant sitting room. 'Is Charles around? There's something important I'd like him to do for me.'

Genevieve, rising, kissed her lightly on both cheeks. 'Sit down, chérie. Charles will be back soon. And I'm perfectly sure he will do anything you ask. And when you look at this' – she waved the piece of paper she had been reading when Kitty had entered the room – 'then you'll see why.'

'What is it?'

Genevieve pulled a pretty, provocative face. 'Guess.'

Kitty dropped her shawl onto a chair, slipped her foot from her shoe and bent to massage a blistered heel. 'I can't. Tell me.'

Genevieve, making the most of her secret, struck an

imperious pose. 'You've heard of course that His Imperial Highness the Czar of All the Russias is visiting our small Exhibition?'

'Of course.' Kitty divested herself of her other shoe.

Genevieve said nothing, but stood waiting. Kitty lifted her head, and at the expression on her friend's face her stomach, as it lately so often had, gave a small queasy lurch.

'He comes to the theatre next week,' Genevieve said. 'He has taken all the boxes. To see you.'

Kitty's hand was at her mouth. 'Oh my God!'

Genevieve threw her arms about her and hugged her, hard. 'What did we not say, chérie? Is not Paris the place for you?'

The Czar's visit was the first of many by the rich, the famous and the aristocratic who had flocked to Paris for the Exhibition. *Le Gamin*, as a popular newspaper had dubbed her, was one of the main attractions of the city during that spring and early summer. Broadsheets of her songs were sold all over Paris, her likeness in her striking masculine clothes on every cover. It was even said that at one of the fabulous costume balls held at the Tuileries Palace, Madame Gorschakoff, a close friend of the Emperor and Empress, appeared dressed as an extravagant Dick the Dipper and spent the evening inexpertly relieving the highest in the land of their pocket watches and jewellery; a compliment of the highest order, as Genevieve pointed out. Kitty herself of course was barred both by her profession and her birth from entry into these dizzy social circles as anything but an artist, though she found herself many times invited to appear at private balls and salons. The splendour of the hotels and apartments she visited on these occasions never failed to astonish her. It was as if all the wealth of Europe were concentrated on these few glittering square miles that were Paris. Inevitably she found herself the centre of a great deal of not always welcome attention. After a particularly trying episode with a corpulent German count she tried to make sure that she was always escorted, sometimes by Charles and Genevieve, but quite frequently by Jem, though he, smilingly stubborn, resisted her idea that she should pay him for the privilege. In fact on the one occasion that she managed to force a few francs upon him she arrived at her dressing room next day to discover it looking even more like a hothouse than usual.

'Jem!' she protested, exasperated. 'Flowers? When you don't know where your next meal's coming from?'

He shook an unrepentant finger repressively under her nose. 'Don't you know it's very bad form to discuss a gentleman's financial affairs? Smell the roses and shut up.'

By utilizing the idea that had come to her when she had first seen Lucette's portrait, however, she did – deviously – manage to put some money in Jem's pocket. At her request Charles arranged for a friend of his, a stranger to Jem, to profess a passion for the 'new art' – and in particular for the portrait – and to buy the picture for a thousand francs, a sum Jem would certainly never ever have accepted from Kitty herself. The stupefied Jem was delighted. Kitty had a great deal of trouble in dissuading him from spending a large part of his unexpected fortune at once by giving them all dinner at the Maison Dorée.

'Jem, don't be ridiculous! Get yourself – and Lucette too – some new clothes. And some food. Buy the canvas you need.'

He lifted a finger and pushed her nose like a button, mockingly. 'What a bore you're becoming in your old age, Kitty Daniels! *Le Gamin* indeed! The latest rage of Paris is nothing but an old stick-in-the-mud.'

She laughed, but shook her head nevertheless. 'Don't squander it, Jem. You need it.'

He shrugged. 'I still think the Dorée's a better idea.' He sobered a little, looking at her. 'And God, girl – you talk about me! You look as if you could do with a good square meal yourself. What have you been doing? You're working too hard. You're losing weight.'

She turned away from him, apparently studying a half-finished painting that was propped against the table. 'I'm all right. It's tough, that's all, and I'm not getting much rest.

But it's only until October. Then' – she hesitated – 'then I thought I might take the winter off. Go away somewhere. Rest a little. Do some thinking. I can afford it now.'

Watching her, understanding in his eyes, he pulled a funny, rueful little face. 'My dear Kitty, don't be absurd. None of us can afford to think –'

Lovely spring moved into summer. The weather became steadily warmer, the life of Paris established itself outdoors in the shaded pavement cafés, in the Bois and in the gardens. Everywhere, it seemed to Kitty, there was music – pavement orchestras, military bands that marched, the Emperor's bright toy soldiers in the Champs Elysées, strains of Strauss and Mozart in the parks and gardens of the city. She had been in Paris for two months, and then three, and her popularity showed no sign of waning.

Breakfasting one morning in the sunlit dining room of the Parisots' apartment, Genevieve frowned a little as she watched Kitty sip black coffee and eat nothing at all. 'Kitty! I insist that you eat something! Are you not well?'

'I'm fine. I'm just not hungry.'

'But you're never hungry! Last night at dinner –'

'I had already eaten at the theatre,' Kitty lied.

Genevieve looked unconvinced. She leaned back in her chair, her elegant silk morning gown draped about her statuesque body in pale folds. Her eyes were fixed worriedly upon Kitty's face. 'You're too thin, chérie,' she said, bluntly.

Kitty shook her head, exasperated. 'For Heaven's sake – you're as bad as Jem. I'm always thin.'

'But not as now. And you have shadows, here –' Genevieve drew her manicured fingers beneath her own dark eyes. 'Charles!' she added, as her husband entered the room, 'you're working Kitty too hard. I believe she is not well.'

'Oh?' Charles glanced sharply at Kitty, concern in his face.

Kitty put her cup down very precisely upon the table, and stood up. 'Nonsense,' she said, firmly. 'I'm perfectly all right. Just a little tired, that's all. Please do stop fussing me.'

Charles, with characteristic readiness to be reassured, beamed. 'But of course, my dear.' About to sit down at the table, he stopped, a hand upraised. 'Oh – I almost forgot. That strange little girl – what's her name? Your American friend's' – he hesitated, shrugged in Gallic fashion – 'friend –'

'Lucette?'

'Ah yes. Lucette. She has come with a message for you. Something about a sketch for a poster –?'

'Of, of course. Jem promised to let me see it today. I had forgotten –' Kitty turned to the door. 'Lucette's in the salon?'

Charles, pouring himself a cup of fragrant, steaming coffee, shook his head. 'I sent her up to your rooms. I did not realize that you had already – Kitty? What is it –?'

The apartment was on two floors. Gathering her skirts about her knees Kitty took the stairs two at a time, stopped abruptly at the top. Lucette stood like a statue at the open door of her little sitting room, watching her.

'Lucette!' Kitty said, urgently, 'please – don't tell him? He needed the money – you know he did. I couldn't think of another way to get him to accept it –'

In the two months since they had met Lucette had addressed hardly one direct word to Kitty. From the very first Kitty had sensed, and had been utterly unable to appease, the other girl's resentment, her total misconstruction of the strong bond of friendship that lay between her American lover and this affluent, unwelcome interloper from England. Kitty did not even know just how much English the other girl understood and, her own sketchy French having for the moment deserted her, she stood helplessly now before the implacable and bitter dislike that showed in the slanting eyes and thin face.

'Lucette – please – you must understand –'

Lucette made a small, unpleasant and contemptuous sound. Then she spat very precisely upon the shining waxed floorboards at Kitty's feet and, with no word, brushed past her and ran swiftly down the stairs to the front door. Watching her go, Kitty's anger was tempered by understanding.

Lucette's relationship with Jem was, they all knew, already sadly one-sided. She adored him. To him, however, although he was truly fond of her, she was just one of many who had come and gone in his life since he had come to Paris. He neither expected nor wanted permanence in their relationship. She was a warm body, a willing drudge, a free model. And that, despite poor Lucette's devotion, was about as far as it went. Kitty wondered now how Jem would take the news that Lucette had for him. Silently she cursed herself for not hiding that damned picture.

She went into her room. The portrait of Lucette that she had so deviously purchased stood propped against the wall. It was ruined, the canvas ripped and slashed. Beside it on the floor lay a small pencil sketch of herself, the one presumably that Jem had done as part of the poster layout and had asked Lucette to deliver. It too was torn, straight across the middle. Kitty sighed, and dropped dispiritedly into a chair. In the mirror on the opposite wall she saw her own tired pallor, the shadows beneath her eyes that Genevieve had mentioned. She sat so for a long moment, staring at the white-faced image in the mirror. Almost she had decided to speak to Jem — confide in him — ask his advice. She sighed again. The likelihood of a sympathetic ear seemed slight now. She closed her eyes for a moment, leaning her head against the back of the chair. Then, with a determined movement she stood and made for the bedroom, her dressing table and the cosmetic box wherein lay the means to disguise all ills. For the moment at least.

She did not, as she had half expected, hear from Jem that day, nor the next. With some difficulty she restrained herself from rushing across the river to the Latin Quarter to discover if his silence bespoke anger, indifference or perhaps even ignorance. The hope began to grow in her that Lucette had not, after all, betrayed her secret. Then, on the third day, he turned up at the theatre after the performance, very much the worse for wear, his face doleful.

'Lucette's gone.'

She stared at him. 'Gone?' she repeated, stupidly. 'Gone where?'

He shrugged elaborately, and nearly fell over. 'Who knows?' He looked around vaguely. 'Have you got anything around here to drink?'

Kitty shook her head.

He dropped into a chair. 'Gone,' he said again. 'Vamoosed. Done a bunk.'

'Why?' Kitty asked, faintly. 'Did she say?'

'Nope. Just upped and left.' Gloomily he rubbed his unshaven face with paint-stained fingers. 'Good riddance,' he muttered, none too certainly, 'she was more trouble than she was worth anyway.'

Wisely Kitty said nothing to that. She looked at him for a long moment. 'How long since you've eaten?'

He shrugged.

'Marie-Claire?'

The little dresser turned from where she was hanging Kitty's costumes carefully in the wardrobe. '*Oui, Mam'selle?*'

Kitty was scribbling a swift note. 'Take this for me please to the gentleman you'll find waiting at the stage door – a tall, thin man with a rose in his buttonhole and a gold-topped cane. Tell him – with apologies of course – that I am unexpectedly indisposed and cannot after all dine with him. Then you can go home.'

'*Oui, Mam'selle.* Thank you, *Mam'selle.*'

Kitty took Jem by the hand and pulled him to his feet. He stood swaying a little and blinking owlishly. 'Where are we going?'

'Somewhere you'll get a square meal and sober up. I'm afraid I have a confession to make, and I'm not doing it while you're in that state. Come on.'

In a little street not far from the Parisots' apartment was Kitty's favourite restaurant, Le Chat Gris. Simple, relatively unknown, it was not a fashionable venue, but it was friendly and quiet and the food was superb. She had eaten there often with Charles and Genevieve, and knew herself in her new-found fame to be sure of a warm welcome.

'Mam'selle Kitty –' Monsieur Aurin, le patron, raised faintly questioning eyebrows at Jem's dishevelled and undoubtedly Bohemian appearance, but made no comment.

Kitty smiled her sweetest. 'Could we have the table in the corner?'

He conducted them to a small table at the far side of the room, secluded by a screen of plants. They ordered soup, Monsieur Aurin's famous chicken in Burgundy and a bottle of wine. Jem drank his first glass at a thirsty gulp. Kitty tutted, and handed him hers; watched as he lifted it to his lips, hesitated, then set it untouched, a little sheepishly, back upon the table.

'I'm sorry about Lucette,' she said.

'So am I.' He tilted the glass and gazed into the sparkling liquid. 'In fact,' he said, 'I find I'm a hell of a lot sorrier than I thought I'd be. Serves me right, I suppose.'

'And – she gave you no idea why she was leaving?'

'No.'

Kitty hesitated. She was playing with Jem's empty glass, running her finger around the wet rim. The glass sang faintly. 'It was my fault,' she said, abruptly.

He shook his head. 'Yours? Don't be daft. Of course it wasn't.'

'It was. Lucette came to the apartment a couple of days ago. She saw –'

'Saw what?'

'She saw the painting. The portrait of her, that you sold for a thousand francs. I bought it.'

Even when mildly drink-befuddled Jem was no one's fool. He did not ask her to repeat the words. 'You,' he said.

'Yes.' She would not look at him. 'You wouldn't let me help you, and I knew you wouldn't have let me pay that much for the painting – so –'

'So you set me up.' He was staring at her, his expression an extraordinary mixture of disbelief, exasperation and a faintly dawning, self-mocking laughter. He shook his head slowly. 'Oh, boy. What an idiot. Why didn't I guess? Who in their right mind'd want to pay a thousand francs for one of my daubs?'

She lifted her head sharply. 'You mustn't say that! You mustn't think it! It was a lovely painting –' She stopped.

He picked up the word. 'Was?'

'Lucette slashed it,' she admitted, miserably.

He nodded, unsurprised.

'Oh, Jem, I'm so very sorry. I did it for the best, truly I did. I never dreamed Lucette would find out – and I never dreamed that if she did she'd take it so badly –'

'It doesn't matter.'

'But yes, of course it does!' The soup had arrived. Kitty leaned back as hers was served. Savoury steam rose. She pushed her plate away, her skin suddenly pale as pearl and sheened with the perspiration of nausea. Jem did not notice. She dabbed at her mouth with her starched white napkin. 'I feel terrible about it now. It never occurred to me that she'd actually leave if she found out.' She hesitated. 'I'm not sure I understand now why she did,' she added, honestly.

Jem smiled, that smile that had not changed with the years, gentle and warm. 'Kitty, you're such an innocent! Don't you know how most of Paris lives? Don't you realize what Lucette thought that you were buying with that money? She almost certainly assumed that I knew. That you and I had entered into some – arrangement – behind her back. Oh, Lord I'm sorry – I've upset you now –' He was by her side, supporting her as she swayed sickly in her chair.

She took a deep, shaky breath. 'I'm all right.'

'You aren't. You're as pale as a ghost. I'd no right to –'

'No, no! Truly, I'm all right.' She sat bolt upright, touching her napkin to her face. 'I'm tired, that's all, and not very hungry. The smell of food turned my stomach.' She tried a smile, not altogether successfully. 'You'll just have to eat mine as well as your own, or M'sieu will never forgive me. If I could just have a glass of water?'

He signalled to a waiter. When the water came she drank it thirstily. 'I'm better now.'

'You're sure?'

'I'm sure. And, oh, Jem, I am so sorry about Lucette. It was stupid and clumsy of me. Perhaps – perhaps she'll come back?'

He shook his head. 'No.'

'But – she loves you.'

He looked at her then with such compassion that she thought he knew; knew of her terrors, of the battle she fought each day. 'Dear Kitty – what has that to do with it? You of all people –' He paused. 'Will you go back?'

She felt the rise of weak tears behind her eyes. Despising herself she shook her head, clenching her teeth. 'No.'

He said no more, but with a small gesture of affection reached for her hand across the table. They sat so for a moment in silence. 'We may not be very good at choosing our lovers, you and I,' he said at last, with a funny, rueful little smile, 'but we sure as hell know a good friend when we see one, wouldn't you say?'

It was only a moment before she managed to collect herself enough to smile at that.

(iii)

Not in the wildest of moments had it occurred to Kitty that Luke would come to Paris: that he should appear with a glowing Lottie upon his arm and with fat Moses the apparent picture of a complaisant husband trotting behind staggered her. Confronted by them unexpectedly when a beaming Charles escorted them to her dressing room before the start of the show she was reduced to total wordlessness by the shock.

'Kitty – chérie! – see what a surprise I have for you! Some old friends from London –'

Nothing had changed. The sight of Luke had, as always, the effect of a physical blow. Despite the manner of their parting she had to admit that not a day had gone by without thought of him; how, then, had she forgotten the force of his presence, the compulsion of those narrowed, wary eyes?

He stood easily, gracefully handsome, faultlessly dressed, his expression pleasant and entirely unreadable. One might almost believe, a bemused Kitty thought, that there could be no possible connection between this self-possessed and charming man and the drunken brute she had faced at their last meeting. Lottie clung prettily to his arm, a picture in lavender and violet silk. Moses, it seemed to Kitty, had in the past months become even more obese: he was sweating profusely, his great belly thrusting through his open jacket, the fleshy rolls of his neck scarlet folds above his high white collar. He had grown an absurd if fashionable Imperial, and the neat moustaches and beard sat upon the moon of his face like scribbling on a child's drawing.

'We heard rumours,' Luke said gently, in the face of her stunned silence, 'of a sensation in Paris. We thought we should investigate.'

'A sensation indeed, M'sieu!' Charles flourished his small, manicured hand. 'The Czar – the German Chancellor – the Emperor himself –'

Kitty shook her head. Her eyes had not left Luke's face since he had entered the room, nor his hers. Yet so great was the shock of seeing him, so totally unprepared was she, that it was as if she were rooted to the spot, her tongue locked speechless. She should say something. She must.

Charles babbled on.

His eyes questioned, cool and expectant. He had come this far. Hers was the move now.

The temptation was to run to him, fling herself into his arms, to give up the awful struggle, lean on his strength –

Then, looking at the calm, smiling face, she saw it suddenly as she had last seen it and as she had no doubt it would be again; brutal, drunken, terrifying.

She said absolutely nothing, nor did she make any move.

A very small smile curved Lottie's pretty mouth. Her hand moved very slightly, gently caressingly, within the crook of Luke's arm. 'Well, well.' Moses, his habitual malevolence veiled by a – to Kitty – revolting affability, chuckled, pleased. 'So here we are, eh? Making quite a name for ourselves, too. A long way from the poor old Song and Supper Rooms, eh?'

'Yes.' She felt her face bloodless. Her tongue barely obeyed her.

'Always knew you had it in you. Always said so –' With characteristic and blatant disregard for the self-evident hypocrisy of his words Moses beamed at her in avuncular fashion. 'The moment you stepped on that stage that night I said it. Ain't that right, Luke?'

Luke half-smiled but said nothing. His eyes were still on Kitty. 'How are you?'

'I'm fine. Yes. I'm fine.' She saw the dark, observant eyes flicker over her face. 'Why – why didn't you let me know you were coming?' They were talking to each other like strangers. Constraint hung between them like a meshed curtain of steel. But then – what else could he have expected, turning up without warning and in such company? She felt fatal anger stir, and tried to quell it.

'We didn't know ourselves,' Luke said. 'It was a – sudden decision' – he grinned that familiar, crooked little smile and her heart lurched – 'taken, perhaps I should add, after several magnums of excellent champagne had been consumed.' He stepped away from Lottie, who released his arm with some reluctance; yet still it seemed to Kitty that the limpid blue eyes held a hint of triumphant challenge, a smug and malicious gleam of satisfaction: here I am, and with him, they said; make what you will of it.

She struggled to order her thoughts, to break the strange threads of tension that seemed to bind the room like the web of an unseen spider. 'Nothing much has changed then?' she found herself saying, knowing the provocation of the words.

Luke said nothing, but the line of his mouth hardened infinitesimally.

There was a small, awkward silence. Charles looked from one to the other enquiringly, even he sensing the strain.

'How's Matt?' she asked then and was startled by a sharply explosive breath from Moses, a small flicker of warning in Luke's eyes.

Moses it was who answered, falsely jocular. 'How d'you expect that young whipper-snapper to be? Too big for his boots as usual, and causing as much trouble as a barrel-load of monkeys. How else? Pity you couldn't have found him a job here. Saved us all a lot of pain.'

Kitty looked at him and then at Luke. 'Has something happened?'

Luke shook his dark head. 'No more than you'd expect. Matt and Moses don't see eye to eye over the matter of a certain young lady, that's all. Nothing to worry about.'

'The same young lady?'

'The very same.'

'He hasn't written. I've not heard a word from him since I got here.'

'You didn't expect it?'

'No. I suppose not.'

Before he could say more there came a sharp rap upon the door and a sing-song call.

Kitty picked up the Dipper's cap and turned it a little nervously in her hands. 'That's me,' she said. 'Five minutes.'

'You'll dine with us afterwards,' Luke said, and it was not a question. 'We'll pick you up.'

Her mouth tightened a little at the arrogance of it. 'I'm – very tired,' she found herself saying, coolly.

She saw the quick flash of anger in his eyes. 'We won't keep you out late, don't worry.' It came to her that whatever Luke had expected of his surprise visit it had not been this. Again her own irritation stirred to match his. How in Heaven's name had he thought she would react? Did he even now honestly not know what he had done?

Charles bustled about them. 'Come – you have my own box. A special occasion, yes –?'

Luke turned and followed him without a word, the straight back and the tilt of his head making Kitty's leaden heart sink even further. If he had come alone – if he had attempted to apologize – to understand – if, if, if –

The audience was not a good one that night. They jeered the comic, drowned the ventriloquist with hoots and boos, cheered when the tightrope walker slipped and all but broke his neck. It took every ounce of willpower that Kitty possessed to get her onto the stage, and every ounce of energy to claim and keep their attention. But she did it. Her act now was polished and professional; she would not disappoint her audience. As always she threw herself heart and soul into her performance, and her reward at the end was a bombardment of flowers – which she knew might well have been rather more bruising missiles – and several curtain calls, the fickle crowd rising to their feet and refusing to let her go. She should, she knew, be pleased that she had triumphed, and on such a night – but in fact she was exhausted. She fled to her dressing room and was very sick indeed. Marie-Claire clucked about her, concerned.

'I'm all right. Truly I am. I just need to rest.' But no hope of that. The thought of facing – and outfacing – Luke sapped what little courage and confidence she had left. Resolution and hard-fought decision trembled weakly upon the brink.

She drank the brandy that the concerned Marie-Claire offered her at one gulp, and asked for another. With that inside her she struggled into a gown of emerald silk, let Marie-Claire deck her short, swinging hair with flowers, small feathered plumes and a pearl clip. Pearls, too, gleamed about her throat and her narrow wrist, the gems no paler, no more translucent than her skin. She was quiet when she met the others, allowing herself to be shepherded to a waiting carriage, speaking when spoken to, volunteering nothing. During the slow journey to the restaurant, however, her silence was not marked, for Lottie's voluble enthusiasm for Paris – addressed, Kitty noted, almost exclusively to Luke – filled the silence and exacerbated the thunderous headache that assaulted Kitty each time the carriage swayed. Lottie's apparently quite genuine love-affair with the city saw them too through the first part of the meal. Her voice, bright and sharp, rattled in Kitty's brain like pebbles in a can. She watched Luke, watched the dark face, the hard mouth whose remembered touch even now stilled her heart, the long, lean hands. Tired anger swept her again.

What were they doing here listening to Lottie's silly chatter? If he had wanted a reconciliation, surely he would have come alone – did not the circumstances of their last parting demand that at least? And if he did not, why be so cruel as to come at all? She watched him. He was listening now to a rambling story from Moses, head tilted to one side. Not once had he glanced at her, not once indicated that he too found the presence of the other two irksome, that he and she might have something more than inanities to speak of. With a swift movement she emptied her glass. Her head swam a little, then resumed its rhythmic pounding. Why had he come? Curiosity? A desire to hurt? To get his own back? What was it that horrible man at the Grange had said about a man never forgetting or forgiving an injury to his pride? And was not Luke the very personification of the kind of man of whom he had been speaking? Illogically, and with no word passed between them, her anger was fuelled again.

The meal dragged on. An orchestra had taken the small stage, and the gentle strains of Strauss lifted above the clatter of cutlery and the voices of the diners. Lottie tapped her foot, looking hopefully at Luke. Luke ignored her. Kitty stared miserably at the exotically dressed *poussin* she was making no attempt to eat.

'Shall we?'

She looked up. Luke was standing over her, unsmiling, a commanding hand held out to her. As she had done everything else this evening she allowed herself as if with no volition to be drawn onto the small dance floor. His arms were about her, his body, so familiar, warm and strong against hers. There was little or no room to waltz: the couples swayed, turned, clung in the half-light like lovers beneath the bridges of the Seine. She felt his cheek against her hair. The strength of the hand that held hers, the feel of his body, even the smell of him was painfully, intolerably familiar. Stupid tears burned in her eyes. She blinked them away.

'Well,' he said, quietly. 'Aren't you going to say anything at all?'

She tilted her head to look at him. The past months had been too much for her. Her mind and her heart were numbed. She could say nothing, for the simple reason that she still did not know in truth what she wanted to say.

'Aren't you glad to see me?'

She hesitated. Then, 'I don't know,' she said, honestly. 'It was such a surprise – and with them –' She glanced to where Moses and Lottie sat in apparently heated conversation at the table.

She felt him stiffen. Knowing his pride she knew she was handling the situation badly. Knowing her own she knew she could handle it no other way.

'What did you expect?' he asked, dangerously softly. 'That I should come alone, and cap in hand?'

'I didn't expect anything.'

'And didn't hope for anything? Didn't care?'

What was he trying to make her say? She was silent.

'Kitty, for Christ's sake' – his voice was sharp – 'say something!'

'Say what?' she flared back. 'What do you want me to say? You turn up here with no warning – and in company that you know I detest –'

'They're my friends,' he said, stubbornly.

Rushing on, she ignored that. 'And having apparently had to get drunk before you even managed that. And expect what? That I should throw myself into your arms? Beg you to stay? In front of them?' She jerked her head once more towards the table. 'How little you know me, Luke. After all this time, how very little.'

'Oh, for God's sake – what does it matter who I come with? I'm here –'

'And for that I should be grateful?' she snapped, scornfully.

He gritted his teeth. She could feel the anger in his tense body. 'You aren't being very constructive.'

Almost with relief she let her temper flare, the pent-up misery and anger of the evening loosening her tongue. 'As

I remember it, your behaviour last time we met could hardly have been described as constructive either.'

His shrug was impatient, dismissive; infuriating. He turned to go back to the table. She caught his arm. 'Oh, no you don't. You can't just ignore it, Luke. You want me to forget what happened? Pretend it was nothing? And what of next time – and the next? It's true what I said – nothing's changed, has it? Nothing. I see it in your eyes, hear it in your voice – Yes, you want me back – but on your terms. You won't change. You can't. Look at you now. You'd hit me if you could. Wouldn't you? Wouldn't you –?' Her voice was rising hysterically. She knew how she was goading him, was helpless to stop herself.

He stood very still. For a moment, looking into his eyes, she was afraid. Then she saw the effort he made to control himself. The music had stopped. They stood alone. Glances were directed at them, curious, amused. 'What do you want me to tell you?' he asked, softly. 'That I'll never lose my temper again? What is it that you want? A milksop to tag along by your apron strings? Is that what Paris has done for you? Well, think again, my lady. No one changes Luke Peveral. No one.'

She did not recognize the root of his anger any more than she had recognized his reasons for coming as he had, accompanied and unannounced. All she saw was the unreason and, lurking beneath it, that endless potential for violence that she so hated. She stepped back from him, fighting tears, temper and the inevitable nausea.

He turned his straight back on her and walked away.

She watched him for a long moment, unaware of the watching eyes. He reached the table. Moses spoke. Lottie pealed prettily into laughter.

Very composedly Kitty turned and beckoned to a worriedly hovering waiter. 'My cloak, please,' she said, and was surprised at the steadiness of her own voice. It did not last. By the time she had hailed a cab and given him halting directions she was in tears. As the ancient vehicle wheeled and set off towards the Left Bank she was huddled in the back seat sobbing as if her heart would break.

Despite the lateness of the hour Jem was working when Kitty arrived. He stared at her. 'Good God! Kitty – my dear, what is it? What's happened? Oh, Lord – come in. Sit down –'

She sank onto one of the uncomfortable wooden chairs, put her elbows on the table, buried her face in her hands and sobbed utterly uncontrollably. The floodgates of misery were open and she could not shut them. Jem watched her helplessly for a moment, then picked up a bottle from the floor where it had been standing beside him as he worked, wiped the top and stood it on the table. Then, hunting through the shambles of a room he found two glasses, peered at them a little doubtfully, wiped them, too, on his shirt tail, set them by the bottle and then sat in the chair across the table from her and waited for the storm to ease a little. After some moments the wild sobbing quietened, but Kitty did not lift her head. Hopelessly miserable, she sat, huddled into herself, the gleam of pearl and of emerald silk incongruous in the dark and squalid little room.

'Well, now. What's this?' The concern in Jem's soft voice almost brought tears again. Kitty scrubbed at her reddened eyes and nose with a sodden, tattered piece of lace that had once been a handkerchief, and sniffed noisily.

Jem poured a generous splash of absinthe into a glass and pushed it to her.

She shook her head.

'Doctor's orders,' he said.

She picked it up shakily, sipped it, almost choked.

'Now. Tell me.'

It came in all but incoherent bursts, the story not just of Luke's unexpected appearance and the awful evening, but her fear, her confusion, her agony of indecision, of love, and of hatred. Like a lost child she sobbed and hiccoughed her way through her unhappiness and uncertainty. And as she spoke Jem, watching her, picking up a word here, a word there, frowned as an awful suspicion took root. He stopped her at last, with a hand upon hers. 'Kitty –'

She lifted eyes so swollen and tear-filled that she could barely see.

'You aren't saying – trying to say that –?'

Her breath catching in her throat, she stared at him, sniffing. She had to say it, she knew – to make the unspeakable real at last by speaking it. 'I'm pregnant,' she said and the tears ran again, helplessly. 'I'm carrying Luke's child.'

2

(i)

'Chérie –' practical Genevieve said, for at least the dozenth time, 'you either have to get rid of it or you have to tell him –'

'No.'

'But –'

'*No!*' They were in Kitty's small, pretty sitting room. The day was hot and the shutters were closed beyond the long, elegant lace curtains. Daggers of golden light pierced the cool shadows, and dustmotes danced. Kitty restlessly stood and walked to the hall windows, parting the curtains and pushing one of the shutters with her hand so that it swung a little open, letting in the sound and light of a bright Parisian morning. 'No,' she said again, more calmly. 'I can't do either of those things. Do you think I haven't thought of it? God! I seem to have thought of nothing else for weeks! I will not kill my baby. I won't. I can't. And if I tell Luke' – she turned from the window, her face desperate – 'he'll never let me go. Never. And I won't have the strength to resist him. And the child will be brought up in violence and in fear, and in the shadow of the gallows.'

'Perhaps he'll change, chérie?' Genevieve suggested, gently. 'You say he would want this child – perhaps fatherhood would –'

She was interrupted and struck to silence by the sharp and bitter little sound that Kitty made. 'Change? Luke? As soon expect the sun to set in the east this evening! He as good as said so himself last night. Jem – you know him – tell her. Tell her what he's like –'

Jem it had been who had very sensibly insisted that she

confide in Genevieve, for whom over the past weeks he had
conceived no small respect, and in whose affection for Kitty
he had justifiable faith. He had been sitting in silence for
some time. Now he ran stained fingers through his fair,
shaggy hair and shook his head. 'Kitty's right, I'm afraid.
The man won't change. Not that much. Not enough. And
she's right too when she says that if he finds out he'll never
let her go.'

'He'd kill me first,' Kitty said, bleakly.

Genevieve made a small, protesting, negative gesture at
that. Jem said nothing. Genevieve stood and walked gracefully to where Kitty stood dejectedly fingering the fine lace
of the curtains, slid an arm about her waist. 'Kitty, my dear,
I won't have you looking so very sad. It isn't the end of the
world.'

'Isn't it?'

'But no.' Briskly and comfortingly Genevieve kissed
her cheek and then, her brow pensive, began to pace the
room, talking almost as if to herself, counting off the
points she made on long, slender fingers. 'You cannot tell
him. *Eh bien*, we will for the moment accept that. You
will not accept a doctor's help –' She paused in her
pacing and looked compassionately into Kitty's white
face. 'You are sure, chérie? I know of a very good, a very
reputable –'

'No!'

Genevieve shrugged. '*Eh bien*,' she said again, 'so that too
is out of the question. So. With what are we left?'

'Kitty has the baby –' Jem said.

'– and is ruined by the scandal,' Kitty finished. 'And then
Luke will find out anyway and – oh, God, what a mess!
What a bloody, horrible mess!'

'*Mais non*.' Genevieve was sucking her lip thoughtfully.
She resumed her pacing. 'Let me think.'

The other two watched her, Jem curiously, Kitty with
affection and no trace of hope. She herself was beyond
thought, almost beyond worry. The past weeks, and especially the past few days had exhausted her.

Genevieve had stopped in front of her, and was eyeing her contemplatively. 'It does not show.'

Kitty shook her head. 'Not at all. In fact – as you've all been pointing out so often – I've actually lost weight. It must be something to do with the way I'm built.'

'When is the baby due?'

'I think, so far as I can be sure – Christmas.'

Genevieve was again counting on her fingers. 'So you are – four months gone?'

'About that.'

'Your contract with Charles is until October?'

'Yes.'

She counted again. 'Three months. It is too long.'

'Too long for what?'

'Too long to hide it.'

'But – Genevieve – how can I possibly –?'

'Hush now. Listen. We embark, we three' – she included Jem in the warmth of her smile – 'upon a small conspiracy. Come' – she took Kitty's hand – 'sit down. We'll talk. Jem, would you be kind enough to ring for fresh coffee?'

'What kind of conspiracy? What good would it do? In a couple of months at the latest I'll start to show –'

'*Exactement*. A couple of months. The end of September. If we can keep your secret until then, then we might be able to keep it for ever. It depends upon you. Can you manage it? Can you keep on working for another couple of months?'

'Yes, I think so. Physically I'm fine. Even the sickness is passing. I think it's the worry that's been making me ill –'

'Precisely. So – if we make a plan, and you no longer need to worry, then all will be well, yes?'

Kitty shrugged doubtfully. 'I suppose so.'

'But of course. So. This is what we do –' Genevieve stopped as the door opened and a little maid in neat black dress and crisp white apron and cap entered carrying a silver tray upon which was set a steaming coffee pot and three delicate china cups. They sat in silence as she set it upon the table. '*Merci*, Lisa,' Genevieve said pleasantly. The girl left the room. Unhurriedly Genevieve poured the coffee and handed out the cups. '*Eh bien*. I was saying. This is what we do. First – absolutely nothing for a month. Kitty works as if all is well. You can do that?'

Kitty nodded.

'Good. Then – towards the end of August you complain a little of tiredness, of lack of appetite, of inability to sleep. To Charles I shall speak – delicately – of a *crise de nerfs*, of women's weakness – he will be sympathetic. All of Paris will be sympathetic. We shall enlist the help of our favourite journalists – a word here, a word there. By the end of September no one will be surprised if you have to break the contract with Charles and go home to rest, to nurse your poor overwrought nerves and repair the damage done to a delicate constitution by so much hard work –'

Kitty had to laugh at that. 'Me? A delicate constitution?'

'There, you see? You feel better already, *non*?'

Kitty sat thoughtfully for a moment. 'We don't tell Charles?'

'Pouf! Tell Charles? Don't be absurd. You know what a terrible gossip he is! He couldn't keep a secret if his life depended upon it! No. We don't tell Charles. We don't tell anybody. The less people who know, the better. And also – you don't go to England. You stay here, in France, where I can keep an eye on you and this – Luke – cannot find you. If he comes – he gets the same story as everyone else. We get you away to the country where for a few months you become a poor bereaved widow about to give birth to your first child. No one will know, chérie. In January – February, perhaps – you will return. And no one will be any the wiser.'

'Might they not guess?' Jem ventured, not wishing to deflate such positive optimism.

Genevieve waved an airy hand. 'So they guess? What can they do? What do they know? Kitty – this is the only way. Between us we will manage it.'

Kitty cleared her throat. 'And – the child?' she asked, hesitantly.

Genevieve looked at her in surprise and with a trace of

exasperation. 'Why – it will be adopted, of course. It's the only sensible thing.'

'I – yes. I suppose so.'

'Don't worry, my dear. I will arrange everything. You just get through the next couple of months.'

Kitty's face had cleared a little, the lines of strain relaxed. Impulsively she leaned forward and took Genevieve's hand. 'I don't know how to thank you. Why didn't I tell you before? It's been so horrible –'

Genevieve patted her hand comfortingly. 'Well it isn't over yet, but at least you are no longer alone. Now, one question remains. Where shall you go to have the baby? It must be in the south, I think –'

'There's a chance I might be able to help there,' Jem said, unexpectedly.

The two women looked at him in surprise.

Jem thought for a moment before continuing. 'There's a place I know in the Lot valley. It's very quiet – miles from anywhere, in fact. Just a small village and – about a kilometre downriver – a ruined watermill called La Source. The mill belongs to the family of a friend of mine. The mill itself is ruined, but the house is fine – they use it each summer for a month or so. Apart from that they're only too pleased to let Gaston's friends borrow it. The valley is a wonderful place to paint, and I think they rather like the idea of lording it as patrons of Gaston's penniless artist friends. In the autumn and winter there's never anyone there. I'm sure I could get them to let us have it. It would be perfect –'

'But – alone? In the heart of the country? When she does not have the language?' Genevieve shook her head vigorously. 'I had in mind a small town – somewhere civilized, with shops, and –'

'And people to ask questions,' Jem put in. 'Like – why should an English widow with very little French choose to have her child anywhere but England?'

'That we must risk. We cannot bury poor Kitty in the middle of nowhere alone –'

Jem hesitated for just one second. Then, 'She won't be alone,' he said quietly, 'I'll be with her. If she'll have me for the duration, that is –'

Kitty stared at him in astonishment. 'Jem! I couldn't impose on you so!'

'But why ever not? I shouldn't have offered if I didn't want to do it. There's nothing for me in Paris at the moment. I can as easily paint at the mill – easier, perhaps. There'll be fewer fatal distractions. No bars. No cafés –'

'No absinthe,' Kitty said.

He laughed. 'Well – just a little perhaps. You can't expect me to go without the delights of civilization entirely! Don't you see, Kitty – we'd be helping each other. You have to get away, and it would be better for me to leave the temptations of Paris for a while before they ruin me entirely. La Source is the perfect answer for both of us. There'd be no questions asked – the locals have long since got used to the comings and goings of Gaston's eccentric artist friends. And anyway, what is more natural than a penniless American and his pregnant English wife escaping from Paris for the winter?'

Genevieve was staring at him in dawning delight. 'But it's wonderful!' she breathed. 'Wonderful!' She turned to Kitty. 'You see? Between us we have arranged it all –'

Kitty looked from one to the other, blinking, her heart too full for words. Jem and Genevieve, an unlikely enough alliance, smiled at each other well satisfied. 'More coffee, I think,' Genevieve said.

Never, Kitty thought, had the old adage of shared troubles being halved been proved to be truer. With the strain of facing alone an uncertain future that had seemed to threaten nothing but trouble and eventual ruin eased, she immediately felt better. Under Genevieve's watchful eye she rested more, ate more sensibly, and her health improved. The terrible and until now all but constant nausea eased. Her energy returned; she no longer felt drained at the end of each performance. She was confident that Genevieve's practical timetable would work. She could last out until the end of September. Luke she did not see again. With no word or sign he had apparently returned to London as abruptly as he had come, a fact for which in her present state of mind she could feel nothing but thankful. She thought of writing to Pol with her news, but resisted the temptation, knowing Genevieve to be right when she said that the fewer people who knew the secret the better. There was, in any case, nothing Pol could have done but worry, and in that there was little point. She would tell her later, when it was all over; hopefully her friend would be too involved with her new husband to spare too many thoughts for Kitty. Her real remaining problem – what was to become of the child once it was born, a problem she declined to share with Genevieve who so blithely assumed adoption – she put determinedly to the back of her mind. She would have months in which to decide – months of peace and of quiet. The secret now, she was sure, was to take life one step at a time. And the first step was simply to get through to September.

With the help of Genevieve and of Jem it proved quite surprisingly easy. She was strong and she was healthy. Her rangy build continued to abet her deception – although as the weeks passed and a blazing August drew to a close she began to realize that even she could not retain her boyish shape forever and both she and Genevieve spent a feverish day or so unpicking and stitching, adding a little here, a little there, to encompass her expanding waistline and abdomen. And then, as September wore on, still very hot and muggy, it was not difficult to enact the scenario with which Genevieve had presented her. Her temper really was short, and she really did find herself tiring easily. Charles, worried by the change in her and totally deceived by his wife's connivances, agreed readily, if with regret, that the summer had been too hard for her and she should take a rest. With a concerned alacrity that shamed her he agreed to waive the last month of her contract. And so, in the last week of September she found herself at last safe out of the public gaze and on a train with Jem heading south to the River Lot and the little village of St Sauvin.

(ii)

The months that followed were the most peaceful and the most contented that Kitty had known since her Suffolk childhood. From the moment she first saw it, set within its sylvan valley, glowing now with the first fire-colours of autumn, the broad and tranquil River Lot enchanted her. On the day that they arrived and were driven the fifteen or so kilometres from the station to the village of St Sauvin in a rattling farmcart the dipping sun lit a sky of molten gold and glittered through the trees as they rode, dazzling their eyes. Small stone houses were scattered along the rutted road. At each wayside home dogs barked, chickens ran squawking from the great plodding hooves of the carthorse and dark-eyed children watched gravely as they passed. The lovely, slow-flowing river gleamed intermittently as it meandered between its willowed banks beside them. Paris – and for that matter London – the traffic, the bustling crowds, the ever-present noise and movement belonged, it seemed, not just to another world, but to another life.

'Jem – it's lovely! Truly lovely!'

He smiled, pleased. 'You're all right?'

She nodded. She was tired, certainly, after the trying journey, and her back stabbed pain with each lurch of the unsprung cart, but the sunlit countryside, the sight of the calm and beautiful river, fed strength and hope into her wearied bones. Not for the first time in the past few days she felt herself relax into a strangely fatalistic and far from unpleasant mood: the thing was done, the die cast. The baby grew steadily within her and nothing now could change the course of the next few months. So be it. She had struggled for long enough. The time had come to accept – accept the inevitable, enjoy each day as it presented itself. Let tomorrow's worries wait upon tomorrow. Today's concern would be wasted upon them anyway.

'There's the village,' Jem said.

The cluster of stone and timber houses, sited at the southern end of an ancient, narrow bridge that spanned the gently flowing river from one thickly wooded bank to the other, apparently dozed in the late afternoon sunshine. As they rolled from rutted mud onto a short stretch of noisy cobblestones curious children stared, a goat lifted an inquisitive head, steadily chewing, and a toothless ancient, ensconced comfortably with a carafe of dark wine at a table beneath a canopy of full-fruiting vines, watched them, deep-lined face impassive. They passed the handful of houses and wound their slow and steady way through the fertile valley bottom – cultivated land on the whole, dotted here and there with stonebuilt farmhouses. In some fields a late harvest was being gathered, others lay ready for the plough and the seed. At last Jem leaned forward and spoke in his rapid French to the driver. The man – who had spoken not a dozen words in as many kilometres – grunted.

'We're nearly there,' Jem said. 'There – the roof through the trees. Do you see?'

Kitty strained her eyes against the low, dazzling sun. Within a great stand of trees by the river, some distance from the lane, she caught a glimpse of terracotta tiles and a golden stone wall. Then the cart had turned ponderously into a long, rutted drive that curved within a tunnel of branches. Sunlight glittered and dappled the cart as it rolled across the first-fallen of the turning leaves. Through an arch of branches ahead she could see a tumble of buildings – sun-coloured stone walls, small windows, moss-grown clay-tiled roofs. As they rode closer she could see that some of them – those closest to the river bank – were in a bad state of disrepair. But as they turned and creaked into the mill clearing she saw that the sturdy, four-square house had been well repaired and renovated. New shutters guarded the windows, the stonework was clean and cleared of moss.

She stared at the house in unfeigned delight. 'Jem! It's beautiful!'

Jem surveyed the buildings, smiling a little. 'You couldn't be seeing it at a better time. The colours are wonderful, aren't they? There's a spring there – beyond the house – where the bamboo is growing, d'you see? It feeds the pool

that once fed the old mill race. Wait till you see the pool —
it's as blue as the sky, and never cold.' He vaulted lightly
from the cart and then turned to hand her down more
carefully. 'Welcome to La Source.'

The river glittered beyond the picturesquely derelict mill
buildings. A single bird called, piercingly sweet on the
autumn-scented air. The sun had dipped suddenly lower,
gleaming red upon the tree-obscured horizon. She stood
quite still, savouring the moment, absorbing the peace and
the beauty.

'You like it?' Jem asked, softly.

'I love it,' she said.

She never changed her opinion; on the contrary, in the
ensuing months she came to love the place in the truest
sense of the word. At first she walked every day, exploring
the countryside and the river's banks, delighting in the
gentle autumn weather, the shades of red and gold that
flamed about the splendid trees. Physically — to her surprise
after those first, difficult months — she had never felt better.
As her body thickened and her pace necessarily slowed so
it seemed to her that her mind and her soul quietened. She
had time at last — time to watch a bird as it flittered through
the branches of a tree, time to listen to its song, time to sit
in the great stand of feather-leafed bamboo, planted by some
imaginative unknown hand years before, beside the opaque,
miraculously blue, spring-fed pool that gave the mill its
name, and watch through the trees the cool, steady flow of
the waters of the Lot as they moved tranquilly on to the
distant sea. She woke with delight to the first morning of
rain and walked still, cloak and hood drawn close about her,
savouring the freshness of the air, the living, fragrant scent
of it. As the nights closed in and began to chill they would
light a fire each evening in the great rustic sitting room,
each curled into a favourite chair, reading, or talking, or
simply enjoying a companionable silence as she sewed for
the coming child and he drew out the inevitable sketch pad
and pencil.

She did not question their rapport, as she did not question anything else. In that place, at that time, it seemed the most natural thing in the world that they should live so, in friendship and in peace. It was as if, together with the other troubles of the outside world, the exhausting conflict, the extremes of feeling that so often characterized the more common relationship between man and woman had been for this short space of time suspended. They lived in harmony, each looking to the other's comfort and happiness and demanding nothing. Perhaps, Kitty reflected a little wryly one day as she sat upon the river bank beside a stand of gracefully weeping willows, they had both needed this rest from the rigours of passion more than they had themselves realized. She half-smiled at the thought. It was a delightfully mild, damp, sweet-smelling late autumn day. The narrow, gold-green leaves of the willows fluttered to the dark waters and drifted lazily downstream. Within her the child stirred and she laid her hand soothingly upon the mound of her belly in the age-old gesture of pregnancy. She hummed quietly to herself, and then found herself singing softly aloud, to the river, to the trees, to the stirring life within her –

    'All round my hat I will wear the green willow –
    All round my hat for a twelvemonth and a day –'

Pictures flickered in her mind. Faces long dead, or long forgotten, faces that no longer held over her the power of pain, but whose memories were transmuted now to a sweetly sad nostalgia.

    'Oh, young men are false and they are so deceitful,
    Young men are false and they seldom prove true –'

On the opposite bank she saw movement and a flash of colour beneath the trailing branches of the trees. She did not move, nor did she stop her singing.

    'For rambling and ranging, their minds always changing,

They're always a-looking for some girl that's true –'

The branches moved again. She lifted a hand and waved, smiling. There was a sudden, smothered squeal of giggling and two little girls in muddy homespun, their plaited hair tangled with leaves and twigs, scampered from their concealment and disappeared into the woodland, laughing and calling, casting impish glances over their shoulders at the strange foreigner who sat by their river and sang.

Kitty watched them go, smiling. Their skin was sunbrowned and their dark eyes bright with a childish mischief. She felt her own child stir again, impatiently. A daughter, she thought, with a sudden, irresistible rise of longing – it would be wonderful to have a daughter. She pulled herself up sharply. Don't think of it. Not now. Not yet. She clambered awkwardly to her feet and strolled back towards the mill, her wide-brimmed hat dangling from her fingers, her voice echoing still through the quiet woods,

'My love it grows older, but never will grow colder,
I wish 'twould fade away like the morning dew –'

Halfway through November the inevitable happened and a spell of wild, windy and wet weather set in, signalling the true approach of winter. The last of the bright leaves were stripped from the branches by the gale, the river muttered sullenly as it swirled, muddily high, against its banks. Kitty heard its murmur as it rushed against the great broken wheel of the mill, and moved her chair a little closer to the dancing flames of the enormous fire that burned upon the deep hearth. The wind blew gusts of rain against the windows and tossed the treetops wildly against the storm-dark sky, yet here, within the solid stone walls the sound was muted and the damp and cold kept at bay. Jem had walked into the village – with his command of the language it was he who shopped, picked up the occasional letter from Genevieve, visited the tiny bar and took a glass of the local wine with the men in the village. Kitty had had no contact with the

village at all – even the arrangements for the attendance of
the midwife at her lying-in had had to be made through Jem.
The thought, as despite herself it did more and more often
lately, caused a small frisson of anxiety that she tried to
ignore, but could not. Remembering Martha Isherwood's
anguish and near-death, the birth itsclf was something she
did not care to contemplate at too great length – but as the
days and the weeks passed and her burden swelled and grew
it became more and more difficult not to dwell on the ordeal
ahead. With Jem's cheerful presence in the house it was
easier, but alone sometimes she found herself brooding, a
little fearfully, upon the inevitable and unknown trial the
future – the near future now – must hold. She stood now
and wandered restlessly to the tiny window that overlooked
the drive, rubbing away the condensation, peering through
the bare, waving branches to the lane. And there Jem came,
whistling, apparently oblivious of the rain and wind, his
wet hair plastered across his face, in his arms a parcel of
provisions. She smiled at the sight, her fears fading, and
hurried to the scullery to set the kettle upon the stove.

It never got really cold in that clement southern valley.
Even December, with mists and drizzle, did not bring the
bite of a northern winter. As Christmas approached, Kitty
decked the house with evergreen and sent Jem off to the
village for the provisions for the seasonal feast. In the long
hours spent by the fireside she sewed him a new shirt,
hiding it when Jem appeared, enjoying the small, childish
excitement of secrecy. On Christmas Eve she tidied and
baked with a surge of energy that neither of them were
experienced enough to recognize.

In the dark early hours of Christmas morning her pains
started.

She lay alone, fighting fear and pain and waiting for Jem
to bring the midwife. The great, griping pain seized her
again, and she clenched against it, bringing blood to her
knuckles with her teeth, refusing to cry out into the desolate
silence of the deserted house.

In God's name, where were they? Why didn't they come?

She seemed to have been lying so, alone and waiting, for hours –

The pain receded a little. In the relief of the aftermath she almost slept, only to be awakened again by a fresh fierce clutch of agony, fiery pincers that gripped her back and her belly, and then at its unbearable peak receded, leaving her panting with effort and drenched in sweat. She dozed again, a half-sleep peopled with the demons of a child's nightmare. Then – at last! – voices, and light. Jem's worried face bending over her, a woman's voice, brusque and confident. Firm hands shook her. She moaned and tried to turn away. The pain came again, taking her unawares, drawing from her a shriek that blanched Jem's face. She reached for and clutched the hands that held her. The woman's voice crooned, soothing her. But when the pain receded the briskness was back.

'She wants to know how often the pains are coming,' Jem said.

Kitty shook her head on the pillow, her hair plastered in strands across her face. 'I don't know. Often.'

'She says you should walk a little, if you can. She says it will help –' Jem's face was taut with fear, his voice strange.

Beyond him, through the mists of pain, Kitty saw a small, shapelessly plump woman with the lined face of a peasant and sharp dark eyes. The woman rattled totally incomprehensible French at her and held out her hand. Kitty took it and struggled to sit up. There was a shocking, hot gush of liquid between her legs, a momentary easing of pain.

The woman spoke again, sharply, pushed her back onto the bed.

Jem disentangled his hand from hers. 'I have to get hot water –' he said, and the helpless anxiety of his expression brought the wan shadow of a smile to her face. 'Hurry,' she whispered. 'All the things I've prepared – they're in the scullery. In the warm cupboard, by the stove –'

'I'll get them.'

The pain assaulted her again, and with it this time came an overwhelming need to push, to expel the agony, to be finished with it. The midwife caught her hand and spoke urgently, shaking her head fiercely. Somehow the meaning of the words communicated itself to Kitty. She forced herself to relax, to ride the pain, not to struggle, her breath shallow gasps in her throat. The agony ebbed. She was vaguely aware of Jem back again, of the woman's hands upon her, of Jem's anxious eyes. She reached a hand to him. 'Don't go.'

'I won't.'

She knew later what it cost him, and never forgot it. But for the moment the urgency of pain and of the immense and exhausting effort of birth took her and she only knew that a familiar hand held hers as she struggled, shrieking, to deliver herself of her burden.

And then it was over. Incredibly, and with the greatest sense of relief that she had ever experienced, she felt the child slide suddenly into the world and the tearing pain was gone. She lay panting, utterly exhausted, drenched in sweat. The midwife's busy hands worked about her. There came another small pain, an echo only of the earlier agony. And then, reedily and strange to the ear, a small, wailing cry, swiftly hushed. Kitty blinked open sweat-slick eyes. Jem knelt before her, his face a transformation of wonder.

'Kitty – see – your son. Born on Christmas Day. A lovely little boy –'

'A boy –' She lifted a weak hand to the bundle that Jem held, parted the swaddling with a finger. Jet-black hair plastered to the tiny wet skull, eyes as dark as night, unsighted in the wrinkled, new-born face. Luke. She closed her eyes for a moment, fighting a wave of exhausted disappointment, the weakness of tears. Not a daughter, then.

The midwife took the baby from Jem and shooed him from the room. Kitty lay still as death, eyes closed, as the woman cleaned her and made her comfortable. Then, slowly, she felt the weakness in her limbs ebbing. She was aware of the dull ache in abused muscles and bones, but despite it, and despite that initial, bitter disappointment the first faint stirrings of a triumphant happiness surprised her. She had done it. She – no one else – had come through that ordeal and had given birth to a new life. Luke's son. She sat up. The woman, smiling and talking, plumped up the pillow at her back. The baby lay in a wooden drawer laid on the floor beside the bed. Kitty leaned to look down at him. The woman restrained her, bent herself to pick up the child and laid him in Kitty's arms. Kitty stared down at him. Her son. The midwife leaned forward and tugged at the ribbons that held Kitty's gown together at the neck. Kitty frowned for a moment, uncomprehending. The baby mewed a little, soft red mouth opening and closing like a little, hungry bird's. The midwife cupped her own ample breast in her hand, graphically, and pointed to the child. Slowly Kitty unlaced her nightgown. Her breasts, usually so small, were swollen and blue-veined, the nipples taut and dark. A little clumsily she drew the child to her. He turned his head and the tiny, greedy mouth fastened upon the nipple. There came a momentary, dagger-sharp pain and then an intense pleasure. The dark, downy head was heavy upon her arm. She leaned back against the pillows tiredly, letting contentment rise within her like the winter-swollen waters of the river beyond the window.

She had, she supposed, always known.

This was her son.

She would not give him up.

'What are you going to call him?' Jem asked, later, when the midwife had left, well compensated for her spoiled Christmas, and he sat by the bed watching the child asleep beside Kitty. 'Do you know?'

'I thought – Michael. After my father.' She hesitated, lifted a defiant head. 'Michael Daniels. It sounds well, doesn't it?'

He glanced at her, his face startled.

'I'm going to keep him,' she said, flatly.

He did not, she thought, look as surprised or as shocked as she had imagined he would be. And yet there was a flicker of something in his eyes that she could not identify. 'I suppose I always thought there was at least an even chance that you might,' he said after a moment.

'He's mine. I won't give him away. I can't. I'll manage

somehow. I could foster him, perhaps – buy a little cottage in the country somewhere – no one need ever know –'

He looked at her, his face sombre. 'Not even Luke?'

'Least of all Luke.'

He shook his head. 'You can't do that.'

'I can. I'm going to.' Her voice was very calm.

'If he found out –'

'Who'll tell him?' She lifted a challenging head, a tigress defending her young. 'You?'

He shook his head.

'I'll manage it,' she said again, as if in the repetition she would convince herself. Then her voice softened, and she held out a hand to him. 'Jem – thank you. For everything. For now, and for the past months. For bringing me here. For giving me time.'

He ducked his head. 'It's nothing.'

'It's everything,' she said, firmly. 'I couldn't have done it without you. And look at him – isn't he worth it?' Gently she fondled the soft, baby head. 'Jem, if – when – I have Michael christened – would you stand as his godfather?'

He looked at her for a long moment, on his face that same baffling flicker of emotion. Then he smiled. 'Of course. I'd love to.'

It was not until after he had left her alone to feed the child that it came to her with a shock of surprise that what she had seen in his face had come very close to pain. And then she dismissed the silly thought. Motherhood was making her fanciful.

She recovered quickly from the birth. Within a few days she was up and a few days later was active again. The child absorbed her totally. She carried him with her everywhere, resting in a sling that Jem had contrived for her of canvas and linen, which she slung around her neck so that the baby rested securely against her breasts. He was a contented child, rarely crying, and he grew very fast. Inexperienced as she was in such matters yet still Kitty could see that he was a fine child, healthy and strong. In the weeks that followed she devoted herself to him utterly, feeding him, watching him, playing with him, talking to him, singing for him. Jem watched, strangely quiet and with a sadness in his eyes that she was too absorbed to notice. There was a cold snap in January that kept them within doors, though still it was not the bitter weather that they were both used to at that time of the year. Even on the coldest days the spring-fed pool kept its warm and steady temperature and the grass grew green as emerald on its wooded banks. The place was idyllic, and in its peace Kitty grew strong again, nursing her child, noting with pleasure that apart from her milk-swollen breasts her figure had returned completely to its normal, boyish shape.

Of the future she simply refused to think, though once or twice and more often as the month drew to its close Jem questioned her. She would think about it tomorrow – next week ... The baby needed time, time to grow and to strengthen. She would make plans soon. But not now. Not right now.

Time drifted on. January slid into February almost unnoticed. At the back of her mind she was aware of it, as she was aware that she must eventually leave this enchanted place and face the world once more; but again and again she pushed the thought away. When she discovered a tiny cluster of fragile snowdrops upon the banks of the pool her pleasure at their beauty was marred by a pang of something close to panic. She could not stay here for ever: yet she could not – she could not! – yet face the thought of leaving.

In the end her indecision proved to be for the worst, for the world, too long ignored, came to her and the shock was the greater.

It was a chill, sunny day in mid-February. With Michael in his sling, safe and warm within her woollen cloak, she had walked the little way to the pool and then followed the path past the derelict mill buildings to the curve of the river's bank. There she stood for a while watching the swirling, cold-looking waters that glimmered in the pale winter sunshine. She would have liked to walk further, but the bank path was muddy and treacherous in places and with her precious burden she would not take the risk. Instead she struck out at an angle through the wet grass around the front of the house to the rutted drive. In the distance a horse and cart plodded along the lane. She narrowed her eyes against the bright light; earlier that morning Jem had set off for the market in the nearby town of Fumel. It was surely too early for him to be returning yet?

Michael stirred sleepily at her breast. Her eyes still idly upon the approaching cart, she rocked him gently, making small, soothing noises.

The cart had stopped, and through the trees Kitty saw a small figure clamber awkwardly from it before it set off again, continuing along the lane. The lone figure stood for a moment looking about him. From this distance she could see nothing familiar about him. It most certainly was not Jem.

Curious, she strolled towards him, half her attention still upon the restless baby.

The small man, head down, shoulders hunched, was trudging up the drive towards the house.

She recognized him while he was still yards away and before he had seen her at all. She stood stock still, dry-mouthed, feeling as if every drop of blood had drained from her heart. Of all the people she had thought to see, this incongruous figure was the last, and oddly the most ominous.

He stopped when he saw her, stood for a moment, taken back by her unexpected appearance. He wiped his dirty coat sleeve across his nose, sniffing.

She could not speak. Her heart that the moment before had seemed to stop entirely was pounding now, taking her breath with fear. Luke. Something terrible had happened to Luke. He was dead. Imprisoned. What –?

'Spider,' she said, and her voice sounded strange, lost in the dry winter's air. 'What are you doing here? What's happened?'

'I bin lookin' fer you fer weeks, miss,' the little man said, unsmiling and with no greeting. 'No one knew where you were –'

'How did you find me?'

'Found a girl named Lucette. Friend of Jem's 'ad told 'er 'e was 'ere. It was 'er guess you were with 'im.'

'What's happened?' Her voice was dull. Her sudden grip upon the child had startled him. He started to whimper. She saw Spider's eyes open wide in his wrinkled face. She caught his arm. 'It's Luke, isn't it? Something's happened to Luke?'

He shook his head, his bemused eyes still on the child where the smooth dark head appeared in the opening of Kitty's cloak. 'It ain't the Guv'nor, miss, no. It's yer brother. It's Matt. They got 'im in Newgate. They say 'e murdered Moses Smith. They're goin' ter top 'im for it –'

3

The journey back to England was a nightmare. The weather was appalling, the trains crowded and uncomfortable. The baby – his regular and peaceful regime so arbitrarily disturbed – was fretful and difficult. Afraid to spend money that might somehow be used to help Matt, she travelled second class together with the uncommunicative Spider and Jem, who had insisted upon accompanying her as far as the Channel.

After a dozen attempts to drag a coherent story from Spider and after the dozenth reiteration of '– the Guv'nor knows what 'appened. 'E'll tell yer –' she gave up, trying unsuccessfully to govern a raging and fear-filled impatience. The facts that she did elicit were basic; Moses was dead, his throat cut in one of the bedrooms at the Song and Supper Rooms, and Matt had been taken and charged with the crime. And – to add to her frantic worry – all this had happened months ago, at the beginning of November, whilst she had been contentedly wandering the autumn woodlands of the Lot. Genevieve's plan to protect her had worked all too well – Luke had sent Spider to Paris to find her, and the unprepossessing little man had, until the stroke of luck that had taken him to Lucette and her accurate if ill-founded guess, met with a wall of silence. It had taken him nearly three months to track her down. And Kitty now had to face the thought that during that time anything might have happened; she might already be too late.

On the way through Paris she called upon Genevieve, a flying visit to tell her what little she knew herself of what had happened, and to tell her too of her decision with regard to Michael. Genevieve gestured with milk-white hands, helplessly philosophic. 'It must be as you wish, of course, my Kitty. But I tell you – you will not be able to hide the child – especially now, with such trouble come upon you. If they hang your brother the newspapers will –'

'They won't! Don't say it! He didn't do it. He couldn't have done it. I know him. There's been some terrible mistake, that's all.'

'Of course, chérie, I'm sorry –' Genevieve was soothing, but her voice was unconvinced.

And for all her brave words Kitty herself suffered the most agonized misgivings as once more they sped northwards, towards the Channel. As she sat, rigidly sleepless and uncomfortable beside the dozing Jem, Michael's small head a cramping weight upon her arm, it seemed to her that the rhythmically clicking wheels mocked as they rode – and the words they used she had heard before, and never forgotten since they had been spoken that day that their troubles had begun: Are you familiar, Matt Daniels – the humming wheels spoke in the light, supercilious tones of Sir Percy Bowyer – with the saying that those who are born to hang will never drown – never drown – never drown – And then Luke's voice – we're the other kind – born to hang – born to hang – She could not stop the words that hammered in her brain.

She said goodbye to Jem at Boulogne almost peremptorily, her mind abstracted with anxiety, her every thought concentrated on her need to get home to Matt. The crossing was rough and Spider was miserably sick. Kitty, determinedly, was not. She sat huddled on a cold and windblown bench, her child clasped to her, and tried to think coherently, to make some sensible plan. Until now she had thought of nothing but getting back to London as swiftly as possible. Now it came to her that in a very few hours she would be there. She had to make up her mind what she intended to do. But first she had to try to ensure Spider's silence upon the matter of Michael.

She tackled him with misgiving as they waited, cold and

depressed, for the train that would take them on the final leg of their journey.

'Spider – I wanted to – ask you something. A favour.'

The little man looked at her, his face blank to the point of hostility.

With sinking heart she struggled on. 'The child –' She hesitated. 'You must have wondered why I ran away from Paris? Why I hid?'

'It's nothin' ter do with me.'

'But it is. Because you know about the child. And – I want you to keep it a secret.' She cuddled the baby to her, hiding the dark hair, the huge, black eyes. Spider had hardly glanced at the child, had shown in fact no interest at all after the first shock. Please God, he had not marked the resemblance. 'The child – isn't Luke's. That's why I hid. I was afraid. And, Spider – surely you can see that we've all got quite enough trouble to contend with at the moment? If Luke should find out . . .' She let the words die between them, miserably. Their breath hung, chill mist upon the bleak, dark air. With a huff of steam the great engine was pulling into the platform.

'Spider – please?' she said, urgently, hating the need to beg.

'It's nothin' ter do with me,' he said again, shrugging.

'You mean – you won't tell him?' She despised the desperation in her own voice but could neither disguise nor prevent it.

He made an irritated, dismissive half gesture with which she had to be satisfied. They spoke only once more before reaching London, when Kitty roused herself to ask him if he knew where Pol was living and Spider muttered that she and Barton Wesley had rented a house in Pascal Road, just three doors from where Amy was living. Kitty relaxed a little – that at least was good news.

At Victoria Station Spider left her, ungraciously ignoring her halting attempts to thank him. She stood alone with the child, surrounded by what luggage she had brought with her – the rest Genevieve was sending on from Paris.

'Cab, lady?'

With relief she nodded. 'Yes, please.'

'Where to?'

She hitched the child tiredly onto her hip. 'Paddington,' she said. 'Pascal Road.'

Early darkness had fallen by the time she reached the address that Spider had given her. With relief she saw that lights gleamed behind the lace curtains of the small windows. The cab driver deposited her luggage upon the pavement, then cheerfully held the child as she hunted for the coins to pay him. Then he flicked a finger to his cap, swung expertly back up onto his high driving seat and at a touch of his long whip the horse ambled off into the gathering darkness. Mist hung about the street lights, smudged darkly with the soot of winter fires. It was bitterly cold. Kitty stepped to the door and knocked loudly.

She heard Pol's voice before the door was opened. ' 'Oo the blazes is that at this time of the day? Bart? Bart – you there? There's someone at the door! Oh, all right. Might 'ave known. If yer want somethin' done, do it yerself –' Grumbling good-naturedly she swung the door open. 'Yes? Oo is it?' She stood, plump and solid, outlined against the light, garish hair like a nimbus of fire about her head – so familiar, so dear, that for a moment Kitty, clutching Michael to her breast, could not speak.

'Well, dearie?' Pol peered into her shadowed face. 'What can I –?' She stopped. There was a moment's incredulous silence. 'Kitty? It can't be – *Kitty*!'

'Yes. It's me.'

'Kitty!' Pol threw herself upon her, arms stretched to hug her. Kitty felt her stiffen and then draw back. Kitty followed her into the light. Michael whimpered. 'Gawd Almighty,' Pol said, very softly. 'Great Gawd Almighty. So that's it?'

Wordless, Kitty nodded.

Sober-faced Pol parted the shawl that protected the tiny head.

'Pol,' Kitty said, and was appalled at the helpless wobble

in her voice. 'Oh, Pol!' she was crying then, crying and babbling, her face buried awkwardly in the other girl's shoulder. 'Oh, Pol, I'm so glad to be home – I never thought I'd get here – I'm so frightened – what's happened? How's Matt –?'

Pol held her for a long moment, comfortingly, including the baby in her embrace, patting Kitty's shoulder, making wordless, soothing noises.

Kitty drew back at last, sniffing. 'I'm sorry. It's just – it was such a shock – about Matt, I mean. And it's been such a horrible journey.'

''Course, love. I understand. But you're 'ere now. Nice cup of tea. That's what's called for – Bart!' She raised her voice to a muted shriek that might have been heard at the far end of the street. 'Bart! Come down 'ere! Look 'oo's come 'ome to us!'

Barton Wesley, obviously alerted by the commotion, had already appeared at the top of the stairs. 'By cracky! Kitty!' He came down the stairs like a small avalanche, gave her a smacking kiss on her tear-wet cheek then, as Pol had done and with much the same expression, stood back to survey her whimpering burden. 'Whew!' he whistled softly, and exchanged a glance with Pol.

'No questions,' Pol said, firmly. 'Not till later. Let's get you in an' make the babe comfy. Then we'll talk.'

Kitty allowed herself to be enveloped by the brisk ministrations of her friend. Tea was made, baggage brought in from the pavement. Settled in peace and warmth by the fire in the tiny parlour, she fed Michael and made him comfortable, settling him securely in the depths of a massive armchair which she pushed against the wall. Then she took her empty tea cup and went out into the hall, following the sound of voices to the half-open kitchen door.

'A kid, eh?' Pol was saying, her voice edged clearly with anxiety. 'What a turn up for the book. As if she 'asn't got enough on 'er plate!'

'Is it 'is, d'you think?' Barton asked.

Pol snorted. 'You blind as well as daft? 'Course it is. Gawd 'elp the poor little bugger.'

'Well – it's just – all them stories that went around –'

'All them lies, more like.'

'What lies?'

Pol spun to where Kitty stood at the doorway. 'What lies, Pol?' Kitty asked again, quietly.

Pol opened her mouth, hesitated, then said flatly, 'Word was that you'd gorn orf with some feller. Some rich Froggy count or somethin', Lottie said.'

'Lottie?' Kitty cut in.

'Lottie,' Pol repeated, grimly. 'She said that when they saw you in Paris you were knee-deep in Russky princes an' flashy French aristos. An' 'is Lordship certainly came 'ome with a flea in 'is ear, anyone could see that. So – well, when you disappeared word was that you'd found yourself a nicely feathered little nest somewhere –'

Kitty stared, appalled. 'And you believed that?'

Pol shrugged. 'Didn't 'ave much reason not to.'

'And – Luke? He believed it too?'

Another shrug.

Kitty sat down hard upon a wooden chair. Here was a complication she had not envisaged.

Pol poured her another cup of tea. 'Gawd, what a mess! Still, when 'e sees the bairn –'

'No!'

They both blinked, startled at her vehemence.

'No,' she said again, determinedly. 'He's not to know. I don't want him near Michael. I don't want him anywhere near my baby.' Tears were close again. She shook her head angrily.

'But – you can't do that! 'E's bound ter find out sooner or later.'

'Not necessarily. Not if you'll help me. You will help me, won't you? We can hide him – I can find someone to look after him for me – he's mine, Pol. I won't give him up and I won't have Luke take him from me. When this awful business with Matt is sorted out –' She had been talking feverishly. At the flicker of pain that crossed Pol's open face at the mention of Matt's name she stopped. Dead silence fell. She looked from one to the other. Barton could not meet her eyes but stared gloomily into his empty cup. The compassion in Pol's face brought a wave of panic, fluttering suddenly in Kitty's throat, all but stopping her breath. 'What's happened?' she whispered through dry lips.

Pol shook her head slowly. 'The trial's over, love. For what it was worth.' Disgust and distrust for the law and all its works harshened the last words.

'And?' Kitty asked.

'Guilty,' Pol said, and the quiet word hung in the air between them like the hangman's noose. 'An' the appeal turned down.'

'Oh, no! Oh, God! No!' Kitty buried her face in her hands, trembling. It was a very long time before, white-faced, she lifted her head. 'What happened? Tell me. I don't know what happened.' She was suddenly and unnaturally calm.

Pol cast her a worried look. 'Drink yer tea.' She pushed the steaming cup to Kitty and watched as she made a gallant effort to sip it. Then she took a long breath. 'There was bad blood – real bad blood – between Moses an' Matt after you left –'

'Over the girl? What's her name? Sally-Anne?'

'That's right. Seems Matt was more smitten than any of us realized. 'E wanted the girl out of The 'Ouse. Moses didn't care much fer that –'

'But still – Matt surely wouldn't have killed him?'

'Someone sure as 'ell did,' Pol said, sombrely. 'And Matt it was that they caught not yards from the body with the knife in 'is 'and an' Moses' blood all over 'im.'

'What?'

'You didn't know?'

She shook her head tiredly. 'I don't know anything.'

'Matt's story was that 'e'd seen a note from Moses sayin' that 'e'd be at the Song an' Supper Rooms that afternoon –'

Kitty frowned. 'A note? Why would Moses send Matt a note?'

Pol and Barton exchanged a quick glance. 'The note wasn't to Matt,' Pol said. 'It was to Luke.'

'Then how did Matt come by it? And why did he go to the Rooms?'

'The kid that took the note couldn't find Luke. So 'e asked Matt to deliver it for 'im,' Pol said. 'Matt wanted to talk to Moses about the girl. Moses 'ad refused point blank to discuss it – seems that Matt thought this'd be a good opportunity.'

'So he never gave the note to Luke?'

'Luke wasn't around.'

'So – what happened?'

'Matt swears 'e don't know. 'E says someone was waitin' for 'im at the Rooms, someone with a bloody great truncheon or somethin'. When 'e came to 'e was in the bedroom with Moses' corpse, smothered in blood and with a knife in 'is 'and. An' the place crawlin' with bleedin' coppers. He tried to get away, but they caught 'im, knife, blood an' all. 'E didn't stand a chance. Overwhelming circumstantial evidence, the judge called it.'

'But – who called the police? What were they doing there?'

''Oo knows?'

'And – why in Heaven's name was he still carrying the knife? Surely – he could have got rid of it – left it?'

There was a short, uncomfortable silence. She looked from one to the other, frowning. 'Well? What is it?'

'The knife –' Pol said.

'Yes?'

'It belonged to Luke. Matt recognized it – yer must 'ave seen it yerself. 'E carries it everywhere with 'im.'

'I've seen it.' Her voice was bleak.

'Well – seems it occurred to Matt that if the knife was found Luke'd be in trouble – so 'e tried to get it away.'

Very slowly Kitty sat back in her chair. 'Luke again,' she said, her voice oddly flat.

Pol said nothing.

'A note to Luke. Luke's knife. And my brother is to hang?'

Hard-faced, Kitty shook her head. 'I don't believe it. I just don't believe it.'

'Kitty –'

'You say there was bad blood between Matt and Moses?'

'Yes.'

'And that, of course, came out at the trial?'

'They made quite somethin' of it.'

'I'll bet they did,' Kitty said bitterly. A picture had risen in her mind – a picture of Luke in her dressing room at the Moulin d'Or, Lottie's small hand possessively on his arm. 'And Luke and Moses?' she asked softly, 'there was no bad blood there?'

The tense silence fairly shrieked an answer.

'And – was that made much of at the trial as well?'

Pol shook her head.

'I thought not.' Kitty stood up composedly. 'Would you give an eye to Michael for me? He's fed and sleeping – he shouldn't be any trouble. He's absolutely exhausted.' She reached for her coat, that Pol had hung behind the kitchen door.

'Kit – leave it – at least for tonight. Give yourself a chance to rest.'

Kitty paused, the coat slung halfway about her shoulders, looking at Pol levelly. 'Rest? You think I could rest before I've heard the truth? Luke knows. Doesn't he?'

'There are rumours –'

'Are there indeed?' Kitty set her small fur hat upon her head and deftly slid the long hatpin into place.

'Where are you going?' Barton asked, worriedly. Exasperated, Pol cast her eyes to the ceiling.

'To find Luke Peveral,' Kitty said, and her voice was grim.

The cab driver flatly refused to venture into the maze of alleys that led down to the canal and the derelict church. 'Not likely, love. You want ter get yer throat cut – that's all right wiv me – but I don't 'ave ter 'ang about an' watch, do I? Let alone 'ave mine slit along a yours.' He eyed her curiously.

She had until that moment all but forgotten her changed appearance. It suddenly seemed a very long time since she had ventured into this dark warren of streets. 'Oh, very well – here.' Smouldering anger had brought her this far. She would, she had told herself, see Luke Peveral if Lucifer and all his angels stood in her way. But after she had paid the cabbie, and watched as the lights of the vehicle disappeared into the darkness she stood alone in the narrow street, collar turned up against the swirling fingers of soot-laden fog, her confidence wavering. The houses leaned above her, menacing. Familiar, awful smells assaulted her nostrils – the foul odours of disease, of poverty, of neglect and of filth. A nearby shadow moved, startling her: a youth's thin, rat's face glimmered at her in the fitful light of a street lamp. Across the road she could see a familiar alleyway. It led, she knew, to the lane where stood the derelict church. She had come too far now to give up. Hands in pockets, hunching her shoulders against the cold, she hurried across the street, willing herself not to turn to see if the rat-faced youth were following, her ears strained for an echo of footsteps behind her. It suddenly seemed unbelievable to her that for so long she had walked these streets with no real fear; in those days she had been a part of them, ragged, threadbare, no target for anyone. She cursed herself for her foolishness – a cab, a fur hat and fur-lined collar. The past year had softened and sheltered her, and suddenly she was afraid. Foolhardy to have allowed her ungovernable anger to bring her so far!

And then the vision rose in her mind of Matt, alone in Newgate Gaol, living in the shadow of the most terrible of deaths, and she gritted her teeth and hurried on. There must be something she could do. There must be! And instinct told her that the only place to start was at Luke Peveral's door.

But he was not there.

At the top of the winding, narrow staircase a lamp burned steadily outside his door, holding out the hope at least of some return, but the door was firmly locked and the room beyond quiet as the grave. Fighting tears of frustration, disappointment and something she did not like to admit might be fear, she crouched, shivering, upon the top step and set herself to wait.

The only thing that kept her there, finally, as the hours passed and dark evening became darker night was the knowledge that as she had waited so the menace of the streets had increased a hundredfold. To venture out alone now would be rash to the point of foolishness – so, stubbornly, she waited, frozen to the marrow and near-distraught with anxiety, knowing that, save for the danger of freezing to death it was now safer to stay than to leave. Sooner or later he must come. She huddled closer to the lamp, leaned her head upon her folded arms and, shivering, uncomfortable, but exhausted, she slept.

She woke from nightmares to find him standing above her, his face deep-cast in shadow as he looked down at her. How long he had stood so, watching her, she did not know: long enough, certainly, for her to have lost any advantage of surprise. She it was who jumped, and gasped, and scrambled to her feet, heart pounding with a nerve-wracking combination of fright, relief and anger. He stepped past her with no word and unlocked the door. She followed him in silence, eyes still blurred with sleep. The room was freezing, the unlit fire laid ready for a match. With the graceful economy of movement that was so much a part of his attraction he turned up the lamps, lit the fire, splashed brandy into two glasses and – still in silence – handed one to her as she stood, stone cold and shivering in the middle of the familiar room.

She shook her head.

'Drink it.' They were the first words he had spoken.

She brought the glass to her lips with trembling fingers. Her lips were almost too cold to feel the strong liquid as it trickled onto her tongue. The fire of it burned her throat and spread in her stomach. Her muscles were stiff and aching. He shifted a deep armchair closer to the fire. 'Here. Sit down.' The words were brusque.

She perched on the edge of the chair, holding hands pinched and translucent with cold to the pale, blossoming flames that as yet held little warmth. In silence still Luke tossed back his brandy in one movement, poured himself another large measure, then came to sit in the armchair opposite hers by the fire. As he passed, a faint, pungent perfume drifted to her nostrils – a perfume she had smelled before. Lottie, she remembered detachedly, had been wearing it in Paris. A sudden sense of weariness overcame her. What in God's name was she doing here – tired, worried, sick with anger? Of all the men to face at such a disadvantage, this must be the worst –

He eyed her coolly. 'And where, for Christ's sake, have you been?'

The chill hostility of the words, oddly, far from intimidating her served to bring her to herself where a softer approach might not have done. She stiffened. 'I've been unwell.'

He waited for long enough for the silence to be insultingly disbelieving. 'I see. May an old friend ask – where you've spent all this time being – unwell?'

She kept her voice even. 'A friend took me to the country.'

'A friend.'

'A mutual friend.' She watched his face. 'Jem O'Connell.'

That shook him, and she was savagely pleased to have caught him off balance. 'Jem?'

'Jem.' She let the single word hang between them, made no attempt to explain or qualify. Let him think what he would.

He rolled his glass between his long fingers. 'What was the matter with you?'

She made a small, impatient sound. 'Oh, for Heaven's sake – does that matter now? I'd been overworking. I had a – nervous collapse. Jem knew a place where I could rest. That's all. It isn't what I came to talk about.'

'No,' he said. 'I didn't for a moment suppose that it was.'

She lifted her head. 'I want to know what happened,' she said quietly. 'And I want the truth.'

He looked into the crackling fire.

'Luke?'

His face was in shadow and she could discern no expression. 'How much do you know?'

'I know,' she said, very softly, 'that Moses Smith was murdered with your knife. I know that someone trapped Matt into taking the blame. I know that you' – she paused, chose the word very deliberately – 'reek – of Lottie Smith's perfume.'

There was a long, long silence. 'You're wrong,' he said at last. 'I didn't kill Moses.'

'Neither did Matt.'

'No.'

'Then – who?'

He took a long breath and leaned back in his chair. 'I'm not sure you'll believe me if I tell you.'

'You do know, then?'

'Yes.'

'Then in God's name why is my brother lying in the condemned cell at Newgate!' For the first time the violence of her emotion showed in her voice, raw and passionate.

'Because the trap was laid too well! Because what we know and what we can prove are two different things! Because we live on the wrong side of the law, and the creatures of the law are not interested in justice for the likes of us!' His tone matched and surpassed hers in violence. 'If there had been anything I could do to save Matt – do you think I would have left it undone?'

She lifted her head, looked at him with a cool, level gaze. 'If in doing it you might have incriminated yourself? Yes, I do.'

He took a sharp, angry breath. She sensed his battle for self-control.

'You spoke of a trap,' she said. 'What trap? Who would wish to trap Matt?'

He drained his glass, held it before him, watching the flames through the distorting glass. 'The trap was not laid for Matt,' he said at last. 'It was laid for me.'

'By whom?'

He leaned back in his chair. For the first time, she saw the tiredness in him. 'By Oliver Fogg,' he said.

For a moment her mind was blank. 'Fogg?' The name was only faintly familiar. Then from some hidden recess of her memory rose a face – a cadaver's face, sharp-boned and ugly. 'But, I don't understand – what has Fogg to do with all this? You said that he was a policeman. That he was after you –'

'And so he was. What none of us knew was that he was after Moses too. He wanted me behind bars.' He turned his dark head and stared into the fire. 'He wanted Moses dead.'

'But, in Heaven's name, why?'

He sat for a moment in silence, then spoke quietly. 'A couple of years ago – just before you and Matt came – a young girl that Moses had working in The House killed herself.' He held his empty glass before him, watching the distorted flames through it. 'She was Oliver Fogg's daughter. His only child.'

'What!'

'Sally-Anne knew her. Knew who she was. Knew the story all along. It just never occurred to her to tell anyone.'

'But what was a respectable girl doing in The House?'

He smiled, bitterly. 'A respectable young man got her into trouble, and her respectable father threw her out. How else? Don't tell me you've not heard the story before.'

'Then it was Fogg's own fault that she was there?'

'Of course. But he didn't see it that way. After she died, eaten up with guilt, he vowed revenge. He tried first to stay on the right side of the law – watching Moses, trying to gather some kind of evidence that would put him behind bars or, preferably, hang him. You remember what happened – Moses, thinking he was protecting me, applied the screws and Fogg was warned off. That was when he decided to take the law into his own hands. He planned and he waited. He wanted Moses dead, and he had a score to settle with me. When rumours reached his ears that Moses and I weren't exactly on the best of terms he knew his time had come.

He stole my knife and killed Moses with it, then sent me a
note, ostensibly from Moses, to get me to the Song and
Supper Rooms.'

'But it was Matt who saw the note, and Matt who went –'

'Exactly. So Fogg took second best. He needed a murderer,
and one that the law would be only too pleased to take.
Since I had not obliged, he substituted Matt.'

'And Matt made things worse for himself by taking the
knife because he recognized it as yours –'

There was the smallest of silences. 'Yes.'

She looked at him, a small puzzled frown on her face.
'How do you know all this?'

The silence this time was much, much longer.

'Luke?'

He rolled the empty glass between long fingers. 'Fogg told
me,' he said, 'just before he died.'

He might have struck her. She gasped, staring, speechless.
He did not look at her. She swallowed noisily. 'What have
you done?' she whispered at last.

'What had to be done.'

'What had to be done? What had to be done?' She was
trembling with rage and grief. 'You killed Fogg? The man
who might have been able to clear Matt's name? You killed
him? And now there's no hope –'

'There was never any hope.' His voice cut across hers like
a pistol shot. 'From the moment Matt was taken, yards from
the body, covered in blood, the murder weapon in his hand
there was never any hope. Matt himself knew it. The trial
was a travesty. No one ever intended it to be anything else.
A criminal murdered by a criminal. Two birds with one
stone. He never stood a chance.'

'But –'

'But nothing! You want justice? You have it – the only
justice you'll get. Fogg's dead.'

'I don't want anyone dead! I want Matt out of there –
alive –!'

He said nothing. She sustained his dark, direct gaze for
a moment, then with a sudden movement buried her

face in her hands. 'I don't believe this. I don't believe any of it.'

He neither spoke nor moved to comfort her. She was trembling again, violently. She felt him remove the empty glass from her nerveless fingers, heard his movements as he refilled it. When he returned she lifted her head, took the glass and swallowed a mouthful of the fiery liquid. The cold knot of nausea in her stomach resisted it. 'What made you suspect Fogg?' she asked, dully. 'How did you know it was him?'

'He was in charge of the policemen who captured Matt. Sally recognized his name at the trial, and told me about the girl. It had already struck me as being fishy – his being so conveniently on hand. I decided that perhaps we should have a little talk.'

'And he admitted it.'

'He took some persuading.'

She turned from him, sickened. 'This is your fault,' she whispered at last. 'All your fault. If Matt hadn't become involved with you – if I hadn't become involved with you – none of it would have happened.'

'Do you think I don't know it?' His voice was bitter and pain-filled, but she was a long way past any sympathy for him. He dropped into the chair again, sat hunched, elbows on knees, dark hair falling forward across his forehead, shadowing his eyes. The flames leapt and danced in the fireplace, limning the bowed head in light.

'Is there truly nothing we can do?' she asked of the silence.

'Nothing.'

Are you familiar, Matt Daniels, with the saying that those born to hang will never drown?

'Oh, God,' she said. And then: 'When?'

His voice rasped. 'Next Thursday.'

'I want to see him.'

'Of course.'

'Tomorrow?'

'I'll take you.'

She opened her mouth to protest, closed it again. What did it matter? What did anything matter? Oddly, the thought brought Michael to mind. She stood up abruptly. 'I have to go.'

He looked up at her in tired surprise.

'Pol will be worried,' she said.

'She won't expect you back at this hour, surely?'

She looked at him tiredly. 'You think she'd expect me to stay?' She made no attempt to disguise the weary bitterness of her tone.

He watched her for a moment, his face inscrutable. Then he reached for his coat. 'I'll walk you to the cab.'

The silence that fell between them as they walked the lanes of Whitechapel that night lasted into the following morning when Luke came to collect her from Pol's. It was as if what had happened stood between them like a wall, precluding any possibility of communication. Through the dark hours of an anguished and sleepless night her suspicions of Luke and of his motives had grown and festered. A note to Luke, supposedly not received. Luke's knife, so conveniently stolen. Luke and Lottie through all the time she had known them. And then, most damning of all, it seemed to her, Fogg dead, executed, and by Luke's hand, and only his word for the justice of the action. She sat wordless in the jolting cab beside him, unable to bring herself in her anger and distrust to speak, and though she was sure that he sensed what she felt he too said nothing. For the moment anyway, as the hansom rolled along Holborn, past the church of St Sepulchre's and into Newgate Street itself, the street dominated by the grim granite fortress that was the prison, her every sense, every nerve was taut, strung like wire against the ordeal to come. She had no energy to fight Luke, nor to fling at him the questions that needed to be answered. With dread as they drew near she surveyed the massive, windowless stone walls of Newgate, the forbidding arched gateway.

'They won't let me come with you to see him,' Luke said,

breaking their strained silence for the first time as they approached the iron-bound door. 'Visiting is restricted. Even bribes don't work all the time – it was all I could do to get you in.'

She nodded. For all the use it was at the moment her tongue might have been cloven to the roof of her mouth. After the early spring sunlight of the street the stone and iron half-light of the prison struck her like the shadow of death. The rank smell of urine pervaded the place; the very walls, chill and grey, seemed to reek of it. Sound was muted – the distant clang of a metal door, a single, smothered shout, the echo of a footstep. It was a different, nightmare world and she felt the force of its hatred and suffering pressing upon her like a physical weight. She heard Luke's voice, low and persuasive as he spoke to the guardian of the massive gate and, remembering his words of a moment ago, for the first time it occurred to her that they might not let her see Matt – and the despicable, irresistible surge of relief that the thought brought with it almost nauseated her. She was ice-cold, her body taut as a bow, teeth gritted, bones aching as if pressured in a vice. Her bowels grumbled uncomfortably.

Luke touched her arm. 'Go with him. I'll wait for you outside.'

Numbly she followed the grim-faced uniformed warden along what seemed like endless miles of chill, foul-smelling corridors punctuated by countless clanging iron doors, to be led at last to a small room within which stood something akin to a wooden sentry box, a tiny window in its back, barred and grilled with fine mesh. The silent warden indicated that she should seat herself upon the wooden stool that was set within the box. For the first time then it came to her that she would not of course be allowed to see her brother alone – to touch him, even. She began to tremble violently. Almost she collapsed onto the stool, then hunched her shoulders tightly, clamping her hands together in her lap to still their shaking, fighting for some small armour of self-possession before Matt should appear.

When he came, if she had not known, she would not have recognized him. A tall, very thin figure shambled to the other side of the grille, heavy, ill-fitting boots dragging upon the floor to the clink of chain. Through the distorting mesh she saw the haggard face, the shorn head, the coarse, arrow-marked clothes that might have been made for a man twice the size. Then the gaunt apparition smiled, and despite the ageing lines and the prison pallor that might already have been the pallor of death, she knew her brother. She put a trembling hand to the grille, as if to touch him through it, though such a thing would certainly have been impossible.

'Don't touch the grille, miss.' The warden's voice, though sharp, was not unkind.

She let her hand drop into her lap.

'Well, moi owd gal. Here's a to-do – eh?' It seemed to her that even his voice had changed; it was dry and husky, as if he spoke with difficulty. 'I'd hoped you wouldn't hear,' he said, 'until it was over. I told the Guv'nor not to try to find you.'

She found her own voice then. 'How could you? If only I'd been here – I might have been able to help.'

He shook his head slowly. 'No, Kit. Not this time. Here's a mess not even you can fish me out of.'

'But – you didn't do it! There must be some way to show them?'

A glimmer of the old, feckless laughter shone in the thin face. 'Remember where you are – this is Newgate, Kitty – we're all innocent here, didn't you know that? Not one of us but isn't wrongly imprisoned. Isn't that so, Mr Wilkins?'

The warder who sat beside him listening nodded, stone-faced.

'But you really are! And we can't give up –'

He shook his head and shifted a little on the stool. She saw the man he had called Wilkins stiffen very slightly, watching him.

'But –'

'Leave it, Kitty. Believe me, there's nothing anyone can do. We have to face that.'

She stared at him, a wave of helpless misery stilling her tongue.

'Well, now,' he said, gently, 'tell me about Paris.'

She saw then the tears that stood, stubbornly unshed in his eyes. 'It was wonderful,' she found herself saying, shakily. 'Absolutely wonderful. You'd have loved it –' She stopped, swallowing noisily.

'I heard tell you were a great success?'

She shrugged a little. 'They've probably forgotten all about me by now.'

He shook his head. They were watching each other with a strange intensity, eyes fixed each upon the other's face as if in some communication other than speech. There was a long, oddly speaking silence. 'Do you remember the beach at Dunwich?' he asked, suddenly and softly. 'So wide, and windy, and empty, and free?'

It seemed to her that the vowels of Suffolk had crept back into his Londoner's voice. 'And the birds,' she said, 'the gulls, and the kittiwakes –'

He leaned forward a little and once more she saw his guardian's wary movement. 'And your voice, singing in the wind – what was that song that you and Anne were always singing? Something about green willow?'

Oh young men are false and they are so deceitful. Her throat constricted. She shook her head. 'I don't remember.'

He sat back. 'It all seems so very far away.'

'Yes.'

'You'll go back, I expect, one day,' he said, unexpectedly. 'Oh, not to the Grange, or to Dunwich – but somewhere like it. The city isn't right for you.'

She shook her head. 'No. It isn't.'

'Wasn't all that right for me either.' Again there was an echo of the old, graceless Matt in the words.

'No,' she said, the word husky.

He watched her for a moment. 'Kitty? Will you do something for me?'

'Of course.'

'Don't blame the Guv'nor. It isn't his fault.'

'I think it is,' she said, and her voice was suddenly hard. 'And I do blame him. I'll always blame him.'

He sighed. 'I don't want that.'

'I can't help it.'

They fell to silence again, a difficult silence this time. Simply to break it Kitty asked, 'Is there anything I can do? Anything you need?'

He half-smiled, bleakly. 'I'm in prison, Kit. Not hospital. No – there's nothing I need – nothing they'd let you give me. Don't worry – I'm not treated badly. The food's almost decent now they've decided to hang me, and I get all the baccy I want. Don't I, Mr Wilkins?' he asked, softly.

Still impassive, the other man nodded again.

Now they've decided to hang me – the words, spoken in a brittle, matter-of-fact tone, hit her like a blow, and she gasped at them. She was shaking uncontrollably, a violent, distressed trembling that seemed to emanate from somewhere deep within her body and which she could not suppress. It was as if a chill of misery, of helplessness, of terror had invaded her very bones.

'– and they make sure that I'm not lonely, too, don't you, Mr Wilkins? Always someone in my cell, day or night – and lots of visits from parsons and rectors and hymn-singing ladies who want to save my poor, damned soul –'

The sudden despair that threaded his voice twisted in her like the blade of a knife. 'Matt!'

'Not even when I die,' he said, softly bitter, 'not even then will I be alone. They tell me that soon – soon – there'll be no more public executions. Soon,' he repeated, shaking his head. 'But not soon enough. Eh, Mr Wilkins?'

Here was a horror she had not even contemplated. Public execution. She clenched her mind against such abomination.

He lifted his voice sharply. 'Promise me something.'

She lifted her head, struggling with tears.

'Don't come. Don't be there. I couldn't stand that. Promise me.'

'I promise.'

In the silence that followed the warder who had brought her said gruffly, 'Two more minutes.'

They looked at each other in sudden desperation. Two more minutes? In lieu of a lifetime? She had stopped trying to stem the flood of tears. They flowed disregarded in silence down her ice-cold face, dripped dark as blood onto the soft velvet of her skirt. 'Isn't there anything I can do?' she asked.

'Look after Sally-Anne for me?'

'Of course I will.'

'And – the Guv'nor. He needs you, Kitty, though he'd never admit it. What's happened isn't his fault –'

'Whose then?' The words were bitter.

He shook his head.

'You know what he did?' she asked, low and violent. 'You know how he –' She stopped, glancing at the silent prison officer. Unforgiveable treachery, even in extremes of anger, to betray Luke to these hostile listeners. If nothing else, Matt would die hating her, and she could not have stood that.

He shot her a fierce, warning look. 'Yes. I know. He was right.'

'How do we know? We only have his word!'

'That's good enough for me.' His voice was even, now. 'Leave it, Kitty. It's all too late.'

'You don't think that he –?' She could not say it, but she saw from his eyes that he had understood her question.

'No,' he said. 'I don't. Kitty – I was there. You weren't. Accept what he tells you. It's what happened.'

She said nothing.

He smiled at her, gently. 'Tell me something – was Lottie right? Were you really hobnobbing with some handsome French aristo?'

She opened her mouth to lie, automatically. Shut it again. She could not.

His eyes were curious. 'Kitty? It doesn't matter – if you don't want to tell me?'

And then it came to her that this was, after all, something she could give him. The truth – and a truth that carried with it hopefully some small grain of comfort, some promise of immortality.

'Time to go, miss,' the warder said.

'Wait. Just a moment.' She leaned to the grille, speaking urgently. 'Matt – listen – I had a baby. A little boy. He's dark, and he's going to be tall, just like you. I called him Michael – after Father. He's healthy, and he's wonderful, and I'm going to keep him safe. I'm going to get him away from here, and I'm going to keep him safe –' She stopped. 'Michael,' she said again, seeing his tears and knowing that he could not speak. 'After Father. He'll grow up strong and happy, I promise you. He'll never know any of this.'

'Come along, miss. Please.' Surprisingly gently the grim-faced warder took her arm. 'Time's up.'

'Matt?' she whispered, stricken.

He lifted a hand. His guardian stepped to his side and helped him from the stool upon which he sat. In silence and with no word of farewell he allowed himself to be led away.

She stood like stone staring after him.

'Can't stay 'ere, miss,' the prison officer said. 'Won't do no good. Come along, now.'

As she followed him back along the oppressive maze of stone corridors she heard in the distance the ominous and heavy clang of a single door shutting.

Two days later, at the gates of Newgate, Matt Daniels was hanged for murder. There was a good turnout to watch the spectacle, and a brisk trade in the penny leaflets that told of the brash young thief's scandalously wicked road to ruin and his just deserts. The lad bore himself well, the old hands had to admit, though for some a death met with dignity and courage was a disappointment. The spectators were as one that the impending cessation of such edifying entertainment was nothing short of an outrage. Nothing could take the place of a good turn-off.

Matt Daniels died just one month short of his nineteenth birthday.

4

Kitty wondered, afterwards, that she did not lose her mind that day. After a night entirely without sleep she sat with Pol in a despairing silence, their hands clasped across the scrubbed wooden table in Pol's kitchen, watching the clock with agonized intensity as the hour grew close. She tried to pray, and found that she could not – her bitterness was so great that it turned any prayer to a savage reproach that could serve no possible purpose. As at last the relentless hour chimed she buried her face in her hands, trying in vain to blot out the picture that seared in her mind, to control a pain that was almost beyond bearing. And then as the morning ticked endlessly past with no message, no sign, she had at last to admit the final truth; no last-minute reprieve had saved her brother from the scaffold. Matt was dead, and in such a manner as to haunt her for ever.

She struggled through the day, automatically caring for Michael, sitting for long hours before the fire, the sleeping baby in her lap, her head filled with the memories that were all she now had of her young brother. That Pol hastily hid the newspaper that Barton brought home she noted but did not question. The tears she wanted to shed refused to come and, denied their relief, she stared dry-eyed and silent into the dying fire. Throughout the day a worried, red-eyed Pol tended her, hovering about her, helplessly offering tea that she could not drink, food that choked her and comfort that both knew was, with the best will in the world, utterly without substance. In the end, however, it was Pol who finally roused her, falling through the door, her face a picture of alarm.

'Kitty – quick! The baby – get 'im out of 'ere! Luke's comin' up the street!'

Kitty lifted a tired head. 'What?'

Pol was frantic. 'Luke! Bart just saw 'im turn the corner! You'd better get the babe upstairs – quick!'

Kitty jumped to her feet, jolting the child, who woke and gave a small, angry squeal at the sudden movement. Desperately Kitty rocked him: 'Sh-sh! There, hush, now –' But the baby's small face was turning an ominous red and the tiny toothless mouth opened in a roar of rage.

''Ere – 'urry up – give 'im to me –' Quick-witted Pol snatched the child from her, wrapped the shawl firmly about him. 'I'll take 'im out the back an' along the alley to Amy's. Don't worry. Just get rid of Luke as fast as you can –' The baby in one arm, she was swooping around the room picking up, one-handed, the detritus of babyhood that littered it – a small silver rattle, a comforter, a long white nightdress.

'But' – automatically Kitty helped her, gathering the things she had been using to tend the baby and piling them into Pol's arms – 'I don't want to see him. I can't –'

Pol, already halfway to the door, paused for a moment, her face grim. 'You think you got a choice?'

She was right. Barton's half-hearted attempts to keep Luke from Kitty were as effective as might be a child's attempt to deter a tiger from its intent. But at least by the time he came into the room all traces of Michael had been removed, and Kitty sat, rigid and still as stone beside the fire. She glanced at him as he entered, turned her eyes both from him and from the small bundle that he carried and stared into the flames.

There was a very long silence. She heard him close the door quietly, sensed him move across the floor towards her, tensed herself against his touch.

'Kitty,' he asked quietly, at last, 'are you all right?'

The sound she made, and the sharp movement of her head were softly bitter, and needed no words.

He sat in the chair opposite her and waited, patient as a cat.

He knew her too well; she could not remain silent. 'You were there?'

'Yes.'

She looked down at her clasped hands, concentrating fiercely upon a small ring that glinted upon the little finger of her right hand. She had bought it in Paris during a happy shopping expedition with Genevieve. She remembered now the colourful crowds that had thronged the vast new many-floored store with its great glass dome and its sweeping staircase. She had thought it a palace . . .

'He was very brave.'

The opal glimmered, palely beautiful, within its circle of diamonds. She had thought herself outrageously extravagant, but Genevieve had waved an airy hand. 'Pouf! Extravagant, yes – to spend your own money! A month – two months – and the gentlemen will be queuing to buy such baubles!'

'Kitty?'

She raised her head dully, but said nothing. There seemed at that moment to be nothing to say.

'They gave me these at the prison. I thought you would want them.' The sad little bundle lay at his feet.

'Thank you.'

He took a long breath. His face was haggard, his dark eyes deeply shadowed. She looked back at the gleaming ring, turning it nervously on her finger.

'Is there anything I can do –?' The words were spoken with difficulty.

She shook her head, suddenly and fiercely. 'Luke – please – go away.' For the first time she lifted her eyes to his, painfully direct. 'Please. Just go away.'

He looked at her for a long moment, and it seemed to her that he might have been about to say something. Then, very abruptly, he stood. 'Of course. I'll see you in a few days. When you've had a chance to –'

'I don't want to see you again.' She heard the flat words with a kind of detached surprise, as if a stranger had spoken them in her voice. He loomed above her, his presence so powerful that it was like a cloak of darkness around her. She hunched herself against it, as a child might hunch against the cold. 'Leave me alone,' she whispered miserably, and at last the tears had started, easing a little the ache in her burning eyes and the suffocating constriction about her heart. 'Leave me – alone!' She would not break in front of him. She fought it, clenched against it, flinched as he dropped to one knee beside her, his movements as always smoothly graceful, his eyes on a level with hers.

'I can't do that now,' he said at last, his voice oddly harsh, 'can I?' and was gone, leaving her to the desolate relief of tears.

That the possible and ominous significance of those words did not immediately strike her was in the circumstances understandable. Three months later she had cause to remember them, and to understand their meaning but at the time, and for the weeks that immediately followed that awful day she lived in an imprisoning daze of misery that precluded logical thought and cut her off from her fellows and from the comfort they tried to offer. Only Michael was any consolation to her – him she tended, fiercely and devotedly, and as he lay sleeping in her arms or gazed at her, wakeful, with dark, innocent eyes she searched for and found the resemblance she longed to see. Matt was not dead but reborn; here in her arms with a new life and a new chance: and this time she would protect him. This time he would be happy.

Inevitably, however, the worst of the agony passed and in the end the night came when, exhausted, she slept at last. A week after that came the day that her first waking thought was not for her brother. Like a nerve-pain in an amputated limb the anguish of Matt's loss – and particularly of the manner of it – would never leave her. But she could – she knew she must – learn to live with it. Very gradually her life returned to something resembling normality. To Amy Buckley's delight Kitty and Michael moved in with her – they could not, after all, trespass on Pol and Barton's hospitality for ever. The arrangement worked remarkably well – Amy adored Michael from the start and was more than happy to help care for him, Kitty's child in a way making up for the lack of her own. And so Kitty, who had long ago abandoned her first thoughts of having Michael fostered somewhere away from her, was able to consider picking up again the threads of her life and her career, knowing the child to be always safe and cared for.

The first message that had come from Pat Kenny she had ignored – not with any thought of deliberate discourtesy but simply because she received it whilst her unhappiness was deepest, very soon after Matt's death. By the time he approached her again, however, a month later, she had already begun to recognize the necessity of a return to work. Her savings had dwindled alarmingly. For Michael's sake, if for nothing else, she must make an effort to renew old contacts and step back onto a stage before a fickle public forgot her existence altogether.

And so at his second invitation she visited Pat Kenny in his impressive new office in Leicester Square and discovered that her sojourn in Paris had done – from a professional point of view at least – nothing but good. She was surprised at the favourable terms Kenny offered – until a couple of days later when, twice in a space of three days, other music hall owners approached her, each eager to be the one to bring *Le Gamin* back to the London stage, and she realized to her surprise that she could in fact have demanded more. 'Well, there'll be no worry about money anyway,' she told Amy with some relief. 'I need new costumes, of course, and there are other expenses – but there'll be plenty left over.' She reached a finger to Michael who lay, quiet and content, in his day cot by the fireside. Nearly four months old now, he was a sturdy child, well-tempered and rarely ruffled – as indeed, with his entire world peopled with the devoted slaves that were Kitty, Amy and Pol, he had good reason to be. He reached with an uncertain, pudgy fist, gurgling in his throat. So far as Kitty knew no one had discovered his existence and so far as she could see there seemed no reason to suppose anyone ever should. To the outside world he could safely and anonymously be presented as Amy's child.

'When do you start?' Amy also indulgently offered a small, work-calloused finger and Michael grasped it eagerly.

'In six weeks. At the Hippodrome.' The Hippodrome was one of the largest of Kenny's newly acquired theatres in the heart of London. 'We start rehearsals in ten days.' Kitty ran a finger, gently regretful, down the smoothly soft baby cheek. 'I'll have to wean him, I suppose.'

'He'll be all right,' Amy said. 'He's as strong as an ox and perfectly happy. He'll come to no harm.'

Kitty, hearing in her friend's voice her pleasure in the thought that now the baby would be wholly hers to care for, quickly suppressed a small, unworthy twinge of possessive jealousy. 'You're sure you won't mind looking after him for me?'

'Oh, of course not! We'll do very well together, won't we, little man? Eh? Won't we –?' She tickled the child under the chin and he chuckled richly.

Kitty smiled a little sadly. 'I'm sure you will.'

She started rehearsals ten days later and the small menage very soon settled into a comfortable and happy routine. At first she found the strenuous rehearsals appallingly hard work, as muscles that had not been used for many long months protested painfully at this sudden and energetic baptism of fire. Her voice too had lost a little of its power and long hours were spent each morning with a voice-coach, an irascible old man who clearly believed that his time could be better spent than in training a flibbertigibbet girl to sing outrageous popular songs. However, he knew his business well and although more than once Kitty had to restrain herself from flinging the nearest moveable object at his testy, disapproving head she knew that those expensive, patience- and temper-testing hours were well spent. Her voice improved and strengthened as, with the endless, exhausting rehearsals, did her muscles and her stamina. As the first night approached she discovered at last that poor Matt's death had slipped if not entirely to the back of her mind at least to a small corner where it could rest in peace, the pain transmuted to an ache of loss that she knew she could bear, if not easily, at least without damage to herself.

Late one afternoon, on her way home from the rehearsal hall, she called at Pol's and was more than a little disconcerted to discover Lottie drinking tea in the kitchen as Pol busied herself at the stove. With Lottie was her daughter, Poppy, a small angel of a child, lovely as her mother must have been at her age and with apparently nothing of her dead father in her at all. She sat at the table beside her mother, subdued and docile, eyes downcast, small hands, nails bitten down to the quick, forever at her mouth despite the number of times Lottie with absent and automatic sharpness slapped them away. Taken aback and unwilling – or perhaps, she had to admit to herself, unable – to face the other girl's overt dislike and hostility, Kitty made hasty excuses and, despising herself, retreated, hearing – as she well knew she was intended to hear – Lottie's voice clearly behind her before she closed the door – 'Hoity toity! Some people think 'emselves just too good ter live in this world, eh?'

Strangely the brief encounter disturbed her more than she liked to admit, reminding her as it inevitably did of the one person she struggled not to think of: Luke Peveral. He had not been near her since the day of Matt's execution. She did not, she told herself fiercely, want him near her – and then found herself miserably wondering if Lottie and her angel-faced child lived with him now in his bell-tower eyrie. She was troubled that night with dreams of him that startled her awake in the darkness, her body betraying her, aching for the touch of him, who had not touched her in a year. Yet with the daylight her stubborn resolution renewed itself. She had meant what she had said – for Michael's sake and her own, she had meant it. She never wanted to see him again.

She might have known, she told herself later, what self-deluding folly it was to have believed that her wishes in that as in anything else could possibly carry any weight with Luke Peveral.

He came a week to the day after her successful opening for Kenny at the Hippodrome. Tired to exhaustion, yet filled as always with the strange tension of energy that a performance on stage inevitably produced in her, she let herself into the little house in Pascal Street to find waiting for her a strained and white-faced Amy who, fearful but stubborn, had kept silent company with the intimidating visitor who had forced his way with steely courtesy into her home an hour or so before and now waited calmly by the parlour fire.

Kitty it was who broke the silence, savage anger in her voice. 'What do you think you're doing here?'

Amy cast a quick, worried look to the ceiling, above which lay the room in which Michael slept.

Luke, who had stood when she entered the room, regarded her, cold and unsmiling. 'We have to talk.'

'No,' she said, flatly. 'We don't.'

'Oh yes, we do.'

Something in the tone, in the cool, relentless eyes brought a small throb of fear to her heart. She stared at him, stone-faced. In the silence poor Amy, flustered, looked from one to the other. 'I'd – better leave you together?' she asked hesitantly, looking almost pleadingly at Kitty.

'If you wouldn't mind?' The courtesy was caustic. Kitty levelled at him a look that might have killed.

'Kitty?' Amy asked, uncertainly.

'There's no need,' she said, the brusque words harsh, 'he's leaving. We've nothing to say to each other that hasn't already been said.'

From above their heads came the thin thread of a child's cry. Amy froze. By not so much as the flicker of an eyelash did Luke betray surprise. Neither did Kitty's expression change; from the moment she had seen him somehow she had guessed.

'You know,' she said.

'Of the child? Yes.'

'Spider?'

His hesitation was barely noticeable. He shook his head. 'No.'

'Who then?' As she said it she knew, and the shock was like a physical blow.

'Matt,' he said, his voice absolutely devoid of emotion.

Michael cried again.

'I'd better go to him.' Amy cast one worried look at Kitty then scuttled from the room, closing the door behind her. They heard her bustle up the stairs, the clip of her footsteps on the floorboards above them. The crying stopped.

'You have absolutely no right to be here,' Kitty said, steadily enough, though her heart was pounding as if she had run a mile. 'You have no rights over me. No rights over him.'

'I disagree.'

It seemed to her that the two implacable, passionless words were the most threatening she had ever heard. She held herself still, head up, eyes steady.

'He is my son,' he said.

Breath would be wasted denying it, and she knew it; instead, sudden anger bolstering her courage, she said, very softly but very clearly, 'And one day you will be taken, as Matt was taken, but with better cause. Shall your son and I visit you then, in the condemned cell? Is that what you want?'

Violence lay deep in his eyes, but his voice was controlled. 'Would you keep him from me entirely? Would you deny me my son?'

'Yes,' she said, flatly.

She saw the dangerous flare of volatile temper, forced herself not to flinch from it. 'A boy needs a father,' he said.

'A father such as you?' In her terror for her child she made no attempt to disguise her scorn.

'Is surely better than none?'

She lifted her chin. 'I doubt it.'

She saw then his control snap, saw the violence of his movement towards her and in the confined space of the small room could not avoid it. He caught her shoulders in a savagely painful grip. Despite herself she cried out sharply. The pressure of his fingers did not lessen. 'Listen to me!' He shook her, fiercely. 'Listen, damn you! We'll be married. The child will have a name. A home. Isn't that what you want for him?'

Despite the pain the sudden surge of outrage at his words all but choked her. 'What name?' Her voice matched his in savagery. 'What home? He has a name! Michael Daniels. My father's name. An honourable name. And he has a home. What better would you offer him? Are you mad? Do you think that after what's happened I'd let you within a mile of my – *my* – child?'

'*Our* child!' He shook her violently again, and his face was murderous.

She was too furious now, too fearful for her child to be cowed. 'No. Never that. Never *our* son, Luke. *My* son. Carried alone and borne alone –'

'Your fault, not mine! You should have told me!' He almost threw her from him. She staggered. He turned from her, his tall silhouette limned darkly forbidding in the lamplight, and when he spoke his voice was ice-hard. 'I'll have him, Kitty. Whether you will it or not.'

She caught his arm, and, surprised at her own furious strength, spun him to face her. 'Kill me first,' she said, 'for it's the only way.'

'Don't tempt me!' he snapped harshly. 'I've done worse for less.'

She stepped back from him. For a long moment they glared at each other, and in the raging silence all hope of harmony died.

Above their heads the floorboards creaked as Amy rocked the disturbed child to sleep.

With no further word then he turned and left her, the slamming of the door behind him reverberating through the fabric of the little house. She stood where she was, shaking, her hands to her face, teeth gritted against tears.

'Kitty –?'

She did not know how long she had stood so, shuddering, her face buried in her spread hands. She lifted her head.

'Are you all right?' Worried, Amy hovered by the door, small face a picture of concern and fright.

'I'm – yes, I'm all right.'

Amy glanced a little fearfully over her shoulder. 'Has he gone?'

'Yes.'

'Well' – the little woman made a gallant attempt at a smile – 'that's a relief anyway.'

Kitty dropped, suddenly and weakly, into the nearest armchair. 'Short-lived, I'm afraid,' she said, grimly weary. 'He'll be back.'

(ii)

It was beyond doubt that Luke Peveral did indeed have every intention of returning to the house in Pascal Road, beyond doubt too, Kitty knew, that his clear intention was to possess his son no matter what she might try to do to stop him. But in the event, and almost as if she had wished the ill-luck upon him, Fate, in the shape of the law that he had so long and so cavalierly flouted, stepped in, and it was a very long time before anyone but Spider or Lottie saw him again.

It was Pol who broke the news to Kitty that he had been taken. 'They'll put 'im away fer sure this time,' she said, not without some grim satisfaction. ''E won't talk 'is way out o' this one so easy, you mark my words. Taken red 'anded 'e was – it'll be a stretch in the steel fer matey this time, you see if it isn't. Ten years, I shouldn't wonder. Shame they've stopped shippin' 'em out to Botany Bay if you ask me – that'd 'ave solved a few problems, eh?'

Kitty was surprised at her own reaction; after an initial wave of relief, of which she was quickly ashamed, she found herself horrified for Luke. For all their differences, for all her changed feelings towards Luke, she never would have wished this upon him. Ten years' imprisonment would kill him or drive him insane, she was sure – or at the very least harden and embitter him beyond redemption. She remembered the day he had spoken of his hatred – his fear – of prison life and shuddered. Better if they had killed him as they had Matt. She heard only once directly from him – a brusque message delivered through Spider that he wanted her under no circumstances either to attend the trial or at any time to attempt to visit him. Through Lottie via Pol she heard some weeks later that in fact the worst fears had not been realized – judicious bribery had ensured if not an escape from punishment at least a more lenient sentence than had been expected. Luke Peveral was to spend two years in gaol.

Upon hearing the news, Kitty was once more victim to a confusion of feeling. For Luke she cried; but then, looking at Michael, who gurgled happily in Pol's arms, she could not deny a lift of pure relief. Two years' reprieve. Two years of safety. Two years in which to decide what to do for the best. And surely, in those years Luke might come round to seeing that what she wanted for the child was for the best?

She took it as a good sign that he did not want to see her – she knew through Pol that on the rare occasions that permission for visits could be obtained Lottie it was that went with Spider. She was astonished and disgusted with herself at the faint stab of jealousy she found that could still cause. And though the thought of Luke incarcerated, humiliated, probably – for she knew too well his pride and his temper – ill-treated, haunted her, yet still that small glimmer of relief burned steadily. Though she would not have had it for such a reason, he was kept from her and from Michael, and for that she could only be grateful. As the months passed the imminent threat of him faded. Almost she persuaded herself of what she wanted to believe – this was the turning point, this would show him that she was right and he wrong. Luke Peveral, now, was surely out of her life for ever. Meanwhile once again she was doing very well. Hardly a month went by without the offer of an engagement. Barton set to work on some new songs and one of them, the saucy story of a raffish young sailor with a girl or two in every port, rivalled *The Dipper* in popularity and the broadsheets sold in the streets of London outside every theatre.

By Christmas and Michael's first birthday she was once more well established upon the London stage and starting the long climb back. In January Charles paid a fleeting visit but she would not at that moment be tempted back to Paris. By all accounts *La Ville Lumière* was as glittering and as enticing as ever – yet she was surprised to hear of strikes and unrest, of ragged marchers in Haussmann's wide boulevards and of effigies hung from lamp posts as to the strains of *The Blue Danube* the cream of Paris society still danced beneath the brilliant chandeliers of The Tuileries.

Charles dismissed it all, as he dismissed the growing unneighbourliness of a unified and belligerent Prussia, with a characteristic shrug and a dismissive click of his fingers. 'What do they know, the rabble? No, chérie – Paris has no worries, France has no worries – if that opéra-comique German Bismarck sticks his fat belly over our borders we will stick him like the pig he is and send him back to his Emperor. Come back to Paris, Kitty – she waits with open arms.'

But Kitty would not be tempted. Indeed there was more than one very good reason for her to stay in London. Michael was settled and happy, she herself was gaining very quickly an immense popular following, and – most exciting of all – Patrick Kenny, who by now was doing extremely well for himself, was talking of commissioning a musical play, the very latest in popular entertainment, with Kitty playing one of her already well-loved characters in the leading role. The lure was irresistible.

By the summer of 1869, a year after the bombshell of Luke's arrest, plans were well under way and Kitty, nervously excited, was busy preparing herself for the venture that could be the final making of her. Once again she was financially independent – almost obsessively she saved every penny she could, for her own future and for Michael's. Eventually she planned to buy a small house in Hampstead for herself, Amy and the boy; but for now she was content with Pascal Road and the gruelling work of preparing for the new show.

The play – a musical adaptation of a vastly popular book about a gutter-urchin whose unlikely generosity to an old beggar-woman led him on to even more unlikely fame, fortune and the hand of a duke's younger daughter – opened in September to faint praise from the critics and standing room only in the theatre. The audiences loved it. The critics might say what they liked, night after night the house was packed and the curtain came down to roaring, stamping pandemonium. Patrick Kenny had a runaway success on his hands, and he was astute enough to know who to thank for it.

All at once the world was at Kitty Daniels' feet. She was wined and dined and squired about town as again the 'Johnnies' queued at her door. On only a couple of occasions did her loneliness and the physical needs that she so stubbornly tried to ignore get the better of her common sense. The first was a light-hearted affair involving a baronet's penniless and utterly charming second son who persuaded her one evening to join him in a splendid meal for which he had not the means to pay and then – having accepted with guileless grace her offer to foot the bill – amused her so well that, happily and just once, they made love on the floor of his garret amidst champagne and laughter.

The second was of rather more moment and taught her a lesson she did not quickly forget. A handsome young actor, tall and dark, joined the company, and within weeks his attentions and apparently slavish devotion had aroused emotions she had foolishly believed long dead. For an infatuated month she imagined herself in love with him, and though she found their first lovemaking obscurely disappointing, still she could not take her eyes from the dark, handsome face, nor her attention from the movement of his long, slender hands. For weeks she blinded herself to weakness and petulance, to self-centredness and sheer unkindness – until the day when, with a shock that took her breath away, she recognized the root of her infatuation in his physical resemblance to Luke, which she had not allowed herself to see before, and the young man's short reign was over. She was much more careful after that.

The show ran through Christmas and into the spring. As a treat for Michael's second birthday she took him, with Amy, to the Zoological Gardens in Regent's Park, a treat that was really a little beyond his baby years but which entirely enthralled both Kitty and Amy. They peered up at the bizarre giraffes and down at the gruff sealions, exclaimed at the hippopotamus, declared the anteater magnificently ugly and were astounded by the great African elephants, Alice and Jumbo, who had for the last eighteen months been the zoo's greatest attractions. As they laughed at the antics of the chimpanzees a woman recognized Kitty, and as a small crowd gathered she was prevailed upon to stand on a bench and lead them all in the Great Vance's popular music hall song, *Walking in the Zoo is the OK Thing to Do*. As she sang, at the back of the crowd she saw a tall dark man, a child of about Michael's age sitting astride his shoulders, tiny hands buried fast in the father's hair as gently the man's hands steadied the boy. She brushed impatiently aside the small twinge of pain that the sight brought, but yet was subdued as the hansom clopped steadily back to Paddington through the gaily decorated and crowded Christmas streets. It was Luke's second Christmas in prison. The question could not be had he changed, but – how had he changed? And somehow, the innocent joy was gone from the day at the thought. And yet, for all her regrets, her resolve remained. Luke should not have Michael. The child was hers. He was growing into a bright, happy, handsome little boy. Never – never – would she allow the stain of Luke's father-hood to shadow his life or his future.

And when she prayed, which admittedly was not often, she prayed, often with a lamentable lack of faith, that Luke would accept that.

The one disappointment in a life that on the whole moved on smoothly and successfully was that she heard not one word from Jem. She wrote several letters, none of which were answered. Neither Charles nor Genevieve, with whom she corresponded regularly, had seen or heard anything from or of him. It was as if the man she had kissed so perfunctorily and left on the quayside that day, the man who had shared with her those strange, magically timeless months by the slow-moving waters of the Lot, had disappeared without trace. For months she worried, and then, caught in the exigencies of a frantically busy life, gradually she forgot. Jem had turned up unexpectedly before, undoubtedly he would do so again. But yet she was a little hurt that such a good friend should so desert her.

It happened that Lottie too, in Luke's enforced absence, had had some small measure of success and for that, despite their mutual dislike, Kitty was glad. She knew from Pol, who often cared for Poppy, that whilst Luke was in prison Lottie was living in his idiosyncratic home – and no doubt, Kitty thought acidly, had every intention of remaining there when at last he returned. Kitty noticed Lottie's name occasionally on the supporting list of a handbill of one or other of the smaller theatres, but professionally their paths never crossed, and for that she was profoundly grateful.

There was, too, an unwritten law concerning the small world of Pol's kitchen – if Pol 'happened' to mention to Kitty that Lottie intended to visit Kitty made sure she was elsewhere at the given time. Yet, strangely and ironically, their two children were fast friends, since on many occasions it would happen that Pol with Poppy and Amy with Michael would spend a happy day together.

'It's a downright pleasure to see them kids together,' wise Pol said one day to Kitty. 'Get on like an 'ouse on fire they do. Brings little Poppy right out of 'erself it does. Poor young mite. Proper little mother she is, given 'alf a chance –'

And so, living from day to day and with a growing sense of security, Kitty found that life had settled into a happy and successful routine.

Until Luke came home.

It seemed to her that, contrary to all her hopes and expectations, he came straight to her, the stink of Newgate clinging to him still. His changed appearance was a shock in itself: always slim, he was now skeletal. Against the grey prison-pallor of his swarthy skin the angry red welt of a scarce-healed new scar cut across his left cheekbone. The long soft hair was gone and in its place a dark cap of shorn bristles that starkly outlined the shape of his skull. There were new, bitter lines too in his face, etched deeply at the corners of his mouth. And yet still, undeniably, the immediate and maddening magnetism of the man was there, despite his forbidding appearance and the obviously now habitual grim expression on his face. The first sight of him stopped her breath and set her heart thumping erratically in her throat. He came to the little house in Pascal Road on a June morning when she was playing with Michael in the sunshine of the tiny back garden that Amy kept as neatly and tidily as she kept the parlour. On sturdy little legs the child toddled after the ball she threw, tumbling like a puppy on the grass, squealing with delight as she swept him up into her arms.

'Little tinker! Don't try to run so fast! You'll –' She stopped, frozen, clutching the child, who struggled impatiently to be put down.

She fought her treacherous emotions, and won. 'Luke,' she said, very calmly, and took not one step towards him.

He stood in the shadows of the kitchen doorway, Amy hovering anxiously behind him. His eyes were fixed upon the child in Kitty's arms.

'Down!' Michael squealed, imperatively. 'Down, Mama!'

Very, very carefully she set him upon his uncertain feet, but kept his hand protectively in hers. Catching sight of Luke he drew back, clinging to his mother's skirts, his dark eyes huge, wary, but not altogether unfriendly. In his small world very little had ever actually threatened him.

'He looks like Matt,' Luke said, his voice oddly remote. 'And – a little – like me.'

She swallowed. 'Yes.'

He stepped into the sunlight and with an unexpected stab of pain she saw the brutal changes in him; saw too the harsher line of mouth, the savagely stubborn set of jaw and knew with sinking heart that prison had neither weakened nor gentled Luke Peveral. She took a deep breath, trying to quell the fear that rose in a cold tide within her, and in defence against it spoke crisply, as if this disturbing near-stranger were a casual acquaintance she had seen mere days before. 'How are you?'

He half-shrugged, his eyes still upon the child. 'As you see,' he said, indifferently.

In the tree above them a bird sang, the sound cascading about them, sweet as honey, piercing through the traffic sounds from the road outside.

She stood in silence, waiting, her hand fondling her son's dark head.

He lifted his eyes to her at last. 'You look well.'

She nodded.

'Mama —?' One eye still upon the tall, intriguing stranger, Michael swung upon her hand, sure of her attention. With the deft easy movement of much practice she swung him onto her hip. Once safe in his mother's arms the child stuck his thumb in his mouth and regarded Luke with large, curious eyes, no longer intimidated.

'Time for your rest,' Kitty said firmly, and stepped past the intently watching Luke to Amy. 'Amy — would you take him for me?'

''Course.' With manifest relief Amy relieved her of the child, and with one swift apprehensive glance at Luke disappeared into the house.

Kitty turned. 'Would you like a cup of tea?' she asked with commendable composure, aware of the absurdity of the everyday question in this far from everyday situation.

The faintest glimmer of the old wry amusement crossed his face and was gone. 'No,' he said, and then, 'thank you,' awkwardly enough for Kitty to wonder how long it was since he had spoken those words.

'We have a little port if you would prefer? I'm afraid we don't keep anything stronger in the house.'

He shook his head, faint impatience in the movement.

'So.' She folded her arms across her breast, forced herself to look steadily into the intolerant eyes. 'Tell me. What do you want?'

'We have to talk.'

She let a small silence develop, her eyes steady. 'About what?'

'About the child.'

She shook her head. 'No.'

'And I say yes.' Face and voice were implacable. The dark cloak of violence hung about him. To Kitty it seemed that his every movement, his every glance, threatened danger. 'He's my son.'

'In no one's eyes but your own.'

'You cannot keep him from me.'

Fool she had been! To believe he might change, that he might listen to the voice of reason — why, oh why, hadn't she taken Michael away while the going was good?

From the alleyway that ran behind the wall at the bottom of the garden came the sound of voices, laughter, hurrying footsteps.

'I say what I said before.' She kept her voice low. 'You shan't have him. He's mine.' Try as she might she could not keep the betraying tremor from her words.

He stepped to her, catching her wrist, his grip calculatingly and cruelly painful. 'Listen to me. I will have him. And you with him. No child of mine shall be called bastard. You'll save yourself a lot of sorrow if you admit it now rather than later. I'll see you dead — you hear me? — dead — before you escape me. You think you can fight me? Try it —'

Roughly, and before she suspected his intention he pulled her to him, grinding his mouth savagely upon hers, kissing her with no trace of tenderness, no attempt at gentleness, but with the awful, pent-up hunger of two long, harrowing years. For a fatal moment she could not fight him, caught helpless on the sudden and shockingly unexpected wave of a desire that equalled his. For the briefest of moments she acknowledged her body's craving for him and gave way to the bitter excitement of his angry embrace.

Neither of them heard the back gate open, but they heard the deliberate slam of its shutting. Luke stepped back from Kitty, his face still a white blaze of rage and hunger.

'Well,' Lottie said, quietly vicious, 'so now we know, do we?' Pol stood beside her, her good-natured face a picture of bemused disbelief, Poppy's small hand in hers.

Kitty licked her bruised lower lip and tasted the salt taste of blood. In a spasm of self-disgust she dashed her hand across her face, scrubbing at it.

'Well?' Lottie's hard-held control was breaking. 'Bloody well?'

No one answered.

Fury lending her an unusual courage, Lottie flew at Luke, screaming like one demented. 'What d'you think yer doin'? Eh? You think yer can throw me over now – fer *that*?' She all but spat the word in Kitty's direction. 'Oh, no yer don't! Not now – not after all this! I sticks by you, an' this is what I get fer it? Oh, no! Not this time! I'll tell you this – I'll see you with yer throat cut – you 'ear me? – I'll see you dead an' buried – before I'll see you go to 'er!'

For a moment Kitty thought Luke would strike the shrieking girl, and she took a swift half-step forward. But Luke, simply and violently, brushed past Lottie, sending her reeling into Kitty before he strode with no backward glance through the gate, leaving it swinging gently in the soft breeze behind him.

In the stunned silence left by his going, Poppy sobbed incoherently, clinging for comfort to Pol's hand.

Pol dropped to one knee beside her, put an arm about the child. 'All right. It's all right. The bogeyman's gone.' She sent a look of dry dislike towards the gate that still swung slowly upon its hinges.

Kitty had caught Lottie to steady her. Now the girl tore herself from her hands and turned on her like a small, frenzied animal. Kitty saw her arm go back but was unable to avoid the wild blow the girl aimed at her, and Lottie's open hand cracked painfully across her already bloodied mouth.

'Oh, no!' Pol left the crying child and leapt forward, dragging Lottie back. 'We'll 'ave none o' that, my girl! Ease off there –'

Lottie struggled for a moment but was no match for plump Pol's strength. She subsided at last, spitting hatred at Kitty. 'You wait! You just wait! I'll get you – you an' your bleedin' brat – if it's the last thing I do on this earth! You shan't 'ave 'im! You shan't! Luke Peveral's mine, if 'e knows it or not –'

'Lottie, for God's sake –'

' 'E's mine – you 'ear?'

'Lottie – I don't want Luke.'

Lottie stared at her, the lovely face made ugly by spite and hysteria. ' 'Oo you tryin' to kid, me or yerself? I got eyes, ain't I? I bloody saw you! If that's the way you are when you don't want 'em, you slut, what do you do when you do? Bleedin' eat 'em?'

'Lottie!' Pol exclaimed.

But Lottie was far beyond hearing. 'You bin nothin' but soddin' trouble since the day you came – you an' that no-good bastard brother of yours –' Kitty was horrified at the depths of loathing in the blazing eyes; it seemed to her to verge upon madness. 'Walkin' in, makin' out yer don't shit the way the rest of us do – takin' my friend – takin' my job – takin' my Luke!' Tears were streaming down the ravaged face as she sobbed out the venom of her rage and jealousy. 'Well yer soddin' brother finished up dancin' on air, an' good riddance, an' so will you!'

'Lottie! Stop this!' Truly concerned, Pol swung her to face her, shaking her a little. 'Stop it!' Poppy was crying again, her frightened sobs mingling with her mother's.

Lottie was beyond control. 'I 'ate 'er! Yer 'ear me? I 'ate 'er!' The words were almost incoherent. With a glance at the white-faced Kitty, Pol put a gentle arm about Lottie's shoulders and drew her close. Lottie sobbed on into her shoulder. 'It ain't fair! It ain't! 'Oo stuck by 'im these two stinkin' years? ''Oo went to see ''im in that filthy 'ole? I'd 'a' done anythin' – gone anywhere – don't 'e know that? Don't 'e care?' The words were threaded with pure despair. Kitty felt the cold and sticky trickle of blood upon her chin. Her cut lip throbbed. She took a tentative step towards the sobbing girl, but Pol shook her head fiercely, and she stepped back. Lottie lifted her head, and nothing had ever struck such a chill to Kitty's heart as the look in the great violet eyes. 'Watch yer back from now on, you,' Lottie said, almost choking with rage. 'You ain't safe. You 'ear me? You ain't safe from me – an' nor's that bastard brat o' yours.'

'That's enough, Lot.' Gently but firmly Pol ushered the sobbing girl back to the gate, throwing a quick look of helpless commiseration over her shoulder to Kitty. Kitty stood for a long time after they had gone, the echoes of hatred, of Lottie's unbalanced hostility ringing like the knell of death in her ears. In the warm sunshine she shivered, and it seemed to her that the garden was strangely shadowed.

Kitty could not rid herself of the memory of that scene, nor of the apprehension that Lottie's almost deranged hatred had engendered in her. She could not forget the girl's threats, especially where they concerned Michael; and her concern was not the slightest abated by the news that Lottie and Luke were estranged.

'But – I thought she was living with him? What happened?'

Pol shrugged gloomily. 'What d'yer think? Silly little fool couldn't let the dead lie. 'Ad ter keep on about it. Luke told 'er –' She stopped, glanced at Kitty sharply then corrected herself. 'Luke threw 'er out.'

'Luke told her what?' Kitty asked, quietly.

Pol said nothing.

'Pol! What?'

' 'E said,' Pol said reluctantly, 'that it was you 'e was goin' to 'ave. You an' the boy. An' no one – not 'er an' not you – was goin' ter stop 'im.'

Distractedly Kitty rubbed her forehead with her hand. 'I

have to get away, Pol. Oh, God! Why didn't I do it before?
Away from Luke. Away from London –'

'Where would yer go?'

Kitty shook her head. 'I don't know. I don't know! Pat
would let me go to the provinces if I wanted, though he
wouldn't like it, but if I'm going to earn a living it has to be
as Kit Daniels, and if I go as Kit Daniels then Luke can find
me whenever he wants. Oh, Lord, what a mess I've made of
things.'

Quickly and with genuine sympathy Pol laid a hand over
hers. 'Don't be daft. It ain't your fault that Luke Peveral's
nothin' but trouble an' never 'as bin. Nor yet that Lottie's
flipped 'er lid –'

'You think it's as bad as that?'

'Well she ain't normal, that's fer sure,' Pol said, the short-
ness of the words disguising her concern.

Kitty frowned worriedly. 'Pol – you don't think she'd –
well – do anything silly?'

'Seems ter me she's done enough yer could call silly
already,' Pol said grimly.

'You know what I mean. Michael – she threatened him –'

The kitchen clock chimed the hour, flatly strident.

'Pol?' Kitty asked, uncertainly, as the sound died.

Pol shook her head. 'No. 'Course not.' The words, after
the pause, were unconvincingly quick.

Dejectedly Kitty sat down and leaned her elbows on the
scrubbed kitchen table, resting her chin on her hands. 'She
really hates me,' she said.

Pol said nothing. In the silence the clock ticked on. Lightly
she touched Kitty's shoulder. Kitty lifted her head. Pol's
smile was as warm as ever it had been. 'Don't worry so. It'll
all blow over.'

Kitty smiled back, but shook her head.

'Let's 'ave a cup o' tea,' Pol said.

No matter how she tried Kitty could not get the thought
of Lottie Smith's unbalanced malevolence out of her mind.
She found herself jumping at shadows, worrying constantly
at her son's whereabouts and well-being. 'Watch yer back,'

Lottie had said. 'You ain't safe – an' neither's that bastard brat o' yours.' Once or twice Kitty was certain that she saw the other girl, once in the street outside the house, another time standing on the pavement outside the theatre after the show, in her face the most implacable hatred, but when she mentioned it to Pol, Pol dismissed her fears as ridiculous. 'You're gettin' as bad as she is! Ferget it, I tell yer! She'll get over it.'

Luke was another problem. Within as many weeks he called upon her three times, his manner surprisingly conciliatory, his physical appearance less menacing with each passing day of freedom. Kitty was adamant. She would not marry him. He would not have Michael. Each time Luke smiled, spoke courteously and left her, with no sign of the fury he had shown at that first meeting. She detested and distrusted this new patience of his: it strung nerves already taut almost to breaking point. Each day she woke with a dull feeling of dread. Something was going to happen. She knew it. They could not go on like this. Yet the days ticked by and spring advanced into summer, and nothing did happen. When a week went by with no visit from Luke she began to relax a little. Perhaps after all sensible Pol was right; she was overwrought and making mountains out of molehills.

In the middle of May, Amy came down with a fierce and feverish cold that all but prostrated her. Over her faint protests Kitty tucked her into her bed and brewed her a hot lemon drink flavoured with honey and laced liberally with brandy before going to the theatre. 'It's all right, don't worry – I'll take Michael with me tonight. He sleeps perfectly well in my dressing room, and Pol will be there to care for him.'

'But, Kitty – there's no need. I'll hear him if he wakes –'

Firmly Kitty shook her head. 'Absolutely not. You need to rest, not to lie here fretting about him. It'll be much better for you if we take him with us. It doesn't do him any harm just once in a while. You know how he enjoys it.'

Pale and red-nosed, Amy asked a little tentatively, 'But –

if you take him with you too often, won't people suspect – well –'

'That he's mine?' Kitty shrugged, picked up her gloves and pulled them on. 'I don't know. To be truthful I don't think I much care any more. We've put it about that he's an orphan Pol's fostered – but I don't know who believes that.'

'But – supposing – ?'

Kitty dropped a light kiss on her damp forehead. 'Suppose nothing, my dear. Get yourself better. I'll see you later.'

And so a delighted Michael was transported to the theatre with Kitty and Pol and installed in a day cot that Kitty kept in her dressing room for that purpose. Kitty played with him until the long dark lashes were drooping tiredly upon the still rounded baby cheeks, then tucked him in tenderly before changing for her first spot of the evening. 'There, little man. Sleep tight.'

She was performing twice that evening, once in the first half and once, a slightly longer spot, in the second. The audience was good and warmly responsive. Her first song went down well, the applause was enthusiastic, the Master of Ceremonies beamed happily. As always she felt herself relaxing, buoyed up by the happiness of being on stage. When she returned to her dressing room to change Michael was sleeping the sleep of the dead in the cot, totally oblivious to the noise and movement around him as Kitty, with Pol's help, changed into stylishly cut tailcoat and trousers. Pol stood back to admire the finished toilette. 'Bloody stunnin',' she said, satisfied. 'The best yet, I reckon. They'll love yer.'

'I'm trying out Bart's new song tonight.'

'So 'e said. 'E's out front. I'll pop up an' watch fer five minutes while yer on.' She did not miss Kitty's flickering glance at the sleeping child. 'All right, don't worry,' she said, soothingly, 'I'll get one o' the other girls in ter sit with 'im while I'm gone.'

Standing in the wings a few minutes later Kitty felt the familiar rise of excitement that always preceded a performance. The theatre was packed, the air very close and thick with cigarette smoke. She could see the faces of the first few rows of the audience, highlighted in the glow of the footlights, enthralled, watching the Great Romanski as he chained his scantily clad, tiny assistant inside the small, straw-filled box to which, in a moment, he would apply a flaming torch. Kitty did not much like this trick, the climax of Romanski's act, and had thought more than once that she would not have liked to take the chances that the fragile-looking girl assistant took each evening. She knew that as the flamboyant illusionist made a few florid passes with the lit torch the girl would be quickly and efficiently slipping the manacles from wrists and ankles before pressing the hidden spring that released the trapdoor beneath the false bottom of the box. What might happen if one day the trapdoor refused to open Kitty hated to think. Then in a spectacular flare of stage-flame the straw in the box was incinerated. A moment later, to a roar of applause, the tough little beauty was being handed from a tall, lacquered cupboard on the opposite side of the stage. Not for the first time Kitty wondered a little uncomfortably how many of the wildly applauding audience waited with bated breath hoping that this time the trick might go wrong.

'And now, ladies and gentlemen –'

She grabbed her hat and cane, took a swift sip of water.

'With a brand new song, straight from Gay Paree –'

Whistles and stamping from the audience. Smoke still drifted across the stage. Kitty wrinkled her nose and cleared her throat.

'Your own – your very own – Miss Kit Daniels –'

The roar of applause carried her, smiling, onto the stage. Through it she heard the orchestra strike up. She stepped to the footlights, had to wait several seconds before the enthusiastic greeting died. 'Who do you see in Mayfair, Strolling with the girls –'

By the second chorus they were singing it with her, and she caught sight of Bart's grinning face, his lifted thumb. It was a simple, catchy tune, one of his best. In the wings she saw Pol, beaming. When the song ended it was to another great roar of applause. The orchestra leader signalled to her again. The orchestra led once more into the opening bars of the song. The audience quieted. Kitty cleared her throat. The smoke from the illusionist's trick had hung about the stage for longer than usual tonight. 'Who do you see in Mayfair, Strolling with the girls –'

There was a quick flutter of subdued commotion in the wings. The smell of smoke was stronger. There was a sudden strange and restless stir in the audience, like the ripple of wind through a standing field of corn. Backstage, someone shouted urgently. Kitty's voice dried in her throat and she stopped, coughing. The orchestra played on raggedly for a moment then died to bewildered and bewildering silence. The cry came again, and this time the urgency of the message was unmistakable.

'Fire!'

The panic was immediate. At the back of the auditorium someone screamed. The great mass of people before the stage began to move, scrambling from their seats, fighting to get to the exits. The theatre manager, a mild-mannered man of no great presence rushed past Kitty to the front of the stage. 'Please! Ladies and gentlemen – please! Keep your seats –'

No one took the slightest notice. Smoke now seeped from the stage into the auditorium. Choking and coughing, people fought each other to escape it. Horrified, Kitty saw a woman go down, screaming terribly, beneath the stampeding feet. And then her confused brain started to function again and she remembered. Michael! She turned. Great, terrifying billows of smoke rolled towards her. People – stagehands, and performers still in their costumes streamed past her, buffeting her as she stood. 'Get out!' A brawny young man grabbed her arm and dragged her with him, 'Hurry, Miss Daniels! The side door –!'

'No!' She struggled free of him. Where was Pol? Where was Michael? A panic-stricken girl, eyes starting from her head, cannoned blindly into her and sent her reeling. The theatre was filled with sounds that might have come straight from Bedlam – screams and moans and a fury of shouting as people jammed the aisles, the stairs and the doorways in their attempts to escape. Someone jumped from the circle, desperate to avoid the lifting, roiling smoke, uncaring of the people below. Another followed, and another. A woman screamed, piercingly. Now, behind the stage, was the unmistakable and lurid lick of flame. She tried to fight her way against the streaming tide of humanity and was almost swamped by it. Terrified, she fought to stay on her feet, knowing that once down she would be trampled to death. Someone caught her arm, trying to force her towards the door. Again, frantically, she fought free. A great choking cloud of smoke boiled across the stage, cutting off the air in her lungs and she gagged, choking. Flames licked higher, blood red in the darkness. The curtains smouldered.

'Get 'er the 'ell out of 'ere fer Gawd's sake!'

Weakly she fought the hands that unceremoniously grabbed her. Her throat was raw, her lungs felt as if they were on fire. 'Door's blocked,' someone said, hoarsely. ''Ere, give 'er to me –' She felt herself half-dragged, half-carried through nightmare darkness shot with flame. Then with miraculous suddenness she was in the clear night air, and other hands took her. 'Michael!' she shrieked, '*Michael!*' Her voice was like the hoarse sobbing of an exhausted child.

'Where?' The hands that caught her then were not gentle, the demanding voice cool and hard as ice. 'Where is he?' She lifted her head. Luke's blurred face wavered before her, his head haloed in a nimbus of ghastly flame. He shook her again, hard. '*Where?*'

She was trying to rub the streaming tears from her stinging eyes. 'In my dressing room. Oh, Luke –!'

He let her go and she fell. She heard someone shout. In the distance bells rang, urgently, above the terrible roar of the fire. The fabric of the old theatre was burning like tinder, the flames bright and beautiful and savagely destructive.

'What's that bloody madman up to? 'Ere – stop 'im! Catch 'im, someone!'

'Luke!' she screamed, tears streaming down her blackened face, and then again, *'Luke!'* the sound tearing painfully from her damaged throat. She staggered to her feet, rubbing her burning eyes. Flame lovingly licked the ornate façade of the building, streamed from the broken windows, blackening the stonework. Heat billowed, scorching the air about her. She staggered forward.

'Stop her!' someone snapped, and she was imprisoned, struggling weakly.

'Luke,' she said, rasping upon a cough, 'my baby –'

The stranger's voice was soothing. 'It's all right. The engines are here. They'll be all right. It'll be out in a tick now –'

But it was not. Nothing now could stop the monster from devouring its prey. Shivering and stunned with shock, she watched the building burn. The crowd about her jostled her and almost she fell. Someone tried to usher her away but she shook them off fiercely, her eyes fixed upon the lurid flames. Her throat and lungs were raw. Her left arm hung oddly awkwardly and throbbed with each breath she took. As she stood, a wave of flame-shot darkness lifted about her, threatening to engulf her. She struggled against it. She must not move. She must not. If she waited they would come. Of course they would come.

'Kitty – Kitty, darlin' – please –'

As if from a distance she recognized Pol's anguished voice but was too intent upon her purpose to respond to it. She must not look away. She must wait, and they would come.

'Kitty – your arm's all burned. You must let someone see to it –'

She looked down, surprised. The sleeve of her jacket was charred and still smouldering. 'Wait a minute,' she said very calmly. 'Wait until they come.'

The inside of the building was an inferno, the glowing cave of the image of hell.

'Look out! The roof's going!'

Hands pulled her back. With something like an explosion the roof collapsed, sending a great torch of sparks to the heavens. Someone screamed. She felt a tearing pain in her throat. Pol's face, tear-drenched, swam before her and was lost in the darkness that at last engulfed her.

5

It was a week before she truly believed what they told her – that Luke was dead, and Michael with him. Almost mindless with grief, she lay for days unspeaking and uncaring of her own injury. She was indeed only vaguely aware of her surroundings, of the painful ministrations to her badly burned left arm. As often as was possible Pol would come, sitting by the bed, holding Kitty's uninjured hand as she drifted in and out of a drug-induced sleep that was as troubled with nightmares as were her waking moments with grief. Her love for Luke had long ago been defeated by her fear of him, for herself and for Michael: but his death in this sudden and terrible way was a horror she would never have wanted nor even envisaged. That her child too was gone, dead with the father he had never known, was a loss so deep she could barely comprehend it. For a time the enormity of it filled her mind and her heart to the exclusion of all else and though her body began to heal it seemed at first as if her spirit never would.

Released from hospital, she allowed herself to be taken back to Pascal Road by Pol and Barton. Once there, however, in familiar surroundings and amongst friends the strange anaesthetic of shock wore off, and for days she could neither eat nor sleep as the tears she had been until now unable to shed came in an endless flood. Patiently and with love Pol tended her, knowing instinctively that the storm of grief, healingly released at last, would eventually ease. And so it proved. A couple of weeks after leaving hospital, though almost unendurable sadness haunted her days Kitty was able at last rationally to face the fact of Luke's and Michael's deaths, even if still she could not reconcile herself to the loss.

It was on a day of sunshine and birdsong that Inspector Ian MacAdam unexpectedly called at the house in Pascal Road. Shown into the parlour, after effecting dourly brief introductions he came directly to the point.

'I feel you should know, Miss Daniels, that we're now as certain as we can be that the fire at the New Palace Theatre – in which, as you know, twenty-eight people died – was no accident. It was deliberately set.' The Inspector was a lowland Scot, staunchly Presbyterian and no great admirer of women unless they be of the pattern of his own rigorously righteous, mouse-plain wife. He eyed Kitty repressively and with no great compassion, the weight of his disapproval of all things theatrical in his severe gaze. She sat stiffly upon a high-backed dining chair nursing, more from habit than from necessity, her still-bandaged left arm with her right hand.

'Deliberately set?' She frowned, shook her head. 'Surely not, Inspector?'

His mouth tightened irritably. 'I tell you, Miss Daniels, that we know it to be true.'

'But – who would do such an awful thing?'

Pol, sitting in a chair by the flower-filled summer grate, stirred, and was still.

Self-importantly the man cleared his throat. 'You are, I believe, Miss Daniels, acquainted with a woman named Charlotte Smith?'

'Charlotte?' All vestiges of colour were draining from Kitty's already pale face, leaving it chalk-white. Beneath the flared brows the dark eyes were horrified. 'Lottie?' she whispered. 'You can't think –?' She stopped.

He watched her dispassionately. 'We have clear reason to believe, Miss Daniels, that she not only would but she did. The fire did not start on or near the stage as was originally believed. It began in your dressing room –'

For one moment Kitty's iron control almost broke. She shut her eyes tightly, jaw clenched, then drew a deep breath and sat straighter, hands clasped in her lap, watching him steadily. 'You have proof?'

'We have a witness.'

Kitty heard Pol's small, shocked intake of breath. She turned. 'Pol –'

'Miss Daniels.' The Inspector interrupted her, his voice brusque, his eyes sharp and totally unsympathetic. 'There is talk of a child.'

Kitty, despite herself, flinched. 'Yes.'

'You know no body was found?'

'Yes.'

With the sudden energy of fury Pol jumped from her chair and ran to Kitty, laying a protective arm about her shoulders, glaring angry and open dislike at the man. 'Fer Gawd's sake! What yer tryin' ter to do 'er?'

The Inspector coldly ignored her. His experience in the police force had encouraged him to draw uncharitable conclusions about Pol from the moment she had opened the door to him. 'Miss Daniels, as I said, twenty-eight people died in that fire and the panic that followed it –'

'Yes. I know.'

'Two of the recovered bodies were children's. Both have now been identified by their families. Yet I understand you to believe that another child died in the flames?'

'There was a child in my dressing room. I tried to get to him after the fire broke out – but – I couldn't.' The helpless tears that always rose at thought of Michael were threatening to get the better of her again. She blinked fiercely and cleared her throat. Pol squeezed her shoulders hard.

'The man' – the Inspector glanced at his notebook – 'Luke Peveral' – the tone in which the name was spoken left no doubt that enquiries had been made and Luke's criminal identity established – 'was the child's father?'

'Yes.'

'And that was why he entered the burning building?'

'Yes.'

He looked up from the book. 'His body was, as you know, recovered and identified.'

'Yes. I know.' Kitty's voice was becoming desperate. She brushed a hand across her eyes. 'Inspector – please – I don't understand why we must go through all this again?'

'Because a witness has come forward, Miss Daniels, and new evidence has come to light.'

'What kind of new evidence?'

He did not reply to her directly. 'To make clear the position and to facilitate enquiries – indeed to ensure that I am speaking to the right person – I should like in the first place to establish the identity of the child who is missing.'

'For Christ's sweet sake,' Pol burst out. 'What diff'rence does it make? The kid's dead, ain't 'e?'

Inspector MacAdam addressed Kitty, his voice steely. 'Miss Daniels, would you ask your – companion' – he emphasized the word with dry contempt – 'to hold her tongue or to leave the room?'

He could not have chosen a better way to stiffen Kitty's back and dry her eyes. A sharp spur of anger goaded her back to sharp self-possession. 'I'll do no such thing, Inspector. Pol has nothing but my welfare at heart, whereas you, it seems, are simply intent upon opening old wounds. However – if you insist –' She met his eyes levelly with her own. 'As I suspect you already know, the child is' – she stopped, corrected herself painfully – 'was – the child was mine. His name was Michael Daniels. He was two and a half years old. He was born in France at Christmas in 1867. As I have already told you, Luke Peveral was his father. Now – is there anything else you need to know?' Only the slightest tremor in her voice betrayed her.

The expression on his face did not change. 'Tell me, Miss Daniels –' The emphasis on her unmarried title brought the faintest flush of colour to her face despite herself. 'You and the woman Charlotte Smith – you were not on the best of terms?'

'No.' The word was short.

'You had in fact quarrelled?'

'Yes.'

'And she had threatened you?'

'Yes.'

'And your child?'

'Yes.'

He looked at her thoughtfully. The silence ticked on.

'Inspector —' she began, a fraught edge of desperation back in her voice.

He stopped her with a brusque lift of his hand. 'I think you should know, Miss Daniels' — still he could not resist that faint, scornful emphasis — 'that we have good reason to believe that your son did not in fact die in the fire.'

Had she been standing she would have fallen. As it was she swayed in her seat and Pol, her face as dumbstruck as Kitty's own, caught her with strong hands.

Inspector MacAdam stood and walked to the fireplace, turned to face them, hands clasped behind his back. For the first time he directly addressed Pol. 'You were in charge of the child?'

'Yes.'

'And you left him to go and see Miss Daniels perform on stage?'

'That's right. We'd arranged it. I'd asked —'

'You had asked a young woman — Betty Dyson by name — to take care of the child while you were gone?'

Pol eyed him warily. 'That's right. If you know, why ask?'

'What you did not know was that Miss Dyson had' — he lifted sardonic brows — 'affairs of her own to arrange with a certain young man; an acrobat, I believe' — he pronounced the word as if it had been in a foreign and unintelligible language — 'and she left the child alone in Miss Daniels' dressing room.'

'I'll murder 'er,' Pol said, conversationally.

Not by the flicker of an eyelid did he indicate that he had heard her. 'Miss Dyson it was who saw Mrs Smith come from your room, Miss Daniels. And who then saw the smoke, and flames —'

'She raised the alarm?'

'No. Unfortunately she did not. She panicked, and she ran away. She has, it would appear, a very possessive husband.

She was afraid of the consequences of explanations. She isn't a very intelligent young woman, I'm afraid. If she had raised the alarm immediately many lives would probably have been saved.'

'Then why has she come forward now?'

'Conscience, Miss Daniels, is a strange thing. She could not sleep.'

'And – you say she actually saw Lottie set the fire?'

'She saw Charlotte Smith hurry from your dressing room, which was by that time well alight.' He paused for a moment. 'Miss Dyson says that she was carrying the child.'

For a moment the words hardly registered. Kitty stared at him. Then, 'Are you – is she – sure?' Her voice was a stranger's.

'She has sworn to it.'

'Lottie's got Michael?' Pol whispered. She was staring at the man as if he had been a ghost risen to haunt her. Suddenly Kitty was galvanized into action. She leapt from the chair and caught the man's arm, almost shaking him. 'Where is she? Where is she?'

He removed his arm from her clutching fingers. 'Precisely? We don't know. Too much time has elapsed and the bird has flown, I fear. She has left the country.'

'Oh, no!' Kitty flung her head back in a sudden furious gesture of frustration.

'And gone where?' Pol asked, steadily, an arm once more about Kitty's trembling shoulders.

'We traced her to France –'

Kitty stilled. 'France?' she asked, sharply. 'Where abouts in France?'

'We think possibly to Paris – we traced her so far, then I'm afraid we lost her. Twenty-eight people died in that fire, Miss Daniels. She had good reason to hide.'

'Luke,' Pol said softly, as if the name had only just occurred to her. 'She killed Luke. Jesus Christ.'

Kitty's mind, emerging with sudden, shocking clarity from the daze of shock that had shackled it, said quickly, 'She's been to Paris before, Inspector, do you know that?'

He shook his head. 'No.'

'Surely there must be some way to trace her whereabouts? The French police –?'

'– couldn't find a pig in its sty in broad daylight,' the man said, sourly. For the first time in this interview his expression was slightly less than granite hard. 'I have to tell you, Miss Daniels, that I fear it's hopeless. To look for one woman in a city of two million souls is a hard enough task at any time – to attempt it now, with hostilities about to break out and Paris the centre of France's war activity . . . No, I'm afraid I must tell you that I didn't come here to offer you hope of the child's recovery, but simply to inform you that he is at least, we believe, still alive.'

Kitty was staring at him blankly. 'Hostilities? War? What war?'

In the act of picking up his hat and gloves from the table the man stopped. 'My dear Miss Daniels – surely you must have seen something of what is going on? Prussia and France have been intent upon picking a quarrel for months, and now it seems the pretext has arrived. War it will be, sooner or later.' His expression was stern again. 'And I know I'm not alone in hoping that our German cousins will teach that harlot nation a lesson they will never forget. Sin brings its own rewards, Miss Daniels, and I dinna doubt that Paris, like Sodom and Gomorrah before her, is likely at last to reap her just deserts in the coming conflict. I give you good day.'

The door closed behind his sanctimonious back onto dead silence.

'Bloody 'ell,' Pol said at last, profound and inexpressible feeling in the two words. 'Why didn't I see? Why didn't I guess? God Almighty – she told me! She bloody as good as *told* me –'

'What? What are you talking about?' Kitty's voice was trembling slightly.

Pol closed her eyes, searching her memory. 'The day before the fire Lot was 'ere. She was laughin' – 'appy – just like old times. I 'adn't seen 'er like it in years. I asked 'er what was up. She said – she said it was a secret. 'Er secret.

An' then she said –' Pol screwed up her face ferociously. 'Gawd, if I could just remember exactly! – somethin' about Luke comin' to 'er. She said if she could give 'im the thing 'e most wanted in the world 'e'd never leave 'er. She said 'e'd come to 'er when she 'ad 'is son. Kitty – may I be struck dead, I swear I thought she was pregnant!'

'But – she meant my son. Michael! She intended to steal him – offer him to Luke in return for – oh, no! It's mad! Unbalanced! It's horrible –'

Pol nodded, a sickness in her eyes.

'But – the fire! Why the fire?'

Pol shrugged. ''Oo knows? P'raps she did it to create a diversion. Could even 'ave bin an accident. But once she realized she'd bin seen – that the police'd be after 'er –'

'She made a run for it. To the only place she knows outside London. The only place far enough away for her to feel safe. Paris.'

Suddenly very calm, Kitty walked back to the chair in which she had been sitting and stood behind it, holding on to the high back as if for support. 'Think,' she said, softly. 'We have to think. Where would she go?'

Pol was at her side in a moment. 'Kitty, love, no! Don't fool yourself! That jackass was right about that at least. It'd be like lookin' fer a blinkin' needle in an 'aystack! An' you'll get no 'elp from the coppers, that's obvious –'

'I shan't ask for any.'

'But – s'pose – like 'e said – s'pose there is a war?'

'I don't care. I've got to try. Pol – Michael's alive! He's alive!' Small, feverish spots of colour had appeared on Kitty's pale cheeks. Unnoticed, tears rolled down her thin face and dripped disregarded onto the pale silk of her dress. 'He's alive!' she whispered again, and almost in one movement they stepped into each other's embrace, hugging, rocking, laughing and crying together. When at last they drew away, Pol mopped her face with a large handkerchief.

'Pol,' Kitty said, urgently. 'Please – think! Try to remember everything Lottie ever told you about that stay in Paris. Where did they go? What did they do? What did she like best? Most important of all – did she make any friends?'

'Oh, yes,' Pol said immediately, 'she made a friend all right. Couldn't stop talkin' about 'er. An' English girl 'oo'd bin over there some time. Done quite well for 'erself by all accounts.'

'Doing what?'

Pol lifted caustic brows. 'Whorin', what else? Oh – she 'ad some fancy Frenchification for it, but whorin' was what she did.'

'What was her name?'

Sadly Pol shook her head.

'Oh, Pol – please! You must remember!'

Pol concentrated ferociously, an intent frown creasing her brow. Then she shook her brassy head in quick self-impatience. 'No. 'S'no good. If I ever knew it, it's gone. Tell you what, though' – she brightened suddenly – 'I've got a picture of 'er somewhere, with Lot. Some street artist drew 'em sittin' at a table at a bar near this girl's 'ouse. Lot gave it to me as a keepsake. P'raps the girl's name's on it?'

'Where is it?'

'Upstairs somewhere.' Pol, followed closely by Kitty, was already halfway to the door.

It was a full, frustrating hour later that Pol, with a quick, profanely triumphant exclamation, pulled a crumpled piece of paper from the back of a drawer. ''Ere it is!' She laid the picture, a smudged pencil sketch, on the dressing table and carefully smoothed the creases. A remarkably faithfully drawn Lottie laughed from beneath an open parasol. She was seated at a small table upon which were set a bottle of wine and two glasses. Beside her sat an attractive dark girl with wide, cat-like eyes and a full, pouting mouth. Behind them a fountain played, the water cascading from the mouth of a dolphin upon whose back a plump cherub rode, one arm upraised and the hand missing. Beyond that were sketched tall, shuttered houses, their front doors opening straight onto the pavement of what looked like a typical, slightly seedy Parisian square.

'No. No name. Blast!' Disappointed, Pol made to refold the picture.

Kitty snatched it from her. 'It doesn't matter! At least it's a start! If I could find that statue –'

Pol was staring at her. 'You gone bleedin' potty? You can't go ter Paris on a wild goose chase like that! Didn't you 'ear what the man said? They're goin' ter be shootin' at each other over there! An' besides – Kitty, love, I don't like ter be a wet blanket, but aren't you addin' two an' two an' makin' bloody twenty-one? You don't know fer sure Lot's in Paris. You don't know she's still got Michael with 'er. You don't know –'

'I don't care! Oh, Pol, you must see – I've got to try! I've got to! While there's a chance – the faintest chance – that Michael's alive, I've got to try.' She stood for a moment, thinking, clicking her fingers. 'What was the name of that boring man from the Foreign Office – you know, the one that kept sending me those terrible poems? Hogarth? Howard? No – Howarth! Lord Howarth! That's it!' Turning, she flew from the room and clattered at risk to her neck down the narrow stairs.

'Where the 'ell you goin'?' Pol followed her onto the landing and hung over the bannisters.

Kitty was struggling into her light summer cloak, wincing as she strained her damaged arm. 'To Whitehall. To find the poetic Lord Howarth. And if he won't help me – then I'll find someone else.' She lifted her face, white and determined in the half-dark. 'I'm going to Paris, Pol. War or no war. Not the whole damned Prussian army will stop me. Michael's in Paris. I know he is. And I'm going to find him. I have friends to help me – Jem, if I can find him, Charles, Genevieve –'

'But –'

Kitty's movements stilled. Her face as she looked up at Pol was strangely sympathetic. 'Don't "but" me, Pol. It won't do any good. Try to understand. I'm not stupid – I know I'm clutching at straws – but what else do I have?' The shadowed dark eyes glittered. 'I lay in that hospital bed and I prayed to die, Pol – as they had died; Matt, Luke, Michael. I thought I had nothing to live for. Now I have. Don't try to stop me. I'm going to Paris.'

The words, of course, were easier said than the journey made. Inspector MacAdam had been right; war between a France sadly deluded as to her own strength and support and the newly united German states was imminent, and the massive guns that Herr Krupp had exhibited so proudly at the Paris Exhibition three short years before were about to be turned in anger upon their erstwhile hosts. Opinion in England was divided, but not evenly; while for a few the idea of the barbaric Prussians daring to threaten the very heart of European civilization was unthinkable, a far greater proportion of the jingoistic British public were far from put out at the prospect of the old, arrogant enemy being given the trouncing it was felt they so richly deserved. Few saw the dangers inherent in an over-strong and unified Germany that might dominate the European mainland for a century to come: fewer still saw this as the first signs of a conflict that would engender generations of destruction, terror and death.

For Kitty, anyway, none of the raging arguments signified. She did not care for cause nor for effect. Her every thought, every effort, was bent upon getting herself, over all protests, to Paris. And with the help of the fortunately still besotted – if unfortunately still as boring – Lord Howarth, she did it. Passes and passports, the transfer of a large sum of money and the acquisition of an equally large sum in French currency in case of emergency – the brainwave of a friendly Under Secretary who had known people who had been caught in such situations before – the obliging Lord Howarth took care of it all. Pol, tutting still, but constitutionally unable to refuse her aid, helped to sew the cash securely into a cotton petticoat, made sure that the necessities of life found their way into Kitty's trunk and issued many a dire warning about the problems a woman might encounter travelling alone. 'Especially with them damn' Froggies about,' she muttered for at least the hundredth time as she sat heavily upon the trunk lid while Kitty pulled the strap tight and buckled it. 'You can't trust 'em, you know, not an inch!' Even Pol, Kitty noticed with some amusement, who had never set foot outside London let alone the country, seemed to have caught the prevailing anti-French feeling.

She straightened. 'I'll be all right. I can take care of myself. And anyway, I'm not travelling alone. Lord Howarth has discovered a worthy and very dull young man named John Babbercombe who is travelling to Paris to join the Embassy there, and he's offered to escort me. The only danger I shall be in is that of dying of boredom. So stop worrying!' With the knowledge that her son was, after all, alive, and with the prospect of positive action, however uncertain its outcome, Kitty had taken a new lease on life. She would not look back; finding Michael was her one and only aim – how it was to be achieved she had no clear idea, but the possibilities of failure she refused to consider. She had determined to take it step by step, and the idea had rooted, deep as superstition in her mind. The first step was to get to Paris, what was to follow would become clear then.

She left London in the blaze of a summer dawn in the middle of July. On the already crowded Victoria Station, as she said her goodbyes to an openly worried Pol they both saw the placards that shouted news of a final affront to French pride that must surely herald war.

'Somethin' about a telegram –' Pol said. 'Kit – don't yer think yer should just wait a bit – see what's goin' to 'appen?'

'No.' The word brooked no argument. Briskly Kitty kissed her. 'Now I'll have to go, for I have to find my seat and Mr John Babbercombe, Heaven help us. I expect he'll know what's going on. And will tell me – at length!' She pulled a comic face which cut no ice with Pol at all. 'Oh, Pol dear, do try to crack a smile. I'll be back in no time, I promise – and Michael with me!'

''Course you will.' Pol, valiantly as she tried, totally failed to hide her lack of conviction. 'You'll write, won't you? Let me know what's 'appenin'?'

'I will.' A train whistle shrieked to the steel-girded roof. 'I'll have to go,' Kitty said again. 'Porter!'

The last she saw of Pol as the train pulled, snorting steam, from the platform, was a handkerchief, bravely fluttering until it was blocked from view by a curve in the track; whereupon, Kitty thought a little guiltily, it would probably be put to its more proper use. She directed a weakly polite smile at the studious-looking Mr Babbercombe, who had in the first moments of re-acquaintance proved himself every bit as dull as she had remembered, and prayed that the journey might be accomplished as speedily as possible.

In that, however, she was to be disappointed. By the time she set foot on French soil, after a smooth crossing, war had been declared and, despite a sweltering and ennervating heatwave, the whole country had run mad with joy. Here was the Imperial dream again – victory and glory, La Belle France the true ruler of Europe as God had so clearly intended. The upstart, comic-opera Prussians would be taught a lesson they would not quickly forget.

Meanwhile the roads and railways were in utter chaos.

The train crawled from station to station, was shunted into sidings, stood still, it seemed to a Kitty wild with impatience and half dead from the heat, for much longer periods than it actually moved. The journey, which should have taken ten hours, in the end took fifteen and it was full darkness before the train steamed wearily at last into Paris and the Gare du Nord, and more scenes of national jubilation. Kitty, her brain cudgelled almost to a stupor by the heat and the tiring journey – to say nothing of the effort of fifteen hours of sporadic conversation with the tedious Mr Babbercombe – leaned eagerly from the window. Charles had been informed of her intended arrival and, late or no, would surely be there to meet her. The vast station was crowded, the atmosphere high-strung and celebratory as Mardi Gras. One might have believed, she thought, scanning the singing crowds, that a holiday rather than a war had been declared.

'Are you sure you'll be all right, Miss Daniels?' The

commendably concerned John Babbercombe, sweating profusely, handed her down to the platform.

'Oh, yes. I'm being met – ah! There he is – Charles! Charles!' Catching sight of Charles Parisot's face, handsome as ever if a little heavier, she waved energetically.

He pushed his way through the crowds, hugged her with unreserved, Gallic pleasure. 'Kitty, my Kitty! What a day to choose to arrive!' Even he seemed affected by the euphoria that had swept aside the good sense of a nation. Introductions were effected, Mr Babbercombe gratefully accepted the offer of a lift in the Parisot carriage as far as the Embassy, Kitty's trunk was located and collected, and they were at last on their way. A scant half hour later, at last, she was in the so-well-remembered, elegant apartment on the Rue de Rivoli, clasped in Genevieve's happy, expansively perfumed embrace. 'But, chérie, it's so good to see you! And so good to have someone here who will talk some sense instead of this ridiculous shouting of war! Oh – we should lock up all the generals, French and German – British too, perhaps! – and then we shall have a bit of peace, *non*? Come in, chérie, come in. Everything is prepared, and a bath is waiting –'

More tired than she would admit, Kitty allowed herself to be led along by the other woman's affectionate efficiency. A short while later she lay in a soothing, sweet-smelling bath, soaking out the sweat and frustration of a trying day, whilst in the room beyond Genevieve's maid, Jeanne-Marie, unpacked her trunk. Yet even now her brain refused to rest. The first step was taken, the second must now be determined. It was with some surprise that she realized suddenly, as she lay, eyes half closed in a state of blessed somnolence, that in fact her next task was as clear-cut as the first had been. She was in Paris; and, as she had suspected would happen, the Parisots had failed to recognize the location of the dolphin statue. The next step was clear.

She must find Jem O'Connell.

The streets of Paris were chaos. Kitty, pushing her way towards the Pont d'Arcole, found her progress hindered by

yet another detachment of marching soldiers; they were
everywhere, it seemed. She watched as they shambled by,
grinning, raggedly out of step, waving at the pretty faces in
the crowd, and reflected not for the first time since she had
arrived in Paris that to all outward appearances the French
forces might be going on a picnic rather than marching to
war. In the two days since her arrival she had watched
groups such as these parade endlessly up and down the Rue
de Rivoli, cheered on by crowds perhaps too wildly patriotic
to be taken seriously. At her openly expressed puzzlement
at the holiday atmosphere that still prevailed in the city
Genevieve had shaken an impatiently disgusted head.
'They're mad. All of them. They hear the trumpets, they
see the flags and they go crazy. Phut! Do they care that our
army is scattered all over the country, that our generals are
too busy fighting each other to have time for any other
enemy, that our Emperor is a sick man?'

Kitty, aware that beneath her friend's fashionable chic
and charm there lurked an astute brain and shrewd grasp of
affairs, had been surprised at her outburst. 'Oh, surely –
things aren't that bad?'

Genevieve had shrugged angrily and turned from the window and the sight of the carnival crowds and the marching
men. 'Look at them. Half of them don't know out of which
end of the rifle the bullet comes. The other half don't have
a rifle. Most of the officers have more experience in the
bedchamber than on the battlefield. Oh, they are brave,
there's no doubt. They'll storm the Prussian guns with
sabres. What good will that do?' She shook her head
sombrely. 'France is not prepared for war, Kitty. The army
is disorganized, communications are in chaos, the railway
system all but broken down under the strain of mobiliz-
ation.'

'How do you know all this? The papers are saying –'

'The papers? Oh, Kitty, don't make me laugh! The papers
say what they are told to say – all but a few, that are branded
left-wing revolutionary – what do you say? – rags? The
country, and especially Paris, wanted war. It has war. It

doesn't want to hear the truth. I spoke to a young officer yesterday, the son of a good friend of mine and a young man of sense. Through the incompetence of his superiors he had lost – physically lost! – a whole battalion of men. He had been told to join them in one place – when he got there – phut! – no men! And no one knew which train they had been put on or where they were. Tell me – does that sound like an army that is likely to win a war?'

She had lifted her head then, and looked directly at Kitty, her expression worried and compassionate. 'Kitty – it's so lovely to see you – but you should not be here! To look for a woman and a child under normal circumstances would be hard enough. But now? Impossible. And – supposing the worst happens? If our army cannot hold these barbarians – these savages! – who knows what will happen to my poor Paris?'

Kitty had been horrified at the gleam of tears in the other woman's eyes. Remembering the uncharacteristic outburst now, she felt a renewed stirring of unease, quickly suppressed. Of course Paris could be in no danger; the idea was absurd. And of course, eventually, somehow, she would find Lottie and through her, Michael. She must. For now, though, her task was to find Jem. He knew Paris better than did most native Parisians. Perhaps he would know the square with the dolphin statue. If not, he would help her to find it. She knew he would.

She passed the great Hôtel de Ville, pushed her way across the bridge, passed beneath the massive shadow of Notre Dame, hurried across the Ile and over the Pont au Double to the Left Bank of the river. She remembered well the way to Jem's apartment and in ten minutes was standing in the familiar narrow street with its tall, shabby, shuttered tenements and disreputable bars. As she climbed the dark stairs she could no longer deny her anxiety. It had been to this apartment that she had written, but he had never replied. She could now no longer suppress the worrying thought that the reason for his neglect might have been other than his preoccupation with his own full and disorganized life. He might have left the apartment and so never have received her letters . . .

The door was opened by a brute of a man in a dirty vest and ragged trousers held across his vast belly by a piece of string. His breath as he grunted a suspicious and slurred enquiry was foul. Behind him she could see the familiar room, squalid and filthy and with no sign of the artist's clutter that had always characterized it, no strong, acrid smell of paint and varnish.

Her heart sank within her. 'Er – *pardon, M'sieu – je – je cherche* Jem O'Connell?'

The man grunted, shook his head and made to close the door.

'Oh – please! *S'il vous plaît* – Jem O'Connell! He – he used to live here –' Despairingly she was aware that every word of French she knew – a pitiful enough store at the best of times – had fled her memory. 'Jem O'Connell,' she repeated. 'An American. *Un Américain. Ici!*' She stabbed a finger to the floor. The ugly head shook again, the dull eyes unhelpful and uncomprehending. The door shut in her face.

She stared at the blank door in a frustration of anger and disappointment. She would not – could not – give up that easily. She lifted her fist to rap again, stopped at a quiet call from the stairs above her. 'Mam'selle?'

She looked up. A thin-faced girl, shabbily dressed, leaned over the rickety bannister. '*Vous cherchez* Jem O'Connell?'

'Yes – er *oui*! You know where he is?'

The girl lifted a finger, smiling a little. 'The American. Yes. Wait a moment, please.' The words were so strongly accented that it took a moment for Kitty to realize that they were spoken in English. She waited as the girl disappeared up the stairs, heard a door bang. It was hot and airless on the dismally filthy landing and the smell – that familiar stink of poverty-stricken, overcrowded humanity that she so hated – was vile. She swallowed, a faint sheen of sweat breaking out on her face. Her burned arm throbbed very slightly. From behind the door that had been Jem's came the sound of raised voices and a crash.

'*Voilà!*' The girl was back, a grubby piece of paper in her hand which she proffered eagerly to Kitty. 'The – American – leeves – 'ere –' The mangled words were spoken with pride and Kitty heard in the rolled 'r's and the long vowels the echoes of Jem's teaching. She glanced at the paper, upon which in faded writing that she recognized as Jem's was scrawled an address.

'Ees een Montmartre,' the girl said. 'You know? Montmartre.'

'Yes. I know Montmartre. Thank you. Thank you very much.'

The girl watched her, her eyes expectant. Kitty fumbled in her pocket and produced a couple of coins. '*Merci.*'

A small grubby hand snatched the coins and the ragged skirt was hauled up as the girl secreted her prize.

Kitty waved the paper. 'How long – since he left?'

The girl frowned, puzzled.

She tried again. 'How long – *combien de* –?' She struggled over the words, then held up her fingers, counting, '*Un? Deux? Trois?*'

'Ah!' Comprehension brightened the pinched little face. The girl held up a dirty finger and thumb. '*Deux.*'

In the unpredictable way of such things the word for 'months' popped into Kitty's brain. '*Deux mois?*' she asked.

The girl laughed and shook her head. '*Deux années!*'

Two years! The address she held was two years old! In a city such as Paris and a nomadic life such as Jem lived that might as well be a lifetime.

Dejectedly – for though a part of her had known all along that this might happen yet still her hopes had been unrealistically high – Kitty stepped out into the hammering sun of a summer that was being spoken of as the hottest in living memory and, nursing her faintly throbbing arm, made her way back to the Rue de Rivoli.

Montmartre, with its windmills, its tiny garden vineyards, and its ancient jumble of winding streets, perched upon its hill above Paris like a turret above a castle, part of the city

since the fields that had once divided them had disappeared
under the inexorable march of the city streets and buildings
into the countryside, and yet separate too, by virtue of its
position and its distinctive village character. Kitty had never
been there before, and even in her somewhat distracted state
of mind she could not help but notice as she climbed the
steep, pretty lanes how picturesque were the tumbledown
cottages with their little gardens and brightly painted doors,
dwarfed by the great windmills, disused now, or converted
into places of entertainment, that towered over them. There
were one or two larger and more prosperous-looking houses
and a few small tenements, but little industry; the steep
nature of the terrain upon which the original village had
been built not lending itself to the building of factories.

Following the directions Charles had given her, she toiled
on up the hill to where a narrow lane crossed the one she
walked. The disappointment she had felt two days before at
not having found Jem at the first attempt still nagged her –
a disappointment that she had been forced on reflection to
admit was rooted in more than the simple and obvious
causes. She had told herself that she had wanted to find him
for purely practical reasons – his intimate knowledge of
Paris, his facility with the language, his wide and varied
circle of acquaintances. But the setback of two days ago had
shown her that her reasons for wanting to find him did not
in fact stop there; she had not realized until that moment
of disappointment how much she had looked forward to
seeing again that fair, boyish, warm-smiling face, to hearing
the attractively slow-drawling voice. How very much she
had counted upon the unquestioning support and encouragement that she was sure he would afford her. Strangely it
seemed to her that finding Jem had now become every bit
as important to her as finding Lottie and Michael, a surprising fact that she did her best not to examine too closely.

She turned into the lane, counted the houses. Number
twelve was, if anything, more tumbledown and in need of
several licks of paint than its neighbours. The gate stood
wide open, as it obviously had for some considerable time,

leaning at a wild angle, its lower bar tangled in the wilderness of weeds that rioted through the tiny front garden and grew even within the cracked brickwork of the building itself. She picked her way to the sun-faded, peeling front door. Somewhere a dog barked, fiercely, and was quieted. In the blazing sun warmth radiated from the broken paving stones at her feet, from the heavy door, from the very fabric of the building. In the absence of bell-pull or knocker she lifted her fist and thumped upon the door.

Nothing happened.

She knocked again, as hard as she could, and this time somewhere within she heard movement, a woman's bad-tempered muttering, heavy, shuffling footsteps.

The apparition that opened the door was the most fearsome she had ever seen. A squat, enormously fat woman, dressed even on this sweltering day in the many-layered dark, voluminous clothes of a country peasant and with a patriotically red, white and blue knitted cap perched ridiculously upon an iron-grey, untidy head, scowled at her fiercely. By her side, held not very securely by the scruff of its neck, a great red-eyed mastiff snarled, no better tempered from its looks than its mistress. Kitty felt the hairs of her neck stir beneath the twin, baleful glares.

'Er – *pardon, Madame* –' she stammered, stepping back a little. The mastiff growled menacingly at the movement and she froze. Sweat trickled uncomfortably between her breasts, soaking her bodice. '*Je – je cherche* M'sieu O'Connell. M'sieu Jem O'Connell –?'

The name brought a remarkable and quite terrifying reaction. The woman's heavy face convulsed with rage and she spat a torrent of obviously abusive French, spittle running obscenely from the corner of her mouth. Desperately Kitty resisted an overwhelming urge to turn and run. This was her only hope.

'*S'il vous plaît – lentement – je ne comprends pas* –' she managed as the woman paused for breath at last.

The woman's head jerked menacingly. '*Américaine?*'

Kitty shook her head. 'English.'

The clouds of fury gathered again in the woman's face. She spat very accurately at Kitty's feet. 'English? Pigs. All of them. They desert us, eh?' The surprising English, like the girl's a couple of days previously, was heavily accented and bore the unmistakable stamp of Jem's own speech. On a faint lift of hysteria Kitty found herself wondering if Jem had set himself to teaching his native tongue to the whole of the female population of Paris. 'They think we lose this war, eh?' The apparition stepped forward threateningly and the dog snarled again. '*Eh bien!* After we slit Bismarck's fat belly we come to England, eh?'

Kitty found herself shaking her head a little wildly. She had been warned by a worried Charles of the growing anti-British feeling in the city but this was the first time she had actually encountered it. 'I'm – I'm sure that most British people are most sympathetic to your cause, Madame –'

The woman snorted, pushed her ugly face closer to Kitty's. Kitty this time stubbornly stood her ground. 'Please – I'm looking for Jem O'Connell. Does he still live here?'

There was a short, expressive silence. 'O'Connell,' the fearsome woman said then, very clearly, having marshalled her linguistic reserves to the attack, 'is a no-good son of bitches. A lying, double-cross bastard –' She pronounced the last word in the French way, but there was no mistaking her meaning or her malice.

The expletives lost none of their force for being spoken in the incongruous, distorted English, yet Kitty found herself fighting suddenly a manic desire to laugh. She had heard stories in those long-gone days of a Suffolk schoolroom of the harpies who had sat at the foot of Madame Guillotine with their knitting as the heads rolled into the baskets; this, surely, must be a direct descendant of one of them. She swallowed hard, fighting down the dangerous possibility of hysterical laughter; she did not for a moment think she would find it funny if the awful woman chose to release the even more awful dog. The tirade had slipped into French now. She waited until the woman ran out of words before asking, 'What did he do?'

That brought a further stream of unintelligible outrage. Kitty concentrated, trying to make some sense of the words. Then, still screeching, the woman extended her free hand and rubbed thumb and forefinger together in an age-old gesture, and all become clear.

'He owes you money?' Kitty held up her hand to stop the excited flow of words. 'How much?'

The two short words brought a sudden silence. Crafty eyes squinted at her, taking in the good clothes and the jewellery and resting in sudden greed upon the gold chain that hung about Kitty's neck. 'Two 'undred francs.'

Kitty knew the sum must be outrageously exaggerated, but she did not argue. She unfastened the chain and held it out, swinging and glittering in the sunshine. 'Would this cover it?'

A rapacious, filthy hand reached out. Quicker, Kitty snatched the chain behind her back. 'Only if you tell me where he is,' she said, knowing as she said it her danger. If the woman chose simply to release her dog . . .

The sly eyes regarded her unblinking. The massive shoulders lifted. 'I don' know where 'e live.' There was no denying the careless truth of the words, Kitty knew that instinctively, her buoyed-up hopes collapsing. Then, 'But I know where 'e drinks –' the woman said.

The bar of *Le Mouchoir Rouge* was the converted front room of a Montmartre cottage, crowded, thick-hung with smoke, cheerfully noisy as a monkey-house. Kitty stood on the threshold trying to adjust her eyes to the gloom. The place was filled to bursting and echoed with chatter and laughter. Predominantly the customers were men, and Kitty recognized with lifting heart the hallmarks of the artistic fraternity – canvases were propped against the wooden tables, paint-stained hands waved in Gallic conversation, or lifted glasses to be swiftly drained and as swiftly refilled. The scattering of women among the customers had a look she recognized also – striking if not always pretty girls with the challenging poise of the professional model. The walls were covered in paintings of that school that Jem termed realist, and so admired. Ignoring the curiosity and unwelcome interest in the eyes of a group of men who stood close by the door she stood on tiptoe and surveyed the crowd.

'*Bonjour, Mam'selle* –' A young man had sidled close to her. She ignored him. He laughed, making a quick aside to his watching friends that brought a gale of laughter.

And then she saw him. Jem sat at a bare wooden table in a corner, a vociferous part of the rowdiest group in the room. He was smiling that wide, vivid smile that she found she remembered so well as a young man of florid complexion and flamboyant dress declaimed passionately, his hand on his heart. Other members of the party were chipping in noisily, obviously good-temperedly baiting the young man. As Kitty watched, a girl moved from her place at Jem's side, languidly draped a long arm about the passionate speaker's shoulders and kissed him long and hard upon the lips, thus forcibly stemming the stream of words to thunderous laughter and applause. At that moment, laughing, Jem turned and his eyes met hers. To her astonishment, knowing her own face to be alight with delight and greeting, she saw for a split second the laughter leave his face as if turned off by a switch, in its place a look of stunned and not altogether joyful surprise. Then the brilliant smile was back and he was across the room to her, hugging her, standing her from him to look at her, hugging her again, and she thought she must have imagined that strange moment of almost painful shock.

'Kitty! By all that's holy! What are you doing here? How on earth did you find me? Good God, girl, don't you know there's a war on?' She allowed herself to be swept to the table, acknowledged unheard introductions, clinging to his hand as if to her hope of salvation. She had found Jem. Against all the odds she had found him. Now everything would be all right.

'Luke dead. Jesus Christ.' Jem stood by the window of the airless and stifling attic that was his home, looking out with unseeing eyes across the wide and lovely vista of the roofs and spires of Paris to where the distant trees of the Bois shimmered in the heat. 'Dead,' he said again, and shook his shaggy fair head in a sharp movement, like a dog emerging from water, bemused disbelief and a muted grief in his eyes. 'And in such a way.'

Kitty said nothing. She had told her story steadily and without tears. Now she felt tired, drained of energy, almost without feeling.

'My God!' Jem came back to the table, splashed dark wine into a cracked cup, lifted the bottle questioningly to Kitty. She shook her head. He tossed the drink back, poured more, then lifted his light eyes to Kitty's. 'And you've come here – despite the war – to look for the child?'

'Yes.' Kitty put her hand in the pocket of her skirt and pulled out the crackling paper of the pencil sketch. 'This is all I have to go on.' She held it out to him, watching with suddenly bated breath as he smoothed the creases thoughtfully and moved back to the light of the window. 'Do you recognize it?'

He looked for a long moment, then shook his head. 'No.'

Obstinately she suppressed once again the dreary rise of disappointment. 'Would you – would you help me try to find it?'

He watched her in silence for a surprisingly long time, his face sombre. Then that well-remembered smile came again, fleetingly, warm and entirely charming. 'I sure will. I guess needles have been found in haystacks before.'

She pulled a face. 'You sound like Pol. And Genevieve. And Charles. Do you really think it's that bad?'

He shrugged a little. 'Who knows? We won't know until we try, will we? Have you tried the cab drivers?'

She stared at him. The simplest answer; and she had not thought of it. 'Oh, Jem – how stupid of me – no, I haven't.'

'Right.' He smiled again, and her heart lifted with hope. He toasted her with the battered cup, and for a moment it seemed to her that the gesture was wry, strangely self-mocking. 'That's where we'll start.'

* * *

But yet again her hopes were doomed to disappointment. Try as they might over the next few days as they wandered the chaotic city streets that were a shambles of military vehicles and personnel, of wheeled gun carriages, ponderous cannon, marching men and heaped wagons of supplies, they could find no one who recognized Kitty's picture. At last, on the day that they stood with the rest of cheering Paris and watched a tired-looking Louis Napoleon ride out of the city at the head of his colourfully uniformed army, they had to admit that the idea, good as it had been, had produced no positive result.

'But at least,' Jem pointed out as they watched the gallant cavalry parade past, colours bravely flying, 'we do know something.'

'What?'

He turned to look at her. 'If the cab drivers of the city don't know the place, then it isn't in fashionable Paris, is it?'

She shook her head. 'I suppose not.'

'I know Montmartre like the back of my hand. It isn't there either, I'll stake the price of my next meal on that. So – at least we've narrowed the field a bit –' He glanced at her again, grinning like a boy. 'How do your feet feel?'

'Fine. Why?'

He ran his hand through his untidy hair, tossing it back from his eyes. 'Because from now on, little Songbird, we walk.' The use of the old nickname was entirely natural. She was astonished at the small stab of pain it brought. 'We'll pound the pavements of Paris and we'll find that confounded statue if it's the last thing we do.'

They quartered the city, poring over a map that Charles had produced for them. Genevieve looked on in sympathetic exasperation, her practical nature outraged by the whole venture. 'But – Kitty! Chérie! You cannot comb the whole of the city!'

'Oh, yes I can.' Kitty straightened, pushing the heavy dark

hair from her eyes, drawing a small sharp breath as a hot needle of pain stabbed at her injured arm. 'Michael's out there. I'm going to find him.'

Jem had glanced at her quickly. 'You okay?'

She nodded, though the sudden angry pain in her arm had taken her breath away. Impatiently she tried to ignore it; the arm had been all but healed when she left England – why should it be bothering her now? 'I'm fine.'

He looked at her for a moment longer, probing. She turned from him, back to the map. 'Where do we start?'

But in the days that followed, as they tramped the streets of the city and as the war news swung in a few short, disastrous days from victory at Saarbrucken to terrible and bloody defeat for the French army at Wissenbourg and Spicheren, the pain in her arm worsened. Beneath the bandages the skin was inflamed and burning. As the war news, all bad, filtered back to the city a new, darker mood engulfed Paris. The gay, improvident enthusiasm of those first days was gone entirely, and in its place a dangerous and unsettling disaffection, fostered and encouraged as always by the extreme Republicans for whom this city, the very cradle of violent revolution, had always been a breeding ground. A long, dispiriting retreat by the bulk of the French army had begun, falling back towards Paris. Suddenly the monstrous possibility of a Prussian army at the gates of the city became more than a nightmare with which to frighten children. Chanting mobs roamed the streets and packed the squares; street orators, who had waited, patiently, upon the hour, came from their attics and their cellars to whip up anti-government feeling and to preach righteous revolution. By the end of the second week in August passions were at white heat and it had become dangerous for any foreigner to be found on the street by the unstable, excited mobs. Jem himself was relatively safe – his French, though slightly accented, could pass as native. But Kitty had no such safeguard.

'It's no good,' Jem said, firmly, 'we'll have to give up for a while. Give them a chance to settle down. I'm not risking having you walk into a mob that mistakes you for Madame Bismarck. They all but lynched a woman in the Rue Royale yesterday. And anyway' – he held up a narrow hand to still her protest – 'you're looking done in. You need a rest.'

In fact she needed rather more than that, and in the end she had to admit it. When she at last shamefacedly showed Genevieve her swollen and obviously infected arm her friend was horrified and justifiably angry. 'You idiot! How long has it been like that? *Mon Dieu!* You could lose the arm!' The Parisots had over the past weeks become increasingly worried over the situation in the city, and the strain showed on Genevieve's face and in her shortened temper. The theatres had closed. Kitty knew her friend were contemplating leaving the city, suspected a little guiltily that she was the main reason for their staying. 'I'll send for a doctor at once,' Genevieve said briskly and, with a quick glance that Kitty did not miss, added, 'You cannot think of travelling with such an arm.'

Kitty lifted her head sharply. 'Travelling? Travelling where?'

Genevieve was already halfway to the door. She spoke over her shoulder. 'We are going to the south – and of course you must come with us. We cannot wait here to be trapped like rats by the Prussians, or murdered in our beds by revolutionaries. You've heard the news? That there's insurrection in the city?' She did not wait for a reply. 'And more defeats. Bazaine's retreat has been cut off. There is no one – no one! – to protect us.'

'Gené –' Kitty cut in, desperately.

Genevieve rushed on. 'God only knows what will happen to Paris now. So you see – we must go. All of us. But first – a doctor for your arm.'

In the silence left by her going Kitty, nursing her now agonizingly painful arm, crossed to the window and looked out. The wide, beautiful boulevard was all but deserted, though beneath the window lay a broken placard and some leaflets, remnants of a noisy demonstration an hour or so earlier. On the pavement opposite, sitting on the kerb, his

feet in the gutter, sat a dispirited-looking soldier, his rifle
discarded beside him, his uniform filthy and his cap gone,
in its place a bloodstained bandage. He seemed to Kitty to
personify the broken hopes of that gallant army that had
marched from the city, colours flying and bands playing,
such a very short time before. As she watched, a file of
Zouaves shambled by in the charge of a mounted officer.
Their flamboyant uniforms were worn and dirty; they
walked like men sleepwalking. The man on the pavement
did not even lift his head to watch them pass. For the first
time and through a rising haze of fever Kitty found herself
in the grip of dread. It did not need an experienced eye to
perceive that these were the harbingers of disaster, the
remnants of a defeated and impotent army. She had at last
to accept the truth, that she had steadily ignored for so long:
the enemy, any day, might indeed be at the gates of Paris.
And Michael was somewhere here in the city, unprotected.
Her head thumped. The skin of her face burned drily. She
would not leave Paris. She could not. Not until she had
found her son.

Genevieve and the doctor found her an hour later
crouched upon Genevieve's elegant chaise-longue, trembling with fever, her skin on fire. Muttering and protesting
incoherently she was put to bed, cool damp cloths laid upon
her blazing body, the infected arm lanced and bandaged,
bitter medicine forced down her throat. The next many
hours were lost to her completely, in pain and delirium.
Luke came to her and she called to him, desperate, as he
turned from her. Michael played upon the bed, his dear,
sunny little face turned brightly to her before crumpling to
heartrending tears as unknown hands tore him from her.
She fell then it seemed into a pit of darkness shot with
flame. For an endless time she struggled, calling on Luke,
on Jem, on someone – anyone – to help her. And then at
last help came. A firm, cool hand held hers, a voice spoke,
calmly and encouragingly. 'Luke,' she said. 'Thank God.'
And she lasped into healing sleep.

She woke to dust-motes dancing in the gleams of sunlight

that knifed through the gaps in the closed shutters. It was very hot. Through the half-open door she could hear sounds of near-frantic activity in the apartment. She moved her head a little. Beside her, asleep in the chair, his fair head lolling at a painful angle, his sharp-boned face in shadow, was Jem. At her movement he started awake and leaned forward. 'Kitty? You're awake?'

'Yes.' The whispered word surprised her by its weakness and by the effort it took to speak.

'Are you feeling better?' With the efficiency of practice he laid his cool hand on her forehead.

'Yes, thank you, doctor.'

That brought a slight smile, yet still it seemed to her that a faint shadow lay across his face as he looked at her. 'The fever's gone, thank God. I'll call Gené.'

He left her for a moment. She lay taking careful stock of herself – of her appalling weakness, of the faint soreness still in her arm, although the awful knife-point pain of infection had gone, of the dryness of her cracked lips. She closed her eyes for a moment, and when she opened them again Genevieve was there, smiling.

'How long – have I been ill?'

'Two days. Nearly three.' As Jem had done Genevieve laid a hand upon her forehead and nodded with satisfaction. 'You'd like a cool drink?'

'Yes. Please. Gené – what's happened?'

Genevieve hesitated. Then she shrugged. 'It's bad, I'm afraid. The Emperor no longer commands the army. Half of our men are besieged within the city of Metz. The other half – who knows? They move, so it is said, towards a place called Sedan. The war is lost, I think. And Paris – Paris seethes.' She sat on the bed, carefully took Kitty's thin hand. 'Kitty, we cannot fool ourselves any longer. In a very short while Paris herself will be in danger. We must leave. We are packing now. We have been waiting for you to recover so that you may travel with us.'

'I'm not coming.'

'Kitty – there is no choice! You cannot stay.'

'I'm not coming.' Her voice was still weak. She shook her head upon the pillow. 'I can't. Don't you see?'

'But you must.'

'No.' The new voice, from the open doorway, was firm. Jem crossed the room, knelt by the bed, laid a gentle hand upon hers. His pale eyes were very serious. 'Kitty. Look at me. Now. You should go. Everything that Gené says is right. It's the only sensible thing. Will you go?'

'No.'

He nodded. 'That's what I thought. Very well. We both stay.'

Inexpressible relief moved in her, and showed upon her face. 'You'll stay with me?'

Genevieve, disbelief and exasperation getting the better of her, jumped to her feet. 'Are you both mad?'

For a long, strange moment Jem held Kitty's eyes with his own, and again she was aware of that inexplicable shadow of sorrow that haunted his face, changing it. He grinned then, and the shadow fled. 'What would I do in the south? It's always raining.'

To the Parisots' concern and continued exasperation, no arguments would change their minds. Genevieve, anxiously tending the still-ailing Kitty whilst her husband made the last-minute arrangements for their departure, threw up her hands at last in despair. 'But what will you do? Where will you go? Charles has given up the lease on the apartment.'

'I know.' Propped amongst the pillows, Kitty was very pale but totally determined. 'I have plenty of money, Gené. Jem has rented me a small apartment in Montmartre, not far from his room. I'll be all right, Gené dear – he'll look after me –'

Genevieve gave her a long look, shaking her head in disbelief then, oddly, laughed suddenly. 'Yes. I'm sure he will.'

Two days later, with news spreading through the city that the second of France's battered armies lay besieged and

helpless within Sedan, the Parisots left, having first efficiently supervised Kitty's removal to the small, shabby but
comfortable apartment on the heights of Montmartre that
Jem had found for her. Genevieve's last, thoughtful service
before she left was to acquire for Kitty a little maid, cousin
to her own Jeanne-Marie, whose bright smile, willing nature
and smattering of English promised well. There were tearful
goodbyes, last-minute pleas which Kitty adamantly resisted,
and then her good friends were gone. Kitty sat in bed,
propped upon pillows, and looked out of the window at the
vista of sunlit Paris laid out before her. Michael was there
somewhere. She banished the doubts that crowded her
mind. She knew he was there. As always in such situations
it was the rich who were able to flee – leaving the poor, who
could not, to face the consequences. If Lottie were here with
the children it was unlikely in the extreme that she would
be able to leave. And Kitty would find her. Today, tomorrow,
sometime – she would find her.

It was a week before she was properly on her feet again.
By then Sedan had fallen, the Emperor had been captured
and the French army hardly existed except in scattered
remnants about the country. The capital lay helpless before
the advance of an invader whose new war-cry was '*Nach
Paris!*' Two days after the disaster of Sedan the Republicans
of Paris rose and stormed the Hôtel de Ville, helped by
the Paris National Guard whose democratic ranks were
thoroughly permeated with Republican sympathizers. Amid
scenes of confusion and wild celebration a new national
government was proclaimed – a government, as had happened so often before, constituted in Paris, by Parisians, and
of Parisians, with no note taken of the rest of France. The
Empress Eugénie, hated by the mob, fled the city barely
with her life as the mob stormed the Tuileries and turbulent
history repeated itself yet again. It was victory for the new
Republic with – more by luck than by judgement – not a
single drop of French blood shed.

For a while wild optimism invested the city – the enemy,
surely, had no quarrel with the people of France as they had

had with their Imperial masters? The Emperor was captured, disgraced, deposed – what more could they want? The Prussian armies could now, with honour, withdraw. But, of course, they did not. Sustained by seemingly endless supplies of excellent looted wine, they continued their all-but-unopposed march on Paris. Beaten remnants of the French armies trailed back into the city. Their camps filled the Champs Elysées and the Champ de Mars where a scant three years earlier the triumphant Exhibition had dominated fashionable Paris. By the time, a few days after the coup, Kitty was well enough to venture into the streets she was appalled at what she saw; the city had been turned into a fortress. Sheep grazed in the woods, the gardens and the squares. Fortifications and military encampments were everywhere. The bridges that spanned the Seine were barricaded, the walls of the city were being strengthened and armed as were the forts that ringed them. In the sweltering heat soldiers, National Guard and civilians laboured side by side: and in the way of such things their work had become a popular entertainment for the sightseers of the city for whom a day out inspecting the fortifications of Paris had become a regular pastime. Day by day as the euphoria once again died the mood of the city became more determined. Paris would never be defeated. With no respite from the heat the defenders worked feverishly to fortify the city that a few months before had been the fabled and fabulous *Ville Lumière*. Kitty, her good common sense restored with her health, drew a considerable amount of her capital from the bank and with the small maid, Louise, embarked upon several extremely tiring but successful shopping expeditions, thinking wryly more than once as she did so of those earlier sprees with Genevieve in the elegant arcades of the Rue de Rivoli. Of course, her reason told her as she surveyed their stock of supplies, the Germans would never reach Paris; the rest of Europe – the world! – would surely not allow that to happen? But, just in case, it was as well to be prepared.

And still the Prussian armies advanced.

On September 15 a train heading north from the Gare du Nord was captured.

Two days later the implacable German pincers closed about the city and Paris – the glittering heart of the civilized world, the jewel of Europe – was under siege.

6

(i)

It was three weeks from the day that Paris was cut off from the rest of the world that Kitty and Jem at last discovered the whereabouts of the square with the dolphin statue – three weeks during which the first battle of the siege was fought and lost to the demoralization of beleaguered citizens and soldiery alike. As the French attack failed in face of superior Prussian arms and military discipline, deserters from the defending army fled back to the city in their hundreds. Panic spread through the streets and the wildest of rumours flew. The National Government had surrendered – had fled the city – were treating for peace – had been shot out of hand. When the disastrous two days of the sortie were over, Parisians found themselves facing the simple, grim fact that nothing had changed; except that they, and their government, were more tightly penned in than ever – two million souls encircled by the iron and fire of one of the most efficient military machines the century could produce, an army that with the short sight of supreme self-confidence the French had publicly laughed to scorn just three years before. On 20 September, Prussian Uhlans took Versailles with no shot fired, and the fearsome encirclement was complete. There were after that a few skirmishes of no great import except to those who were killed in them. In the last days of the month as the oddly peaceful streets and boulevards still sweltered beneath a blazing sun a strange quiet descended on the city, a quiet disturbed only by the optimistic stir caused three days after the fall of Versailles by the successful launching of the hot air balloon *Neptune* in a triumphant attempt to communicate with the outside world. Kitty and Jem were among the crowds that cheered the gallant Douroff as he lifted from the high ground at the foot of the Solferino Tower in Montmartre, his hastily patched balloon gracefully bobbing in the clear air as it drifted in proud defiance over the flabbergasted enemy encampments.

Within days a new industry had blossomed in the besieged city as in the now useless and silent vast station buildings of Paris men, women and children laboured to produce more balloons and to patch up those others existing in the city – most of them sad souvenirs of the Great Exhibition. In a remarkably short time a 'balloon post' was established, with balloons flying two or three times a week: and if it could not be denied that their destinations were uncertain – for no one had devised a way to guide the things – the effect on the morale of the city's defenders was understandably substantial. Paris was not, after all, totally cut off from the civilized world, even though the traffic was entirely one-way. On 8 October Léon Gambetta, Minister of the Interior, bravely volunteered to be ballooned out of the city to help organize resistance in the rest of France and effect the raising of the siege. As the balloon *Armand Barbès* lifted, the unstable basket spinning and swinging, Gambetta unfurled the gallant banner of the Tricolor and the watching crowds cheered him to the echo. But then once more the silence of siege descended and, as it became increasingly obvious that the Prussians had no intention of wasting men and resources in trying to take the city by direct assault, the boredom of anti-climax and forced incarceration depressed spirits and once more lowered morale. The theatres were closed and a ten o'clock curfew imposed upon the dark and all but deserted streets of what had been just a few months before acknowledged as the gayest city in the world. Troops cooped up in barracks and temporary encampments with nothing more to do but endlessly reinforce the city's defences and to keep watch over an enemy well dug-in, secure and apparently perfectly happy, drank and gambled and quarrelled and listened in idleness to the left-wing agitators for whom such a captive audience was the answer to a prayer. On the day in October that Jem burst into Kitty's apartment, the tattered sketch in one hand and what proved to be a bottle of very fine champagne in the other, disaffected National Guards and enraged citizens had marched for the second time in seven days upon the Hôtel de Ville to demand action – any action – from the government of General Trochu, who not for the first and most certainly not for the last time was faced with as much of a threat from within as without the city.

Kitty, standing by the window, turned in surprise at Jem's obvious excitement. 'Champagne? Jem – what on earth are you up to?' She stopped, her eyes wide. 'Jem! You haven't – you haven't found something?'

'I have, my Songbird, I have, I have, I have! And in such a way that I could kick both of us for not having thought of it before! Fetch the glasses.'

Kitty ran to the tiny kitchen, returned with two glasses. 'What? Oh, Jem – don't be a beast! – what?'

The champagne cork popped loudly. With a flourish Jem poured the foaming stuff into the glasses. Smiling teasingly, he offered her a glass. Uncharacteristically she all but stamped her foot in wild impatience. 'Jem! If you don't want this poured down your silly neck –'

He lifted his glass, still grinning. 'A toast,' he said, 'to Miss Lily Daltrey.'

'Who's –' She stopped. 'You haven't discovered her name?'

'Her name – and where she lives. The square with the dolphin statue is over the river, in Montparnasse, near the cemetery. So far as my informant knows, the lovely Miss Daltrey still resides there. Your champagne's going flat.'

Staring at him, she had not even tasted it. 'How? How did you find her?'

'I went to *Le Chat Fou*, off St Germain. Idiot I was not to have thought of it before! It's a great hang-out of the street-artists. I asked around and – *voilà!* Sure enough someone recognized the style. A guy called Hugo Sanchon drew the picture. I found him and he remembered the ladies very well. Especially the lovely Lily. She was his model for a while. And more, I suspect. Lord, woman, don't expect me to buy you champagne again! It's wasted on you!'

Laughing, she sipped the sparkling drink and in her excitement almost choked. 'Champagne! With the Prussians camped on our doorsteps! It's ridiculous!'

· 'Outrageous. But very Parisian, *non*?' He topped up her glass and his own, ran a hand through his thick, untidy hair. 'Butter – if you can discover any – may be upwards of ten francs a pound, we may be eating horsemeat, fresh vegetables may have run out already; but the city, thank God for His mercy, is absolutely awash with alcohol. The story is that we've food for six weeks and alcohol for six months – so the outlook isn't so bad after all, is it? It might have been the other way round – perish the thought!' With that boyish, incorrigibly cheerful smile he tossed back the drink in his glass, took a quick swig from the bottle. 'Get your coat. We've got a call to make.'

She entered the small, shabby square with an odd and unexpected shock of recognition. She had studied its image so frequently, imagined the moment of finding it so often that it seemed to her that the place was as well known to her as her own back garden. The face, too, of the young woman who opened the door to Jem's jaunty rapping was uncannily familiar; the wide, feline eyes, the pouting mouth, the luxurious, heavy hair – the artist had captured her beauty perfectly. What he had not succeeded in getting onto paper – perhaps indeed he had not tried – was the hard, rapacious set of that luscious mouth, the calculating look in the light, heartless eyes.

'*Oui?*' Her look was suspicious.

'Miss Daltrey?' Jem turned on his most spectacular smile, 'Miss Lily Daltrey?' Half exasperated, Kitty noted the faint, charming exaggeration of his already attractive accent, saw the gleam of interest in the cat-like eyes.

''Oo's askin'?' The girl's voice was unpleasantly and incongruously harsh.

'My name's Jem O'Connell. This is Miss Daniels. We wondered – could you spare us a moment of your valuable time?'

The girl did not move. Nor did the calculating gaze flicker. 'What for?'

'We're looking for someone,' Kitty said. 'A – mutual friend I think – Lottie Smith?'

The girl did not conceal well enough the flicker of wariness that crossed her face. 'Never 'eard of 'er.'

'Oh, but surely –' Jem, still pleasantly smiling and radiating the most irresistible charm, moved a foot to block the closing door. He fished in the inner pocket of his jacket, pulled out the battered sketch and held it out to her. 'I spoke to Hugo just this morning. He remembers you as being the best of friends –'

'Sod Hugo,' she said. 'What's it got ter do with 'im? Or you?'

'We're looking for Lottie,' Kitty said. 'She's in Paris. We thought she might have got in touch with you?' She had reached into her pocket and pulled out a small roll of banknotes, stood tapping them idly with the tips of her fingers.

Lily Daltrey shook her head, but her eyes displayed interest.

'What a pity.' Very deliberately Kitty fingered the notes, then made as if to tuck them back into her pocket.

'Wait. You might as well come in.' Ungraciously the girl moved back to let them pass. 'Straight on. Through the curtain.'

As they entered the small sitting room Kitty and Jem exchanged a swift, half-amused glance. The room was like a cheap and gaudy stage set for *The Arabian Nights*. Garishly coloured shawls were flung across low divans, an enormous, moth-eaten tigerskin rug, the head glaring lopsidedly with one filmed glass eye, lay upon the floor. Long-fringed lamps and beaded curtains completed the bizarre illusion. 'What you buyin'?' the girl asked from behind them, bluntly.

'What are you selling?'

She eyed first Jem, then Kitty. 'Somethin' you want I guess.' She held out a flat, shapely hand.

Ignoring Jem's quickly-cast, warning look Kitty peeled a note from the roll and laid it upon the girl's open palm. The long fingers curled, signalling greedily. Kitty peeled off another note. Both disappeared without trace into the shadowed cleft between the girl's full breasts. Kitty saw Jem watching the deft movement with interest.

Lily Daltrey lifted her head. 'All right. Yer entitled to what bit I know. Yes. She came 'ere. 'Er an' them bleedin' nippers.'

'Nippers?' Kitty asked sharply, trying to quell the sudden, shocking turmoil in her stomach. 'What nippers?'

''Er nippers. Girl an' a boy. 'Ere – I thought yer said yer knew 'er?' She peered at Kitty suspiciously.

'We do.' It was all that Kitty could do to control her shaking voice. 'The little girl – Poppy?'

'Yeah. That's right.'

'And the little boy? Is it – Michael?'

The girl nodded. 'Mick they call 'im.'

Kitty thought for a moment that she might faint. Relief and terror fought within her – relief that, through it all, she had been right, Lottie was with Michael in Paris – and terror that after coming so close something still might prevent her from finding her son.

Jem slid a light supporting arm about her waist. 'Where are they now?' he asked, quietly.

It seemed an age before the girl answered. 'I dunno,' she said.

Kitty caught a shocked breath. 'But – surely! Please! You must know! I'll pay you! Anything you want!'

The girl shook her head, the mercenary regret in her eyes obviously and shatteringly genuine.

'What happened?' Jem asked.

She shrugged. 'They stayed 'ere for a bit. It was all right

at first, though the kids was a nuisance. It's difficult 'avin' nippers about when yer tryin' ter earn a decent livin' – fellers don't like knowin' there's kids in the place. But then she got sick.'

'Lottie?'

'Yeah – well – I wasn't 'avin' that, was I?' The lovely face was the very picture of injured innocence. 'I mean – I could 'a' caught somethin', couldn't I? An' I've got a livin' to earn. Gotta be careful, you know? An' what with 'er gettin' so thin an' all – she looked a bleedin' bag o' bones. Wasn't bringin' in a sou. An' I mean – I'm not a bleedin' charitable institution, am I?'

'You threw her out,' Kitty said.

'Yeah – well, I 'ad to, didn't I? Like I said, I got meself ter think about. Be sure no other bugger does –'

'When?' Kitty asked.

The girl considered. 'Oh, I dunno – two, three weeks ago – somethin' like that. Just after the bleedin' pickle-stickers arrived.'

'Pickle-stickers?'

'The Germans,' Jem supplied. His eyes on her face were full of sympathy.

She tightened her jaw. In her head, furiously, beat the knowledge that Michael had been here – here in this very apartment – whilst she had been hunting on the other side of the city. The thought almost physically nauseated her. 'Have you no idea where she went?'

'Nope.' The girl made a brief, sour grimace that might have been a smile. 'We didn't exactly part the best o' friends. She didn't leave no forwardin' address.'

'Did she have any money?'

Lily shook her head, and rightly interpreting Kitty's look of bleak anger lifted her shoulders in a shrug. 'Ain't my fault, is it?'

'You threw her out, sick, with two children to care for and no money?'

'Seems like it, don't it?'

Appalled, Kitty recognized in the girl's attitude not bravado but an injured certainty that she was in the right, an absolute lack of anything of regret or conscience.

Jem took her arm. His face was shadowed with disgust. 'Come on, Kit. We'll get nothing else here.'

She pulled away from him, still facing the girl. 'The little boy – Michael – was he all right?'

Lily eyed her curiously. 'Last time I saw 'im – yeah, 'e was fine.'

'If you hear or see anything of them – anything! – will you come to me?' Kitty was hastily scribbling her address on a corner of the sketch. She tore if off and handed it to the girl. 'If you help us find them I promise I'll make it worth your while.'

''Ow much?'

Kitty did not hesitate. 'Fifteen hundred francs.'

The girl whistled between her teeth. 'You really want 'em, don't you?'

'Just one more thing. If you do see Lottie – I don't want her to know. I want to – to surprise her.'

The girl smiled, craftily. 'That's all right by me.'

Blindly and with no farewell Kitty turned and pushed her way back through the beaded curtain to the front door.

This time the disappointment was crushing; for now there were no more straws, no more flimsy hopes to cling to. Yet she would not, could not, give up. Michael was here, in the beleaguered city, in the charge of a sick and penniless woman; and though she knew that her chances of finding him had surely plummeted to nothing, doggedly and despite Jem's fiercely worried warnings she walked the blighted streets, ignoring the dangers. She visited the overcrowded convents where scores of lost and homeless children had found refuge, she loitered outside schools, hunted through the all but empty market places, but all, of course, to no avail. As she walked the unnaturally quiet streets she found herself scanning the faces that passed her. The cry of a child would set her heart racing, her eyes searching for that one small gypsy-dark head.

The weather now had broken at last, and broken with a vengeance. In the place of the blazing heat a chill cold had enveloped the hard-pressed city, unseasonably early. Time trickled on, and the strange, nervous strain of inaction and ever present threat strung tempers to breaking point once again. Acting too late, in mid-October the government at last rationed meat – but by now supplies were so low that only a hundred grammes a week could be allowed. Jem, Kitty and the little Louise ate frugally of the supplies Kitty had laid in, supplementing them wherever possible with food bought from outside. When Kitty was not engaged on her obstinate and hopeless search for the child, she and Louise stood in endless queues in the damp, bone-chilling cold while Jem, in a remarkably short time, became adept at being the first to track down a black market source for meat, or fish, for fresh vegetables or even, on one memorable occasion, for fresh milk, which few people in Paris had tasted since the siege had begun. In the way of such things, despite disaster and extraordinary circumstance, life assumed a pattern that oddly parodied normality; by day the simple necessities of existence took up most of their combined time and effort, in the evening after Louise had left to join her own family – usually with some small supplement for their store cupboard – Jem and Kitty, in a happy echo of those peaceful times at La Source, would sit before the meagre fire in Kitty's apartment and play cards, or talk, sipping the wine of which there still seemed to be an unending supply – indeed, it was as Jem had predicted the only thing in the city of which there was no shortage.

Often Jem would sketch as they talked and, over her laughing protests, his thick pad soon became filled with a succession of pictures of Kitty – curled into an armchair, huddled against the cold, laughing, frowning, talking, staring pensively into the flames of the small, precious fire. The life of Paris too, despite the exigencies of a besieged city – the shortages, the barricades, the lack of freedom, the tensely quiet streets – paralleled their own and had achieved a strange sense of normalcy. Some of the theatres had re-opened. The cafés were full again. The smarter restaurants even still managed to produce passable meals and varied menus – though it did not pay for the squeamish to enquire too far into the ingredients of the more exotic dishes. As always it was the poor who suffered most as prices soared and winter closed in. Beyond the ring of defending forts smoke from the enemy camp fires rose, whilst within the walls the strange combination of stress and tedium was disturbed only by the usual wild rumours that everyone had on the highest authority. The Prussians were about to shell the city. A French army was advancing from the south – the north – the east – the west. The Reds were planning open revolution.

Beneath the surface disaffection and dissatisfaction with the 'popular' government that had been swept to power in the coup of less than two months before was growing. Resentment in the working areas at the comparative affluence of the better-off flickered like a small, angry fire in undergrowth tinder-dry and ready to flare. At the end of October the boredom and frustration felt by the besieged forces were personified by an idiotic attack upon the village of Le Bourget. The attack – on an indefensible and strategically useless hamlet occupied a little shakily by the Prussian army under the French guns of the Forts de l'Est and Aubervilliers – was ordered by a brigadier so ambitious to achieve personal glory and advancement – and to ease the crushing boredom of inaction – that he did not bother to inform the government of his intended action. The result was disaster; an early, comparatively easy victory turning to punitive and ignominious defeat. From their eyrie above the city Kitty and Jem watched the distant flicker of flame, the rise of smoke, listened to the echo of cannon and rifle fire. As reports of the atrocious casualties sustained by the French reached the city, fury at the waste and incompetence blazed and, once again, in one of those troubled and bewildering swings so characteristic of Parisian politics rebellion flared and the chanting mobs were on the streets again.

'For Heaven's sake!' Kitty said to Jem, helplessly, 'I just

don't believe it! They're all on the same side, aren't they? I mean – the Germans are at the very gates of the city – and still they fight amongst themselves?' She shook her head. 'I'll never understand it.'

'Change is never easy to understand.' Jem was on his knees by the fireplace, feeding into the flickering flames slithers of a precious packing case that he had – Kitty had not enquired too deeply how – acquired for fuel. 'The politics of the world are close to upheaval, Kitty – and the roots of that upheaval are right here in Paris. The working people here have learned their lessons in a hard school. They have learned not to trust their masters. They have learned – a little – their own strength, and that is the most dangerous of all. And in Paris itself they have learned that if you rule the streets you rule the city, and if you take the city you take the country.' He sat back on his heels, rubbing his dirty hands thoughtfully together. 'One day,' he said, 'there will be a revolution somewhere that will change the balance of the world.'

She looked at him, surprised at his unusual solemnity. 'Here. Now?'

He shook his head. 'I shouldn't think so, though they might try. But it's too early. There are no real leaders. And perhaps, too, a nation that has experienced the trauma of one bloodbath in the name of equality and freedom is reluctant, underneath it all, to instigate another.'

'What is going to happen then? Now, I mean?'

He pulled a funny, rueful face. 'My dear girl, if I knew that then I'd make a fortune as a clairvoyant!'

What did happen was that another chanting, screaming mob marched yet again on the seat of government, the Hôtel de Ville, and – after charge and counter-charge, threat and counter-threat, betrayal and counter-betrayal – there was yet another mob-inspired change of government. On Tuesday 1 November Paris woke up on a dismal, streaming morning to another day of siege and privation and a new set of masters. On the same day the grim news – several times vehemently and officially denied over the past few days –

was confirmed that Metz had been starved into submission, another French army was captured and more Prussian troops were free to join those encamped in comfort about Paris. It was on that day that Jem announced his entirely unexpected decision to serve with the American Ambulance, the field hospital that had been, with strange foresight, purchased lock, stock and barrel and kept in the city by a rich and philanthropic American after its showing at the Paris Exhibition. Its reputation was fabled: it was said that half the ranks and most of the officers of the defending forces carried into battle cards to the effect that, if wounded, they would be happier surrendered to the ministrations of the American Ambulance than of some other rather less efficient medical establishment.

'But –' Kitty, unexpectedly, found herself shamingly piqued that he should consider doing such a thing. The Ambulance would take his time, would be bound to distract him from – from what? From her. The plangent voice of honesty, long ignored in the matter of her relationship with Jem, suddenly refused to quiet. 'But won't it be awfully dangerous?' she asked, a little lamely; not at all what she had started to say.

He shook his head. There was a new lightness in his step, a new purpose in his boyish voice. Fiercely, and she had to admit thoroughly unreasonably, she found she resented it. 'It's only dangerous if there's a real battle. And the way things stand at the moment that doesn't seem very likely.'

Irritated, she did not miss the tinge of dissatisfaction at that state of affairs. 'Well don't sound so put out about that,' she snapped. 'You'd rather get yourself killed?' Her voice was irrationally tart. She flushed. 'I'm sorry,' she said quickly, unsuccessfully attempting a smile. 'Siege nerves.'

He looked at her for a long moment, and once again, as so often despite his apparent openness and charm, the strange shadow of reserve that she found herself so frequently and usually successfully having to ignore lay between them.

The days that followed were days of bitter cold, of a noticeable diminution of supplies of all kinds, of communal depression and of the beginnings of a new fear. In the first week in November smallpox claimed five hundred lives in the city. Other diseases too had begun to attack the weakened population. Food was running out; the meat ration – when it could be obtained at all – was reduced by half. Prices had become outrageous. Kitty, as with others rather better-off than their fellows, still managed not to deplete her emergency store too severely: the way things were going, who knew how vital those provisions might eventually become? And, always and without let, the thought of Michael – increasingly of Lottie, Poppy and Michael – haunted her. Where were they? How were they surviving? Were they even still alive? Smallpox. Typhoid. Pneumonia. Starvation.

On Christmas Day Michael would be three years old.

Jem's duties with the Ambulance turned out in fact not to be too demanding, and she still saw him frequently. In mid-November, as belated news reached the city of an isolated victory for French arms west of Orléans, just seventy miles from the beleaguered capital, and the weary population defiantly found the energy to celebrate, Kitty, determinedly, bought her first skilfully butchered and pre-pared cat and they ate more satisfyingly than they had for weeks.

'I can't help hating the thought of it,' she admitted ruefully to Jem. 'Though why pretending it's lamb should have made it easier to cook and eat I really don't know! What's the difference, for Heaven's sake, between a poor little dead lamb and a cat! Still, I must say that somehow – I don't know why – I just don't ever see myself being able to eat dog, no matter how hungry I get.'

He grinned, and quite suddenly she noticed how thin his face had become. For the first time it occurred to her to wonder about her own looks. Her fingers strayed to her face, sensed the drawn skin, the sharp line of bone. 'I'm sorry –?'

'I said, "You English!" You and your dogs! You treat them better than you treat your –' He stopped, the teasing laughter leaving his face.

She looked down at her plate, eyes blurring.

'Kitty! – Oh, damn it! – Kitty – I'm sorry –' He was beside her in a moment, his arm about her shoulders.

She shook her head. 'It's all right. It's just –'

'God, when will I ever learn to keep my big mouth shut! Of all the stupid, insensitive –'

'No.' In a perfectly natural gesture of affection she leaned her head against his shoulder, lifted her hand to stroke his face. 'No, you aren't –'

She sensed the change in him, the stiffening, the drawing away. She lifted her head, hurt in her eyes. 'Jem?'

He stood up, dropped a quick, brotherly kiss onto the top of her head and stepped back. 'I have to go. I'm on duty at eight.'

She had to face it. And, huddled miserably in bed that night, cold to the bone, shivering, alone, she finally did. In the past weeks her feelings for Jem, slowly, almost imperceptibly, had changed. Until that moment this afternoon she had not herself suspected the extent of that change: in face of his adamant refusal to acknowledge it had not, perhaps, wanted to admit to it. But it was there, and she could no longer ignore it. Over these past few weeks of close contact with Jem had grown a longing for more than his friendship, more than the easy camaraderie that they had shared for so many years. She closed her eyes, tried to think honestly. She was lonely, and she was frightened. Out there in the darkness lurked, horribly, the permanent threat of violence; of bombardment, of attack, of God knew what nightmares. Somewhere in the city her small son starved – might indeed already be dead. The anguish of that was a constant in her life. She knew the danger of those pressures, understood the influence they may well have had on her feelings for Jem. But she knew also, very certainly, that although they may, like the warmth of a hothouse, have forced the swifter growth of something that under normal circumstances might have taken more time, in no way were they the root cause of her feelings. She wanted Jem, wanted him beside her; thin, warm body, thin strong hands, thin dearly loved face –

But he did not want her.

There was no denying it now, in the honesty of the bleak, dark small hours of a November morning. Incident after incident, stubbornly ignored, proved it – a hand withdrawn, a touch deflected, that infuriating, light, friendly kiss. Always the gentle, considerate withdrawal from her.

She turned restlessly, stared into darkness, the tears icecold on her cheeks before they ever reached the pillow.

(ii)

When Jem arrived the next day she found herself looking at him with new eyes. Always slight, he was now downright thin, though that in her eyes in no way detracted from his physical attraction. The privations of the past few weeks had in fact produced a wiry toughness which had never been in evidence before. The boyish looks, enhanced as they were by the thatch of invariably untidy hair were, she knew, deceptive. The wide, sensitive mouth, that still smiled so readily, had yet firmed and hardened since those first days she had known him in London, when they had danced in the Cremorne Gardens on the night of Luke Peveral's birthday. Covertly now she watched him as, like a brigand with his loot, he displayed the results of his latest foray.

'*Violà!* Potatoes – one, two, three – what do you think of that?'

'Wonderful!'

'And – two carrots and a cabbage. A cabbage?' He held up the sorry-looking object, grimacing comically, then shrugged philosophically. 'A cabbage.'

'Where on earth did you get these?'

Secretively, he touched the side of his bony nose with an equally bony finger. 'I know a man.'

She laughed.

He put his hand into the sack again. 'Sugar. Just a few spoonfuls.' He gently laid the precious twist of paper on the table, then shook the sack. 'That's the lot.' He tousled his hair in a characteristic gesture, then stopped suddenly, snapping his fingers. 'Say – I've just thought of something I kept meaning to ask –'

'Mmm?' She was watching him again, hardly listening, watching the play of winter light from the window on the long, straight, fair lashes that shaded his light eyes.

'That old feller that used to shadow Luke – what was his name? The one with a face like a walnut –?'

She blinked. 'Spider?'

'That's the one.' He unwound his long, threadbare scarf from about his neck, rubbed his rough, reddened hands briskly together in front of the small fire. 'Tell me – he likely to be in Paris, would you think?'

'Spider? In Paris? Of course not.'

He hunkered in front of the fire, trying to warm himself. 'That's what I thought. I must have been mistaken. Yet – I'd have sworn it was him.'

'Where?'

'In the road outside. I was past him before it struck me who he reminded me of.'

'You didn't speak to him?'

'Nope. When I went back, he'd gone.'

'You must have been mistaken.'

'Guess so.' He eyed the vegetables hungrily. 'Looks like the makings of some fine warm soup there?'

She gathered them into her apron. 'Better get used to a vegetarian diet – they've issued the last of the fresh meat, so the butcher said.'

He grinned. 'Not quite.'

'What do you mean?'

He quirked a fair eyebrow. 'When did you last visit the zoo?'

She stared at him in fascinated dismay. 'Oh, no!'

'Oh, yes! Elephant – camel – rhinoceros – all on next week's menu, Madame!'

Her face was a picture of almost comic repugnance. 'Jem! I couldn't!'

He nodded, undisturbed. 'Oh, yes you could. If you were hungry enough.'

The laughter died a little. 'And – do you think we will be?'

He lifted a shoulder. 'Who knows?'

'But – it can't go on for much longer, surely? Everyone's saying that something big's going to happen very soon – that the army's going to break out and join up with the reinforcements coming with Gambetta –'

His movements stilled. 'Where in hell's name did you hear about that?'

'It's all over the city. The butcher told me. Jem – do you know anything about it?'

He turned back to the fire. 'The Ambulance has been told to stand by for the twenty-ninth. It's supposed to be a secret.'

'There's no such thing as a secret in Paris.'

'Ain't that the simple truth?' Shaking his head he stood up and walked to the window, stood looking, sombrely thoughtful, across the frost-covered roofs to the enemy lines in the distance. 'If you know,' he said after a moment, 'and I know, and the butcher knows, and presumably the best part of Paris knows – I guess it's too much to hope that our Prussian visitors haven't heard?'

The operation known as the Great Sortie began on a foul-weathered day at the end of October in an atmosphere of the wildest confidence and optimism and in forty-eight hours collapsed in a welter of mismanagement, incompetence and sheer bad luck. From the start the Fates were against it. The message sent to Gambetta from the city was entrusted to the balloon the *Ville d'Orléans* – no one could possibly have foreseen that, incredibly, it would land not in unoccupied France but would fly nonstop across the face of northern Europe to distant, inaccessible Norway – so ensuring that Gambetta and his forces would not discover until too late where and when the breakout from the city was to take place. The lines of communication to the Prussian camp, however – as Jem had suspected – suffered from no such disadvantage as adverse winds and capricious air currents. Days before the Great Sortie was due to begin Prussian troops were quietly redeployed to face it. Even the weather proved to be on the Prussian side as torrential rain washed away the pontoon bridges by which the French were to have crossed the River Marne. At the last moment, uneasily, the French High Command considered calling off the whole operation; the uncertain temper and high expectations of the Paris mobs, however, proved forceful if mistaken arguments against that. On the night of 28 November a tremendous cannonade shook the city as the forts opened fire on the German entrenchments, and the Prussian guns replied in kind. Kitty stood at the window and looked through rain that was showing signs of turning to driving snow to the small, flickering spots of flame that were the cannon mouths, listened to the faint, reverberating crash of the bombardment and the frantic barking of the city's dogs and thought of Jem, standing by with the others of the American Ambulance awaiting the morning and the blood and bone and broken bodies that would be the inevitable consequence of it. She thought too, with the dull pain of an old wound, of Michael, somewhere there beneath her in the rain-drenched city. Was he afraid? Was he hungry? Was he, even, alive?

In the two days that it took for the attempted break-out to collapse in blood and terror and sheer, demoralized panic she saw nothing of Jem. Whilst the sounds of battle raged to the north, the city lay with bated breath beneath a bitter blanket of cloud that had turned rain to snow and froze the wounded to death where they fell. Little news was allowed to filter back to the city but, as always, rumour was rife and the steady flow of desperately wounded men and terror-stricken deserters through the chaotic streets did little to reassure the civilian population. Kitty hardly went out. There seemed no point. The shops were closed, the weather bitter and for the moment even the dreary everyday routine of siege life had been suspended. And anyway, Jem might come. She stood for hours at the window, staring out in the direction of the battle, apparent from where she stood as a harmless echo of sound, faint puffs of smoke on the horizon. Jem was out there, on the battlefield – not fighting, of course, but in the thick of the shells and the flying bullets. Did a piece of shrieking, hot metal know the difference between a combatant and a non-combatant? she found herself wondering, bleakly, and remembered that when she had first met him he had been a refugee from a war of his own, a war in which he had found it impossible to fight. The irony would be cruel indeed if his humane services in this war – a conflict in which he had no concern at all – should end his life.

He came late on the third afternoon, with cold early darkness closing upon the city. Louise had just left, having spent the afternoon scouring the streets for bread and for news. No, she had reported, no one knew how the battle had gone, but the guns were silent and the general feeling was that the silence was ominous. The mood in the city was not cheerful.

The first Kitty knew of Jem's arrival was the oddly uncertain sound of a key searching for the doorlock. All afternoon she had huddled in layers of clothing and an old army greatcoat that Jem had acquired for her – the fuel shortage in Paris was now critical and she had but one hoarded bucket of coal and a small stack of what looked suspiciously like chopped up furniture, again the product of one of Jem's scavenging expeditions. The apartment was as cold as an ice-cave, her breath clouding the air, ice patterning the inside of the windows. A single, precious candle flickered upon the mantelpiece. A chill, somehow threatening silence enveloped the city beyond the window. Finally, shivering, she had laid a tiny fire and set a match to it. If she could just get warm – perhaps heat the last of the soup – then she could crawl into bed and conserve both heat and energy. At the sound of the key fumbling at the lock she bent to put a couple of pieces of the priceless coal on the fire, straightening as Jem finally managed to open the door.

The first sight of him stopped her breath in her throat.

Beneath his carelessly open, filthy greatcoat his shirt and trousers were bloodsoaked, stain upon old stain, brick to vermilion. His hands were blue with cold, his face gaunt and stone-white. The blue shadows beneath his eyes were like the mark of death. He looked utterly exhausted.

'Jem!'

As he stepped uncertainly towards her he staggered, and she flew to him. 'Jem – you're hurt!'

He shook his head. 'No. Not hurt. No. All right,' he mumbled, the words a little slurred.

Close to him she could smell it; he was as drunk as a lord. He stood watching her, swaying, frowning in fierce concentration.

'It's a good job,' she said, her eyes uncertain, her voice tart, 'that I don't have a rolling pin to hand.'

'Cold,' he said, shivering suddenly. 'Jesus bloody Christ, I'm cold.'

'Come to the fire.' She pushed the chair she had been sitting in even closer to the flames, profligately shovelled more coal upon the fire. He huddled in the chair, hands extended to the sudden welcome blaze. He was trembling so violently that he could not hold them still. A wave of compassion all but choked her; what in God's name had happened to bring him to this state? Almost without thought she leaned forward and brushed back the tousled, dirty hair from his forehead. One of his hands, so cold and clawlike it barely felt human, imprisoned hers. The nails were dark with blood, the skin stained. Fiercely he pressed his forehead against their clenched hands. His grip was painful. It was a full minute before she realized with a shock that the burning upon the chill skin of her wrist was his tears. He wept helplessly and soundlessly. She fought back the tears that rose in sympathy. He had begun to shake his head a little, his forehead still pressed against her hand, back and forth, back and forth, an endless denial, a desperate negation of what he had seen and done over the past days. 'God!' he whispered at last, 'Oh, God! Oh, God! Oh, God!' A monotonous chant of failure and despair.

She put her arms about him as he sat, rigid and shivering, held him with every ounce of strength she possessed, her cheek pressed hard against the shaggy thatch of his hair. At last the trembling eased a little. She felt him take a great, gulping breath. She sat back on her heels, holding his hands firmly in hers. 'Do you want to tell me?'

Tears welled again in his reddened eyes. He looked away, shaking his head dumbly.

'Then – can I get you something?' Despite all her efforts her voice shook.

'A drink,' he said.

In silence she stood and walked to a cupboard on which stood an open bottle of wine and some glasses. She poured some for him, then after a moment's hesitation a glass for herself and carried them back to the fireside.

He drank thirstily, half the glass in a gulp.

'There's a little soup left,' she said, 'if you'd like it?'

'Later.'

She nodded, knelt beside him again, taking his hand in hers. He clutched her fingers, crushing them painfully, driving the blood from them. She did not move. He carried her hand to his face, rested his cheek upon their linked hands.

She waited.

'Carnage,' he muttered. 'Bloody carnage.'

She said nothing. She was sitting on the wrong side of the armchair, away from the fire, and she had begun to shiver with cold, yet she could not bring herself to move.

He drank again.

A coal slipped in the grate sending a shower of sparks up the narrow, soot-stained chimney.

'The look on their faces –' Abruptly he let go of her hand and dashed his knuckles across his eyes, shaking his head sharply, like a dog shaking free of water. 'Not enough doctors. Not enough drugs. Not enough stretchers – They were dying in filth and fear on the bare ground. Boys. Christ Almighty, they were just boys –' He shuddered, drank the rest of his wine at a draught. Unspeaking she held out her own untouched glass. He reached for it. Stopped. Shook his head. 'No. I've had enough.'

'Could you eat the soup?'

He lifted his tousled head. Sucked his lower lip. Tears stood still in his eyes. He shook his head again.

An irresistible impulse of compassion brought her up on her knees, and she took his thin face between her two hands. He made no attempt to escape her, nor to hide the weariness and pain. Very, very gently she kissed him, tasting the wine, the salt of their mingled tears.

He sat for a moment, very still, eyes closed, lips cool and soft and totally passionless beneath hers. Then slowly she sensed a change. His mouth hardened hungrily. She felt his hands upon her shoulders, almost demented in their sudden strength. She closed her eyes. Without taking his mouth from hers he stood up, roughly pulling her to her feet with him. His hands were under the heavy greatcoat, brutal upon her breasts, sliding to her buttocks, clamping her body to his. She felt a brief flash of fear; this was not the Jem she knew, but an urgent, savage stranger. And then she touched his tear-wet face with her cold fingertips and all doubts were drowned in a surge of mixed desire and pity that was as hurtful and as lovely as flame. Whatever he had seen, whatever horrors he had endured he was here now, and he needed her. Tenderness would surely come later. She slid her fingers into the dirty, wind-tangled hair and pulled his mouth down harder upon hers. He groaned against her open lips. His hands were again roughly at the bodice of her dress. Still within the vice of his arms and careless for the moment of the bitter cold, she shrugged the greatcoat from her shoulders. Her breasts were bare, nipples rigid in the cold. He forced her back, his hungry mouth at her nakedness and she shuddered, afraid again at the violence in him. Yet as he pressed her down onto the rug before the flickering fire she did not resist. Pity was gone; her need rose now to match his. She it was who pulled the revolting, blood-stained shirt from him, who held him to her, arms and legs entwined fiercely about him, her hands moving frenziedly upon his thin back. The slight weight of his body was ice-cold against hers. His savage strength surprised her. The exquisite explosion of pleasure it engendered within her body brought helpless tears; and deep, deep within her happiness moved, warm and certain. He was hers. He loved her. She knew it.

In that moment she would have died for him.

She moved her head, resting her wet cheek upon his shoulder as he sprawled, exhausted, across her.

The abruptness of his movement as he flung himself from her shocked her more than anything that had come before.

She sat up, pulling the crumpled greatcoat about her bare, cold shoulders. 'Jem –?'

He did not look at her. Vicious with haste he hauled the filthy shirt back over his head.

Stunned, she watched his movements in the flickering candlelight. Climbing into his trousers, standing on one leg, he lost his balance and almost fell; and with a cold premonition of utter disaster she at last realized just how drunk he was. She scrambled to her feet, the coat clutched about her naked body. 'Jem – what are you doing?' Her voice was sharp with anxiety.

Still he kept his eyes turned from her. His face was set in a deadly mask of distaste and self-disgust. She bit her lip, stepped forward and touched his arm.

He froze, his head bowed. 'Don't!'

She dropped her hand as if it had been burned. Stepped back from him. 'Jem!'

He turned and looked at her at last. 'I'm sorry. I acted like an animal. It was unforgiveable.' He almost choked on the words.

'No!'

He talked blindly on, the words blurred with weariness and drink and remembered evils. He was swaying a little on his feet. 'I swore I wouldn't. Years ago I swore it. Luke's. You're Luke's and always will be.'

'No!' she shouted again and as if in nightmare realized that he hardly heard the word, let alone registered its meaning.

'You came to me as a friend and I – oh, God!' In despair

he swung away from her and hit the wall with the flat of his open hand.

She flinched from the violence. 'Jem, please! Listen to me –' She reached for him again.

He shook her off fiercely.

She was crying now, and trembling with cold and with shock. He stumbled awkwardly towards the door.

'Jem,' she whispered. 'Please don't go. Don't leave me –'

He turned unsteadily to face her. His face was hard as rock and shadowed with misery. 'Don't fool yourself, Kitty,' he said, 'and don't think to fool me. You don't want *me*,' and, stumbling, he left her there, bereft in a world as bleak and hopeless as death itself.

She slept at last, that night, for a few uncomfortable, restless hours, her face still tear-stained. She had lain for hours awake going over, minute by minute, the horrible scene with Jem, alternately shedding tears of misery and – more often as time moved on – burning with shame and humiliation. She had done nothing to stop him; worse, she had thrown herself at him, all but begged him to take her – she remembered the sound of her own voice, pleading, and her cheeks flamed again; God! How could she have so acted the whore? He at least had had the excuse – such as it was – of drunkenness and distress. She had none: and now, in face of his brutal rejection, the episode seemed sordid and shameful. Time and again his face rose before her eyes and she heard the faint and, it seemed to her now, contemptuous emphasis on the last pronoun when he had thrown those last words at her. 'You don't want *me* –'

What in God's sweet name had he meant by that? Did he really believe that she had used him for some selfish purpose of her own?

Until the exhausted small hours she swung on a pendulum of unstable emotion. Tomorrow she would go to him. Convince him. Go on her knees if she must. She would make him see her love, her need of him.

Then damaged pride stirred. Damn him! Why should she?

How dare he treat her so? Was that what he expected – what he wanted? That she would crawl to him – beg him? Freezing cold, curled tense as a steel spring beneath the damp bed-clothes that seemed themselves to radiate cold rather than heat, she clenched her hands, bruising her palms with her fingernails. She would not. She bloody well would not. She'd die first.

She drifted in and out of sleep. Once she woke to a far-away crackle of gunfire, and then silence. She was a little warmer, but her feet were frozen and her back was cold. She was aware of a faint worm of hunger. Her eyes and her head ached. She took a long breath, staring into darkness. Tomorrow she would go to him. Sober, he would be more rational. His brutality this evening, his physical savagery, had obviously been brought on by drink. She would not beg, nor would she cry. She would explain to him, and the man she knew, the kind, sensitive, joyous Jem she knew would understand.

She went to sleep a little comforted and woke to broad daylight, a dead fire, frost-rimed windows and a tentative tapping on the door.

Jem. He had come back. Of course.

She scrambled from bed, pushed her arms into the cold sleeves of the greatcoat that she had been using as an extra blanket and ran to the door, smiling. He would be contrite, and hung over and very very sorry for himself of course. And she would not forgive him straight away –

Lily Daltrey stood at the door, thinner than Kitty remembered her, the heavy hair untidy, blue shadows beneath the cat-like eyes. She gave no greeting as Kitty stood, gawping in astonishment. 'That fifteen 'undred francs still on offer?' she asked, flatly.

(iii)

Lottie was alive and so were both the children: at least, Lily said, sourly cynical, they had been the day before. What had happened since was none of her business.

'Came beggin',' she said, succinctly. 'Looked in a bad way.'

'And the children?'

She shrugged. 'Didn't see 'em. But Lot said they was both still with 'er.' Her eyes slid about the small apartment, probing, calculating. 'Comfortable enough 'ere, ain't yer?'

'Where are they?' Kitty asked.

In answer a long, flat palm was held out.

Kitty hesitated. Then she walked to the kitchen door and opened it. 'Would you mind waiting in here?'

Unconcernedly, eyes everywhere, the girl sauntered at her own pace through the open door. Kitty shut it sharply behind her and ran to the suitcase that stood in the corner behind the door. With cold, clumsy fingers she pulled out the white cotton petticoat and ripped at Pol's firm, neat stitching. A few minutes later she opened the kitchen door. Lily was standing with her back to her, looking out of the window. As she turned Kitty saw with a twinge of irritation that she had rifled the precious stores and was nibbling a small, sweet biscuit she had taken from a tin that lay open on the table. The sheer gall of the girl almost took Kitty's breath away.

'You got it?' Lily asked, unconcernedly helping herself to another biscuit. 'Gawd, 'ow in 'ell's name did yer got 'old o' these?'

'Where are they?'

'Over the river. The Left Bank.' The hand extended again and the wide eyes watched expectantly.

Kitty hesitated for only one second longer. She had to trust the unlovable Miss Daltrey – she had no alternative. She pulled the money from her pocket and put it in the long white hand. 'Where?'

'Rue Devine. Off the Boulevard St Germain. Across the Pont St Michel, towards the university –'

'Yes. Yes, I know where it is –' Kitty's heart was thumping erratically, and the sickness of excitement stirred her empty stomach.

''Ere.' Lily handed her a slip of paper. 'That's the address.

I wrote it down. Bet yer didn't think I could write, eh? Comes of me 'igh class connections.' She took another biscuit, put it in her pocket, then pushed past Kitty into the other room.

Kitty caught her arm as she passed. 'You didn't tell her?'

Lily shook her lovely head. 'Nah. None o' my business, is it?'

'No. It isn't.' Kitty opened the outside door for her. A surprised Louise stood, key poised.

'Mornin',' Lily said, pleasantly. 'An' ta –' she added to Kitty, tapping her pocket, 'Ta very much. That'll see me through fer a bit –'

'They'd better be there,' Kitty said. 'Or the police will hear something of it.'

The girl shrugged nonchalantly. 'They'll be there. They won't be in good shape, but they'll be there.'

She knew how perverse it was to decide not to tell Jem, but in the cold light of day his behaviour of the night before rankled badly, and hurt pride and feelings did not dictate prudence. Why should she run to him now, as if she could not do without him? There was faint, bitter satisfaction in the thought of succeeding alone where they had failed together. If – when – he came back to apologize, as he surely would, what triumph to have Michael here, hers again –

Kitty feverishly threw on layers of heavy clothing – fashion and elegance had long ago given way before the onslaught of the dreadful weather – issuing instructions to the bemused Louise as she did so. 'Louise – I have to go out. I won't be long, I hope. I want you to light a small fire in – oh, about an hour or so. I know we haven't much fuel, but light it anyway. There's some of that packing case left, and if it comes to the worst we can do without that rickety chest of drawers in the bedroom. There's nothing in it anyway. I want a fire, a warm fire, to come home to. You understand?'

'Yes, Mam'selle.' Clearly Louise did not. It had been many days since they had allowed themselves the luxury of a fire in the morning.

Kitty headed off the inevitable questions. 'My hat. Where's my hat?'

'In the bedroom, Mam'selle.' The girl brought it, watched as Kitty slapped it on her hastily pinned-up hair. 'Mam'selle?'

Raging to go, Kitty stopped. 'Yes?'

'If M'sieu Jem comes –?'

'Tell him –' Hand on the door, Kitty paused. Then, 'Tell him nothing,' she said, grimly.

As she hurried through the city it seemed to Kitty, even in her distracted state, that the smell of defeat hung about the streets as the winter mists, clinging and cold, hung low above the river. The setbacks of the past few days had been the worst of the siege – if the much vaunted Great Sortie had failed, what now could save Paris from the barbarians? With the battle over, the population had once more emerged onto the streets to pursue their own endless battle for survival; there were queues everywhere, long, sullen, straggling lines of people who stood in numbed silence or muttered, aggressively ill-tempered, of profiteers and the inequality of suffering. She crossed the Pont St Michel against a flow of wounded coming into the city, those that could walk supported by their fellows or staggering on improvised crutches, those who could not carried ashen-faced on makeshift stretchers. Their filthy bandages were blood- and pus-stained; empty sleeves and trouser legs flapped in the biting wind like the clothes of scarecrows. The faces were grim and grey and filled with a despair that chilled her heart as the wind chilled her body. Suddenly and brutally the memory of Jem's terrible distress came back to her, but obstinately, as she turned her face from the pathetic procession and pushed on past the barricades across the bridge, she turned her mind from any softening towards Jem. No matter what he had suffered, no matter what he had seen, his treatment of her had been unforgivable. She would not think of him. She was going to find her son.

The Rue Devine was, as Lily had said, a small side road

off the Boulevard St Germain. It was narrow as a canyon and straight as a ruled line, the buildings tall on either side. People hurried past, their collars turned up against the arctic weather – surely, Kitty thought bitterly, remembering Inspector MacAdam's righteous, Presbyterian tirade against the hedonistic sins of the glittering, opulent Paris that now seemed a lifetime removed from the suffering city of today, the odious man must have been right in his opinion that God must be on the Prussian side, for after the hottest summer in living memory had followed the most punishing winter. She counted the houses. Stopped. Number twelve. She glanced at the piece of paper. Number twelve, Rue Devine. Her heart had taken up an awful erratic, sickly thumping; worse, much worse than any stage fright she had ever known. Blindly she stepped towards the door and was almost bowled over by a uniformed figure in the scarlet and blue of the National Guard as she stepped heedlessly in front of him. The man stumbled and cursed.

'Pardon!' she gasped, startled. 'Pardon!'

The man scowled and snarled a curse. His uniform was motley – a worker's shirt beneath the uniform jacket, a bright, if filthy, canary-yellow cummerbund gathering in the voluminous waistband of trousers made for a man several sizes larger than he. He strode on, scowling.

With slightly trembling hand Kitty jerked on the ancient bell-pull of number twelve.

Nothing happened.

She waited a moment, then pushed the tall, peeling door tentatively. Protesting a little it opened halfway and then stuck. She slid through the gap and found herself in an open courtyard, the cobblestones littered and dirty, an uncovered drain running down its centre. Flakes of snow were beginning to drift, whirling, down the tall shaft of buildings beneath which the yard lay, lightless and cheerless. On each side of the courtyard steep flights of wooden steps ran in the open from landing to landing. From a floor high above a voice called and a door slammed. She stood for a moment, nonplussed; the place was a warren. Then, determinedly, she made for the nearest flight of steps. If she had to break down every damned door in the place she would find Lottie Smith.

Her sharp knock on the door of the first floor landing produced no results at all. The sound echoed emptily. From nowhere a small child had sidled up behind her. She glanced at him sharply. Dirty face, sly grey eyes, tow-coloured hair. Catching her eye he stuck his tongue out and made an obscenely filthy gesture. He was, she estimated, all of five years old.

She set off up the next flight of ramshackle stairs.

A woman answered her knock this time, a slattern with a gaggle of half-clothed children at her ragged skirts and an infant at suck at her lined and sagging breast. She stared vacantly at Kitty's stumbling questions, shook her head, shut the door in Kitty's face.

Several more urchins had now joined the filthy, tow-headed child – as she set off for the third landing Kitty reflected with grim humour that she made a strange Pied Piper and had perhaps better keep a weather eye out for rats. In this place there certainly did not look to be any shortage – she stopped dead.

Sitting on the stair above her, watching her solemnly, sat a small figure, raggedly dressed, sturdily built. His jet-black hair was shaggily unkempt as a pony's mane, his dark eyes, wide and warily interested, showed no sign of recognition whatsoever. He had a very dirty thumb in his mouth.

Michael.

She knew it was he; there was no doubt. She opened her mouth to speak his name, and could not. She cleared her throat. 'Michael?'

At the sound of her soft voice the velvet-dark eyes widened a little, but the thumb stayed put and the child did not move.

She took a tentative step towards him, held out her hand. Like a small animal he was off the step and scampering away in one movement, disappearing through the door behind him, lost in the darkness beyond.

One of the children behind her giggled, another sniffed noisily and cuffed his nose. She turned and stamped a foot. 'Shoo!'

They retreated two steps then stopped, watching her with interested, rapacious small eyes.

She took a breath and walked to the door through which Michael had disappeared. It opened at her touch. She stepped into the darkness that made the dismal stairwell seem as bright as a summer's day and for a moment completely blinded her. Then as her eyes adjusted she discovered herself to be standing alone in an all but empty room. In one corner, on the floor, lay a large, dirty mattress. There was a small, stained table and a wooden chair. The fireplace was empty and cold, and the place smelled of damp and of decay. On the floor near the mattress, abandoned and oddly pathetic, a tattered rag doll stared at her with one wide blue eye. The walls were running water, the ceiling stained and peeling. There was no sign of Michael.

'Hello?' she called, sharply. 'Hello – is anyone there? Lottie –?'

There was a door in the wall opposite. Kitty watched it. 'Hello?' she called again, insistently.

Cold air blew through the open door at her back.

Very slowly then, the door she was watching opened. Framed in it stood a woman with two children clinging to her skirts. Michael's thumb was still in his mouth. The little girl, who must be Poppy, her frail and delicate beauty obvious even beneath the ragged clothes, the ingrained dirt, the sores about her mouth, nervously clung to her mother's heavy skirt with both hands. Lottie Smith – emaciated, haggard-faced, no longer beautiful, stared at Kitty in weary defiance edged with implacable hatred. In her hand she held a long, vicious-looking knife.

'Get out,' she said.

Kitty shook her head.

The woman took a step forward. The change in her was shocking; the bones stood from her face like a death's head, the skin was sallow and covered in sores. Even from where

Kitty stood she could see the woman's deathly struggle for every breath. 'Get out,' she said again, harshly, 'or I'll stick yer, I swear it.' The words ended on a cough, half-suppressed.

'No.' Kitty felt oddly calm. Her eyes were on Michael, who stared back at her with eyes still heartbreakingly devoid of recognition. 'I've come for Michael. Nothing else. I won't harm you.'

'No!' The woman reached for the boy and dragged him fiercely to her. 'No!'

'He's my son.'

A skeletal, red-rough hand grasped the boy's shoulder possessively. 'Luke's son,' Lottie said. 'Never yours. He'll thank me. You see. I saved him for him –'

Kitty stared at her. 'Lottie!' She heard the tiny sound behind her at the very moment that Lottie, her glance flicking past Kitty, brought the knife up swift as a flash, her face contorted.

'So – that's it, is it? All right. I'll take on the both of yer –'

Kitty turned – and for a moment it seemed that her wits had deserted her entirely.

There was a long, tense silence.

'Spider!' Kitty said, faintly.

He did not look at or acknowledge her. ''Ello, Lot,' he said, and the two words, softly rasped, were infinitely threatening. Kitty felt the small hairs on her neck rise.

Lottie said nothing.

'Bin lookin' for yer,' Spider said, gently.

Kitty stepped forward. 'Spider – what are you doing here? How did you find this place?'

For a moment the little man's eyes flicked to her and then away, warily back to Lottie and her knife. 'Bin follerin' yer. Reckoned sooner or later yer'd run 'er down.'

'But – why?'

'I'm gonna break 'er bleedin' neck,' he said, unemotionally.

Lottie moved a little. The knife glittered wickedly in the half-light. 'Try it,' she said.

He nodded. 'I will.'

Kitty looked from one to the other. Too late she saw her foolishness in coming here alone. 'Spider —'

Spider, ignoring her, lifted a wizened hand and levelled a small, pointed, brown-stained finger at Lottie. 'You killed my Guv'nor,' he said, his voice utterly calm and the more threatening for that. 'You ain't gettin' away with that.'

The effect of the words was astonishing. Lottie, who had been crouched defensively, the knife held before her, very slowly and in the manner of one dazed by a blow straightened up, staring at Spider, the hand holding the knife dropping to her side. Her sallow face had taken on the colour of the dead ashes that lay in the hearth. 'What d'yer mean?'

In the silence, Poppy caught her breath in a small sob.

'Luke?' Lottie asked, faintly, and then again, 'Luke?' And then Kitty knew for certain what she had begun to suspect a moment before Spider's unexpected entrance; Lottie Smith had not known, had never discovered, that her madness had caused her lover's death.

'He died in the fire,' Kitty said, quietly, 'trying — he thought — to rescue Michael.'

Lottie shook her head. 'No! Oh — no!' Still moving in that odd, frozen manner she brought her two hands to her face. 'Oh, no!' she said again. She still held the knife, forgotten in her hand. Its blade gleamed lethally against the death-mask of her emaciated face.

Poppy had begun openly to cry. Michael, uncertainly, had moved closer to the little girl and had gathered a handful of her dirty dress in his small fist. His thumb was still in his mouth.

'Luke,' Lottie whispered, and the pain in the single word was so terrible that despite herself Kitty felt the beginnings of pity stir within her.

Not so Spider. 'Luke Peveral.' He stepped forward, crouching menacingly, hands crooked. 'The best cracksman, and the greatest gentleman that ever drew breath. The best Guv'nor a man could ask for. An' you done fer 'im, you stinkin' little bitch. Like I'm gonna do fer you.' And still the total absence of any obvious emotion in his voice added strange and threatening emphasis to his words.

Lottie had begun to tremble uncontrollably. The knife clattered to the floor. She wrapped her arms about her own thin body, shaking her head in despair and grief. 'Not Luke, oh not Luke – I didn't know – didn't know 'e was there –'

Spider lunged. Lottie made no attempt to defend herself. Kitty, sensing the man's move, had no opportunity to shield Lottie – Poppy, screaming in terror was between the snarling Spider and her mother. Kitty threw herself forward and grabbed the child, hauling her out of the way as Spider and Lottie crashed to the floor, Spider's hands locked about the woman's thin throat.

Michael, still holding, limpet-like, his fistful of Poppy's dress, was pulled over by the violence of Kitty's action and, around his thumb, began to wail dismally. The two thrashing bodies on the floor rolled over, crashing into them. Poppy was by now screaming hysterically, white-faced, her eyes glazed. Lottie had somehow broken Spider's hold and had scrambled free of him. As Spider grabbed for her she came to her feet at a run and dashed for the open door, hampered by her heavy skirt. Kitty, desperately trying to protect the terrified children, saw Spider's hand reach out swift as a striking snake and catch the woman's flying hair. Frantically Kitty tried to disengage small, clinging hands. Brutally Spider jerked Lottie from her feet. The woman screamed with pain. Then with vicious strength and murderous intent the little man began to push Lottie towards the rickety bannisters of the landing.

'No! No, Spider! Don't –' Kitty leapt forward, reaching for Lottie's flailing hand.

She was just a second too late.

With a final, terrible effort Spider almost bodily threw Lottie's slight frame into the rotten bannisters that snapped like matchwood and showered down with the tumbling, screaming body to scatter in the snow in the sudden awful silence that followed its landing.

Poppy's screams, distracted and hysterical, were renewed.

Doors opened. Voices called. But it was for the most part in silence that the inhabitants of number twelve Rue Devine gathered on their landings to peer into the dimly lit well at the body that sprawled beneath them in the snow.

Spider, with no glance at Kitty, walked calmly down the three flights of steps to the door. He looked back, once, at the broken figure of Lottie Smith before slipping through the door to the street.

No one made any attempt to stop him.

In the filthy yard Lottie lay like a broken doll, limbs grotesquely twisted, blood seeping, half-hidden by the thickening, swirling snow.

7

(i)

Astonishingly – and tragically for her – Lottie was not dead. Profoundly unconscious, she was carried to her room and laid upon the mattress. Poppy and Michael huddled beside the still body, shocked and silent. For the moment Kitty could do nothing for them. A woman from the floor above offered to fetch a doctor, and Kitty, sitting by Lottie's side, watching the faint rise and fall of the pathetically scrawny chest and hopelessly trying to stem the flow of blood where shattered bone had pieced the flesh of her leg, commandeered the brightest-looking urchin from the interested group that refused to disperse from the open doorway and sent her to Montmartre with a note for Louise, hastily scribbled upon a scrap of dirty paper.

It seemed half a lifetime before the doctor put in an appearance. He was an elderly, tired-looking man with the florid complexion and dull eyes of a heavy drinker. He shook his head discouragingly over the unconscious Lottie – seemed indeed ready to give up before he had ever properly examined her. The woman would die anyway, he said – what was the point of wasting his time?

Even Kitty's poor French was up to understanding that – the attitude, if not a translation word for word. She was outraged. 'But – she must go to hospital! She must!'

He looked at her pityingly, spread none-too-clean hands. Hospital? Impossible. The hospitals were all packed to the doors with sick and wounded. There would be no place for a dying woman. Anyway – there were few medicines and fewer drugs. There was a war on.

Kitty, raging, pointed to the shattered leg. 'At least you

can do something about that, can't you? You can't leave her to bleed to death!' Cursing herself for not having thought of it before she produced money from her small bag, waving it beneath the red-veined nose. 'Money – I have money. For God's sake do something for her! I can pay –'

By the time Louise came, breathless and nervously wide-eyed, led to the Rue Devine by the girl who had taken the note, the doctor had nearly finished his ministrations, such as they were, to the still unconscious Lottie. Relieved at last to have someone to translate, Kitty questioned him. The man shrugged. It was amazing that the – accident – had not been fatal. It was unlikely in any case that the woman would regain consciousness. If she did she would certainly be at least partly paralysed and in great pain. He had done his best. He would call again tomorrow, if the woman lived. Apart from the ironically significant pause upon the word 'accident', which even Kitty picked up, he showed no curiosity about the nature of Lottie's injuries.

'Doesn't he have something he can give her? Something to ease the pain?'

Louise shook a helpless head. 'He says such things are very scarce. And very expensive.'

Kitty glanced at the ashen face upon the dirty pillow. 'Tell him I'll pay.'

With a great show of reluctance the doctor opened his bag once more and produced a tiny phial. Kitty took it, thrusting a roll of notes into the man's shaking hand, and thankfully closed the latchless door behind him, ramming the back of the single chair under the doorknob to keep it closed. Lottie lay unmoving upon the mattress, to all outward appearances lifeless already. Beside her, huddled in the corner Poppy and Michael sat, Michael enclosed by the circle of the little girl's thin arms.

'Louise' – the sight of the children spurred Kitty from the numbness of shock – 'we need some things from the apartment – blankets, food, clothing. And fuel for the fire – we can't move her, so we have to make her comfortable here.'

'But Mam'selle – how?'

Kitty restrained herself from shaking her. 'I don't know how! But somehow! Find someone to help you. Here –' She thrust a couple of notes at the girl. 'There must be some man who's willing to earn a few francs! Go! And be quick!'

As the door shut behind the bemused Louise she shoved the chair back under the knob and looked around helplessly, seeing almost for the first time the utter poverty in which Lottie and the children had been living. There was nothing of comfort in the two bare rooms at all. Her own warm cloak was all, apart from a threadbare blanket, that covered Lottie as she lay. In the small kitchen there was no food apart from a stale half loaf of the almost inedible grey bread known as *pain Ferry*. She went back into the main room. Lottie still lay as quiet as death. The eyes of the children followed her, fearfully. They had resisted every move she had made towards them.

She knelt beside them, seeing Poppy flinch from her. 'It's all right,' she said, softly, 'I won't hurt you I promise. Don't you – don't you remember me?'

Poppy blinked, owl-like. Michael did not move. His thumb was in his mouth, his free hand tangled in Poppy's tattered skirt. Very, very gently Kitty held out a hand. 'Michael. It's Mama. Don't you remember me? Your Mama –' The unshed tears of reaction, of shock, of desperate disappointment sounded in her voice. In all the times she had imagined this reunion she had never imagined it so, never believed that in six short months he could forget her.

The little boy shifted a little, pressing closer to Poppy.

'S'true, little Mick,' Poppy said, unexpectedly. 'She is your Ma! I remember 'er.'

Great tears formed in the younger child's dark eyes. With a small, strange sound he turned from Kitty and buried his head in Poppy's lap. The little girl, very gently, laid a roughened hand upon the unkempt dark hair, looking at Kitty with empty eyes.

Beside them Lottie made the faintest sound, then lapsed again to stillness and silence.

Kitty sat back on her heels. Every instinct she possessed urged her to touch Michael – to pick him up, hug him to her, reassure him of her love. Yet she knew she must not. He was confused and terrified. To frighten him further now, to demand too much of him, would be to jeopardize their relationship for ever. He must be won round, with calm and gentleness. And the other child, too. She glanced at Poppy, nursing Michael, her eyes upon her unconscious, dying mother and a great surge of pity for the child brought fresh tears welling to her eyes. Absurdly, she had thought that finding Michael would be the end of her troubles. Sitting here now in the dark room that was cold and bare as a tomb she perceived clearly the foolishness of that.

It was thirty-six hours before Lottie regained consciousness, during which time the doctor grudgingly returned, shook his head, grumbling, changed the dressing on her leg, accepted his fee and left; and Louise and Kitty between them transformed the two rooms to something with at least some semblance of comfort. There was another large mattress, to accommodate Kitty and the two children, there were blankets and pillows and for the children warm clothes, bought from Louise's family. There was food in the kitchen and a fire in the stove, albeit a small one. Poppy and Michael sat beside it for hours, staring at the flames, refusing to move even to eat. Kitty, watching the pinched faces that were lit by the meagre flames, wondered how long it was since they had known such comfort. Warming to her task, Louise had enlisted the help of two of her brawny brothers, and the main room now boasted a couple of battered armchairs and a rug on the floor.

Also – most important of all in this, neither the most salubrious of districts nor the safest to demonstrate possession of rather more than one's penurious neighbours – a sturdy bar was set across the door, for the night time when Kitty and the children were alone. For almost in those first moments Kitty had seen that this was the only way. Lottie could not be moved, and she could not be abandoned. In any case Poppy would not have left her mother, and Michael would not have left Poppy. So she, Kitty, was bound there too, whilst Lottie's shallow breathing, the fitful beating of her heart showed still that she preserved her tenuous hold on life. Kitty tended to her as best she could, inexperienced as she was, and spent long hours sitting beside her, watching for change that never happened. Her advances to the children were at first disappointingly and determinedly rejected. They took what she offered by way of food and comfort, but gave nothing in return, speaking only when spoken to, refusing utterly to respond to any small gesture of affection. Poppy, obviously, was old enough to reason that her mother's condition, if not exactly Kitty's doing, was certainly connected with her arrival on the scene. And Michael took his cue from Poppy, whose side he never left.

As the darkness of the December evening, the second of her vigil, closed in and Louise, protesting dutifully but obviously anxious to return to her family, had left, Kitty settled down in the armchair that was nearest to Lottie and rested her head tiredly against the battered and threadbare wing. She was aware of the possibility of the wish fathering the thought, but it seemed to her that the sick woman's breathing was just a little easier than it had been. She half-closed her eyes. For economy's sake she had put out the candle and let the fire die a little, bitterly cold though it was. It glimmered redly now, casting smudged shadows. In the far corner the two children slept, dark head and fair head close together. A simple tune, remembered from childhood, slipped unexpectedly into Kitty's head. She hummed it softly, then sang, very quietly, in the deceptively peaceful room. 'Go to sleep, go to sleep, While the bright stars do peep –' The pretty little lullaby soothed her, eased the worries that had been nagging at her waking hours – Now that she had found them, what was she to do about Lottie and the children? How long could she support them all? How long before the food and fuel in the city ran out altogether? Without Jem and his contacts, how far would her money carry them? She had spent an awful lot; how much longer might it last? How long before the Prussians grew tired of this terrible waiting, and bombarded the city –? 'Mother's a milkmaid, Father's a king, They can bring baby everything. Go to sleep, go to sleep –' Eyes still half closed, she became faintly aware of movement. In the shadows of the far corner a small figure had rolled off the mattress and come to its feet, staggering.

Kitty did not move. 'Mother is pretty and Father is rich, Sister baby's cap does stitch –'

Michael toddled sleepily towards her. She watched him come, her heart in her throat, a catch in her voice. 'Go to sleep, go to sleep –'

He stopped, knuckling his eyes and watching her. Very slowly she turned her head, still singing softly, and smiled, lifting her arms in invitation. He hesitated for just one moment longer and then climbed into her lap as if it were the most natural thing in the world. She rested her cheek against the tangled dark hair, feeling the living warmth of her son's small body in her arms at last. 'Go to sleep, go to sleep –' She sang the lullaby through again and then, reluctant to break the spell of enchantment that held them, she slipped to another song, one she had sung many times, the words as clear in memory as the pictures they conjured: winter evenings with the Bowyers about the fire at the Grange, the piano in the parlour on Mersea Island, Amos' eyes upon her, his voice lifting with hers. 'All round my hat I will wear the green willow –' The peaceful Lot, in those magic months with Jem. Michael sighed and burrowed deeper into her lap. Then Kitty became aware of another small figure in the shadows. Poppy, the battered rag doll clutched under one arm, stood just beyond the range of the firelight, the expression on her face indiscernible. Kitty lifted a hand, extended it, open, in invitation. Very, very slowly the girl came forward, hesitated just out of Kitty's reach, her eyes moving from Michael's dozing face to Kitty's tentatively smiling one. Kitty stretched her hand a little, curling fingers in invitation. Just one more step – she prayed – just one little step –

'Oh, young men are false, and they are so deceitful, Young men are false and they seldom prove true –'

The great violet eyes, so like her mother's had once been, blinked. Then Lottie's daughter stepped forward into the circle of Kitty's arm and leaned there, her head resting on her shoulder, her small hand lightly upon Michael's knee.

As the last note of Kitty's song died Lottie moved her head a little, muttered and lapsed once more into unconsciousness.

The next day Lottie woke at last, and the doctor's gloomy predictions were confirmed. She was almost completely paralysed. She could move neither her legs nor her right arm. The movements of her left arm she could barely control. She was in terrible pain. She said little as Kitty tended her, only her eyes following the other girl's movements, bleak and bitter with pain. Poppy sat beside her mother, holding her left hand, her eyes fixed fiercely on the skeletal face. Halfway through the morning Louise arrived with a basket of provisions from the store at the Montmartre apartment. She was talking as she entered the door. '– nothing to be had anywhere! And have you heard –? There's been another battle. Oh, Mam'selle, it's terrible – the wounded are everywhere! M'sieu' – she glanced at Kitty quickly and hastily covered her mistake – *'mon père*, he says there is no more hope. Paris will surrender –'

'Surrender?' Kitty looked at her sharply. It was almost the first time she had heard the word, and oddly it shocked her.

Louise grimaced. *'Mais oui.* Before the people starve. For us there is no meat, no cheese, no butter, no milk. They hunt the rats in the sewers. And even the rats are too thin to eat. On the Champs Elysées they eat elephant and camel from the Jardin des Plantes, and they make a great joke of it, yes? The restaurants – so one hears – have fresh meat and vegetables. What do they eat in Bellevue? I tell you. They eat nothing.' Muttering still, almost to herself, she continued to unpack the basket. It did not escape Kitty that this was the first such outburst she had ever heard from the docile Louise, and she was aware, uneasily, that the girl was probably not alone in her uncharacteristic and growing resentment. 'The butchers – *zut!*' The small sound was illustrative of total disgust. 'They are – what is it? That sucks the blood?'

'Leeches.'

'*Oui*. Leeches. They should beware; the profits they make will do them no good when they dangle from a lamp post –'

'Louise?' Kitty said, sharply, holding up a tin.

'And now the government talks of rationing bread!'

'Louise!'

The girl stopped in surprise.

'What's this?' Kitty held up the tin.

Louise shrugged, avoiding her eyes. 'I don't know. I just take what is there.'

'But this wasn't.'

The girl looked at her, blankly.

Kitty read from the label. 'Hominy and grits. Home cooking in a tin.' She looked back at Louise. 'Hominy and grits?' she asked gently.

The girl shrugged again.

'Jem,' Kitty said.

Louise turned and busied herself at the sink.

'Louise!'

Reluctantly the little maid turned back. Kitty waved at the goods that were stacked on the table. 'Potted meat? And the label in English? Some of this is from the American Legation, isn't it?'

Louise, discomfited, nodded.

'I told you to tell Jem nothing.'

Louise sighed, her face the personification of injured martyrdom. 'You say this, M'sieu Jem say that – how do I know –?'

'You told him.'

'Yes.' The word was reluctant.

'Then you can tell him this,' Kitty said, grimly, fighting the spurt of near-hysterical laughter that the sight of the hominy and grits had brought on. 'Tell him under no circum-

stances do I want to see him here. Tell him I don't want –
don't need – his help.'

'Mam'selle!' Louise was shocked. Clearly in her world
one did not tell young men such things.

'Tell him –' Kitty stopped. Clearly as if he had been
standing beside her she heard his laughter, saw the quick
lift of his head, the mischievous gleam in his eyes, pale and
clear as sunlit water. Lord, she'd missed him over these past
days! 'Tell him,' she said, 'that he's obviously got no more
sense than he ever had. What for Heaven's sake are hominy
and grits? Are we supposed to eat them or light the fire with
them? Tell him that if he wants to help he'll have to help
sensibly; we've children here – we need milk, and eggs, and
decent bread –'

'Mam'selle, they are not to be had.'

Kitty grinned at her, her heart suddenly and absurdly
light. 'You think not? Tell Jem O'Connell that. He'll prove
you wrong.'

He came the next day.

For the first time the children had gone to rejoin their
playmates on the landings and stairs of the tenement. Kitty
had determinedly suppressed her own misgivings at the
thought of letting them out of her sight and allowed them
to go – such signs of normality were encouraging and the
children had already been cooped up for too long. Louise
had left early that morning, basket over her arm and with a
purseful of the francs that were becoming more worthless
with each passing day, in a brave but probably futile attempt
to find a queue less than a mile long at a shop that might,
eventually, open. Lottie, Kitty having dressed her inflamed
injured legs as the doctor had shown her, slept restlessly,
soothed by a drop from the precious phial. Kitty opened the
door to a jaunty, rhythmic tap, her face wary. Her expression
did not change at sight of her visitor.

'Mornin', ma'am,' Jem said.

Kitty said nothing.

'Heard tell you were short of a few things?'

She stepped back. Breezily he stepped past her. She barred

the door behind him and led the way in silence into the kitchen.

'Eggs,' he said. 'Only three I'm afraid, but the best I could do at short notice. Butter. No milk. I'm working on it.'

She stood rigid by the closed door for a moment longer. The mere sight of him had roused feelings she had spent the past harrowing days denying. Hurt. Humiliation. Fierce, physical need. 'Where on earth did you get them?' Her voice was perfectly cool and steady.

'The Legation. Our Mr Washburne's a generous man. Where's Michael?'

'Out playing.'

He glanced towards the door. 'And Lottie? How is she?'

'Bad. The doctor gives her no chance. But she's alive and I can't leave her. And Poppy won't leave her mother and Michael won't leave Poppy, so we're all stuck here for a while. What's happening outside?'

'Nothing good.' The words were succinct. She did not pursue them.

They stood for several moments in strangely communicative silence.

'Friends again?' he asked at last, tentatively. 'I forgot to bring the sackcloth and ashes, but if you insist –?'

She shook her head. 'It was my fault as much as yours.' She gritted her teeth. My fault? Your fault? What were they talking about? Where lay the fault in love?

He shook his head. 'I was drunk. Pissed as a newt. It was unforgiveable.'

She smiled very faintly. 'It's forgiven.' Did he even remember the really unforgiveable thing? – Not the taking, but the rejection of love? She thought probably not.

He spat on his right palm, held it out. She slapped it lightly with her own, her heart aching.

He perched on the edge of the table. 'So – here's a mess. It was Spider, Louise said?'

'Yes. He'd been following me. He attacked her. Threw her off the balcony.'

'The police?'

She shook her head. 'Of course not. Who'd send for the police round here? And what good would it do? Lottie herself's a wanted criminal remember. They wouldn't be as gentle as we've been. And if they moved her she'd die.'

He looked at her, contemplatively, for a very long time and, strangely, she found herself blushing. He stood up. 'You're one hell of a girl, Kitty Daniels,' he said quietly, and reaching into the capacious pocket of his greatcoat produced, like a rabbit from a hat, a bottle of cognac. 'Essential supplies,' he said, soberly, 'for the nursing staff. Now, if you'll excuse me, I have to see a man about a cow.'

That bottle remained unbroached until the day several days later when Kitty ventured into the streets only to find herself caught up in the riots caused by the threat to ration bread – that last staple, life-preserver of the poor. The rich might still, by whatever means, find it possible to dine in some style: for the poor of Paris hunger had now turned to the threat of famine, and their children were dying. Kitty struggled home, frightened, avoiding the rioting mobs, and did not feel safe until she had dropped the heavy bar across the door and tucked the children into their bed.

Lottie watched her. 'What's – goin' on?' Her speech was slurred and difficult, but Kitty, looking into those implacable eyes, knew that the brain behind them was as sharp and hate-filled as ever.

'They're rioting in the streets. The government are talking of rationing bread.'

'Bastards.'

Kitty tidied the bedclothes, plumped the pillows. 'Are you comfortable? Can I get you anything?'

'Comfortable?' Lottie repeated, bitterly.

Kitty sucked her lip, turned to stoke the fire.

'What yer burnin'?'

Kitty inspected the sack of wood. 'Looks like piano. Jem got it from somewhere. God only knows where.'

For a moment there was no sound but that of Lottie's difficult breathing. Then, 'What 'appened – to that – little shit – Spider?' she asked, evenly.

Kitty straightened, a hand to her aching back. 'Nothing. He got away.' She turned. 'There was nothing I could do, Lottie. How could I have stopped him?'

Her only reply was the tremulous breathing. Kitty turned towards the kitchen door.

'Kitty?'

Something in the tone stopped her. 'Yes?' She approached the mattress, perched on the edge.

Lottie's face was working. 'What 'e said – that right? Luke's – dead?'

Kitty nodded.

'In the fire?'

'Yes.'

Lottie turned her head on the pillow. A tear trickled and then slid swiftly down the emaciated cheek.

Kitty could not find it in her heart to comfort her. 'Jem brought some brandy,' she said. 'I'll open it.'

Christmas approached and still Lottie clung to life, if such an existence of pain and paralysis could be described so. Kitty tended her, and the children, with the help of Louise and occasionally of Jem, of whom however she saw relatively little, although his gifts, via Louise, continued to sustain them. The weather was brutal, unremittingly and searingly cold, as if still the elements themselves threw their weight behind the city's enemies. At the beginning of the last week of December another attack on Le Bourget, dogged again by poor planning and poorer security, ended in disaster. As the news trickled back to the city Kitty waited for Jem, but he did not come. Sleepless, she lay imagining him wounded, dying, dead. Or in the arms of someone able to comfort him better than she had done. On Christmas Eve, unannounced, he arrived. He was unhurt and in remarkably good spirits. He made no mention of the battle. From beneath his greatcoat, with the air of a practised

magician, he produced presents – an almost-new doll for
Poppy, a wooden toy soldier for Michael, two bottles of
wine, a bag of frost-blackened potatoes and – wonder of
wonders – a skinny chicken.

'Jem! You must have done murder!'

He shook his head. 'Nope. Just asked nicely. The Legation's still well supplied.'

'You'll come for dinner tomorrow?'

Avoiding her eyes he shook his head. 'Sorry. I volunteered
for duty with the Ambulance.'

She did not know whether to believe him or not.

That evening she and the children sang together the carols
she had taught them and she saw again the gleam of tears
on Lottie's face. Outside, the city was silent, as were the
guns on this holiest of nights. Kitty wondered that the
Prussian invaders about their campfires could be worship-
ping that same child of peace to whom hymns were being
sung and precious candles lit within the besieged city that
they were trying to starve into submission. Tomorrow –
Michael's birthday, as well as the Christ Child's – the
slaughter would begin again. Suddenly the whole thing
seemed monstrously pointless. What madness in man produced such bloodsoaked lunacy?

She had no present for Michael for his third birthday,
except to sing for him that special *Green Willow* song that
had become his favourite. 'Next year,' she said, hugging
him, 'you shall have two presents. Two big presents,' and
she tried to ignore the forebodings. Next year? How could
she promise for next year when she could not begin to guess
what might happen tomorrow?

And so the strange Christmas passed; and now there were
whispers, frightening whispers, that the encircling army had
come to the end of its patience. The rumours grew and the
rumours were strong. Paris was to be bombarded.

Louise brought the first, disturbing gossip. '*Mon Dieu*,
mam'selle! – they mean to kill us in our beds!'

'Calm yourself, Louise! We've heard such rumours before.'

'But – the guns, they can be seen! And didn't you hear last night! Already they bombard the Avron Plateau –'

'The guns are always there. And the Plateau's a military target. They wouldn't dare bombard the city. It's barbaric! They'd lose all support in Europe. In the world.'

Louise, unconvinced, sniffed in injured fashion. 'I hope you're right, mam'selle.'

Within two days Kitty had more immediate things to worry about. A day or so after this most unpromising new year had arrived, with no warning Lottie's temperature suddenly soared and her breath rattled frighteningly in her chest. It was hours before Louise could track down the doctor. When he came at last, smelling strongly of spirits, he shook his head. Pneumonia. More people were dying of it than were being killed by the god-forsaken Prussians. In Lottie's weakened state there was nothing to be done. He shrugged. Perhaps it was a blessing.

'Louise – for tonight, would you stay and care for the children?' Kitty's own head ached and her limbs were heavy with weariness. For nights on end she had barely slept. 'Move the other mattress into the kitchen for them. Use the last of the wood to light the stove.' She looked down in pity at Lottie's fever-bright face. 'There's no need to conserve it now –'

She settled down beside Lottie, watching with helpless compassion the painful struggle for every breath. She remembered Lottie, fair and beautiful, standing upon the stage of the Song and Supper Rooms; remembered her, too, lovely and laughing, hanging onto Luke's arm, utter devotion in her eyes. Almost as if the thought had reached her, Lottie's eyes fluttered open. 'You there?'

'Yes.'

'Luke's dead.' The whisper was so faint Kitty could barely hear it.

'Yes.'

'In – in the fire.'

'Yes.'

'It was an accident – the fire – I didn't mean to –'

'Lottie – please – don't talk. I don't think it can be good for you.'

'Only meant to take little Mick, yer see – Luke's kid –'

'Lottie –'

'I – knocked over a lamp. It sort of exploded –'

Kitty waited. She could hear the fatal rattle of the other girl's breath in her chest.

'Then – when I realized – all them folk dead! I – well, I 'ad ter get away, didn't I? Away from London, till the fuss died down, an' I could let Luke know –' Shining tears slid down the parched, thin face. 'Paris was – the on'y place I'd ever been outside London. An' Lily – I remembered my friend Lily –' She stopped a moment, gasping. 'Some friend!'

'Lottie – please! You must stop.'

'Didn't mean to kill – anyone –' Her breath was coming in agonizing gasps. Through the rattle in poor Lottie's chest Kitty was aware of a strange new sound, a distant, shrill whistle. 'I wanted little Mick' – Lottie gasped – 'for Luke – 'E should 'a bin mine.' Her voice lifted. ''E should 'a bin mine!'

The explosion was terrifying in its unexpectedness. It seemed close enough to be in the street outside. The candle flickered. Instinctively Kitty threw herself forward, covering Lottie's body with her own. In the next room one of the children shrieked, and Louise screamed. There came another explosion, and another. The world rocked, and settled.

'God Almighty,' Kitty said, dazed, 'they're shelling the city.'

Lottie had not relinquished her superhumanly strong grip upon Kitty's hand. She seemed not to have noticed the explosions. She pulled Kitty to her, half sat, gasping for breath. 'Poppy,' she said.

Kitty forced her gently back onto the pillow. The children were crying. The night air sang again with the menace of death. 'I'll look after her. I promise. As my own.'

Lottie's eyes were glazed. She let out a great sob. 'I've always hated you. I still – hate you!'

'I know.'

Lottie fell back onto the pillow, letting go of Kitty's hand, the last of her dying strength deserting her. 'I loved 'im,' she said. 'That was my trouble. I bloody loved 'im –' and, as an explosion in the street outside rocked the building to its foundations and glass flew, Lottie Smith died.

'Mam'selle! Oh, mam'selle –' Louise was shrieking hysterically, in English and in French. *'Nous sommes morts! Oh, mon Dieu!* They bomb us –!'

Kitty was through the door and into the kitchen in three strides, her feet crunching on shattered glass. 'Louise! Shut up or I'll slap you! Now – help me! Quickly! The table –' She dragged the heavy table clear of the window, grabbed a blanket from the mattress. Glass tinkled. 'Michael! Poppy! Get under the table!' The terrified children crawled under the sturdy table. Kitty threw the heavy blanket over it. 'There. You're safe now. In a little house, you see? Oh, Louise! For God's sake calm yourself.'

'But, mam'selle –' Louise's protest was cut off by another shattering explosion. Smoke and the stinging smell of high explosives drifted through the dark opening of the window. Louise screamed.

'If you do that again,' Kitty warned grimly, 'I will slap you. Hard. I swear it. Now – give me a hand with this mattress. Rest it against the table, so. There. That makes a shelter for us. We can just squeeze in, and it's extra protection for the children –' The words were cut off by the vicious whine of another shell. 'Get down!'

They huddled in the shelter of the mattress and the table, clinging to each other, the children curled like small frightened animals in their laps. In the courtyard outside Bedlam reigned. They could hear shouts and screams, children crying.

'We must stay here,' Kitty said, determinedly. 'It's ridiculous to run around in the open. We're safer here. It can't last long. We'll be all right.' She prayed her voice sounded firmer and more convinced in the others' ears than it did in her own.

The night hours passed like endless days. The bombardment eased, then renewed itself with brutal vigour.

'They seem to be landing further away,' Kitty said at last.
'Michael – do stop wriggling! You're kicking me black and
blue!'

'Want to pee,' Michael said.

'Oh, Lord. Wait a minute.' She scrambled from her refuge
and fetched the bucket from the corner. With the glass gone
from the window the room was bitterly cold. Through the
glassless gap snow swirled, and she could see a square of
sky, the heavy snowclouds lit blood red with the flash of
the shells and the reflection of fire. 'Here. Be quick.'

Remarkably cheerfully, Michael did what was necessary
then crawled back under the table again. With the resilience
of childhood he seemed already to have lost his fear. 'Pretty
lights,' he said.

'Where's Ma?' Poppy's voice, desolate. 'Where's my Ma?
Is she all right?'

Kitty gathered the child to her in the darkness.

Outside, the cannonade errupted again in fire and fury
as Paris huddled, all but defenceless, beneath the rain of
death.

Jem arrived with first light, and Kitty had never been so
pleased to see anyone in her whole life.

'Lottie or no Lottie we're getting out of here –' He stopped,
his eyes taking in, in the half dark of a January dawn, the
tableau of the sheet-covered corpse, Poppy crying quietly
beside it.

'We can't leave her –' Kitty began.

'You can. And you will. No more harm can come to her.
Which is more than can be said for you. I'll come back later
to see about the arrangements for burial. For now we need
to get you out. Over the river. The Right Bank hasn't been
touched – it looks as if the Prussian guns don't have the
range to reach across the river. You can't stay here. The
apartment in Montmartre is safe. Now – come on! The
bombardment's stopped, for the time being anyway – but

it's chaos out there. The bridges are blocked solid. Well –
at least we don't have to worry about the goods and chattels.
Leave everything. What you stand up in is what you bring.
Kitty – do you think you can manage Michael?'

'Yes.' Kitty swung the child up onto her hip.

'Right. I'll take Poppy.' Infinitely gently he bent beside
the sobbing child and took her hand. 'Poppy – you must
come away. To somewhere you'll be safe. You understand
that, don't you? Your Ma would have wanted it.'

With the utter trust she had shown in Jem from the first
meeting, the child did not demur. Silent and docile, her
tear-stained face a mask of grief she allowed herself, like a
lifeless doll, to be dressed in her warm outdoor clothes and
hoisted pick-a-back onto Jem's back.

'Right,' he said then, 'stay close to me, Kitty. Louise –
you follow Mam'selle and stay close. *Comprenez?* Ready?
Off we go –'

As they set off, gingerly, down the rickety, glass-strewn
steps the door banged eerily in the wind behind them,
Lottie's only companion.

The streets of the bombarded Left Bank were a shambles.
Refugees fleeing their threatened homes dragged carts and
barrows piled high with possessions, crying children clinging to the adults, their parents on the whole silent as grimly
they trudged through the thick, new-fallen snow towards
the bridges that spanned the Seine. Men and women with
burdens of a poverty-stricken lifetime stumbled in the uncertain footing, the hems of the women's skirts heavy and
clinging with the moisture of melted snow. Kitty saw an
old woman, hobbling, grumbling, buffeted by the crowds,
and grown children, fearless and excited, dashed about with
uncaring exuberance, cursed by those slower and more bur-
dened than they. Their party was indeed lucky, Kitty
realized, to be able to abandon possessions and travel encumbered only by the light weight of two half-starved children. They forged on, Jem spearheading their progress with
a grim determination that made it a struggle to keep pace
with him. Around them the signs of the night's bombard-

ment were clear, scarce covered by the new-fallen snow. Smoking craters in the road, fire-damaged, windowless houses, abandoned, their doors standing open in parody of welcome, left so as their inhabitants fled. Here and there small gangs were looting, ignored by the stream of fleeing humanity that made steadily for the bridges. Sickened, Kitty averted her eyes: surely even animals would not behave so to their own kind at a time of common disaster?

They reached the bridge of St Michel, where on that first day Kitty had encountered the columns of wounded coming back into the city. Now the bridge was again packed with streams of moving humanity as the refugees fought to cross to safety. Michael's light weight had grown heavy in her arms. The strain and the sleepless nights dragged at her heels like lead. Jem turned back and caught her eye, grinning encouragingly. Heartened, she hefted the child more firmly onto her hip and smiled back.

Just as they reached the safety of the Right Bank the guns opened up again, the crash and whine of the shells filling the winter air with a menace of sound that, despite herself, made Kitty flinch as if from physical pain. Dear God, she thought as she plodded on through the trampled snow, how long will we have to put up with this? I'll never get used to it. Never.

But, together with the rest of Paris, she did. The decision finally made to bombard the city, the Prussians did the deed with their usual efficiency. Rarely did a day or a night pass that was not disturbed by the cannonade as three hundred, sometimes four hundred shells a day were hurled into the suffering city. Yet, remarkably, both Paris and her inhabitants withstood the bombardment remarkably well. It was starvation that was the spectre now, and in the poorer parts of the city disease and death were taking a far greater toll of the very young and the very old than were the Prussian shells. In fact, had the invaders but known it, the bombardment was, from the besiegers' point of view, downright counterproductive. Resistance stiffened at this open attack, and folk who had the week before been ready to surrender for the promise of bread, and meat and milk for the children now were ready once more to spit in the face of the enemy and soldier on. But such an attitude, in face of the overwhelming fear of starvation, the intense cold and the almost total disappearance of any kind of fuel, could not last. One could somehow face the thought of annihilation in a shell-blast; to watch one's children starve and freeze to death was a different matter entirely. Unrest stirred again. Red posters plastered the city's walls overnight.

'What is a Commune?' Kitty asked Jem, reading from the kitchen window the poster which had appeared on the wall across the street, depicting struggling workers bearing a triumphantly streaming red banner above a barricade in a recognizably Parisian street.

'Rule of the people by the people,' Jem said. 'A workers' state, I suppose you'd call it.'

'But –' Kitty grimaced, confused. 'They're at it again, aren't they? – Fighting amongst themselves while the wolf that's actually at the door waits to pick up the pieces?'

'Looks like it, doesn't it?' Jem had been out scavenging for fuel, not very successfully. The small sack of wood that he carried – a part of someone's prize dining-room table, looted and chopped up – he had managed to obtain in barter for two tins of meat. It was the first such transaction he had been able to make for three days. In fact the fuel shortage was their greatest problem, Kitty's carefully hoarded supplies, supplemented by the help Jem was able to obtain from the American Legation, being perfectly adequate to feed them all for at least another few weeks. When they had first arrived at the Montmartre apartment the children had not been able to believe their eyes at the sight of the full store cupboards. Their faces as they had tasted their first small, sweet biscuit had been a picture of delight that Kitty was never likely to forget. But the cold was harder to fight. Like almost everyone else in the city they wore almost every stitch they possessed, and the luxury of a fire in the week since the bombardment began was becoming rarer. On at least two occasions Kitty had not had the fuel to light the cooking stove and they had had to eat their meals unheated. Yet despite the hardships she thought the children were looking better as their improved diet of the past weeks took effect. The sores had disappeared from Poppy's pretty, melancholy little face and Michael was almost his sturdy small self again. Poppy hardly ever mentioned her mother, who had been buried with little ceremony in a communal grave that had taken the other victims of that first night's bombardment. Jem had quietly handled all the arrangements and no awkward questions had been asked. None of them had been there to see Lottie Smith's earthly remains finally put to rest, and to Kitty that somehow seemed sadly fitting. There was, after all, no one but poor Poppy truly to grieve at her passing.

As the cold month crept on, shortages grew worse and unrest in the city became more open each day. When rations had to be cut again by half and the Red revolutionaries of Bellevue reappeared to lead the riots in the streets it became clear that the situation could not for much longer be contained. In a desperate bid to placate the rising anger of the people General Trochu's shaky government planned one last all-out attack upon the besieging forces.

'We're to stand by for the eighteenth,' Jem said, his face sombre. 'God only knows what will come of this.'

Kitty watched him. Their relationship, since he had brought them back to Montmartre ten days before, had slipped back outwardly almost to the old, easy friendship: almost, but not quite, and the difference, the hidden change evident only to them was absolutely basic. They had in fact seen little of each other, and hardly ever alone – Jem spending most of his time scavenging for what could be had in the city or serving his duties at the field hospital, Kitty totally engrossed in caring for the children and in building her relationship with them. And that, she had more than once reflected as she had sat through the bitter evenings and watched their sleeping faces, was an unexpected and odd thing – she never, now, thought in terms of Michael alone as before, almost obsessively, she had. In the past weeks Lottie and Moses Smith's pathetic orphaned little girl had come to mean as much to her as her own son – a gentle irony that she found somehow eased the pain that memories of the past could still bring. Her determination now was that both should be safe and both should be happy, so that in some way, in her own heart at least, some sense might be made of the loss of those other lives – Matt's, Luke's, Lottie's. That their situation might seem close to desperate now – marooned as they were within a besieged city apparently on the point of revolution – did not dismay her. They were alive and they were well. They would survive. And if it came to the worst, as Jem had pointed out, between them their contacts at the Foreign Office and at the American Legation should see them safe once the siege was lifted. No. What dismayed Kitty now as she watched Jem's wildly shaggy head silhouetted against the winter light of the window, was that even in such extreme circumstances as these pride and stubbornness could estrange two people to the point where they could not even bring themselves to discuss what had gone so very wrong between them. Bleakly and certainly she knew that if the siege were to be lifted tomorrow and she and the children should be spirited to safety in England she would never see Jem O'Connell again. She would have to go, and he would let her, without making the painful attempt to breach the barrier that had risen between them.

'You think this sortie will fail?' she asked.

'I know it will.' He turned from the window. 'And if – when – it does, Paris is lost. I want you to promise me something.'

'What?'

'I want you and the children on the first train out of Paris. Whatever happens. When the city surrenders – and I can see no end to it but that – God only knows what may happen. In arming the people's National Guard this government have armed the people.'

'You mean – revolution?'

'I mean a bloodbath,' he said, grimly.

She stared at him. 'And you?' she asked at last, very quietly. 'What will you do?'

In the other room Michael and Poppy were playing, Michael's gurgling laughter sounding over Poppy's quieter voice.

He jerked his head, flicking his hair from eyes that had become suddenly, hatefully guarded. 'I don't know.'

'Come with us.' She had spoken the words before her brain had told her she should not. 'Come to England! Jem – if you're right it'll be terribly dangerous here –' She broke off.

He was shaking his head. 'It's no good, Kitty.'

In the silence that followed they both understood that he was speaking of more than the simple suggestion that he should accompany them to England.

Unexpectedly anger suddenly boiled in Kitty, a flash of that temper that over the years she had thought she had learned to control. As he made to turn from her she caught his arm. 'Oh, no you don't! You're not going to walk out again, just like that! This time we'll talk about it –'

He shook his head wearily.

'And I say yes! What's the matter with you? What are you so afraid of?'

She saw his jaw tighten at that, but he said nothing.

She still had her hand on his arm. Angrily using all her force, she swung him to face her. 'Jem' – her voice all at once was openly pleading and she made no attempt to conceal it – 'that night – you were drunk – and terribly distressed. It was perfectly understandable. You did things, said things, that you didn't mean. But, don't you see –?'

He did not allow her to go on. 'No,' he said. 'What I did – yes – that was unforgiveable. What I said I meant.'

Luke's. You're Luke's and always will be.

'No,' she said.

He watched her in silence.

She took a breath. 'You can't hold it against me for the rest of our lives that I loved Luke Peveral before I loved you.' She saw the small flick of shock in his eyes. Colour rose in her cheeks, but she faced him steadily. 'Did you hear what I said?'

'I heard.' He made no move towards her. His expression barely changed.

She lifted her chin. 'I love you,' she said, 'not more than I once loved Luke, but as much, and in a different way. A better way. A more worthwhile way. And if you can't accept that, it's your weakness, not mine. If my life were my own I'd stay – I'd do anything – to convince you. But it isn't, and I can't. I have the children to think of. They have to be the first consideration. And if, as you say, civil war is likely I can't keep them here at risk. So you're right. I do have to go. And if I go and you stay we'll never see each other again. Will we?'

He did not speak.

'For God's sake,' she said, bitterly, 'at least do me the courtesy of answering!'

He bit his lip. Shook his head. 'You don't understand.'

'What don't I understand? Tell me.' She was astonished at her own calm. A great part of her wanted to scream at him, to shake him. To cry. To throw herself, begging, at his feet. 'Tell me,' she said, again, quietly insistent.

He lifted his head then. His face was pale, his clear eyes pain-filled. 'I've always loved you. From the first time I saw you – an awkward, frightened, brave little girl with a lovely voice and a rapscallion brother to fight for –'

'You never said anything.'

'You wouldn't have heard if I had. Even before you knew it yourself Luke was there, blinding you, deafening you to anyone else. I don't chase rainbows, Kitty. I knew then you weren't for me, and never could be. Why do you think I left London that time – without seeing you, without saying goodbye? Why do you think I never answered your letters? Oh – I'm not pretending it broke my young heart. I've more sense than that. And I've long ago learned to live without the things others won't or can't give me.'

She remembered his embittered mother, his sister. 'But – Jem –'

'As long as I stayed away from you I was all right. But then things changed. At La Source they changed. When you were having Michael. When, almost, it seemed that you could be mine –'

'Yet again you never said anything!'

'I was afraid,' he said, simply. 'I knew that Luke was there still.'

'No!'

'Yes. Always. There between us. And then you left me –'

'For Matt! Not for Luke!'

'So you said.'

In a frustration of anger she turned from him. 'Whatever I say you won't believe me, will you? You've made up your mind, and that's that. Well – listen to me – hear what I say – it was over between me and Luke before I ever knew I was expecting the baby. Even at the end it was his son he wanted – not me. Can't you see that? And I – oh, Jem, I'd seen long before that what had been between us couldn't possibly last. It was too destructive. Too violent. I would never have gone back to him. If you can't accept that then it's both our loss, but it isn't my fault. I'd go on my knees to you if I thought it would make any difference. But it wouldn't, would it? Because when it comes down to it, what I'm fighting, what's keeping us apart, is your pride, isn't it? Your stupid, stubborn pride! What woman stands a chance against that? You won't bend an inch, and you'll ruin us both.'

She put her head back, trying to ease the tension in her neck. Tired tears were very close. 'A man once told me – the man who, as God is just, will carry to his grave the blame for what has happened to me and to Matt, though he knows nothing of it – he told me that a woman affronted a man's pride at her peril. I should have thanked him for the hard lesson. I should have taken heed. He's been proved right more than once. But Jem – oh, Jem – I thought better of you.' There was a small catch in her voice. She swallowed. 'I thought better of you,' she said again, quietly.

Behind her the door closed softly. She heard Jem's farewell to the children. She leaned against the table, her face in her hands, fighting weak tears.

Outside the guns had started again.

(ii)

She did not see him again until after the grotesquely mismanaged débâcle of the sortie of the eighteenth and nineteenth of January. Knee-deep in mud caused by a sudden thaw that was in its way as much of a calamity as had been the bitter weather that had preceded it, the wrecked armies of Paris broke, fled and were slaughtered. The field of Buzenval was littered with French dead and wounded, and it was all for nothing. In thick fog the city, bludgeoned again by misfortune, watched its beaten soldiers return and knew the end to be near. After four brutal, suffering months the truth had to be faced: Paris was lost. A large proportion of her population was on the edge of starvation, fuel had all but run out, disease was rife. And revolution stalked the battered streets, lurked around each fog-wreathed corner. As the shattered National Guard streamed back through the streets of the city the old cry was heard, muttered in a thousand throats: *'Nous sommes trahis'* – we are betrayed. The casualty figures spoke for themselves – for only seven hundred Prussian casualties, the French forces had sustained four thousand dead and wounded, and almost half of them had come from the National Guard, the people's army that had been thrown into battle so ill-equipped, ill-trained and ill-led. The population of Paris came onto the streets, silent, watching, anger smouldering beneath the surface as they waited for the tidings that they sensed could only mean final disaster. By the twenty-first of the month the worst of the news had been confirmed and for a while the silence of utter defeat fell upon the city. It was Jem who brought to the apartment in Montmartre the news that Trochu's government had been forced to resign and the way to negotiations with the Prussian invaders was open.

'There's bad trouble brewing.' He leaned against the door, gaunt and exhausted. 'Don't go out. Not for anything. The Reds have taken over the streets.'

Since he had left five days before they had heard nothing of him, but he had not for a moment been out of Kitty's thoughts. When she was busy with the children during the day it had been a nagging worry, nibbling at the back of her mind like a rat at a bone. In the frozen, sleepless small hours of the night it had been a nightmare, a conviction of mutilation or death. Her relief at seeing him whole, if apparently half-dead with exhaustion, expressed itself, since she could not indulge her first impulse to fling herself into his arms, in an idiotic wave of bossy solicitude.

'Lord God, just look at you. Come inside and sit down. Poppy – help me move the chair to the fire. No, don't take your coat off yet, Jem – it isn't warm enough in here. I'll build up the fire. Louise managed to buy a sackful of logs – real logs! – from a man down the road. Lord knows where they came from. I don't think there can be a tree left in the Bois! Michael – fetch a log from the box, there's a good boy. Now, Jem, what would you like? We've tea – no milk of course – and some absolutely dreadful coffee. Are you hungry –?'

He shook his head tiredly, subsided gratefully into the chair. 'I ate before I came away. You've heard about Buzenval?'

She kept her voice bright. 'The defeat? Yes. Louise told us.'

'It was murder,' he said. 'Sheer bloody murder. The medical services were completely overwhelmed. God, I'm tired. I could sleep for a week.' Poppy had sidled up shyly and stood now, leaning by his chair, watching him. Smiling faintly, he lifted his hand and tugged at the lovely, fair curls. 'Hello, Princess.'

The child smiled – Jem, Kitty had noted before, was one of the only people that could bring forth that rare, lovely smile – and knelt beside him, her head on his knee. Jem tousled her hair again, lifted clear, tired eyes to Kitty. 'You wouldn't have a wee drop of that brandy left?'

'I'll get it.' She left him sitting, his head back, eyes closed, one hand fondling Poppy's bright, golden head. As she poured the brandy she sent up a small prayer of thanks. He was exhausted, but he was whole and undamaged – whatever might happen now between them, even if it meant, as she feared, the pain of parting, she would never cease to give thanks for that.

When she re-entered the room he lay exactly as she had left him, fast asleep.

He stayed with them for the next few days as something close to civil war raged in the streets of the city. A few days after the defeat at Buzenval the Hôtel de Ville was attacked and stormed once again, but this time not without deaths and casualties. In a terrible foretaste of the future, Frenchmen had shed French blood and a fatal step had been taken. Kitty told a frightened Louise to stay with her family. A well-recovered Jem went out each morning, foraging for supplies and for news and she was on tenterhooks each day until he returned. Dense fog still enveloped the city, rolling against the windows, enwrapping and enclosing the streets, eerily disorientating. The snippets of news that Jem brought back were even more eagerly awaited than the supplies he brought from the Legation. So-called secret armistice talks were being held with the Prussians. And though the German guns still belched and bellowed the feeling was strong that the end must be near.

From the very first night, by tacit agreement, Jem had laid a mattress in the warmth of the kitchen, whilst Kitty continued to share the bedroom with the children. Kitty, all but exhausted herself by the efforts to fill the extra mouths, made no more mention to Jem of her feelings for him. She realized that she had failed. If the strange, complicated, sensitive Jem decided himself to meet her halfway, then so be it. Almost above all else, she wanted peace, and freedom, and safety for the children.

The heartache would come later, she knew.

On the day that the guns at last fell silent it was Michael who saw it first. 'Jemby!' he said, tugging imperiously at Jem's tattered coattails. 'No more bang!'

Kitty looked up from her efforts to teach earnest small Poppy, smiling at Michael's use of the silly nickname he had given Jem. 'No, there isn't.'

Jem was sitting on the floor with Michael, overcoat on, and a scarf wrapped several times about his neck, fingerless gloves warming his hands as he sketched his godchild. He tilted his head, listening, his face alert. 'I wonder for how long?'

'I don't know.' Kitty laughed, a little shakily. 'How silly of us not to have noticed. Jem – do you think –?'

'Wait. We can't be sure.'

The day crept by in silence. Mist still wreathed the roadway and a strange half-light added to the eerie stillness. At length, abruptly, Jem threw down his pencil and leapt to his feet. 'It's no good. I'm going out to see what's going on.'

'Be careful.'

'I will.'

She settled Poppy, caught up with Jem at the door, handed him a second scarf. He took it and wound it about his neck. Then with a quick, helpless gesture that touched her almost to tears, very swiftly and gently, he kissed her. He stood for a moment, looking at her, his open face the picture of baffled unhappiness. 'I'm sorry,' he said. 'I know I love you. I can't seem to make myself –'

'– forget Luke?' she finished for him.

Despite his obvious unhappiness his jaw was stubborn, the line of his mouth tight. 'I won't be – I can't be – second best. Can't you see that?'

'You wouldn't be.' Her voice was steady.

He shook his head.

'Come home with us,' she said.

He turned away, ran swiftly down the stairs and out into the street. Kitty dashed the tears from her eyes and turned to the children.

Two long hours later she heard his step on the stairs. She was up and at the door before he had reached it. She closed the door behind him, and leaned against it. He turned. His movements were oddly slow, almost awkard. 'It's over,' he said.

She swallowed. Said nothing.

'A hundred and thirty days,' he said. 'I just worked it out. A hundred and thirty days. And now it's over.'

The most extraordinary emotions were warring in Kitty's brain; excitement, overwhelming relief, a strange, bitter sadness. 'Poor Paris,' she said, softly.

He lifted his head. Nodded. There was an odd moment of silent mourning. Then, 'It's over!' he shouted, exultantly, '*over*! Get the children. We're going to the Legation.'

'Now?'

'Now.' He took a breath, smiled his wide, warm smile. 'You're safe, Songbird, all of you. The trains will be running again. And you're going home –'

(iii)

The Gare du Nord, its recent history graphically illustrated by hastily stacked remnants of the balloon factory it had become during the siege, was teeming with anxious, jostling people. Eli Washburne, the popular American Legate who had done so much for the people of Paris over the past months, proved every bit as helpful and influential as Jem had claimed he was. The train that Kitty and the children were about to board might not be the first one that had left the stricken city – that had in fact left an hour or two earlier – but his swift efficiency in obtaining passes, travel papers and seats had left Kitty almost breathlessly thankful. The courteous and helpful Mr Washburne had been delighted, he had assured her, to help. Dazed as she was at the sudden speed of events, his obvious admiration had come for Kitty as a strange reminder of a life she had all but forgotten and to which she was, astoundingly, returning.

'Charmed, Miss Daniels, absolutely charmed!' he had said, warmly. 'I had the very great pleasure of attending some of your performances at the Moulin d'Or some time ago. I shall be taking this rascal to task for keeping you under his hat!' He had grinned at the abashed Jem. 'If we'd known you were here, we could have arranged some very pleasant entertainment –'

She had smiled, and nodded.

Eli Washburne had turned back to Jem. 'You'll be deserting us too, no doubt? Don't blame you, m'boy, don't blame you a bit –' And Kitty had turned away from Jem's shaken head, his muttered explanations, aware of the old man's shrewd eyes flicking from Jem's red face to her own wooden one. 'Well,' he had said then, 'I've said it before and I'll say it again. There's no fool like a young fool, Miss Daniels, no sir,' and she had had to smile, and agree, wanting nothing so much as to get away, to finish it.

And now here they were. She clung tightly to the children's hands. Their luggage was aboard, so the young American who had escorted her to the train had assured her, though to be honest so anxious was she to be on her way that she would quite cheerfully have abandoned it in the middle of the crowded platform if it had been necessary to do so.

Where was Jem? She had thought she had not wanted to see him – had told him, indeed, how much she detested goodbyes, and he had sensibly agreed, but now the moment had come, she wanted so much to see him once more that it hurt.

'This way, ma'am. It's going to be rather crowded, I fear – but at least Mr Washburne secured seats for you and the children –'

'Thank you. And – please – thank Mr Washburne again for me.'

'I will, ma'am.'

Where was Jem?

The young man, clean-cut and deferential, handed her into a carriage already almost full. Kitty squeezed herself and Poppy into the seat, took Michael onto her lap. The young man touched his cap and left them. She stared out of the window. She felt tired to the point of exhaustion – deflated and irritable, with disappointingly none of the elation that she had always anticipated would accompany this moment. There was still no sign of Jem. He was going to let her go without even saying goodbye –

Michael wriggled on her lap. 'Where's Jemby?' he asked, suddenly, with the uncanny sixth sense of the very young.

The sound of that silly nickname almost released the pent-up tears. Why hadn't he come? For all that she had said, she had expected him. He must have been afraid of what she might say, what she might do to try to persuade him to come with them. Afraid of what? Afraid of the hurt? Or simply – humiliatingly – the embarrassment? She did not know. Would never know. She remembered once saying to him that he was in love with Paris – that no woman would stand a chance of taking him from the city. Self evidently she had been right.

'Want Jemby,' Michael said, stubbornly.

The carriage had filled to bursting point. Not just passengers, but their luggage took up every square inch of space. A large man stood in front of her, leaning uncomfortably upon her cramped knees, blocking the light, his suitcase jammed painfully against her foot. Michael squirmed again. She held him firmly, trying not to think of the long haul north to the Channel port of Boulogne. Boulogne. Dear God, how long it seemed –

'Where's Jemby?' the child asked, again fretfully.

The train jerked. The huge man staggered, stumbling painfully upon her foot.

'There 'e is,' Poppy said, calmly. 'There's Jem.'

'What? Where?' Frantically Kitty craned her neck, looking out of the window. A whistle shrieked. The train jerked again and began, infinitely slowly, to move. The platform was empty but for a few uniformed officials and two Prussian guards. '*Where?*'

Poppy giggled, tugging her sleeve. 'There.'

Kitty followed the line of the small, pointing finger. The engine screeched again and slowly the carriages clanked over points long unused. The passengers swayed with the movement. The corridor outside the carriage was packed. People leaned upon the handrails that ran along the windows, or sat upon suitcases and trunks. Jem was wedged uncomfortably between a man with a huge untidy bundle in his arms and an enormous woman wearing an unlikely, flamboyant flower-trimmed hat. He was watching Kitty. Catching her eye, he gave a small, self-mocking smile and lifted his shoulders – in fact the only part of him he could reasonably attempt to move – in a wryly graphic shrug. Here I am, it said, make what you will of it –

She blinked.

'There's Jemby,' Michael said, satisfied, and thrust his thumb into his mouth, burrowing into her lap.

'Yes, dear,' she said.

'On the puffer,' he said, sleepily, around his thumb.

'On the train,' she corrected him. 'Jemby's on the train.'

A small hand crept into hers. Poppy smiled, and nestled closer. Magically the world had changed. A small, capricious snatch of tune hummed in her mind. 'Who d'you see in Mayfair, Strolling with the girls –' For the first time in months she allowed herself to remember the brilliance and excitement of the London stage.

Trailing its plume of smoke, the train rattled northward, through the encampments of the enemy, away from a city that after four months of privation and violence seethed now on the brink of doomed and bloody revolution.

Ahead lay England, home and safety.

Poppy was watching Jem. He pulled a sudden, silly, mock-ferocious face, and she giggled. Then his eyes moved to Kitty and the gleam of mockery died. For a long, wary moment they watched each other. And then, together, they smiled; and the shadow was gone. His eyes not leaving Kitty's face, Jem began to push his way through the crush to her side.

Fontana's Family Sagas

Molly
Teresa Crane

Molly is a spirited young woman who escapes poverty in Ireland for a new life in Victorian London. Courageous and passionate, she fights the prejudice against her sex and her class — and wins.   A compelling story.

The Cavendish Face
Jane Barry

A love story to sweep you off your feet. Set in London of the 1920s and '30s, it tells of a young woman's struggle against the stifling conventions and corrupt morals around her and how she seeks a way to love freely the only man who has ever had a place in her life.   A captivating novel.

Futures
Freda Bright

Caro Harmsworth is the perfect twentieth-century woman — young, liberated, independent, and determined to be a success in the high financial world of Wall Street. A strong contemporary story of love and success — and of the woman who has to chose between the two. . .

FONTANA PAPERBACKS

Belva Plain

– the best-loved bestseller –

Evergreen

The tempestuous story of Anna Friedman, the beautiful, penniless Jewish girl who arrives in New York from Poland at the turn of the century and survives to become the matriarch of a powerful dynasty.

Random Winds

The poignant story of a family of doctors – Dr Farrell, the old-fashioned country doctor who dies penniless and exhausted, his son Martin who becomes a famous brain surgeon but is haunted by his forbidden love for a woman, and Martin's daughter Claire, headstrong and modern, whose troubled romance provides a bitter-sweet ending.

Eden Burning

A romantic saga set against the backdrop of New York, Paris and the Caribbean. The island of St Felice holds many secrets, one of which is the secret of the passionate moment of abandon that threatened to destroy the life of beautiful Teresa Francis. A story of violence, political upheaval and clandestine love.

Crescent City

Miriam Raphael leaves the ghettoes of Europe to become a belle of New Orleans. Trapped in a bad marriage she begins a turbulent, forbidden love affair with dangerous, attractive André Perrin. But the horrors of the Civil War sweep away the old splendour, and Miriam must rebuild her own and her family's life from the ashes.

FONTANA PAPERBACKS

Catherine Gaskin

'Catherine Gaskin is one of the few big talents now engaged in writing historical romance.'

Daily Express

'A born story-teller.' *Sunday Mirror*

THE SUMMER OF THE SPANISH WOMAN
ALL ELSE IS FOLLY
BLAKE'S REACH
DAUGHTER OF THE HOUSE
EDGE OF GLASS
A FALCON FOR A QUEEN
THE FILE ON DEVLIN
FIONA
THE PROPERTY OF A GENTLEMAN
SARA DANE
THE TILSIT INHERITANCE
FAMILY AFFAIRS
CORPORATION WIFE
I KNOW MY LOVE
THE LYNMARA LEGACY
PROMISES

FONTANA PAPERBACKS

Winston Graham

'One of the best half-dozen novelists in this country.' *Books and Bookmen*.

'Winston Graham excels in making his characters come vividly alive.' *Daily Mirror*.

'A born novelist.' *Sunday Times*.

The Poldark Saga, his famous story of eighteenth-century Cornwall

ROSS POLDARK
DEMELZA
JEREMY POLDARK
WARLEGGAN
THE BLACK MOON
THE FOUR SWANS
THE ANGRY TIDE
THE STRANGER FROM THE SEA
THE MILLER'S DANCE
THE LOVING CUP

His immensely popular suspense novels include

THE WALKING STICK
MARNIE
THE SLEEPING PARTNER

Historical novel

THE FORGOTTEN STORY

FONTANA PAPERBACKS

Rhanna
Christine Marion Fraser

A rich, romantic, Scottish saga set
on the Hebridean island of Rhanna

Rhanna

The poignant story of life on the rugged and tranquil island
of Rhanna, and of the close-knit community for whom it
is home.

Rhanna at War

Rhanna's lonely beauty is no protection against the horrors
of war. But Shona Mackenzie, home on leave, discovers
that the fiercest battles are those between lovers.

Children of Rhanna

The four island children, inseparable since childhood, find
that growing up also means growing apart.

Return to Rhanna

Shona and Niall Mackenzie come home to find Rhanna
unspoilt by the onslaught of tourism. But then tragedy
strikes at the heart of their marriage.

Song of Rhanna

Ruth is happily married to Lorn. But the return to Rhanna
of her now famous friend Rachel threatens Ruth's
happiness.

'Full-blooded romance, a strong, authentic setting'
Scotsman

FONTANA PAPERBACKS

Fontana Paperbacks: Fiction

Fontana is a leading paperback publisher of both non-fiction, popular and academic, and fiction. Below are some recent fiction titles.

You can buy Fontana paperbacks at your local bookshop or newsagent. Or you can order them from Fontana Paperbacks, Cash Sales Department, Box 29, Douglas, Isle of Man. Please send a cheque, postal or money order (not currency) worth the purchase price plus 22p per book for postage (maximum postage required is £3.00 for orders within the UK).

NAME (Block letters) _____

ADDRESS _____

_____

_____